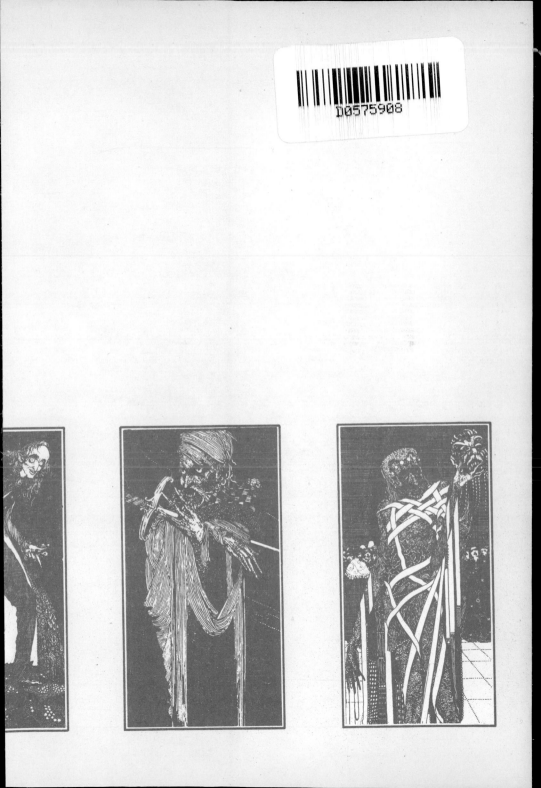

FORTY-TWO TALES

INCLUDING

THE FALL OF THE HOUSE OF USHER
THE MURDERS IN THE RUE MORGUE
THE PIT AND THE PENDULUM

EDGAR ALLAN POE

FORTY-TWO TALES

INCLUDING

THE FALL OF THE HOUSE OF USHER
THE MURDERS IN THE RUE MORGUE
THE PIT AND THE PENDULUM

ILLUSTRATIONS BY

HARRY CLARKE

OCTOPUS

Edgar Allen Poe was born in Boston, Mass. in 1809 but on the death of his parents was adopted by John Allan and his wife from Richmond in Virginia. They travelled to England and Edgar was sent to school at Stoke Newington for five years; on their return to America he was noted as a brilliant pupil at Richmond school, and then at the University of Virginia. On his eighteenth birthday he published *Tamerlane and Other Poems*. He was dismissed from the Military Academy after two years, quarrelled with the Allans and turned to journalism without initial success. He worked for various periodicals in Baltimore, Virginia and New York where he published the first of his stories, but it was not until he settled in Philadelphia that he gained a reputation as a writer and his work became popular.

Tragedy struck with the illness and subsequent death of his wife which affected Poe very seriously; he took to drink and died in 1849.

This edition first published in Great Britain in 1979 by
Octopus Books Limited
59 Grosvenor Street London W1

ISBN 0 7064 1053 X

Filmset in Great Britain by
Northumberland Press Ltd, Gateshead, Tyne and Wear

Printed in Czechoslovakia

Illustrations first appeared in
Tales of Mystery and Imagination by E. A. Poe,
and reproduced here, by courtesy of
George G. Harrap and Company Ltd.

50370

Contents

List of Illustrations

MS. Found in a Bottle

Qui n'a plus qu'un moment a vivre
N'a plus rien a dissimuler.   *Quinault – Atys.*

Of my country and of my family I have little to say. Ill-usage and length of years have driven me from the one, and estranged me from the other. Hereditary wealth afforded me an education of no common order, and a contemplative turn of mind enabled me to methodise the stores which early study very diligently garnered up. Beyond all things, the works of the German moralists gave me great delight; not from any ill-advised admiration of their eloquent madness, but from the ease with which my habits of rigid thought enabled me to detect their falsities. I have often been reproached with the aridity of my genius; a deficiency of imagination has been imputed to me as a crime; and the Pyrrhonism of my opinions has at all times rendered me notorious. Indeed, a strong relish for physical philosophy has, I fear, tinctured my mind with a very common error of this age – I mean the habit of referring occurrences, even the least susceptible of such reference, to the principles of that science. Upon the whole, no person could be less liable than myself to be led away from the severe precincts of truth by the *ignes fatui* of superstition. I have thought proper to premise this much, lest the incredible tale I have to tell should be considered rather the raving of a crude imagination than the positive experience of a mind to which the reveries of fancy have been a dead letter and a nullity.

After many years spent in foreign travel, I sailed in the year 18—, from the port of Batavia, in the rich and populous island of Java, on a voyage to the Archipelago of the Sunda Islands. I went as passenger – having no other inducement than a kind of nervous restlessness which haunted me as a fiend.

Our vessel was a beautiful ship of about four hundred tons, copper-fastened, and built at Bombay of Malabar teak. She was freighted with cotton-wool and oil, from the Lachadive Islands. We had also on board coir, jaggeree, ghee, cocoa-nuts, and a few cases of opium. The stowage was clumsily done, and the vessel consequently crank.

We got under way with a mere breath of wind, and for many days stood along the eastern coast of Java, without any other incident to beguile the monotony of our course than the occasional meeting with some of the small grabs of the Archipelago to which we were bound.

One evening, leaning over the taffrail, I observed a very singular isolated cloud to the N.W. It was remarkable, as well for its colour as from its being the first we had seen since our departure from Batavia. I watched it attentively until sunset, when it spread all at once to the eastward and westward, girting in the horizon with a narrow strip of vapour, and looking like a long line of low beach. My notice was soon afterwards attracted by the dusky-red appearance of the moon, and the peculiar character of the sea. The latter was undergoing a rapid change, and the water seemed more than usually transparent. Although I could distinctly see the bottom, yet, heaving the lead, I found the ship in fifteen fathoms. The air now became intolerably hot, and was loaded with spiral exhalations similar to those arising from heated iron. As night came on, every breath of wind died away, and a more entire calm it is impossible to conceive. The flame of a candle burned upon the poop without the least perceptible motion, and a long hair, held between the finger and thumb, hung without the possibility of detecting a vibration. However, as the captain said he could perceive no indication of danger, and as we were drifting in bodily to shore, he ordered the sails to be furled, and the anchor let go. No watch was set, and the crew, consisting principally of Malays, stretched themselves deliberately upon deck. I went below – not without a full presentiment of evil. Indeed, every appearance warranted me in apprehending a simoom. I told the captain my fears; but he paid no attention to what I said, and left me without deigning to give a reply. My uneasiness, however, prevented me from sleeping, and about midnight I went upon deck. As I placed my foot upon the upper step of the companion-ladder, I was startled by a loud, humming noise, like that occasioned by the rapid revolution of a mill-wheel, and before I could ascertain its meaning, I found the ship quivering to its centre. In the next instant, a wilderness of foam hurled us upon our beam-ends, and, rushing over us fore and aft, swept the entire decks from stem to stern.

The extreme fury of the blast proved, in a great measure, the salvation of the ship. Although completely water-logged, yet, as her masts had gone by the board, she rose, after a minute, heavily from the sea, and, staggering awhile beneath the immense pressure of the tempest, finally righted.

By what miracle I escaped destruction it is impossible to say. Stunned by the shock of the water I found myself, upon recovery, jammed in between the stern-post and rudder. With great difficulty I gained my feet, and, looking dizzily around, was at first struck with the idea of our being among breakers; so terrific, beyond the wildest imagination, was the whirlpool of mountainous and foaming ocean within which we were engulfed. After a while, I heard the voice of an old Swede, who had shipped with us at the moment of our leaving port. I hallooed to him with all my strength, and presently he came reeling aft. We soon discovered that we were the sole survivors of the accident. All on deck, with the exception of ourselves, had been swept overboard; the captain and mates must have perished as they slept, for the cabins were deluged with water. Without assistance, we could expect to do little for the security of the ship, and our exertions were at first paralysed by the momentary expectation of going down. Our cable had, of course, parted like pack-thread, at the first breath of the hurricane, or we should have been instantaneously overwhelmed. We scudded with frightful velocity before the sea, and the water made clear breaches over us. The framework of our stern was shattered excessively, and in almost every respect we had received considerable injury; but to our extreme joy we found the pumps unchoked, and that we had made no great shifting of our ballast. The main fury of the blast had already blown over, and we apprehended little danger from the violence of the wind; but we looked forward to its total cessation with dismay; well believing, that in our shattered condition, we should inevitably perish in the tremendous swell which would ensue. But this very just apprehension seemed by no means likely to be soon verified. For five entire days and nights – during which our only subsistence was a small quantity of jaggeree, procured with great difficulty from the forecastle – the hulk flew at a rate defying computation, before rapidly succeeding flaws of wind, which without equalling the first violence of the simoom, were still more terrific than any tempest I had before encountered. Our course for the first four days was, with trifling variations, S.E. and by S.; and we must have run down the coast of New Holland. On the fifth day the cold became extreme, although the wind had hauled round a point more to the northward. The sun arose with a sickly yellow lustre, and clambered a very few degrees above the horizon – emitting no decisive light. There were no clouds apparent, yet the wind was upon the increase, and blew with a fitful and unsteady fury. About noon, as nearly as we could guess, our attention was again arrested by the appearance of the sun. It gave out no light, properly so called, but a dull and sullen glow without reflection, as if all its rays were polarised. Just before sinking within the turgid sea, its central fires suddenly went out, as if hurriedly extinguished by some unaccountable power. It was a dim, silver-like rim, alone, as it rushed down the unfathomable ocean.

We waited in vain for the arrival of the sixth day – that day to me has not arrived – to the Swede never did arrive. Thenceforward we were enshrouded in pitchy darkness, so that we could not have seen an object at twenty paces from the ship. Eternal night continued to envelop us, all unrelieved by the phosphoric sea-brilliancy to which we had been accustomed in the tropics. We observed too, that, although the tempest continued to rage with unabated violence, there was no longer to be discovered the usual appearance of surf, or foam, which had hitherto attended us. All around were horror, and thick gloom, and a black sweltering desert of ebony. Superstitious terror crept by degrees into the spirit of the old Swede, and my own soul was wrapped up in silent wonder. We neglected all care of the ship as worse than useless, and securing ourselves, as well as possible, to the stump of the mizen-mast, looked out bitterly into the world of ocean. We had no means of calculating time, nor could we form any guess of our situation. We were, however, well aware of having made farther to the southward than any previous navigators, and felt great amazement at not meeting with the usual impediments of ice. In the meantime every moment threatened to be our last – every mountainous billow hurried to overwhelm us. The swell surpassed anything I had imagined possible, and that we were not instantly buried is a miracle. My companion spoke of the lightness of our cargo, and reminded me of the excellent qualities of our ship; but I could not help feeling the utter hopelessness of hope itself, and prepared myself gloomily for that death which I thought nothing could defer beyond an hour, as, with every knot of way the ship made, the swelling of the black stupendous seas became more dismally appalling. At times we gasped for breath at an elevation beyond the albatross – at times became dizzy with the velocity of our descent into some watery hell, where the air grew stagnant, and no sound disturbed the slumbers of the kraken.

We were at the bottom of one of the abysses, when a quick scream from my companion broke fearfully upon the night. 'See! see!' cried he, shrieking in my ears, 'Almighty God! see! see!' As he spoke, I became aware of a dull, sullen glare of red light which streamed down the sides of the vast chasm where we lay, and threw a fitful brilliancy upon our deck. Casting my eyes upwards, I beheld a spectacle which froze the current of my blood. At a terrific height directly above us, and upon the very verge of the precipitous descent, hovered a gigantic ship, of perhaps four thousand tons. Although upreared upon the summit of a wave more than a hundred times her own altitude, her apparent size still exceeded that of any ship of the line or East Indiaman in existence. Her huge hull was of a deep dingy black unrelieved by any of the customary carvings of a ship. A single row of brass cannon protruded from her open ports, and dashed from their polished surfaces the fires of innumerable battle-lanterns, which swung to and fro about her rigging. But what mainly inspired us with horror and atonishment was, that she bore up under a press of sail in the very teeth of that supernatural sea, and of that ungovernable hurricane. When we first discovered her, her bows were alone to be seen, as she rose slowly from the dim and horrible gulf beyond her. For a moment of intense terror she paused upon the giddy pinnacle, as if in contemplation of her own sublimity, then trembled and tottered, and – came down.

At this instant, I know not what sudden self-possession came over my spirit. Staggering as far aft as I could, I awaited fearlessly the ruin that was to overwhelm. Our own vessel was at length ceasing from her struggles, and sinking with her head to the sea. The shock of the descending mass struck her, consequently, in that portion of her frame which was already under water, and the inevitable result was to hurl me, with irresistible violence, upon the rigging of the stranger.

As I fell, the ship hove in stays, and went about; and to the confusion ensuing I attributed my escape from the notice of the crew. With little difficulty I made my way, unperceived, to the main hatchway, which was partially open, and soon found an opportunity of secreting myself in the hold. Why I did so I can hardly tell. An indefinite sense of awe, which at first sight of the navigators of the ship had taken hold of my mind, was perhaps the principle of my concealment. I was unwilling to trust myself with a race of people who had offered, to the cursory glance I had taken, so many points of vague novelty, doubt, and apprehension. I therefore thought proper to contrive a hiding-place in the hold. This I did by removing a small portion of the shifting-boards, in such manner as to afford me a convenient retreat between the huge timbers of the ship.

I had scarcely completed my work, when a footstep in the hold forced me to make use of it. A man passed by my place of concealment with a feeble and unsteady gait. I could not see his face, but had an opportunity of observing his general appearance. There was about it an evidence of great age and infirmity. His knees tottered beneath a load of years, and his entire frame quivered under the burden. He muttered to himself, in a low broken tone, some words of a language which I could not understand, and groped in a corner among a pile of singular-looking instruments, and decayed charts of navigation. His manner was a wild mixture of the peevishness of second childhood and the solemn dignity of a God. He at length went on deck, and I saw him no more.

A feeling, for which I have no name, has taken possession of my soul – a sensation which will admit of no analysis, to which the lessons of bygone time are inadequate, and for which I fear futurity itself will offer me no key. To a mind constituted like my own, the latter consideration is an evil. I shall never – I know that I shall never – be satisfied with regard to the nature of my conceptions. Yet it is not wonderful that these conceptions are indefinite, since they have their origin in sources so utterly novel. A new sense – a new entity is added to my soul.

It is long since I first trod the deck of this terrible ship, and the rays of my destiny are, I think, gathering to a focus. Incomprehensible men! Wrapped up in meditations of a kind which I cannot divine, they pass me by unnoticed. Concealment is utter folly on my part, for the people *will not* see. It was but just now that I passed directly before the eyes of the mate; it was no long while ago that I ventured into the captain's own private cabin, and took thence the materials with which I write, and have written. I shall from time to time continue this journal. It is true that I may not find an opportunity of transmitting it to the world, but I will not fail to make the endeavour. At the last moment I will enclose the MS. in a bottle and cast it within the sea.

An incident has occurred which has given me new room for meditation. Are such things the operation of ungoverned chance? I had ventured upon deck and thrown myself down, without attracting any notice, among a pile of ratlin-stuff and old sails, in the bottom of the yawl. While musing upon the singularity of my fate, I unwittingly

'Incomprehensible men! Wrapped up in meditations of a kind which I
cannot divine, they pass me by unnoticed'

daubed with a tar-brush the edges of a neatly-folded studding-sail which lay near me on a barrel. The studding-sail is now bent upon the ship, and the thoughtless touches of the brush are spread out into the word DISCOVERY.

I have made many observations lately upon the structure of the vessel. Although well armed, she is not, I think, a ship of war. Her rigging, build, and general equipment, all negative a supposition of this kind, what she *is not* I can easily perceive; what she *is*, I fear it is impossible to say. I know not how it is, but in scrutinising her strange model and singular cast of spars, her huge size and overgrown suits of canvas, her severely simple bow and antiquated stern, there will occasionally flash across my mind a sensation of familiar things, and there is always mixed up with such indistinct shadows of recollection an unaccountable memory of old foreign chronicles and ages long ago.

I have been looking at the timbers of the ship. She is built of a material to which I am a stranger. There is a peculiar character about the wood which strikes me as rendering it unfit for the purpose to which it has been applied. I mean its extreme *porousness*, considered independently of the worm-eaten condition which is a consequence of navigation in these seas, and apart from the rottenness attendant upon age. It will appear perhaps an observation somewhat over-curious, but this wood would have every characteristic of Spanish oak, if Spanish oak were distended by any unnatural means.

In reading the above sentence, a curious apothegm of an old weather-beaten Dutch navigator comes full upon my recollection. 'It is as sure,' he was wont to say when any doubt was entertained of his veracity, 'as sure as there is a sea where the ship itself will grow in bulk like the living body of the seaman.'

About an hour ago, I made bold to thrust myself among a group of the crew. They paid me no manner of attention, and, although I stood in the very midst of them all, seemed utterly unconscious of my presence. Like the one I had first seen in the hold, they all bore about them the marks of a hoary old age. Their knees trembled with infirmity; their shoulders were bent double with decrepitude; their shrivelled skins rattled in the wind; their voices were low, tremulous, and broken; their eyes glistened with the rheum of years; and their grey hairs streamed terribly in the tempest. Around them, on every part of the deck, lay scattered mathematical instruments of the most quaint and obsolete construction.

I mentioned some time ago the bending of a studding-sail. From that period, the ship, being thrown dead off the wind, has continued her terrific course due south, with every rag of canvas packed upon her, from her trucks to her lower studding-sail booms, and rolling every moment her top-gallant yard-arms into the most appalling hell of water which it can enter into the mind of man to imagine. I have just left the deck, where I find it impossible to maintain a footing, although the crew seem to experience little inconvenience. It appears to me a miracle of miracles that our enormous bulk is not swallowed up at once and for ever. We are surely doomed to hover continually upon the brink of eternity, without taking a final plunge into the abyss. From billows a thousand times more stupendous than any I have ever seen, we glide away with the facility of the arrowy sea-gull; and the colossal waters rear their heads above us like demons of the deep, but like demons confined to simple threats and forbidden to destroy. I am led to attribute these frequent escapes to the only natural cause which can account for such effect. I must suppose the ship to be within the influence of some strong current, or impetuous under-tow.

I have seen the captain face to face, and in his own cabin – but, as I expected, he paid me no attention. Although in his appearance there is, to a casual observer, nothing which might bespeak him more or less than man, still a feeling of irrepressible reverence and awe mingled with the sensation of wonder with which I regarded him. In stature, he is nearly my own height; that is, about five feet eight inches. He is of a well-knit and compact frame of body, neither robust nor remarkable otherwise. But it is the singularity of the expression which reigns upon the face – it is the intense, the wonderful, the thrilling evidence of old age, so utter, so extreme, which excites within my spirit a sense – a sentiment ineffable. His forehead, although little wrinkled, seems to bear upon it the stamp of a myriad of years. His grey hairs are records of the past, and his greyer eyes are sibyls of the future. The cabin floor was thickly strewn with strange, iron-clasped folios, and mouldering instruments of science, and obsolete long-forgotten charts. His head was bowed down upon his hands, and he pored with a fiery unquiet eye over a paper which I took to be a commission, and which, at all events, bore the signature of a monarch. He muttered to himself – as did the first seaman whom I saw in the hold – some low peevish syllables of a foreign tongue; and although the speaker was close at my elbow, his voice seemed to reach my ears from the distance of a mile.

The ship and all in it are imbued with the spirit of Eld. The crew glide to and fro like the ghosts of buried centuries; their eyes have an eager and uneasy meaning; and when their figures fall athwart my path in the wild glare of the battle-lanterns, I feel as I have never felt before, although I have been all my life a dealer in antiquities, and have imbibed the shadows of fallen columns at Balbec, and Tadmor, and Persepolis, until my very soul has become a ruin.

When I look around me I feel ashamed of my former apprehensions. If I trembled at the blast which has hitherto attended us, shall I not stand aghast at a warring of wind and ocean, to convey any idea of which the words tornado and simoom are trivial and ineffective? All in the immediate vicinity of the ship is the blackness of eternal night, and a chaos of foamless water; but, about a league on either side of us, may be seen, indistinctly and at intervals, stupendous ramparts of ice towering away into the desolate sky, and looking like the walls of the universe.

As I imagined, the ship proves to be in a current – if that appellation can properly be given to a tide which, howling and shrieking by the white ice, thunders on to the southward with a velocity like the headlong dashing of a cataract.

To conceive the horror of my sensations is, I presume, utterly impossible; yet a curiosity to penetrate the mysteries of these awful regions predominates even over my despair, and will reconcile me to the most hideous aspect of death. It is evident that we are hurrying onwards to some exciting knowledge – some never-to-be-imparted secret, whose attainment is destruction. Perhaps this current leads us to the southern pole itself. It must be confessed that a supposition apparently so wild has every probability in its favour.

The crew pace the deck with unquiet and tremulous step; but there is upon their countenances an expression more of the eagerness of hope than of the apathy of despair.

In the meantime the wind is still in our poop, and as we carry a crowd of canvas the ship is at times lifted bodily out of the sea! Oh, horror upon horror! – the ice opens suddenly to the right, and to the left, and we are whirling dizzily, in immense concentric circles, round and round the borders of a gigantic amphitheatre, the summit of whose walls is lost in the darkness and the distance. But little time will be left me to ponder upon my destiny! The circles rapidly grow small – we are plunging madly within the grasp of the whirlpool – and amid a roaring, and bellowing, and thundering of ocean and of tempest, the ship is quivering – Oh God! and – going down!

Note. – The 'MS. found in a Bottle' was originally published in 1831, and it was not until many years afterwards that I became acquainted with the maps of Mercator, in which the ocean is represented as rushing, by four mouths, into the (northern) Polar Gulf, to be absorbed into the bowels of the earth; the Pole itself being represented by a black rock towering to a prodigious height.

X-ing a Paragrab

As it is well-known that the 'wise men' came 'from the East,' and as Mr.
Touch-and-go Bullet-Head came from the East, it follows that Mr.
Bullet-Head was a wise man; and if collateral proof of the matter be
needed, here we have it – Mr. B. was an editor. Irascibility was his sole
foible; for in fact the obstinacy of which men accused him was
anything but his *foible*, since he justly considered it his forte. It was his
strong point – his virtue; and it would have required all the logic of a
Brownson to convince him that it was 'anything else.'

I have shown that Touch-and-go Bullet-Head was a wise man; and
the only occasion on which he did not prove infallible, was when,
abandoning that legitimate home for all wise men, the East, he
migrated to the city of Alexander-the-Great-o-nopolis, or some place
of a similar title, out West.

I must do him the justice to say, however, that when he made up
his mind finally to settle in that town, it was under the impression that
no newspaper, and consequently no editor, existed in that particular
section of the country. In establishing 'The Tea-Pot,' he expected to
have the field all to himself. I feel confident he never would have
dreamed of taking up his residence in Alexander-the-Great-o-nopolis,
had he been aware that in Alexander-the-Great-o-nopolis there lived a

gentleman named John Smith (if I rightly remember), who, for many years, had there quietly grown fat in editing and publishing the 'Alexander-the-Great-o-nopolis Gazette.' It was solely, therefore, on account of having been misinformed, that Mr. Bullet-Head found himself in Alex——suppose we call it 'Nopolis,' for short – but, as he *did* find himself there, he determined to keep up his character for obst – for firmness, and remain. So remain he did; and he did more; he unpacked his press, type, etc. etc., rented an office exactly opposite to that of the 'Gazette,' and, on the third morning after his arrival, issued the first number of 'The Alexan' – that is to say of 'The Nopolis Tea-Pot:' as nearly as I can recollect this was the name of the new paper.

The leading article, I must admit, was brilliant – not to say severe. It was especially bitter about things in general – and as for the editor of 'The Gazette,' he was torn all to pieces in particular. Some of Bullet-Head's remarks were really so fiery that I have always, since that time, been forced to look upon John Smith, who is still alive, in the light of a salamander. I cannot pretend to give *all* the 'Tea-Pot's' paragraphs *verbatim*, but one of them runs thus:

'Oh, yes! Oh! we perceive! Oh, no doubt! The editor over the way is a genius – Oh, my! Oh, goodness gracious! – what *is* this world coming to? *Oh, tempora! Oh, Moses!*'

A philippic at once so caustic and so classical alighted like a bombshell among the hitherto peaceful citizens of Nopolis. Groups of excited individuals gathered at the corners of the streets. Every one awaited, with heart-felt anxiety, the reply of the dignified Smith. Next morning it appeared as follows:–

'We quote from "The Tea-Pot" of yesterday the subjoined paragraph – "*Oh*, yes! *Oh*, we perceive! *Oh*, no doubt! *Oh*, my! *Oh*, goodness! *Oh*, tempora! *Oh*, Moses!" Why the fellow is all O! That accounts for his reasoning in a circle, and explains why there is neither beginning nor end to him, nor to anything that he says. We really do not believe the vagabond can write a word that hasn't an O in it. Wonder if this O-thing is a habit of his? By-the-bye, he came away from Down-East in a great hurry. Wonder if he O's as much there as he does here? *O!* it is pitiful.'

The indignation of Mr. Bullet-Head at these scandalous insinuations, I shall not attempt to describe. On the eel-skinning
principle, however, he did not seem to be so much incensed at the
attack upon his integrity as one might have imagined. It was the sneer
at his *style* that drove him to desperation. What! – *he*, Touch-and-go
Bullet-head! – not able to write a word without an O in it! He would
soon let the jackanapes see that he was mistaken. Yes! he would let him
see how *much* he was mistaken, the puppy! He, Touch-and-go Bullet-
Head, of Frogpondium, would let Mr. John Smith perceive that he,
Bullet-Head, could indite, if it so pleased him, a whole paragraph – ay!
a whole article – in which that contemptible vowel should not *once* –
not even *once* – make its appearance. But no; – that would be yielding a
point to the said John Smith. *He*, Bullet-Head, would make *no*
alteration in his style to suit the caprices of any Mr. Smith in
Christendom. Perish so vile a thought! The O for ever! He would
persist in the O. He would be as O-wy as O-wy could be.

Burning with the chivalry of this determination, the great Touch-
and-go, in the next 'Tea-Pot,' came out merely with this simple but
resolute paragraph, in reference to this unhappy affair:–

'The editor of the "Tea-Pot" has the *honour* of advising the editor
of the "Gazette," that he (the "Tea-Pot") will take an opportunity in
to-morrow morning's paper of convincing him (the "Gazette") that he
(the "Tea-Pot") both can and will be *his own master* as regards style – he
(the "Tea-Pot") intending to show him (the "Gazette") the supreme,
and indeed the withering contempt with which the criticism of him (the
"Gazette") inspires the independent bosom of him (the "Tea-Pot"),
by composing for the especial gratification (?) of him (the "Gazette") a
leading article of some extent in which the beautiful vowel – the
Emblem of Eternity – yet so offensive to the hyper-exquisite delicacy
of him (the "Gazette"), shall most certainly *not be avoided* by his (the
"Gazette's") most obedient, humble servant, the "Tea-Pot." "So
much for Buckingham!"'

In fulfilment of the awful threat thus darkly intimated rather than
decidedly enunciated, the great Bullet-Head, turning a deaf ear to all
entreaties for 'copy,' and simply requesting his foreman to 'go to the

d—l,' when he (the foreman) assured him (the 'Tea-Pot!') that it was high time to 'go to press;' turning a deaf ear to everything, I say, the Great Bullet-Head sat up until day-break, consuming the midnight oil, and absorbed in the composition of the really unparalleled paragraph which follows:

'So ho, John! how now? Told you so, you know. Don't crow another time before you're out of the woods! Does your mother *know* you're out? Oh, no, no – so go home at once, now, John, to your odious old woods of Concord! Go home to your woods, old owl, – go! You won't? Oh, poh, poh, John, don't do so! You've *got* to go, you know! so go at once, and don't go slow; for nobody owns you here, you know. Oh, John, John, if you *don't* go you're no *homo* – no! You're only a fowl, an owl; a cow, a sow; a doll, a poll; a poor old good-for-nothing-to-nobody, log, dog, hog, or frog, come out of a Concord bog. Cool, now – cool! *Do* be cool, you fool! None of your crowing, old cock! Don't frown so – don't. Don't hollo, nor howl, nor growl, nor bow-wow-wow! Good Lord, John, how you *do* look! Told you so, you know – but stop rolling your goose of an old poll about so, and go and drown your sorrows in a bowl!'

Exhausted, very naturally, by so stupendous an effort, the great Touch-and-go could attend to nothing further that night. Firmly, composedly, yet with an air of conscious power, he handed his MS. to the devil in waiting, and then walking leisurely home, retired with ineffable dignity to bed.

Meantime the devil to whom the copy was entrusted ran up-stairs to his 'case' in an unutterable hurry, and forthwith made a commencement at 'setting' the MS. 'up.'

In the first place, of course, – as the opening word was 'So' – he made a plunge into the capital S hole, and came out in triumph with a capital S. Elated by this success, he immediately threw himself upon the little *o* box with a blindfold impetuosity – but who shall describe his horror when his fingers came up without the anticipated letter in their clutch? who shall paint his astonishment and rage at perceiving, as he rubbed his knuckles, that he had been only thumping them to no purpose against the bottom of an *empty* box. Not a single little *o* was in the little *o* hole; and glancing fearfully at the Capital O partition, he found *that*, to his extreme terror, in a precisely similar predicament. Awe-stricken, his first impulse was to rush to the foreman.

'Sir!' said he, gasping for breath, 'I can't never set up nothing without no o's.'

'*What* do you mean by that?' growled the foreman, who was in a very ill-humour at being kept up so late.

'Why, sir, there bean't an *o* in the office, neither a big un nor a little un!'

'What – what the d—l has become of all that were in the case?'

'*I* don't know, sir,' said the boy, 'but one of them ere G'zette devils is bin prowling bout here all night, and I spect *he's* gone and cabbaged 'em every one.'

'Dod rot him! I haven't a doubt of it,' replied the foreman, getting purple with rage – 'but I tell you what you do, Bob, that's a good boy – you go over the first chance you get and hook every one of their i's and (d—n them!) their izzards.'

'Jist so,' replied Bob, with a wink and a frown – '*I'll* be into 'em, *I'll* let 'em know a thing or two; but in de meantime, that ere paragrab? *Mus* go in to-night, you know – else there'll be the d—l to pay and'——

'And not a *bit* of pitch hot,' interrupted the foreman, with a deep sigh and an emphasis on the 'bit.' 'Is it a *very* long paragraph, Bob?'

'Shouldn't call it a *wery* long paragrab,' said Bob.

'Ah, well then! do the best you can with it! we *must* get to press,' said the foreman, who was over head and ears in work; 'just stick in some other letter for *o*, nobody's going to read the fellow's trash, any-how.'

'*Wery* well,' replied Bob, 'here goes it!' and off he hurried to his case; muttering as he went – 'Considdeble vell, them ere expressions, perticcler for a man as doesn't swar. So I's to gouge out all their eyes, eh? and d—n all their gizzards! Vell! this here's the chap as is jist able *for* to do it.' The fact is, that although Bob was but twelve years old and four feet high, he was equal to any amount of fight, in a small way.

The exigency here described is by no means of rare occurrence in printing offices; and I cannot tell how to account for it, but the fact is indisputable, that when the exigency *does* occur, it almost always happens that *x* is adopted as a substitute for the letter deficient. The true reason, perhaps, is that *x* is rather the most superabundant letter in the cases, or at least *was* so in old times – long enough to render the substitution in question a habitual thing with printers. As for Bob, he would have considered it heretical to employ any other character in a case of this kind than the *x* to which he had been accustomed.

'I *shell* have to *x* this ere paragrab,' said he to himself, as he read it over in astonishment, 'but it's jest about the awfullest *o*-wy paragrab I ever *did* see:' so *x* it he did, unflinchingly, and to press it went *x*-ed.

Next morning the population of Nopolis were taken all aback by reading in 'The Tea-Pot,' the following extraordinary leader:

'Sx hx Jxhn! hxw nxw? Txld yxu sx, yxu knxw. Dxn't crxw anxther time befxre yxu're xut xf the wxxds! Dxes yxur mxther *knxw* yxu're xut? Xh, nx, nx! – sx gx hxme at xnce nxw, Jxhn, tx yxur xdixus xld wxxds xf Cxncxrd! Gx hxme tx yxur wxxds xld xwl, – gx! Yxu wxn't? Xh, pxh, pxh, Jxhn, dxn't dx sx! Yxu've *gxt* tx gx, yxu knxw! sx gx at xnce, and dxn't gx slxw; fxr nxbxdy xwns yxu here, yxu knxw. Xh, Jxhn, Jxhn, if yxu *dxn't* gx yxu're nx hxmx – nx! Yxu're xnly, a fxwl, an xwl, a cxw, a sxw; a dxll, a pxll; a pxxr xld gxxd-fxr-nxthing-tx-nxbxdy lxg, dxg, hxg xr frxg, cxme xut xf a Cxncxrd bxg. Cxxl, nxw – cxxl! Dx be cxxl, yxu fxxl! Nxne xf yxur crxwing xld cxck! Dxn't frxwn sx – dxn't! Dxn't hxllx, nxr hxwl, nxr grxwl, nxr bxw-wxw-wxw! Gxxd Lxrd, Jxhn, hxw yxu *dx* lxxk! Txld yxu sx, yxu knxw, but stxp rxlling yxur gxxse xf an xld pxll abxut sx and gx and drxwn yxur sxrrxws in a bxwl!'

The uproar occasioned by this mystical and cabalistical article is not to be conceived. The first definite idea entertained by the populace was that some diabolical treason lay concealed in the hieroglyphics; and there was a general rush to Bullet-Head's residence for the purpose of riding him on a rail, but that gentleman was nowhere to be found. He had vanished, no one could tell how; and not even the ghost of him has ever been seen since.

Unable to discover its legitimate object, the popular fury at length subsided, leaving behind it by way of sediment quite a medley of opinion about this unhappy affair.

One gentleman thought the whole an X-ellent joke.

Another said that, indeed, Bullet-Head had shown much X-uberance of fancy.

A third admitted him X-entric but no more.

A fourth could only suppose it the Yankee's design to X-press, in a general way, his X-asperation.

'Say rather to set an X-ample to posterity,' suggested a fifth.

That Bullet-Head had been driven to an X-tremity was clear to all; and in fact, since *that* editor could not be found there was some talk about lynching the other one.

The more common conclusion, however, was that the affair was simply X-traordinary and in-X-plicable. Even the town mathematician confessed that he could make nothing of so dark a problem. X, everybody knew, was an unknown quantity; but in this case (as he properly observed) there was an unknown quantity of X.

The opinion of Bob the devil (who kept dark about his having 'X-ed the paragrab') did not meet with so much attention as I think it deserved, although it was very openly and very fearlessly expressed. He said that for his part, he had no doubt about the matter at all, that it was a clear case, that Mr. Bullet-Head never *could* be persvaded fur to drink like other folks, but vas *con*tinually a-svigging o' that ere blessed XXX ale, and as a naiteral consekvence, it just puffed him up savage, and made him X (cross) in the X-treme.

Lionizing

all people went
Upon their ten toes in wild wonderment.

Bishop Hall's Satires.

I am, that is to say I *was*, a great man, but I am neither the author of
Junius nor the Man in the Iron Mask, for my name, I believe, is
Robert Jones, and I was born somewhere in the city of Fum-Fudge.

The first action of my life was the taking hold of my nose with both
hands. My mother saw this and called me a genius, my father wept for
joy and presented me with a treatise on Nosology. This I mastered
before I was breeched.

I now began to feel my way in the science, and soon came to
understand that, provided a man had a nose sufficiently conspicuous
he might, by merely following it, arrive at a Lionship. But my
attention was not confined to theories alone. Every morning I gave my
proboscis a couple of pulls and swallowed a half-dozen of drams.

When I came of age my father asked me one day if I would step
with him into his study.

'My son,' said he, when we were seated, 'what is the chief end of
your existence?'

'My father,' I answered, 'it is the study of Nosology.'

'And what, Robert,' he inquired, 'is Nosology?'

'Sir,' I said, 'it is the Science of Noses.'

'And can you tell me,' he demanded, 'what is the meaning of a
nose?'

'A nose, my father,' I replied, greatly softened, 'has been variously defined by about a thousand different authors. (Here I pulled out my watch.) 'It is now noon or thereabouts; we shall have time enough to get through with them all before midnight. To commence then: the nose, according to Bartholinus, is that protuberance – that bump – that excrescence – that——'

'Will do, Robert,' interrupted the good old gentleman. 'I am thunderstruck at the extent of your information – I am positively – upon my soul.' (Here he closed his eyes and placed his hand upon his heart.) 'Come here!' (Here he took me by the arm.) 'Your education may now be considered as finished – it is high time you should scuffle for yourself – and you cannot do a better thing than merely follow your nose – so – so – so.'—— (Here he kicked me down stairs and out of the door) – 'so get out of my house, and God bless you!'

As I felt within me the divine *afflatus* I considered this accident rather fortunate than otherwise. I resolved to be guided by the paternal advice. I determined to follow my nose. I gave it a pull or two upon the spot, and wrote a pamphlet on Nosology forthwith.

All Fum-Fudge was in an uproar.

'Wonderful genius!' said the Quarterly.

'Superb physiologist!' said the Westminster.

'Clever fellow!' said the Foreign.

'Fine writer!' said the Edinburgh.

'Profound thinker!' said the Dublin.

'Great man!' said Bentley.

'Divine soul!' said Fraser.

'One of us!' said Blackwood.

'Who can he be?' said Mrs. Bas-Bleu.

'What can he be?' said big Miss Bas-Bleu.

'Where can he be?' said little Miss Bas-Bleu. But I paid these people no attention whatever – I just stepped into the shop of an artist.

The Duchess of Bless-my-Soul was sitting for her portrait; the Marquis of So-and-So was holding the Duchess's poodle; the Earl of This-and-That was flirting with her salts; and his Royal Highness of Touch-me-Not was leaning upon the back of her chair.

I approached the artist and turned up my nose.

'Oh, beautiful!' sighed her Grace.

'Oh my!' lisped the Marquis.

'Oh, shocking!' groaned the Earl.

'Oh, abominable!' growled his Royal Highness.

'What will you take for it?' asked the artist.

'For his *nose*!' shouted her Grace.

'A thousand pounds,' said I, sitting down.

'A thousand pounds?' inquired the artist, musingly.

'A thousand pounds,' said I.

'Beautiful!' said he, entranced.

'A thousand pounds,' said I.

'Do you warrant it?' he asked, turning the nose to the light.

'I do,' said I, blowing it well.

'Is it *quite* original?' he inquired, touching it with reverence.

'Humph!' said I, twisting it to one side.

'Has *no* copy been taken?' he demanded, surveying it through a microscope.

'None,' said I, turning it up.

'*Admirable!*' he ejaculated, thrown quite off his guard by the beauty of the manoeuvre.

'A thousand pounds,' said I.

'A *thousand* pounds?' said he.

'Precisely,' said I.

'A thousand *pounds*!' said he.

'Just so,' said I.

'You shall have them,' said he. 'What a piece of *virtu*!' So he drew me a cheque upon the spot, and took a sketch of my nose. I engaged rooms in Jermyn Street, and sent her Majesty the ninety-ninth edition of the 'Nosology,' with a portrait of the proboscis. That sad little rake the Prince of Wales invited me to dinner.

We were all lions and *recherchés*.

There was a modern Platonist. He quoted Porphyry, Iamblicus, Plotinus, Proclus, Hierocles, Maximus Tyrius, and Syrianus.

There was a human perfectability man. He quoted Turgôt, Price,

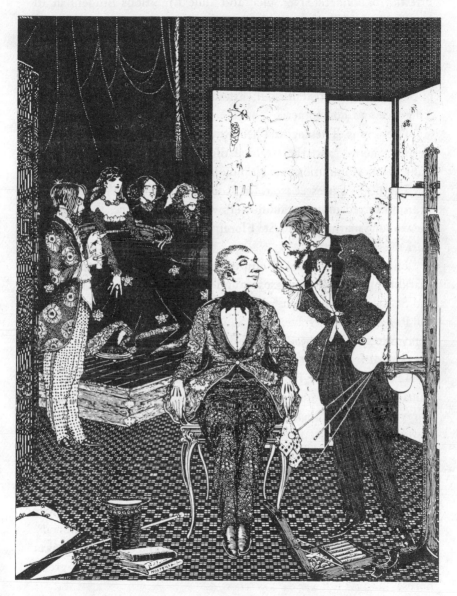

'Has no copy been taken?' he demanded, surveying it through a microscope

Priestley, Condorcet, De Staël, and 'The Ambitious Student in Ill Health.'

There was Sir Positive Paradox. He observed that all fools were philosophers, and that all philosophers were fools.

There was Æstheticus Ethix. He spoke of fire, unity, and atoms; bi-part and pre-existent soul; affinity and discord; primitive intelligence and homoömeria.

There was Theologos Theology. He talked of Eusebius and Arianus; heresy and the Council of Nice; Puseyism and consubstantialism; Homousios and Homoiousios.

There was Fricassée from the Rocher de Cancale. He mentioned Muriton of red tongue; cauliflowers with *velouté* sauce: veal *à la* St. Menehoult; marinade *à la* St. Florentin; and orange jellies *en mosaïques*.

There was Bibulus O'Bumper. He touched upon Latour and Markbrünnen; upon Mousseaux and Chambertin; upon Richbourg and St. George; upon Haubrion, Leonville, and Medoc; upon Barac and Preignac; upon Grâve, upon Sauterne, upon Lafitte, and upon St. Peray. He shook his head at Clos de Vougeot, and told with his eyes shut the difference between Sherry and Amontillado.

There was Signor Tintontintino from Florence. He discoursed of Cimabué, Arpino, Carpaccio, and Argostino – of the gloom of Caravaggio, of the amenity of Albano, of the colours of Titian, of the frowns of Rubens, and of the waggeries of Jan Steen.

There was the President of the Fum-Fudge University. He was of opinion that the moon was called Bendis in Thrace, Bubastis in Egypt, Dian in Rome, and Artemis in Greece.

There was a Grand Turk from Stamboul. He could not help thinking that the angels were horses, cocks, and bulls; that somebody in the sixth heaven had seventy thousand heads; and that the earth was supported by a sky-blue cow with an incalculable number of green horns.

There was Delphinus Polyglott. He told us what had become of the eighty-three lost tragedies of Æschylus; of the fifty-four orations of Isæus; of the three hundred and ninety-one speeches of Lysias; of the hundred and eighty treatises of Theophrastus; of the eighth book of the conic sections of Apollonius; of Pindar's hymns and dithyrambics; and of the five and forty tragedies of Homer Junior.

There was Ferdinand Fitz-Fossillus Feltspar. He informed us all about internal fires and tertiary formations; about aëriforms, fluidiforms, and solidiforms; about quartz and marl; about schist and schorl; about gysum and trap; about talc and calc; about blende and horn-blende; about mica-slate and pudding-stone; about cyanite and lepidolite; about hæmatite and tremolite; about antimony and calcedony; about manganese, and whatever you please.

There was myself. I spoke of myself; – of myself, of myself, of myself; – of Nosology, of my pamphlet, and of myself. I turned up my nose, and I spoke of myself.

'Marvellous clever man!' said the Prince.

'Superb!' said his guests – and next morning her Grace of Bless-my-Soul paid me a visit.

'Will you go to Almack's, pretty creature?' she said, tapping me under the chin.

'Upon honour,' said I.

'Nose and all?' she asked.

'As I live,' I replied.

'Here then is a card, my life. Shall I say you *will* be there?'

'Dear Duchess, with all my heart.'

'Pshaw, no! – but with all your nose?'

'Every bit of it, my love,' said I:– so I gave it a twist or two, and found myself at Almack's.

The rooms were crowded to suffocation.

'He is coming!' said somebody on the staircase.

'He is coming!' said somebody farther up.

'He is coming!' said somebody farther still.

'He is come!' exclaimed the Duchess. 'He is come, the little love!' – and seizing me firmly by both hands, she kissed me thrice upon the nose.

A marked sensation immediately ensued.

'*Diavolo!*' cried Count Capricornutti.

'*Dios guarda!*' muttered Don Stiletto.

'*Mille tonnerres!*' ejaculated the Prince de Grenouille.

'*Tausand teufel!*' growled the Elector of Bluddennuff.

It was not to be borne. I grew angry. I turned short upon Bluddennuff.

'Sir!' said I to him, 'you are a baboon.'

'Sir,' he replied, after a pause, '*Donner und Blitzen!*'

This was all that could be desired. We exchanged cards. At chalk-Farm, the next morning, I shot off his nose – and then called upon my friends.

'*Bête!*' said the first.

'Fool!' said the second.

'Dolt!' said the third.

'Ass!' said the fourth.

'Ninny!' said the fifth.

'Noodle!' said the sixth.

'Be off!' said the seventh.

At all this I felt mortified, and so called upon my father.

'Father,' I asked, 'what is the chief end of my existence?'

'My son,' he replied, 'it is still the study of nosology; but in hitting the Elector upon the nose you have overshot your mark. You have a fine nose, it is true, but then Bluddennuff has none. You are damned, and he has become the hero of the day. I grant you that in Fum-Fudge the greatness of a lion is in proportion to the size of his proboscis – but, good heavens! there is no competing with a lion who has no proboscis at all.'

Three Sundays in a Week

'You hard-hearted, dunder-head, obstinate, rusty, crusty, musty, fusty old savage!' said I, in fancy, one afternoon, to my grand uncle Rumgudgeon – shaking my fist at him in imagination.

Only in imagination. The fact is, some trivial discrepancy *did* exist, just then, between what I said and what I had not the courage to say – between what I did and what I had half a mind to do.

The old porpoise, as I opened the drawing-room door, was sitting with his feet upon the mantelpiece, and a bumper of port in his paw, making strenuous efforts to accomplish the ditty

> Remplis ton verre vide!
> Vide ton verre plein!

'My *dear* uncle,' said I, closing the door gently, and approaching him with the blandest of smiles, 'you are always so *very* kind and considerate, and have evinced your benevolence in so many – so *very* many ways – that – that I feel I have only to suggest this little point to you once more to make sure of your acquiescence.'

'Hem!' said he, 'good boy! go on!'

'I am sure, my dearest uncle (you confounded old rascal!) that you have no design really, seriously, to oppose my union with Kate. This is

merely a joke of yours, I know – ha! ha! ha! how *very* pleasant you are at
times.'

'Ha! ha! ha!' said he, 'curse you! yes!'

'To be sure – of course! I *knew* you were jesting. Now, uncle, all
that Kate and myself wish at present, is that you would oblige us with
your advice as – as regards the *time – you* know, uncle – in short, when
will it be most convenient for yourself, that the wedding shall – shall
come off, you know?'

'Come off, you scoundrel! – what do you mean by that? – Better
wait till it goes on.'

'Ha! ha! ha! – he! he! he! – hi! hi! hi! – ho! ho! ho! – hu! hu! hu! – oh,
that's good! – oh that's capital – *such* a wit! But all we want just *now*,
you know, uncle, is that you would indicate the time precisely.'

'Ah! – precisely?'

'Yes, uncle – that is, if it would be quite agreeable to yourself.'

'Wouldn't it answer, Bobby, if I were to leave it at random – some
time within a year or so, for example? – *must* I say precisely?'

'*If* you please, uncle – precisely.'

'Well then, Bobby, my boy – you're a fine fellow, aren't you? –
since you *will* have the exact time, I'll – why, I'll oblige you for once.'

'Dear uncle!'

'Hush, sir!' (drowning my voice) – 'I'll oblige you for once. You
shall have my consent – and the *plum*, we mustn't forget the plum – let
me see! when shall it be? To-day's Sunday – isn't it? Well then, you
shall be married precisely – *precisely*, now mind! – *when three Sundays
come together in a week!* Do you hear me, sir! *What* are you gaping at? I
say, you shall have Kate and her plum when three Sundays come
together in a week – but not *till* then – you young scapegrace – not *till*
then, if I die for it. You know me – *I'm a man of my word* – now be off!'
Here he swallowed his bumper of port, while I rushed from the room
in despair.

A very 'fine old English gentleman,' was my grand-uncle
Rumgudgeon, but unlike him of the song, he had his weak points. He
was a little, pursy, pompous, passionate, semicircular somebody, with
a red nose, a thick skull, a long purse, and a strong sense of his own

consequence. With the best heart in the world, he contrived, through a predominant whim of *contradiction*, to earn for himself, among those who only knew him superficially, the character of a curmudgeon. Like many excellent people, he seemed possessed with a spirit of *tantalisation*, which might easily, at a casual glance, have been mistaken for malevolence. To every request, a positive 'No!' was his immediate answer; but in the end – in the long, long end – there were exceedingly few requests which he refused. Against all attacks upon his purse he made the most sturdy defence; but the amount extorted from him at last was generally in direct ratio with the length of the siege and the stubbornness of the resistance. In charity no one gave more liberally or with a worse grace.

For the fine arts, and especially for the belles lettres, he entertained a profound contempt. With this he had been inspired by Casimir Perier, whose pert little query '*A quoi un poëte est il bon?*' he was in the habit of quoting, with a very droll pronunciation, as the *ne plus ultra* of logical wit. Thus my own inkling for the Muses had excited his entire displeasure. He assured me one day, when I asked him for a new copy of Horace, that the translation of '*Poeta nascitur non fit*' was 'a nasty poet for nothing fit' – a remark which I took in high dudgeon. His repugnance to 'the humanities' had also much increased of late, by an accidental bias in favour of what he supposed to be natural science. Somebody had accosted him in the street, mistaking him for no less a personage than Doctor Dubble L. Dee, the lecturer upon quack physics. This set him off at a tangent; and just at the epoch of this story – for story it is getting to be after all – my grand-uncle Rumgudgeon was accessible and pacific only upon points which happened to chime in with the caprioles of the hobby he was riding. For the rest, he laughed with his arms and legs, and his politics were stubborn and easily understood. He thought, with Horsley, that 'the people have nothing to do with the laws but to obey them.'

I had lived with the old gentleman all my life. My parents, in dying, had bequeathed me to him as a rich legacy. I believe the old villain loved me as his own child – nearly if not quite as well as he loved Kate – but it was a dog's existence that he led me after all. From my first year until my fifth, he obliged me with very regular floggings. From five to fifteen, he threatened me hourly with the House of Correction. From fifteen to twenty, not a day passed in which he did not promise to cut me off with a shilling. I was a sad dog, it is true – but then it was a part of my nature – a point of my faith. In Kate, however, I had a firm friend, and I knew it. She was a good girl, and told me very sweetly that I might have her (plum and all) whenever I could badger my grand-uncle Rumgudgeon into the necessary consent. Poor girl! – she was barely fifteen, and without this consent her little amount in the funds was not come-at-able until five immeasurable summers had 'dragged their slow length along.' What then, to do? At fifteen, or even at twenty-one (for I had now passed my fifth olympiad) five years in prospect are very much the same as five hundred. In vain we besieged the old gentleman with importunities. Here was a *pièce de résistance* (as Messieurs Ude and Carême would say) which suited his perverse fancy to a T. It would have stirred the indignation of Job himself to see how much like an old mouser he behaved to us two poor wretched little mice. In his heart he wished for nothing more ardently than our union. He had made up his mind to this all along. In fact, he would have given ten thousand pounds from his own pocket (Kate's plum was *her own*) if he could have invented anything like an excuse for complying with our very natural wishes. But then we had been so imprudent as to broach the subject *ourselves*. Not to oppose it under such circumstances, I sincerely believe was not in his power.

I have said already that he had his weak points; but in speaking of these I must not be understood as referring to his obstinacy, which was one of his strong points – '*assurement ce n'était pas sa foible.*' When I mention his weakness I make allusion to a *bizarre* old womanish superstition which beset him. He was great in dreams, portents, *et id genus omne* of rigmarole. He was excessively punctilious, too, upon small points of honour, and, after his own fashion, was a man of his word, beyond doubt. This was, in fact, one of his hobbies. The *spirit* of his vows he made no scruple of setting at naught, but the *letter* was a bond inviolable. Now it was this latter peculiarity in his disposition, of which Kate's ingenuity enabled us one fine day, not long after our interview in the dining-room, to take a very unexpected advantage; and, having thus, in the fashion of all modern bards and orators, exhausted in *prolegomena*, all the time at my command, and nearly all the room at my disposal, I will sum up in a few words what constitutes the whole pith of the story.

It happened then – so the Fates ordered it – that among the naval acquaintances of my betrothed were two gentlemen who had just set foot upon the shores of England, after a year's absence each in foreign travel. In company with these gentlemen, my cousin and I, preconcertedly, paid Uncle Rumgudgeon a visit on the afternoon of Sunday, October the tenth, – just three weeks after the memorable decision which had so cruelly defeated our hopes. For about half-an-hour the conversation ran upon ordinary topics; but at last, we contrived, quite naturally, to give it the following turn:–

Capt. Pratt. 'Well, I have been absent just one year. Just one year to-day, as I live – let me see! yes! – this is October the tenth. You remember, Mr. Rumgudgeon, I called this day year to bid you good-bye. And by the way, it *does* seem something like a coincidence, does it not – that our friend Captain Smitherton, here, has been absent exactly a year also – a year to-day?'

Smitherton. 'Yes! just one year to a fraction. You will remember, Mr. Rumgudgeon, that I called with Captain Pratt on this very day last year, to pay my parting respects.'

Uncle. 'Yes, yes, yes – I remember it very well – very queer indeed! Both of you gone just one year. A very strange coincidence, indeed! Just what Doctor Dubble L. Dee would denominate an extraordinary concurrence of events. Doctor Dub——'

Kate. (*Interrupting*.) 'To be sure, papa, it *is* something strange; but then Captain Pratt and Captain Smitherton didn't go altogether the same route, and that makes a difference you know.'

Uncle. 'I don't know any such thing, you huzzy! How should I? I think it only makes the matter more remarkable. Doctor Dubble L. Dee'——

Kate. 'Why, papa, Captain Pratt went round Cape Horn, and Captain Smitherton doubled the Cape of Good Hope.'

Uncle. 'Precisely! – the one went east and the other went west, you jade, and they both have gone quite round the world. By-the-bye, Doctor Dubble L. Dee'——

Myself (*hurriedly*). 'Captain Pratt, you must come and spend the evening with us to-morrow – you and Smitherton – you can tell us all about your voyage, and we'll have a game of whist, and——'

Pratt. 'Whist, my dear fellow. You forget. To-morrow will be Sunday. Some other evening'——

Kate. 'Oh, no, fie! – Robert's not *quite* so bad as that. *To-day's* Sunday.'

Uncle. 'To be sure – to be sure!'

Pratt. 'I beg both your pardons – but I can't be so much mistaken. I know to-morrow's Sunday, because'——

Smitherton (*much surprised*). 'What *are* you all thinking about! Wasn't *yesterday* Sunday, I should like to know?'

All. 'Yesterday, indeed! you *are* out!'

Uncle. 'To-day's Sunday, I say – don't *I* know?'

Pratt. 'Oh no! – to-morrow's Sunday.'

Smitherton. 'You are *all* mad – every one of you. I am as positive that yesterday was Sunday, as I am that I sit upon this chair.'

Kate (*jumping up eagerly*). 'I see it – I see it all. Papa, this is a judgment upon you, about – about you know what. Let me alone, and I'll explain it all in a minute. It's a very simple thing, indeed. Captain Smitherton says that yesterday was Sunday: so it was; he is right. Cousin Bobby, and uncle and I, say that to-day is Sunday: so it is; we are right. Captain Pratt maintains that to-morrow will be Sunday: so it will; he is right, too. The fact is, we are all right, and thus *three Sundays have come together in a week*.'

Smitherton (*after a pause*). 'By-the-bye, Pratt, Kate has us completely. What fools we two are! Mr. Rumgudgeon, the matter stands thus: the earth you know is twenty-four thousand miles in circumference. Now this globe of the earth turns upon its own axis – revolves – spins round – these twenty-four thousand miles of extent, going from west to east, in precisely twenty-four hours. Do you understand, Mr. Rumgudgeon?'

Uncle. 'To be sure – to be sure – Doctor Dub——'

Smitherton (*drowning his voice*). 'Well, sir; that is at the rate of one thousand miles per hour. Now, suppose that I sail from this position a thousand miles east. Of course, I anticipate the rising of the sun here at London by just one hour. I see the sun rise one hour before you do. Proceeding in the same direction yet another thousand miles, I anticipate the rising by two hours – another thousand, and I anticipate it by three hours, and so on, until I go entirely round the globe, and back to this spot, when, having gone twenty-four thousand miles east, I anticipate the rising of the London sun by no less than twenty-four hours; that is to say, I am a day *in advance* of your time. Understand, eh?'

Uncle. 'But, Dubble L. Dee'——

Smitherton (*speaking very loud*). 'Captain Pratt, on the contrary, when he had sailed a thousand miles west of this position, was an hour, and when he had sailed twenty-four thousand miles west, was twenty-four hours, or one day *behind* the time at London. Thus, with me, yesterday was Sunday – thus, with you, to-day is Sunday – and thus, with Pratt, to-morrow will be Sunday. And what is more, Mr. Rumgudgeon, it is positively clear that we are *all right*; for there can be no philosophical reason assigned why the idea of one of us should have preference over that of the other.'

Uncle. 'My eyes! – well, Kate – well, Bobby! this *is* a judgment upon me, as you say. But I am a man of my word – *mark that!* you shall have her, boy (plum and all), when you please. Done up, by Jove! Three Sundays all in a row! I'll go and take Dubble L. Dee's opinion upon *that*.'

The Assignation

Stay for me there! I will not fail
To meet thee in that hollow vale.

Exequy on the death of his wife, by Henry King, Bishop of Chichester.

Ill-fated and mysterious man! bewildered in the brilliancy of thine own imagination, and fallen in the flames of thine own youth! Again in fancy I behold thee! Once more thy form hath risen before me! – not – O not as thou art in the cold valley and shadow – but as thou *shouldst be* – squandering away a life of magnificent meditation in that city of dim visions, thine own Venice – which is a star-beloved Elysium of the sea, and the wide windows of whose Palladian palaces look down with a deep and bitter meaning upon the secrets of her silent waters. Yes! I repeat it – as thou *shouldst be*. There are surely other worlds than this – other thoughts than the thoughts of the multitude – other speculations than the speculations of the sophist. Who then shall call thy conduct into question? who blame thee for thy visionary hours, or denounce those occupations as a wasting away of life, which were but the overflowings of thine everlasting energies?

It was at Venice, beneath the covered archway there called the *Ponte di Sospiri*, that I met for the third or fourth time the person of whom I speak. It is with a confused recollection that I bring to mind the circumstances of that meeting. Yet I remember – ah! how should I forget? – the deep midnight, the Bridge of Sighs, the beauty of woman, and the Genius of Romance, that stalked up and down the narrow canal.

It was a night of unusual gloom. The great clock of the Piazza had sounded the fifth hour of the Italian evening. The square of the Campanile lay silent and deserted, and the lights in the old Ducal Palace were dying fast away. I was returning home from the Piazetta by way of the Grand Canal. But as my gondola arrived opposite the mouth of the canal San Marco, a female voice from its recesses broke suddenly upon the night in one wild, hysterical, and long-continued shriek. Startled at the sound, I sprang upon my feet: while the gondolier, letting slip his single oar, lost it in the pitchy darkness beyond a chance of recovery, and we were consequently left to the guidance of the current which here sets from the greater into the smaller channel. Like some huge and sable-feathered condor, we were slowly drifting down towards the Bridge of Sighs, when a thousand flambeaux flashing from the windows, and down the staircases of the Ducal Palace, turned all at once that deep gloom into a livid and preternatural day.

A child, slipping from the arms of its own mother, had fallen from an upper window of the lofty structure into the deep and dim canal. The quiet waters had closed placidly over their victim; and although my own gondola was the only one in sight, many a stout swimmer, already in the stream, was seeking in vain upon the surface the treasure which was to be found, alas! only within the abyss. Upon the broad black marble flagstones at the entrance of the palace, and a few steps above the water, stood a figure which none who then saw can have ever since forgotten. It was the Marchesa Aphrodite – the adoration of all Venice – the gayest of the gay – the most lovely where all were beautiful – but still the young wife of the old and intriguing Mentoni, and the mother of that fair child, her first and only one, who now, deep beneath the murky water, was thinking in bitterness of heart upon her sweet caresses, and exhausting its little life in struggles to call upon her name.

She stood alone. Her small, bare, and silvery feet gleamed in the black marble beneath her. Her hair, not as yet more than half loosened for the night from its ballroom array, clustered amid a shower of diamonds round and round her classical head, in curls like those of the

It was the Marchesa Aphrodite – the adoration of all Venice

'*I had myself no power to move from the upright position I had assumed*'

young hyacinth. A snowy-white and gauze-like drapery seemed to be nearly the sole covering to her delicate form; but the mid-summer and midnight air was hot, sullen, and still, and no motion in the statue-like form itself stirred even the folds of that raiment of very vapour which hung around it as the heavy marble hangs around the Niobe. Yet – strange to say! – her large lustrous eyes were not turned downwards upon that grave wherein her brightest hope lay buried – but riveted in a widely different direction! The prison of the Old Republic is, I think, the stateliest building in all Venice; but how could that lady gaze so fixedly upon it, when beneath her lay stifling her own child? Yon dark gloomy niche, too, yawns right opposite her chamber window – what then *could* there be in its shadows, in its architecture, in its ivy-wreathed and solemn cornices – that the Marchesa di Mentoni had not wondered at a thousand times before? Nonsense! – Who does not remember, that at such a time as this, the eye, like a shattered mirror, multiplies the images of its sorrow, and sees in innumerable far-off places, the woe which is close at hand?

Many steps above the Marchesa, and within the arch of the water-gate, stood, in full dress, the Satyr-like figure of Mentoni himself. He was occasionally occupied in thrumming a guitar, and seemed *ennuyé* to the very death, as at intervals he gave directions for the recovery of his child. Stupefied and aghast, I had myself no power to move from the upright position I had assumed upon first hearing the shriek, and must have presented to the eyes of the agitated group a spectral and ominous appearance, as with pale countenance and rigid limbs I floated down among them in that funereal gondola.

All efforts proved in vain. Many of the most energetic in the search were relaxing their exertions, and yielding to a gloomy sorrow. There seemed but little hope for the child (how much less then for the mother!) but now, from the interior of that dark niche which has been already mentioned as forming a part of the Old Republican prison, and as fronting the lattice of the Marchesa, a figure muffled in a cloak stepped out within reach of the light, and pausing a moment upon the verge of the giddy descent, plunged headlong into the canal. As in an instant afterwards he stood with the still living and breathing child within his grasp upon the marble flagstones by the side of the Marchesa, his cloak heavy with the drenching water became unfastened, and, falling in folds about his feet, discovered to the wonder-stricken spectators the graceful person of a very young man, with the sound of whose name the greater part of Europe was then ringing.

No word spoke the deliverer. But the Marchesa! She will now receive her child – she will press it to her heart – she will cling to its little form, and smother it with her caresses. Alas! *another's* arms have taken it from the stranger – *another's* arms have taken it away, and borne it afar off, unnoticed, into the palace! And the Marchesa! Her lip – her beautiful lip trembles: tears are gathering in her eyes – those eyes which, like Pliny's acanthus, are 'soft and almost liquid.' Yes! tears are gathering in those eyes – and see! the entire woman thrills throughout the soul, and the statue has started into life! The pallor of the marble countenance, the swelling of the marble bosom, the very purity of the marble feet, we behold suddenly flushed over with a tide of ungovernable crimson; and a slight shudder quivers about her delicate frame, as a gentle air at Napoli about the rich silver lilies in the grass.

Why *should* that lady blush? To this demand there is no answer – except that having left, in the eager haste and terror of a mother's heart, the privacy of her own *boudoir*, she has neglected to enthral her tiny feet in their slippers, and utterly forgotten to throw over her Venetian shoulders that drapery which is their due. What other possible reason could there have been for her so blushing? – for the glance of those wild appealing eyes? – for the unusual tumult of that throbbing bosom? – for the convulsive pressure of that trembling hand? – that hand which fell, as Mentoni turned into the palace, accidentally, upon the hand of the stranger. What reason could there have been for the low – the singularly low tone of those unmeaning words which the lady uttered hurriedly in bidding him adieu? 'Thou hast conquered,' she said, or the murmurs of the water deceived me; 'thou hast conquered – one hour after sunrise – we shall meet – so let it be!'

The tumult had subsided, the lights had died away within the palace, and the stranger whom I now recognised stood alone upon the flags. He shook with inconceivable agitation, and his eye glanced around in search of a gondola. I could not do less than offer him the service of my own; and he accepted the civility. Having obtained an oar at the water-gate, we proceeded together to his residence, while he rapidly recovered his self-possession, and spoke of our former slight acquaintance in terms of great apparent cordiality.

There are some subjects upon which I take pleasure in being minute. The person of the stranger – let me call him by this title, who to all the world was still a stranger – the person of the stranger is one of these subjects. In height he might have been below rather than above the medium size: although there were moments of intense passion when his frame actually *expanded* and belied the assertion. The light, almost slender symmetry of his figure, promised more of that ready activity which he evinced at the Bridge of Sighs, than of that Herculean strength which he has been known to wield without an effort, upon occasions of more dangerous emergency. With the mouth and chin of a deity – singular, wild, full, liquid eyes, whose shadows varied from pure hazel to intense and brilliant jet – and a profusion of curling black hair, from which a forehead of unusual breadth gleamed forth at intervals all light and ivory – his were features than which I have seen none more classically regular, except, perhaps, the marble ones of the Emperor Commodus. Yet his countenance was, nevertheless, one of those which all men have seen at some period of their lives, and have never afterwards seen again. It had no peculiar – it had no settled predominant expression to be fastened upon the memory; a countenance seen and instantly forgotten – but forgotten with a vague and never-ceasing desire of recalling it to mind. Not that the spirit of each rapid passion failed, at any time, to throw its own distinct image upon the mirror of that face – but that the mirror, mirror-like, retained no vestige of the passion when the passion had departed.

Upon leaving him on the night of our adventure, he solicited me, in what I thought an urgent manner, to call upon him *very* early the next morning. Shortly after sunrise I found myself accordingly at his Palazzo, one of those huge structures of gloomy, yet fantastic pomp, which tower above the waters of the Grand Canal in the vicinity of the Rialto. I was shown up a broad winding staircase of mosaics into an apartment whose unparalleled splendour burst through the opening door with an actual glare, making me blind and dizzy with luxuriousness.

I knew my acquaintance to be wealthy. Report had spoken of his possessions in terms which I had even ventured to call terms of ridiculous exaggeration. But as I gazed about me, I could not bring myself to believe that the wealth of any subject in Europe could have supplied the princely magnificence which burned and blazed around.

Although, as I say, the sun had arisen, yet the room was still brilliantly lighted up. I judge from this circumstance, as well as from an air of exhaustion in the countenance of my friend, that he had not retired to bed during the whole of the preceding night. In the architecture and embellishments of the chamber, the evident design had been to dazzle and astound. Little attention had been paid to the *decora* of what is technically called *keeping*, or to the proprieties of nationality. The eye wandered from object to object, and rested upon none – neither the *grotesques* of the Greek painters, nor the sculptures of the best Italian days, nor the huge carvings of untutored Egypt. Rich draperies in every part of the room trembled to the vibration of low, melancholy music, whose origin was not to be discovered. The senses were oppressed by mingled and conflicting perfumes, reeking up from strange convolute censers, together with multitudinous flaring and flickering tongues of emerald and violet fire. The rays of the newly risen sun poured in upon the whole, through windows, formed each of a single pane of crimson-tinted glass. Glancing to and fro, in a thousand reflections, from curtains which rolled from their cornices like cataracts of molten silver, the beams of natural glory mingled at length fitfully with the artificial light, and lay weltering in subdued masses upon a carpet of rich, liquid-looking cloth of Chili gold.

'Ha! ha! ha – ha! ha! ha!' – laughed the proprietor, motioning me to a seat as I entered the room, and throwing himself back at full length upon an ottoman. 'I see,' said he, perceiving that I could not immediately reconcile myself to the *bienseance* of so singular a welcome

– 'I see you are astonished at my apartment – at my statues – my pictures – my originality of conception in architecture and upholstery! absolutely drunk, eh, with my magnificence? But pardon me, my dear sir' (here his tone of voice dropped to the very spirit of cordiality), 'pardon me for my uncharitable laughter. You appeared so *utterly* astonished. Besides, some things are so completely ludicrous that a man *must* laugh or die. To die laughing must be the most glorious of all glorious deaths! Sir Thomas More – a very fine man was Sir Thomas More – Sir Thomas More died laughing, you remember. Also in the *Absurdities* of Ravisius Textor there is a long list of characters who came to the same magnificent end. Do you know, however,' continued he, musingly, 'that at Sparta (which is now Palæochori), at Sparta, I say, to the west of the citadel, among a chaos of scarcely visible ruins, is a kind of *socle* upon which are still legible the letters ΛΑΞΜ. They are undoubtedly part of ΓΕΛΑΞΜΑ. Now, at Sparta were a thousand temples and shrines to a thousand different divinities. How exceedingly strange that the altar of Laughter should have survived all the others! But in the present instance,' he resumed, with a singular alteration of voice and manner, 'I have no right to be merry at your expense. You might well have been amazed. Europe cannot produce anything so fine as this my little regal cabinet. My other apartments are by no means of the same order – mere *ultras* of fashionable insipidity. This is better than fashion – is it not? Yet this has but to be seen to become the rage –' that is with those who could afford it at the cost of their entire patrimony. I have guarded, however, against any such profanation. With one exception you are the only human being, besides myself and my *valet*, who has been admitted within the mysteries of these imperial precincts since they have been bedizened as you see!'

I bowed in acknowledgment – for the overpowering sense of splendour, and perfume, and music, together with the unexpected eccentricity of his address and manner, prevented me from expressing in words my appreciation of what I might have construed into a compliment.

'Here,' he resumed, arising and leaning on my arm as he sauntered

around the apartment, 'here are paintings from the Greeks to
Cimabue, and from Cimabue to the present hour. Many are chosen, as
you see, with little deference to the opinions of Virtu. They are all,
however, fitting tapestry for a chamber such as this. Here, too, are
some *chef d'œuvres* of the unknown great; and here unfinished
designs by men celebrated in their day, whose very names the
perspicacity of the academies has left to silence and to me. What think
you,' said he, turning abruptly as he spoke – 'what think you of this
Madonna della Pieta?'

'It is Guido's own,' I said with all the enthusiasm of my nature, for
I had been poring intently over its surpassing loveliness. 'It is Guido's
own! – how *could* you have obtained it? she is undoubtedly in painting
what the Venus is in sculpture.'

'Ha!' said he thoughtfully, 'the Venus – the beautiful Venus? – the
Venus of the Medici? – she of the diminutive head and the gilded hair?
Part of the left arm (here his voice dropped so as to be heard with
difficulty) and all the right are restorations; and in the coquetry of that
right arm lies, I think, the quintessence of all affectation. Give *me* the
Canova! Apollo, too, is a copy – there can be no doubt of it – blind fool
that I am who cannot behold the boasted inspiration of the Apollo! I
cannot help – pity me! – I cannot help preferring the Antinous. Was it
not Socrates who said that the statuary found his statue in the block
of marble? Then Michael Angelo was by no means original in his
couplet –

> 'Non ha l'ottimo artista alcun concetto
> Che un marmo solo in se non circunscriva.'

It has been or should be remarked that in the manner of the true
gentleman we are always aware of a difference from the bearing of the
vulgar, without being at once precisely able to determine in what such
difference consists. Allowing the remark to have applied in its full
force to the outward demeanour of my acquaintance, I felt it on that
eventful morning still more fully applicable to his moral temperament
and character. Nor can I better define that peculiarity of spirit which

seemed to place him so essentially apart from all other human beings, than by calling it a *habit* of intense and continual thought pervading even his most trivial actions – intruding upon his moments of dalliance, and interweaving itself with his very flashes of merriment – like adders which writhe from out the eyes of the grinning masks in the cornices around the temples of Persepolis.

I could not help, however, repeatedly observing through the mingled tone of levity and solemnity with which he rapidly descanted upon matters of little importance, a certain air of trepidation – a degree of nervous *unction* in action and in speech – an unquiet excitability of manner which appeared to me at all times unaccountable, and upon some occasions even filled me with alarm. Frequently, too, pausing in the middle of a sentence whose commencement he had apparently forgotten, he seemed to be listening in the deepest attention as if either in momentary expectation of a visitor, or to sounds which must have had existence in his imagination alone.

It was during one of these reveries or pauses of apparent abstraction, that, in turning over a page of the poet and scholar Politian's beautiful tragedy, 'The Orfeo' (the first native Italian tragedy), which lay near me upon an ottoman, I discovered a passage underlined in pencil. It was a passage towards the end of the third act – a passage of the most heart-stirring excitement – a passage which although tainted with impurity no man shall read without a thrill of novel emotion – no woman without a sigh. The whole page was blotted with fresh tears; and upon the opposite interleaf were the following English lines, written in a hand so very different from the peculiar characters of my acquaintance, that I had some difficulty in recognising it as his own:–

Thou wast that all to me, love,
　　For which my soul did pine –
A green isle in the sea, love,
　　A fountain and a shrine,
All wreathed with fairy fruits and flowers;
　　And all the flowers were mine.

Ah, dream too bright to last!
　　Ah, starry Hope, that didst arise
But to be overcast!
　　A voice from out the Future cries,
'Onward!' – but o'er the past
　　(Dim gulf!) my spirit hovering lies,
Mute – motionless – aghast!

For alas! alas! with me
　　The light of life is o'er.
'No more – no more – no more,'
　　(Such language holds the solemn sea
To the sands upon the shore),
　　Shall bloom the thunder-blasted tree,
Or the stricken eagle soar!

Now all my hours are trances;
　　And all my nightly dreams
Are where thy dark eye glances,
　　And where thy footstep gleams –
In what ethereal dances –
　　By what Italian streams!

Alas! for that accursed time
　　They bore thee o'er the billow,
From Love to titled age and crime,
　　And an unholy pillow! –
From me, and from our misty clime,
　　Where weeps the silver willow!

That these lines were written in English – a language with which I
had not believed their author acquainted – afforded me little matter
for surprise. I was too well aware of the extent of his acquirements, and
of the singular pleasure he took in concealing them from observation,
to be astonished at any similar discovery; but the place of date I must

confess occasioned me no little amazement. It had been originally written in *London*, and afterwards carefully overscored – not, however, so effectually as to conceal the word from a scrutinising eye. I say this occasioned me no little amazement; for I well remember that, in a former conversation with my friend, I particularly inquired if he had at any time met in London the Marchesa di Mentoni, (who for some years previous to her marriage had resided in that city), when his answer, if I mistake not, gave me to understand that he had never visited the metropolis of Great Britain. I might as well here mention that I have more than once heard (without, of course, giving credit to a report involving so many improbabilities) that the person of whom I speak, was not only by birth, but in education, an *Englishman*.

'There is one painting,' said he, without being aware of my notice of the tragedy – 'there is still one painting which you have not seen.' And throwing aside a drapery, he discovered a full-length portrait of the Marchesa Aphrodite.

Human art could have done no more in the delineation of her superhuman beauty. The same ethereal figure which stood before me the preceding night upon the steps of the Ducal Palace, stood before me once again. But in the expression of the countenance, which was beaming all over with smiles, there still lurked (incomprehensible anomaly!) that fitful strain of melancholy which will ever be found inseparable from the perfection of the beautiful. Her right arm lay folded over her bosom. With her left she pointed downward to a curiously fashioned vase. One small, fairy foot, alone visible, barely touched the earth; and, scarcely discernible in the brilliant atmosphere which seemed to encircle and enshrine her loveliness, floated a pair of the most delicately imagined wings. My glance fell from the painting to the figure of my friend, and the vigorous words of Chapman's *Bussy D'Ambois* quivered instinctively upon my lips:

> 'He is up
> There like a Roman statue! He will stand
> Till Death hath made him marble!'

'Come,' he said at length, turning towards a table of richly enamelled and massive silver, upon which were a few goblets fantastically stained, together with two large Etruscan vases, fashioned in the same extraordinary model as that in the foreground of the portrait, and filled with what I supposed to be Johannisberger. 'Come,' he said abruptly, 'let us drink! It is early – but let us drink. It is *indeed* early,' he continued, musingly, as a cherub with a heavy golden hammer made the apartment ring with the first hour after sunrise: 'it is *indeed* early – but what matters it? let us drink! Let us pour out an offering to yon solemn sun which these gaudy lamps and censers are so eager to subdue!' And, having made me pledge him in a bumper, he swallowed in rapid succession several goblets of the wine.

'To dream,' he continued, resuming the tone of his desultory conversation, as he held up to the rich light of a censer one of the magnificent vases – 'to dream has been the business of my life. I have therefore framed for myself, as you see, a bower of dreams. In the heart of Venice could I have erected a better? You behold around you, it is true, a medley of architectural embellishments. The chastity of Ionia is offended by antediluvian devices, and the sphynxes of Egypt are outstretched upon carpets of gold. Yet the effect is incongruous to the timid alone. Proprieties of place, and especially of time, are the bugbears which terrify mankind from the contemplation of the magnificent. Once I was myself a decorist; but that sublimation of folly has palled upon my soul. All this is now the fitter for my purpose. Like these arabesque censers, my spirit is writhing in fire, and the delirium of this scene is fashioning me for the wilder visions of that land of real dreams whither I am now rapidly departing.' He here paused abruptly, bent his head to his bosom, and seemed to listen to a sound which I could not hear. At length, erecting his frame, he looked upwards, and ejaculated the lines of the Bishop of Chichester:

'Stay for me there! I will not fail
To meet thee in that hollow vale.'

In the next instant, confessing the power of the wine, he threw himself at full length upon an ottoman.

A quick step was now heard upon the staircase, and a loud knock at the door rapidly succeeded. I was hastening to anticipate a second disturbance, when a page of Mentoni's household burst into the room, and faltered out, in a voice choking with emotion, the incoherent words, 'My mistress! – my mistress! – Poisoned! – poisoned! Oh, beautiful – oh, beautiful Aphrodite!'

Bewildered, I flew to the ottoman, and endeavoured to arouse the sleeper to a sense of the startling intelligence. But his limbs were rigid – his lips were livid – his lately beaming eyes were riveted in *death*. I staggered back towards the table – my hand fell upon a cracked and blackened goblet – and a consciousness of the entire and terrible truth flashed suddenly over my soul.

The Angel of the Odd

An Extravaganza

It was a chilly November afternoon. I had just consummated an unusually hearty dinner, of which the dyspeptic *truffe* formed not the least important item, and was sitting alone in the dining-room with my feet upon the fender and at my elbow a small table which I had rolled up to the fire, and upon which were some apologies for dessert, with some miscellaneous bottles of wine, spirit and *liqueur*. In the morning I had been reading Glover's 'Leonidas,' Wilkie's 'Epigoniad,' Lamartine's 'Pilgrimage,' Barlow's 'Columbiad,' Tuckerman's 'Sicily,' and Griswold's 'Curiosities;' I am willing to confess, therefore, that I now felt a little stupid. I made effort to arouse myself by a frequent aid of Lafitte, and all failing, I betook myself to a stray newspaper in despair. Having carefully perused the column of 'houses to let,' and the column of 'dogs lost,' and then the two columns of 'wives and apprentices runaway,' I attacked with great resolution the editorial matter, and reading it from beginning to end without understanding a syllable, conceived the possibility of its being Chinese, and so re-read it from the end to the beginning, but with no more satisfactory result. I was about throwing away in disgust

This folio of four pages, happy work
Which not even critics criticise,

when I felt my attention somewhat aroused by the paragraph which follows:–

'The avenues to death are numerous and strange. A London paper mentions the decease of a person from a singular cause. He was playing at "puff the dart," which is played with a long needle inserted in some worsted, and blown at a target through a tin tube. He placed the needle at the wrong end of the tube, and drawing his breath strongly to puff the dart forward with force, drew the needle into his throat. It entered the lungs, and in a few days killed him.'

Upon seeing this I fell into a great rage, without exactly knowing why. 'This thing,' I exclaimed, 'is a contemptible falsehood – a poor hoax – the lees of the invention of some pitiable penny-a-liner, of some wretched concocter of accidents in Cocaigne. These fellows knowing the extravagant gullibility of the age set their wits to work in the imagination of improbable possibilities, of odd accidents as they term them, but to a reflecting intellect (like mine,' I added, in parenthesis, putting my forefinger unconsciously to the side of my nose), 'to a contemplative understanding such as I myself possess, it seems evident at once that the marvellous increase of late in these "odd accidents" is by far the oddest accident of all. For my own part, I intend to believe nothing henceforward that has anything of the "singular" about it.'

'Mein Gott, den, vat a vool you bees for dat!' replied one of the most remarkable voices I ever heard. At first I took it for a rumbling in my ears – such as a man sometimes experiences when getting very drunk – but upon second thought, I considered the sound as more nearly resembling that which proceeds from an empty barrel beaten with a big stick; and, in fact, this I should have concluded it to be, but for the articulation of the syllables and words. I am by no means naturally nervous, and the very few glasses of Lafitte which I had sipped served to embolden me a little, so that I felt nothing of trepidation, but merely uplifted my eyes with a leisurely movement and looked carefully around the room for the intruder. I could not, however, perceive any one at all.

'Humph!' resumed the voice as I continued my survey, 'you mus pe so dronk as de pig den for not zee me as I zit here at your zide.'

Hereupon I bethought me of looking immediately before my nose, and there, sure enough, confronting me at the table sat a personage nondescript, although not altogether indescribable. His body was a winepipe or a rum puncheon, or something of that character, and had a truly Falstaffian air. In its nether extremity were inserted two kegs, which seemed to answer all the purposes of legs. For arms there dangled from the upper portion of the carcase two tolerably long bottles with the necks outward for hands. All the head that I saw the monster possessed of was one of those Hessian canteens which resemble a large snuff-box with a hole in the middle of the lid. This canteen (with a funnel on its top like a cavalier cap slouched over the eyes) was set on edge upon the puncheon, with the hole towards myself; and through this hole, which seemed puckered up like the mouth of a very precise old maid, the creature was emitting certain rumbling and grumbling noises which he evidently intended for intelligible talk.

'I zay,' said he, 'you mos pe dronk as de pig, vor zit dare and not zee me zet ere; and I zay, doo, you mos pe pigger vool as de goose, vor to dispelief vat is print in de print. 'Tis de troof – dat it iz – ebery vord ob it.'

'Who are you, pray?' said I with much dignity, although somewhat puzzled; 'how did you get here? and what is it you are talking about?'

'As vor ow I com'd ere,' replied the figure, 'dat is none of your pizziness; and as vor vat I pe talking apout, I be talk apout vat I tink proper; and as vor who I be, vy dat is de very ting I com'd here for to let you zee for yourself.'

'You are a drunken vagabond,' said I, 'and I shall ring the bell and order my footman to kick you into the street.'

'He! he! he!' said the fellow, 'hu! hu! hu! dat you can't do.'

'Can't do!' said I, 'what do you mean? – I can't do what?'

'Ring de pell,' he replied, attempting a grin with his little villainous mouth.

Upon this I made an effort to get up in order to put my threat into execution, but the ruffian just reached across the table very deliberately, and hitting me a tap on the forehead with the neck of one of the long bottles, knocked me back into the armchair from which I had half arisen. I was utterly astounded, and for a moment was quite at a loss what to do. In the meantime he continued his talk.

'You zee,' said he, 'it iz te bess vor zit still; and now you shall know who I pe. Look at me! zee! I am te *Angel ov te Odd*.'

'And odd enough, too,' I ventured to reply; 'but I was always under the impression that an angel had wings.'

'Te wing!' he cried, highly incensed, 'vat I pe do mit te wing? Mein Gott! do you take me for a shicken?'

'No – oh no!' I replied, much alarmed, 'you are no chicken – certainly not.'

'Well, den, zit still and pehabe yourself, or I'll rap you again mid me vist. It iz de shicken ab te wing, und te owl ab te wing, und te imp ab te wing, und te head-teuffel ab te wing. Te angel ab *not* te wing, and I am te *Angel ov te Odd*.'

'And your business with me at present is – is'——

'My pizziness!' ejaculated the thing, 'vy vat a low bred buppy you mos pe vor to ask a gentleman und an angel apout his pizziness!'

This language was rather more than I could bear, even from an angel; so, plucking up courage, I seized a salt-cellar which lay within reach, and hurled it at the head of the intruder. Either he dodged, however, or my aim was inaccurate; for all I accomplished was the demolition of the crystal which protected the dial of the clock upon the mantelpiece. As for the Angel, he evinced his sense of my assault by giving me two or three hard consecutive raps upon the forehead as before. These reduced me at once to submission, and I am almost ashamed to confess that, either through pain or vexation there came a few tears into my eyes.

'Mein Gott!' said the Angel of the Odd, apparently much softened at my distress; 'mein Gott, te man is eder ferry dronk or ferry zorry. You mos not trink it so strong – you mos put te water in te wine. Here, trink dis, like a goot veller, and don't gry now – don't!'

Hereupon the Angel of the Odd replenished my goblet (which was about a third full of port) with a colourless fluid that he poured from one of his hand-bottles. I observed that these bottles had labels about their necks, and that these labels were inscribed 'Kirschenwässer.'

The considerate kindness of the Angel mollified me in no little measure; and, aided by the water with which he diluted my port more than once, I at length regained sufficient temper to listen to his very extraordinary discourse. I cannot pretend to recount all that he told me, but I gleaned from what he said that he was the genius who presided over the *contretemps* of mankind, and whose business it was to bring about the *odd accidents* which are continually astonishing the sceptic. Once or twice, upon my venturing to express my total incredulity in respect to his pretensions, he grew very angry indeed, so that at length I considered it the wiser policy to say nothing at all, and let him have his own way. He talked on, therefore, at great length, while I merely leaned back in my chair with my eyes shut, and amused myself with munching raisins and filliping the stems about the room. But, by-and-by, the Angel suddenly construed this behaviour of mine into contempt. He arose in a terrible passion, slouched his funnel down over his eyes, swore a vast oath, uttered a threat of some character, which I did not precisely comprehend, and finally made me a low bow and departed, wishing me, in the language of the archbishop of Gil Blas, *'beaucoup de bonheur et un peu plus de bon sens.'*

His departure afforded me relief. The *very* few glasses of Lafitte that I had sipped had the effect of rendering me drowsy, and I felt inclined to take a nap of some fifteen or twenty minutes, as is my custom after dinner. At six I had an appointment of consequence, which it was quite indispensable that I should keep. The policy of insurance for my dwelling-house had expired the day before; and some dispute having arisen, it was agreed that, at six, I should meet the board of directors of the company and settle the terms of a renewal. Glancing upward at the clock on the mantelpiece (for I felt too drowsy to take out my watch), I had the pleasure to find that I had still twenty-five minutes to spare. It was half-past five; I could easily walk to the insurance office in five minutes; and my usual siestas had never been known to exceed five-and-twenty. I felt sufficiently safe, therefore, and composed myself to my slumbers forthwith.

Having completed them to my satisfaction, I again looked towards the time-piece, and was half inclined to believe in the possibility of odd accidents when I found that, instead of my ordinary fifteen or twenty minutes, I had been dozing only three; for it still wanted seven-and-twenty of the appointed hour. I betook myself again to my nap, and at length a second time awoke, when, to my utter amazement, it *still* wanted twenty-seven minutes of six. I jumped up to examine the clock, and found that it had ceased running. My watch informed me that it was half-past seven; and of course, having slept two hours, I was too late for my appointment. 'It will make no difference,' I said: 'I can call at the office in the morning and apologise; in the meantime what can be the matter with the clock?' Upon examining it I discovered that one of the raisin stems which I had been filliping about the room during the discourse of the Angel of the Odd, had flown through the fractured crystal, and lodged, singularly enough, in the key-hole, with an end projecting outward, had thus arrested the revolution of the minute hand.

'Ah!' said I, 'I see how it is. This thing speaks for itself. A natural accident, such as *will* happen now and then!'

I gave the matter no further consideration, and at my usual hour retired to bed. Here, having placed a candle upon a reading-stand at the bed head, and having made an attempt to peruse some pages of the 'Omnipresence of the Deity,' I unfortunately fell asleep in less than twenty seconds, leaving the light burning as it was.

My dreams were terrifically disturbed by visions of the Angel of the Odd. Methought he stood at the foot of the couch, drew aside the curtains, and in the hollow, detestable tones of a rum puncheon, menaced me with the bitterest vengeance for the contempt with which I had treated him. He concluded a long harangue by taking off his funnel-cap, inserting the tube into my gullet, and thus deluging me with an ocean of Kirschenwässer, which he poured in a continuous flood, from one of the long-necked bottles that stood him instead of an arm. My agony was at length insufferable, and I awoke just in time to perceive that a rat had run off with the lighted candle from the stand, but *not* in season to prevent his making his escape with it through the hole. Very soon a strong suffocating odour assailed my nostrils; the house, I clearly perceived, was on fire. In a few minutes the blaze broke forth with violence, and in an incredibly brief period the entire building was wrapped in flames. All egress from my chamber, except through a window, was cut off. The crowd, however, quickly procured and raised a long ladder. By means of this I was descending rapidly, and in apparent safety, when a huge hog, about whose rotund stomach, and indeed about whose whole air and physiognomy, there was something which reminded me of the Angel of the Odd – when this hog, I say, which hitherto had been quietly slumbering in the mud, took it suddenly into his head that his left shoulder needed scratching, and could find no more convenient rubbing-post than that afforded by the foot of the ladder. In an instant I was precipitated, and had the misfortune to fracture my arm.

This accident, with the loss of my insurance, and with the more serious loss of my hair, the whole of which had been singed off by the fire, predisposed me to serious impressions, so that, finally, I made up my mind to take a wife. There was a rich widow disconsolate for the loss of her seventh husband, and to her wounded spirit I offered the balm of my vows. She yielded a reluctant consent to my prayers. I knelt at her feet in gratitude and adoration. She blushed and bowed her luxuriant tresses in close contact with those supplied me temporarily by Grandjean. I know not how the entanglement took place, but so it was I arose with a shining pate, wigless; she in disdain and wrath, half-buried in alien hair. Thus ended my hopes of the widow by an accident which could not have been anticipated, to be sure, but which the natural sequence of events had brought about.

Without despairing, however, I undertook the siege of a less implacable heart. The fates were again propitious for a brief period; but again a trivial incident interfered. Meeting my betrothed in an avenue thronged with the *élite* of the city, I was hastening to greet her with one of my best considered bows, when a small particle of some foreign matter lodging in the corner of my eye rendered me for the moment completely blind. Before I could recover my sight, the lady of my love had disappeared – irreparably affronted at what she chose to consider my premeditated rudeness in passing her by ungreeted. While I stood bewildered at the suddenness of this accident (which might have happened, nevertheless, to any one under the sun), and while I still continued incapable of sight, I was accosted by the Angel of the Odd, who proffered me his aid with a civility which I had no reason to expect. He examined my disordered eye with much gentleness and skill, informed me that I had a drop in it, and (whatever a 'drop' was) took it out, and afforded me relief.

I now considered it high time to die (since fortune had so determined to persecute me), and accordingly made my way to the nearest river. Here, divesting myself of my clothes (for there is no reason why we cannot die as we were born), I threw myself headlong into the current; the sole witness of my fate being a solitary crow that had been seduced into the eating of brandy-saturated corn, and so had staggered away from his fellows. No sooner had I entered the water than this bird took it into his head to fly away with the most indispensable portion of my apparel. Postponing, therefore, for the present, my suicidal design, I just slipped my nether extremities into the sleeves of my coat, and betook myself to a pursuit of the felon with all the nimbleness which the case required and its circumstances would admit. But my evil destiny attended me still. As I ran at full speed, with my nose up in the atmosphere, and intent only upon the purloiner of my property, I suddenly perceived that my feet rested no longer upon *terra firma*; the fact is, I had thrown myself over a precipice, and should inevitably have been dashed to pieces but for my good fortune in grasping the end of a long guide-rope, which depended from a passing balloon.

As soon as I sufficiently recovered my senses to comprehend the terrific predicament in which I stood or rather hung, I exerted all the power of my lungs to make that predicament known to the aeronaut overhead. But for a long time I exerted myself in vain. Either the fool could not, or the villain would not perceive me. Meanwhile the machine rapidly soared, while my strength even more rapidly failed. I was soon upon the point of resigning myself to my fate, and dropping quietly into the sea, when my spirits were suddenly revived by hearing a hollow voice from above, which seemed to be lazily humming an opera air. Looking up, I perceived the Angel of the Odd. He was leaning, with his arms folded, over the rim of the car; and with a pipe in his mouth, at which he puffed leisurely, seemed to be upon excellent terms with himself and the universe. I was too much exhausted to speak, so I merely regarded him with an imploring air.

For several minutes, although he looked me full in the face, he said nothing. At length, removing carefully his meerschaum from the right to the left corner of his mouth, he condescended to speak.

'Who pe you,' he asked, 'and what der teuffel you be do dare?'

To this piece of impudence, cruelty, and affectation, I could reply only by ejaculating the monosyllable, 'Help!'

'Elp!' echoed the ruffian, 'not I. Dare iz te pottle – elp yourself, und pe tam'd!'

With these words he let fall a heavy bottle of Kirschenwässer, which, dropping precisely upon the crown of my head, caused me to imagine that my brains were entirely knocked out. Impressed with this idea, I was about to relinquish my hold and give up the ghost with a good grace, when I was arrested by the cry of the Angel, who bade me hold on.

''Old on!' he said: 'don't pe in te urry – don't. Will you pe take de odder pottle, or ave you pe got zober yet and come to your zenzes?'

I made haste, hereupon, to nod my head twice – once in the negative, meaning thereby that I would prefer not taking the other bottle at present; and once in the affirmative, intending thus to imply that I *was* sober and *had* positively come to my senses. By these means I somewhat softened the Angel.

'Und you pelief, ten,' he inquired, 'at te last? You pelief, ten, in te possibility of te odd?'

I again nodded my head in assent.

'Und you ave pelief in *me*, te Angel of te Odd?'

I nodded again.

'Und you acknowledge tat you pe to blink dronk und te vool?'

I nodded once more.

'Put your right hand into your left hand preeches pocket, ten, in token ov your vull submission unto te Angel ov te Odd.'

This thing, for very obvious reasons, I found it quite impossible to do. In the first place, my left arm had been broken in my fall from the ladder, and therefore, had I let go my hold with the right hand I must have let go altogether. In the second place, I could have no breeches until I came across the crow. I was therefore obliged, much to my regret, to shake my head in the negative, intending thus to give the Angel to understand that I found it inconvenient, just at that moment, to comply with his very reasonable demand! No sooner, however, had I ceased shaking my head than –

'Go to der teuffel, ten!' roared the Angel of the Odd.

In pronouncing these words he drew a sharp knife across the guide-rope by which I was suspended, and as we then happened to be precisely over my own house (which, during my peregrinations, had been handsomely rebuilt), it so occurred that I tumbled headlong down the ample chimney and lit upon the dining-room hearth.

Upon coming to my senses (for the fall had very thoroughly stunned me) I found it about four o'clock in the morning. I lay outstretched where I had fallen from the balloon. My head grovelled in the ashes of an extinguished fire, while my feet reposed upon the wreck of a small table, overthrown, and amid the fragments of a miscellaneous dessert, intermingled with a newspaper, some broken glasses and shattered bottles, and an empty jug of the Schiedam Kirschenwässer. Thus revenged himself the Angel of the Odd.

King Pest

A Tale containing an Allegory

The gods do bear and well allow all kings
The things which they abhor in rascal routes.
                    BUCKHURST'S *Tragedy of Ferrex and Porrex.*

About twelve o'clock one night in the month of October, during the chivalrous reign of the third Edward, two seamen belonging to the crew of the *Free and Easy*, a trading schooner plying between Sluys and the Thames, and then at anchor in that river, were much astonished to find themselves seated in the tap-room of an ale-house in the parish of St. Andrew's, London – which ale-house bore for sign the portraiture of a 'Jolly Tar.'

The room, although ill-contrived, smoke-blackened, low-pitched, and in every other respect agreeing with the general character of such places at the period – was nevertheless, in the opinion of the grotesque groups scattered here and there within it, sufficiently well adapted to its purpose.

Of these groups our two seamen formed, I think, the most interesting, if not the most conspicuous.

The one who appeared to be the elder, and whom his companion addressed by the characteristic appellation of 'Legs,' was at the same time much the taller of the two. He might have measured six feet and a half, and an habitual stoop in the shoulders, seemed to have been the necessary consequence of an altitude so enormous. Superfluities in height were, however, more than accounted for by deficiencies in other respects. He was exceedingly thin; and might, as his associates asserted, have answered, when drunk, for a pennant at the mast-head, or, when sober, have served for a jib-boom. But these jests, and others of a similar nature, had evidently produced at no time any effect upon the cachinnatory muscles of the tar. With high cheek-bones, a large hawk-nose, retreating chin, fallen under-jaw, and huge protruding white eyes, the expression of his countenance, although tinged with a species of dogged indifference to matters and things in general, was not the less utterly solemn and serious beyond all attempts at imitation or description.

The younger seaman was, in all outward appearance, the converse of his companion. His stature could not have exceeded four feet. A pair of stumpy bow-legs supported his squat, unwieldy figure, while his unusually short and thick arms, with no ordinary fists at their extremities, swung off dangling from his sides like the fins of a sea-turtle. Small eyes, of no particular colour, twinkled far back in his head. His nose remained buried in the mass of flesh which enveloped his round, full, and purple face; and his thick upper-lip rested upon the still thicker one beneath with an air of complacent self-satisfaction, much heightened by the owner's habit of licking them at intervals. He evidently regarded his tall shipmate with a feeling half-wondrous, half-quizzical; and stared up occasionally in his face as the red setting sun stares up at the crags of Ben Nevis.

Various and eventful, however, had been the peregrinations of the worthy couple in and about the different tap-houses of the neighbourhood during the earlier hours of the night. Funds even the most ample, are not always everlasting; and it was with empty pockets our friends had ventured upon the present hostelrie.

At the precise period, then, when this history properly commences, Legs, and his fellow, Hugh Tarpaulin, sat, each with both elbows resting upon the large oaken table in the middle of the floor, and with a hand upon either cheek. They were eyeing, from behind a huge flagon of unpaid-for 'humming-stuff,' the portentous words 'No Chalk,' which to their indignation and astonishment were scored over the doorway by means of that very mineral whose presence they purported to deny. Not that the gift of deciphering written characters – a gift among the commonalty of that day considered little less cabalistical than the art of inditing – could, in strict justice, have been laid to the charge of either disciple of the sea; but there was, to say the truth, a certain twist in the formation of the letters – an indescribable lee-lurch about the whole – which foreboded, in the opinion of both seamen, a long run of dirty weather; and determined them at once, in the allegorical words of Legs himself, to 'pump ship, clew up all sail, and scud before the wind.'

Having accordingly disposed of what remained of the ale, and looped up the points of their short doublets, they finally made a bolt for the street. Although Tarpaulin rolled twice into the fireplace, mistaking it for the door, yet their escape was at length happily effected – and half after twelve o'clock found our heroes ripe for mischief, and running for life down a dark alley in the direction of St. Andrew's Stair, hotly pursued by the landlady of the 'Jolly Tar.'

At the epoch of this eventful tale, and periodically for many years before and after, all England, but more especially the metropolis, resounded with the fearful cry of 'Plague!' The city was in a great measure depopulated – and in those horrible regions in the vicinity of the Thames, where amid the dark, narrow, and filthy lanes and alleys, the Demon of Disease was supposed to have had his nativity, Awe, Terror, and Superstition were alone to be found stalking abroad.

By authority of the king such districts were placed *under ban*, and all persons forbidden, under pain of death, to intrude upon their dismal solitude. Yet neither the mandate of the monarch, nor the huge barriers erected at the entrances of the streets, nor the prospect of that loathsome death which, with almost absolute certainty, overwhelmed the wretch whom no peril could deter from the adventure, prevented the unfurnished and untenanted dwellings from being stripped by the hand of nightly rapine, of every article, such as iron, brass, or lead-work, which could in any manner be turned to a profitable account.

Above all, it was usually found, upon the annual winter opening of the barriers, that locks, bolts, and secret cellars, had proved but slender protection to those rich stores of wines and liquors which, in consideration of the risk and trouble of removal, many of the numerous dealers having shops in the neighbourhood had consented to trust, during the period of exile, to so insufficient a security.

But there were very few of the terror-stricken people who attributed these doings to the agency of human hands. Pest-spirits, plague-goblins, and fever-demons were the popular imps of mischief; and tales so blood-chilling were hourly told, that the whole mass of forbidden buildings was at length enveloped in terror as in a shroud, and the plunderer himself was often scared away by the horrors his own depredations had created; leaving the entire vast circuit of prohibited district to gloom, silence, pestilence, and death.

It was by one of the terrific barriers already mentioned, and which indicated the region beyond to be under the Pest-ban, that in scrambling down an alley, Legs and the worthy Hugh Tarpaulin found their progress suddenly impeded. To return was out of the question, and no time was to be lost, as their pursuers were close upon their heels. With thorough-bred seamen to clamber up the roughly fashioned plank-work was a trifle; and, maddened with the twofold excitement of exercise and liquor, they leaped unhesitatingly down within the enclosure, and holding on their drunken course with shouts and yellings, were soon bewildered in its noisome and intricate recesses.

Had they not, indeed, been intoxicated beyond moral sense their reeling footsteps must have been palsied by the horrors of their situation. The air was cold and misty. The paving-stones, loosened from their beds, lay in wild disorder amid the tall, rank grass, which sprang up around their feet and ankles. Fallen houses choked up the streets. The most fetid and poisonous smells everywhere prevailed; and by the aid of that ghastly light which, even at midnight, never fails to emanate from a vapoury and pestilential atmosphere, might be discerned lying in the bye-paths and alleys, or rotting in the windowless habitations, the carcase of many a nocturnal plunderer arrested by the hand of the plague in the very perpetration of his robbery.

But it lay not in the power of images, or sensations, or impediments such as these, to stay the course of men who, naturally brave, and at that time especially brimful of courage and of 'humming-stuff,' would have reeled, as straight as their condition might have permitted, undauntingly into the very jaws of Death. Onward – still onward stalked the grim Legs, making the desolate solemnity echo and re-echo with yells like the terrific war-whoop of the Indian: and onward, still onward rolled the dumpy Tarpaulin, hanging on to the doublet of his more active companion, and far surpassing the latter's most strenuous exertions in the way of vocal music, by bull-roarings *in basso*, from the profundity of his stentorian lungs.

They had now evidently reached the stronghold of the pestilence. Their way at every step or plunge grew more noisome and more horrible – the paths more narrow and more intricate. Huge stones and beams falling momently from the decaying roofs above them, gave evidence, by their sullen and heavy descent, of the vast height of the surrounding houses; and while actual exertion became necessary to force a passage through frequent heaps of rubbish, it was by no means seldom that the hand fell upon a skeleton or rested upon a more fleshy corpse.

Suddenly, as the seamen stumbled against the entrance of a tall and ghastly-looking building a yell more than usually shrill from the throat of the excited Legs, was replied to from within, in a rapid succession of wild, laughter-like, and fiendish shrieks. Nothing daunted at sounds which, of such a nature, at such a time, and in such a place, might have curdled the very blood in hearts less irrevocably on fire, the drunken couple rushed headlong against the door, burst it open, and staggered into the midst of things with a volley of curses.

The room within which they found themselves proved to be the shop of an undertaker; but an open trap-door, in a corner of the floor near the entrance, looked down upon a long range of wine-cellars, whose depths the occasional sound of bursting bottles proclaimed to be well stored with their appropriate contents. In the middle of the room stood a table, in the centre of which again arose a huge tub of what appeared to be punch. Bottles of various wines and cordials, together with jugs, pitchers, and flagons of every shape and quality, were scattered profusely upon the board. Around it, upon coffin-tressels, was seated a company of six. This company I will endeavour to delineate one by one.

Fronting the entrance, and elevated a little above his companions, sat a personage who appeared to be the president of the table. His stature was gaunt and tall, and Legs was confounded to behold in him a figure more emaciated than himself. His face was as yellow as saffron – but no feature excepting one alone, was sufficiently marked to merit a particular description. This one consisted in a forehead so unusually and hideously lofty, as to have the appearance of a bonnet or crown of flesh super-added upon the natural head. His mouth was puckered and dimpled into an expression of ghastly affability, and his eyes, as indeed the eyes of all at table, were glazed over with the fumes of intoxication. This gentleman was clothed from head to foot in a richly embroidered black silk-velvet pall, wrapped negligently around his form after the fashion of a Spanish cloak. His head was stuck full of sable hearse-plumes, which he nodded to and fro with a jaunty and knowing air; and, in his right hand, he held a huge human thigh-bone, with which he appeared to have been just knocking down some member of the company for a song.

Opposite him, and with her back to the door, was a lady of no whit the less extraordinary character. Although quite as tall as the person just described, she had no right to complain of his unnatural emaciation. She was evidently in the last stage of a dropsy; and her figure resembled nearly that of a huge puncheon of October beer which stood, with the head driven in, close by her side, in a corner of the chamber. Her face was exceedingly round, red, and full; and the same peculiarity, or rather want of peculiarity, attached itself to her countenance, which I before mentioned in the case of the president – that is to say, only one feature of her face was sufficiently distinguished to need a separate characterisation: indeed the acute Tarpaulin immediately observed that the same remark might have applied to each individual person of the party; every one of whom seemed to possess a monopoly of some particular portion of physiognomy. With the lady in question this portion proved to be the mouth. Commencing at the right ear, it swept with a terrific chasm to the left – the short pendants which she wore in either auricle continually bobbing into the aperture. She made, however, every exertion to keep her mouth closed and look dignified, in a dress consisting of a newly starched and ironed shroud coming up close under her chin, with a crimpled ruffle of cambric muslin.

At her right hand sat a diminutive young lady whom she appeared to patronise. This delicate little creature, in the trembling of her wasted fingers, in the livid hue of her lips, and in the slight hectic spot which tinged her otherwise leaden complexion, gave evident indication of a galloping consumption. An air of extreme *haut ton*, however, pervaded her whole appearance; she wore in a graceful and *dégagé* manner, a large and beautiful winding-sheet of the finest Indian lawn; her hair hung in ringlets over her neck; a soft smile played about her mouth; but her nose, extremely long, thin, sinuous, flexible, and pimpled, hung down far below her under lip, and in spite of the delicate manner in which she now and then moved it to one side or the other with her tongue, gave to her countenance a somewhat equivocal expression.

Over against her, and upon the left of the dropsical lady, was seated a little puffy, wheezing, and gouty old man, whose cheeks reposed upon the shoulders of their owner, like two huge bladders of Oporto wine. With his arms folded, and with one bandaged leg deposited upon the table, he seemed to think himself entitled to some consideration. He evidently prided himself much upon every inch of his personal appearance, but took more especial delight in calling attention to his gaudy-coloured surtout. This, to say the truth, must have cost him no little money, and was made to fit him exceedingly well – being fashioned from one of the curiously embroidered silken covers appertaining to those glorious escutcheons which, in England and elsewhere, are customarily hung up in some conspicuous place upon the dwellings of departed aristocracy.

Next to him, and at the right hand of the president, was a gentleman in long white hose and cotton drawers. His frame shook in a ridiculous manner with a fit of what Tarpaulin called 'the horrors.' His jaws, which had been newly shaved, were tightly tied up by a bandage of muslin; and his arms being fastened in a similar way at the wrists, prevented him from helping himself too freely to the liquors upon the table – a precaution rendered necessary, in the opinion of Legs, by the peculiarly sottish and wine-bibbing cast of his visage. A pair of prodigious ears, nevertheless, which it was no doubt found impossible to confine, towered away into the atmosphere of the apartment, and were occasionally pricked up in a spasm at the sound of the drawing of a cork.

Fronting him, sixthly and lastly, was situated a singularly stiff-looking personage, who, being afflicted with paralysis, must, to speak seriously, have felt very ill at ease in his unaccommodating habiliments. He was habited somewhat uniquely, in a new and handsome mahogany coffin. Its top or head-piece pressed upon the skull of the wearer, and extended over it in the fashion of a hood, giving to the entire face an air of indescribable interest. Arm-holes had been cut in the sides, for the sake not more of elegance than of convenience, but the dress, nevertheless, prevented its proprietor from sitting as erect as his associates; and as he lay reclining against his tressel, at an angle of forty-five degrees, a pair of huge goggle eyes rolled up their awful whites towards the ceiling in absolute amazement at their own enormity.

Before each of the party lay a portion of a skull, which was used as a drinking cup. Overhead was suspended a human skeleton by means of a rope tied round one of the legs and fastened to a ring in the ceiling. The other limb confined by no such fetter, stuck off from the body at right angles, causing the whole loose and rattling frame to dangle and twirl about at the caprice of every occasional puff of wind which found its way into the apartment. In the cranium of this hideous thing lay a quantity of ignited charcoal, which threw a fitful but vivid light over the entire scene; while coffins, and other wares appertaining to the shop of an undertaker, were piled high up around the room and against the windows, preventing any ray from escaping into the street.

At sight of this extraordinary assembly, and of their still more extraordinary paraphernalia, our two seamen did not conduct themselves with that degree of decorum which might have been expected. Legs, leaning against the wall near which he happened to be standing, dropped his lower jaw still lower than usual, and spread open his eyes to their fullest extent; while Hugh Tarpaulin, stooping down so as to bring his nose upon a level with the table, and spreading out a palm upon either knee, burst into a long, loud, and obstreperous roar of very ill-timed and immoderate laughter.

Without, however, taking offence at behaviour so excessively rude, the tall president smiled very graciously upon the intruders – nodded to them in a dignified manner with his head of sable plumes – and, arising, took each by an arm, and led him to a seat which some others of the company had placed in the meantime for his accommodation. Legs to all this offered not the slightest resistance, but sat down as he was directed; while the gallant Hugh, removing his coffin tressel from its station near the head of the table to the vicinity of the little consumptive lady in the winding sheet, plumped down by her side in high glee, and pouring out a skull of red wine, quaffed it to their better acquaintance. But at this presumption the stiff gentleman in the coffin seemed exceedingly nettled; and serious consequences might have ensued, had not the president, rapping upon the table with his truncheon, diverted the attention of all present to the following speech:–

'It becomes our duty upon the present happy occasion'——

'Avast there!' interrupted Legs, looking very serious, 'avast there a bit, I say, and tell us who the devil ye all are, and what business ye have here, rigged off like the foul fiends, and swilling the snug blue ruin stowed away for the winter by my honest shipmate, Will Wimble the undertaker!'

At this unpardonable piece of ill-breeding, all the original company half-started to their feet, and uttered the same rapid succession of wild fiendish shrieks which had before caught the

'Avast there a bit, I say, and tell us who the devil ye all are!'

attention of the seamen. The president, however, was the first to recover his composure, and at length, turning to Legs with great dignity, recommended:

'Most willingly will we gratify any reasonable curiosity on the part of guests so illustrious, unbidden though they be. Know then that in these dominions I am monarch, and here rule with undivided empire under the title of "King Pest the First."

'This apartment, which you no doubt profanely, suppose to be the shop of Will Wimble the undertaker – a man whom we know not, and whose plebeian appellation has never before this night thwarted our royal ears – this apartment, I say, is the Dais-Chamber of our Palace, devoted to the councils of our kingdom, and to other sacred and lofty purposes.

'The noble lady who sits opposite is Queen Pest, our Serene Consort. The other exalted personages whom you behold are all of our family, and wear the insignia of the blood-royal under the respective titles of "His Grace the Archduke Pest-Iferous" – "His Grace the Duke Pest-Ilential" – "His Grace the Duke Tem-Pest" – and "Her Serene Highness the Archduchess Ana-Pest."

'As regards,' continued he, 'your demand of the business upon which we sit here in council, we might be pardoned for replying that it concerns and concerns *alone*, our own private and regal interest, and is in no manner important to any other than ourself. But, in consideration of those rights to which as guests and strangers you may feel yourselves entitled, we will furthermore explain that we are here this night, prepared by deep research and accurate investigation, to examine, analyse, and thoroughly determine the indefinable spirit – the incomprehensible qualities and nature – of those inestimable treasures of the palate, the wines, ales, and liqueurs of this goodly metropolis: by so doing to advance not more our own designs than the true welfare of that unearthly sovereign whose reign is over us all, whose dominions are unlimited, and whose name is "Death."'

'Whose name is Davy Jones!' ejaculated Tarpaulin, helping the lady by his side to a skull of liqueur, and pouring out a second for himself.

'Profane varlet!' said the president, now turning his attention to the worthy Hugh, 'profane and execrable wretch! – we have said that in consideration of those rights which, even in thy filthy person, we feel no inclination to violate, we have condescended to make reply to thy rude and unseasonable inquiries. We nevertheless, for your unhallowed intrusion upon our councils, believe it our duty to mulct thee and thy companion each in a gallon of Black Strap – having imbibed which to the prosperity of our kingdom – at a single draught – and upon your bended knees – ye shall be forthwith free either to proceed upon your way, or remain and be admitted to the privileges of our table, according to your respective and individual pleasures.'

'It would be a matter of utter impossibility,' replied Legs, whom the assumptions and dignity of King Pest the First had evidently inspired with some feelings of respect, and who arose and steadied himself by the table as he spoke – 'it would, please your majesty, be a matter of utter impossibility to stow away in my hold even one-fourth part of that same liqueur which your majesty has just mentioned. To say nothing of the stuffs placed on board in the forenoon by way of ballast, and not to mention the various ales and liqueurs shipped this evening at various seaports, I have at present a full cargo of 'humming-stuff' taken in and duly paid for at the sign of the "Jolly Tar." You will therefore, please your majesty, be so good as to take the will for the deed – for by no manner of means either can I or will I swallow another drop – least of all a drop of that villainous bilge-water that answers to the hail of "Black Strap."'

'Belay that!' interrupted Tarpaulin, astonished not more at the length of his companion's speech than at the nature of his refusal –'Belay that, you lubber! – and I say, Legs, none of your palaver! *My* hull is still light, although I confess you yourself seem to be a little top-heavy; and as for the matter of your share of the cargo, why rather than raise a squall I would find stowage-room for it myself, but'——

'This proceeding,' interposed the president, 'is, by no means in accordance with the terms of the mulct or sentence, which is in its nature Median, and not to be altered or recalled. The conditions we have imposed must be fulfilled to the letter, and that without a moment's hesitation – in failure of which fulfilment we decree that you do here be tied neck and heels together, and duly drowned as rebels in yon hogshead of October beer!'

'A sentence! – a sentence! – a righteous and just sentence! – a glorious decree! – a most worthy and upright and holy condemnation!' shouted the Pest family altogether. The king elevated his forehead into innumerable wrinkles; the gouty little old man puffed like a pair of bellows; the lady of the winding-sheet waved her nose to and fro; the gentleman in the cotton drawers pricked up his ears; she of the shroud gasped like a dying fish; and he of the coffin looked stiff and rolled up his eyes.

'Ugh! ugh! ugh!' chuckled Tarpaulin, without heeding the general excitation, 'ugh! ugh! ugh! – ugh! ugh! ugh! – ugh! ugh! ugh! – I was saying,' said he, 'I was saying when Mr. King Pest poked in his marlin-spike, that as for the matter of two or three gallons more or less of Black Strap, it was a trifle to a tight sea-boat like myself not overstowed – but when it comes to drinking the health of the devil (whom God assoilzie) and going down upon my marrow bones to his ill-favoured majesty there, whom I know, as well as I know myself to be a sinner, to be nobody in the whole world but Tim Hurlygurly the stage-player! – why! I guess it's quite another sort of a thing, and utterly and altogether past my comprehension.'

He was not allowed to finish this speech in tranquillity. At the name of Tim Hurlygurly the whole assembly leaped from their seats.

'Treason!' shouted his Majesty King Pest the First.

'Treason!' said the little man with the gout.

'Treason!' screamed the Archduchess Ana-Pest.

'Treason!' muttered the gentleman with his jaws tied up.

'Treason!' growled he of the coffin.

'Treason! treason!' shrieked her majesty of the mouth; and, seizing by the hinder part of his breeches the unfortunate Tarpaulin, who had just commenced pouring out for himself a skull of liquor, she lifted him high into the air, and let him fall without ceremony into the huge open puncheon of his beloved ale. Bobbing up and down for a few seconds like an apple in a bowl of toddy, he at length finally disappeared amid the whirlpool of foam which, in the already effervescent liquor, his struggles easily succeeded in creating.

Not tamely, however, did the tall seaman behold the discomfiture of his companion. Jostling King Pest through the open trap, the valiant Legs slammed the door down upon him with an oath, and strode towards the centre of the room. Here tearing down the skeleton which swung over the table, he laid it about him with so much energy and good will, that, as the last glimpses of light died away within the apartment, he succeeded in knocking out the brains of the little gentleman with the gout. Rushing then with all his force against the fatal hogshead full of October ale and Hugh Tarpaulin, he rolled it over and over in an instant. Out burst a deluge of liquor so fierce – so impetuous – so overwhelming – that the room was flooded from wall to wall – the loaded table was overturned – the tressels were thrown upon their backs – the tub of punch into the fireplace – and the ladies into hysterics. Piles of death-furniture floundered about. Jugs, pitchers, and carboys mingled promiscuously in the *mêlée*, and wicker flagons encountered desperately with bottles of junk. The man with the horrors was drowned upon the spot – the little stiff gentleman floated off in his coffin – and the victorious Legs, seizing by the waist the fat lady in the shroud, rushed out with her into the street, and made a bee-line for the *Free and Easy*, followed under easy sail by the redoubtable Hugh Tarpaulin, who, having sneezed three or four times, panted and puffed after him with the Archduchess Ana-Pest.

The Duc De L'Omelette

And stepped at once into a cooler clime. – *Cowper*.

Keats fell by a criticism. Who was it died of '*The Andromache*'?*
Ignoble souls! – De l'Omelette perished of an ortolan. *L'histoire en est
brève*. Assist me, Spirit of Apicius!

A golden cage bore the little winged wanderer, enamoured,
melting, indolent, to the *Chaussée D'Antin*, from its home in far Peru.
From its queenly possessor La Bellissima, to the Duc de l'Omelette,
six peers of the empire conveyed the happy bird.

That night the Duc was to sup alone. In the privacy of his bureau
he reclined languidly on that ottoman for which he sacrificed his
loyalty in outbidding his king – the notorious ottoman of Cadêt.

He buries his face in the pillow. The clock strikes! Unable to
restrain his feelings, his Grace swallows an olive. At this moment the
door gently opens to the sound of soft music, and lo! the most delicate
of birds is before the most enamoured of men! But what inexpressible
dismay now overshadows the countenance of the Duc? – '*Horreur!* –

* Montfleury. The author of the *Parnasse Réformé* makes him speak in
Hades:– '*L'Homme donc qui voudrait savoir ce dont je suis mort, qu'il ne
demande pas s'il fût de fievre ou de podagre ou d'autre chose, mais qu'il entende
que ce fut de "L'Andromache."*'

chien! – Baptiste! – l'oiseau! ah, bon Dieu! cet oiseau modeste que tu as deshabillé de ses plumes, et que tu as servi sans papier!' It is superfluous to say more:– the Duc expired in a paroxysm of disgust. * * * * * *

'Ha! ha! ha!' said his Grace on the third day after his decease.

'He! he! he!' replied the devil faintly, drawing himself up with an air of *hauteur.*

'Why, surely you are not serious,' retorted De l'Omelette. 'I have sinned – *c'est vrai* – but, my good sir, consider! – you have no actual intention of putting such – such – barbarous threats into execution.'

'No *what?*' said his majesty – 'come, sir, strip!'

'Strip, indeed! – very pretty i' faith! – no, sir, I shall *not* strip. Who are you, pray, that I, Duc de l'Omelette, Prince de Foie-Gras, just come of age, author of the "Mazurkiad" and Member of the Academy, should divest myself at your bidding of the sweetest pantaloons ever made by Bourdon, the daintiest *robe-de-chambre* ever put together by Rombêrt – to say nothing of the taking my hair out of paper – not to mention the trouble I should have in drawing off my gloves!'

'Who am I? – ah, true! I am Baal-Zebub, Prince of the Fly. I took thee, just now, from a rose-wood coffin inlaid with ivory. Thou wast curiously scented, and labelled as per invoice. Belial sent thee – my Inspector of Cemeteries. The pantaloons, which thou sayest were made by Bourdon, are an excellent pair of linen drawers, and thy *robe-de-chambre* is a shroud of no scanty dimensions.'

'Sir!' replied the Duc, 'I am not to be insulted with impunity! – Sir! I shall take the earliest opportunity of avenging this insult! – Sir! you shall hear from me! In the meantime *au revoir!*' – and the Duc was bowing himself out of the Satanic presence when he was interrupted and brought back by a gentleman in waiting. Hereupon his Grace rubbed his eyes, yawned, shrugged his shoulders, reflected. Having become satisfied of his identity, he took a bird's-eye view of his whereabouts.

The apartment was superb. Even De l'Omelette pronounced it *bien comme il faut.* It was not its length nor its breadth – but its height –

ah, that was appalling! – there was no ceiling – certainly none – but a dense whirling mass of fiery-coloured clouds. His Grace's brain reeled as he glanced upwards. From above hung a chain of an unknown blood-red metal, its upper end lost, like the city of Boston, *parmi les nues.* From its nether extremity swung a large cresset. The Duc knew it to be a ruby; but from it there poured a light so intense, so still, so terrible, Persia never worshipped such – Gheber never imagined such – Mussulman never dreamed of such – when, drugged with opium, he has tottered to a bed of poppies, his back to the flowers, and his face to the god Apollo. The Duc muttered a slight oath, decidedly approbatory.

The corners of the room were rounded into niches. Three of these were filled with statues of gigantic proportions. Their beauty was Grecian, their deformity Egyptian, their *tout ensemble* French. In the fourth niche the statue was veiled; it was *not* colossal. But then there was a taper ankle, a sandalled foot. De l'Omelette pressed his hand upon his heart, closed his eyes, raised them, and caught his Satanic Majesty – in a blush.

But the paintings! – Kupris! Astarte! Astoreth? – a thousand and the same! And Rafaelle has beheld them! Yes, Rafaelle has been here; for did he not paint the——? and was he not consequently damned? The paintings! – the paintings! O luxury! O love! – who, gazing on those forbidden beauties, shall have eyes for the dainty devices of the golden frames that besprinkled, like stars, the hyacinth and porphyry walls?

But the Duc's heart is fainting within him. He is not, however, as you suppose, dizzy with magnificence, nor drunk with the ecstatic breath of those innumerable censers. *C'est vrai que de toutes ces choses il a pensé beaucoup – mais!* The Duc de l'Omelette is terror-stricken; for, through the lurid vista which a single uncurtained window is affording, lo! gleams the most ghastly of all fires!

Le pauvre Duc! He could not help imagining that the glorious, the voluptuous, the never-dying melodies which pervaded that hall, as they passed filtered and transmuted through the alchemy of the enchanted window-panes, were the wailings and the howlings of the hopeless and the damned! And there, too! – there! – upon that ottoman! – who could *he* be? – he, the *petit maitre* – no, the Deity – who sat as if carved in marble, *et qui sourit* with his pale countenance, *si amèrement*!

Mais il faut agir, – that is to say, a Frenchman never faints outright. Besides, his Grace hated a scene – De l'Omelette is himself again. There were some foils upon a table – some points also. The Duc had studied under B——; *il avait tué ses six hommes.* Now, then, *il peuts s'échapper.* He measures two points, and, with a grace inimitable, offers his Majesty the choice. *Horreur!* his Majesty does not fence!

Mais il joue? – how happy a thought! – but his Grace had always an excellent memory. He had dipped in the '*Diable*' of the Abbé Gualtier. Therein it is said '*que le Diable n'ose pas refuser un jeu d'écarté.*'

But the chances – the chances! True – desperate; but scarcely more desperate than the Duc. Besides, was he not in the secret? – had he not skimmed over Père le Brun? was he not a member of the Club Vingt-un? '*Si je perds,*' said he, '*je serai deux fois perdu* – I shall be doubly damned – *voila tout!* (Here his Grace shrugged his shoulders.) *Si je gagne, je reviendrai à mes ortolans – que les cartes soient préparées!*'

His Grace was all care, all attention – his Majesty all confidence. A spectator would have thought of Francis and Charles. His Grace thought of his game. His Majesty did not think; he shuffled. The Duc cut.

The cards are dealt. The trump is turned – it is – it is – the king! No – it was the queen. His Majesty cursed her masculine habiliments. De l'Omelette placed his hand upon his heart.

They play. The Duc counts. The hand is out. His Majesty counts heavily, smiles, and is taking wine. The Duc slips a card.

'*C'est à vous à faire,*' said his Majesty, cutting. His Grace bowed, dealt, and arose from the table *en presentant le Roi.*

His Majesty looked chagrined.

Had Alexander not been Alexander, he would have been Diogenes; and the Duc assured his antagonist in taking leave, '*que s'il n'eût pas été De l'Omelette il n'aurait point a'objection d'être le Diable.*'

A Tale of Jerusalem

Intensos rigidam in frontem ascendere canos
Passus erat...

LUCAN – *De Catone*.

...a bristly *bore*. – *Translation*.

'Let us hurry to the walls,' said Abel-Phittim to Buzi-Ben-Levi and
Simeon the Pharisee, on the tenth day of the month Thammuz, in the
year of the world three thousand nine hundred and forty-one – 'let us
hasten to the ramparts adjoining the gates of Benjamin, which is in the
city of David, and overlooking the camp of the uncircumcised, for it is
the last hour of the fourth watch, being sunrise; and the idolaters, in
fulfilment of the promise of Pompey, should be awaiting us with the
lambs for the sacrifices.'

Simeon, Abel-Phittim, and Buzi-Ben-Levi, were the Gizbarim, or
sub-collectors of the offering, in the holy city of Jerusalem.

'Verily,' replied the Pharisee, 'let us hasten; for this generosity in
the heathen is unwonted; and fickle-mindedness has ever been an
attribute of the worshippers of Baal.'

'That they are fickle-minded and treacherous is as true as the
Pentateuch,' said Buzi-Ben-Levi, 'but that is only towards the people
of Adonai. When was it ever known that the Ammonites proved

wanting to their own interests? Methinks it is no great stretch of generosity to allow us lambs for the altar of the Lord, receiving in lieu thereof thirty silver shekels per head!'

'Thou forgettest, however, Ben-Levi,' replied Abel-Phittim, 'that the Roman Pompey, who is now impiously besieging the city of the Most High, has no security that we apply not the lambs thus purchased for the altar, to the sustenance of the body, rather than of the spirit.'

'Now, by the five corners of my beard,' shouted the Pharisee, who belonged to the sect called The Dashers (that little knot of saints whose manner of *dashing* and lacerating the feet against the pavement was long a thorn and a reproach to less zealous devotees – a stumbling block to less gifted perambulators) – 'by the five corners of that beard which as a priest I am forbidden to shave! – have we lived to see the day when a blaspheming and idolatrous upstart of Rome shall accuse us of appropriating to the appetites of the flesh the most holy and consecrated elements? Have we lived to see the day when'——

'Let us not question the motives of the Philistine,' interrupted Abel-Phittim, 'for to-day we profit for the first time by his avarice or by his generosity; but rather let us hurry to the ramparts, lest offerings should be wanting for that altar whose fire the rains of heaven cannot extinguish, and whose pillars of smoke no tempest can turn aside.'

That part of the city to which our worthy Gizbarim now hastened, and which bore the name of its architect King David, was esteemed the most strongly fortified district of Jerusalem; being situated upon the steep and lofty hill of Zion. Here a broad, deep, circumvallatory trench, hewn from the solid rock, was defended by a wall of great strength erected upon its inner edge. This wall was adorned, at regular interspaces, by square towers of white marble; the lowest sixty, and the highest one hundred and twenty cubits in height. But, in the vicinity of the gate of Benjamin, the wall arose by no means from the margin of the fosse. On the contrary, between the level of the ditch and the basement of the rampart, sprang up a perpendicular cliff of two hundred and fifty cubits; forming part of the precipitous Mount Moriah. So when Simeon and his associates arrived on the summit of

the tower called Adoni-Bezek – the loftiest of all the turrets around
about Jerusalem, and the usual place of conference with the besieging
army – they looked down upon the camp from an eminence excelling
by many feet that of the Pyramid of Cheops, and by several, that of the
temple of Belus.

'Verily,' sighed the Pharisee, as he peered dizzily over the
precipice, 'the uncircumcised are as the sands by the sea-shore – as the
locusts in the wilderness! The valley of The King hath become the
valley of Adommin.'

'And yet,' added Ben-Levi, 'thou canst not point me out a
Philistine – no, not one – from Aleph to Tau – from the wilderness to
the battlements – who seemeth any bigger than the letter Jod!'

'Lower away the basket with the shekels of silver!' here shouted a
Roman soldier in a hoarse, rough voice, which appeared to issue from
the regions of Pluto – 'lower away the basket with the accursed coin
which it has broken the jaw of a noble Roman to pronounce! Is it thus
you evince your gratitude to our master Pompeius, who, in his
condescension, has thought fit to listen to your idolatrous importunities? The god Phœbus, who is a true god, has been charioted for an
hour – and were you not to be on the ramparts by sunrise? Ædepol! do
you think that we, the conquerors of the world, have nothing better to
do than stand waiting by the walls of every kennel to traffic with the
dogs of the earth? Lower away! I say – and see that your trumpery be
bright in colour, and just in weight!'

'El Elohim!' ejaculated the Pharisee, as the discordant tones of the
centurion rattled up the crags of the precipice, and fainted away
against the temple – 'El Elohim! – *who* is the God Phœbus? – *whom*
doth the blasphemer invoke? Thou, Buzi-Ben-Levi! who art read in
the laws of the Gentiles, and hast sojourned among them who dabble
with the Teraphim! – is it Nergal of whom the idolater speaketh? – or
Ashimah? – or Nibhaz? – or Tartak? – or Adramalech? – or
Anamalech? – or Succoth-Benith? – or Dagon? – or Belial? – or Baal-
Perith? – or Baal-Peor? – or Baal-Zebub?'

'Verily it is neither – but beware how thou lettest the rope slip too
rapidly through thy fingers; for should the wicker-work chance to

hang on the projection of yonder crag, there will be a woeful outpouring of the holy things of the sanctuary.'

By the assistance of some rudely constructed machinery, the heavily laden basket was now carefully lowered down among the multitude; and, from the giddy pinnacle, the Romans were seen gathering confusedly round it; but owing to the vast height and the prevalence of a fog, no distinct view of their operations could be obtained.

Half-an-hour had already elapsed.

'We shall be too late,' sighed the Pharisee, as at the expiration of this period, he looked over into the abyss – 'we shall be too late! we shall be turned out of office by the Katholim.'

'No more,' responded Abel-Phittim, 'no more shall we feast upon the fat of the land – no longer shall our beards be odorous with frankincense – our loins girded up with fine linen from the Temple.'

'Raca!' swore Ben-Levi, 'Raca! do they mean to defraud us of the purchase-money? or, Holy Moses! are they weighing the shekels of the tabernacle?'

'They have given the signal at last,' cried the Pharisee, 'they have given the signal at last! – pull away, Abel-Phittim! – and thou, Buzi-Ben-Levi, pull away! – for verily the Philistines have either still hold upon the basket, or the Lord hath softened their hearts to place therein a beast of good weight!' And the Gizbarim pulled away, while their burden swung heavily upwards through the still increasing mist.

'Booshoh he!' – as, at the conclusion of an hour, some object at the extremity of the rope became indistinctly visible – 'Booshoh he!' was the exclamation which burst from the lips of Ben-Levi.

'Booshoh he! – for shame! – it is a ram from the thickets of Engedi, and as rugged as the valley of Jehosaphat!'

'It is a firstling of the flock,' said Abel-Phittim, 'I know him by the bleating of his lips, and the innocent folding of his limbs. His eyes are more beautiful than the jewels of the Pectoral, and his flesh is like the honey of Hebron.'

'It is a fatted calf from the pastures of Bashan,' said the Pharisee, 'the heathen have dealt wonderfully with us! – let us raise up our voices in a psalm! – let us give thanks on the shawm and on the psaltery – on the harp and on the huggab – on the cythern and on the sackbut!'

It was not until the basket had arrived within a few feet of the Gizbarim, that a low grunt betrayed to their perception a *hog* of no common size.

'Now, El Emanu!' slowly and with upturned eyes ejaculated the trio, as, letting go their hold, the emancipated porker tumbled headlong among the Philistines, 'El Emanu! – God be with us! – *it is the unutterable flesh!*'

The Gold-Bug

What ho! what ho! this fellow is dancing mad?
He hath been bitten by the Tarantula.

All in the Wrong.

Many years ago I contracted an intimacy with a Mr. William Legrand. He was of an ancient Huguenot family, and had once been wealthy; but a series of misfortunes had reduced him to want. To avoid the mortification consequent upon his disasters, he left New Orleans, the city of his forefathers, and took up his residence at Sullivan's Island, near Charleston, South Carolina.

This island is a very singular one. It consists of little else than the sea sand, and is about three miles long. Its breadth at no point exceeds a quarter of a mile. It is separated from the mainland by a scarcely perceptible creek, oozing its way through a wilderness of reeds and slime, a favourite resort of the marsh-hen. The vegetation, as might be supposed, is scant, or at least dwarfish. No trees of any magnitude are to be seen. Near the western extremity, where Fort Moultrie stands, and where are some miserable frame buildings, tenanted, during summer, by the fugitives from Charleston dust and fever, may be found, indeed, the bristly palmetto; but the whole island, with the exception of this western point, and a line of hard, white beach on the sea-coast, is covered with a dense undergrowth of the sweet myrtle, so much prized by the horticulturists of England. The shrub here often attains the height of fifteen or twenty feet, and forms an almost impenetrable coppice, burdening the air with its fragrance.

In the inmost recesses of this coppice, not far from the eastern or more remote end of the island, Legrand had built himself a small hut, which he occupied when I first, by mere accident, made his acquaintance. This soon ripened into friendship – for there was much in the recluse to excite interest and esteem. I found him well educated, with unusual powers of mind, but infected with misanthropy, and subject to perverse moods of alternate enthusiasm and melancholy. He had with him many books, but rarely employed them. His chief amusements were gunning and fishing, or sauntering along the beach and through the myrtles, in quest of shells or entomological specimens:– his collection of the latter might have been envied by a Swammerdamm. In these excursions he was usually accompanied by an old negro, called Jupiter who had been manumitted before the reverses of the family, but who could be induced, neither by threats nor by promises, to abandon what he considered his right of attendance upon the footsteps of his young 'Massa Will'. It is not improbable that the relatives of Legrand, conceiving him to be somewhat unsettled in intellect, had contributed to instil this obstinacy into Jupiter, with a view to the supervision and guardianship of the wanderer.

The winters in the latitude of Sullivan's Island are seldom very severe, and in the fall of the year it is a rare event indeed when a fire is considered necessary. About the middle of October, 18—, there occurred, however, a day of remarkable chilliness. Just before sunset I scrambled my way through the evergreens to the hut of my friend, whom I had not visited for several weeks – my residence being at that time in Charleston, a distance of nine miles from the island, while the facilities of passage and re-passage were very far behind those of the present day. Upon reaching the hut I rapped, as was my custom, and getting no reply, sought for the key where I knew it was secreted, unlocked the door and went in. A fine fire was blazing upon the hearth. It was a novelty, and by no means an ungrateful one. I threw off an overcoat, took an armchair by the crackling logs, and awaited patiently the arrival of my hosts.

Soon after dark they arrived, and gave me a most cordial welcome. Jupiter, grinning from ear to ear, bustled about to prepare some marsh-hens for supper. Legrand was in one of his fits – how else shall I term them? – of enthusiasm. He had found an unknown bivalve, forming a new genus, and, more than this, he had hunted down and secured, with Jupiter's assistance, a *scarabæus* which he believed to be totally new, but in respect to which he wished to have my opinion on the morrow.

'And why not to-night?' I asked, rubbing my hands over the blaze, and wishing the whole tribe of *scarabæi* at the devil.

'Ah, if I had only known you were here!' said Legrand, 'but it's so long since I saw you; and how could I foresee that you would pay me a visit this very night of all others? As I was coming home I met Lieutenant G——, from the fort, and, very foolishly, I lent him the bug; so it will be impossible for you to see it until the morning. Stay here to-night, and I will send Jup down for it at sunrise. It is the loveliest thing in creation!'

'What! – sunrise?'

'Nonsense! no! – the bug. It is of a brilliant gold colour – about the size of a large hickory-nut – with two jet black spots near one extremity of the back, and another, somewhat longer, at the other. The *antennæ* are'——

'Dey aint *no* tin in him, Massa Will, I keep a tellin on you,' here interrupted Jupiter; 'de bug is a goole bug, solid, ebery bit of him, inside and all, sep him wing – neber feel half so hebby a bug in my life.'

'Well, suppose it is, Jup,' replied Legrand, somewhat more earnestly, it seemed to me, than the case demanded, 'is that any reason for your letting the birds burn? The colour' – here he turned to me – 'is really almost enough to warrant Jupiter's idea. You never saw a more brilliant metallic lustre than the scales emit – but of this you cannot judge till to-morrow. In the meantime I can give you some idea of the shape.' Saying this, he seated himself at a small table, on which were a pen and ink, but no paper. He looked for some in a drawer, but found none.

'Never mind,' said he at length, 'this will answer;' and he drew from his waistcoat pocket a scrap of what I took to be very dirty foolscap, and made upon it a rough drawing with the pen. While he did this, I retained my seat by the fire, for I was still chilly. When the design was complete, he handed it to me without rising. As I received it, a loud growl was heard, succeeded by a scratching at the door. Jupiter opened it, and a large Newfoundland, belonging to Legrand, rushed in, leaped upon my shoulders, and loaded me with caresses; for I had shown him much attention during previous visits. When his gambols were over, I looked at the paper, and, to speak the truth, found myself not a little puzzled at what my friend had depicted.

'Well!' I said, after contemplating it for some minutes, 'this *is* a strange *scarabæus*, I must confess: new to me: never saw anything like it before – unless it was a skull, or a death's-head – which it more nearly resembles than anything else that has come under my observation.'

'A death's-head!' echoed Legrand – 'Oh – yes – well, it has something of that appearance upon paper, no doubt. The two upper black spots look like eyes, eh? and the longer one at the bottom like a mouth – and then the shape of the whole is oval.'

'Perhaps so,' said I; 'but, Legrand, I fear you are no artist. I must wait until I see the beetle itself, if I am to form any idea of its personal appearance.'

'Well, I don't know,' said he, a little nettled, 'I draw tolerably – *should* do it at least – have had good masters, and flatter myself that I am not quite a blockhead.'

'But, my dear fellow, you are joking then,' said I; 'this is a very passable *skull* – indeed, I may say that it is a very *excellent* skull, according to the vulgar notions about such specimens of physiology – and your *scarabæus* must be the queerest *scarabæus* in the world if it resembles it. Why, we may get up a very thrilling bit of superstition upon this hint. I presume you will call the bug *scarabæus caput hominis*, or something of that kind – there are many similar titles in the Natural Histories. But where are the *antennæ* you spoke of?'

'The *antennæ!*' said Legrand, who seemed to be getting unaccountably warm upon the subject; 'I am sure you must see the *antennæ.* I made them as distinct as they are in the original insect, and I presume that is sufficient.'

'Well, well,' I said, 'perhaps you have – still I don't see them;' and I handed him the paper without additional remark, not wishing to ruffle his temper; but I was much surprised at the turn affairs had taken; his ill-humour puzzled me – and, as for the drawing of the beetle, there were positively *no antennæ* visible, and the whole *did* bear a very close resemblance to the ordinary cuts of a death's-head.

He received the paper very peevishly, and was about to crumple it, apparently to throw it in the fire, when a casual glance at the design seemed suddenly to rivet his attention. In an instant his face grew violently red – in another as excessively pale. For some minutes he continued to scrutinise the drawing minutely where he sat. At length he arose, took a candle from the table, and proceeded to seat himself upon a sea-chest in the farthest corner of the room. Here again, he made an anxious examination of the paper; turning it in all directions. He said nothing, however, and his conduct greatly astonished me; yet I thought it prudent not to exacerbate the growing moodiness of his temper by any comment. Presently he took from his coat pocket a wallet, placed the paper carefully in it, and deposited both in a writing-desk, which he locked. He now grew more composed in his de-meanour; but his original air of enthusiasm had quite disappeared. Yet he seemed not so much sulky as abstracted. As the evening wore away he became more and more absorbed in reverie, from which no sallies of mine could arouse him. It had been my intention to pass the night at the hut, as I had frequently done before, but, seeing my host in this mood, I deemed it proper to take leave. He did not press me to remain, but, as I departed, he shook my hand with even more than his usual cordiality.

It was about a month after this (and during the interval I had seen nothing of Legrand) when I received a visit, at Charleston, from his man, Jupiter. I had never seen the good old negro look so disspirited, and I feared that some serious disaster had befallen my friend.

'Well, Jup,' said I, 'what is the matter now? – how is your master?'

'Why, to speak de troof, massa, him not so berry well as mought be.'

'Not well! I am truly sorry to hear it. What does he complain of?'

'Dar! dat's it! – him nebber plain of notin – but him berry sick for all dat.'

'*Very* sick, Jupiter! – why didn't you say so at once? Is he confined to bed?'

'No dat he aint! – he aint find nowhar – dat's just whar de shoe pinch – my mind is got to be berry hebby bout poor Massa Will.'

'Jupiter, I should like to understand what it is you are talking about. You say your master is sick. Hasn't he told you what ails him?'

'Why, massa, taint worf while for to git mad about de matter – Massa Will say nuffin at all aint de matter wid him – but den what make him go about looking dis here way, wid he head down and he soldiers up, and as white as a gose? And den he keeps a syphon all de time' –

'Keeps a what, Jupiter?'

'Keeps a syphon wide de figgurs on de slate – de queerest figgurs I ebber did see. Ise gitten to be skeered, I tell you. Hab for to keep mighty tight eye pon him noovers. Todder day he gib me slip fore de sun up, and was gone de whole ob de blessed day. I had a big stick ready cut for to gib him deuced good beating when he did come – but Ise sich a fool dat I hadn't de heart after all – he look so berry poorly.'

'Eh? – what? – ah yes! – upon the whole I think you had better not be too severe with the poor fellow – don't flog him, Jupiter – he can't very well stand it – but can you form no idea of what has occasioned this illness, or rather this change of conduct? Has anything unpleasant happened since I saw you?'

'No, massa, dey aint bin noffin onpleasant *since* den – 'twas *fore* den, I'm feared – 'twas de berry day you was dare.'

'How? what do you mean?'

'Why, massa, I mean de bug – dare now.'

'The what?'

'De bug – I'm berry sertain dat Massa Will bin bit somewhere bout de head by dat goole-bug.'

'And what cause have you, Jupiter, for such a supposition?'

'Claws enuff, massa, and mouff too. I nebber did see sich a deuced bug – he kick and he bite ebery ting what cum near him. Massa Will cotch him fuss, but had for to let him go gin mighty quick, I tell you – den was de time he must ha got de bite. I didn't like de look ob de bug mouff, myself, no how, so I wouldn't take hold ob him wid my finger, but I cotch him wid a piece ob paper dat I found. I rap him up in de paper and stuff piece ob it in he mouff – dat was de way.'

'And you think, then, that your master was really bitten by the beetle, and that the bite made him sick?'

'I don't tink noffin about it – I nose it. What make him dream bout de goole so much, if taint cause he bit by de goole-bug? Ise heerd bout dem goole-bugs fore dis.'

'But how do you know he dreams about gold?'

'How I know? why, cause he talk about it in he sleep – dat's how I nose.'

'Well, Jup, perhaps you are right; but to what fortunate circumstance am I to attribute the honour of a visit from you to-day?'

'What de matter, massa?'

'Did you bring any message from Mr. Legrand?'

'No, massa, I bring dis here pissel;' and here Jupiter handed me a note which ran thus:

MY DEAR——

Why have I not seen you for so long a time? I hope you have not been so foolish as to take offence at any little *brusquerie* of mine; but no, that is improbable.

Since I saw you I have had great cause for anxiety. I have something to tell you, yet scarcely know how to tell it, or whether I should tell it at all.

I have not been quite well for some days past, and poor old Jup annoys me, almost beyond endurance, by his well-meant attentions. Would you believe it? – he had prepared a huge stick the other day, with which to chastise me for giving him the slip, and spending the day, *solus*, among the hills on the main land. I verily believe that my ill looks alone saved me a flogging.

I have made no addition to my cabinet since we met.

If you can in any way make it convenient, come over with Jupiter. *Do* come. I wish to see you *to-night*, upon business of importance. I assure you that it is of the *highest* importance. – Ever yours,

WILLIAM LEGRAND.

There was something in the tone of this note which gave me great uneasiness. Its whole style differed materially from that of Legrand. What could he be dreaming of? What new crochet possessed his excitable brain? What 'business of the highest importance' could *he* possibly have to transact? Jupiter's account of him boded no good. I dreaded lest the continued pressure of misfortune had, at length, fairly unsettled the reason of my friend. Without a moment's hesitation, therefore, I prepared to accompany the negro.

Upon reaching the wharf, I noticed a scythe and three spades, all apparently new, lying in the bottom of the boat in which we were to embark.

'What is the meaning of all this, Jup?' I inquired.

'Him syfe, massa, and spade.'

'Very true; but what are they doing here?'

'Him de syfe and de spade what Massa Will sis pon my buying for him in de town, and de debbil's own lot of money I had to gib for em.'

'But what, in the name of all that is mysterious, is your "Massa Will" going to do with scythes and spades?'

'Dat's more dan *I* know, and debbil take me if I don't believe 'tis more dan he know too. But it's all cum ob de bug.'

Finding that no satisfaction was to be obtained of Jupiter, whose whole intellect seemed to be absorbed by 'de bug,' I now stepped into the boat and made sail. With a fair and strong breeze we soon ran into the little cove to the northward of Fort Moultrie, and a walk of some two miles brought us to the hut. It was about three in the afternoon when we arrived. Legrand had been awaiting us in eager expectation. He grasped my hand with a nervous *empressement* which alarmed me and strengthened the suspicions already entertained. His countenance was pale even to ghastliness, and his deep-set eyes glared with unnatural lustre. After some inquiries respecting his health, I asked him, not knowing what better to say, if he had yet obtained the *scarabæus* from Lieutenant G——

'Oh, yes,' he replied, colouring violently, 'I got it from him the next morning. Nothing should tempt me to part with that *scarabæus*. Do you know that Jupiter is quite right about it!'

'In what way?' I asked, with a sad foreboding at heart.

'In supposing it to be a bug of *real gold*.' He said this with an air of profound seriousness, and I felt inexpressibly shocked.

'This bug is to make my fortune,' he continued, with a triumphant smile, 'to reinstate me in my family possessions. Is it any wonder, then, that I prize it? Since Fortune has thought fit to bestow it upon me, I have only to use it properly and I shall arive at the gold of which it is the index. Jupiter, bring me that *scarabæus*!'

'What! de bug, massa? I'd rudder not go fer trubble dat bug – you mus git him for your own self.' Hereupon Legrand arose, with a grave and stately air, and brought me the beetle from a glass case in which it was enclosed. It was a beautiful *scarabæus*, and, at that time, unknown to naturalists – of course a great prize in a scientific point of view. There were two round black spots near one extremity of the back, and a long one near the other. The scales were exceedingly hard and glossy, with all the appearance of burnished gold. The weight of the insect was very remarkable, and, taking all things into consideration, I could hardly blame Jupiter for his opinion respecting it; but what to make of Legrand's concordance with that opinion, I could not, for the life of me, tell.

'I sent for you,' said he, in a grandiloquent tone, when I had completed my examination of the beetle, 'I sent for you, that I might have your counsel and assistance in furthering the views of Fate and of the bug'——

'My dear Legrand,' I cried, interrupting him, 'you are certainly unwell, and had better use some little precautions. You shall go to bed, and I will remain with you a few days, until you get over this. You are feverish and'——

'Feel my pulse,' said he.

I felt it, and, to say the truth, found not the slightest indication of fever.

'But you may be ill and yet have no fever. Allow me this once to prescribe for you. In the first place, go to bed. In the next'——

'You are mistaken,' he interposed; 'I am as well as I can expect to be under the excitement which I suffer. If you really wish me well, you will relieve this excitement.'

'And how is this to be done?'

'Very easily. Jupiter and myself are going upon an expedition into the hills, upon the main land, and, in this expedition, we shall need the aid of some person in whom we can confide. You are the only one we can trust. Whether we succeed or fail, the excitement which you now perceive in me will be equally allayed.'

'I am anxious to oblige you in any way,' I replied; 'but do you mean to say that this infernal beetle has any connection with your expedition into the hills?'

'It has.'

'Then, Legrand, I can become a party to no such absurd proceeding.'

'I am sorry – very sorry – for we shall have to try it by ourselves.'

'Try it by yourselves! the man is surely mad! – but stay! – how long do you propose to be absent?'

'Probably all night. We shall start immediately, and be back, at all events, by sunrise.'

'And will you promise me upon your honour, that when this freak of yours is over, and the bug business (good God!) settled to your satisfaction, you will then return home and follow my advice implicitly, as that of your physician?'

'Yes; I promise; and now let us be off, for we have no time to lose.'

With a heavy heart I accompanied my friend. We started about four o'clock – Legrand, Jupiter, the dog, and myself. Jupiter had with him the scythe and spades – the whole of which he insisted upon carrying – more through fear, it seemed to me, of trusting either of the implements within reach of his master, than from any excess of industry or complaisance. His demeanour was dogged in the extreme, and 'dat deuced bug' were the sole words which escaped his lips during the journey. For my own part, I had charge of a couple of dark lanterns, while Legrand contented himself with the *scarabæus*, which he carried attached to the end of a bit of whip-cord; twirling it to and fro, with the air of a conjuror, as he went. When I observed this last plain evidence of my friend's aberration of mind I could scarcely refrain from tears. I thought it best, however, to humour his fancy, at least for the present, or until I could adopt some more energetic measures with a chance of success. In the meantime I endeavoured, but all in vain, to sound him in regard to the object of the expedition. Having succeeded in inducing me to accompany him, he seemed unwilling to hold conversation upon any topic of minor importance, and to all my questions vouchsafed no other reply than 'We shall see!'

We crossed the creek at the head of the island by means of a skiff, and, ascending the high grounds on the shore of the main land, proceeded in a north-westerly direction, through a tract of country excessively wild and desolate, where no trace of a human footstep was to be seen. Legrand led the way with decision; pausing only for an instant, here and there, to consult what appeared to be certain landmarks of his own contrivance upon a former occasion.

In this manner we journeyed for about two hours, and the sun was just setting when we entered a region infinitely more dreary than any yet seen. It was a species of tableland, near the summit of an almost inaccessible hill, densely wooded from base to pinnacle, and interspersed with huge crags that appeared to lie loosely upon the soil, and in many cases were prevented from precipitating themselves into the valleys below, merely by the support of the trees against which they reclined. Deep ravines, in various directions, gave an air of still sterner solemnity to the scene.

The natural platform to which we had clambered was thickly overgrown with brambles, through which we soon discovered that it would have been impossible to force our way but for the scythe; and Jupiter, by direction of his master, proceeded to clear for us a path to the foot of an enormously tall tulip-tree, which stood, with some eight or ten oaks, upon the level, and far surpassed them all, and all other trees which I had then ever seen, in the beauty of its foliage and form, in the wide spread of its branches, and in the general majesty of its appearance. When we reached this tree, Legrand turned to Jupiter, and asked him if he thought he could climb it. The old man seemed a little staggered by the question, and for some moments made no reply. At length he approached the huge trunk, walked slowly round it, and examined it with minute attention. When he had completed his scrutiny, he merely said.

'Yes, massa, Jup climb any tree he ebber see in he life.'

'Then up with you as soon as possible, for it will soon be too dark to see what we are about.'

'How far mus go up, massa?' inquired Jupiter.

'Get up the main trunk first, and then I will tell you which way to go – and here – stop! take this beetle with you.'

'De bug, Massa Will! – de goole bug!' cried the negro, drawing back in dismay – 'what for mus tote de bug way up de tree? – d – n if I do!'

'If you are afraid, Jup, a great big negro like you, to take hold of a harmless little dead beetle, why you can carry it up by this string – but if you do not take it up with you in some way, I shall be under the necessity of breaking your head with this shovel.'

'What de matter now, massa?' said Jup, evidently shamed into compliance; 'always want to raise fuss wid old nigger. Was only funnin any how. *Me* feered de bug! what I keer for de bug?' Here he took cautiously hold of the extreme end of the string, and, maintaining the insect as far from his person as circumstances would permit, prepared to ascend the tree.

In youth, the tulip-tree, or *Liriodendron tulipiferum*, the most magnificent of American foresters, has a trunk peculiarly smooth, and often rises to a great height without lateral branches; but, in its riper age, the bark becomes gnarled and uneven, while many short limbs make their appearance on the stem. Thus the difficulty of ascension, in the present case, lay more in semblance than in reality. Embracing the huge cylinder, as closely as possible, with his arms and knees, seizing with his hands some projections, and resting his naked toes upon others, Jupiter, after one or two narrow escapes from falling, at length wriggled himself into the first great fork, and seemed to consider the whole business as virtually accomplished. The *risk* of the achievement was, in fact, now over, although the climber was some sixty or seventy feet from the ground.

'Which way mus go now, Massa Will?' he asked.

'Keep up the largest branch – the one on this side,' said Legrand. The negro obeyed him promptly, and apparently with but little trouble; ascending higher and higher, until no glimpse of his squat figure could be obtained through the dense foliage which enveloped it. Presently his voice was heard in a sort of halloo.

'How much fudder is got for go?'

'How high up are you?' asked Legrand.

'Ebber so fur,' replied the negro; 'can see de sky fru de top ob de tree.'

'Never mind the sky, but attend to what I say. Look down the trunk and count the limbs below you on this side. How many limbs have you passed?'

'One, two, three, four, fibe, – I done pass fibe big limb, massa, pon dis side.'

'Then go one limb higher.'

In a few minutes the voice was heard again, announcing that the seventh limb was attained.

'Now, Jup,' cried Legrand, evidently much excited, 'I want you to work your way out upon that limb as far as you can. If you see anything strange, let me know.'

By this time what little doubt I might have entertained of my poor friend's insanity was put finally at rest. I had no alternative but to conclude him stricken with lunacy, and I became seriously anxious about getting him home. While I was pondering upon what was best to be done, Jupiter's voice was again heard.

'Mos feerd for to ventur pon dis limb berry far – tis dead limb putty much all de way.'

'Did you say it was a *dead* limb, Jupiter?' cried Legrand in a quavering voice.

'Yes, massa, him dead as de door-nail – done up for sartain – done departed dis here life.'

'What in the name of heaven shall I do?' asked Legrand, seemingly in the greatest distress.

'Do!' said I, glad of an opportunity to interpose a word, 'why come home and go to bed. Come now! – that's a fine fellow. It's getting late, and, besides, you remember your promise.'

'Jupiter,' cried he, without heeding me in the least, 'do you hear me?'

'Yes, Massa Will, hear you ebber so plain.'

'Try the wood well, then, with your knife, and see if you think it *very* rotten.'

'Him rotten, massa, sure nuff,' replied the negro in a few moments, 'but not so berry rotten as mought be. Mought ventur out leetle way pon de limb by myself, dat's true.'

'By yourself! – What do you mean?'

'Why, I mean de bug. 'Tis *berry* hebby bug. Spose I drop him down fuss, and den de limb won't break wid just de weight ob one nigger.'

'You infernal scoundrel!' cried Legrand, apparently much relieved, 'what do you mean by telling me such nonsense as that? As sure as you drop that beetle I'll break your neck. Look here, Jupiter, do you hear me?'

'Yes, massa, needn't hollo at poor nigger dat style.'

'Well! now listen! if you will venture out on the limb as far as you think safe, and not let go the beetle, I'll make you a present of a silver dollar as soon as you get down.'

'I'm gwine, Massa Will – deed I is,' replied the negro very promptly – 'mos out to the eend now.'

'*Out to the end!*' here fairly screamed Legrand, 'do you say you are out to the end of that limb?'

'Soon be to de eend, massa, – o o-o-o-oh! Lor-gol-a-marcy! what *is* dis here pon de tree?'

'Well,' cried Legrand, highly delighted, 'what is it?'

'Why, taint noffin but a skull – somebody bin lef him head up de tree, and de crows done gobble every bit ob de meat off.'

'A skull, you say! – very well! – how is it fastened to the limb? – what holds it on?'

'Sure nuff, massa; mus look. Why dis berry curious sarcumstance, pon my word – dare's a great big nail in de skull, what fastens ob it on to de tree.'

'Well now, Jupiter, do exactly as I tell you – do you hear?'

'Yes, massa.'

'Pay attention, then! – find the left eye of the skull.'

'Hum! hoo! dat's good! why dare aint no eye lef at all.'

'Curse your stupidity! do you know your right hand from your left?'

'Yes, I nose dat – nose all bout dat – 'tis my lef hand what chops de wood wid.'

'To be sure! you are left-handed; and your left eye is on the same side as your left hand. Now, I suppose, you can find the left eye of the skull, or the place where the left eye has been. Have you found it?'

Here was a long pause. At length the negro asked,

'Is de lef eye of de skull pon de same side as de lef hand of de skull, too? – cause de skull aint got not a bit ob a hand at all – nebber mind! I got de lef eye now – here de lef eye! what mus do wid it?'

'Let the beetle drop through it, as far as the string will reach – but be careful and not let go your hold of the string.'

'All dat done, Massa Will; mighty easy ting for to put de bug fru de hole – look out for him dare below!'

During this colloquy no portion of Jupiter's person could be seen; but the beetle, which he had suffered to descend, was now visible at the end of the string, and glistened, like a globe of burnished gold, in the last rays of the setting sun, some of which still faintly illuminated the eminence upon which we stood. The *scarabæus* hung quite clear of any branches, and, if allowed to fall, would have fallen at our feet. Legrand immediately took the scythe, and cleared with it a circular space, three or four yards in diameter, just beneath the insect, and, having accomplished this, ordered Jupiter to let go the string and come down from the tree.

Driving a peg, with great nicety, into the ground, at the precise spot where the beetle fell, my friend now produced from his pocket a tape-measure. Fastening one end of this at that point of the trunk of the tree which was nearest the peg, he unrolled it till it reached the peg, and thence farther unrolled it, in the direction already established by the two points of the tree and the peg, for the distance of fifty feet – Jupiter clearing away the brambles with the scythe. At the spot thus attained a second peg was driven, and about this, as a centre, a rude circle, about four feet in diameter, described. Taking now a spade himself, and giving one to Jupiter and one to me, Legrand begged us to set about digging as quickly as possible.

To speak the truth, I had no especial relish for such amusement at any time, and, at that particular moment, would most willingly have declined it; for the night was coming on, and I felt much fatigued with the exercise already taken; but I saw no mode of escape, and was fearful of disturbing my poor friend's equanimity by a refusal. Could I have depended, indeed, upon Jupiter's aid, I would have had no hesitation in attempting to get the lunatic home by force; but I was too well assured of the old negro's disposition, to hope that he would assist me, under any circumstances, in a personal contest with his master. I made no doubt that the latter had been infected with some of the innumerable Southern superstitions about money buried, and that his fantasy had received confirmation by the finding of the *scarabæus*, or, perhaps, by Jupiter's obstinacy in maintaining it to be 'a bug of real gold.' A mind disposed to lunacy would readily be led away by such suggestions – especially if chiming in with favourite preconceived ideas – and then I called to mind the poor fellow's speech about the beetle's being 'the index of his fortune.' Upon the whole, I was sadly vexed and puzzled, but, at length, I concluded to make a virtue of necessity – to dig with a good will, and thus the sooner to convince the visionary, by ocular demonstration, of the fallacy of the opinions he entertained.

The lanterns having been lit, we all fell to work with a zeal worthy a more rational cause; and, as the glare fell upon our persons and implements, I could not help thinking how picturesque a group we composed and how strange and suspicious our labours must have appeared to any interloper who, by chance, might have stumbled upon our whereabouts.

We dug very steadily for two hours. Little was said; and our chief embarrassment lay in the yelpings of the dog, who took exceeding interest in our proceedings. He at length became so obstreperous, that we grew fearful of his giving the alarm to some stragglers in the vicinity; or, rather, this was the apprehension of Legrand; – for myself, I should have rejoiced at any interruption which might have enabled me to get the wanderer home. The noise was, at length, very effectually silenced by Jupiter, who, getting out of the hole with a dogged air of deliberation, tied the brute's mouth up with one of his suspenders, and then returned, with a grave chuckle, to his task.

When the time mentioned had expired, we had reached a depth of five feet, and yet no signs of any treasure became manifest. A general pause ensued and I began to hope that the farce was at an end. Legrand, however, although evidently much disconcerted, wiped his brow thoughtfully and recommenced. We had excavated the entire circle of four feet diameter, and now we slightly enlarged the limit, and went to the farther depth of two feet. Still nothing appeared. The gold-seeker, whom I sincerely pitied, at length clambered from the pit, with the bitterest disappointment imprinted upon every feature, and proceeded, slowly and reluctantly, to put on his coat, which he had thrown off at the beginning of his labour. In the meantime I made no remark. Jupiter, at a signal from his master, began to gather up his tools. This done, and the dog having been unmuzzled, we turned in profound silence towards home.

We had taken, perhaps, a dozen steps in this direction, when, with a loud oath, Legrand strode up to Jupiter, and seized him by the collar. The astonished negro opened his eyes and mouth to the fullest extent, let fall the spades, and fell upon his knees.

'You scoundrel,' said Legrand, hissing out the syllables from between his clenched teeth – 'you infernal black villain! – speak, I tell you! – answer me this instant, without prevarication! – which – which is your left eye?'

'Oh, my golly, Massa Will! aint dis here my lef eye for sartain?' roared the terrified Jupiter, placing his hand upon his *right* organ of vision, and holding it there with a desperate pertinacity, as if in immediate dread of his master's attempt at a gouge.

'I thought so! – I knew it! hurrah!' vociferated Legrand letting the negro go, and executing a series of curvets and caracols, much to the astonishment of his valet, who, arising from his knees, looked mutely from his master to myself, and then from myself to his master.

'Come! we must go back,' said the latter; 'the game's not up yet;' and he again led the way to the tulip-tree.

'Jupiter,' said he, when he reached its foot, 'come here! was the skull nailed to the limb with the face outwards, or with the face to the limb?'

'De face was out, massa, so dat de crows could get at de eyes good, widout any trouble.'

'Well, then, was it this eye or that through which you dropped the beetle?' – here Legrand touched each of Jupiter's eyes.

''Twas dis eye, massa – de lef eye – jis as you tell me,' and here it was his right eye that the negro indicated.

'That will do – we must try it again.'

Here my friend, about whose madness I now saw, or fancied that I saw, certain indications of method, removed the peg which marked the spot where the beetle fell, to a spot about three inches to the westward of its former position. Taking, now, the tape-measure from the nearest point of the trunk to the peg, as before, and continuing the extension in a straight line to the distance of fifty feet, a spot was indicated, removed by several yards from the point, at which we had been digging.

Around the new position a circle, somewhat larger than in the former instance, was now described, and we again set to work with the spades. I was dreadfully weary, but scarcely understanding what had occasioned the change in my thoughts, I felt no longer any great aversion from the labour imposed. I had become most unaccountably interested – nay, even excited. Perhaps there was something, amid all the extravagant demeanour of Legrand – some air of forethought, or of deliberation, which impressed me. I dug eagerly, and now and then caught myself actually looking, with something that very much resembled expectation, for the fancied treasure, the vision of which had demented my unfortunate companion. At a period when such vagaries of thought most fully possessed me, and when we had been at work perhaps an hour and a half, we were again interrupted by the violent howlings of the dog. His uneasiness, in the first instance, had been, evidently, but the result of playfulness or caprice, but he now assumed a bitter and serious tone. Upon Jupiter's again attempting to muzzle him, he made furious resistance, and, leaping into the hole, tore up the mould frantically with his claws. In a few seconds he had uncovered a mass of human bones, forming two complete skeletons, intermingled with several buttons of metal, and what appeared to be the dust of decayed woollen. One or two strokes of a spade upturned the blade of a large Spanish knife, and, as we dug farther, three or four loose pieces of gold and silver coin came to light.

At the sight of these the joy of Jupiter could scarcely be restrained, but the countenance of his master wore an air of extreme disappointment. He urged us, however, to continue our exertions, and the words were hardly uttered when I stumbled and fell forward, having caught the toe of my boot in a large ring of iron that lay half-buried in the loose earth.

We now worked in earnest, and never did I pass ten minutes of more intense excitement. During this interval we had fairly unearthed an oblong chest of wood, which from its perfect preservation and wonderful hardness, had plainly been subjected to some mineralising process – perhaps that of the bichloride of mercury. This box was three feet and a half long, three feet broad, and two and a half feet deep. It was firmly secured by bands of wrought iron, riveted, and forming a kind of open trellis-work over the whole. On each side of the chest, near the top, were three rings of iron – six in all – by means of which a firm hold could be obtained by six persons. Our utmost united endeavours served only to disturb the coffer very slightly in its bed. We at once saw the impossibility of removing so great a weight. Luckily, the sole fastenings of the lid consisted of two sliding bolts.

There flashed upward a glow and a glare

These we drew back – trembling and panting with anxiety. In an instant, a treasure of incalculable value lay gleaming before us. As the rays of the lanterns fell within the pit, there flashed upwards a glow and a glare, from a confused heap of gold and of jewels, that absolutely dazzled our eyes.

I shall not pretend to describe the feelings with which I gazed. Amazement was, of course, predominant. Legrand appeared exhausted with excitement, and spoke very few words. Jupiter's countenance wore, for some minutes, as deadly a pallor as it is possible, in the nature of things, for any negro's visage to assume. He seemed stupefied – thunderstricken. Presently he fell upon his knees in the pit, and, burying his naked arms up to the elbows in gold, let them there remain, as if enjoying the luxury of a bath. At length, with a deep sigh, he exclaimed, as if in a soliloquy,

'And dis all cum ob de goole-bug? de putty goole-bug! de poor little goole-bug what I boosed in dat sabage kind ob style! Aint you shamed ob yourself, nigger? – answer me dat!'

It became necessary, at last, that I should arouse both master and valet to the expediency of removing the treasure. It was growing late, and it behoved us to make exertion, that we might get everything housed before daylight. It was difficult to say what should be done, and much time was spent in deliberation – so confused were the ideas of all. We finally, lightened the box by removing two-thirds of its contents, when we were enabled, with some trouble, to raise it from the hole. The articles taken out were deposited among the brambles, and the dog left to guard them, with strict orders from Jupiter neither, upon any pretence, to stir from the spot, nor to open his mouth until our return. We then hurriedly made for home with the chest; reaching the hut in safety, but after excessive toil, at one o'clock in the morning. Worn out as we were, it was not in human nature to do more immediately. We rested until two, and had supper; starting for the hills immediately afterwards, armed with three stout sacks, which, by good luck, were upon the premises. A little before four we arrived at the pit, divided the remainder of the booty, as equally as might be, among us, and, leaving the holes unfilled, again set out for the hut, at which, for the second time, we deposited our golden burdens, just as the first faint streaks of the dawn gleamed from over the tree-tops in the East.

We were now thoroughly broken down; but the intense excitement of the time denied us repose. After an unquiet slumber of some three or four hours' duration, we arose, as if by preconcert, to make examination of our treasure.

The chest had been full to the brim, and we spent the whole day, and the greater part of the next night, in a scrutiny of its contents. There had been nothing like order or arrangement. Everything had been heaped in promiscuously. Having assorted all with care, we found ourselves possessed of even vaster wealth than we had at first supposed. In coin there was rather more than four hundred and fifty thousand dollars – estimating the value of the pieces, as accurately as we could, by the tables of the period. There was not a particle of silver. All was gold of antique date and of great variety – French, Spanish, and German money, with a few English guineas, and some counters, of which we had never seen specimens before. There were several very large and heavy coins, so worn that we could make nothing of their inscriptions. There was no American money. The value of the jewels we found more difficulty in estimating. There were diamonds – some of them exceedingly large and fine – a hundred and ten in all, and not one of them small; eighteen rubies of remarkable brilliancy; – three hundred and ten emeralds, all very beautiful; and twenty-one sapphires, with an opal. These stones had all been broken from their settings and thrown loose in the chest. The settings themselves, which we picked out from among the other gold, appeared to have been beaten up with hammers, as if to prevent identification. Besides all this, there was a vast quantity of solid gold ornaments; – nearly two hundred massive finger and ear-rings; – rich chains – thirty of these, if I remember; – eighty-three very large and heavy crucifixes; – five gold censers of great value; – a prodigious golden punch-bowl, ornamented with richly chased vine-leaves and Bacchanalian figures; with two sword-handles exquisitely embossed, and many other smaller articles which I cannot recollect. The weight of these valuables exceeded three hundred and fifty pounds avoirdupois; and in this estimate I have not included one hundred and ninety-seven superb gold watches, three of the number being worth each five hundred dollars, if one. Many of them were very old, and as time-keepers valueless; the works having suffered, more or less, from corrosion – but all were richly jewelled, and in cases of great worth. We estimated the entire contents of the chest, that night, at a million and a half dollars; and, upon the subsequent disposal of the trinkets and jewels (a few being retained for our own use), it was found that we had greatly undervalued the treasure.

When, at length, we had concluded our examination, and the intense excitement of the time had in some measure subsided, Legrand, who saw that I was dying with impatience for a solution of this most extraordinary riddle, entered into a full detail of all the circumstances connected with it.

'You remember,' said he, 'the night when I handed you the rough sketch I had made of the *scarabæus*. You recollect also, that I became quite vexed at you for insisting that my drawing resembled a death's head. When you first made this assertion I thought you were jesting; but afterwards I called to mind the peculiar spots on the back of the insect, and admitted to myself that your remark had some little foundation in fact. Still, the sneer at my graphic powers irritated me – for I am considered a good artist – and, therefore, when you handed me the scrap of parchment, I was about to crumple it up and throw it angrily into the fire.'

'The scrap of paper, you mean,' said I.

'No; it had much of the appearance of paper, and at first I supposed it to be such, but when I came to draw upon it, I discovered it, at once, to be piece of very thin parchment. It was quite dirty, you remember. Well, as I was in the very act of crumpling it up, my glance fell upon the sketch at which you had been looking, and you may imagine my astonishment when I perceived, in fact, the figure of a death's-head just where, it seemed to me, I had made the drawing of the beetle. For a moment I was too much amazed to think with accuracy. I knew that my design was very different in detail from this –

although there was a certain similarity in general outline. Presently I took a candle, and seating myself at the other end of the room, proceeded to scrutinise the parchment more closely. Upon turning it over, I saw my own sketch upon the reverse, just as I had made it. My first idea, now, was mere surprise at the really remarkable similarity of outline – at the singular coincidence involved in the fact, that unknown to me, there should have been a skull upon the other side of the parchment, immediately beneath my figure of the *scarabæus*, and that this skull, not only in outline, but in size, should so closely resemble my drawing. I say the singularity of this coincidence absolutely stupefied me for a time. This is the usual effect of such coincidences. The mind struggles to establish a connection – a sequence of cause and effect – and, being unable to do so, suffers a species of temporary paralysis. But when I recovered from this stupor, there dawned upon me gradually a conviction which startled me even far more than the coincidence. I began distinctly, positively, to remember that there had been *no* drawing upon the parchment when I made my sketch of the *scarabæus*. I became perfectly certain of this; for I recollected turning up first one side and then the other, in search of the cleanest spot. Had the skull been then there, of course I could not have failed to notice it. Here was indeed a mystery which I felt it impossible to explain; but, even at that early moment, there seemed to glimmer, faintly, within the most remote and secret chambers of my intellect, a glow-worm-like conception of that truth which last night's adventure brought to so magnificent a demonstration. I arose at once, and putting the parchment securely away, dismissed all further reflection until I should be alone.

'When you had gone, and when Jupiter was fast asleep, I betook myself to a more methodical investigation of the affair. In the first place I considered the manner in which the parchment had come into my possession. The spot where we discovered the *scarabæus* was on the coast of the mainland, about a mile eastward of the island, and but a short distance above high-water mark. Upon my taking hold of it, it gave me a sharp bite, which caused me to let it drop. Jupiter, with his accustomed caution, before seizing the insect, which had flown towards him, looked about him for a leaf, or something of that nature, by which to take hold of it. It was at this moment that his eyes, and mine also, fell upon the scrap of parchment, which I then supposed to be paper. It was lying half buried in the sand, a corner sticking up. Near the spot where we found it, I observed the remnants of the hull of what appeared to have been a ship's long boat. The wreck seemed to have been there for a very great while; for the resemblance to boat timbers could scarcely be traced.

'Well, Jupiter picked up the parchment, wrapped the beetle in it, and gave it to me. Soon afterwards we turned to go home, and on the way met Lieutenant G——. I showed him the insect, and he begged me to let him take it to the fort. Upon my consenting, he thrust it forthwith into his waistcoat pocket, without the parchment in which it had been wrapped, and which I had continued to hold in my hand during his inspection. Perhaps he dreaded my changing my mind, and thought it best to make sure of the prize at once; you know how enthusiastic he is on all subjects connected with Natural History. At the same time, without being conscious of it, I must have deposited the parchment in my own pocket.

'You remember that when I went to the table, for the purpose of making a sketch of the beetle, I found no paper where it was usually kept. I looked in the drawer, and found none there. I searched my pockets, hoping to find an old letter, when my hand fell upon the parchment. I thus detail the precise mode in which it came into my possession; for the circumstances impressed me with peculiar force.

'No doubt you will think me fanciful – but I had already established a kind of *connection*. I had put together two links of a great chain. There was a boat lying upon a sea-coast, and not far from the boat was a parchment – *not a paper* – with a skull depicted upon it. You will, of course, ask "Where is the connection?" I reply that the skull, or death's-head, is the well-known emblem of the pirate. The flag of the death's-head is hoisted in all engagements.

'I have said that the scrap was parchment, and not paper. Parchment is durable – almost imperishable. Matters of little moment are rarely consigned to parchment; since, for the mere ordinary purposes of drawing or writing, it is not nearly so well adapted as paper. This reflection suggested some meaning – some relevancy – in the death's-head. I did not fail to observe, also, the *form* of the parchment. Although one of its corners had been, by some accident, destroyed, it could be seen that the original form was oblong. It was just such a slip, indeed, as might have been chosen for a memorandum – for a record, of something to be long remembered and carefully preserved.'

'But,' I interposed, 'you say that the skull was *not* upon the parchment when you made the drawing of the beetle. How then do you trace any connection between the boat and the skull – since this latter, according to your own admission, must have been designed (God only knows how or by whom) at some period subsequent to your sketching the *scarabæus?*'

'Ah, hereupon turns the whole mystery; although the secret, at this point, I had comparatively little difficulty in solving. My steps were sure, and could afford but a single result. I reasoned, for example, thus: When I drew the *scarabæus*, there was no skull apparent upon the parchment. When I had completed the drawing I gave it to you, and observed you narrowly until you returned it. *You*, therefore, did not design the skull, and no one else was present to do it. Then it was not done by human agency. And nevertheless it was done.

'At this stage of my reflections I endeavoured to remember, and *did* remember, with entire distinctness, every incident which occurred about the period in question. The weather was chilly (oh rare and happy accident!), and a fire was blazing upon the hearth. I was heated with exercise and sat near the table. You, however, had drawn a chair close to the chimney. Just as I placed the parchment in your hand, and as you were in the act of inspecting it, Wolf, the Newfoundland, entered, and leaped upon your shoulders. With your left hand you caressed him and kept him off, while your right, holding the parchment, was permitted to fall listlessly between your knees, and in close proximity to the fire. At one moment I thought the blaze had caught it, and was about to caution you, but, before I could speak, you had withdrawn it, and were engaged in its examination. When I considered all these particulars, I doubted not for a moment that *heat* had been the agent in bringing to light, upon the parchment, the skull which I saw designed upon it. You are well aware that chemical preparations exist, and have existed time out of mind, by means of which it is possible to write upon either paper or vellum, so that the characters shall become visible only when subjected to the action of fire. Zaffre, digested in *aqua regia*, and diluted with four times its weight of water, is sometimes employed; a green tint results. The regulus of cobalt, dissolved in spirit of nitre, gives a red. These colours disappear at longer or shorter intervals after the material written upon cools, but again become apparent upon the re-application of heat.

'I now scrutinised the death's head with care. Its outer edges – the edges of the drawing nearest the edge of the vellum – were far more *distinct* than the others. It was clear that the action of the caloric had been imperfect, or unequal. I immediately kindled a fire, and subjected every portion of the parchment to a glowing heat. At first, the only effect was the strengthening of the faint lines in the skull; but, upon persevering in the experiment, there became visible at the corner of the slip, diagonally opposite to the spot in which the death's-head was delineated, the figure of what I at first supposed to be a goat. A closer scrutiny, however, satisfied me that it was intended for a kid.'

'Ha! ha!' said I, 'to be sure. I have no right to laugh at you – a million and a half of money is too serious a matter for mirth – but you are not about to establish a third link in your chain – you will not find any especial connection between your pirates and a goat – pirates, you know, have nothing to do with goats; they appertain to the farming interest.'

'But I have said that the figure was *not* that of a goat.'

'Well, a kid then – pretty much the same thing.'

'Pretty much, but not altogether,' said Legrand. 'You may have heard of one *Captain* Kidd. I at once looked upon the figure of the animal as a kind of punning or hieroglyphical signature. I say signature; because its position upon the vellum suggested this idea. The death's-head at the corner diagonally opposite, had, in the same manner, the air of a stamp, or seal. But I was sorely put out by the absence of all else – of the body to my imagined instrument – of the text for my context.'

'I presume you expected to find a letter between the stamp and the signature.'

'Something of that kind. The fact is, I felt irresistibly impressed with a presentiment of some vast good fortune impending. I can scarcely say why. Perhaps, after all, it was rather a desire than an actual belief; but do you know that Jupiter's silly words, about the bug being of solid gold, had a remarkable effect upon my fancy? And then the series of accidents and coincidences – these were so *very* extraordinary. Do you observe how mere an accident it was that these events should have occurred upon the *sole* day of all the year in which it has been, or may be, sufficiently cool for fire, and that without the fire, or without the intervention of the dog at the precise moment in which he appeared, I should never have become aware of the death's-head, and so never the possessor of the treasure?'

'But proceed – I am all impatience.'

'Well; you have heard, of course, the many stories current – the thousand vague rumours afloat about money buried, somewhere upon the Atlantic coast, by Kidd and his associates. These rumours must have had some foundation in fact. And that the rumours have existed so long and so continuous, could have resulted, it appeared to me, only from the circumstances of the buried treasure still *remaining* entombed. Had Kidd concealed his plunder for a time, and afterwards reclaimed it, the rumours would scarcely have reached us in their present unvarying form. You will observe that the stories told are all about money-seekers, not about money-finders. Had the pirate recovered his money, there the affair would have dropped. It seemed to me that some accident – say the loss of a memorandum indicating its locality – had deprived him of the means of recovering it, and that this accident had become known to his followers, who otherwise might never have heard that treasure had been concealed at all, and who, busying themselves in vain, because unguided attempts, to regain it, had given first birth, and then universal currency, to the reports which are now so common. Have you ever heard of any important treasure being unearthed along the coast?'

'Never.'

'But that Kidd's accumulations were immense is well known. I took it for granted, therefore, that the earth still held them; and you will scarcely be surprised when I tell you that I felt a hope, nearly amounting to certainty, that the parchment so strangely found, involved a lost record of the place of deposit.'

'But how did you proceed?'

'I held the vellum again to the fire, after increasing the heat; but nothing appeared. I now thought it possible that the coating of dirt might have something to do with the failure; so I carefully rinsed the parchment by pouring warm water over it, and, having done this, I placed it in a tin pan, with the skull downwards, and put the pan upon a furnace of lighted charcoal. In a few minutes, the pan having become thoroughly heated, I removed the slip and to my inexpressible joy, found it spotted, in several places, with what appeared to be figures arranged in lines. Again I placed it in the pan and suffered it to remain another minute. Upon taking it off, the whole was just as you see it now.'

Here Legrand, having re-heated the parchment, submitted it to my inspection. The following characters were rudely traced, in a red tint, between the death's-head and the goat:

53‡‡†305))6*;4826)4‡.)4‡);806*;48†8¶60))85;1‡(;:‡*8†83
(88)5*†;46(;88*96*?;8)*‡(;485);5*†2:*‡(;4956*2(5*—4)8¶8*;
4069285);)6†8)4‡‡;1(‡9;48081;8:8‡1;48†85;4)485†528806*81
(‡9;48;(88;4(‡?34;48)4‡;161;:188;‡?;

'But,' said I, returning him the slip, 'I am as much in the dark as ever. Were all the jewels of Golconda awaiting me upon my solution of this enigma, I am quite sure that I should be unable to earn them.'

'And yet,' said Legrand, 'the solution is by no means so difficult as you might be led to imagine from the hasty inspection of the charcters.

These characters, as any one might readily guess, form a cipher – that is to say, they convey a meaning: but then, from what is known of Kidd, I could not suppose him capable of constructing any of the more abstruse cryptographs. I made up my mind, at once, that this was of a simple species – such, however, as would appear, to the crude intellect of the sailor, absolutely insoluble without the key.'

'And you really solved it?'

'Readily; I have solved others of an abstruseness ten thousand times greater. Circumstances, and a certain bias of mind, have led me to take interest in such riddles, and it may well be doubted whether human ingenuity can construct an enigma of the kind which human ingenuity may not by proper application, resolve. In fact, having once established connected and legible characters, I scarcely gave a thought to the mere difficulty of developing their import.

'In the present case – indeed in all cases of secret writing – the first question regards the *language* of the cipher; for the principles of solution, so far, especially, as the more simple ciphers are concerned, depend upon, and are varied by, the genius of the particular idiom. In general, there is no alternative but experiment (directed by probabilities) of every tongue known to him who attempts the solution, until the true one be attained. But, with the cipher now before us, all difficulty was removed by the signature. The pun upon the word "Kidd" is appreciable in no other language than the English. But for this consideration I should have begun my attempts with the Spanish and French, as the tongues in which a secret of this kind would most naturally have been written by a pirate of the Spanish main. As it was, I assumed the cryptograph to be English.

'You observe there are no divisions between the words. Had there been divisions, the task would have been comparatively easy. In such case I should have commenced with a collation and analysis of the shorter words, and had a word of a single letter occurred, as is most likely (*a* or *I*, for example), I should have considered the solution as assured. But, there being no division, my first step was to ascertain the predominant letters, as well as the least frequent. Counting all, I constructed a table thus:

Of the character 8 there are 33.

,	„	26.
4	„	19.
‡)	„	16.
*	„	13.
5	„	12.
6	„	11.
†1	„	8.
0	„	6.
92	„	5.
:3	„	4.
?	„	3.
¶	„	2.
—.	„	1.

'Now, in English, the letter which most frequently occurs is *e*. Afterwards, the succession runs thus: *a o i d h n r s t u y c f g l m w b k p q x z*. *E* predominates so remarkably that an individual sentence of any length is rarely seen, in which it is not the prevailing character.

'Here, then, we have, in the very beginning, the groundwork for something more than a mere guess. The general use which may be made of the table is obvious – but in this particular cipher we shall only very partially require its aid. As our predominant character is 8, we will commence by assuming it as the *e* of the natural alphabet. To verify the supposition, let us observe if the 8 be seen often in couples – for *e* is doubled with great frequency in English – in such words, for example, as "meet," "fleet," "speed," "seen," "been," "agree," etc. In the present instance we see it doubled no less than five times, although the cryptograph is brief.

'Let us assume 8 then, as *e*. Now, of all *words* in the language, "the" is the most usual; let us see, therefore, whether there are not repetitions of any three characters, in the same order of collocation, the last of them being 8. If we discover repetitions of such letters, so arranged, they will most probably represent the word "the." Upon inspection, we find no less than seven such arrangements, the characters being ;48. We may, therefore, assume that ; represents *t*, 4 represents *h*, and 8 represents *e* – the last being now well confirmed. Thus a great step has been taken.

'But, having established a single word, we are enabled to establish a vastly important point; that is to say, several commencements and terminations of other words. Let us refer, for example, to the last instance but one, in which the combination ;48 occurs – not far from the end of the cipher. We know that the ; immediately ensuing is the commencement of a word, and of the six characters succeeding this "the," we are cognisant of no less than five. Let us set these characters down, thus, by the letters we know them to represent, leaving a space for the unknown –

t eeth

'Here we are enabled, at once, to discard the "*th*," as forming no portion of the word commencing with the first *t* ; since, by experiment of the entire alphabet for a letter adapted to the vacancy, we perceive that no word can be formed of which this *th* can be a part. We are thus narrowed into

t ee,

and, going through the alphabet, if necessary, as before, we arrive at the word "tree," as the sole possible reading. We thus gain another letter, *r*, represented by (with the words "the three," in juxtaposition.

'Looking beyond these words, for a short distance, we again see the combination ;48, and employ it by way of *termination* to what immediately precedes. We have thus this arrangement:

the tree ;4(‡?34 the,

or, substituting the natural letters, where known, it reads thus:

the tree thr‡?3h the.

'Now, if, in place of the unknown characters, we leave blank spaces, or substitute dots, we read thus:

the tree thr...h the,

when the word "*through*" makes itself evident at once. But this discovery gives us three new letters, *o*, *u*, and *g*, represented by ‡ ? and 3.

'Looking now, narrowly, through the cipher for combinations of known characters, we find, not very far from the beginning, this arrangement,

83(88, or egree,

which, plainly, is the conclusion of the word "degree," and gives us another letter, *d*, represented by †.

'Four letters beyond the word "degree," we perceive the combination.

;46(;88

'Translating the known characters, and representing the unknown by dots, as before, we read thus:

th. rtee.

an arrangement immediately suggestive of the word "thirteen," and again furnishing us with two new characters *i* and *n*, represented by 6 and *.

'Referring, now, to the beginning of the cryptograph, we find the combination,

53‡‡†.

'Translating, as before, we obtain

. good.

which assures us that the first letter is *A*, and that the first two words are "A good."

'It is now time that we arrange our key, as far as discovered, in a tabular form, to avoid confusion. It will stand thus:

5	represents	a
†	„	d
8	„	e
3	„	g
4	„	h
6	„	i
*	„	n
‡	„	o
(	„	r
,	„	t

'We have, therefore, no less than ten of the most important letters represented, and it will be unnecessary to proceed with the details of the solution. I have said enough to convince you that ciphers of this nature are readily soluble, and to give you some insight into the *rationale* of their development. But be assured that the specimen before us appertains to the very simplest species of cryptograph. It now only remains to give you the full translation of the characters upon the parchment as unriddled. Here it is:

"'A good glass in the bishop's hostel in the devil's seat forty-one degrees and thirteen minutes northeast and by north main branch seventh limb east side shoot from the left eye of the death's head a bee line from the tree through the shot fifty feet out."'

'But,' said I, 'the enigma seems still in as bad a condition as ever. How is it possible to extort a meaning from all this jargon about "devil's seats," "death's-heads," and "bishop's hotels?"'

'I confess,' replied Legrand, 'that the matter still wears a serious aspect, when regarded with a casual glance. My first endeavour was to divide the sentence into the natural division intended by the cryptographist.'

'You mean to punctuate it?'

'Something of that kind.'

'But how was it possible to effect this?'

'I reflected that it had been a *point* with the writer to run his words together without division, so as to increase the difficulty of solution. Now, a not over-acute man, in pursuing such an object, would be nearly certain to overdo the matter. When, in the course of his composition, he arrived at a break in his subject which would naturally require a pause, or a point, he would be exceedingly apt to run his characters, at this place, more than usually close together. If you will observe the MS. in the present instance you will easily detect five such cases of unusual crowding. Acting upon this hint, I made the division thus:

"'A good glass in the bishop's hostel in the devil's seat – forty-one degrees and thirteen minutes – north east and by north – main branch seventh limb east side – shoot from the left eye of the death's head – a bee line from the tree through the shot fifty feet out."'

'Even this division,' said I, 'leaves me still in the dark.'

'It left me also in the dark,' replied Legrand, 'for a few days; during which I made diligent inquiry, in the neighbourhood of Sullivan's Island, for any building which went by the name of the "Bishop's Hotel;" for, of course, I dropped the obsolete word "hostel." Gaining no information on the subject, I was on the point of extending my sphere of search, and proceeding in a more systematic manner, when, one morning, it entered into my head, quite suddenly, that this "Bishop's Hostel" might have some reference to an old family, of the name of Bessop, which, time out of mind, had held possession of an ancient manor-house, about four miles to the northward of the Island. I accordingly went over to the plantation, and re-instituted my inquiries among the older negroes of the place. At length one of the most aged of the women said that she had heard of such a place as *Bessop's Castle*, and thought that she could guide me to it, but that it was not a castle, nor a tavern, but a high rock.

'I offered to pay her well for her trouble, and, after some demur, she consented to accompany me to the spot. We found it without much difficulty, when, dismissing her I proceeded to examine the place. The "castle" consisted of an irregular assemblage of cliffs and rocks – one of the latter being quite remarkable for its height as well as for its insulated and artificial appearance. I clambered to its apex, and then felt much at a loss as to what should be next done.

'While I was busied in reflection, my eyes fell upon a narrow ledge in the eastern face of the rock, perhaps a yard below the summit upon which I stood. This ledge projected about eighteen inches, and was not more than a foot wide, while a niche in the cliff just above it gave it a rude resemblance to one of the hollow-backed chairs used by our ancestors. I had no doubt that here was the "devil's seat" alluded to in the MS., and now I seemed to grasp the full secret of the riddle.

'The "good glass," I knew, could have reference to nothing but a telescope: for the word "glass" is rarely employed in any other sense by seamen. Now here, I at once saw, was a telescope to be used, and a definite point of view, *admitting no variation*, from which to use it. Nor did I hesitate to believe that the phrases, "forty-one degrees and thirteen minutes," and "northeast and by north," were intended as directions for the levelling of the glass. Greatly excited by these discoveries, I hurried home, procured a telescope, and returned to the rock.

'I let myself down to the ledge, and found that it was impossible to retain a seat upon it except in one particular position. This fact confirmed my preconceived idea. I proceeded to use the glass.

'Of course, the "forty-one degrees and thirteen minutes" could allude to nothing but elevation above the visible horizon, since the horizontal direction was clearly indicated by the words, "northeast and by north." This latter direction I at once established by means of a pocket-compass; then, pointing the glass as nearly at an angle of forty-one degrees of elevation as I could do it by guess, I moved it cautiously up or down, until my attention was arrested by a circular rift or opening in the foliage of a large tree that overtopped its fellows in the distance. In the centre of this rift I perceived a white spot, but could not, at first, distinguish what it was. Adjusting the focus of the telescope, I again looked, and now made it out to be a human skull.

'Upon this discovery I was so sanguine as to consider the enigma solved; for the phrase "main branch, seventh limb, east side," could refer only to the position of the skull upon the tree, while "shoot from the left eye of the death's head," admitted also of but one interpretation, in regard to a search for buried treasure. I perceived that the design was to drop a bullet from the left eye of the skull, and that a bee-line, or, in other words, a straight line, drawn from the nearest point of the trunk through "the shot," (or the spot where the bullet fell), and thence extended to a distance of fifty feet, would indicate a definite point – and beneath this point I thought it at least *possible* that a deposit of value lay concealed.'

'All this,' I said, 'is exceedingly clear, and, although ingenious, still simple and explicit. When you left the Bishop's Hotel, what then?'

'Why, having carefully taken the bearings of the tree, I turned homewards. The instant that I left the "devil's seat," however, the circular rift vanished nor could I get a glimpse of it afterwards, turn as I would. What seems to me the chief ingenuity in this whole business is the fact (for repeated experiment has convinced me it *is* a fact) that the circular opening in question is visible from no other attainable point of view than that afforded by the narrow ledge upon the face of the rock.

'In this expedition to the "Bishop's Hotel," I had been attended by Jupiter, who had no doubt observed for some weeks past the abstraction of my demeanour, and took especial care not to leave me alone. But, on the next day, getting up very early, I contrived to give him the slip, and went into the hills in search of the tree. After much toil I found it. When I came home at night my valet proposed to give me a flogging. With the rest of the adventure I believe you are as well acquainted as myself.'

'I suppose,' said I, 'you missed the spot, in the first attempt at digging, through Jupiter's stupidity in letting the bug fall through the right instead of through the left eye of the skull.'

'Precisely. This mistake made a difference of about two inches and a half in the "shot" – that is to say, in the position of the peg nearest the tree; and had the treasure been *beneath* the "shot," the error would have been of little moment; but the "shot," together with the nearest point of the tree, were merely two points for the establishment of a line of direction; of course the error, however trivial in the beginning, increased as we proceeded with the line, and by the time we had gone fifty feet, threw us quite off the scent. But for my deep-seated impressions that treasure was here somewhere actually buried, we might have had all our labour in vain.'

'But your grandiloquence, and your conduct in swinging the beetle – how exceedingly odd! I was sure you were mad. And why did you insist upon letting fall the bug, instead of a bullet, from the skull?'

'Why, to be frank, I felt somewhat annoyed by your evident suspicions touching my sanity, and so resolved to punish you quietly, in my own way, by a little bit of sober mystification. For this reason I swung the beetle, and for this reason I let it fall from the tree. An observation of yours about its great weight suggested the latter idea.'

'Yes, I perceive; and now there is only one point which puzzles me. What are we to make of the skeletons found in the hole?'

'That is a question I am no more able to answer than yourself.

There seems, however, only one plausible way of accounting for them – and yet it is dreadful to believe in such atrocity as my suggestion would imply. It is clear that Kidd – if Kidd indeed secreted this treasure, which I doubt not – it is clear that he must have had assistance in the labour. But this labour concluded, he may have thought it expedient to remove all participants in his secret. Perhaps a couple of blows with a mattock were sufficient, while his coadjutors were busy in the pit; perhaps it required a dozen – who shall tell?'

Diddling

Considered as one of the Exact Sciences

Hey, diddle diddle,
The cat and the fiddle.

Since the world began there have been two Jeremys. The one wrote a Jeremiad about usury, and was called Jeremy Bentham. He has been much admired by Mr. John Neal, and was a great man in a small way. The other gave name to the most important of the Exact Sciences, and was a great man in a *great* way – I may say, indeed, in the very greatest of ways.

Diddling – or the abstract idea conveyed by the verb to diddle – is sufficiently well understood. Yet the fact, the deed, the thing *diddling*, is somewhat difficult to define. We may get, however, at a tolerably distinct conception of the matter in hand, by defining – not the thing diddling in itself – but man as an animal that diddles. Had Plato but hit upon this, he would have been spared the affront of the picked chicken.

Very pertinently it was demanded of Plato why a picked chicken, which was clearly 'a biped without feathers,' was not, according to his own definition, a man? But I am not to be bothered by any similar query. Man is an animal that diddles, and there is *no* animal that diddles *but* man. It will take an entire hen-coop of picked chickens to get over that.

What constitutes the essence, the nature, the principle of diddling is, in fact, peculiar to the class of creatures that wear coats and pantaloons. A crow thieves; a fox cheats; a weasel outwits; a man diddles. To diddle is his destiny. 'Man was made to mourn,' says the poet. But not so – he was made to diddle. This is his aim – his object – his *end*. And for this reason when a man's diddled we say he's '*done*.'

Diddling, rightly considered, is a compound, of which the ingredients are minuteness, interest, perseverance, ingenuity, audacity, *nonchalance*, originality, impertinence, and *grin*.

Minuteness:– Your diddler is minute. His operations are upon a small scale. His business is retail for cash, or approved paper at sight. Should he ever be tempted into magnificent speculation, he then, at once, loses his distinctive features, and becomes what we term 'financier.' This latter word conveys the diddling idea in every respect except that of magnitude. A diddler may thus be regarded as a banker *in petto* – a 'financial operation,' as a diddle at Brobdignag. The one is to the other as Homer to 'Flaccus' – as a mastodon to a mouse – as the tail of a comet to that of a pig.

Interest:– Your diddler is guided by self-interest. He scorns to diddle for the mere *sake* of the diddle. He has an object in view – his pocket – and yours. He regards always the main chance. He looks to Number One. You are Number Two, and must look to yourself.

Perseverance:– Your diddler perseveres. He is not readily discouraged. Should even the banks break, he cares nothing about it. He steadily pursues his end, and,

Ut canis a corio nunquam absterrebitur uncto,

so he never lets go of his game.

Ingenuity:– Your diddler is ingenious. He has constructiveness large. He understands plot. He invents and circumvents. Were he not Alexander, he would be Diogenes. Were he not a diddler, he would be a maker of patent rat-traps, or an angler for trout.

Audacity:– Your diddler is audacious – He is a bold man. He carries the war into Africa. He conquers all by assault. He would not fear the daggers of the Frei Herren. With a little more prudence Dick

Turpin would have made a good diddler: with a trifle less blarney, Daniel O'Connell; with a pound or two more brains, Charles the Twelfth.

Nonchalance:– Your Diddler is *nonchalant*. He is not at all nervous. He never *had* any nerves. He is never seduced into a flurry. He is never put out – unless put out of doors. He is cool – cool as a cucumber. He is calm – 'calm as a smile from Lady Bury.' He is easy – easy as an old glove, or the damsels of ancient Baiæ.

Originality:– Your diddler is original – conscientiously so. His thoughts are his own. He would scorn to employ those of another. A stale trick is his aversion. He would return a purse, I am sure, upon discovering that he had obtained it by an unoriginal diddle.

Impertinence:– Your diddler is impertinent. He swaggers. He sets his arms akimbo. He thrusts his hands in his trousers' pockets. He sneers in your face. He treads on your corns. He eats your dinner, he drinks your wine, he borrows your money, he pulls your nose, he kicks your poodle, and he kisses your wife.

Grin:– Your *true* diddler winds up all with a grin. But this nobody sees but himself. He grins when his daily work is done – when his allotted labours are accomplished – at night in his own closet, and altogether for his own private entertainment. He goes home. He locks his door. He divests himself of his clothes. He puts out his candle. He gets into bed. He places his head upon the pillow. All this done, and your diddler *grins*. This is no hypothesis. It is a matter of course. I reason *a priori*, and a diddle would be *no* diddle without a grin.

The origin of the diddle is referrable to the infancy of the Human Race. Perhaps the first diddler was Adam. At all events, we can trace the science back to a very remote period of antiquity. The moderns, however, have brought it to a perfection never dreamed of by our thick-headed progenitors. Without pausing to speak of the 'old saws,' therefore, I shall content myself with a compendious account of some of the more 'modern instances.'

A very good diddle is this. A housekeeper in want of a sofa, for instance, is seen to go in and out of several cabinet warehouses. At length she arrives at one offering an excellent variety. She is accosted, and invited to enter, by a polite and voluble individual at the door. She finds a sofa well adapted to her views, and upon inquiring the price, is surprised and delighted to hear a sum named at least twenty per cent. lower than her expectations. She hastens to make the purchase, gets a bill and receipt, leaves her address, with a request that the article be sent home as speedily as possible, and retires amid a profusion of bows from the shopkeeper. The night arrives, and no sofa. The next day passes, and still none. A servant is sent to make inquiry about the delay. The whole transaction is denied. No sofa has been sold – no money received – except by the diddler, who played shopkeeper for the nonce.

Our cabinet warehouses are left entirely unattended, and thus afford every facility for a trick of this kind. Visitors enter, look at furniture, and depart unheeded and unseen. Should anyone wish to purchase, or to inquire the price of an article, a bell is at hand, and this is considered amply sufficient.

Again, quite a respectable diddle is this. A well-dressed individual enters a shop; makes a purchase to the value of a dollar; finds, much to his vexation, that he has left his pocket-book in another coat pocket; and so says to the shopkeeper – 'My dear sir, never mind! – just oblige me, will you, by sending the bundle home? But stay! I really believe that I have nothing less than a five dollar bill even *there*. However, you can send four dollars in change *with* the bundle, you know.' 'Very good, sir,' replies the shopkeeper, who entertains at once a lofty opinion of the high-mindedness of his customer. 'I know fellows,' he says to himself, 'who would just have put the goods under their arm, and walked off with a promise to call and pay the dollar as they came by in the afternoon.'

A boy is sent with the parcel and change. On the route, quite accidentally, he is met by the purchaser, who exclaims:

'Ah! this is my bundle, I see – I thought you had been home with it, long ago. Well, go on! My wife, Mrs. Trotter, will give you the five dollars – I left instructions with her to that effect. The change you might as well give to *me* – I shall want some silver for the Post-Office. Very good! One, two, is this a good quarter? – three, four – quite right!

Say to Mrs. Trotter that you met me, and be sure now, and *do* not loiter on the way.'

The boy does not loiter at all – but he is a very long time in getting back from his errand – for no lady of the precise name of Mrs. Trotter is to be discovered. He consoles himself, however, that he has not been such a fool as to leave the goods without the money, and re-entering his shop with a self-satisfied air, feels sensibly hurt and indignant when his master asks him what has become of the change.

A very simple diddle, indeed, is this. The captain of a ship which is about to sail is presented by an official-looking person with an unusually moderate bill of city charges. Glad to get off so easily, and confused by a hundred duties pressing upon him all at once, he discharges the claim forthwith. In about fifteen minutes, another and less reasonable bill is handed him by one who soon makes it evident that the first collector was a diddler, and the original collection a diddle.

And here, too, is a somewhat similar thing. A steamboat is casting loose from the wharf. A traveller, portmanteau in hand, is discovered running towards the wharf at full speed. Suddenly, he makes a dead halt, stoops and picks up something from the ground in a very agitated manner. It is a pocket-book, and – 'Has any gentleman lost a pocket-book?' he cries. No one can say that he has exactly lost a pocket-book; but a great excitement ensues, when the treasure trove is found to be of value. The boat, however, must not be detained.

'Time and tide, wait for no man,' says the captain.

'For God's sake, stay only a few minutes,' says the finder of the book – 'the true claimant will presently appear.'

'Can't wait!' replies the man in authority; 'cast off there, d'ye hear?'

'What *am* I to do?' asks the finder, in great tribulation.

'I am about to leave the country for some years, and I cannot conscientiously retain this large amount in my possession. I beg your pardon, sir' (here he addresses a gentleman on shore), 'but you have the air of an honest man. *Will* you confer upon me the favour of taking charge of this pocket-book – I *know* I can trust you – and of advertising it? The notes, you see, amount to a very considerable sum. The owner will, no doubt, insist upon rewarding you for your trouble'——

'*Me!* – no, *you!* – it was *you* who found the book.'

'Well, if you *must* have it so – I will take a small reward – just to satisfy your scruples. Let me see – why, these notes are all hundreds – bless my soul, a hundred is too much to take – fifty would be quite enough, I am sure'——

'Cast off there!' says the captain.

'But then I have no change for a hundred, and upon the whole, you had better'——

'Cast off there!' says the captain.

'Never mind!' cries the gentleman on shore, who has been examining his own pocket-book for the last minute or so – 'never mind; I can fix it – here is a fifty on the Bank of North America – throw me the book.'

And the over-conscientious finder takes the fifty with marked reluctance, and throws the gentleman the book, as desired, while the steamboat fumes and fizzes on her way. In about half-an-hour after her departure the 'large amount' is seen to be a 'counterfeit present-ment,' and the whole thing a capital diddle.

A bold diddle is this. A camp-meeting, or something similar, is to be held at a certain spot which is accessible only by means of a free bridge. A diddler stations himself upon this bridge, respectfully informs all passers-by of the new county law which establishes a toll of one cent for foot-passengers, two for horses and donkeys, and so forth, and so forth. Some grumble but all submit, and the diddler goes home a wealthier man by some fifty or sixty dollars well earned. This taking a toll from a great crowd of people is an excessively troublesome thing.

A neat diddle is this. A friend holds one of the diddler's promises to pay, filled up and signed in due form, upon the ordinary blanks printed in red ink. The diddler purchases one or two dozen of these blanks, and every day dips one of them in his soup, makes his dog jump for it, and finally gives it to him as a *bonne bouche*. The note arriving at maturity, the diddler, with the diddler's dog, calls upon the friend, and the promise to pay is made the topic of discussion. The friend produces it from his *escritoire*, and is in the act of reaching it to the diddler, when up jumps the diddler's dog, and devours it forthwith. The diddler is not only surprised but vexed and incensed at the absurd behaviour of his dog, and expresses his entire readiness to cancel the obligation at any moment when the evidence of the obligation shall be forthcoming.

A very minute diddle is this. A lady is insulted in the street by a diddler's accomplice. The diddler himself flies to her assistance, and, giving his friend a comfortable thrashing, insists upon attending the lady to her own door. He bows, with his hand upon his heart and most, respectfully bids her adieu. She entreats him, as her deliverer, to walk in and be introduced to her big brother and her papa. With a sigh he declines to do so. 'Is there no way, then, sir,' she murmurs, 'in which I may be permitted to testify my gratitude?'

'Why, yes, madam, there is. Will you be kind enough to lend me a couple of shillings?'

In the first excitement of the moment the lady decides upon fainting outright. Upon second thought, however, she opens her purse-strings and delivers the specie. Now this, I say, is a diddle minute – for one entire moiety of the sum borrowed has to be paid to the gentleman who had the trouble of performing the insult, and who had then to stand still and be thrashed for performing it.

Rather a small, but still a scientific diddle is this. The diddler approaches the bar of a tavern, and demands a couple of twists of tobacco. These are handed to him, when, having slightly examined them, he says:

'I don't much like this tobacco. Here, take it back, and give me a glass of brandy-and-water in its place.'

The brandy-and-water is furnished and inbibed, and the diddler makes his way to the door. But the voice of the tavern-keeper arrests him.

'I believe, sir, you have forgotten to pay for your brandy-and-water.'

'Pay for my brandy-and-water! – didn't I give you the tobacco for the brandy-and-water? What more would you have?'

'But, sir, if you please, I don't remember that you paid for the tobacco.'

'What do you mean by that, you scoundrel? – Didn't I give you back your tobacco? Isn't *that* your tobacco lying *there*! Do you expect me to pay for what I did not take?'

'But, sir,' says the publican, now rather at a loss what to say, 'but, sir'——

'But me no buts, sir,' interrupts the diddler, apparently in very high dudgeon, and slamming the door after him as he makes his escape – 'but me no buts, sir, and none of your tricks upon travellers.'

Here again is a very clever diddle, of which the simplicity is not its least recommendation. A purse or pocket-book, being really lost, the loser inserts in *one* of the daily papers of a large city a fully descriptive advertisement.

Whereupon our diddler copies the *facts* of this advertisement, with a change of heading, of general phraseology, and *address*. The original, for instance, is long and verbose, is headed, 'A Pocket-Book Lost!' and requires the treasure, when found, to be left at No. 1 Tom Street. The copy is brief, and being headed 'Lost' only, indicates No 2 Dick, or No 3 Harry Street, as the locality at which the owner may be seen. Moreover it is inserted in at least five or six of the daily papers of the day, while in point of time it makes its appearance only a few hours after the original. Should it be read by the loser of the purse, he would hardly suspect it to have any reference to his own misfortune. But, of course, the chances are five or six to one that the finder will repair to the address given by the diddler, rather than to that pointed out by the rightful proprietor. The former pays the reward, pockets the treasure, and decamps.

Quite an analogous diddle is this. A lady of *ton* has dropped, somewhere in the street, a diamond ring of very unusual value. For its recovery, she offers some forty or fifty dollars reward – giving, in her advertisement, a very minute description of the gem and of its settings, and declaring that, upon its restoration to No. so and so, in such and such Avenue, the reward will be paid *instantly*, without a single question being asked. During the lady's absence from home, a day or two afterwards, a ring is heard at the door of No. so and so, in such and such Avenue; a servant appears; the lady of the house is asked for and is declared to be out, at which astounding information the visitor expresses the most poignant regret. His business is of importance and concerns the lady herself. In fact he had the good fortune to find her diamond ring. But perhaps it would be as well that he should call again. 'By no means!' says the servant; and 'By no means!' say the lady's sister and the lady's sister-in-law, who are summoned forthwith. The ring is clamorously identified, the reward is paid, and the finder nearly thrust out of doors. The lady returns, and expresses some little dissatisfaction with her sister and sister-in-law because they happen to have paid forty or fifty dollars for a *facsimile* of her diamond ring – a *facsimile* made out of real pinchbeck and unquestionable paste.

But as there is really no end to diddling, so there would be none to this essay, were I even to hint at half the variations or inflections of which this science is susceptible. I must bring this paper, perforce, to a conclusion, and this I cannot do better than by a summary notice of a very decent but rather elaborate diddle of which our own city was made the theatre not very long ago, and which was subsequently repeated with success in other still more verdant localities of the Union. A middle-aged gentleman arrives in town from parts unknown. He is remarkably precise, cautious, staid, and deliberate in his demeanour. His dress is scrupulously neat, but plain, unostentatious. He wears a white cravat, and ample waistcoat, made with an eye to comfort alone; thick-soled cosy-looking shoes, and pantaloons without straps. He has the whole air, in fact, of your well-to-do, sober-sided, exact, and respectable 'man of business,' *par excellence* – one of the stern and outwardly hard, internally soft, sort of people that we see in the crack high comedies – fellows whose words are so many bonds, and who are noted for giving away guineas in charity with the one hand, while, in the way of mere bargain, they exact the uttermost fraction of a farthing with the other.

He makes much ado before he can get suited with a boarding-house. He dislikes children. He has been accustomed to quiet. His habits are methodical – and then he would prefer getting into a private and respectable small family, piously inclined. Terms, however, are no object – only he must insist upon settling his bill on the first of every month (it is now the second), and begs his landlady, when he finally obtains one to his mind, *not* on any account to forget his instructions upon this point, but to send in a bill *and* receipt precisely at ten o'clock on the *first* day of every month, and under no circumstances to put it off to the second.

These arrangements made, our man of business rents an office in a reputable rather than a fashionable quarter of the town. There is nothing he more despises than pretence. 'Where there is much show,' he says, 'there is seldom anything very solid behind' – an observation which so profoundly impresses his landlady's fancy that she makes a pencil memorandum of it forthwith in her great family Bible, on the broad margin of the Proverbs of Solomon.

The next step is to advertise, after some such fashion as this, in the principal business sixpennies of this city – the pennies are eschewed as not 'respectable' – and as demanding payment for all advertisements in advance. Our man of business holds it as a point of his faith that work should never be paid for until done.

WANTED.– The advertisers, being about to commence extensive business operations in this city, will require the services of three or four intelligent and competent clerks, to whom a liberal salary will be paid. The very best recommendations, not so much for capacity as for integrity, will be expected. Indeed, as the duties to be performed involve high responsibilities, and large amounts of money must necessarily pass through the hands of those engaged, it is deemed advisable to demand a deposit of fifty dollars from each clerk employed. No person need apply, therefore, who is not prepared to leave this sum in the possession of the advertisers, and who cannot furnish the most satisfactory testimonials of morality. Young gentlemen piously inclined will be preferred. Application should be made between the hours of ten and eleven a.m., and four and five p.m., of Messrs Bogs, Hogs, Logs, Frogs, & Co.

No. 110 Dog Street.

By the thirty-first day of the month this advertisement has brought to the office of Messrs Bogs, Hogs, Logs, Frogs, and Company, some fifteen or twenty young gentlemen piously inclined. But our man of business is in no hurry to conclude a contract with any – no man of business is *ever* precipitate – and it is not until the most rigid catechism in respect to the piety of each young gentleman's inclination, that his services are engaged and his fifty dollars receipted for, *just* by way of proper precaution, on the part of the respectable firm of Bogs, Hogs, Logs, Frogs, and Company. On the morning of the first day of the next month, the landlady does *not* present her bill according to promise – a piece of neglect for which the comfortable head of the house ending in *ogs* would no doubt have chided her severely could he have been prevailed upon to remain in town a day or two for that purpose.

As it is, the constables have had a sad time of it, running hither and thither, and all they can do is to declare the man of business most emphatically 'a hen knee high' – by which some persons imagine them to imply that, in fact, he is N. E. I. – by which again the very classical phrase *non est inventus* is supposed to be understood. In the meantime the young gentlemen, one and all, are somewhat less piously inclined than before, while the landlady purchases a shilling's worth of the best Indian rubber, and very carefully obliterates the pencil memorandum that some fool has made in her great family Bible, on the broad margin of the Proverbs of Solomon.

William Wilson

What say of it? what says CONSCIENCE grim,
That spectre in my path?

Chamberlain's Pharronida.

Let me call myself, for the present, William Wilson. The fair page now lying before me need not be sullied with my real appellation. This has been already too much an object for the scorn, for the horror, for the detestation of my race. To the uttermost regions of the globe have not the indignant winds bruited its unparalleled infamy? O outcast of all outcasts most abandoned! to the earth art thou not for ever dead? to its honours, to its flowers, to its golden aspirations? – and a cloud, dense, dismal, and limitless, does it not hang eternally between thy hopes and heaven?

I would not, if I could, here or to-day, embody a record of my later years of unspeakable misery and unpardonable crime. This epoch – these later years – took unto themselves a sudden elevation in turpitude, whose origin alone it is my present purpose to assign. Men usually grow base by degrees. From me in an instant all virtue dropped bodily as a mantle. From comparatively trivial wickedness I passed, with the stride of a giant, into more than the enormities of an Elagabalus. What chance – what one event brought this evil thing to pass, bear with me while I relate. Death approaches, and the shadow which foreruns him has thrown a softening influence over my spirit. I long in passing through the dim valley for the sympathy, I had nearly said for the pity, of my fellow-men. I would fain have them believe that

I have been in some measure the slave of circumstances beyond human control. I would wish them to seek out for me, in the details I am about to give, some little oasis of *fatality* amid a wilderness of error. I would have them allow, what they cannot refrain from allowing, that although temptation may have erewhile existed as great, man was never *thus* at least tempted before, certainly never *thus* fell. And is it therefore that he has never thus suffered? Have I not indeed been living in a dream? And am I not now dying a victim to the horror and the mystery of the wildest of all sublunary visions?

I am the descendant of a race whose imaginative and easily excitable temperament has at all times rendered them remarkable; and in my earliest infancy I gave evidence of having fully inherited the family character. As I advanced in years it was more strongly developed, becoming for many reasons a cause of serious disquietude to my friends, and of positive injury to myself. I grew self-willed, addicted to the wildest caprices, and a prey to the most ungovernable passions. Weak-minded, and beset with constitutional infirmities akin to my own, my parents could do but little to check the evil propensities which distinguished me. Some feeble and ill-directed efforts resulted in complete failure on their part, and of course in total triumph on mine. Thenceforward my voice was a household law, and at an age when few children have abandoned their leading-strings, I was left to the guidance of my own will, and became in all but name the master of my own actions.

My earliest recollections of a school-life are connected with a large rambling Elizabethan house, in a misty-looking village of England, where were a vast number of gigantic and gnarled trees, and where all the houses were excessively ancient. In truth, it was a dream-like and spirit-soothing place, that venerable old town. At this moment, in fancy, I feel the refreshing chilliness of its deeply-shadowed avenues, inhale the fragrance of its thousand shrubberies, and thrill anew with indefinable delight at the deep hollow note of the church-bell, breaking each hour with sullen and sudden roar upon the stillness of the dusky atmosphere in which the fretted Gothic steeple lay imbedded and asleep.

It gives me perhaps as much pleasure as I can now in any manner experience to dwell upon minute recollections of the school and its concerns. Steeped in misery as I am – misery, alas! only too real – I shall be pardoned for seeking relief, however slight and temporary, in the weakness in a few rambling details. These, moreover, utterly trivial, and even ridiculous in themselves, assume to my fancy adventitious importance, as connected with a period and a locality when and where I recognise the first ambiguous monitions of the destiny which afterwards so fully overshadowed me. Let me then remember.

The house, I have said, was old and irregular. The grounds were extensive, and a high and solid brick wall, topped with a bed of mortar and broken glass, encompassed the whole. This prison-like rampart formed the limit of our domain: beyond it we saw but thrice a week, once every Saturday afternoon, when, attended by two ushers, we were permitted to take brief walks in a body through some of the neighbouring fields; and twice during Sunday, when we were paraded in the same formal manner to the morning and evening service in the one church of the village. Of this church the principal of our school was pastor. With how deep a spirit of wonder and perplexity was I wont to regard him from our remote pew in the gallery, as with step solemn and slow he ascended the pulpit! This reverend man, with countenance so demurely benign, with robes so glossy and so clerically flowing, with wig so minutely powdered, so rigid and so vast – could this be he who, of late, with sour visage, and in snuffy habiliments, administered, ferule in hand, the Draconian laws of the academy? O gigantic paradox, too utterly monstrous for solution!

At an angle of the ponderous wall frowned a more ponderous gate. It was riveted and studded with iron bolts, and surmounted with jagged iron spikes. What impressions of deep awe did it inspire! It was never opened save for the three periodical egressions and ingressions already mentioned; then in every creak of its mighty hinges we found a plenitude of mystery, a world of matter for solemn remark, or for more solemn meditation.

The extensive enclosure was irregular in form, having many capacious recesses. Of these, three or four of the largest constituted the playground. It was level, and covered with fine hard gravel. I well remember it had no trees nor benches, nor anything similar within it. Of course it was in the rear of the house. In front lay a small parterre, planted with box and other shrubs, but through this sacred division we passed only upon rare occasions indeed, such as a first advent to school or final departure thence, or perhaps, when a parent or friend having called for us, we joyfully took our way home for the Christmas or Midsummer holidays.

But the house! – how quaint an old building was this! to me how veritably a palace of enchantment! There was really no end to its windings, to its incomprehensible subdivisions. It was difficult, at any given time, to say with certainty upon which of its two stories one happened to be. From each room to every other there were sure to be found three or four steps either in ascent or descent. Then the lateral branches were innumerable, inconceivable, and so returning in upon themselves that our most exact ideas in regard to the whole mansion were not very far different from those with which we pondered upon infinity. During the five years of my residence here I was never able to ascertain with precision in what remote locality lay the little sleeping apartment assigned to myself and some eighteen or twenty other scholars.

The school-room was the largest in the house, I could not help thinking, in the world. It was very long, narrow, and dismally low, with pointed Gothic windows and a ceiling of oak. In a remote and terror-inspiring angle was a square enclosure of eight or ten feet, comprising the *sanctum*, 'during hours,' of our principal, the Reverend Dr. Bransby. It was a solid structure, with massy door, sooner than open which in the absence of the 'dominie' we would all have willingly perished by the *piene forte et dure*. In other angles were two other similar boxes, far less reverenced, indeed, but still greatly matters of awe. One of these was the pulpit of the 'classical' usher, one of the 'English and mathematical.' Interspersed about the room, crossing and recrossing in endless irregularity, were innumerable benches and desks, black, ancient, and time-worn, piled desperately with much-bethumbed books, and so beseamed with initial letters, names at full length, grotesque figures, and other multiplied efforts of the knife, as to have entirely lost what little of original form might have been their portion in days long departed. A huge bucket with water stood at one extremity of the room, and a clock of stupendous dimensions at the other.

Encompassed by the massy wall of this venerable academy, I passed, yet not in a tedium or disgust, the years of the third lustrum of my life. The teeming brain of childhood requires no external world of incident to occupy or amuse it; and the apparently dismal monotony of a school was replete with more intense excitement than my riper youth has derived from luxury, or my full manhood from crime. Yet I must believe that my first mental development had in it much of the uncommon – even much of the *outré*. Upon mankind at large the events of very early existence rarely leave in mature age any definite impression. All is grey shadow – a weak and irregular remembrance – an indistinct regathering of feeble pleasures and phantasmagoric pains. With me this is not so. In childhood I must have felt with the energy of a man what I now find stamped upon memory in lines as vivid, as deep, and as durable as the *exergues* of the Carthaginian medals.

Yet in fact – in the fact of the world's view – how little was there to remember! The morning's awakening, the nightly summons to bed; the connings, the recitations; the periodical half-holidays, and perambulations; the play-ground with its broils, its pastimes, its intrigues; – these, by a mental sorcery long forgotten, were made to involve a wilderness of sensation, a world of rich incident, a universe of varied emotion; of excitement the most passionate and spirit-stirring. *'Oh le bon temps, que ce siècle de fer?'*

In truth, the ardour, the enthusiasm, and the imperiousness of my disposition, soon rendered me a marked character among my school-mates, and by slow but natural gradations gave me an ascendancy over all not greatly older than myself – over all with a single exception. This exception was found in the person of a scholar, who, although no relation, bore the same Christian and surname as myself, a circum-stance, in fact, little remarkable; for notwithstanding a noble descent, mine was one of those every-day appellations which seem, by prescriptive right, to have been, time out of mind, the common property of the mob. In this narrative I have therefore designated myself as William Wilson – a fictitious title not very dissimilar to the real. My namesake alone, of those who in school phraseology constituted 'our set,' presumed to compete with me in the studies of the class – in the sports and broils of the play-ground – to refuse implicit belief in my assertions, and submission to my will – indeed, to interfere with my arbitrary dictation in any respect whatsoever. If there is on earth a supreme and unqualified despotism, it is the despotism of a mastermind in boyhood over the less energetic spirits of its companions.

Wilson's rebellion was to me a source of the greatest embarrassment: the more so as, in spite of the bravado with which in public I made a point of treating him and his pretensions, I secretly felt that I feared him, and could not help thinking the equality which he maintained so easily with myself a proof of his true superiority, since not to be overcome cost me a perpetual struggle. Yet this superiority – even this equality – was in truth acknowledged by no one but myself; our associates, by some unaccountable blindness, seemed not even to suspect it. Indeed, his competition, his resistance, and especially his impertinent and dogged interference with my purposes, were not more pointed than private. He appeared to be destitute alike of the ambition which urged, and of the passionate energy of mind which enabled me to excel. In his rivalry he might have been supposed actuated solely by a whimsical desire to thwart, astonish, or mortify myself; although there were times when I could not help observing, with a feeling made up of wonder, abasement, and pique, that he mingled with his injuries, his insults, or his contradictions, a certain most inappropriate, and assuredly most unwelcome *affectionateness* of manner. I could only conceive this singular behaviour to arise from a consummate self-conceit assuming the vulgar airs of patronage and protection.

Perhaps it was this latter trait in Wilson's conduct, conjoined with our identity of name, and the mere accident of our having entered the school upon the same day, which set afloat the notion that we were brothers among the senior classes in the academy. These do not usually inquire with much strictness into the affairs of their juniors. I have before said, or should have said, that Wilson was not, in the most remote degree, connected with my family. But assuredly if we *had* been brothers we must have been twins; for, after leaving Dr. Bransby's, I casually learned that my namesake was born on the nineteenth of January 1813 – and this is a somewhat remarkable coincidence, for the day is precisely that of my own nativity.

It may seem strange that in spite of the continual anxiety occasioned me by the rivalry of Wilson, and his intolerable spirit of contradiction, I could not bring myself to hate him altogether. We had, to be sure, nearly every day a quarrel, in which, yielding me publicly the palm of victory, he in some manner contrived to make me feel that it was he who had deserved it, yet a sense of pride on my part and a veritable dignity on his own, kept us always upon what are called 'speaking terms,' while there were many points of strong congeniality in our tempers, operating to awake in me a sentiment which our position alone, perhaps, prevented from ripening into friendship. It is difficult indeed to define or even to describe my real feelings towards him. They formed a motley and heterogeneous admixture; some petulant animosity, which was not yet hatred, some esteem, more respect, much fear, with a world of uneasy curiosity. To the moralist it will be unnecessary to say in addition that Wilson and myself were the most inseparable of companions.

It was no doubt the anomalous state of affairs existing between us which turned all my attacks upon him (and they were many, either open or covert) into the channel of banter or practical joke (giving pain while assuming the aspect of mere fun), rather than into a more serious and determined hostility. But my endeavours on this head were by no means uniformly successful, even when my plans were the most wittily concocted; for my namesake had much about him in character of that unassuming and quiet austerity which, while enjoying the poignancy of its own joke, has no heel of Achilles in itself, and absolutely refuses to be laughed at. I could find indeed but one vulnerable point, and that lying in a personal peculiarity, arising perhaps from constitutional disease, would have been spared by any antagonist less at his wit's end than myself; my rival had a weakness in the faucial or guttural organs which precluded him from raising his voice at any time *above a very low whisper*. Of this defect I did not fail to take what poor advantage lay in my power.

Wilson's retaliations in kind were many; and there was one form of his practical wit that disturbed me beyond measure. How his sagacity first discovered at all that so petty a thing would vex me is a question I never could solve, but having discovered, he habitually practised the annoyance. I had always felt aversion to my uncourtly patronymic and its very common, if not plebeian prænomen. The words were venom in my ears; and when, upon the day of my arrival, a second William Wilson came also to the academy, I felt angry with him for bearing the name, and doubly disgusted with the name because a stranger bore it, who would be the cause of its twofold repetition, who would be constantly in my presence, and whose concerns, in the ordinary routine of the school business, must inevitably, on account of the detestable coincidence, be often confounded with my own.

The feeling of vexation thus engendered grew stronger with every circumstance tending to show resemblance, moral or physical, between my rival and myself. I had not then discovered the remarkable fact that we were of the same age; but I saw that we were of the same height, and I perceived that we were even singularly alike in general contour of person and outline of feature. I was galled, too, by the rumour touching a relationship, which had grown current in the upper forms. In a word, nothing could more seriously disturb me (although I scrupulously concealed such disturbance), than any allusion to a similarity of mind, person, or condition existing between us. But, in truth, I had no reason to believe that (with the exception of the matter of relationship, and in the case of Wilson himself) this similarity had ever been made a subject of comment or even observed at all by our schoolfellows. That *he* observed it in all its bearings, and as fixedly as I, was apparent; but that he could discover in such circumstances so fruitful a field of annoyance can only be attributed, as

I said before, to his more than ordinary penetration.

His cue, which was to perfect an imitation of myself, lay both in words and in actions, and most admirably did he play his part. My dress it was an easy matter to copy; my gait and general manner were without difficulty appropriated; in spite of his constitutional defect, even my voice did not escape him. My louder tones were of course unattempted, but then the key, it was identical; *and his singular whisper, it grew the very echo of my own.*

How greatly this most exquisite portraiture harassed me (for it could not justly be termed a caricature), I will not now venture to describe. I had but one consolation – in the fact that the imitation, apparently, was noticed by myself alone, and that I had to endure only the knowing and strangely sarcastic smiles of my namesake himself. Satisfied with having produced in my bosom the intended effect he seemed to chuckle in secret over the sting he had inflicted, and was characteristically disregardful of the public applause which the success of his witty endeavours might have so easily elicited. That the school, indeed, did not feel his design, perceive its accomplishment, and participate in his sneer, was for many anxious months a riddle I could not resolve. Perhaps the *gradation* of his copy rendered it not so readily perceptible, or more possibly I owed my security to the masterly air of the copyist, who, disdaining the letter (which in a painting is all the obtuse can see), gave but the full spirit of his original for my individual contemplation and chagrin.

I have already more than once spoken of the disgusting air of patronage which he assumed towards me, and of his frequent officious interference with my will. This interference often took the ungracious character of advice – advice not openly given but hinted or insinuated. I received it with a repugnance which gained strength as I grew in years. Yet at this distant day, let me do him the simple justice to acknowledge that I can recall no occasion when the suggestions of my rival were on the side of those errors or follies so usual to his immature age and seeming inexperience; that his moral sense, at least, if not his general talents and worldly wisdom, was far keener than my own; and that I might to-day have been a better, and thus a happier man, had I less frequently rejected the counsels embodied in those meaning whispers which I then but too cordially hated and too bitterly despised.

As it was, I at length grew restive in the extreme under his distasteful supervision, and daily resented more and more openly what I considered his intolerable arrogance. I have said that in the first years of our connection as schoolmates, my feelings in regard to him might have been easily ripened into friendship; but, in the latter months of my residence at the academy, although the intrusion of his ordinary manner had, beyond doubt, in some measure abated, my sentiments in nearly similar proportion partook very much of positive hatred. Upon one occasion he saw this, I think, and afterwards avoided, or made a show of avoiding me.

It was about the same period, if I remember aright, that, in an altercation of violence with him, in which he was more than usually thrown off his guard, and spoke and acted with an openness of demeanour rather foreign to his nature, I discovered, or fancied I discovered, in his accent, his air, and general appearance, a something which first startled, and then deeply interested me, by bringing to mind dim visions of my earliest infancy, wild, confused, and thronging memories of a time when memory herself was yet unborn. I cannot better describe the sensation which oppressed me than by saying that I could with difficulty shake off the belief of my having been acquainted with the being who stood before me at some epoch very long ago, some point of the past even infinitely remote. The delusion, however, faded as rapidly as it came, and I mention it at all but to define the day of the last conversation I there held with my singular namesake.

The huge old house, with its countless subdivisions, had several large chambers communicating with each other, where slept the greater number of the students. There were, however (as must necessarily happen in a building so awkwardly planned), many little nooks or recesses, the odds and ends of the structure, and these the economic ingenuity of Dr. Bransby had also fitted up as dormitories, although, being the merest closets, they were capable of accommodating but a single individual. One of these small apartments was occupied by Wilson.

. One night, about the close of my fifth year at the school, and immediately after the altercation just mentioned, finding every one wrapped in sleep, I arose from bed, and, lamp in hand, stole through a wilderness of narrow passages from my own bedroom to that of my rival. I had long been plotting one of those ill-natured pieces of practical wit at his expense in which I had hitherto been so uniformly unsuccessful. It was my intention now to put my scheme in operation, and I resolved to make him feel the whole extent of the malice with which I was imbued. Having reached his closet I noiselessly entered, leaving the lamp, with a shade over it, on the outside. I advanced a step and listened to the sound of his tranquil breathing. Assured of his being alseep, I returned, took the light, and with it again approached the bed. Close curtains were around it, which, in the prosecution of my plan, I slowly and quietly withdrew, when the bright rays fell vividly upon the sleeper, and my eyes, at the same moment, upon his countenance. I looked, and a numbness, an iciness of feeling, instantly pervaded my frame. My breast heaved, my knees tottered, my whole spirit became possessed with an objectless yet intolerable horror. Gasping for breath I lowered the lamp in still nearer proximity to the face. Were these – *these* the lineaments of William Wilson? I saw, indeed, that they were his, but I shook as if with a fit of the ague in fancying they were not. What *was* there about them to confound me in this manner? I gazed, while my brain reeled with a multitude of incoherent thoughts. Not thus he appeared, assuredly not *thus*, in the vivacity of his waking hours. The same name, the same contour of person, the same day of arrival at the academy; and then his dogged and meaningless imitation of my gait, my voice, my habits, and my manner. Was it, in truth, within the bounds of human possibility that *what I now saw* was the result merely of the habitual practice of this sarcastic imitation. Awestricken, and with a creeping shudder, I extinguished the lamp, passed silently from the chamber, and left at once the halls of that old academy, never to enter them again.

After a lapse of some months, spent at home in mere idleness, I found myself a student at Eton. The brief interval had been sufficient to enfeeble my remembrance of the events at Dr. Bransby's, or at least to effect a material change in the nature of the feelings with which I remembered them. The truth, the tragedy, of the drama was no more. I could now find room to doubt the evidence of my senses, and seldom called up the subject at all but with wonder at the extent of human credulity, and a smile at the vivid force of the imagination which I hereditarily possessed. Neither was this species of scepticism likely to be diminished by the character of the life I led at Eton. The vortex of thoughtless folly into which I there so immediately and so recklessly plunged washed away all but the froth of my past hours, engulfed at once every solid or serious impression, and left to memory only the veriest levities of a former existence.

I do not wish, however, to trace the course of my miserable profligacy here – a profligacy which set at defiance the laws, while it eluded the vigilance of the institution. Three years of folly, passed without profit, had but given me rooted habits of vice, and added, in a somewhat unusual degree, to my bodily stature, when, after a week of soulless dissipation, I invited a small party of the most dissolute students to a secret carousal in my chambers. We met at a late hour of the night, for our debaucheries were to be faithfully protracted until morning. The wine flowed freely, and there were not wanting other and perhaps more dangerous seductions, so that the grey dawn had already faintly appeared in the east, while our delirious extravagance was at its height. Madly flushed with cards and intoxication, I was in the act of insisting upon a toast of more than wonted profanity when my attention was suddenly diverted by the violent, although partial, unclosing of the door of the apartment, and by the eager voice of a servant from without. He said that some person, apparently in great haste, demanded to speak with me in the hall.

Wildly excited with wine, the unexpected interruption rather delighted than surprised me. I staggered forward at once, and a few steps brought me to the vestibule of the building. In this low and small room there hung no lamp, and now no light at all was admitted, save that of the exceedingly feeble dawn which made its way through the semicircular window. As I put my foot over the threshold I became aware of the figure of a youth about my own height, and habited in a white kerseymere morning frock, cut in the novel fashion of the one I myself wore at the moment. This the faint light enabled me to perceive, but the features of his face I could not distinguish. Upon my entering he strode hurriedly up to me, and seizing me by the arm with a gesture of petulant impatience, whispered the words 'William Wilson!' in my ear.

I grew perfectly sober in an instant.

There was that in the manner of the stranger, and in the tremulous shake of his uplifted finger, as he held it between my eyes and the light, which filled me with unqualified amazement; but it was not this which had so violently moved me. It was the pregnancy of solemn admonition in the singular, low, hissing utterance, and, above all, it was the character, the tone, *the key*, of those few, simple, and familiar, yet *whispered* syllables, which came with a thousand thronging memories of by-gone days, and struck upon my soul with the shock of a galvanic battery. Ere I could recover the use of my senses he was gone.

Although this event failed not of a vivid effect upon my disordered imagination, yet was it evanescent as vivid. For some weeks, indeed, I busied myself in earnest inquiry, or was wrapped in a cloud of morbid speculation. I did not pretend to disguise from my perception the identity of the singular individual who thus perseveringly interfered with my affairs, and harassed me with his insinuated counsel. But who and what was this Wilson? – and whence came he? – and what were his purposes? Upon neither of these points could I be satisfied – merely ascertaining in regard to him, that a sudden accident in his family had caused his removal from Dr. Bransby's academy on the afternoon of the day in which I myself had eloped. But in a brief period I ceased to think upon the subject, my attention being all absorbed in a contemplated departure for Oxford. Thither I soon went, the uncalculating vanity of my parents furnishing me with an outfit and annual establishment which would enable me to indulge at will in the luxury already so dear to my heart – to vie in profuseness of expenditure with the haughtiest heirs of the wealthiest earldoms in Great Britain.

Excited by such appliances to vice, my constitutional temperament broke forth with redoubled ardour, and I spurned even the common restraints of decency in the mad infatuation of my revels. But it were absurd to pause in the detail of my extravagance. Let it suffice, that among spendthrifts I out-Heroded Herod, and that giving name to a multitude of novel follies, I added no brief appendix to the long catalogue of vices then usual in the most dissolute university of Europe.

It could hardly be credited, however, that I had, even here, so utterly fallen from the gentlemanly estate as to seek acquaintance with the vilest arts of the gambler by profession, and having become an adept in his despicable science, to practise it habitually as a means of increasing my already enormous income at the expense of the weak-minded among my fellow-collegians. Such, nevertheless, was the fact; and the very enormity of this offence against all manly and honourable sentiment proved, beyond doubt, the main, if not the sole reason of the impunity with which it was committed. Who, indeed, among my most abandoned associates would not rather have disputed the clearest evidence of his senses than have suspected of such courses the gay, the frank, the generous William Wilson – the noblest and most liberal commoner at Oxford – him whose follies (said his parasites) were but the follies of youth and unbridled fancy – whose errors but inimitable whim – whose darkest vice but a careless and dashing extravagance?

I had been now two years successfully busied in this way when there came to the university a young *parvenu* nobleman, Glendinning – rich, said report, as Herodes Atticus – his riches, too, as easily acquired. I soon found him of weak intellect, and of course marked him as a fitting subject for my skill. I frequently engaged him in play, and contrived with the gambler's usual art to let him win considerable sums, the more effectually to entangle him in my snares. At length, my schemes being ripe, I met him (with the full intention that this meeting should be final and decisive) at the chambers of a fellow commoner (Mr. Preston) equally intimate with both, but who, to do him justice, entertained not even a remote suspicion of my design. To give to this a better colouring I had contrived to have assembled a party of some eight or ten, and was solicitously careful that the introduction of cards should appear accidental, and originate in the proposal of my contemplated dupe himself. To be brief upon a vile topic, none of the low finesse was omitted, so customary upon similar occasions, that it is a just matter for wonder how any are still found so besotted as to fall its victim.

We had protracted our sitting far into the night, and I had at length effected the manoeuvre of getting Glendinning as my sole antagonist. The game, too, was my favourite *écarté*. The rest of the company, interested in the extent of our play, had abandoned their own cards, and were standing around us as spectators. The *parvenu*, who had been induced by my artifices in the early part of the evening to drink deeply, now shuffled, dealt, or played, with a wild nervousness of manner for which his intoxication I thought might partially but could not altogether account. In a very short period he had become my debtor to a large amount, when, having taken a long draught of port, he did precisely what I had been coolly anticipating – he proposed to double our already extravagant stakes. With a well-feigned show of re-luctance, and not until after my repeated refusal had seduced him into some angry words which gave a colour of *pique* to my compliance, did I finally comply. The result of course did but prove how entirely the prey was in my toils: in less than an hour he had quadrupled his debt. For some time his countenance had been losing the florid tinge lent it by the wine, but now to my astonishment I perceived that it had grown to a pallor truly fearful. I say to my astonishment. Glendinning had been represented to my eager inquiries as immeasurably wealthy; and the sums which he had as yet lost, although in themselves vast, could not, I supposed, very seriously annoy, much less so violently affect him. That he was overcome by the wine just swallowed was the idea which most readily presented itself; and, rather with a view to the preservation of my own character in the eyes of my associates, than from any less interested motive, I was about to insist peremptorily, upon a discontinuance of the play, when some expressions at my elbow from among the company, and an ejaculation evincing utter despair on the part of Glendinning, gave me to understand that I had effected his total ruin under circumstances which, rendering him an object for the pity of all, should have protected him from the ill offices even of a fiend.

What now might have been my conduct it is difficult to say. The pitiable condition of my dupe had thrown an air of embarrassed gloom over all, and for some moments a profound silence was maintained, during which I could not help feeling my cheeks tingle with the many burning glances of scorn or reproach cast upon me by the less abandoned of the party. I will even own that an intolerable weight of anxiety was a brief instant lifted from my bosom by the sudden and extraordinary interruption which ensued. The wide heavy folding-doors of the apartment were all at once thrown open to their full extent, with a vigorous and rushing impetuosity that extinguished, as if by magic, every candle in the room. Their light, in dying, enabled us just to perceive that a stranger had entered, about my own height, and closely muffled in a cloak. The darkness, however, was now total, and we could only *feel* that he was standing in our midst. Before any one of us could recover from the extreme astonishment into which this rudeness had thrown all, we heard the voice of the intruder.

'Gentlemen,' he said, in a low, distinct, and never-to-be-forgotten *whisper* which thrilled to the very marrow of my bones, 'Gentlemen, I make no apology for this behaviour, because in thus behaving I am but fulfilling my duty. You are, beyond doubt, uninformed of the true character of the person who has to-night won at *écarté* a large sum of money from Lord Glendinning. I will therefore put you upon an expeditious and decisive plan of obtaining this very necessary information. Please to examine at your leisure the inner linings of the cuff of his left sleeve, and the several little packages which may be found in the somewhat capacious pockets of his embroidered morning wrapper.'

While he spoke, so profound was the stillness that one might have heard a pin drop upon the floor. In ceasing, he departed at once, and as abruptly as he had entered. Can I – shall I describe my sensations? Must I say that I felt all the horrors of the damned? Most assuredly I had little time for reflection. Many hands roughly seized me upon the spot, and lights were immediately re-procured. A search ensued. In the lining of my sleeve were found all the court cards essential in *écarté*, and in the pockets of my wrapper a number of packs, facsimiles of those used at our sittings, with the single exception that mine were of the species called, technically, *arrondées*; the honours being slightly convex at the ends, the lower cards slightly convex at the sides. In this disposition, the dupe who cuts, as customary, at the length of the pack, will invariably find that he cuts his antagonist an honour; while the gambler, cutting at the breadth, will as certainly cut nothing for his victim which may count in the records of the game.

Any burst of indignation upon this discovery would have affected me less than the silent contempt, or the sarcastic composure, with which it was received.

'Mr. Wilson,' said our host, stooping to remove from beneath his feet an exceedingly luxurious cloak of rare furs, 'Mr. Wilson, this is your property.' (The weather was cold; and, upon quitting my own room, I had thrown a cloak over my dressing wrapper, putting it off upon reaching the scene of play.) 'I presume it is supererogatory to seek here (eyeing the folds of the garment with a bitter smile) for any further evidence of your skill. Indeed, we have had enough. You will see the necessity, I hope, of quitting Oxford – at all events, of quitting instantly my chambers.'

Abased, humbled to the dust as I then was, it is probable that I should have resented this galling language by immediate personal violence, had not my whole attention been at the moment arrested by a fact of the most startling character. The cloak which I had worn was of a rare description of fur; how rare, how extravagantly costly, I shall not venture to say. Its fashion, too, was of my own fantastic invention, for I was fastidious to an absurd degree of coxcombry in matters of this frivolous nature. When, therefore, Mr. Preston reached me that which he had picked up upon the floor, and near the folding doors of the apartment, it was with an astonishment nearly bordering upon terror, that I perceived my own already hanging on my arm (where I had no doubt unwittingly placed it), and that the one presented me was but its exact counterpart in every, in even the minutest, possible particular.

The singular being who had so disastrously exposed me had been muffled, I remembered, in a cloak, and none had been worn at all by any of the members of our party with the exception of myself. Retaining some presence of mind, I took the one offered me by Preston, placed it unnoticed over my own, left the apartment with a resolute scowl of defiance, and next morning, ere dawn of day, commenced a hurried journey from Oxford to the Continent in a perfect agony of horror and of shame.

I fled in vain. My evil destiny pursued me as if in exultation, and proved indeed that the exercise of its mysterious dominion had as yet only begun. Scarcely had I set foot in Paris ere I had fresh evidence of the detestable interest taken by this Wilson in my concerns. Years flew while I experienced no relief. Villain! – at Rome, with how untimely, yet with how spectral an officiousness, stepped he in between me and my ambition! At Vienna, too – at Berlin – and at Moscow! Where, in truth, had I *not* bitter cause to curse him within my heart? From his inscrutable tyranny did I at length flee, panic-stricken, as from a pestilence; and to the very ends of the earth *I fled in vain*.

And again and again, in secret communion with my own spirit, would I demand the questions 'Who is he? – whence came he? – and what are his objects?' But no answer was there found. And now I scrutinised with a minute scrutiny, the forms, and the methods, and the leading traits of his impertinent supervision. But even here there was very little upon which to base a conjecture. It was noticeable, indeed, that in no one of the multiplied instances in which he had of late crossed my path had he so crossed it except to frustrate those schemes, or to disturb those actions, which, if fully carried out, might have resulted in bitter mischief. Poor justification this, in truth, for an authority so imperiously assumed! Poor indemnity for natural rights of self-agency so pertinaciously, so insultingly denied!

I had also been forced to notice that my tormentor for a very long period of time (while scrupulously and with miraculous dexterity maintaining his whim of an identity of apparel with myself) had so contrived it, in the execution of his varied interference with my will, that I saw not any moment the features of his face. Be Wilson what he might, *this* at least was but the veriest of affectation or of folly. Could he for an instant have supposed that in my admonisher at Eton— in the destroyer of my honour at Oxford – in him who thwarted my ambition at Rome, my revenge at Paris, my passionate love at Naples, or what he falsely termed my avarice in Egypt, – that in this, my arch-enemy and evil genius, I could fail to recognise the William Wilson of my school-boy days, – the namesake, the companion, the rival, – the hated and dreaded rival at Dr. Bransby's? Impossible! – But let me hasten to the last eventful scene of the drama.

Thus far I had succumbed supinely to this imperious domination. The sentiment of deep awe with which I habitually regarded the elevated character, the majestic wisdom, the apparent omnipresence and omnipotence of Wilson, added to a feeling of even terror, with which certain other traits in his nature and assumptions inspired me, had operated hitherto to impress me with an idea of my own utter weakness and helplessness, and to suggest an implicit, although bitterly reluctant submission to his arbitrary will. But of late days I had given myself up entirely to wine, and its maddening influence upon my hereditary temper rendered me more and more impatient of control. I began to murmur, – to hesitate, – to resist. And was it only fancy which induced me to believe that, with the increase of my own firmness, that of my tormentor underwent a proportional diminution? Be this as it may, I now began to feel the inspiration of a burning hope, and at length nurtured in my secret thoughts a stern and desperate resolution that I would submit no longer to be enslaved.

It was at Rome, during the Carnival of 18—, that I attended a masquerade in the palazzo of the Neapolitan Duke Di Broglio. I had indulged more freely than usual in the excesses of the wine-table, and now the suffocating atmosphere of the crowded rooms irritated me beyond endurance. The difficulty, too, of forcing my way through the mazes of the company contributed not a little to the ruffling of my temper; for I was anxiously seeking (let me not say with what unworthy motive) the young, the gay, the beautiful wife of the aged and doting Di Broglio. With a too unscrupulous confidence she had previously communicated to me the secret of the costume in which she would be habited, and now, having caught a glimpse of her person, I was hurrying to make my way into her presence. At this moment I felt a light hand placed upon my shoulder, and that ever-remembered low, damnable *whisper* within my ear.

In an absolute frenzy of wrath I turned at once upon him who had thus interrupted me, and seized him violently by the collar. He was attired, as I had expected, in a costume altogether similar to my own; wearing a Spanish cloak of blue velvet, begirt about the waist with a crimson belt sustaining a rapier. A mask of black silk entirely covered his face.

'Scoundrel!' I said, in a voice husky with rage, while every syllable I uttered seemed as new fuel to my fury; 'scoundrel! imposter! accursed villain! you shall not – you *shall not* dog me unto death! Follow me, or I stab you where you stand!' and – I broke my way from the ball-room into a small ante-chamber adjoining, dragging him unresistingly with me as I went.

Upon entering, I thrust him furiously from me. He staggered against the wall, while I closed the door with an oath, and commanded him to draw. He hesitated but for an instant; then, with a slight sigh, drew in silence, and put himself upon his defence.

The contest was brief indeed. I was frantic with every species of wild excitement, and felt within my single arm the energy and power of a multitude. In a few seconds I forced him by sheer strength against the wainscoting, and thus, getting him at mercy, plunged my sword, with brute ferocity, repeatedly through and through his bosom.

At that instant some person tried the latch of the door. I hastened to prevent an intrusion, and then immediately returned to my dying antagonist. But what human language can adequately portray *that* astonishment, *that* horror which possessed me at the spectacle then presented to view? The brief moment in which I averted my eyes had been sufficient to produce apparently a material change in the arrangements at the upper or farther end of the room. A large mirror – so at first it seemed to me in my confusion – now stood where none had been perceptible before; and, as I stepped up to it in extremity of terror, mine own image, but with features all pale and dabbled in

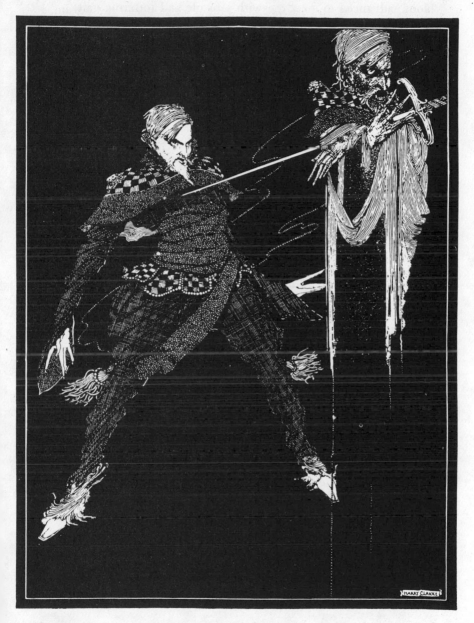

'In my death, see by this image, which is thine own, how utterly thou hast murdered thyself'

blood, advanced to meet me with a feeble and tottering gait.

Thus it appeared, I say, but was not. It was my antagonist – it was Wilson who then stood before me in the agonies of his dissolution. His mask and cloak lay where he had thrown them upon the floor. Not a thread in all his raiment – not a line in all the marked and singular lineaments of his face which was not, even in the most absolute identity, *mine own!*

It was Wilson; but he spoke no longer in a whisper, and I could have fancied that I myself was speaking while he said:

'*You have conquered and I yield. Yet, henceforward art thou also dead – dead to the World, to Heaven, and to Hope! In me didst thou exist – and, in my death, see by this image, which is thine own, how utterly thou hast murdered thyself.*'

The Purloined Letter

Nil sapientiæ odiosius acumina nimio. – *Seneca*.

At Paris, just after dark one gusty evening in the autumn of 18——, I was enjoying the twofold luxury of meditation and a meerschaum, in company with my friend C. Auguste Dupin, in his little back library, or book-closet, *au troisième, No. 33 Rue Dunôt, Faubourg St. Germain.* For one hour at least we had maintained a profound silence: while each, to any casual observer, might have seemed intently and exclusively occupied with the curling eddies of smoke that oppressed the atmosphere of the chamber. For myself, however, I was mentally discussing certain topics which had formed matter for conversation between us at an earlier period of the evening; I mean the affair of the Rue Morgue, and the mystery attending the murder of Marie Rogêt. I looked upon it, therefore, as something of a coincidence, when the door of our apartment was thrown open and admitted our old acquaintance, Monsieur G——, the Prefect of the Parisian police.

We gave him a hearty welcome; for there was nearly half as much of the entertaining as of the contemptible about the man, and we had not seen him for several years. We had been sitting in the dark, and Dupin now arose for the purpose of lighting a lamp, but sat down again, without doing so, upon G.'s saying that he had called to consult us, or rather to ask the opinion of my friend, about some official business which had occasioned a great deal of trouble.

'If it is any point requiring reflection,' observed Dupin, as he forebore to enkindle the wick, 'we shall examine it to better purpose in the dark.'

'That is another of your odd notions,' said the Prefect, who had a fashion of calling everything 'odd' that was beyond his comprehension, and thus lived amid an absolute legion of 'oddities.'

'Very true,' said Dupin, as he supplied his visitor with a pipe, and rolled towards him a comfortable chair.

'And what is the difficulty now?' I asked. 'Nothing more in the assassination way, I hope?'

'Oh no; nothing of that nature. The fact is, the business is *very* simple indeed, and I make no doubt that we can manage it sufficiently well ourselves; but then I thought Dupin would like to hear the details of it, because it is so excessively *odd*.'

'Simple and odd,' said Dupin.

'Why, yes; and not exactly that either. The fact is, we have all been a good deal puzzled because the affair *is* so simple, and yet baffles us altogether.'

'Perhaps it is the very simplicity of the thing which puts you at fault,' said my friend.

'What nonsense you *do* talk!' replied the Prefect, laughing heartily.

'Perhaps the mystery is a little *too* plain,' said Dupin.

'Oh, good heavens! who ever heard of such an idea?'

'A little *too* self-evident.'

'Ha! ha! ha! – ha! ha! ha! – ho! ho! ho!' roared our visitor, profoundly amused, 'Oh, Dupin, you will be the death of me yet!'

'And what, after all, *is* the matter on hand?' I asked.

'Why, I will tell you,' replied the Prefect, as he gave a long, steady, and contemplative puff, and settled himself in his chair. 'I will tell you in a few words; but, before I begin, let me caution you that this is an affair demanding the greatest secrecy, and that I should most probably lose the position I now hold were it known that I confided it to any one.'

'Proceed,' said I.

'Or not,' said Dupin.

'Well, then; I have received personal information, from a very high quarter, that a certain document of the last importance has been purloined from the royal apartments. The individual who purloined it is known; this beyond a doubt; he was seen to take it. It is known, also, that it still remains in his possession.'

'How is this known?' asked Dupin.

'It is clearly inferred,' replied the Prefect, 'from the nature of the document, and from the non-appearance of certain results which would at once arise from its passing *out* of the robber's possession; – that is to say, from his employing it as he must design in the end to employ it.'

'Be a little more explicit,' I said.

'Well, I may venture so far as to say that the paper gives its holder a certain power in a certain quarter where such power is immensely valuable.' The Prefect was fond of the cant of diplomacy.

'Still I do not quite understand,' said Dupin.

'No? Well; the disclosure of the document to a third person, who shall be nameless, would bring in question the honour of a personage of most exalted station; and this fact gives the holder of the document an ascendancy over the illustrious personage whose honour and peace are so jeopardised.'

'But this ascendancy,' I interposed, 'would depend upon the robber's knowledge of the loser's knowledge of the robber. Who would dare –'

'The thief,' said G——, 'is the Minister D——, who dares all things, those unbecoming as well as those becoming a man. The method of the theft was not less ingenious than bold. The document in question – a letter to be frank – had been received by the personage robbed while alone in the royal *boudoir*. During its perusal she was suddenly interrupted by the entrance of the other exalted personage from whom especially it was her wish to conceal it. After a hurried and vain endeavour to thrust it in a drawer, she was forced to place it, open as it was, upon a table. The address, however, was uppermost, and the contents thus unexposed, the letter escaped notice. At this juncture enters the Minister D——. His lynx eye immediately perceives the paper, recognises the handwriting of the address, observes the confusion of the personage addressed, and fathoms her secret. After some business transactions, hurried through in his ordinary manner, he produces a letter somewhat similar to the one in question, opens it, pretends to read it, and then places it in close juxtaposition to the other. Again he converses for some fifteen minutes upon the public affairs. At length, in taking leave, he takes also from the table the letter to which he had no claim. Its rightful owner saw, but, of course, dared not call attention to the act, in the presence of the third personage who stood at her elbow. The minister decamped; leaving his own letter – one of no importance – upon the table.'

'Here then,' said Dupin to me, 'you have precisely what you demand to make the ascendancy complete – the robber's knowledge of the loser's knowledge of the robber.'

'Yes,' replied the Prefect; 'and the power thus attained has, for some months past, been wielded for political purposes to a very dangerous extent. The personage robbed is more thoroughly convinced every day of the necessity of reclaiming her letter. But this of course cannot be done openly. In fine, driven to despair, she has committed the matter to me.'

'Than whom,' said Dupin, amid a perfect whirlwind of smoke, 'no more sagacious agent could, I suppose, be desired, or even imagined.'

'You flatter me,' replied the Prefect; 'but it is possible that some such opinion may have been entertained.'

'It is clear,' said I, 'as you observe, that the letter is still in possession of the minister; since it is this possession, and not any employment of the letter, which bestows the power. With the employment the power departs.'

'True,' said G——; 'and upon this conviction I proceeded. My first care was to make thorough search of the minister's hotel; and here my chief embarrassment lay in the necessity of searching without his knowledge. Beyond all things, I have been warned of the danger which would result from giving him reason to suspect our design.'

'But,' said I, 'you are quite *au fait* in these investigations. The

Parisian police have done this thing often before.'

'O yes; and for this reason I did not despair. The habits of the minister gave me, too, a great advantage. He is frequently absent from home all night. His servants are by no means numerous. They sleep at a distance from their master's apartment, and being chiefly Neapolitans, are readily made drunk. I have keys, as you know, with which I can open any chamber or cabinet in Paris. For three months a night has not passed, during the greater part of which I have not been engaged, personally, in ransacking the D—— Hotel. My honour is interested, and, to mention a great secret, the reward is enormous. So I did not abandon the search until I had become fully satisfied that the thief is a more astute man than myself. I fancy that I have investigated every nook and corner of the premises in which it is possible that the paper can be concealed.'

'But is it not possible,' I suggested, 'that although the letter may be in possession of the minister, as it unquestionably is, he may have concealed it elsewhere than upon his own premises?'

'This is barely possible,' said Dupin. 'The present peculiar condition of affairs at court, and especially of those intrigues in which D—— is known to be involved, would render the instant availability of the document – its susceptibility of being produced at a moment's notice – a point of nearly equal importance with its possession.'

'Its susceptibility of being produced?' said I.

'That is to say of being *destroyed*,' said Dupin.

'True,' I observed; 'the paper is clearly then upon the premises. As for its being upon the person of the minister, we may consider that as out of the question.'

'Entirely,' said the Prefect. 'He has been twice waylaid, as if by footpads, and his person rigorously searched under my own inspection.'

'You might have spared yourself this trouble,' said Dupin. 'D——, I presume, is not altogether a fool, and, if not, must have anticipated these waylayings as a matter of course.'

'Not *altogether* a fool,' said G—— 'but then he's a poet, which I take to be only one remove from a fool.'

'True,' said Dupin, after a long and thoughtful whiff from his meerschaum, 'although I have been guilty of certain doggerel myself.'

'Suppose you detail,' said I, 'the particulars of your search.'

'Why the fact is, we took our time, and we searched *everywhere*. I have had long experience in these affairs. I took the entire building, room by room; devoting the nights of a whole week to each. We examined, first, the furniture of each apartment. We opened every possible drawer; and I presume you know that, to a properly trained police-agent, such a thing as a *secret* drawer is impossible. Any man is a dolt who permits a "secret" drawer to escape him in a search of this kind. The thing is *so* plain. There is a certain amount of bulk – of space – to be accounted for in every cabinet. Then we have accurate rules. The fiftieth part of a line could not escape us. After the cabinets we took the chairs. The cushions we probed with the fine long needles you have seen me employ. From the tables we removed the tops.'

'Why so?'

'Sometimes the top of a table, or other similarly arranged piece of furniture, is removed by the person wishing to conceal an article; then the leg is excavated, the article deposited within the cavity, and the top replaced. The bottoms and tops of bedposts are employed in the same way.'

'But could not the cavity be detected by sounding?' I asked.

'By no means, if, when the article is deposited, a sufficient wadding of cotton be placed around it. Besides, in our case, we were obliged to proceed without noise.'

'But you could not have removed – you could not have taken to pieces *all* articles of furniture in which it would have been possible to make a deposit in the manner you mention. A letter may be compressed into a thin spiral roll, not differing much in shape or bulk from a large knitting-needle, and in this form it might be inserted into the rung of a chair, for example. You did not take to pieces all the chairs?'

'Certainly not; but we did better – we examined the rungs of every chair in the hotel, and, indeed, the jointings of every description of furniture, by the aid of a most powerful microscope. Had there been any traces of recent disturbance we should not have failed to detect it instantly. A single grain of gimlet-dust, for example, would have been as obvious as an apple. Any disorder in the glueing – any unusual gaping in the joints – would have sufficed to insure detection.'

'I presume you looked to the mirrors, between the boards and the plates, and you probed the beds and the bedclothes, as well as the curtains and carpets.'

'That of course; and when we had absolutely completed every particle of the furniture in this way then we examined the house itself. We divided its entire surface into compartments, which we numbered, so that none might be missed; then we scrutinised each individual square inch throughout the premises, including the two houses immediately adjoining, with the microscope, as before.'

'The two houses adjoining?' I exclaimed; 'you must have had a great deal of trouble.'

'We had; but the reward offered is prodigious.'

'You include the *grounds* about the houses?'

'All the grounds are paved with brick. They gave us comparatively little trouble. We examined the moss between the bricks, and found it undisturbed.'

'You looked among D——'s papers, of course, and into the books of the library?'

'Certainly; we opened every package and parcel; we not only opened every book, but we turned over every leaf in each volume, not contenting ourselves with a mere shake, according to the fashion of some of our police-officers. We also measured the thickness of every book-*cover*, with the most accurate admeasurement, and applied to each the most jealous scrutiny of the microscope. Had any of the bindings been recently meddled with, it would have been utterly impossible that the fact should have escaped observation. Some five or six volumes, just from the hands of the binder, we carefully probed, longitudinally, with the needles.'

'You explored the floors beneath the carpets?'

'Beyond doubt. We removed every carpet, and examined the boards with the microscope.'

'And the paper on the walls?'

'Yes.'

'You looked into the cellars?'

'We did.'

'Then,' I said, 'you have been making a miscalculation, and the letter is *not* upon the premises, as you suppose.'

'I fear you are right there,' said the Prefect. 'And now, Dupin, what would you advise me to do?'

'To make a thorough re-search of the premises.'

'That is absolutely needless,' replied G——. 'I am not more sure that I breathe than I am that the letter is not at the hotel.'

'I have no better advice to give you,' said Dupin. 'You have, of course, an accurate description of the letter?'

'Oh yes!' – And here the Prefect producing a memorandum-book, proceeded to read aloud a minute account of the internal, and especially of the external appearance of the missing document. Soon after finishing the perusal of this description, he took his departure more entirely depressed in spirits than I had ever known the good gentleman before.

In about a month afterwards he paid us another visit, and found us occupied very nearly as before. He took a pipe and a chair, and entered into some ordinary conversation. At length I said,

'Well, but G——, what of the purloined letter? I presume you have at last made up your mind that there is no such thing as overreaching the minister?'

'Confound him, say I – yes; I made the re-examination, however, as Dupin suggested – but it was all labour lost, as I knew it would be.'

'How much was the reward offered, did you say?' asked Dupin.

'Why, a very great deal – a *very* liberal reward – I don't like to say how much, precisely; but one thing I *will* say, that I wouldn't mind giving my individual cheque for fifty thousand francs to any one who would obtain me that letter. The fact is, it is becoming of more and more importance every day; and the reward has been lately doubled. If it were trebled, however, I could do no more than I have done.'

'Why, yes,' said Dupin, drawlingly, between the whiffs of his meerschaum, 'I really – think, G——, you have not exerted yourself – to the utmost in this matter. You might – do a little more, I think, eh?'

'How? – in what way?'

'Why – puff, puff – you might – puff, puff – employ counsel in the matter, eh? – puff, puff, puff. Do you remember the story they tell of Abernethy?'

'No; hang Abernethy!'

'To be sure! hang him and welcome. But, once upon a time, a certain rich miser, conceived the design of sponging upon this Abernethy for a medical opinion. Getting up, for this purpose, an ordinary conversation in a private company, he insinuated the case to his physician as that of an imaginary individual.

'"We will suppose," said the miser, "that his symptoms are such and such; now, doctor, what would *you* have directed him to take?"

'"Take!" said Abernethy, "why, take *advice*, to be sure."'

'But,' said the Prefect, a little discomposed, '*I* am *perfectly* willing to take advice, and to pay for it. I would *really* give fifty thousand francs to any who would aid me in the matter.'

'In that case,' replied Dupin, opening a drawer, and producing a cheque-book, 'you may as well fill me up a cheque for the amount mentioned. When you have signed it, I will hand you the letter.'

I was astounded. The Prefect appeared absolutely thunder-stricken. For some minutes he remained speechless and motionless, looking incredulously at my friend with open mouth, and eyes that seemed starting from their sockets; then, apparently recovering himself in some measure, he seized a pen, and after several pauses and vacant stares, finally filled up and signed a cheque for fifty thousand francs, and handed it across the table to Dupin. The latter examined it carefully, and deposited it in his pocket-book; then, unlocking an *escritoire*, took thence a letter and gave it to the Prefect. This functionary grasped it in a perfect agony of joy, opened it with a trembling hand, cast a rapid glance at its contents and then scrambling and struggling to the door, rushed at length unceremoniously from the room and from the house, without having uttered a syllable since Dupin had requested him to fill up the cheque.

When he had gone my friend entered into some explanations.

'The Parisian police,' he said, 'are exceedingly able in their way. They are persevering, ingenious, cunning, and thoroughly versed in the knowledge which their duties seem chiefly to demand. Thus, when G—— detailed to us his mode of searching the premises at the Hotel D——, I felt entire confidence in his having made a satisfactory investigation, so far as his labours extended.'

'So far as his labours extended?' said I.

'Yes,' said Dupin. 'The measures adopted were not only the best of their kind, but carried out to absolute perfection. Had the letter been deposited within the range of their search, these fellows would, beyond question, have found it.'

I merely laughed, but he seemed, quite serious in all that he said.

'The measures then,' he continued, 'were good of their kind, and well executed; their defect lay in their being inapplicable to the case, and to the man. A certain set of highly ingenious resources are with the Prefect a sort of Procrustean bed, to which he forcibly adapts his designs. But he perpetually errs by being too deep or to shallow for the matter in hand, and many a schoolboy is a better reasoner than he. I knew one about eight years of age, whose success at guessing in the game of "even and odd" attracted universal admiration. This game is simple, and is played with marbles. One player holds in his hand a number of these toys, and demands of another whether that number is even or odd. If the guess is right the guesser wins one, if wrong, he loses one. The boy to whom I allude won all the marbles of the school. Of course he had some principle of guessing, and this lay in mere observation and admeasurement of the astuteness of his opponents. For example, an arrant simpleton is his opponent, and holding up his closed hand asks, "are they even or odd?" Our schoolboy replies "odd," and loses, but upon the second trial he wins, for he then says to himself, "the simpleton had them even upon the first trial, and his amount of cunning is just sufficient to make him have them odd upon the second, I will therefore guess odd," he guesses odd, and wins. Now with a simpleton a degree above the first he would have reasoned thus: "This fellow finds that in the first instance I guessed odd, and in the second he will propose to himself upon the first impulse, a simple variation from even to odd, as did the first simpleton, but then a second thought will suggest that this is too simple a variation, and finally he will decide upon putting it even as before. I will therefore guess even," he guesses even, and wins. Now this mode of reasoning in the schoolboy, whom his fellows termed "lucky," what in its last analysis is it?'

'It is merely,' I said, 'an identification of the reasoner's intellect with that of his opponent.'

'It is,' said Dupin, 'and upon inquiring of the boy by what means he effected the *thorough* identification in which his success consisted, I received answer as follows: "When I wish to find out how wise, or how stupid, or how good, or how wicked, is any one, or what are his thoughts at the moment, I fashion the expression of my face as accurately as possible in accordance with the expression of his, and then wait to see what thoughts or sentiments arise in my mind or heart, as if to match or correspond with the expression." This response of the schoolboy lies at the bottom of all the spurious profundity which has been attributed to Rochefoucault, to La Bruyère, to Machiavelli, and to Campanella.'

'And the identification,' I said, 'of the reasoner's intellect with that of his opponent depends, if I understand you aright, upon the accuracy with which the opponent's intellect is admeasured.'

'For its practical value it depends upon this,' replied Dupin, 'and the Prefect and his cohort fail so frequently, first, by default of this identification, and secondly, by ill-admeasurement, or rather through non-admeasurement of the intellect with which they are engaged. They consider only their *own* ideas of ingenuity; and in searching for anything hidden, advert only to the modes in which *they* would have hidden it. They are right in this much – that their own ingenuity is a faithful representative of that of *the mass*; but when the cunning of the individual felon is diverse in character from their own, the felon foils them of course. This always happens when it is above their own, and very usually when it is below. They have no variation of principle in their investigations; at best, when urged by some unusual emergency, by some extraordinary reward, they extend or exaggerate their old modes of *practice*, without touching their principles. What, for example, in this case of D—— has been done to vary the principle of action? What is all this boring, and probing, and sounding, and scrutinising with the microscope, and dividing the surface of the building into registered square inches – what is it all but an exaggeration *of the application* of the one principle or set of principles of search, which are based upon the one set of notions regarding human ingenuity, to which the Prefect in the long routine of his duty has been accustomed? Do you not see he has taken it for granted that *all* men proceed to conceal a letter – not exactly in a gimlet-hole bored in a chair-leg – but, at least, in *some* out-of-the-way hole or corner suggested by the same tenor of thought which would urge a man to secrete a letter in a gimlet-hole bored in a chair-leg? And do you not see also that such *recherché* nooks for concealment are adapted only for ordinary occasions, and would be adopted only by ordinary intellects; for in all cases of concealment, a disposal of the article concealed – a disposal of it in this *recherché* manner – is in the very first instance presumable and presumed; and thus its discovery depends, not at all upon the acumen, but altogether upon the mere care, patience, and determination of the seekers; and where the case is of importance, or what amounts to the same thing in the political eyes, when the reward is of magnitude, the qualities in question have *never* been known to fail? You will now understand what I meant in suggesting that had the purloined letter been hidden anywhere within the limits of the Prefect's examination – in other words, had the principle of its concealment been comprehended within the principles of the Prefect, its discovery would have been a matter altogether beyond question. This functionary, however, has been thoroughly mystified, and the remote source of his defeat lies in the supposition that the minister is a fool, because he has acquired renown as a poet. All fools are poets, this the Prefect *feels*, and he is merely guilty of a *non distributio medii* in thence inferring that all poets are fools.'

'But is this really the poet?' I asked. 'There are two brothers, I know, and both have attained reputation in letters. The minister, I believe, has written learnedly on the Differential Calculus. He is a mathematician and no poet.'

'You are mistaken; I know him well; he is both. As poet *and* mathematician he would reason well; as mere mathematician he could not have reasoned at all, and thus would have been at the mercy of the Prefect.'

'You surprise me,' I said, 'by these opinions, which have been contradicted by the voice of the world. You do not mean to set at naught the well-digested idea of centuries. The mathematical reason has long been regarded as *the* reason *par excellence*.'

' "*Il y a à parier*," ' replied Dupin, quoting from Chamfort, ' "*que toute idée publique, toute convention reçue, est une sottise, car elle a convenue au plus grand nombre.*' The mathematicians, I grant you, have done their best to promulgate the popular error to which you allude, and which is none the less an error for its promulgation as truth. With an art worthy of a better cause for example, they have insinuated the term "analysis" into application to algebra. The French are the originators of this particular deception, but if a term is of any importance, if words derive any value from applicability, then "analysis" conveys "algebra" about as much as, in Latin, "*ambitus*" implies "ambition," "*religio*" "religion," or "*homines honesti,*" a set of *honourable* men.'

'You have a quarrel on hand, I see,' said I, 'with some of the algebraists of Paris – but proceed.'

'I dispute the availability, and thus the value of that reason which is cultivated in any especial form other than the abstractly logical. I dispute in particular the reason educed by mathematical study. The mathematics are the science of form and quantity, mathematical reasoning is merely logic applied to observation upon form and quantity. The great error lies in supposing that even the truths of what is called *pure* algebra are abstract or general truths. And this error is so egregious that I am confounded at the universality with which it has been received. Mathematical axioms are *not* axioms of general truth. What is true of *relation* – of form and quantity – is often grossly false in regard to morals, for example. In this latter science it is very usually *un*true that the aggregated parts are equal to the whole. In chemistry also the axiom fails. In the consideration of motive it fails, for two motives, each of a given value, have not necessarily a value when united equal to the sum of their values apart. There are numerous other mathematical truths which are only truths within the limits of *relation*. But the mathematician argues from his *finite truths*, through habit, as if they were of an absolutely general applicability – as the world indeed imagines them to be. Bryant, in his very learned "Mythology," mentions an analogous source of error, when he says that "although the Pagan fables are not believed, yet we forget ourselves continually, and make inferences from them as existing realities." With the algebraists, however, who are Pagans themselves, the "Pagan fables" *are* believed, and the inferences are made, not so much through lapse of memory as through an unaccountable addling of the brains. In short, I never yet encountered the mere mathematician who could be trusted out of equal roots, or one who did not clandestinely hold it as a point of his faith that $x^2 + px$ was absolutely and unconditionally equal to q. Say to one of these gentlemen, by way of experiment, if you please, that you believe occasions may occur where $x^2 + px$ is *not* altogether equal to q, and having made him understand what you mean, get out of his reach as speedily as convenient, for beyond doubt he will endeavour to knock you down.

'I mean to say,' continued Dupin, while I merely laughed at his last observations, 'that if the minister had been no more than a mathematician, the Prefect would have been under no necessity of giving me this cheque. I knew him, however, as both mathematician and poet, and my measures were adapted to his capacity, with reference to the circumstances by which he was surrounded. I knew him as a courtier, too, and as a bold *intrigant*. Such a man, I considered, could not fail to be aware of the ordinary policial modes of action. He could not have failed to anticipate – and events have proved that he did not fail to anticipate – the waylayings to which he was subjected. He must have foreseen, I reflected, the secret investigations of his premises. His frequent absences from home at nights, which were hailed by the Prefect as certain aids to his success, I regarded only as *ruses*, to afford opportunity for thorough search to the police, and thus the sooner to impress them with the conviction to which G——, in fact, did finally arrive – the conviction that the letter was not upon the premises. I felt, also, that the whole train of thought which I was at some pains in detailing to you just now, concerning the invariable principle of policial action in searches for articles concealed – I felt that this whole train of thought would necessarily pass through the mind of the minister. It would imperatively lead him to despise all the ordinary *nooks* of concealment. *He* could not, I reflected, be so weak as not to see that the most intricate and remote recess of his hotel would be as open as his commonest closets to the eyes, to the probes, to the gimlets, and to the microscopes of the Prefect. I saw, in fine, that he would be driven, as a matter of course, to *simplicity*, if not deliberately induced to it as a matter of choice. You will remember, perhaps, how desperately the Prefect laughed when I suggested, upon our first interview, that it was just possible this mystery troubled him so much on account of its being so *very* self-evident.'

'Yes,' said I, 'I remember his merriment well. I really thought he would have fallen into convulsions.'

'The material world,' continued Dupin, 'abounds with very strict analogies to the immaterial; and thus some colour of truth has been given to the rhetorical dogma that metaphor or simile may be made to strengthen an argument as well as to embellish a description. The principle of the *vis inertiæ*, for example, seems to be identical in physics and metaphysics. It is not more true in the former that a large body is with more difficulty set in motion than a smaller one, and that its subsequent *momentum* is commensurate with this difficulty, than it is, in the latter, that intellects of the vaster capacity, while more forcible, more constant, and more eventful in their movements than those of inferior grade, are yet the less readily moved, and more embarrassed and full of hesitation in the first few steps of their progress. Again; have you ever noticed which of the street signs over the shop-doors are the most attractive of attention?'

'I have never given the matter a thought,' I said.

'There is a game of puzzles,' he resumed, 'which is played upon a map. One party playing requires another to find a given word – the name of town, river, state, or empire – any word, in short, upon the motley and perplexed surface of the chart. A novice in the game generally seeks to embarrass his opponents by giving them the most minutely lettered names, but the adept selects such words as stretch, in large characters from one end of the chart to the other. These, like the over-largely lettered signs and placards of the street, escape observation by dint of being excessively obvious; and here the physical oversight is precisely analogous with the moral inapprehension by which the intellect suffers to pass unnoticed those considerations which are too obtrusively and too palpably self-evident. But this is a point, it appears, somewhat, above or beneath the understanding of the Prefect. He never once thought it probable, or possible, that the minister had deposited the letter immediately beneath the nose of the whole world, by way of best preventing any portion of that world from perceiving it.

'But the more I reflected upon the daring, dashing, and discriminating ingenuity of D——; upon the fact that the document must always have been *at hand* if he intended to use it to good purpose; and upon the decisive evidence, obtained by the Prefect, that it was not hidden within the limits of that dignitary's ordinary search – the more satisfied I became that, to conceal this letter, the minister had resorted to the comprehensive and sagacious expedient of not attempting to conceal it at all.

'Full of these ideas, I prepared myself with a pair of green spectacles, and called one fine morning, quite by accident, at the ministerial hotel. I found D—— at home, yawning, lounging, and dawdling, as usual, and pretending to be in the last extremity of *ennui*. He is, perhaps, the most really energetic human being now alive – but that is only when nobody sees him.

'To be even with him, I complained of my weak eyes, and lamented the necessity of the spectacles, under cover of which I cautiously and thoroughly surveyed the whole apartment, while seemingly intent only upon the conversation of my host.

'I paid especial attention to a large writing-table near which he sat, and upon which lay confusedly some miscellaneous letters and other papers, with one or two musical instruments and a few books. Here, however, after a long and very deliberate scrutiny, I saw nothing to excite particular suspicion.

'At length my eyes, in going the circuit of the room, fell upon a trumpery filigree card-rack of pasteboard that hung dangling by a dirty blue ribbon from a little brass knob just beneath the middle of the mantelpiece. In this rack, which had three or four compartments, were five or six visiting cards and a solitary letter. This last was much soiled and crumpled. It was torn nearly in two, across the middle – as if a design, in the first instance, to tear it entirely up as worthless, had been altered, or stayed, in the second. It had a large black seal, bearing the D—— cipher *very* conspicuously, and was addressed in a diminutive female hand, to D——, the minister, himself. It was thrust carelessly, and even, as it seemed, contemptuously, into one of the uppermost divisions of the rack.

'No sooner had I glanced at this letter than I concluded it to be that of which I was in search. To be sure, it was to all appearance radically different from the one of which the Prefect had read us so minute a description. Here the seal was large and black, with the D—— cipher; there it was small and red, with the ducal arms of the S—— family. Here the address, to the minister, was diminutive and feminine; there the superscription to a certain royal personage, was markedly bold and decided; the size alone formed a point of correspondence. But, then, the *radicalness* of these differences, which was excessive; the dirt; the soiled and torn condition of the paper, so inconsistent with the *true* methodical habits of D——, and so suggestive of a design to delude the beholder into an idea of the worthlessness of the document; these things, together with the hyper-obtrusive situation of this document, full in the view of every visitor, and thus exactly in accordance with the conclusions to which I had previously arrived: these things, I say, were strongly corroborative of suspicion in one who came with the intention to suspect.

'I protracted my visit as long as possible, and while I maintained a most animated discussion with the minister upon a topic which I knew well had never failed to interest and excite him, I kept my attention really riveted upon the letter. In this examination I committed to memory its external appearance and arrangement in the rack; and also fell, at length, upon a discovery which set at rest whatever trivial doubt I might have entertained. In scrutinising the edges of the paper I observed them to be more *chafed* than seemed necessary. They presented the *broken* appearance which is manifested when a stiff paper, having been once folded and pressed with a folder, is refolded in a reversed direction, in the same creases or edges which had formed the original fold. This discovery was sufficient. It was clear to me that the letter had been turned as a glove, inside out, re-directed and re-sealed. I bade the minister good-morning and took my departure at once, leaving a gold snuff-box upon the table.

'The next morning I called for the snuff-box, when we resumed quite eagerly the conversation of the preceding day. While thus engaged, however, a loud report as if of a pistol, was heard immediately beneath the windows of the hotel, and was succeeded by a series of fearful screams, and the shoutings of a terrified mob. D—— rushed to a casement, threw it open and looked out. In the meantime I stepped to the card-rack, took the letter, put it in my pocket, and replaced it by a *facsimile* (so far as regards externals), which I had carefully prepared at my lodgings – imitating the D—— cipher very readily by means of a seal formed of bread.

'The disturbance in the street had been occasioned by the frantic behaviour of a man with a musket. He had fired it among a crowd of women and children. It proved, however, to have been without ball, and the fellow was suffered to go his way as a lunatic or a drunkard. When he had gone, D—— came from the window, whither I had followed him immediately upon securing the object in view. Soon afterwards I bade him farewell. The pretended lunatic was a man in my own pay.'

'But what purpose had you,' I asked, 'in replacing the letter by a *facsimile*? Would it not have been better at the first visit to have seized it openly, and departed?'

'D——,' replied Dupin, 'is a desperate man and a man of nerve.

His hotel, too, is not without attendants devoted to his interests. Had I made the wild attempt you suggest I might never have left the ministerial presence alive. The good people of Paris might have heard of me no more. But I had an object apart from these considerations. You know my political prepossessions. In this matter, I act as a partisan of the lady concerned. For eighteen months the minister has had her in his power. She now has him in hers – since, being unaware that the letter is not in his possession, he will proceed with his exactions as if it was. Thus will he inevitably commit himself at once to his political destruction. His downfall, too, will not be more precipitate than awkward. It is all very well to talk about the *facilis descensus Averni*, but in all kinds of climbing, as Catalani said of singing, it is far more easy to get up than to come down. In the present instance I have no sympathy – at least no pity – for him who descends. He is that *monstrum horrendum*, an unprincipled man of genius. I confess, however, that I should like very well to know the precise character of his thoughts, when, being defied by her whom the Prefect terms "a certain personage," he is reduced to opening the letter which I left for him in the card-rack.'

'How? did you put anything particular in it?'

'Why – it did not seem altogether right to leave the interior blank – that would have been insulting. D——, at Vienna, once did me an evil turn, which I told him, quite good-humouredly, that I should remember. So, as I knew he would feel some curiosity in regard to the identity of the person who had outwitted him, I thought it a pity not to give him a clue. He is well acquainted with my MS., and I just copied into the middle of the blank sheet the words –

"—— Un dessein si funeste,
S'il n'est digne d'Atrée, est digne de Thyeste."

They are to be found in Crébillon's "Atrée."'

The Spectacles

Many years ago it was the fashion to ridicule the idea of 'love at first sight;' but those who think, not less than those who feel deeply, have always advocated its existence. Modern discoveries, indeed, in what may be termed ethical magnetism or magnetæsthetics, render it probable that the most natural, and, consequently, the truest and most intense of the human affections, are those which arise in the heart as if by electric sympathy – in a word, that the brightest and most enduring of the psychal fetters are those which are riveted by a glance. The confession I am about to make will add another to the already almost innumerable instances of the truth of the proposition.

My story requires that I should be somewhat minute. I am still a very young man – not yet twenty-two years of age. My name, at present, is a very usual and rather plebeian one – Simpson. I say 'at present;' for it is only lately that I have been so called – having legislatively adopted this surname within the last year in order to receive a large inheritance left me by a distant male relative, Adolphus Simpson, Esq. The bequest was conditioned upon my taking the name of the testator:– the family, not the Christian name; my Christian name is Napoleon Bonaparte – or, more properly, these are my first and middle appellations.

I assumed the name Simpson with some reluctance, as in my true patronym, Froissart, I felt a very pardonable pride – believing that I could trace a descent from the immortal author of the 'Chronicles.' While on the subject of names, by-the-by, I may mention a singular coincidence of sound attending the names of some of my immediate predecessors. My father was a Monsieur Froissart of Paris. His wife – my mother, whom he married at fifteen – was a Mademoiselle Croissart, eldest daughter of Croissart the banker; whose wife, again, being only sixteen when married, was the eldest daughter of one Victor Voissart. Monsieur Voissart, very singularly had married a lady of similar name – a Mademoiselle Moissart. She, too, was quite a child when married; and her mother, also Madame Moissart, was only fourteen when led to the altar. These early marriages are usual in France. Here, however, are Moissart, Voissart, Croissart, and Froissart, all in the direct line of descent. My own name, though, as I say, became Simpson by act of legislature, and with so much repugnance on my part, that at one period I actually hesitated about accepting the legacy with the useless and annoying *proviso* attached.

As to personal endowments I am by no means deficient. On the contrary, I believe that I am well-made, and possess what nine-tenths of the world would call a handsome face. In height I am five feet eleven. My hair is black and curling. My nose is sufficiently good. My eyes are large and grey; and although, in fact, they are weak to a very inconvenient degree, still no defect in this regard would be suspected from their appearance. The weakness itself, however, has always much annoyed me, and I have resorted to every remedy – short of wearing glasses. Being youthful and good-looking, I naturally dislike these, and have resolutely refused to employ them. I know nothing, indeed, which so disfigures the countenance of a young person, or so impresses every feature with an air of demureness, if not altogether of sanctimoniousness and of age. An eye-glass, on the other hand, has a savour of downright foppery and affectation. I have hitherto managed as well as I could without either. But something too much of these merely personal details, which, after all, are of little importance. I will content myself with saying, in addition, that my temperament is sanguine, rash, ardent, enthusiastic – and that all my life I have been a devoted admirer of the women.

One night last winter, I entered a box at the P—— Theatre, in company with a friend, Mr. Talbot. It was an opera night, and the bills presented a very rare attraction, so that the house was excessively crowded. We were in time, however, to obtain the front seats which had been reserved for us, and into which, with some little difficulty, we elbowed our way.

For two hours, my companion, who was a musical *fanatico*, gave his undivided attention to the stage; and in the meantime, I amused myself by observing the audience, which consisted, in chief part, of the very *élite* of the city. Having satisfied myself upon this point, I was about turning my eyes to the *prima donna*, when they were arrested and riveted by a figure in one of the private boxes which had escaped my observation.

If I live a thousand years, I can never forget the intense emotion with which I regarded this figure. It was that of a female, the most exquisite I had ever beheld. The face was so far turned towards the stage, that, for some minutes, I could not obtain a view of it – but the form was *divine*; no other word can sufficiently express its magnificent proportion – and even the term 'divine' seems ridiculously feeble as I write it.

The magic of a lovely form in woman – the necromancy of female gracefulness – was always a power which I had found it impossible to resist; but here was grace personified, incarnate, the *beau idéal* of my wildest and most enthusiastic visions. The figure, almost all of which the construction of the box permitted to be seen, was somewhat above the medium height, and nearly approached, without positively reaching the majestic. Its perfect fulness, and *tournure* were delicious. The head, of which only the back was visible, rivalled in outline that of the Greek Psyche, and was rather displayed than concealed by an elegant cap of *gaze aërienne*, which put me in mind of *ventum textilem* of Apuleius. The right arm hung over the balustrade of the box, and thrilled every nerve of my frame with its exquisite symmetry. Its upper portion was draperied by one of the loose open sleeves now in fashion.

This extended but little below the elbow. Beneath it was worn an under one of some frail material, close-fitting, and terminated by a cuff of rich lace which fell gracefully over the top of the hand, revealing only the delicate fingers upon one of which sparkled a diamond ring, which I at once saw was of extraordinary value. The admirable roundness of the wrist was well set off by a bracelet which encircled it and which also was ornamented and clasped by a magnificent aigrette of jewels – telling, in words that could not be mistaken, at once of the wealth and fastidious taste of the wearer.

I gazed at this queenly apparition for at least half-an-hour, as if I had been suddenly converted to stone; and, during this period I felt the full force and truth of all that has been said or sung concerning 'love at first sight.' My feelings were totally different from any which I had hitherto experienced, in the presence of even the most celebrated specimens of female loveliness. An unaccountable, and what I am compelled to consider a *magnetic* sympathy of soul for soul, seemed to rivet not only my vision, but my whole powers of thought and feeling upon the admirable object before me. I saw – I felt – I knew that I was deeply, madly, irrevocably in love – and this even before seeing the face of the person beloved. So intense, indeed, was the passion that consumed me, that I really believe it would have received little if any abatement had the features, yet unseen, proved of merely ordinary character; so anomalous is the nature of the only true love – of the love at first sight – and so little really dependent is it upon the external conditions which only seem to create and control it.

While I was thus wrapped in admiration of this lovely vision, a sudden disturbance among the audience caused her to turn her head partially towards me, so that I beheld the entire profile of the face. Its beauty even exceeded my anticipations – and yet there was something about it which disappointed me without my being able to tell exactly what it was. I said 'disappointed,' but this is not altogether the word. My sentiments were at once quieted and exalted. They partook less of transport and more of calm enthusiams – of enthusiastic repose. This state of feeling arose perhaps from the Madonna-like and matronly air of the face; and yet I at once understood that it could not have arisen entirely from this. There was something else – some mystery which I could not develop – some expression about the countenance which slightly disturbed me while it greatly heightened my interest. In fact, I was just in that condition of mind which prepares a young and susceptible man for any act of extravagance. Had the lady been alone, I should undoubtedly have entered her box and accosted her at all hazards; but, fortunately, she was attended by two companions – a gentleman, and a strikingly beautiful woman, to all appearance a few years younger than herself.

I revolved in my mind a thousand schemes by which I might obtain hereafter an introduction to the elder lady, or for the present, at all events, a more distinct view of her beauty. I would have removed my position to one nearer her own, but the crowded state of the theatre rendered this impossible; and the stern decrees of Fashion had of late imperatively prohibited the use of the operaglass, in a case such as this, even had I been so fortunate as to have one with me – but I had not – and was thus in despair.

At length I bethought me of applying to my companion.

'Talbot,' I said, '*you* have an opera-glass. Let me have it.'

'An opera-glass! – no! – what do you suppose *I* would be doing with an opera-glass?' Here he turned impatiently towards the stage.

'But, Talbot,' I continued, pulling him by the shoulder, 'listen to me, will you? Do you see the stage-box? – there! – no, the next – Did you ever behold as lovely a woman?'

'She is very beautiful, no doubt,' he said.

'I wonder who she can be?'

'Why, in the name of all that is angelic, don't you *know* who she is? "Not to know her, argues yourself unknown." She is the celebrated Madame Lalande – the beauty of the day *par excellence*, and the talk of the whole town. Immensely wealthy, too – a widow – and a great match – has just arrived from Paris.'

'Do you know her?'

'Yes – I have the honour.'

'Will you introduce me?'

'Assuredly – with the greatest pleasure; when shall it be?'

'To-morrow, at one; I will call upon you at B——'s.'

'Very good; and now *do* hold your tongue, *if* you can.'

In this latter respect I was forced to take Talbot's advice; for he remained obstinately deaf to every further question or suggestion, and occupied himself exclusively for the rest of the evening with what was transacting upon the stage.

In the meantime I kept my eyes riveted on Madame Lalande, and at length had the good fortune to obtain a full front view of her face. It was exquisitely lovely: this, of course, my heart had told me before, even had not Talbot fully satisfied me upon the point – but still the unintelligible something disturbed me. I finally concluded that my senses were impressed by a certain air of gravity, sadness, or, still more properly, of weariness, which took something from the youth and freshness of the countenance, only to endow it with a seraphic tenderness and majesty, and thus, of course, to my enthusiastic and romantic temperament, with an interest tenfold.

While I thus feasted my eyes, I perceived, at last to my great trepidation, by an almost imperceptible start on the part of the lady, that she had become suddenly aware of the intensity of my gaze. Still I was absolutely fascinated, and could not withdraw it, even for an instant. She turned aside her face, and again I saw only the chiselled contour of the back portion of the head. After some minutes, as if urged by curiosity to see if I was still looking, she gradually brought her face again around, and again encountered my burning gaze. Her large dark eyes fell instantly, and a deep blush mantled her cheek. But what was my astonishment at perceiving that she not only did not a second time avert her head, but that she actually took from her girdle a double eye-glass – elevated it – adjusted it – and then regarded me through it, intently and deliberately, for the space of several minutes.

Had a thunderbolt fallen at my feet I could not have been more thoroughly astounded – astounded *only* – not offended or disgusted in the slightest degree; although an action so bold in any other woman would have been likely to offend or disgust. But the whole thing was done with so much quietude – so much *nonchalance* – so much repose – with so evident an air of the highest breeding, in short – that nothing of mere effrontery was perceptible, and my sole sentiments were those of admiration and surprise.

I observed that, upon her first elevation of the glass, she had seemed satisfied with a momentary inspection of my person, and was withdrawing the instrument, when, as if struck by a second thought, she resumed it, and so continued to regard me with fixed attention for the space of several minutes – for five minutes at the very least, I am sure.

This action, so remarkable in an American theatre, attracted very general observation, and gave rise to an indefinite movement, or *buzz*, among the audience, which for a moment filled me with confusion, but produced no visible effect upon the countenance of Madame Lalande.

Having satisfied her curiosity – if such it was – she dropped the glass, and quietly gave her attention again to the stage; her profile now being turned towards myself, as before. I continued to watch her unremittingly, although I was fully conscious of my rudeness in so doing. Presently I saw the head slowly and slightly change its position; and soon I became convinced that the lady, while pretending to look at the stage was, in fact, attentively regarding myself. It is needless to say what effect this conduct, on the part of so fascinating a woman, had upon my excitable mind.

Having thus scrutinised me for perhaps a quarter of an hour, the fair object of my passion addressed the gentleman who attended her, and, while she spoke, I saw distinctly, by the glances of both, that the conversation had reference to myself.

Upon its conclusion Madame Lalande again turned towards the stage, and for a few minutes seemed absorbed in the performances. At the expiration of this period, however, I was thrown into an extremity of agitation by seeing her unfold, for the second time, the eye-glass which hung at her side, fully confront me as before, and, disregarding the renewed buzz of the audience, survey me, from head to foot, with the same miraculous composure which had previously so delighted and confounded my soul.

This extraordinary behaviour, by throwing me into a perfect fever of excitement – into an absolute delirium of love – served rather to

embolden than to disconcert me. In the mad intensity of my devotion I
forgot everything but the presence and the majestic loveliness of the
vision which confronted my gaze. Watching my opportunity, when I
thought the audience were fully engaged with the opera, I at length
caught the eyes of Madame Lalande, and, upon the instant, made a
slight but unmistakeable bow.

She flushed very deeply, then averted her eyes, then slowly and
cautiously looked around, apparently to see if my rash action had been
noticed and then leaned over towards the gentleman who sat by her side.

I now felt a burning sense of the impropriety I had committed, and
expected nothing less than instant exposure; while a vision of pistols
upon the morrow floated rapidly and uncomfortably through my
brain. I was greatly and immediately relieved, however, when I saw
the lady merely hand the gentleman a play-bill, without speaking; but
the reader may form some feeble conception of my astonishment – of
my *profound* amazement – my delirious bewilderment of heart and soul
– when, instantly afterwards, having again glanced furtively around,
she allowed her bright eyes to settle fully and steadily upon my own,
and then, with a faint smile, disclosing a bright line of her pearly teeth,
made two distinct, pointed, and unequivocal affirmative inclinations
of the head.

It is useless, of course, to dwell upon my joy – upon my transport –
upon my illimitable ecstasy of heart. If ever man was mad with excess
of happiness, it was myself at that moment. I loved. This was my *first*
love – so I felt it to be. It was love supreme – indescribable. It was
'love at first sight;' and at first sight too it had been appreciated and
returned.

Yes, returned. How and why should I doubt it for an instant?
What other construction could I possibly put upon such conduct, on
the part of a lady so beautiful – so wealthy, evidently so accomplished,
of so high breeding, of so lofty a position in society – in every regard so
entirely respectable as I felt assured was Madame Lalande? Yes, she
loved me – she returned the enthusiasm of my love, with an
enthusiasm as blind, as uncompromising, as uncalculating, as abandoned, and as utterly unbounded as my own! These delicious fancies

and reflections, however, were now interrupted by the falling of the drop-curtain. The audience arose, and the usual tumult immediately supervened. Quitting Talbot abruptly, I made every effort to force my way into closer proximity with Madame Lalande. Having failed in this, on account of the crowd, I at length gave up the chase and bent my steps homewards; consoling myself for my disappointment in not having been able to touch even the hem of her robe, by the reflection that I should be introduced by Talbot in due form upon the morrow.

This morrow at last came; that is to say, a day finally dawned upon a long and weary night of impatience; and then the hours until 'one,' were snail-paced, dreary, and innumerable. But even Stamboul, it is said, shall have an end, and there came an end to this long delay. The clock struck. As the last echo ceased, I stepped into B——'s and inquired for Talbot.

'Out,' said the footman – Talbot's own.

'Out!' I replied, staggering back half-a-dozen paces – 'let me tell you, my fine fellow, that this thing is thoroughly impossible and impracticable; Mr. Talbot is *not* out. What do you mean?'

'Nothing, sir: only Mr. Talbot is not in. That's all. He rode over to S——, immediately after breakfast, and left word that he would not be in town again for a week.'

I stood petrified with horror and rage. I endeavoured to reply, but my tongue refused its office. At length I turned on my heel, livid with wrath, and inwardly consigning the whole tribe of the Talbots to the innermost regions of Erebus. It was evident that my considerate friend, *il fanatico*, had quite forgotten his appointment with myself – had forgotten it as soon as it was made. At no time was he a very scrupulous man of his word. There was no help for it; so smothering my vexation as well as I could, I strolled moodily up the street, propounding futile inquiries about Madame Lalande to every male acquaintance I met. By report she was known, I found, to all – to many by sight – but she had been in town only a few weeks, and there were very few therefore who claimed her personal acquaintance. These few, being still comparatively strangers, could not, or would not, take the liberty of introducing me through the formality of a morning call.

While I stood thus, in despair, conversing with a trio of friends upon the all-absorbing subject of my heart, it so happened that the subject itself passed by.

'As I live, there she is!' cried one.

'Surpassingly beautiful!' exclaimed a second.

'An angel upon earth!' ejaculated a third.

I looked; and in an open carriage which approached us, passing slowly down the street, sat the enchanting vision of the opera, accompanied by the younger lady who had occupied a portion of her box.

'Her companion also wears remarkably well,' said the one of my trio who had spoken first.

'Astonishingly,' said the second: 'still quite a brilliant air; but art will do wonders. Upon my word she looks better than she did at Paris five years ago. A beautiful woman still; — don't you think so, Froissart? — Simpson, I mean.'

'*Still!*' said I, 'and why shouldn't she be? But compared with her friend she is as a rushlight to the evening star — a glow-worm to Antares.'

'Ha! ha! ha! – why Simpson, you have an astonishing tact at making discoveries – original ones, I mean.' And here we separated, while one of the trio began humming a gay *vaudeville*, of which I caught only the lines —

> Ninon, Ninon, Ninon à bas –
> A bas Ninon de l'Enclos!

During this little scene, however, one thing had served greatly to console me, although it fed the passion by which I was consumed. As the carriage of Madame Lalande rolled by our group, I had observed that she recognised me; and more than this, she had blessed me by the most seraphic of all imaginable smiles, with no equivocal mark of the recognition.

As for an introduction, I was obliged to abandon all hope of it until such time as Talbot should think proper to return from the country. In

the meantime I perseveringly frequented every reputable place of
public amusement; and at length, at the theatre, where I first saw her, I
had the supreme bliss of meeting her, and of exchanging glances with
her once again. This did not occur, however, until the lapse of a
fortnight. Every day in the *interim*, I had inquired for Talbot at his
hotel, and every day had been thrown into a spasm of wrath by the
everlasting 'Not come home yet' of his footman.

Upon the evening in question therefore I was in a condition little
short of madness. Madame Lalande, I had been told, was a Parisian –
had lately arrived from Paris – might she not suddenly return? – return
before Talbot came back – and might she not be thus lost to me for
ever? The thought was too terrible to bear. Since my future happiness
was at issue, I resolved to act with a manly decision. In a word, upon
the breaking up of the play, I traced the lady to her residence, noted
the address, and the next morning sent her a full and elaborate letter,
in which I poured out my whole heart.

I spoke boldly, freely – in a word I spoke with passion. I concealed
nothing – nothing even of my weakness. I alluded to the romantic
circumstances of our first meeting – even to the glances which had
passed between us. I went so far as to say that I felt assured of her love;
while I offered this assurance, and my own intensity of devotion, as
two excuses for my otherwise unpardonable conduct. As a third, I
spoke of my fear that she might quit the city before I could have the
opportunity of a formal introduction. I concluded the most wildly
enthusiastic epistle ever penned, with a frank declaration of my
worldly circumstances – of my affluence – and with an offer of my
heart and of my hand.

In an agony of expectation I awaited the reply. After what seemed
the lapse of a century it came.

Yes, *actually came*. Romantic as all this may appear, I really
received a letter from Madame Lalande – the beautiful, the wealthy,
the idolised Madame Lalande. Her eyes – her magnificent eyes – had
not belied her noble heart. Like a true French-woman, as she was, she
had obeyed the frank dictates of her reason – the generous impulses of
her nature – despising the conventional pruderies of the world. She

had *not* scorned my proposals. She had *not* sheltered herself in silence. She had *not* returned my letter unopened. She had even sent me in reply, one penned by her own exquisite fingers. It ran thus:

MONSIEUR SIMPSON ville pardonne me for not compose de butefulle tong of his contrée so vell as might. It is only de late dat I am arrive, and not yet ave de opportunité for to – l'étudier.

Vid dis apologie for the manière, I vill now say dat, hélas! – Monsieur Simpson ave guess but de too true. Need I say de more? Hélas? am I not ready speak de too moshe.

EUGENIE LALANDE.

This noble-spirited note I kissed a million times, and committed, no doubt, on its account a thousand other extravagances that have now escaped my memory. Still Talbot *would* not return. Alas! could he have formed even the vaguest idea of the suffering his absence occasioned his friend, would not his sympathising nature have flown immediately to my relief? Still, however, he came *not*. I wrote. He replied. He was detained by urgent business – but would shortly return. He begged me not to be impatient – to moderate my transports – to read soothing books – to drink nothing stronger than Hock – and to bring the consolations of philosophy to my aid. The fool! if he could not come himself, why, in the name of everything rational, could he not have enclosed me a letter of presentation? I wrote again, entreating him to forward one forthwith. My letter was returned by *that* footman, with the following endorsement in pencil. The scoundrel had joined his master in the country:

Left S—— yesterday for parts unknown – did not say where – or when be back – so thought best to return letter, knowing your handwriting, and as how you is always, more or less, in a hurry. – Yours sincerely, STUBBS.

After this, it is needless to say that I devoted to the infernal deities both master and valet; but there was little use in anger, and no consolation at all in complaint.

But I had yet a resource left in my constitutional audacity. Hitherto it had served me well, and I now resolved to make it avail me to the end. Besides, after the correspondence which had passed between us, what act of mere informality *could* I commit, within bounds, that ought to be regarded as indecorous by Madame Lalande? Since the affair of the letter, I had been in the habit of watching her house, and thus discovered that, about twilight, it was her custom to promenade, attended only by a negro in livery, in a public square overlooked by her windows. Here, amid the luxuriant and shadowing groves, in the grey gloom of a sweet midsummer evening, I observed my opportunity and accosted her.

The better to deceive the servant in attendance, I did this with the assured air of an old and familiar acquaintance. With a presence of mind truly Parisian, she took the cue at once, and, to greet me held out the most bewitchingly little of hands. The valet at once fell into the rear; and now, with hearts full to overflowing, we discoursed long and unreservedly of our love.

As Madame Lalande spoke English even less fluently than she wrote it, our conversation was necessarily in French. In this sweet tongue, so adapted to passion, I gave loose to the impetuous enthusiasm of my nature, and with all the eloquence I could command, besought her consent to an immediate marriage.

At this impatience she smiled, she urged the old story of decorum – that bugbear which deters so many from bliss until the opportunity for bliss has for ever gone by. I had most imprudently made it known among my friends, she observed, that I desired her acquaintance – thus that I did not possess it – thus again, there was no possibility of concealing the date of our first knowledge of each other. And then she adverted, with a blush, to the extreme recency of this date. To wed immediately would be improper – would be indecorous – would be *outré*. All this she said with a charming air of *naïveté* which enraptured while it grieved and convinced me. She went even so far as to accuse me, laughingly, of rashness – of imprudence. She bade me remember that I really even knew not who she was – what were her prospects, her connections, her standing in society. She begged me, but with a sigh, to reconsider my proposal, and termed my love an infatuation – a will o' the wisp – a fancy or fantasy of the moment – a baseless and unstable creation rather of the imagination than of the heart. These things she uttered as the shadows of the sweet twilight gathered darkly and more darkly around us, – and then, with a gentle pressure of her fairy-like hand, overthrew, in a single sweet instant, all the argumentative fabric she had reared.

I replied as best I could – as only a true lover can. I spoke at length and perseveringly of my devotion, of my passion – of her exceeding beauty, and of my own enthusiastic admiration. In conclusion, I dwelt, with a convincing energy, upon the perils that encompass the course of love – that course of true love that never did run smooth, and thus deduced the manifest danger of rendering that course unnecessarily long.

This latter argument seemed finally to soften the rigour of her determination. She relented; but there was yet an obstacle, she said, which she felt assured I had not properly considered. This was a delicate point – for a woman to urge, especially so; in mentioning it, she saw that she must make a sacrifice of her feelings; still, for *me*, every sacrifice should be made. She alluded to the topic of *age*. Was I aware – was I fully aware of the discrepancy between us? That the age of the husband should surpass by a few years – even by fifteen or twenty – the age of the wife, was regarded by the world as admissible, and, indeed, as even proper; but she had always entertained the belief that the years of the wife should *never* exceed in number those of the husband. A discrepancy of this unnatural kind gave rise, too frequently, alas! to a life of unhappiness. Now she was aware that my own age did not exceed two and twenty; and I on the contrary, perhaps, was *not* aware that the years of my Eugènie extended very considerably beyond that sum.

About all this there was a nobility of soul – a dignity of candour – which delighted – which enchanted me – which eternally riveted my chains. I could scarcely restrain the excessive transport which possessed me.

'My sweetest Eugènie,' I cried, 'what is all this about which you are discoursing? Your years surpass in some measure my own. But what then? The customs of the world are so many conventional follies. To those who love as ourselves, in what respect differs a year from an hour? I am twenty-two, you say – granted; indeed you may as well call me, at once, twenty-three. Now you yourself, my dearest Eugènie, can have numbered no more than – can have numbered no more than – no more than – than – than – than——'

Here I paused for an instant, in the expectation that Madame Lalande would interrupt me by supplying her true age. But a French woman is seldom direct, and has always, by way of answer to an embarrassing query, some little practical reply of her own. In the present instance, Eugènie, who for a few moments past, had seemed to be searching for something in her bosom, at length let fall upon the grass a miniature, which I immediately picked up and presented to her.

'Keep it!' she said, with one of her most ravishing smiles. 'Keep it for my sake – for the sake of her whom it too flatteringly represents. Besides, upon the back of the trinket, you may discover, perhaps, the very information you seem to desire. It is now, to be sure, growing rather dark – but you can examine it at your leisure in the morning. In the meantime, you shall be my escort home to-night. My friends are about holding a little musical *levée*. I can promise you, too, some good singing. We French are not nearly so punctilious as you Americans, and I shall have no difficulty in smuggling you in, in the character of an old acquaintance.'

With this, she took my arm, and I attended her home. The mansion was quite a fine one, and, I believe, furnished in good taste. Of this latter point, however, I am scarcely qualified to judge; for it was just dark as we arrived; and in American mansions of the better sort, lights seldom, during the heat of summer, make their appearance at this, the most pleasant period of the day. In about an hour after my arrival, to be sure, a single shaded solar lamp was lit in the principal drawing-room; and this apartment, I could thus see, was arranged with unusual good taste and even splendour; but two other rooms of the suite, and in which the company chiefly assembled, remained, during the whole evening, in a very agreeable shadow. This is a well-conceived custom, giving the party at least a choice of light or shade, and one which our friends over the water could not do better than immediately adopt.

The evening thus spent was unquestionably the most delicious of my life. Madame Lalande had not overrated the musical abilities of her friends; and the singing I here heard I had never heard excelled in any private circle out of Vienna. The instrumental performers were many and of superior talents. The vocalists were chiefly ladies, and no individual sang worse than well. At length, upon a peremptory call for 'Madame Lalande,' she arose at once, without affectation or demur, from the *chaise longue* upon which she had sat by my side, and, accompanied by one or two gentlemen and her female friend of the opera, repaired to the piano in the main drawing-room. I would have escorted her myself; but felt that, under the circumstances of my introduction to the house, I had better remain unobserved where I was. I was thus deprived of her pleasure of seeing, although not of hearing her sing.

The impression she produced upon the company seemed electrical – but the effect upon myself was something even more. I know not how adequately to describe it. It arose in part, no doubt, from the sentiment of love with which I was imbued; but chiefly from my conviction of the extreme sensibility of the singer. It is beyond the reach of art to endow either air or recitative with more impassioned *expression* than was hers. Her utterance of the romance in Otello – the tone with which she gave the words, '*Sul mio sasso,*' in the Capuletti is ringing in my memory yet. Her lower tones were absolutely miraculous. Her voice embraced three complete octaves, extending from the contralto D to the D upper soprano, and, though sufficiently powerful to have filled the San Carlos, executed, with the minutest precision, every difficulty of vocal composition – ascending and descending scales, cadences, or *fiorituri*. In the finale of the Sonnambula, she brought about a most remarkable effect at the words –

Ah! non giunge uman pensiero
Al contento ond' io son piena.

Here, in imitation of Malibran, she modified the original phrase of Bellini, so as to let her voice descend to the tenor G, when, by a rapid transition, she struck the G above the treble stave, springing over an interval of two octaves.

Upon rising from the piano after these miracles of vocal execution, she resumed her seat by my side; when I expressed to her, in terms of the deepest enthusiasm, my delight at her performance. Of my surprise I said nothing, and yet was I most unfeignedly surprised; for a certain feebleness, or rather a certain tremulous indecision of voice in ordinary conversation, had prepared me to anticipate that, in singing, she would not acquit herself with any remarkable ability.

Our conversation was now long, earnest, uninterrupted, and totally unreserved. She made me relate many of the earlier passages of my life, and listened with breathless attention to every word of the narrative. I concealed nothing – I felt that I had a right to conceal nothing from her confiding affection. Encouraged by her candour upon the delicate point of her age, I entered, with perfect frankness, not only into a detail of my many minor vices, but made full confession of those moral and even of those physical infirmities, the disclosure of which, in demanding so much higher a degree of courage, is so much surer an evidence of love. I touched upon my college indiscretions – upon my extravagances – upon my carousals – upon my debts – upon my flirtations. I even went so far as to speak of a slightly hectic cough with which, at one time, I had been troubled – of a chronic rheumatism – of a twinge of hereditary gout – and, in conclusion, of the disagreeable and inconvenient, but hitherto carefully concealed, weakness of my eyes.

'Upon this latter point,' said Madame Lalande, laughingly, 'you have been surely injudicious in coming to confession; for, without the confession, I take it for granted that no one would have accused you of the crime. By-the-by,' she continued, 'have you any recollection' – and here I fancied that a blush, even through the gloom of the apartment, became distinctly visible upon her cheek – 'have you any recollection, *mon cher ami*, of this little ocular assistant which now depends from my neck?'

As she spoke she twirled in her fingers the identical double eye-glass which had so overwhelmed me with confusion at the opera.

'Full well – alas! do I remember it,' I explained, pressing passionately the delicate hand which offered the glasses for my inspection. They formed a complex and magnificent toy, richly chased and filigreed, and gleaming with jewels, which, even in the deficient light, I could not help perceiving were of high value.

'*Eh bien! mon ami,*' she resumed with a certain *empressement* of manner that rather surprised me – '*Eh bien, mon ami,* you have earnestly besought of me a favour which you have been pleased to denominate priceless. You have demanded of me my hand upon the morrow. Should I yield to your entreaties – and, I may add, to the pleadings of my own bosom – would I not be entitled to demand of you a very – a very little boon in return?'

'Name it!' I exclaimed with an energy that had nearly drawn upon us the observation of the company, and restrained by their presence alone from throwing myself impetuously at her feet. 'Name it, my beloved, my Eugènie my own? – name it! – but alas, it is already yielded ere named.'

'You shall conquer then, *mon ami*,' said she, 'for the sake of the Eugènie whom you love, this little weakness which you have last confessed – this weakness more moral than physical – and which, let me assure you, is so unbecoming the nobility of your real nature – so inconsistent with the candour of your usual character – and which, if permitted farther control, will assuredly involve you, sooner or later, in some very disagreeable scrape. You shall conquer, for my sake, this affectation which leads you, as you yourself acknowledge, to the tacit or implied denial of your infirmity of vision. For this infirmity you virtually deny, in refusing to employ the customary means for its relief. You will understand me to say, then, that I wish you to wear spectacles:– ah, hush! – you have already consented to wear them *for my sake*. You shall accept the little toy which I now hold in my hand, and which, though admirable as an aid to vision, is really of no very immense value as a gem. You perceive that, by a trifling modification thus – or thus – it can be adapted to the eyes in the form of spectacles, or worn in the waistcoat pocket as an eye-glass. It is in the former mode, however, and habitually, that you have already consented to wear it *for my sake*.'

This request – must I confess it! – confused me in no little degree. But the condition with which it was coupled rendered hesitation, of course, a matter altogether out of the question.

'It is done!' I cried, with all the enthusiasm that I could muster at the moment. 'It is done – it is most cheerfully agreed. I sacrifice every feeling for your sake. To-night I wear this dear eye-glass, *as* an eye-glass, and upon my heart; but with the earliest dawn of that morning which gives me the pleasure of calling you wife, I will place it upon my – upon my nose – and there wear it ever afterwards, in the less romantic, and less fashionable, but certainly in the more serviceable form which you desire.'

Our conversation now turned upon the details of our arrangements for the morrow. Talbot, I learned from my betrothed, had just arrived in town. I was to see him at once, and procure a carriage. The *soirée* would scarcely break up before two; and by this hour the vehicle was to be at the door: when, in the confusion occasioned by the departure of the company, Madame L. could easily enter it unobserved. We were then to call at the house of a clergyman who would be in waiting; there be married, drop Talbot, and proceed on a short tour to the East; leaving the fashionable world at home to make whatever comments upon the matter it thought best.

Having planned all this, I immediately took leave, and went in search of Talbot, but, on the way, I could not refrain from stepping into a hotel, for the purpose of inspecting the miniature; and this I did by the powerful aid of the glasses. The countenance was a surpassingly beautiful one! Those large luminous eyes! – that proud Grecian nose! – those dark luxuriant curls! – 'Ah!' said I exultingly to myself, 'this is indeed the speaking image of my beloved!' I turned the reverse, and discovered the words – 'Eugènie Lalande – aged twenty-seven years and seven months.'

I found Talbot at home, and proceeded at once to acquaint him with my good fortune. He professed excessive astonishment, of course, but congratulated me most cordially, and proffered every assistance in his power. In a word, we carried out our arrangement to the letter; and, at two in the morning, just ten minutes after the ceremony, I found myself in a close carriage with Madame Lalande – with Mrs. Simpson, I should say – and driving at a great rate out of town, in a direction north-east by north, half-north.

It had been determined for us by Talbot, that, as we were to be up all night, we should make our first stop at C——, a village about twenty miles from the city, and there get an early breakfast and some repose, before proceeding upon our route. At four precisely, therefore, the carriage drew up at the door of the principal inn. I handed my adored wife out, and ordered breakfast forthwith. In the meantime we were shown into a small parlour, and sat down.

It was now nearly if not altogether daylight; and, as I gazed, enraptured, at the angel by my side, the singular idea came all at once into my head that this was really the very first moment, since my acquaintance with the celebrated loveliness of Madame Lalande, that I had enjoyed a near inspection of that loveliness by daylight at all.

'And now, *mon ami*,' said she, taking my hand, and so interrupting this train of reflection, 'and now, *mon cher ami*, since we are indissolubly one – since I have yielded to your passionate entreaties, and performed my portion of our agreement – I presume you have not forgotten that you also have a little favour to bestow – a little promise which it is your intention to keep. Ah! – let me see! Let me remember! Yes; full easily do I call to mind the precise words of the dear promise you made to Eugènie last night. Listen! You spoke thus: "It is done! – it is most cheerfully agreed! I sacrifice every feeling for your sake. To-night I wear this dear eyeglass *as* an eyeglass, and upon my heart; but with the earliest dawn of that morning which gives me the privilege of calling you wife, I will place it upon my – upon my nose – and there wear it ever afterwards, in the less romantic, and less fashionable, but certainly in the more serviceable form which you desire." These were the exact words, my beloved husband, were they not?'

'They were,' I said; 'you have an excellent memory; and assuredly, my beautiful Eugènie, there is no disposition on my part to evade the performance of the trivial promise they imply. See! Behold! They are becoming – rather – are they not?' And here, having arranged the glasses in the ordinary form of spectacles, I applied them gingerly in their proper position; while Madame Simpson, adjusting her cap, and folding her arms, sat bolt upright in her chair, in a somewhat stiff and prim, and indeed, in a somewhat undignified position.

'Goodness gracious me!' I exclaimed almost at the very instant that the rim of the spectacles had settled upon my nose – '*My!* goodness gracious me! – why what *can* be the matter with these glasses?' and taking them quickly off, I wiped them carefully with a silk handkerchief, and adjusted them again.

But if, in the first instance, there had occurred something which occasioned me surprise, in the second this surprise became elevated into astonishment; and this astonishment was profound – was extreme – indeed I may say it was horrific. What, in the name of everything hideous, did this mean? Could I believe my eyes? – *could* I? – that was the question. Was that – was that – was that *rouge?* And were those – and were those – were those *wrinkles*, upon the visage of Eugènie Lalande? And O Jupiter! and every one of the gods and goddesses, little and big! – what – what – what – *what* had become of her teeth? I dashed the spectacles violently to the ground, and, leaping to my feet, stood erect in the middle of the floor, confronting Mrs. Simpson, with my arms set akimbo, and grinning and foaming, but, at the same time utterly speechless and helpless with terror and with rage.

Now I have already said that Madame Eugènie Lalande – that is to say, Simpson – spoke the English language but very little better than she wrote it: and for this reason she very properly never attempted to speak it upon ordinary occasions. But rage will carry a lady to any extreme; and in the present case it carried Mrs. Simpson to the very extraordinary extreme of attempting to hold a conversation in a tongue that she did not altogether understand.

'Vell, Monsieur,' said she, after surveying me, in great apparent astonishment, for some moments – 'Vell, Monsieur! – and vat den? – vat de matter now? Is it de dance of de Saint Vitusse dat you ave? If not like me, vat for vy buy de pig in de poke?'

'You wretch!' said I catching my breath – 'you – you – you villainous old hag!'

'Ag? – ole? – me not so *ver* ole, after all! me not one single day more dan de eighty-doo.'

'Eighty-two!' I ejaculated, staggering to the wall – 'eighty-two hundred thousand baboons! The miniature said twenty-seven years and seven months!'

'To be sure! – dat is so! – ver true! but den de portraite has been take for dese fifty-five years. Ven I go marry my segonde usbande, Monsieur Lalande, at dat time I had de portraite take for my daughter by my first usbande, Monsieur Moissart!'

'Moissart!' said I.

'Yes, Moissart;' said she, mimicking my pronunciation, which, to speak the truth, was none of the best; 'and vat den? Vat *you* know bout de Moissart?'

'Nothing, you old fright! – I know nothing about him at all; only I had an ancestor of that name, once upon a time.'

'Dat name! and vat you ave for say to dat name? 'Tis ver *goot* name; and so is Voissart – *dat* is ver goot name too. My daughter, Mademoiselle Moissart, she marry von Monsieur Voissart; and de name is bote *ver* respectaable name.'

'Moissart!' I exclaimed, 'and Voissart! why what is it you mean?'

'Vat I mean? – I mean Moissart and Voissart; and for de matter of dat, I mean Croissart and Froissart, too, if I only tink proper to mean it. My daughter's daughter Mademoiselle Voissart, she marry von Monsieur Croissart, and den agin, my daughter's grande-daughter, Mademoiselle Croissart, she marry von Monsieur Froissart; and I suppose you say dat *dat* is not *ver* respectaable name.'

'Froissart!' said I, beginning to faint, 'why surely you don't say Moissart, and Voissart, and Croissart, and Froissart?'

'Yes,' she replied, leaning fully back in her chair, and stretching out her lower limbs at great length; 'yes, Moissart, and Voissart, and Croissart, and Froissart. But Monsieur Froissart, he was von *ver* big vat you call fool – he vas von ver great big donce like yourself – for he lef *la belle France* for come to dis stupide Amérique – and ven he get here he vent and ave von *ver* stupide von *ver*, *ver* stupide sonn, so I hear, dough I not yet av ad de plaisir to meet vid him – neither me nor my companion, de Madame Stephanie Lalande. He is name de Napoleon Bonaparte Froissart, and I suppose you say dat *dat*, too, is not von *ver* respectaable name.'

Either the length or the nature of this speech had the effect of working up Mrs. Simpson into a very extraordinary passion indeed: and as she made an end of it, with great labour, she jumped up from her chair like somebody bewitched, dropping upon the floor an entire universe of bustle as she jumped. Once upon her feet, she gnashed her gums, brandished her arms, rolled up her sleeves, shook her fist in my face, and concluded the performance by tearing the cap from her head, and with it an immense wig of the most valuable and beautiful black hair, the whole of which she dashed upon the ground with a yell, and there trampled and danced a fandango upon it, in an absolute ecstasy and agony of rage.

Meantime I sank aghast into the chair which she had vacated. 'Moissart and Voissart!' I repeated thoughtfully, as she cut one of her pigeon-wings, and Croissart and Froissart!' as she completed another – 'Moissart and Voissart and Croissart and Napoleon Bonaparte Froissart! – why, you ineffable old serpent, that's *me* – that's *me* – d'ye hear? – that's *me*' – here I screamed at the top of my voice – 'that's *me-e-e*! *I* am Napoleon Bonaparte Froissart! and if I haven't married my great-great-grandmother, I wish I may be everlastingly confounded!'

Madame Eugènie Lalande, *quasi* Simpson – formerly Moissart – was, in sober fact, my great-great-grandmother. In her youth she had been beautiful, and even at eighty-two retained the majestic height, the sculptural contour of head, the fine eyes and the Grecian nose of her girlhood. By the aid of these, of pearl-powder, of rouge, of false hair, false teeth, and false *tournure*, as well as of the most skilful *modistes* of Paris, she contrived to hold a respectable footing among the beauties *un peu pasées* of the French metropolis. In this respect, indeed, she might have been regarded as little less than the equal of the celebrated Ninon de l'Enclos.

She was immensely wealthy, and being left, for the second time, a widow without children,˙ she bethought herself of my existence in America, and, for the purpose of making me her heir, paid a visit to the United States, in company with a distant and exceedingly lovely relative of her second husband's – a Madame Stephanie Lalande.

At the opera, my great-great-grandmother's attention was arrested by my notice; and, upon surveying me through her eye-glass, she was struck with a certain family resemblance to herself. Thus interested, and knowing that the heir she sought was actually in the city, she made inquiries of her party respecting me. The gentleman who attended her knew my person, and told her who I was. The information thus obtained induced her to renew her scrutiny; and this scrutiny it was which so emboldened me that I behaved in the absurd manner already detailed. She returned my bow, however, under the impression that, by some odd accident, I had discovered her identity. When, deceived by my weakness of vision, and the arts of the toilet, in respect to the age and charms of the strange lady, I demanded so enthusiastically of Talbot who she was, he concluded that I meant the younger beauty, as a matter of course, and so informed me, with perfect truth, that she was 'the celebrated widow, Madame Lalande.'

In the street, next morning, my great-great-grandmother encountered Talbot, an old Parisian acquaintance; and the conversation, very naturally, turned upon myself. My deficiencies of vision were then explained; for these were notorious, although I was entirely ignorant of their notoriety; and my good old relative discovered, much to her chagrin, that she had been deceived in supposing me aware of her identity, and that I had been merely making a fool of myself, in making open love in a theatre, to an old woman unknown. By way of punishing me for this imprudence, she concocted with Talbot a plot. He purposely kept out of my way, to avoid giving me the introduction. My street inquiries about 'the lovely widow, Madame Lalande,' were supposed to refer to the younger lady, of course; and thus the conversation with the three gentlemen whom I encountered shortly after leaving Talbot's hotel, will be easily explained, as also their allusion to Ninon de l'Enclos. I had no opportunity of seeing Madame Lalande closely during daylight, and, at her musical *soirée*, my silly weakness in refusing the aid of glasses, effectually prevented me from making a discovery of her age. When 'Madame Lalande' was called upon to sing, the younger lady was intended; and it was she who arose to obey the call; my great-great-grandmother, to further the deception, arising at the same moment, and accompanying her to the piano in the main drawing-room. Had I decided upon escorting her thither, it had been her design to suggest the propriety of my remaining where I was; but my own prudential views rendered this unnecessary. The songs which I so much admired, and which so confirmed my impression of the youth of my mistress, were executed by Madame Stephanie Lalande. The eye-glass was presented by way of adding a reproof to the hoax − a sting to the epigram of the deception. Its presentation afforded an opportunity for the lecture upon affectation with which I was so especially edified. It is almost superfluous to add that the glasses of the instrument, as worn by the old lady, had been exchanged by her for a pair better adapted to my years. They suited me, in fact, to a T.

The clergyman who merely pretended to tie the fatal knot, was a boon companion of Talbot's, and no priest. He was an excellent 'whip,' however; and having doffed his cassock to put on a great coat, he drove the hack which conveyed the 'happy couple' out of town. Talbot took a seat at his side. The two scoundrels were thus 'in at the death,' and through a half-open window of the back parlour of the inn, amused themselves in grinning at the *dénouement* of the drama. I believe I shall be forced to call them both out.

Nevertheless I am *not* the husband of my great-great-grandmother; and this is a reflection which affords me infinite relief; − but I *am* the husband of Madame Lalande − of Madame Stephanie Lalande − with whom my good old relative, besides making me her sole heir when she dies − if she ever does − has been at the trouble of concocting me a match. In conclusion: I am done for ever with *billets doux*, and am never to be met without SPECTACLES.

The Cask of Amontillado

The thousand injuries of Fortunato I had borne as I best could, but when he ventured upon insult, I vowed revenge. You, who so well know the nature of my soul, will not suppose, however, that I gave utterance to a threat. *At length* I would be avenged; this was a point definitively settled – but the very definitiveness with which it was resolved, precluded the idea of risk. I must not only punish, but punish with impunity. A wrong is unredressed when retribution overtakes its redresser. It is equally unredressed when the avenger fails to make himself felt as such to him who has done the wrong.

It must be understood that neither by word nor deed had I given Fortunato cause to doubt my good will. I continued as was my wont, to smile in his face, and he did not perceive that my smile *now* was at the thought of his immolation.

He had a weak point – this Fortunato – although in other regards he was a man to be respected and even feared. He prided himself on his connoisseurship in wine. Few Italians have the true virtuoso spirit. For the most part their enthusiasm is adopted to suit the time and opportunity to practise imposture upon the British and Austrian *millionaires*. In painting and gemmary, Fortunato, like his countrymen, was a quack, but in the matter of old wines he was sincere. In this respect I did not differ from him materially; I was skilful in the Italian vintages myself, and bought largely whenever I could.

It was about dusk, one evening during the supreme madness of the carnival season, that I encountered my friend. He accosted me with excessive warmth, for he had been drinking much. The man wore motley. He had on a tight-fitting parti-striped dress, and his head was surmounted by the conical cap and bells. I was so pleased to see him, that I thought I should never have done wringing his hand.

I said to him – 'My dear Fortunato, you are luckily met. How remarkably well you are looking to-day! But I have received a pipe of what passes for Amontillado, and I have my doubts.'

'How?' said he, 'Amontillado? A pipe? Impossible? And in the middle of the carnival?'

'I have my doubts,' I replied; 'and I was silly enough to pay the full Amontillado price without consulting you in the matter. You were not to be found, and I was fearful of losing a bargain.'

'Amontillado!'

'I have my doubts.'

'Amontillado!'

'And I must satisfy them.'

'Amontillado!'

'As you are engaged, I am on my way to Luchesi. If any one has a critical turn, it is he. He will tell me'——

'Luchesi cannot tell Amontillado from Sherry.'

'And yet some fools will have it that his taste is a match for your own.'

'Come let us go.'

'Whither?'

'To your vaults.'

'My friend, no; I will not impose upon your good nature. I perceive you have an engagement. Luchesi'——

'I have no engagement; come.'

'My friend, no. It is not the engagement, but the severe cold with which I perceive you are afflicted. The vaults are insufferably damp. They are encrusted with nitre.'

'Let us go, nevertheless. The cold is merely nothing. Amontillado! You have been imposed upon; and as for Luchesi, he cannot distinguish Sherry from Amontillado.'

Thus speaking, Fortunato possessed himself of my arm. Putting on a mask of black silk, and drawing a *roquelaire* closely about my person, I suffered him to hurry me to my palazzo.

There were no attendants at home; they had absconded to make merry in honour of the time. I had told them that I should not return until the morning, and had given them explicit orders not to stir from the house. These orders were sufficient, I well knew, to insure their immediate disappearance, one and all, as soon as my back was turned.

I took from their sconces two flambeaux, and giving one to Fortunato, bowed him through several suites of rooms to the archway that led into the vaults. I passed down a long and winding staircase, requesting him to be cautious as he followed. We came at length to the foot of the descent, and stood together on the damp ground of the catacombs of the Montresors.

The gait of my friend was unsteady, and the bells upon his cap jingled as he strode.

'The pipe,' said he.

'It is farther on,' said I; 'but observe the white webwork which gleams from these cavern walls.'

He turned towards me, and looked into my eyes with two filmy orbs that distilled the rheum of intoxication.

'Nitre?' he asked, at length.

'Nitre,' I replied. 'How long have you had that cough!'

'Ugh! ugh! ugh! – ugh! ugh! ugh! – ugh! ugh! ugh! – ugh! ugh! ugh! – ugh! ugh! ugh!'

My poor friend found it impossible to reply for many minutes.

'It is nothing,' he said, at last.

'Come,' I said, with decision, 'we will go back; your health is precious. You are rich, respected, admired, beloved; you are happy, as once I was. You are a man to be missed. For me it is no matter. We will go back; you will be ill, and I cannot be responsible. Besides, there is Luchesi'——

'Enough,' he said, 'the cough is a mere nothing; it will not kill me. I shall not die of a cough.'

'True – true,' I replied; 'and, indeed, I had no intention of alarming you unnecessarily – but you should use all proper caution. A draught of this Medoc will defend us from the damps.'

Here I knocked off the neck of a bottle which I drew from a long row of its fellows that lay upon the mould.

'Drink,' I said, presenting him the wine.

He raised it to his lips with a leer. He paused and nodded to me familiarly, while his bells jingled.

'I drink,' he said, 'to the buried that repose around us.'

'And I to your long life.'

He again took my arm, and we proceeded.

'These vaults,' he said, 'are extensive.'

'The Montresors,' I replied, 'were a great and numerous family.'

'I forget your arms.'

'A huge human foot d'or, in a field azure; the foot crushes a serpent rampant whose fangs are imbedded in the heel.'

'And the motto?'

'Nemo me impune lacessit.'

'Good!' he said.

The wine sparkled in his eyes and the bells jingled. My own fancy grew warm with the Medoc. We had passed through walls of piled bones, with casks and puncheons intermingling, into the inmost recesses of the catacombs. I paused again, and this time I made bold to seize Fortunato by an arm above the elbow.

'The nitre!' I said: 'see, it increases. It hangs like moss upon the vaults. We are below the river's bed. The drops of moisture trickle among the bones. Come, we will go back ere it is too late. Your cough'——

'It is nothing,' he said; 'let us go on. But first, another draught of the Medoc.'

I broke and reached him a flagon of De Grave. He emptied it at a breath. His eyes flashed with a fierce light. He laughed and threw the bottle upwards with a gesticulation I did not understand.

I looked at him in surprise. He repeated the movement – a grotesque one.

'You do not comprehend?' he said.

'Not I,' I replied.

'Then you are not of the brotherhood.'

'How?'

'You are not of the masons.'

'Yes, yes,' I said, 'yes, yes.'

'You? Impossible! A mason?'

'A mason,' I replied.

'A sign,' he said.

'It is this,' I answered, producing a trowel from beneath the folds of my *roquelaire*.

'You jest,' he exclaimed, recoiling a few paces. 'But let us proceed to the Amontillado.'

'Be it so,' I said, replacing the tool beneath the cloak, and again offering him my arm. He leaned upon it heavily. We continued our route in search of the Amontillado. We passed through a range of low arches, descended, passed on, and descending again, arrived at a deep crypt, in which the foulness of the air caused our flambeaux rather to glow than flame.

At the most remote end of the crypt there appeared another less spacious. Its walls had been lined with human remains piled to the vault overhead, in the fashion of the great catacombs of Paris. Three sides of this interior crypt were still ornamented in this manner. From the fourth the bones had been thrown down, and lay promiscuously upon the earth, forming at one point a mound of some size. Within the wall thus exposed by the displacing of the bones, we perceived a still interior recess, in depth about four feet, in width three, in height six or seven. It seemed to have been constructed for no especial use in itself, but formed merely the interval between two of the colossal supports of the roof of the catacombs, and was backed by one of their circumscribing walls of solid granite.

It was in vain that Fortunato, uplifting his dull torch, endeavoured to pry into the depths of the recess. Its termination the feeble light did not enable us to see.

'Proceed,' I said; 'herein is the Amontillado. As for Luchesi'——

'He is an ignoramus,' interrupted my friend, as he stepped unsteadily forward, while I followed immediately at his heels. In an instant he had reached the extremity of the niche, and finding his progress arrested by the rock, stood stupidly bewildered. A moment more and I had fettered him to the granite. In its surface were two iron staples, distant from each other about two feet, horizontally. From one of these depended a short chain, from the other a padlock. Throwing the links about his waist, it was but the work of a few seconds to secure it. He was too much astounded to resist. Withdrawing the key I stepped back from the recess.

'Pass your hand,' I said, 'over the wall; you cannot help feeling the nitre. Indeed it is *very* damp. Once more let me *implore* you to return. No? Then I must positively leave you. But I must first render you all the little attentions in my power.'

'The Amontillado!' ejaculated my friend, not yet recovered from his astonishment.

'True,' I replied; 'the Amontillado.'

As I said these words I busied myself among the pile of bones of which I have before spoken. Throwing them aside, I soon uncovered a quantity of building stone and mortar. With these materials and with the aid of my trowel, I began vigorously to wall up the entrance of the niche.

I had scarcely laid the first tier of my masonry when I discovered that the intoxication of Fortunato had in a great measure worn off. The earliest indication I had of this was a low moaning cry from the depth of the recess. It was *not* the cry of a drunken man. There was then a long and obstinate silence. I laid the second tier, and the third, and the fourth; and then I heard the furious vibrations of the chain. The noise lasted for several minutes, during which, that I might hearken to it with the more satisfaction, I ceased my labours and sat down upon the bones. When at last the clanking subsided, I resumed the trowel, and finished without interruption the fifth, the sixth, and the seventh tier. The wall was now nearly upon a level with my breast. I again paused, and holding the flambeaux over the mason-work, threw a few feeble rays upon the figure within.

A succession of loud and shrill screams, bursting suddenly from the throat of the chained form, seemed to thrust me violently back. For a brief moment I hesitated – I trembled. Unsheathing my rapier, I began to grope with it about the recess; but the thought of an instant reassured me. I placed my hand upon the solid fabric of the catacombs, and felt satisfied. I reapproached the wall. I replied to the yells of him who clamoured. I re-echoed – I aided – I surpassed them in volume and in strength. I did this, and the clamourer grew still.

It was now midnight, and my task was drawing to a close. I had completed the eighth, the ninth, and the tenth tier. I had finished a portion of the last and the eleventh; there remained but a single stone to be fitted and plastered in. I struggled with its weight; I placed it partially in its destined position. But now there came from out the niche a low laugh that erected the hairs upon my head. It was succeeded by a sad voice, which I had difficulty in recognising as that of the noble Fortunato. The voice said –

'Ha! ha! ha! – he! he! – a very good joke indeed – an excellent jest. We will have many a rich laugh about it at the palazzo – he! he! he! – over our wine – he! he! he!'

'The Amontillado!' I said.

'He! he! he! – he! he! he! – yes, the Amontillado. But is it not getting late? Will not they be awaiting us at the palazzo, the Lady Fortunato and the rest? Let us be gone.'

'Yes,' I said, 'let us be gone.'

'*For the love of God, Montresor!*'

'Yes,' I said, 'for the love of God!'

But to these words I hearkened in vain for a reply. I grew impatient. I called aloud –

'Fortunato!'

No answer. I called again –

'Fortunato!'

No answer still. I thrust a torch through the remaining aperture and let it fall within. There came forth in return only a jingling of the

'For the love of God! Montresor!' '*Yes*,' *I said, 'for the love of God!*'

bells. My heart grew sick – on account of the dampness of the catacombs. I hastened to make an end of my labour. I forced the last stone into its position; I plastered it up. Against the new masonry I re-erected the old rampart of bones. For the half of a century no mortal has disturbed them.

In pace
requiescat!

Metzengerstein

Pestis eram vivus – moriens tua mors ero. – *Martin Luther*

Horror and fatality have been stalking abroad in all ages. Why then give a date to the story I have to tell? Let it suffice to say, that at the period of which I speak, there existed in the interior of Hungary, a settled although hidden belief in the doctrines of the Metempsychosis. Of the doctrines themselves – that is, of their falsity or of their probability – I say nothing. I assert, however, that much of our incredulity (as La Bruyère says of all our unhappiness) '*vient de ne pouvoir être seuls.*'*

But there were some points in the Hungarian superstition which were fast verging to absurdity. They, the Hungarians, differed very essentially from their Eastern authorities. For example – '*The soul,*' said the former – I give the words of an acute and intelligent Parisian – '*ne demeure qu'un seul fois dans un corps sensible: au reste – un cheval, un chien, un homme même, n'est que la ressemblance peu tangible de ces animaux.*'

* Mercier, in '*L'an deux mille quatre cents quarante,*' seriously maintains the doctrines of the Metempsychosis, and I. D'Israeli says that 'no system is so simple and so little repugnant to the understanding.' Colonel Ethan Allen, the 'Green Mountain Boy,' is also said to have been a serious metempsychosist.

The families of Berlifitzing and Metzengerstein had been at variance for centuries. Never before were two houses so illustrious, mutually embittered by hostility so deadly. The origin of this enmity seems to be found in the words of an ancient prophecy – 'A lofty name shall have a fearful fall when, as the rider over his horse, the mortality of Metzengerstein shall triumph over the immortality of Berlifitzing.

To be sure the words themselves had little or no meaning. But more trivial causes have given rise – and that no long while ago – to consequences equally eventful. Besides, the estates, which were contiguous, had long exercised a rival influence in the affairs of a busy government. Moreover, near neighbours are seldom friends; and the inhabitants of the Castle Berlifitzing might look from their lofty buttresses, into the very windows of the Palace Metzengerstein. Least of all had the more than feudal magnificence discovered a tendency to allay the irritable feelings of the less ancient and less wealthy Berlifitzings. What wonder then, that the words, however silly, of that prediction, should have succeeded in setting and keeping at variance two families already predisposed to quarrel by every instigation of hereditary jealousy? The prophecy seemed to imply, if it implied anything, a final triumph on the part of the already more powerful house; and was of course remembered with the more bitter animosity by the weaker and less influential.

Wilhelm, Count Berlifitzing, although loftily descended, was, at the epoch of this narrative, an infirm and doting old man, remarkable for nothing but an inordinate and inveterate personal antipathy to the family of his rival, and so passionate a love of horses, and of hunting, that neither bodily infirmity, great age, nor mental incapacity, prevented his daily participation in the dangers of the chase.

Frederick, Baron Metzengerstein, was, on the other hand, not yet of age. His father, the Minister G——, died young. His mother the Lady Mary, followed him quickly. Frederick was at that time in his eighteenth year. In a city eighteen years are no long period: but in a wilderness – in so magnificent a wilderness as that old principality, the pendulum vibrates with a deeper meaning.

From some peculiar circumstances attending the administration of his father, the young Baron at the decease of the former, entered immediately upon his vast possessions. Such estates were seldom held before by a nobleman of Hungary. His castles were without number. The chief in point of splendour and extent was the 'Palace Metzengerstein.' The boundary line of his dominions were never clearly defined, but his principal park embraced a circuit of fifty miles.

Upon the succession of a proprietor so young, with a character so well known, to a fortune so unparalleled, little speculation was afloat in regard to his probable course of conduct. And indeed for the space of three days, the behaviour of the heir out-Heroded Herod, and fairly surpassed the expectations of his most enthusiastic admirers. Shameful debaucheries – flagrant treacheries – unheard-of atrocities – gave his trembling vassals quickly to understand that no servile submission on their part – no punctilios of conscience on his own – were thenceforward to prove any security against the remorseless fangs of a petty Caligula. On the night of the fourth day, the stables of the Castle Berlifitzing were discovered to be on fire; and the unanimous opinion of the neighbourhood added the crime of the incendiary to the already hideous list of the Baron's misdemeanours and atrocities.

But during the tumult occasioned by this occurrence, the young nobleman himself sat, apparently buried in meditation, in a vast and desolate upper apartment of the family palace of Metzengerstein. The rich although faded tapestry hangings which swung gloomily upon the walls, represented the shadowy and majestic forms of a thousand illustrious ancestors. *Here*, rich ermined priests and pontifical dignitaries, familiarly seated with the autocrat and the sovereign, put a veto on the wishes of a temporal king, or restrained with the fiat of papal supremacy the rebellious sceptre of the Arch-enemy. *There*, the dark tall statures of the Princes Metzengerstein – their muscular war-coursers plunging over the carcases of fallen foes – startled the steadiest nerves with their vigorous expression; and *here* again, the voluptuous and swan-like figures of the dames of days gone by, floated away in the mazes of an unreal dance to the strains of imaginary melody.

But as the Baron listened or affected to listen to the gradually increasing uproar in the stables of Berlifitzing – or perhaps pondered upon some more novel, some more decided act of audacity – his eyes were turned unwittingly to the figure of an enormous and unnaturally coloured horse, represented in the tapestry as belonging to a Saracen ancestor of the family of his rival. The horse itself, in the foreground of the design, stood motionless and statue-like – while further back, its discomfited rider perished by the dagger of a Metzengerstein.

On Frederick's lip arose a fiendish expression as he became aware of the direction which his glance had, without his consciousness, assumed. Yet he did not remove it. On the contrary, he could by no means account for the overwhelming anxiety which appeared falling like a pall upon his senses. It was with difficulty that he reconciled his dreamy and incoherent feelings with the certainty of being awake. The longer he gazed the more absorbing became the spell – the more impossible did it appear that he could ever withdraw his glance from the fascination of that tapestry. But the tumult without becoming suddenly more violent, with a compulsory exertion he diverted his attention to the glare of ruddy light thrown full by the flaming stables upon the windows of the apartment.

The action, however, was but momentary; his gaze returned mechanically to the wall. To his extreme horror and astonishment the head of the gigantic steed had in the meantime altered its position. The neck of the animal, before arched, as if in compassion, over the prostrate body of its lord, was now extended at full length in the direction of the Baron. The eyes, before invisible, now wore an energetic and human expression, while they gleamed with a fiery and unusual red; and the distended lips of the apparently enraged horse left in full view his sepulchral and disgusting teeth.

Stupefied with terror the young nobleman tottered to the door. As he threw it open a flash of red light, streaming far into the chamber, flung his shadow with a clear outline against the quivering tapestry; and he shuddered to perceive that shadow – as he staggered awhile upon the threshold – assuming the exact position, and precisely filling up the contour of the relentless and triumphant murderer of the

Saracen Berlifitzing.

To lighten the depression of his spirits the Baron hurried into the open air. At the principal gate of the palace he encountered three equerries. With much difficulty, and at the imminent peril of their lives, they were restraining the convulsive plunges of a gigantic and fiery-coloured horse.

'Whose horse? Where did you get him?' demanded the youth in a querulous and husky tone, as he became instantly aware that the mysterious steed in the tapestried chamber was the very counterpart of the furious animal before his eyes.

'He is your own property, sire,' replied one of the equerries, 'at least he is claimed by no other owner. We caught him flying, all smoking and foaming with rage, from the burning stables of the Castle Berlifitzing. Supposing him to have belonged to the old Count's stud of foreign horses we led him back as an estray. But the grooms there disclaim any title to the creature, which is strange, since he bears evident marks of having made a narrow escape from the flames.'

'The letters W. V. B. are also branded very distinctly on his forehead,' interrupted a second equerry; 'I supposed them of course to be the initials of Wilhelm Von Berlifitzing – but all at the castle are positive in denying any knowledge of the horse.'

'Extremely singular!' said the young Baron with a musing air, and apparently unconscious of the meaning of his words. 'He is as you say a remarkable horse – a prodigious horse! although, as you very justly observe, of a suspicious and untractable character; let him be mine, however,' he added, after a pause, 'perhaps a rider like Frederick of Metzengerstein may tame even the devil from the stables of Berlifitzing.'

'You are mistaken, my lord; the horse, as I think we mentioned, is *not* from the stables of the Count. If such had been the case, we know our duty better than to bring him into the presence of a noble of your family.'

'True!' observed the Baron, drily: and at that instant a page of the bed-chamber came from the palace with a heightened colour and a precipitate step. He whispered into his master's ear an account of the sudden disappearance of a small portion of the tapestry in an apartment which he designated, entering at the same time into particulars of a minute and circumstantial character; but from the low tone of voice in which these latter were communicated, nothing escaped to gratify the excited curiosity of the equerries.

The young Frederick during the conference seemed agitated by a variety of emotions. He soon, however, recovered his composure, and an expression of determined malignancy settled upon his countenance as he gave peremptory orders that the apartment in question should be immediately locked up, and the key placed in his own possession.

'Have you heard of the unhappy death of the old hunter Berlifitzing?' said one of his vassals to the Baron, as, after the departure of the page, the huge steed which that nobleman had adopted as his own plunged and curvetted with redoubled fury down the long avenue which extended from the palace to the stables of Metzengerstein.

'No!' said the Baron turning abruptly towards the speaker; 'dead! say you?'

'It is indeed true, my lord; and, to the noble of your name, will be, I imagine, no unwelcome intelligence.'

A rapid smile shot over the countenance of the listener. 'How died he?'

'In his rash exertions to rescue a favourite portion of his hunting stud, he has himself perished miserably in the flames.'

'I – n – d – e – e – d – !' ejaculated the Baron, as if slowly and deliberately impressed with the truth of some exciting idea.

'Indeed,' repeated the vassal.

'Shocking!' said the youth calmly, and turned quietly into the palace.

From this date a marked alteration took place in the outward demeanour of the dissolute young Baron Frederick Von Metzengerstein. Indeed, his behaviour disappointed every expectation, and proved little in accordance with the views of many a manœuvring mamma; while his habits and manners, still less than formerly, offered anything congenial with those of the neighbouring aristocracy. He was never to be seen beyond the limits of his own domain, and in this wide and social world was utterly companionless – unless indeed that unnatural, impetuous, and fiery-coloured horse, which he henceforward continually bestrode, had any mysterious right to the title of his friend.

Numerous invitations on the part of the neighbourhood for a long time, however, periodically came in. 'Will the Baron honour our festivals with his presence?' 'Will the Baron join us in a hunting of the boar?' – 'Metzengerstein does not hunt;' 'Metzengerstein will not attend,' were the haughty and laconic answers.

These repeated insults were not to be endured by an imperious nobility. Such invitations became less cordial, less frequent; in time they ceased altogether. The widow of the unfortunate Count Berlifitzing was even heard to express a hope 'that the Baron might be at home when he did not wish to be at home, since he disdained the company of his equals; and ride when he did not wish to ride, since he preferred the society of a horse.' This to be sure was a very silly explosion of hereditary pique, and merely proved how singularly unmeaning our sayings are apt to become when we desire to be unusually energetic.

The charitable, nevertheless, attributed the alteration in the conduct of the young nobleman to the natural sorrow of a son for the untimely loss of his parents; forgetting, however, his atrocious and reckless behaviour during the short period immediately succeeding that bereavement. Some there were, indeed, who suggested a too haughty idea of self-consequence and dignity. Others again (among whom may be mentioned the family physician) did not hesitate in speaking of morbid melancholy and hereditary ill-health, while dark hints of a more equivocal nature were current among the multitude.

Indeed, the Baron's perverse attachment to his lately-acquired charger – an attachment which seemed to attain new strength from every fresh example of the animal's ferocious and demon-like propensities – at length became, in the eyes of all reasonable men, a hideous and unnatural fervour. In the glare of noon – at the dead hour of night – in sickness or in health – in calm or in tempest – the young Metzengerstein seemed riveted to the saddle of that colossal horse, whose intractable audacities so well accorded with his own spirit.

There were circumstances, moreover, which, coupled with late events, gave an unearthly and portentous character to the mania of the rider, and to the capabilities of the steed. The space passed over in a single leap had been accurately measured, and was found to exceed, by an astounding difference, the wildest expectations of the most imaginative. The Baron, besides, had no particular *name* for the animal, although all the rest in his collection were distinguished by characteristic appellations. His stable, too, was appointed at a distance from the rest; and with regard to grooming and other necessary offices, none but the owner in person had ventured to officiate, or even to enter the enclosure of that horse's particular stall. It was also to be observed, that although the three grooms, who had caught the steed as he fled from the conflagration at Berlifitzing, had succeeded in arresting his course by means of a chain-bridle and noose – yet no one of the three could with any certainty affirm that he had, during that dangerous struggle, or at any period thereafter, actually placed his hand upon the body of the beast. Instances of peculiar intelligence in the demeanour of a noble and high-spirited horse are not to be supposed capable of exciting unreasonable attention, but there were certain circumstances which intruded themselves per force upon the most sceptical and phlegmatic; and it is said there were times when the animal caused the gaping crowd who stood around to recoil in horror from the deep and impressive meaning of his terrible stamp – times when the young Metzengerstein turned pale and shrunk away from the rapid and searching expression of his earnest and human-looking eye.

Among all the retinue of the Baron, however, none were found to doubt the ardour of that extraordinary affection which existed on the part of the young nobleman for the fiery qualities of his horse; at least none but an insignificant and misshapen little page, whose deformities were in everybody's way, and whose opinions were of the least possible importance. He (if his ideas are worth mentioning at all) had the effrontery to assert that his master never vaulted into the saddle without an unaccountable and almost imperceptible shudder; and that, upon his return from every long continued and habitual ride, an expression of triumphant malignity distorted every muscle in his countenance.

One tempestuous night Metzengerstein, awaking from heavy slumber, descended like a maniac from his chamber, and mounting in hot haste, bounded away into the mazes of the forest. An occurrence so common attracted no particular attention, but his return was looked for with intense anxiety on the part of his domestics, when, after some hours' absence, the stupendous and magnificent battlements of the Palace Metzengerstein were discovered crackling and rocking to their very foundation under the influence of a dense and livid mass of ungovernable fire.

As the flames, when first seen, had already made so terrible a progress that all efforts to save any portion of the building were evidently futile, the astonished neighbourhood stood idly round in silent, if not apathetic wonder. But a new and fearful object soon riveted the attention of the multitude, and proved how much more intense is the excitement wrought in the feelings of a crowd by the contemplation of human agony than that brought about by the most appalling spectacles of inanimate matter.

Up the long avenue of aged oaks which led from the forest to the main entrance of the Palace Metzengerstein, a steed, bearing an unbonneted and disordered rider, was seen leaping with an impetuosity which outstripped the very Demon of the Tempest.

The career of the horseman was indisputably, on his own part, uncontrollable. The agony of his countenance, the convulsive struggle of his frame, gave evidence of superhuman exertion; but no sound, save a solitary shriek, escaped from his lacerated lips, which were bitten through and through in the intensity of terror. One instant, and the clattering of hoofs resounded sharply and shrilly above the roaring of the flames and the shrieking of the winds – another, and, clearing at a single plunge the gateway and the moat, the steed bounded far up the tottering staircase of the palace, and, with its rider, disappeared amid the whirlwind of chaotic fire.

The fury of the tempest immediately died away, and a dead calm suddenly succeeded. A white flame still enveloped the building like a shroud, and, streaming far away into the quiet atmosphere, shot forth a glare of preternatural light; while a cloud of smoke settled heavily over the battlements in the distinct colossal figure of – *a horse*.

Landor's Cottage

A Pendent to 'the Domain of Arnheim.'

During a pedestrian tour last summer through one or two of the river counties of New York, I found myself as the day declined somewhat embarrassed about the road I was pursuing. The land undulated very remarkably; and my path for the last hour had wound about and about so confusedly in its effort to keep in the valleys, that I no longer knew in what direction lay the sweet village of B——, where I had determined to stop for the night. The sun had scarcely *shone*, strictly speaking, during the day, which nevertheless had been unpleasantly warm. A smoky mist, resembling that of the Indian summer, enveloped all things, and of course added to my uncertainty. Not that I cared much about the matter. If I did not hit upon the village before sunset, or even before dark, it was more than possible that a little Dutch farm-house, or something of that kind, would soon make its appearance, although, in fact, the neighbourhood (perhaps on account of being more picturesque than fertile) was very sparsely inhabited. At all events, with my knapsack for a pillow, and my hound as a sentry, a bivouac in the open air was just the thing which would have amused me. I sauntered on, therefore, quite at ease, Ponto taking charge of my gun, until at length, just as I had begun to consider whether the numerous little glades that led hither and thither were intended to be paths at all, I was conducted by one of the most promising of them into an unquestionable carriage track. There could be no mistaking it. The traces of light wheels were evident; and although the tall shrubberies and overgrown undergrowth met overhead, there was no obstruction whatever below, even to the passage of a Virginian mountain waggon, the most aspiring vehicle, I take it, of its kind. The road, however, except in being open through the wood, if wood be not too weighty a name for such an assemblage of light trees; and except in the particulars of evident wheel-tracks, bore no resemblance to any road I had before seen. The tracks of which I speak were but faintly perceptible, having been impressed upon the firm, yet pleasantly moist surface of what looked more like green Genoese velvet than anything else. It was grass, clearly, but grass such as we seldom see out of England, so short, so thick, so even, and so vivid in colour. Not a single impediment lay in the wheel-rut, not even a chip or a dead twig. The stones that once obstructed the way had been carefully *placed*, not thrown, along the sides of the lane, so as to define its boundaries at bottom with a kind of half-precise, half-negligent, and wholly picturesque definition. Clumps of wild flowers grew everywhere luxuriantly in the interspaces.

What to make of all this, of course I knew not. Here was *art* undoubtedly, *that* did not surprise me, all roads, in the ordinary sense, are works of art; nor can I say there was much to wonder at in the mere *excess* of art manifested; all that seemed to have been done, might have been done *here*, with such natural 'capabilities' (as they have it in the books on Landscape Gardening), with very little labour and expense. No, it was not the amount but the *character* of the art which caused me to take a seat on one of the blossomy stones and gaze up and down this fairylike avenue for half-an-hour or more in bewildered admiration. One thing became more and more evident the longer I gazed: an artist, and one with a most scrupulous eye for form, had superintended all these arrangements. The greatest care had been taken to preserve a due medium between the neat and graceful on the one hand, and the *pittoresque*, in the true sense of the Italian term, on the other. There were few straight and no long uninterrupted lines. The same effect of curvature or of colour appeared twice usually, but not oftener, at any one point of view. Everywhere was variety in uniformity. It was a piece of 'composition,' in which the most fastidiously critical taste could scarcely have suggested an emendation.

I had turned to the right as I entered this road, and now, arising, I continued in the same direction. The path was so serpentine that at no moment could I trace its course for more than two or three paces in advance. Its character did not undergo any material change.

Presently the murmur of water fell gently upon my ear, and in a few moments afterwards, as I turned with the road somewhat more abruptly than hitherto, I became aware that a building of some kind lay at the foot of a gentle declivity just before me. I could see nothing distinctly on account of the mist which occupied all the little valley below. A gentle breeze, however, now arose, as the sun was about descending; and while I remained standing on the brow of the slope, the fog gradually became dissipated into wreaths, and so floated over the scene.

As it came fully into view, thus *gradually* as I describe it, piece by piece, here a tree, there a glimpse of water, and here again the summit of a chimney, I could scarcely help fancying that the whole was one of the ingenious illusions sometimes exhibited under the name of 'vanishing pictures.'

By the time, however, that the fog had thoroughly disappeared, the sun had made its way down behind the gentle hills, and thence, as if with a slight *chassez* to the south, had come again fully into sight, glaring with a purplish lustre through a chasm that entered the valley from the west. Suddenly, therefore, and as if by the hand of magic, this whole valley and everything in it became brilliantly visible.

The first *coup d'œil*, as the sun slid into the position described, impressed me very much as I have been impressed when a boy by the concluding scene of some well-arranged theatrical spectacle or melodrama. Not even the monstrosity of colour was wanting, for the sunlight came out through the chasm, tinted all orange and purple; while the vivid green of the grass in the valley was reflected more or less upon all objects from the curtain of vapour that still hung

Landor's cottage

overhead, as if loth to take its total departure from a scene so enchantingly beautiful.

The little vale into which I thus peered down from under the fog canopy could not have been more than four hundred yards long; while in breadth it varied from fifty to one hundred and fifty, or perhaps two hundred. It was most narrow at its northern extremity, opening out as it tended southwardly, but with no very precise regularity. The widest portion was within eighty yards of the southern extreme. The slopes which encompassed the vale could not fairly be called hills, unless at their northern face. Here a precipitous ledge of granite arose to a height of some ninety feet; and, as I have mentioned, the valley at this point was not more than fifty feet wide; but as the visitor proceeded southwardly from this cliff, he found on his right hand and on his left declivities at once less high, less precipitous, and less rocky. All, in a word, sloped and softened to the south- and yet the whole vale was engirdled by eminences, more or less high, except at two points. One of these I have already spoken of. It lay considerably to the north of west, and was where the setting sun made its way, as I have before described, into the amphitheatre, through a cleanly cut natural cleft in the granite embankment; this fissure might have been ten yards wide at its widest point, so far as the eye could trace it. It seemed to lead up, up, like a natural causeway, into the recesses of unexplored mountains and forests. The other opening was directly at the southern end of the vale. Here, generally, the slopes were nothing more than gentle inclinations, extending from east to west about one hundred and fifty yards. In the middle of this extent was a depression, level with the ordinary floor of the valley. As regards vegetation, as well as in respect to everything else, the scene *softened and sloped* to the south. To the north, on the craggy precipice, a few paces from the verge, up sprang the magnificent trunks of numerous hickories, black walnuts, and chestnuts, interspersed with occasional oak; and the strong lateral branches thrown out by the walnuts especially, spread far over the edge of the cliff. Proceeding southwardly, the explorer saw at first the same class of trees, but less and less lofty and Salvatorish in character; then he saw the gentler elm, succeeded by the sassafras and locust –

these again by the softer linden, redbud, catalpa, and maple – these yet again by still more graceful and more modest varieties. The whole face of the southern declivity was covered with wild shrubbery alone, an occasional silver willow or white poplar excepted. In the bottom of the valley itself (for it must be borne in mind that the vegetation hitherto mentioned grew only on the cliffs or hill sides) were to be seen three insulated trees. One was an elm of fine size and exquisite form; it stood guard over the southern gate of the vale. Another was a hickory, much larger than the elm, and altogether a much finer tree, although both were exceedingly beautiful; it seemed to have taken charge of the north-western entrance, springing from a group of rocks in the very jaws of the ravine, and throwing its graceful body, at an angle of nearly forty-five degrees, far out into the sunshine of the amphitheatre. About thirty yards east of this tree, stood, however, the pride of the valley, and beyond all question the most magnificent tree I have ever seen, unless perhaps among the cypresses of the Itchiatuckanee. It was a triple-stemmed tulip-tree – the *Liriodendron tulipiferum* – one of the natural order of magnolias. Its three trunks separated from the parent at about three feet from the soil, and, diverging very slightly and gradually, were not more than four feet apart at the point where the largest stem shot out into foliage: this was at an elevation of about eighty feet. The whole height of the principal division was one hundred and twenty feet. Nothing can surpass in beauty the form or the glossy vivid green of the leaves of the tulip tree. In the present instance they were fully eight inches wide; but their glory was altogether eclipsed by the gorgeous splendour of the profuse blossoms. Conceive, closely congregated, a million of the largest and most resplendent tulips! Only thus can the reader get any idea of the picture I would convey. And then the stately grace of the clean, delicately-granulated columnar stems, the largest four feet in diameter at twenty from the ground. The innumerable blossoms, mingling with those of other trees scarcely less beautiful, although infinitely less majestic, filled the valley with more than Arabian perfumes.

The general floor of the amphitheatre was *grass* of the same character as that I had found in the road; if anything, more deliciously soft, thick, velvety, and miraculously green. It was hard to conceive how all this beauty had been attained.

I have spoken of the two openings into the vale. From the one to the north-west issued a rivulet, which came gently murmuring and slightly foaming down the ravine, until it dashed against the group of rocks out of which sprang the insulated hickory. Here, after encircling the tree, it passed on a little to the north of east, leaving the tulip tree. some twenty feet to the south, and making no decided alteration in its course until it came near the midway between the eastern and western boundaries of the valley. At this point, after a series of sweeps, it turned off at right angles, and pursued a generally southern direction, meandering as it went, until it became lost in a small lake of irregular figure (although roughly oval) that lay gleaming near the lower extremity of the vale. This lakelet was, perhaps, a hundred yards in diameter at its widest part. No crystal could be clearer than its waters. Its bottom, which could be distinctly seen, consisted altogether of pebbles brilliantly white. Its banks, of the emerald grass already described, *rounded*, rather than sloped, off into the clear heaven below; and *so* clear was this heaven, so perfectly at times did it reflect all objects above it that where the true bank ended and where the mimic one commenced, it was a point of no little difficulty to determine. The trout, and some other varieties of fish, with which this pond seemed to be almost inconveniently crowded, had all the appearance of veritable flying-fish. It was almost impossible to believe that they were not absolutely suspended in the air. A light birch canoe, that lay placidly on the water, was reflected in its minutest fibres with a fidelity unsurpassed by the most exquisitely polished mirror. A small island, fairly laughing with flowers in full bloom, and affording little more space than just enough for a picturesque little building, seemingly a fowl-house – arose from the lake not far from its northern shore – to which it was connected by means of an inconceivably light-looking and yet very primitive bridge. It was formed of a single broad and thick plank of the tulip wood. This was forty feet long, and spanned the interval between shore and shore with a slight but very perceptible arch, preventing all oscillation. From the southern extreme of the lake issued a continuation of the rivulet, which, after meandering for perhaps thirty yards, finally passed through the 'depression' (already described) in the middle of the southern declivity, and tumbling down a sheer precipice of a hundred feet, made its devious and unnoticed way to the Hudson.

The lake was deep – at some points thirty feet – but the rivulet seldom exceeded three, while its greatest width was about eight. Its bottom and banks were as those of the pond – if a defect could have been attributed to them, in point of picturesqueness, it was that of excessive *neatness*.

The expanse of the green turf was relieved, here and there, by an occasional showy shrub, such as the hydrangea, or the common snow-ball, or the aromatic seringa; or more frequently by a clump of geraniums blossoming gorgeously in great varieties. These latter grew in pots which were carefully buried in the soil, so as to give the plants the appearance of being indigenous. Besides all this, the lawn's velvet was exquisitely spotted with sheep, a considerable flock of which roamed about the vale, in company with three tamed deer, and a vast number of brilliantly-plumed ducks. A very large mastiff seemed to be in vigilant attendance upon these animals, each and all.

Along the eastern and western cliffs – where, towards the upper portion of the amphitheatre, the boundaries were more or less precipitous – grew ivy in great profusion – so that only here and there could even a glimpse of the naked rock be obtained. The northern precipice, in like manner, was almost entirely clothed by grape-vines of rare luxuriance; some springing from the soil at the base of the cliff, and others from ledges on its face.

The slight elevation which formed the lower boundary of this little domain was crowned by a neat stone wall, of sufficient height to prevent the escape of the deer. Nothing of the fence kind was observable elsewhere; for nowhere else was an artificial enclosure needed: any stray sheep, for example, which should attempt to make its way out of the vale by means of the ravine, would find its progress arrested, after a few yards' advance, by the precipitous ledge of rock over which tumbled the cascade that had arrested my attention as I first drew near the domain. In short, the only ingress or egress was through a gate occupying a rocky pass in the road, a few paces below the point at which I stopped to reconnoitre the scene.

I have described the brook as meandering very irregularly through the whole of its course. Its two *general* directions, as I have said, were first from west to east, and then from north to south. At the *turn*, the stream, sweeping backwards, made an almost circular *loop*, so as to form a peninsula which was *very* nearly an island, and which included about the sixteenth of an acre. On this peninsula stood a dwelling-house – and when I say that this house, like the infernal terrace seen by Vathek, *'etait d'une architecture inconnue dans les annales de la terre,'* I mean merely that its *tout ensemble* struck me with the keenest sense of combined novelty and propriety – in a word, of *poetry* – (for, than in the words just employed, I could scarcely give, of poetry in the abstract, a more rigorous definition) – and I do *not* mean that the merely *outré* was perceptible in any respect.

In fact nothing could well be more simple – more utterly unpretending than this cottage. Its marvellous *effect* lay altogether in its artistic arrangement *as a picture*. I could have fancied, while I looked at it, that some eminent landscape-painter had built it with his brush.

The point of view from which I first saw the valley was not *altogether*, although it was nearly, the best point from which to survey the house. I will therefore describe it as I afterwards saw it – from a position on the stone wall at the southern extreme of the amphitheatre.

The main building was about twenty-four feet long and sixteen broad – certainly not more. Its total height, from the ground to the apex of the roof, could not have exceeded eighteen feet. To the west end of this structure was attached one about a third smaller in all its proportions:– the line of its front standing back about two yards from that of the larger house; and the line of its roof, of course, being considerably depressed below that of the roof adjoining. At right angles to these buildings, and from the rear of the main one – not exactly in the middle – extended a third compartment, very small – being, in general, one third less than the western wing. The roofs of the two larger were very steep – sweeping down from the ridge-beam with a long concave curve, and extending at least four feet beyond the walls in front, so as to form the roofs of two piazzas. These latter roofs, of course, needed no support; but as they had the *air* of needing it, slight and perfectly plain pillars were inserted at the corners alone. The roof of the northern wing was merely an extension of a portion of the main roof. Between the chief building and western wing arose a very tall and rather slender square chimney of hard Dutch bricks, alternately black and red:– a slight cornice of projecting bricks at the top. Over the gables, the roofs also projected very much:– in the main building about four feet to the east and two to the west. The principal door was not exactly in the middle of the main division, being a little to the east – while the two windows were to the west. These latter did not extend to the floor, but were much longer and narrower than usual – they had single shutters like doors – the panes were of lozenge form, but quite large. The door itself had its upper half of glass, also in lozenge panes – a moveable shutter secured it at night. The door to the west wing was in its gable, and quite simple! A single window looked out to the south. There was no external door to the north wing, and it also had only one window to the east.

The blank wall of the eastern gable was relieved by stairs (with a balustrade) running diagonally across it – the ascent being from the south. Under cover of the widely projecting eave these steps gave access to a door leading into the garret, or rather loft – for it was lighted only by a single window to the north, and seemed to have been intended as a store-room.

The piazzas of the main building and western wing had no floors, as is usual; but at the doors and at each window, large, flat, irregular slabs of granite lay imbedded in the delicious turf, affording comfortable footings in all weather. Excellent paths of the same material – not *nicely* adapted, but with the velvety sod filling frequent intervals between the stones, led hither and thither from the house, to a crystal spring about five paces off, to the road, or to one or two out-houses that lay to the north, beyond the brook, and were thoroughly concealed by a few locusts and catalpas.

Not more than six steps from the main door of the cottage stood the dead trunk of a fantastic pear-tree, so clothed from head to foot in the gorgeous bignonia blossoms that one required no little scrutiny to determine what manner of sweet thing it could be. From various arms of this tree hung cages of different kinds. In one, a large wicker cylinder with a ring at top, revelled a mocking bird; in another, an oriole; in a third, the impudent bobalink – while three or four more delicate prisons were loudly vocal with canaries.

The pillars of the piazza were enwreathed in jasmine and sweet honeysuckle, while from the angle formed by the main structure and its west wing in front sprang a grape-vine of unexampled luxuriance. Scorning all restraint, it had clambered first to the lower roof, then to the higher, and along the ridge of this latter it continued to writhe on, throwing out tendrils to the right and left, until at length it fairly attained the east gable, and fell trailing over the stairs.

The whole house, with its wings, was constructed of the old-fashioned Dutch shingles, broad, and with unrounded corners. It is a peculiarity of this material to give houses built of it the appearance of being wider at bottom than at top, after the manner of Egyptian architecture; and in the present instance this exceedingly picturesque effect was aided by numerous pots of gorgeous flowers that almost encompassed the base of the buildings.

The shingles were painted a dull grey, and the happiness with which this neutral tint melted into the vivid green of the tulip tree leaves that partially overshadowed the cottage can readily be conceived by an artist.

From the position near the stone wall, as described, the buildings were seen at great advantage, for the south-eastern angle was thrown forward, so that the eye took in at once the whole of the two fronts, with the picturesque eastern gable, and at the same time obtained just a sufficient glimpse of the northern wing, with parts of a pretty roof to the spring-house, and nearly half of a light bridge that spanned the brook in the near vicinity of the main buildings.

I did not remain very long on the brow of the hill, although long enough to make a thorough survey of the scene at my feet. It was clear that I had wandered from the road to the village, and I had thus good travellers' excuse to open the gate before me and inquire my way at all events; so, without more ado, I proceeded.

The road, after passing the gate, seemed to lie upon a natural ledge, sloping gradually down along the face of the north-eastern cliffs. It led me on to the foot of the northern precipice, and thence over the bridge, round by the eastern gable to the front door. In this progress I took notice that no sight of the outhouses could be obtained.

As I turned the corner of the gable the mastiff bounded towards me in stern silence, but with the eye and the whole air of a tiger. I held him out my hand, however, in token of amity, and I never yet knew the dog who was proof against such an appeal to his courtesy. He not only shut his mouth and wagged his tail, but absolutely offered me his paw, afterwards extending his civilities to Ponto.

As no bell was discernible, I rapped with my stick against the door which stood half open. Instantly a figure advanced to the threshold – that of a young woman about twenty-eight years of age – slender, or rather slight, and somewhat above the medium height. As she approached with a certain *modest decision* of step altogether indescribable, I said to myself, 'Surely here I have found the perfection of natural in contradistinction from artificial *grace*.' The second impression which she made on me, but by far the more vivid of the two, was that of *enthusiasm*. So intense an expression of *romance*, perhaps I should call it, or of unworldliness, as that which gleamed from her deep-set eyes, had never so sunk into my heart of hearts before. I know not how it is, but this peculiar expression of the eye, wreathing itself occasionally into the lips, is the most powerful, if not absolutely the *sole* spell, which rivets my interest in woman. '*Romance*,' provided my readers fully comprehend what I would here imply by the word – 'romance' and 'womanliness' seem to me convertible terms, and after all, what man truly *loves* in woman is simply her *womanhood*. The eyes of Annie (I heard some one from the interior call her 'Annie, darling!') were 'spiritual grey,' her hair a light chestnut; this is all I had time to observe of her.

At her most courteous of invitations I entered, passing first into a tolerably wide vestibule. Having come mainly to *observe*, I took notice that to my right as I stepped in was a window such as those in front of the house, to the left, a door leading into the principal room, while, opposite me, an *open* door enabled me to see a small apartment, just the size of the vestibule arranged as a study, and having a large *bow* window looking to the north.

Passing into the parlour I found myself with *Mr Landor*, for this I afterwards found was his name. He was civil, even cordial, in his manner, but just then I was more intent on observing the arrangements of the dwelling which had so much interested me than the personal appearance of the tenant.

The north wing I now saw was a bedchamber, its door opened into the parlour. West of this door was a single window looking towards the brook. At the west end of the parlour were a fireplace and a door leading into the west wing, probably a kitchen.

Nothing could be more rigorously simple than the furniture of the parlour. On the floor was an ingrain carpet of excellent texture, a white ground spotted with small circular green figures. At the windows were curtains of snowy white jaconet muslin; they were tolerably full, and hung *decisively*, perhaps rather formally, in sharp parallel plaits to the floor – *just* to the floor. The walls were papered with a French paper of great delicacy, a silver ground with a faint green cord running zigzag throughout. Its expanse was relieved merely by three of Julien's exquisite lithographs *a trois crayons*, fastened to the wall without frames. One of these drawings was a scene of Oriental luxury, or rather voluptuousness; another was a 'carnival piece,' spirited beyond compare; the third was a Greek female head: a face so divinely beautiful, and yet of an expression so provokingly indeterminate, as had never before arrested my attention.

The more substantial furniture consisted of a round table, a few chairs (including a large rocking-chair), and a sofa, or rather 'settee;' its material was plain maple painted a creamy white, slightly interstriped with green; the seat of cane. The chairs and table were 'to match,' but the *forms* of all had evidently been designed by the same brain which planned 'the grounds,' it is impossible to conceive anything more graceful.

On the table were a few books, a large, square, crystal bottle of some novel perfume, a plain ground-glass *astral* (not solar) lamp with an Italian shade, and a large vase of resplendently-blooming flowers. Flowers, indeed, of gorgeous colours and delicate odour formed the sole mere *decoration* of the apartment. The fireplace was nearly filled with a vase of brilliant geranium. On a triangular shelf in each angle of the room stood also a similar vase, varied only as to its lovely contents. One or two smaller *bouquets* adorned the mantel, and late violets clustered about the open windows.

It is not the purpose of this work to do more than give in detail, a picture of Mr Landor's residence *as I found it*.

A Tale of the Ragged Mountains

During the fall of the year 1827, while residing near Charlottesville, Virginia, I casually made the acquaintance of Mr. Augustus Bedloe. This young gentleman was remarkable in every respect, and excited in me a profound interest and curiosity. I found it impossible to comprehend him either in his moral or physical relations. Of his family I could obtain no satisfactory account. Whence he came, I never ascertained. Even about his age – although I call him a young gentleman – there was something which perplexed me in no little degree. He certainly *seemed* young – and he made a point of speaking about his youth – yet there were moments when I should have had little trouble in imagining him a hundred years of age. But in no regard was he more peculiar than in his personal appearance. He was singularly tall and thin. He stooped much. His limbs were exceedingly long and emaciated. His forehead was broad and low. His complexion was absolutely bloodless. His mouth was large and flexible, and his teeth were more widely uneven, although sound, than I had ever before seen teeth in a human head. The expression of his smile, however, was by no means unpleasing, as might be supposed; but it had no variation whatever. It was one of profound melancholy – of a phaseless and unceasing gloom. His eyes were abnormally large, and round like those of a cat. The pupils, too, upon any accession or diminution of light, underwent contraction or dilation, just such as is observed in the feline tribe. In moments of excitement the orbs grew bright to a degree almost inconceivable; seeming to emit luminous rays, not of a reflecting, but of an intrinsic lustre, as does a candle or the sun; yet their ordinary condition was so totally vapid, filmy, and dull, as to convey the idea of the eyes of a long-interred corpse.

These peculiarities of person appeared to cause him much annoyance, and he was continually alluding to them in a sort of half-explanatory, half-apologetic strain, which, when I first heard it, impressed me very painfully. I soon, however, grew accustomed to it, and my uneasiness wore off. It seemed to be his design rather to insinuate, than directly to assert that, physically, he had not always been what he was – that a long series of neuralgic attacks had reduced him from a condition of more than usual personal beauty, to that which I saw. For many years past he had been attended by a physican, named Templeton – an old man, perhaps seventy years of age – whom he had first encountered at Saratoga, and from whose attention, while there, he either received, or fancied that he received great benefit. The result was that Bedloe, who was wealthy, had made an arrangement with Doctor Templeton, by which the latter, in consideration of a liberal annual allowance, had consented to devote his time and medical experience exclusively to the care of the invalid.

Doctor Templeton had been a traveller in his younger days, and, at Paris, had become a convert, in great measure, to the doctrines of Mesmer. It was altogether by means of magnetic remedies that he had succeeded in alleviating the acute pains of his patient; and this success had very naturally inspired the latter with a certain degree of confidence in the opinions from which the remedies had been educed. The Doctor, however, like all enthusiasts, had struggled hard to make a thorough convert of his pupil, and finally so far gained his point as to induce the sufferer to submit to numerous experiments. – By a frequent repetition of these, a result had arisen, which of late days has become so common as to attract little or no attention, but which, at the period of which I write, had very rarely been known in America. I mean to say, that between Doctor Templeton and Bedloe there had grown up, little by little, a very distinct and strongly-marked *rapport* or magnetic relation. I am not prepared to assert, however, that this *rapport* extended beyond the limits of the simple sleep-producing power; but this power itself had attained great intensity. At the first attempt to induce the magnetic somnolency, the mesmerist entirely failed. In the fifth or sixth he succeeded very partially and after long continued effort. Only at the twelfth was the triumph complete. After this the will of the patient succumbed rapidly to that of the physician, so that, when I first became acquainted with the two, sleep was brought about almost instantaneously, by the mere volition of the operator, even when the invalid was unaware of his presence. It is only now, in the year 1845, when similar miracles are witnessed daily by thousands, that I dare venture to record this apparent impossibility as a matter of serious fact.

The temperament of Bedloe was, in the highest degree, sensitive, excitable, enthusiastic. His imagination was singularly vigorous and creative; and no doubt it derived additional force from the habitual use of morphine, which he swallowed in great quantity, and without which he would have found it impossible to exist. It was his practice to take a very large dose of it immediately after breakfast, each morning – or rather immediately after a cup of strong coffee, for he ate nothing in the forenoon – and then set forth alone, or attended only by a dog, upon a long ramble among the chain of wild and dreary hills that lie westward and southward of Charlottesville and are there dignified by the title of the Ragged Mountains.

Upon a dim, warm, misty day, towards the close of November, and during the strange *interregnum* of the seasons which in America is termed the Indian Summer, Mr. Bedloe departed as usual for the hills. The day passed, and still he did not return.

About eight o'clock at night, having become seriously alarmed at his protracted absence, we were about setting out in search of him, when he unexpectedly made his appearance, in health no worse than usual, and in rather more than ordinary spirits. The account which he gave of his expedition, and of the events which detained him, was a singular one indeed.

'You will remember,' said he, 'that it was about nine in the morning when I left Charlottesville. I bent my steps immediately to the
mountains, and, about ten, entered a gorge which was entirely new to
me. I followed the windings of this pass with much interest. The
scenery which presented itself on all sides, although scarcely entitled
to be called grand, had about it an indescribable, and to me, a delicious
aspect of dreary desolation. The solitude seemed absolutely virgin. I
could not help believing that the green sods and the grey rocks upon
which I trod, had never been trodden by the foot of a human being. So
entirely secluded, and in fact inaccessible, except through a series of
accidents, is the entrance of the ravine, that it is by no means
impossible that I was indeed the first adventurer – the very first and
sole adventurer – who had ever penetrated its recesses.

'The thick and peculiar mist or smoke which distinguishes the
Indian Summer, and which now hung heavily over all objects, served
no doubt to deepen the vague impressions which these objects created.
So dense was this pleasant fog that I could at no time see more than a
dozen yards of the path before me. This path was excessively sinuous,
and as the sun could not be seen, I soon lost all idea of the direction in
which I journeyed. In the meantime the morphine had its customary
effect – that of enduing all the external world with an intensity of
interest. In the quivering of a leaf – in the hue of a blade of grass – in
the shape of a trefoil – in the humming of a bee – in the gleaming of a
dewdrop – in the breathing of the wind – in the faint odours that came
from the forest – there came a whole universe of suggestion – a gay and
motley train of rhapsodical and immethodical thought.

'Busied in this, I walked on for several hours, during which the
mist deepened around me to so great an extent that at length I was
reduced to an absolute groping of the way. And now an indescribable
uneasiness possessed me – a species of nervous hesitation and tremor,
– I feared to tread, lest I should be precipitated into some abyss. I
remembered, too, strange stories told about these Ragged Hills, and of
the uncouth and fierce races of men who tenanted their groves and
caverns. A thousand vague fancies oppressed and disconcerted me –

fancies the more distressing because vague. Very suddenly my situation was arrested by the loud beating of a drum.

'My amazement was, of course, extreme. A drum in these hills was a thing unknown. I could not have been more surprised at the sound of the trump of the Archangel. But a new and still more astounding source of interest and perplexity arose. There came a wild rattling or jingling sound, as if of a bunch of large keys – and upon the instant a dusky-visaged and half-naked man rushed past me with a shriek. He came so close to my person that I felt his hot breath upon my face. He bore in one hand an instrument composed of an assemblage of steel rings, and shook them vigorously as he ran. Scarcely had he disappeared in the mist, before, panting after him, with open mouth and glaring eyes, there darted a huge beast. I could not be mistaken in the character. It was a hyena.

'The sight of this monster rather relieved than heightened my terrors – for I now made sure that I dreamed, and endeavoured to arouse myself to waking consciousness. I stepped boldly and briskly forward. I rubbed my eyes. I called aloud. I pinched my limbs. A small spring of water presented itself to my view, and here stooping, I bathed my hands and my head and neck. This seemed to dissipate the equivocal sensations which had hitherto annoyed me. I arose, as I thought, a new man, and proceeded steadily and complacently on my unknown way.

'At length quite overcome by exertion, and by a certain oppressive closeness of the atmosphere, I seated myself beneath a tree. Presently there came a feeble gleam of sunshine, and the shadow of the leaves of the tree fell faintly but definitely upon the grass. At this shadow I gazed wonderingly for many minutes. Its character stupified me with astonishment. I looked upward. The tree was a palm.

'I now arose hurriedly, and in a state of fearful agitation – for the fancy that I dreamed would serve me no longer. I saw – I felt that I had perfect command of my senses – and these senses now brought to my soul a world of novel and singular sensation. The heat became all at once intolerable. A strange odour loaded the breeze. – A low continuous murmur, like that arising from a full, but gently flowing river, came to my ears, intermingled with the peculiar hum of multitudinous human voices.

'While I listened in an extremity of astonishment which I need not attempt to describe, a strong and brief gust of wind bore off the incumbent fog as if by the wand of an enchanter.

'I found myself at the foot of a high mountain, and looking down into a vast plain, through which wound a majestic river. On the margin of this river stood an Eastern-looking city, such as we read of in the Arabian Tales, but of a character even more singular than any there described. From my position, which was far above the level of the town, I could perceive its every nook and corner, as if delineated on a map. The streets seemed innumerable and crossed each other irregularly in all directions, but were rather long winding alleys than streets, and absolutely swarmed with inhabitants. The houses were widely picturesque. On every hand was a wilderness of balconies, of verandahs, of minarets, of shrines, and fantastically carved oriels. Bazaars abounded; and in these were displayed rich wares in infinite variety, and profusion – silks, muslins, the most dazzling cutlery, the most magnificent jewels and gems. Besides these things, were seen on all sides, banners and palanquins, litters with stately dames close veiled, elephants gorgeously caparisoned, idols grotesquely hewn, drums, banners, and gongs, spears, silver and gilded maces. And amid the crowd, and the clamour, and the general intricacy and confusion – amid the million of black and yellow men, turbaned and robed, and of flowing beard, there roamed a countless multitude of holy filleted bulls, while vast legions of the filthy but sacred ape clambered, chattering and shrieking, about the cornices of the mosques, or clung to the minarets and oriels. From the swarming streets to the banks of the river descended innumerable flights of steps leading to bathing-places, while the river itself seemed to force a passage with difficulty through the vast fleets of deeply burdened ships that far and wide encumbered its surface. Beyond the limits of the city arose, in frequent majestic groups, the palm and the cocoa, with other gigantic and weird trees of vast age; and here and there might be seen a field of rice, the thatched hut of a peasant, a tank, a stray temple, a gipsy camp, or a solitary graceful maiden taking her way, with a pitcher upon her head, to the banks of the magnificent river.

'You will say now, of course, that I dreamed; but not so. What I saw – what I heard – what I felt – what I thought – had about it nothing of the unmistakeable idiosyncrasy of the dream. All was rigorously self-consistent. At first doubting that I was really awake, I entered into a series of tests which soon convinced me that I really was. Now, when one dreams, and in the dream suspects that he dreams, the suspicion *never fails to confirm itself*, and the sleeper is almost immediately aroused. Thus Novalis errs not in saying that "we are near waking when we dream that we dream." Had the vision occurred to me as I describe it, without my suspecting it as a dream, then a dream it might absolutely have been, but occurring as it did, and suspected and tested as it was, I am forced to class it among other phenomena.'

'In this I am not sure that you are wrong,' observed Dr. Templeton, 'but proceed. You arose and descended into the city.'

'I arose,' continued Bedloe, regarding the Doctor with an air of profound astonishment, 'I arose, as you say, and descended into the city. On my way, I fell in with an immense populace, crowding through every avenue, all in the same direction, and exhibiting in every action the wildest excitement. Very suddenly, and by some inconceivable impulse, I became intensely imbued with personal interest in what was going on. I seemed to feel that I had an important part to play, without exactly understanding what it was. Against the crowd which environed me, however, I experienced a deep sentiment of animosity. I shrank from amid them, and, swiftly, by a circuitous path, reached and entered the city. Here all was the wildest tumult and contention. A small party of men, clad in garments half-Indian, half-European, and officered by gentlemen in a uniform partly British, were engaged, at great odds, with the swarming rabble of the alleys. I joined the weaker party, arming myself with the weapons of a fallen officer, and fighting I knew not whom with the nervous ferocity of despair. We were soon overpowered by numbers, and driven to seek refuge in a species of kiosk. Here we barricaded ourselves, and, for the present, were secure. From a loop-hole near the summit of the kiosk, I perceived a vast crowd, in furious agitation, surrounding and assaulting a gay palace that overhung the river. Presently from an upper window of this palace, there descended an effeminate-looking person, by means of a string made of the turbans of his attendants. A boat was at hand, in which he escaped to the opposite bank of the river.

'And now a new object took possession of my soul. I spoke a few hurried but energetic words to my companions, and, having succeeded in gaining over a few of them to my purpose, made a frantic sally from the kiosk. We rushed amid the crowd that surrounded it. They retreated at first before us. They rallied, fought madly, and retreated again. In the meantime we were borne far from the kiosk, and became bewildered and entangled among the narrow streets of tall overhanging houses, into the recesses of which the sun had never been able to shine. The rabble pressed impetuously upon us, harassing us with their spears, and overwhelming us with flights of arrows. These latter were very remarkable, and resembled in some respects the writhing creese of the Malay. They were made to imitate the body of a creeping serpent, and were long and black, with a poisoned barb. One of them struck me upon the right temple. I reeled and fell. An instantaneous and dreadful sickness seized me. I struggled – I gasped – I died.'

'You will hardly persist *now*,' said I, smiling, 'that the whole of your adventure was not a dream. You are not prepared to maintain that you are dead?'

When I said these words, I of course expected some lively sally from Bedloe in reply; but to my astonishment, he hesitated, trembled, became fearfully pallid, and remained silent. I looked towards Templeton. He sat erect and rigid in his chair – his teeth chattered, and his eyes were starting from their sockets. 'Proceed!' he at length said hoarsely to Bedloe.

'For many minutes,' continued the latter, 'my sole sentiment – my sole feeling – was that of darkness and nonentity, with the consciousness of death. At length, there seemed to pass a violent and sudden shock through my soul, as if of electricity. With it came the sense of elasticity and of light. This latter I felt – not saw. In an instant I seemed to rise from the ground. But I had no bodily, no visible, audible, or palpable presence. The crowd had departed. The tumult had ceased. The city was in comparative repose. Beneath me lay my corpse, with the arrow in my temple, the whole head greatly swollen and disfigured. But all these things I felt – not saw. I took interest in nothing. Even the corpse seemed a matter in which I had no concern. Volition I had none, but appeared to be impelled into motion, and flitted buoyantly out of the city, retracing the circuitous path by which I had entered it. When I had attained that point of the ravine in the mountains at which I had encountered the hyena, I again experienced a shock as of a galvanic battery; the sense of weight, of volition, of substance, returned. I became my original self, and bent my steps eagerly homewards – but the past had not lost the vividness of the real – and not now, even for an instant, can I compel my understanding to regard it as a dream.'

'Nor was it,' said Templeton, with an air of deep solemnity, 'yet it would be difficult to say how otherwise it should be termed. Let us suppose only, that the soul of the man of to-day is upon the verge of some stupendous psychal discoveries. Let us content ourselves with this supposition. For the rest I have some explanation to make. Here is a water-colour drawing which I should have shown you before, but which an unaccountable sentiment of horror has hitherto prevented me from showing!'

We looked at the picture which he presented. I saw nothing in it of an extraordinary character; but its effect upon Bedloe was prodigious. He nearly fainted as he gazed. And yet it was but a miniature portrait – a miraculously accurate one, to be sure – of his own very remarkable features. At least this was my thought as I regarded it.

'You will perceive,' said Templeton, 'the date of this picture – it is here, scarcely visible, in this corner – 1780. In this year was the portrait taken. It is the likeness of a dead friend – a Mr. Oldeb – to whom I became much attached at Calcutta, during the administration of Warren Hastings. I was then only twenty years old. When I first saw you, Mr. Bedloe, at Saratoga, it was the miraculous similarity which existed between yourself and the painting, which induced me to accost you, to seek your friendship, and to bring about those arrangements which resulted in my becoming your constant companion. In accomplishing this point I was urged partly, and perhaps principally, by a regretful memory of the deceased, but also, in part, by an uneasy and not altogether horrorless curiosity respecting yourself.

'In your details of the vision which presented itself to you amid the hills, you have described, with the minutest accuracy, the Indian city of Benares upon the Holy River. The riots, the combats, the massacre, were the actual events of the insurrection of Cheyte Sing, which took place in 1780, when Hastings was put in imminent peril of his life. The man escaping by the string of turbans was Cheyte Sing himself. The party in the kiosk were sepoys and British officers headed by Hastings. Of this party I was one, and did all I could to prevent the rash and fatal sally of the officer who fell, in the crowded alleys, by the poisoned arrow of a Bengalee. That officer was my dearest friend. It was Oldeb. You will perceive by these manuscripts' (here the speaker produced a note-book in which several pages appeared to have been freshly written) 'that at the very period in which you fancied these things amid the hills, I was engaged in detailing them upon paper here at home.'

In about a week after this conversation, the following paragraphs appeared in a Charlottesville paper:

'We have the painful duty of announcing the death of Mr. AUGUSTUS BEDLO, a gentleman whose amiable manners and many virtues have long endeared him to the citizens of Charlottesville.

'Mr. B., for some years past, has been subject to neuralgia, which has often threatened to terminate fatally; but this can be regarded only as the mediate cause of his decease. The proximate cause was one of especial singularity. In an excursion to the Ragged Mountains, a few days since, a slight cold and fever were contracted, attended with great determination of blood to the head. To relieve this, Dr. Templeton resorted to topical bleeding. Leeches were applied to the temples. In a fearfully brief period the patient died, when it appeared that, in the jar containing the leeches, had been introduced, by accident, one of the venomous vermicular sangsues which are now and then found in the neighbouring ponds. This creature fastened itself upon a small artery in the right temple. Its close resemblance to the medicinal leech caused the mistake to be overlooked until too late.

'*N.B.* – The poisonous sangsue of Charlottesville may always be distinguished from the medicinal leech by its blackness, and especially by its writhing or vermicular motions, which very nearly resemble those of a snake.'

I was speaking with the editor of the paper in question, upon the topic of this remarkable accident, when it occurred to me to ask how it happened that the name of the deceased had been given as Bedlo.

'I presume,' said I, 'you have authority for this spelling, but I have always supposed the name to be written with an *e* at the end.'

'Authority? – no,' he replied. 'It is a mere typographical error. The name is Bedlo with an *e*, all the world over, and I never knew it to be spelt otherwise in my life.'

'Then,' said I mutteringly, as I turned upon my heel, 'then indeed has it come to pass that one truth is stranger than any fiction – for Bedlo without the *e*, what is it but Oldeb conversed? And this man tells me it is a typographical error.'

The Black Cat

For the most wild, yet most homely narrative which I am about to pen, I neither expect nor solicit belief. Mad indeed would I be to expect it in a case where my very senses reject their own evidence. Yet mad am I not – and very surely do I not dream. But to-morrow I die, and to-day I would unburthen my soul. My immediate purpose is to place before the world plainly, succinctly, and without comment, a series of mere household events. In their consequences these events have terrified – have tortured – have destroyed me. Yet I will not attempt to expound them. To me they have presented little but horror – to many they will seem less terrible than *barroques*. Hereafter, perhaps, some intellect may be found which will reduce my phantasm to the commonplace – some intellect more calm, more logical, and far less excitable than my own, which will perceive, in the circumstances I detail with awe, nothing more than an ordinary succession of very natural causes and effects.

From my infancy I was noted for the docility and humanity of my disposition. My tenderness of heart was even so conspicuous as to make me the jest of my companions. I was especially fond of animals, and was indulged by my parents with a great variety of pets. With these I spent most of my time, and never was so happy as when feeding and caressing them. This peculiarity of character grew with my growth, and in my manhood I derived from it one of my principal sources of pleasure. To those who have cherished an affection for a faithful and sagacious dog, I need hardly be at the trouble of explaining the nature or the intensity of the gratification thus derivable. There is something in the unselfish and self-sacrificing love of a brute which goes directly to the heart of him who has had frequent occasion to test the paltry friendship and gossamer fidelity of mere *Man*.

I married early, and was happy to find in my wife a disposition not uncongenial with my own. Observing my partiality for domestic pets, she lost no opportunity of procuring those of the most agreeable kind. We had birds, gold-fish, a fine dog, rabbits, a small monkey, and *a cat*.

This latter was a remarkably large and beautiful animal, entirely black, and sagacious to an astonishing degree. In speaking of his intelligence, my wife, who at heart was not a little tinctured with superstition, made frequent allusion to the ancient popular notion which regarded all black cats as witches in disguise. Not that she was ever *serious* upon this point, and I mention the matter at all for no better reason than that it happens just now to be remembered.

Pluto – this was the cat's name – was my favourite pet and playmate. I alone fed him, and he attended me wherever I went about the house. It was even with difficulty that I could prevent him from following me through the streets.

Our friendship lasted in this manner for several years, during which my general temperament and character – through the in-strumentality of the Fiend Intemperance – had (I blush to confess it) experienced a radical alteration for the worse. I grew, day by day, more moody, more irritable, more regardless of the feelings of others. I suffered myself to use intemperate language to my wife. At length, I even offered her personal violence. My pets of course were made to feel the change in my disposition. I not only neglected, but ill-used them. For Pluto, however, I still retained sufficient regard to restrain me from maltreating him, as I made no scruple of maltreating the rabbits, the monkey, or even the dog, when by accident, or through affection, they came in my way. But my disease grew upon me – for what disease is like Alcohol! – and at length even Pluto, who was now becoming old, and consequently somewhat peevish – even Pluto began to experience the effects of my ill-temper.

One night returning home much intoxicated from one of my haunts about town, I fancied that the cat avoided my presence. I seized him, when, in his fright at my violence, he inflicted a slight wound upon my hand with his teeth. The fury of a demon instantly possessed me. I knew myself no longer. My original soul seemed at once to take its flight from my body, and a more than fiendish malevolence, gin nurtured, thrilled every fibre of my frame. I took from my waistcoat-pocket a penknife, opened it, grasped the poor beast by the throat, and deliberately cut one of its eyes from the socket! I blush, I burn, I shudder, while I pen the damnable atrocity.

When reason returned with the morning – when I had slept off the fumes of the night's debauch – I experienced a sentiment half of horror, half of remorse, for the crime of which I had been guilty, but it was at best a feeble and equivocal feeling, and the soul remained untouched. I again plunged into excess, and soon drowned in wine all memory of the deed.

In the meantime the cat slowly recovered. The socket of the lost eye presented, it is true, a frightful appearance, but he no longer appeared to be suffering any pain. He went about the house as usual, but, as might be expected, fled in extreme terror at my approach. I had so much of my old heart left as to be at first grieved by this evident dislike on the part of a creature which had once so loved me. But this feeling soon gave place to irritation. And then came, as if to my final and irrevocable overthrow, the spirit of PERVERSENESS. Of this spirit philosophy takes no account. Yet I am not more sure that my soul lives than I am that perverseness is one of the primitive impulses of the human heart – one of the indivisible primary faculties or sentiments which gave direction to the character of Man. Who has not, a hundred times, found himself commiting a vile or a silly action for no other reason than because he knows he should *not*? Have we not a perpetual inclination, in the teeth of our best judgment, to violate that which is *Law*, merely because we understand it to be such? This spirit of perverseness, I say, came to my final overthrow. It was this unfathomable longing of the soul *to vex itself* – to offer violence to its own nature – to do wrong for the wrong's sake only – that urged me to continue, and finally to consummate the injury I had inflicted upon the unoffending brute. One morning, in cool blood, I slipped a noose about its neck, and hung it to the limb of a tree; – hung it with the tears streaming from my eyes, and with the bitterest remorse at my heart; hung it *because* I knew that it had loved me, and *because* I felt it had given me no reason of offence; hung it *because* I knew that in so doing I was committing a sin – a deadly sin that would so jeopardise my immortal soul as to place it, if such a thing were possible, even beyond the reach of the infinite mercy of the Most Merciful and Most Terrible God.

On the night of the day on which this cruel deed was done, I was aroused from sleep by the cry of fire. The curtains of my bed were in flames. The whole house was blazing. It was with great difficulty that my wife, a servant, and myself made our escape from the conflagration. The destruction was complete. My entire worldly wealth was swallowed up, and I resigned myself thenceforward to despair.

I am above the weakness of seeking to establish a sequence of cause and effect between the disaster and the atrocity. But I am detailing a chain of facts, and wish not to leave even a possible link imperfect. On the day succeeding the fire, I visited the ruins. The walls with one exception had fallen in. This exception was found in a compartment wall, not very thick, which stood about the middle of the house, and against which had rested the head of my bed. The plastering had here in great measure resisted the action of the fire, a fact which I attributed to its having been recently spread. About this wall a dense crowd were collected, and many persons seemed to be examining a particular portion of it with very minute and eager attention. The words 'strange!' 'singular!' and other similar expressions, excited my curiosity. I approached and saw, as if graven in *bas relief* upon the white surface, the figure of a gigantic *cat*. The impression was given with an accuracy truly marvellous. There was a rope about the animal's neck.

When I first beheld this apparition – for I could scarcely regard it as less – my wonder and my terror were extreme. But at length reflection came to my aid. The cat, I remembered, had been hung in a garden adjacent to the house. Upon the alarm of fire this garden had been immediately filled by the crowd, by some one of whom the animal must have been cut from the tree and thrown through an open window into my chamber. This had probably been done with the view of arousing me from sleep. The falling of other walls had compressed the victim of my cruelty into the substance of the freshly-spread plaster; the lime of which, with the flames and the *ammonia* from the carcase, had then accomplished the portraiture as I saw it.

Although I thus readily accounted to my reason, if not altogether to my conscience, for the startling fact just detailed, it did not the less fail to make a deep impression upon my fancy. For months I could not rid myself of the phantasm of the cat, and during this period there came back into my spirit a half-sentiment that seemed, but was not, remorse. I went so far as to regret the loss of the animal, and to look about me among the vile haunts which I now habitually frequented for another pet of the same species, and of somewhat similar appearance, with which to supply its place.

One night as I sat half-stupefied in a den of more than infamy, my attention was suddenly drawn to some black object, reposing upon the head of one of the immense hogsheads of gin or of rum, which constituted the chief furniture of the apartment. I had been looking steadily at the top of this hogshead for some minutes, and what now caused me surprise was the fact that I had not sooner perceived the object thereupon. I approached it, and touched it with my hand. It was a black cat – a very large one – fully as large as Pluto, and closely resembling him in every respect but one. Pluto had not a white hair upon any portion of his body; but this cat had a large, although indefinite splotch of white, covering nearly the whole region of the breast.

Upon my touching him he immediately arose, purred loudly, rubbed against my hand, and appeared delighted with my notice. This then, was the very creature of which I was in search. I at once offered to purchase it of the landlord; but this person made no claim to it – knew nothing of it – had never seen it before.

I continued my caresses, and when I prepared to go home the animal evinced a disposition to accompany me. I permitted it to do so, occasionally stooping and patting it as I proceeded. When it reached the house it domesticated itself at once, and became immediately a great favourite with my wife.

For my own part, I soon found a dislike to it arising within me. This was just the reverse of what I had anticipated, but – I know not how or why it was – its evident fondness for myself rather disgusted and annoyed. By slow degrees these feelings of disgust and annoyance rose into the bitterness of hatred. I avoided the creature; a certain sense of shame, and the remembrance of my former deed of cruelty, preventing me from physically abusing it. I did not, for some weeks, strike or otherwise violently ill use it, but gradually – very gradually – I came to look upon it with unutterable loathing, and to flee silently from its odious presence as from the breath of a pestilence.

What added, no doubt, to my hatred of the beast was the discovery, on the morning after I brought it home, that, like Pluto, it also had been deprived of one of its eyes. This circumstance, however, only endeared it to my wife, who, as I have already said, possessed in a high degree that humanity of feeling which had once been my distinguishing trait, and the source of many of my simplest and purest pleasures.

With my aversion to this cat, however, its partiality for myself seemed to increase. It followed my footsteps with a pertinacity which it would be difficult to make the reader comprehend. Whenever I sat, it would crouch beneath my chair or spring upon my knees, covering me with its loathsome caresses. If I arose to walk it would get between my feet and thus nearly throw me down, or fastening its long and sharp claws in my dress, clamber in this manner to my breast. At such times, although I longed to destroy it with a blow, I was yet withheld from so doing, partly by a memory of my former crime, but chiefly – let me confess it at once – by absolute *dread* of the beast.

This dread was not exactly a dread of physical evil – and yet I should be at a loss how otherwise to define it. I am almost ashamed to own – yes, even in this felon's cell, I am almost ashamed to own – that the terror and horror with which the animal inspired me, had been heightened by one of the merest chimeras it would be possible to conceive. My wife had called my attention more than once to the character of the mark of white hair, of which I have spoken, and which constituted the sole visible difference between the strange beast and the one I had destroyed. The reader will remember that this mark, although large, had been originally very indefinite, but by slow degrees – degrees nearly imperceptible, and which for a long time my reason struggled to reject as fanciful – it had at length assumed a rigorous distinctness of outline. It was now the representation of an object that I shudder to name – and for this above all I loathed and dreaded, and would have rid myself of the monster *had I dared* – it was now, I say the image of a hideous – of a ghastly thing – of the GALLOWS! – O, mournful and terrible engine of horror and of crime – of agony and of death!

And now was I indeed wretched beyond the wretchedness of mere humanity. And *a brute beast* – whose fellow I had contemptuously destroyed – *a brute beast* – to work out for *me* – for me a man, fashioned in the image of the High God – so much of insufferable woe! Alas! neither by day nor by night knew I the blessing of rest any more! During the former the creature left me no moment alone; and in the latter I started hourly from dreams of unutterable fear, to find the hot breath of *the thing* upon my face, and its vast weight – an incarnate night-mare that I had no power to shake off – incumbent eternally upon my *heart*!

Beneath the pressure of torments such as these, the feeble remnant of the good within me succumbed. Evil thoughts became my sole intimates – the darkest and most evil of thoughts. The moodiness of my usual temper increased to hatred of all things and of all mankind; while from the sudden frequent and ungovernable outbursts of a fury to which I now blindly abandoned myself, my uncomplaining wife, alas! was the most usual and the most patient of sufferers.

One day she accompanied me upon some household errand into the cellar of the old building which our poverty compelled us to inhabit. The cat followed me down the steep stairs, and nearly throwing me headlong, exasperated me to madness. Uplifting an axe, and forgetting in my wrath the childish dread which had hitherto stayed my hand, I aimed a blow at the animal, which of course would have proved instantly fatal had it descended as I wished. But this blow was arrested by the hand of my wife. Goaded by the interference into a rage more than demoniacal, I withdrew my arm from her grasp and buried the axe in her brain. She fell dead upon the spot without a groan.

This hideous murder accomplished, I set myself forthwith and with entire deliberation to the task of concealing the body. I knew that I could not remove it from the house, either by day or by night, without the risk of being observed by the neighbours. Many projects entered my mind. At one period I thought of cutting the corpse into minute fragments and destroying them by fire. At another I resolved to dig a grave for it in the floor of the cellar. Again, I deliberated about casting it in the well in the yard – about packing it in a box, as if merchandise, with the usual arrangements, and so getting a porter to take it from the house. Finally I hit upon what I considered a far better expedient than either of these. I determined to wall it up in the cellar – as the monks of the middle ages are recorded to have walled up their victims.

For a purpose such as this the cellar was well adapted. Its walls were loosely constructed and had lately been plastered throughout with a rough plaster, which the dampness of the atmosphere had prevented from hardening. Moreover, in one of the walls was a projection caused by a false chimney or fireplace, that had been filled up and made to resemble the rest of the cellar. I made no doubt that I could readily displace the bricks at this point, insert the corpse, and wall the whole up as before, so that no eye could detect anything suspicious.

And in this calculation I was not deceived. By means of a crow-bar I easily dislodged the bricks, and having carefully deposited the body against the inner wall, I propped it in that position, while with little trouble I re-laid the whole structure as it originally stood. Having procured mortar, sand, and hair with every possible precaution, I prepared a plaster which could not be distinguished from the old, and with this I very carefully went over the new brickwork. When I had finished I felt satisfied that all was right. The wall did not present the slightest appearance of having been disturbed. The rubbish on the floor was picked up with the minutest care. I looked around triumphantly, and said to myself – 'Here at last, then, my labour has not been in vain.'

My next step was to look for the beast which had been the cause of so much wretchedness, for I had at length firmly resolved to put it to death. Had I been able to meet with it at that moment there could have been no doubt of its fate, but it appeared that the crafty animal had been alarmed at the violence of my previous anger, and forebore to present itself in my present mood. It is impossible to describe or to imagine the deep, the blissful sense of relief which the absence of the detested creature occasioned in my bosom. It did not make its appearance during the night – and thus for one night at least since its introduction into the house I soundly and tranquilly slept; ay, *slept* even with the burden of murder upon my soul!

The second and the third day passed, and still my tormentor came not. Once again I breathed as a freeman. The monster, in terror, had fled the premises for ever! I should behold it no more! My happiness was supreme! The guilt of my dark deed disturbed me but little. Some few inquiries had been made, but these had been readily answered. Even a search had been instituted – but of course nothing was to be discovered. I looked upon my future felicity as secured.

Upon the fourth day of the assassination, a party of the police came very unexpectedly into the house, and proceeded again to make rigorous investigation of the premises. Secure, however, in the inscrutability of my place of concealment, I felt no embarrassment whatever. The officers bade me accompany them in their search. They left no nook or corner unexplored. At length, for the third or fourth time, they descended into the cellar. I quivered not in a muscle. My heart beat calmly as that of one who slumbers in innocence. I walked the cellar from end to end. I folded my arms upon my bosom, and

'*I had walled the monster up within the tomb*'

roamed easily to and fro. The police were thoroughly satisfied, and prepared to depart. The glee at my heart was too strong to be restrained. I burned to say if but one word by way of triumph, and to render doubly sure their assurance of my guiltlessness.

'Gentlemen,' I said at last, as the party ascended the steps, 'I delight to have allayed your suspicions. I wish you all health, and a little more courtesy. By-the-by, gentlemen, this – this is a very well constructed house.' (In the rabid desire to say something easily, I scarcely knew what I uttered at all.) – 'I may say an *excellently* well-constructed house. These walls – are you going, gentlemen? – these walls are solidly put together;' and here, through the mere frenzy of bravado, I rapped heavily with a cane which I held in my hand upon that very portion of the brickwork behind which stood the corpse of the wife of my bosom.

But may God shield and deliver me from the fangs of the arch-fiend! No sooner had the reverberation of my blows sunk into silence than I was answered by a voice from within the tomb! – by a cry, at first muffled and broken, like the sobbing of a child, and then quickly swelling into one long, loud, and continuous scream, utterly anomalous and inhuman – a howl – a wailing shriek, half of horror and half of triumph, such as might have arisen only out of hell, conjointly from the throats of the damned in their agony and of the demons that exult in their damnation.

Of my own thoughts it is folly to speak. Swooning, I staggered to the opposite wall. For one instant the party upon the stairs remained motionless, through extremity of terror and of awe. In the next a dozen stout arms were toiling at the wall. It fell bodily. The corpse, already greatly decayed and clotted with gore, stood erect before the eyes of the spectators. Upon its head, with red extended mouth and solitary eye of fire, sat the hideous beast whose craft had seduced me into murder, and whose informing voice had consigned me to the hangman. I had walled the monster up within the tomb!

Hop-Frog

I never knew anyone so keenly alive to a joke as the king was. He seemed to live only for joking. To tell a good story of the joke kind, and to tell it well, was the surest road to his favour. Thus it happened that his seven ministers were all noted for their accomplishments as jokers. They all took after the king, too, in being large, corpulent, oily men, as well as inimitable jokers. Whether people grow fat by joking, or whether there is something in fat itself which predisposes to a joke, I have never been quite able to determine, but certain it is that a lean joker is a *rara avis in terris*.

About the refinements, or, as he called them, the 'ghosts' of wit, the king troubled himself very little. He had an especial admiration for *breadth* in a jest, and would often put up with *length* for the sake of it. Over-niceties wearied him. He would have preferred Rabelais's 'Gargantua,' to the 'Zadig' of Voltaire; and upon the whole, practical jokes suited his taste far better than verbal ones.

At the date of my narrative, professing jesters had not altogether gone out of fashion at court. Several of the great Continental 'powers' still retained their 'fools,' who wore motley, with caps and bells, and who were expected to be always ready with sharp witticisms at a moment's notice, in consideration of the crumbs that fell from the royal table.

Our king, as a matter of course, retained his 'fool.' The fact is, he *required* something in the way of folly – if only to counterbalance the heavy wisdom of the seven wise men who were his ministers – not to mention himself.

His fool, or professional jester, was not *only* a fool, however. His value was trebled in the eyes of the king by the fact of his being also a dwarf and a cripple. Dwarfs were as common at court in those days as fools; and many monarchs would have found it difficult to get through their days (days are rather longer at court than elsewhere) without both a jester to laugh *with* and a dwarf to laugh *at*. But, as I have already observed, your jesters, in ninety-nine cases out of a hundred, are fat, round, and unwieldy – so that it was no small source of self-gratulation with our king that in Hop-Frog (this was a fool's name) he possessed a triplicate treasure in one person.

I believe the name 'Hop-Frog' was *not* that given to the dwarf by his sponsors at baptism, but it was conferred upon him by general consent of the seven ministers on account of his inability to walk as other men do. In fact, Hop-Frog could only get along by a sort of interjectional gait – something between a leap and a wriggle – a movement that afforded illimitable amusement, and of course consolation to the king, for (notwithstanding the protuberance of his stomach and a constitutional swelling of the head) the king, by his whole court, was accounted a capital figure.

But although Hop-Frog, through the distortion of his legs, could move only with great pain and difficulty along a road or floor, the prodigious muscular power which nature seemed to have bestowed upon his arms, by way of compensation for deficiency in the lower limbs, enabled him to perform many feats of wonderful dexterity where trees or ropes were in question, or anything else to climb. At such exercises he certainly much more resembled a squirrel, or a small monkey, than a frog.

I am not able to say with precision from what country Hop-Frog originally came. It was from some barbarous region, however, that no person ever heard of – a vast distance from the court of our king. Hop-Frog, and a young girl very little less dwarfish than himself (although of exquisite proportions and a marvellous dancer), had been forcibly carried off from their respective homes in adjoining provinces, and sent as presents to the king by one of his ever-victorious generals.

Under these circumstances, it is not to be wondered at that a close intimacy arose between the two little captives. Indeed, they soon became sworn friends, Hop-Frog, who, although he made a great deal or sport, was by no means popular, had it not in his power to render Trippetta many services; but *she*, on account of her grace and exquisite beauty (although a dwarf) was universally admired and petted, so she possessed much influence, and never failed to use it whenever she could for the benefit of Hop-Frog.

On some grand state occasion – I forget what – the king determined to have a masquerade; and whenever a masquerade or anything of that kind occurred at our court, then the talents of Hop-Frog and Trippetta were sure to be called in play. Hop-Frog, in especial was so inventive in the way of getting up pageants, suggesting novel characters, and arranging costume for masked balls, that nothing could be done, it seems, without his assistance.

The night appointed for the *fête* had arrived. A gorgeous hall had been fitted up, under Trippetta's eye, with every kind of device which could possibly give *éclat* to a masquerade. The whole court was in a fever of expectation. As for costumes and characters, it might well be supposed that everybody had come to a decision on such points. Many had made up their minds (as to what *rôles* they should assume) a week, or even a month, in advance; and, in fact, there was not a particle of indecision anywhere – except in the case of the king and his seven ministers. Why *they* hesitated I never could tell, unless they did it by way of a joke. More probably they found it difficult, on account of being so fat, to make up their minds. At all events, time flew; and as a last resource, they sent for Trippetta and Hop-Frog.

When the two little friends obeyed the summons of the king, they found him sitting at his wine with the seven members of his cabinet council; but the monarch appeared to be in a very ill humour. He knew that Hop-Frog was not fond of wine; for it excited the poor cripple almost to madness, and madness is no comfortable feeling. But the king loved his practical jokes, and took pleasure in forcing Hop-Frog to drink and (as the king called it) 'to be merry.'

'Come here, Hop-Frog,' said he, as the jester and his friend entered the room: 'swallow this bumper to the health of your absent friends (here Hop-Frog sighed), and then let us have the benefit of your invention. We want characters – *characters*, man – something novel – out of the way. We are wearied with this everlasting sameness. Come, drink! the wine will brighten your wits.'

Hop-Frog endeavoured as usual to get up a jest in reply to these advances from the king, but the effort was too much. It happened to be the poor dwarf's birthday, and the command to drink to his 'absent friends' forced the tears to his eyes. Many large, bitter drops fell into the goblet as he took it humbly, from the hand of the tyrant.

'Ah! ha! ha! ha!' roared the latter, as the dwarf reluctantly drained the beaker. 'See what a glass of good wine can do! Why, your eyes are shining already!'

Poor fellow! his large eyes *gleamed* rather than shone; for the effect of wine on his excitable brain was not more powerful than instantaneous. He placed the goblet nervously on the table, and looked round upon the company with a half-insane stare. They all seemed highly amused at the success of the king's *'joke.'*

'And now to business,' said the prime minister, a *very* fat man.

'Yes,' said the king; 'come, Hop-Frog, lend us your assistance. Characters, my fine fellow; we stand in need of characters – all of us – ha! ha! ha!' and as this was seriously meant for a joke, his laugh was chorused by the seven.

Hop-Frog also laughed, although feebly and somewhat vacantly.

'Come, come,' said the king, impatiently, 'have you nothing to suggest?'

'I am endeavouring to think of something *novel*,' replied the dwarf, abstractedly, for he was quite bewildered by the wine.

'Endeavouring!' cried the tyrant, fiercely; 'what do you mean by *that*? Ah, I perceive. You are sulky, and want more wine. Here, drink this!' and he poured out another goblet full and offered it to the cripple, who merely gazed at it, gasping for breath.

'Drink, I say!' shouted the monster, 'or by the fiends'——

The dwarf hesitated. The king grew purple with rage. The courtiers smirked. Trippetta, pale as a corpse, advanced to the monarch's seat, and, falling on her knees before him, implored him to spare her friend.

The tyrant regarded her for some moments in evident wonder at her audacity. He seemed quite at a loss what to do or say – how most becomingly to express his indignation. At last, without uttering a syllable, he pushed her violently from him and threw the contents of the brimming goblet in her face.

The poor girl got up as best she could, and, not daring even to sigh, resumed her position at the foot of the table.

There was a dead silence for about half-a-minute, during which the falling of a leaf or of a feather might have been heard. It was interrupted by a low, but harsh and protracted *grating* sound which seemed to come at once from every corner of the room.

'What – what – *what* are you making that noise for?' demanded the king, turning furiously to the dwarf.

The latter seemed to have recovered in great measure from his intoxication, and looking fixedly but quietly into the tyrant's face merely ejaculated:

'I – I? How could it have been me?'

'The sound appeared to come from without,' observed one of the courtiers. 'I fancy it was the parrot at the window, whetting his bill upon his cage-wires.'

'True,' replied the monarch, as if much relieved by the suggestion, 'but on the honour of a knight I could have sworn that it was the grinding of this vagabond's teeth.'

Hereupon the dwarf laughed (the king was too confirmed a joker to object to any one's laughing), and displayed a set of large, powerful, and very repulsive teeth. Moreover, he avowed his perfect willingness to swallow as much wine as desired. The monarch was pacified; and having drained another bumper with no very perceptible ill effect, Hop-Frog entered at once and with spirit into the plans for the masquerade.

'I cannot tell what was the association of ideas,' observed he, very tranquilly, and as if he had never tasted wine in his life, 'but *just after* your majesty had struck the girl and thrown the wine in her face – *just after* your majesty had done this, and while the parrot was making that odd noise outside the window, there came into my mind a capital diversion – one of my own country's frolics – often enacted among us at our masquerades, but here it will be new altogether. Unfortunately, however, it requires a company of eight persons, and'——

'Here we *are*!' cried the king laughing at his acute discovery of the coincidence: 'eight to a fraction – I and my seven ministers. Come! what is the diversion!'

'We call it,' replied the cripple, 'the Eight Chained Ourang-Outangs, and it really is excellent sport if well enacted.'

'*We* will enact it,' remarked the king, drawing himself up, and lowering his eyelids.

'The beauty of the game,' continued Hop-Frog, 'lies in the fright it occasions among the women.'

'Capital!' roared in chorus the monarch and his ministry.

'I will equip you as ourang-outangs,' proceeded the dwarf; 'leave all that to me. The resemblance shall be so striking, that the company of masqueraders will take you for real beasts – and of course they will be as much terrified as astonished.'

'Oh, this is exquisite!' exclaimed the king. 'Hop-Frog! I will make a man of you.'

'The chains are for the purpose of increasing the confusion by their jangling. You are supposed to have escaped *en masse*, from your keepers. Your majesty cannot conceive the *effect* produced at a masquerade by eight chained ourang-outangs, imagined to be real ones by most of the company; and rushing in with savage cries among the crowd of delicately and gorgeously habited men and women. The *contrast* is inimitable.'

'It *must* be,' said the king: and the council arose hurriedly (as it was growing late) to put in execution the scheme of Hop-Frog.

His mode of equipping the party as ourang-outangs was very simple, but effective enough for his purposes. The animals in question had, at the epoch of my story, very rarely been seen in any part of the civilised world; and as the imitations made by the dwarf were sufficiently beast-like, and more than sufficiently hideous, their truthfulness to nature was thus thought to be secured. The king and his ministers were first encased in tight fitting stockinet shirts and drawers. They were then saturated with tar. At this stage of the process some one of the party suggested feathers; but the suggestion was at once overruled by the dwarf, who soon convinced the eight, by ocular demonstration, that the hair of such a brute as the ourang-outang was much more efficiently represented by *flax*. A thick coating of the latter was accordingly plastered upon the coating of tar. A long chain was now procured. First, it was passed about the waist of the king, *and tied*; then about another of the party and also tied; then about all successively, in the same manner. When this chaining arrangement was complete, and the party stood as far apart from each other as possible, they formed a circle; and to make all things appear natural, Hop-Frog passed the residue of the chain, in two diameters, at right angles, across the circle, after the fashion adopted at the present day by those who capture Chimpanzees or other large apes in Borneo.

The grand saloon in which the masquerade was to take place was a circular room, very lofty, and receiving the light of the sun only through a single window at the top. At night (the season for which the apartment was especially designed) it was illuminated principally by a large chandelier, depending by a chain from the centre of the sky-light, and lowered or elevated by means of a counterbalance as usual, but (in order not to look unsightly) this latter passed outside the cupola and over the roof.

The arrangements of the room had been left to Trippetta's superintendence; but in some particulars, it seems, she had been guided by the calmer judgment of her friend the dwarf. At his suggestion it was that on this occasion the chandelier was removed. Its waxen drippings (which, in weather so warm, it was quite impossible to prevent) would have been seriously detrimental to the rich dresses of the guests, who, on account of the crowded state of the saloon, could not *all* be expected to keep from out its centre – that is to say, from under the chandelier. Additional sconces were set in various parts of the hall, out of the way; and a flambeau, emitting sweet odour, was placed in the right hand of each of the Caryatides that stood against the wall – some fifty or sixty altogether.

The eight ourang-outangs, taking Hop-Frog's advice, waited patiently until midnight (when the room was thoroughly filled with masqueraders) before making their appearance. No sooner had the clock ceased striking, however, than they rushed, or rather rolled in, all together – for the impediment of their chains caused most of the party to fall, and all to stumble as they entered.

The excitement among the masqueraders was prodigious, and filled the heart of the king with glee. As had been anticipated, there were not a few of the guests who supposed the ferocious-looking creatures to be beasts of *some* kind in reality, if not precisely ourang-outangs. Many of the women swooned with affright; and had not the king taken the precaution to exclude all weapons from the saloon, his party might soon have expiated their frolic in their blood. As it was, a general rush was made for the doors, but the king had ordered them to be locked immediately upon his entrance; and, at the dwarf's suggestion, the keys had been deposited with *him*.

While the tumult was at its height, and each masquerader attentive only to his own safety (for in fact, there was much *real* danger from the pressure of the excited crowd), the chain by which the chandelier ordinarily hung and which had been drawn up on its removal, might have been seen very gradually to descend, until its hooked extremity came within three feet of the floor.

Soon after this, the king and his seven friends, having reeled about the hall in all directions, found themselves at length in its centre, and, of course, in immediate contact with the chain. While they were thus situated, the dwarf, who had followed closely at their heels, inciting them to keep up the commotion, took hold of their own chain at the intersection of the two portions which crossed the circle diametrically and at right angles. Here, with the rapidity of thought, he inserted the hook from which the chandelier had been wont to depend; and in an instant, by some unseen agency, the chandelier-chain was drawn so far upward as to take the hook out of reach, and as an inevitable consequence, to drag the ourang-outangs together in close connection, and face to face.

The masqueraders by this time had recovered in some measure from their alarm, and, beginning to regard the whole matter as a well-contrived pleasantry, set up a loud shout of laughter at the predicament of the apes.

'Leave them to *me*!' now screamed Hop-Frog, his shrill voice making itself easily heard through all the din. 'Leave them to *me*. I fancy *I* know them. If I can only get a good look at them *I* can soon tell who they are!'

Here scrambling over the heads of the crowd, he managed to get to the wall, when, seizing a flambeau from one of the Caryatides, he returned, as he went, to the centre of the room, leaped with the agility of a monkey upon the king's head, and thence clambered a few feet up the chain, holding down the torch to examine the group of ourang-outangs, and still screaming '*I* shall soon find out who they are!'

And now, while the whole assembly (the apes included) were convulsed with laughter, the jester suddenly uttered a shrill whistle, when the chain flew violently up for about thirty feet, dragging with it the dismayed and struggling ourang-outangs, and leaving them suspended in mid-air between the sky-light and the floor. Hop-Frog, clinging to the chain as it rose, still maintained his relative position in respect to the eight maskers, and still (as if nothing were the matter) continued to thrust his torch down towards them as though endeavouring to discover who they were.

So thoroughly astonished were the whole company at this ascent, that a dead silence of about a minute's duration ensued. It was broken by just such a low harsh, *grating* sound, as had before attracted the attention of the king and his councillors when the former threw the wine in the face of Trippetta. But on the present occasion there could be no question as to *whence* the sound issued. It came from the fang-like teeth of the dwarf, who ground them and gnashed them as he foamed at the mouth, and glared with an expression of maniacal rage into the upturned countenances of the king and his seven companions.

'Ah, ha!' said at length the infuriated jester. 'Ah, ha! I begin to see who these people *are* now.' Here, pretending to scrutinise the king more closely, he held the flambeau to the flaxen coat which enveloped him, and which instantly burst into a sheet of vivid flame. In less than half-a-minute the whole eight ourang-outangs were blazing fiercely, amid the shrieks of the multitude who gazed at them from below, horror stricken, and without the power to render them the slightest assistance.

At length the flames, suddenly increasing in virulence, forced the jester to climb higher up the chain to be out of their reach, and as he made this movement the crowd again sank for a brief instant into silence. The dwarf seized his opportunity, and once more spoke:

'I now see *distinctly*,' he said, 'what manner of people these maskers are. They are a great king and his seven privy-councillors – a king who does not scruple to strike a defenceless girl, and his seven councillors who abet him in the outrage. As for myself, I am simply Hop-Frog, the jester, and *this is my last jest*.'

Owing to the high combustibility of both the flax and the tar to which it adhered, the dwarf had scarcely made an end of his brief speech before the work of vengeance was complete. The eight corpses swung in their chains, a fetid, blackened, hideous, and indistinguishable mass. The cripple hurled his torch at them, clambered leisurely to the ceiling, and disappeared through the sky-light.

It is supposed that Trippetta, stationed on the roof of the saloon, had been the accomplice of her friend in his fiery revenge, and that, together, they effected their escape to their own country, for neither was seen again.

The Sphinx

During the dread reign of the cholera in New York, I had accepted the invitation of a relative to spend a fortnight with him in the retirement of his *cottage orné* on the banks of the Hudson. We had here around us all the ordinary means of summer amusement; and what with rambling in the woods, sketching, boating, fishing, bathing, music, and books, we should have passed the time pleasantly enough, but for the fearful intelligence which reached us every morning from the populous city. Not a day elapsed which did not bring us news of the decease of some acquaintance. Then, as the fatality increased, we learned to expect daily the loss of some friend. At length we trembled at the approach of every messenger. The very air from the South seemed to us redolent with death. That palsying thought, indeed, took entire possession of my soul. I could neither speak, think, nor dream of anything else. My host was of a less excitable temperament, and although greatly depressed in spirits, exerted himself to sustain my own. His richly philosophical intellect was not at any time affected by unrealities. To the substances of terror he was sufficiently alive, but of its shadows he had no apprehension.

His endeavours to arouse me from the condition of abnormal gloom into which I had fallen were frustrated in great measure by certain volumes which I had found in his library. These were of a character to force into germination whatever seeds of hereditary superstition lay latent in my bosom. I had been reading these books without his knowledge, and thus he was often at a loss to account for the forcible impressions which had been made upon my fancy.

A favourite topic with me was the popular belief in omens – a belief which, at this one epoch of my life, I was almost seriously disposed to defend. On this subject we had long and animated discussions – he maintaining the utter groundlessness of faith in such matters – I contending that a popular sentiment arising with absolute spontaneity – that is to say, without apparent traces of suggestion – had in itself the unmistakable elements of truth, and was entitled to much respect.

The fact is, that soon after my arrival at the cottage, there had occurred to myself an incident so entirely inexplicable, and which had in it so much of the portentous character, that I might well have been excused for regarding it as an omen. It appalled, and at the same time so confounded and bewildered me, that many days elapsed before I could make up my mind to communicate the circumstance to my friend.

Near the close of an exceedingly warm day I was sitting, book in hand, at an open window, commanding, through a long vista of the river banks, a view of a distant hill, the face of which nearest my position had been denuded, by what is termed a landslide, of the principal portion of its trees. My thoughts had been long wandering from the volume before me to the gloom and desolation of the neighbouring city. Uplifting my eyes from the page, they fell upon the naked face of the hill, and upon an object – upon some living monster of hideous conformation, which very rapidly made its way from the summit to the bottom, disappearing finally in the dense forest below. As this creature came first in sight, I doubted my own sanity – or at least the evidence of my own eyes; and many minutes passed before I succeeded in convincing myself that I was neither mad nor in a dream. Yet when I describe the monster (which I distinctly saw, and calmly surveyed through the whole period of its progress), my readers, I fear, will feel more difficulty in being convinced of these points than even I did myself.

Estimating the size of the creature by comparison with the diameter of the large trees near which it passed – the few giants of the forest which had escaped the fury of the land-slide – I concluded it to be far larger than any ship of the line in existence. I say ship of the line, because the shape of the monster suggested the idea – the hull of one of our seventy-fours might convey a very tolerable conception of the general outline. The mouth of the animal was situated at the extremity of a proboscis some sixty or seventy feet in length, and about as thick as the body of an ordinary elephant. Near the root of this trunk was an immense quantity of black shaggy hair – more than could have been supplied by the coats of a score of buffaloes: and projecting from this hair downwardly and laterally, sprang two gleaming tusks not unlike those of the wild boar, but of infinitely greater dimensions. Extending forward, parallel with the proboscis, and on each side of it, was a gigantic staff, thirty or forty feet in length, formed seemingly of pure crystal, and in shape a perfect prism:– it reflected in the most gorgeous manner the rays of the declining sun. The trunk was fashióned like a wedge with the apex to the earth. From it there were outspread two pairs of wings – each wing nearly one hundred yards in length – one pair being placed above the other, and all thickly covered with metal scales, each scale apparently some ten or twelve feet in diameter. I observed that the upper and lower tiers of wings were connected by a strong chain. But the chief peculiarity of this horrible thing, was the representation of a *Death's Head*, which covered nearly the whole surface of its breast, and which was as accurately traced in glaring white, upon the dark ground of the body, as if it had been there carefully designed by an artist. While I regarded this terrific animal, and more especially the appearance on its breast, with a feeling of horror and awe – with a sentiment of forthcoming evil, which I found it impossible to quell by any effort of the reason, I perceived the huge jaws at the extremity of the proboscis, suddenly expand themselves, and from them there proceeded a sound so loud and so expressive of woe that it struck upon my nerves like a knell, and as the monster disappeared at the foot of the hill, I fell at once, fainting, to the floor.

Upon recovering, my first impulse of course was to inform my friend of what I had seen and heard – and I can scarcely explain what feeling of repugnance it was which in the end operated to prevent me.

At length, one evening, some three or four days after the occurrence, we were sitting together in the room in which I had seen the apparition – I occupying the same seat at the same window, and he lounging on a sofa near at hand. The association of the place and time impelled me to give him an account of the phenomenon. He heard me to the end – at first laughed heartily – and then lapsed into an excessively grave demeanour, as if my insanity was a thing beyond suspicion. At this instant I again had a distinct view of the monster – to which, with a shout of absolute terror, I now directed his attention. He looked eagerly – but maintained that he saw nothing – although I designated minutely the course of the creature, as it made its way down the naked face of the hill.

I was now immeasurably alarmed, for I considered the vision either as an omen of my death, or, worse, as the forerunner of an attack of mania. I threw myself passionately back in my chair, and for some moments buried my face in my hands. When I uncovered my eyes the apparition was no longer visible.

My host, however, had in some degree resumed the calmness of his demeanour, and questioned me very rigorously in respect to the conformation of the visionary creature. When I had fully satisfied him on this head he sighed deeply, as if relieved of some intolerable burden, and went on to talk, with what I thought a cruel calmness, of various points of speculative philosophy, which had heretofore formed subject of discussion between us. I remember his insisting very especially (among other things) upon the idea that the principal source of error in all human investigations lay in the liability of the understanding to under-rate or to over-value the importance of an object, through mere misadmeasurement of its propinquity. 'To estimate properly, for example,' he said, 'the influence to be exercised on mankind at large by the thorough diffusion of Democracy, the distance of the epoch at which such diffusion may possibly be accomplished, should not fail to form an item in the estimate. Yet can you tell me one writer on the subject of government who has ever thought this particular branch of the subject worthy of discussion at all?'

He here paused for a moment, stepped to a bookcase, and brought forth one of the ordinary synopses of natural history. Requesting me then to exchange seats with him, that he might the better distinguish the fine print of the volume, he took my arm-chair at the window, and, opening the book, resumed his discourse very much in the same tone as before.

'But for your exceeding minuteness,' he said, 'in describing the monster, I might never have had it in my power to demonstrate to you what it was. In the first place, let me read to you a school-boy account of the genus *Sphinx*, of the family, *Crepuscularia* of the order *Lepidoptera*, of the class of *Insecta* – or insects. The account runs thus:

'"Four membranous wings covered with little coloured scales of a metallic appearance; mouth forming a rolled proboscis, produced by an elongation of the jaws, upon the sides of which are found the rudiments of mandibles and downy palpi; the inferior wings retained to the superior by a stiff hair; antennæ in the form of an elongated club, prismatic: abdomen pointed. The Death's-headed Sphinx has occasioned much terror among the vulgar at times by the melancholy kind of cry which it utters, and the insignia of death which it wears upon its corslet."'

He here closed the book and leaned forward in the chair, placing himself accurately in the position which I had occupied at the moment of beholding 'the monster.'

'Ah, here it is!' he presently explained: 'it is re-ascending the face of the hill, and a very remarkable looking creature, I admit it to be. Still, it is by no means so large or so distant as you imagined it, for the fact is that, as it wriggles its way up this thread, which some spider has wrought along the window-sash, I find it to be about the sixteenth of an inch in its extreme length, and also about the sixteenth of an inch distant from the pupil of my eye.'

The Facts in the Case of M. Valdemar

Of course I shall not pretend to consider it any matter for wonder that the extraordinary case of M. Valdemar has excited discussion. It would have been a miracle had it not – especially under the circumstances. Through the desire of all parties concerned to keep the affair from the public, at least for the present, or until we had further opportunities for investigation – through our endeavours to effect this – a garbled or exaggerated account made its way into society, and became the source of many unpleasant misrepresentations; and, very naturally, of a great deal of disbelief.

It is now rendered necessary that I give the *facts* – as far as I comprehend them myself. They are, succinctly, these:

My attention for the last three years had been repeatedly drawn to the subject of Mesmerism: and about nine months ago it occurred to me, quite suddenly, that in the series of experiments made hitherto there had been a very remarkable and most unaccountable omission – no person had as yet been mesmerised *in articulo mortis*. It remained to be seen, first, whether, in such condition there existed in the patient any susceptibility to the magnetic influence: secondly, whether, if any existed, it was impaired or increased by the condition: thirdly, to what extent, or for how long a period, the encroachments of Death might be arrested by the process. There were other points to be ascertained, but these most excited my curiosity – the last in especial, from the immensely important character of its consequences.

In looking around me for some subject by whose means I might test these particulars, I was brought to think of my friend, M. Ernest Valdemar, the well-known compiler of the 'Bibliotheca Forensica,' and author (under the *nom de plume* of Issachar Marx) of the Polish versions of 'Wallenstein' and 'Gargantua.' M. Valdemar, who has resided principally at Harlem, N.Y., since the year 1839, is (or was) particularly noticeable for the extreme spareness of his person – his lower limbs much resembling those of John Randolph; and also for the whiteness of his whiskers, in violent contrast to the blackness of his hair – the latter, in consequence, being very generally mistaken for a wig. His temperament was markedly nervous, and rendered him a good subject for mesmeric experiment. On two or three occasions I had put him to sleep with little difficulty, but was disappointed in other results which his peculiar constitution had naturally led me to anticipate. His will was at no period positively or thoroughly under my control, and in regard to *clairvoyance*, I could accomplish with him nothing to be relied upon. I always attributed my failure at these points to the disordered state of his health. For some months previous to my becoming acquainted with him his physicans had declared him in a confirmed phthisis. It was his custom, indeed, to speak calmly of his approaching dissolution as of a matter neither to be avoided nor regretted.

When the ideas to which I have alluded first occurred to me, it was of course very natural that I should think of M. Valdemar. I knew the steady philosophy of the man too well to apprehend any scruples from *him*; and he had no relatives in America who would be likely to interfere. I spoke to him frankly upon the subject, and to my surprise his interest seemed vividly excited. I say to my surprise; for, although he had always yielded his person freely to my experiments, he had never before given me any tokens of sympathy with what I did. His disease was of that character which would admit of exact calculation in respect to the epoch of its termination in death; and it was finally arranged between us that he would send for me about twenty-four hours before the period announced by his physicians as that of his decease.

It is now rather more than seven months since I received, from M. Valdemar himself, the subjoined note:

MY DEAR P——

You may as well come *now*. D—— and F—— are agreed that I cannot hold out beyond to-morrow midnight; and I think they have hit the time very nearly.

VALDEMAR.

I received this note within half-an-hour after it was written, and in fifteen minutes more I was in the dying man's chamber. I had not seen him for ten days, and was appalled by the fearful alteration which the brief interval had wrought in him. His face wore a leaden hue; the eyes were utterly lustreless; and the emaciation was so extreme that the skin had been broken through by the cheek-bones. His expectoration was excessive. The pulse was barely perceptible. He retained, nevertheless, in a very remarkable manner, both his mental power and a certain degree of physical strength. He spoke with distinctness – took some palliative medicines without aid – and, when I entered the room, was occupied in pencilling memoranda in a pocket-book. He was propped up in the bed by pillows. Doctors D—— and F—— were in attendance.

After pressing Valdemar's hand, I took these gentlemen aside, and obtained from them a minute account of the patient's condition. The left lung had been for eighteen months in a semiosseous or cartilaginous state, and was of course entirely useless for all purposes of vitality. The right, in its upper portion, was also partially if not thoroughly ossified, while the lower region was merely a mass of purulent tubercles running one into another. Several extensive perforations existed, and at one point permanent adhesion to the ribs had taken place. These appearances in the right lobe were of comparatively recent date. The ossification had proceeded with very unusual rapidity; no sign of it had been discovered a month before, and the adhesion had only been observed during the three previous days. Independently of the phthisis, the patient was suspected of aneurism of the aorta; but on this point the osseous symptoms rendered an exact diagnosis impossible. It was the opinion of both physicians that M. Valdemar would die about midnight on the morrow (Sunday). It was then seven o'clock on Saturday evening.

On quitting the invalid's bed-side to hold conversation with myself, Doctors D—— and F—— had bidden him a final farewell. It had not been their intention to return; but, at my request, they agreed to look in upon the patient about ten the next night.

When they had gone, I spoke freely with M. Valdemar on the subject of his approaching dissolution, as well as, more particularly, of the experiment proposed. He still professed himself quite willing and even anxious to have it made, and urged me to commence it at once. A male and a female nurse were in attendance; but I did not feel myself altogether at liberty to engage in a task of this character with no more reliable witnesses than these people, in case of sudden accident, might prove. I therefore postponed operations until about eight the next night, when the arrival of a medical student, with whom I had some acquaintance (Mr. Theodore L——l), relieved me from farther embarrassment. It had been my design, originally, to wait for the physicians; but I was induced to proceed, first, by the urgent entreaties of M. Valdemar, and secondly, by my conviction that I had not a moment to lose, as he was evidently sinking fast.

Mr. L——l was so kind as to accede to my desire that he would take notes of all that occurred; and it is from his memoranda that what I now have to relate is, for the most part, either condensed or copied *verbatim*.

It wanted about five minutes of eight when, taking the patient's hand, I begged him to state, as distinctly as he could, to Mr. L——l, whether he (M. Valdemar) was entirely willing that I should make the experiment of mesmerising him in his then condition.

He replied feebly, yet quite audibly, 'Yes, I wish to be mesmerised' – adding immediately afterwards, 'I fear you have deferred it too long.'

While he spoke thus, I commenced the passes which I had already found most effectual in subduing him. He was evidently influenced with the first lateral stroke of my hand across his forehead; but although I exerted all my powers, no farther perceptible effect was induced until some minutes after ten o'clock, when Doctors D—— and F—— called, according to appointment. I explained to them in a few words what I designed, and as they opposed no objection, saying that the patient was already in the death agony, I proceeded without hesitation – exchanging, however, the lateral passes for downward ones, and directing my gaze entirely into the right eye of the sufferer.

By this time his pulse was imperceptible and his breathing was stertorous, and at intervals of half-a-minute.   .

This condition was nearly unaltered for a quarter of an hour. At the expiration of this period, however, a natural although a very deep sigh escaped the bosom of the dying man, and the stertorous breathing ceased – that is to say, its stertorousness was no longer apparent; the intervals were undiminished. The patient's extremities were of an icy coldness.

At five minutes before eleven I perceived unequivocal signs of the mesmeric influence. The glassy roll of the eye was changed for that expression of uneasy *inward* examination which is never seen except in cases of sleep-walking, and which it is quite impossible to mistake. With a few rapid lateral passes I made the lids quiver, as in incipient sleep, and with a few more I closed them altogether. I was not satisfied, however, with this, but continued the manipulations vigorously, and with the fullest exertion of the will, until I had completely stiffened the limbs of the slumberer, after placing them in a seemingly easy position. The legs were at full length; the arms were nearly so, and reposed on the bed at a moderate distance from the loins. The head was very slightly elevated.

When I had accomplished this it was fully midnight, and I requested the gentlemen present to examine M. Valdemar's condition. After a few experiments, they admitted him to be in an unusually perfect state of mesmeric trance. The curiosity of both the physicians was greatly excited. Dr. D—— resolved at once to remain with the patient all night, while Dr. F—— took leave with a promise to return at daybreak. Mr. L——l and the nurses remained.

We left M. Valdemar entirely undisturbed until about three o'clock in the morning, when I approached him and found him in precisely the same condition as when Dr. F—— went away – that is to say, he lay in the same position; the pulse was imperceptible; the breathing was gentle (scarcely noticeable, unless through the application of a mirror to the lips); the eyes were closed naturally; and the limbs were as rigid and as cold as marble. Still, the general appearance was certainly not that of death.

As I approached M. Valdemar I made a kind of half effort to influence his right arm into pursuit of my own, as I passed the latter gently to and fro above his person. In such experiments with this patient, I had never perfectly succeeded before, and assuredly I had little thought of succeeding now; but, to my astonishment, his arm very readily, although feebly, followed every direction I assigned it with mine. I determined to hazard a few words of conversation.

'M. Valdemar,' I said, 'are you asleep?' He made no answer, but I perceived a tremor about the lips, and was thus induced to repeat the question, again and again. At this third repetition, his whole frame was agitated by a very slight shivering: the eyelids unclosed themselves so far as to display a white line of a ball; the lips moved sluggishly, and from between them, in a barely audible whisper, issued the words:

'Yes; – asleep now. Do not wake me! – let me die so!'

I here felt the limbs, and found them as rigid as ever. The right arm, as before, obeyed the direction of my hand. I questioned the sleep-walker again.

'Do you still feel pain in the breast, M. Valdemar?'

The answer now was immediate, but even less audible than before: 'No pain – I am dying.'

I did not think it advisable to disturb him farther just then, and nothing more was said or done until the arrival of Dr. F——, who came a little before sunrise, and expressed unbounded astonishment at finding the patient still alive. After feeling the pulse and applying a mirror to the lips he requested me to speak to the sleep-walker again. I did so, saying:

'M. Valdemar, do you still sleep?'

As before, some minutes elapsed ere a reply was made; and during the interval the dying man seemed to be collecting his energies to speak. At my fourth repetition of the question, he said very faintly, almost inaudibly:

'Yes still asleep – dying.'

It was now the opinion, or rather the wish, of the physicians, that M. Valdemar, should be suffered to remain undisturbed in his present apparently tranquil condition, until death should supervene; and this, it was generally agreed, must now take place within a few minutes. I concluded, however, to speak to him once more, and merely repeated my previous question.

While I spoke, there came a marked change over the countenance of the sleep–walker. The eyes rolled themselves slowly open, the pupils disappearing upwardly; the skin generally assumed a cadaverous hue, resembling not so much parchment as white paper: and the circular hectic spots, which hitherto had been strongly defined in the centre of each cheek, *went out* at once. I use this expression because the suddenness of their departure put me in mind of nothing so much as the extinguishment of a candle by a puff of the breath. The upper lip, at the same time, writhed itself away from the teeth, which it had previously covered completely; while the lower jaw fell with an audible jerk, leaving the mouth widely extended, and disclosing in full view the swollen and blackened tongue. I presume that no member of the party then present had been unaccustomed to death-bed horrors; but so hideous beyond conception was the appearance of M. Valdemar at this moment, that there was a general shrinking back from the region of the bed.

I now feel that I have reached a point of this narrative at which every reader will be startled into positive disbelief. It is my business, however, simply to proceed.

There was no longer the faintest sign of vitality in M. Valdemar; and, concluding him to be dead, we were consigning him to the charge of the nurses, when a strong vibratory motion was observable in the tongue. This continued for perhaps a minute. At the expiration of this period, there issued from the distended and motionless jaw a voice – such as it would be madness in me to attempt describing. There are, indeed, two or three epithets which might be considered as applicable to it in part; I might say, for example, that the sound was harsh, and broken and hollow; but the hideous whole is indescribable, for the simple reason that no similar sounds have ever jarred upon the ear of humanity. There were two particulars, nevertheless, which I thought then, and still think, might fairly be stated as characteristic of the intonation – as well adapted to convey some idea of its unearthly peculiarity. In the first place, the voice seemed to reach our ears – at least mine – from a vast distance, or from some deep cavern within the earth. In the second place, it impressed me (I fear, indeed, that it will be impossible to make myself comprehended) as gelatinous or glutinous matters impress the sense of touch.

I have spoken both of 'sound' and of 'voice.' I mean to say that the sound was one of distinct – of even wonderfully, thrillingly, distinct syllabification. M. Valdemar *spoke* – obviously in reply to the question I had propounded to him a few minutes before. I had asked him, it will be remembered, if he still slept. He now said:

'Yes; – no; – I *have been sleeping* – and now – now – *I am dead.*'

No person present even affected to deny, or attempted to repress, the unutterable, shuddering horror which these few words thus uttered, were so well calculated to convey, Mr. L——l (the student) swooned. The nurses immediately left the chamber, and could not be induced to return. My own impressions I would not pretend to render intelligible to the reader. For nearly an hour we busied ourselves silently – without the utterance of a word – in endeavours to revive Mr. L——l. When he came to himself we addressed ourselves again to an investigation of M. Valdemar's condition.

It remained in all respects as I have last described it, with the exception that the mirror no longer afforded evidence of respiration. An attempt to draw blood from the arm failed. I should mention, too, that this limb was no farther subject to my will. I endeavoured in vain to make it follow the direction of my hand. The only real indication, indeed, of the mesmeric influence was now found in the vibratory movement of the tongue, whenever I addressed M. Valdemar a question. He seemed to be making an effort to reply, but had no longer sufficient volition. To queries put to him by any other person than myself he seemed utterly insensible – although I endeavoured to place each member of the company in mesmeric *rapport* with him. I believe that I have now related all that is necessary to an understanding of the sleep-walker's state at this epoch. Other nurses were procured; and at ten o'clock I left the house in company with the two physicians and Mr. L——l.

In the afternoon we all called again to see the patient. His condition remained precisely the same. We had now some discussion as to the propriety and feasibility of awakening him; but we had little difficulty in agreeing that no good purpose would be served by so doing. It was evident, that, so far, death (or what is usually termed death) had been arrested by the mesmeric process. It seemed clear to us all that to awaken M. Valdemar would be merely to insure his instant, or at least his speedy dissolution.

From this period until the close of last week – *an interval of nearly seven months* – we continued to make daily calls at M. Valdemar's house, accompanied now and then by medical and other friends. All this time the sleep-walker remained *exactly* as I have last described him. The nurses' attentions were continual.

It was on Friday last that we finally resolved to make the experiment of awakening, or attempting to awaken him; and it is the (perhaps) unfortunate result of this latter experiment which has given rise to so much discussion in private circles – to so much of what I cannot help thinking unwarranted popular feeling.

For the purpose of relieving M. Valdemar from the mesmeric trance, I made use of the customary passes. These, for a time, were unsuccessful. The first indication of revival was afforded by a partial descent of the iris. It was observed, as especially remarkable, that this lowering of the pupil was accompanied by the profuse out-flowing of a yellowish ichor (from beneath the lids) of a pungent and highly offensive odour.

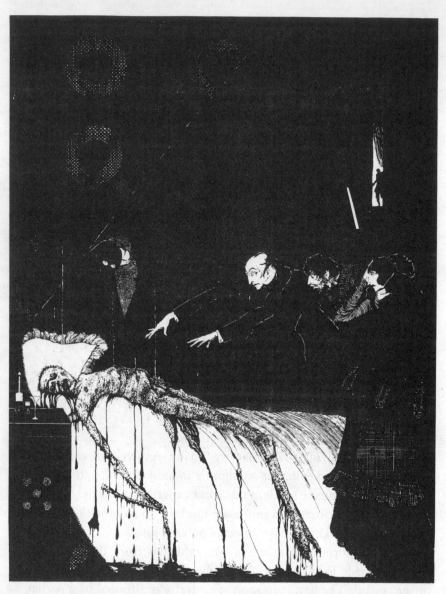

Upon the bed lay a nearly liquid mass of loathsome – of detestable putridity

It was now suggested that I should attempt to influence the patient's arm, as heretofore. I made the attempt and failed. Dr. F——— then intimated a desire to have me put a question. I did so, as follows:

'M. Valdemar, can you explain to us what are your feelings or wishes now?'

There was an instant return of the hectic circles on the cheeks: the tongue quivered, or rather rolled violently in the mouth (although the jaws and lips remained rigid as before); and at length the same hideous voice which I have already described broke forth:

'For God's sake! – quick! – quick! – put me to sleep – or, quick! – waken me! – quick! – *I say to you that I am dead*!'

I was thoroughly unnerved, and for an instant remained undecided what to do. At first I made an endeavour to recompose the patient; but, failing in this through total abeyance of the will, I retraced my steps and as earnestly struggled to awaken him. In this attempt I soon saw that I should be successful – or at least I soon fancied that my success would be complete; and I am sure that all in the room were prepared to see the patient awaken.

For what really occurred, however, it is quite impossible that any human being could have been prepared.

As I rapidly made the mesmeric passes, amid ejaculations of 'dead! dead!' absolutely *bursting* from the tongue and not from the lips of the sufferer, his whole frame at once – within the space of a single minute, or even less, shrunk – crumbled, absolutely *rotted* away beneath my hands. Upon the bed, before the whole company, there lay a nearly liquid mass of loathsome – of detestable putrescence.

Bon-Bon

Quand un bon vin meuble mon estomac,
Je suis plus savant que Balzac,
Plus sage que Pibrac;
Mon bras seul faisant l'attaque
De la nation Cossaque;
La mettroit au sac;
De Charon je passerois le lac
En dormant dans son bac;
J'irois au fier Eac,
Sans que mon cœur fit tic ni tac,
Presenter du tabac.

French Vaudeville.

That Pierre Bon-Bon was a *restaurateur* of uncommon qualifications, no man who, during the reign of ——, frequented the little Café in the *cul-de-sac* Le Febvre at Rouen, will, I imagine, feel himself at liberty to dispute. That Pierre Bon-Bon was, in an equal degree, skilled in the philosophy of that period is, I presume, still more especially undeniable. His *pâtés à la fois* were beyond doubt immaculate; but what pen can do justice to his essays *sur la Nature* – his thoughts *sur l'Ame* – his observations *sur l'Esprit*? If his *omelettes* – if his *fricandeaux* were inestimable, what *littérateur* of that day would not have given twice as much for an '*Idée de Bon-Bon*' as for all the trash of all the '*Idées*' of all the rest of the *savants*? Bon-Bon had ransacked libraries which no other man had ransacked – had read more than any other would have entertained a notion of reading – had understood more than any other would have conceived the possibility of understanding; and although, while he flourished, there were not wanting some authors at Rouen to assert 'that his *dicta* evinced neither the purity of the Academy, nor the depth of the Lyceum' – although, mark me, his doctrines were by no means very generally comprehended, still it did not follow that they were difficult of comprehension. It was, I think, on account of their self-evidency that many persons were led to consider them abstruse. It is to Bon-Bon – but let this go no farther – it is to Bon-Bon that Kant himself is mainly indebted for his meta-physics. The former, was indeed not a Platonist, nor strictly speaking an Aristotelian – nor did he, like the modern Leibnitz, waste those precious hours which might be employed in the invention of a *fricasée*, or *facili gradu*, the analysis of a sensation, in frivolous attempts at reconciling the obstinate oils and waters of ethical discussion. Not at all. Bon-Bon was Ionic – Bon-Bon was equally Italic. He reasoned *a priori* – reasoned also *a posteriori*. His ideas were innate – or otherwise. He believed in George of Trebizond – he believed in Bossarion. Bon-Bon was emphatically a – Bon-Bonist.

I have spoken of the philosopher in his capacity of *restaurateur*. I would not, however, have any friend of mine imagine that, in fulfilling his hereditary duties in that line, our hero wanted a proper estimation of their dignity and importance. Far from it. It was impossible to say in which branch of his profession he took the greater pride. In his opinion the powers of the intellect held intimate connection with the capabilities of the stomach. I am not sure, indeed, that he greatly disagreed with the Chinese, who hold that the soul lies in the abdomen. The Greeks, at all events, were right, he thought, who employed the same word for the mind and the diaphragm.* By this I do not mean to insinuate a charge of gluttony, or indeed any other serious charge to the prejudice of the metaphysician. If Pierre Bon-

* φρενες.

Bon had his failings – and what great man has not a thousand? – if
Pierre Bon-Bon, I say, had his failings they were failings of very little
importance – faults indeed which, in other tempers, have often been
looked upon rather in the light of virtues. As regards one of these
foibles, I should not even have mentioned it in this history but for the
remarkable prominency – the extreme *alto rilievo* – in which it jutted
out from the plane of his general disposition. – He could never let slip
an opportunity of making a bargain.

Not that he was avaricious – no. It was by no means necessary to
the satisfaction of the philosopher that the bargain should be to his
own proper advantage. Provided a trade could be effected – a trade of
any kind, upon any terms, or under any circumstances – a triumphant
smile was seen for many days thereafter to enlighten his countenance,
and a knowing wink of the eye to give evidence of his sagacity.

At any epoch it would not be very wonderful if a humour so
peculiar as the one I have just mentioned should elicit attention and
remark. At the epoch of our narrative, had this peculiarity *not* attracted
observation, there would have been room for wonder indeed. It was
soon reported that, upon all occasions of the kind, the smile of Bon-
Bon was wont to differ widely from the downright grin with which he
would laugh at his own jokes or welcome an acquaintance. Hints were
thrown out of an exciting nature, stories were told of perilous bargains
made in a hurry and repented of at leisure; and instances were
adduced of unaccountable capacities, vague longings, and unnatural
inclinations implanted by the author of all evil for wise purposes of his
own.

The philosopher had other weaknesses, but they are scarcely
worthy our serious examination. For example, there are few men of
extraordinary profundity who are found wanting in an inclination for
the bottle. Whether this inclination be an exciting cause or rather a
valid proof of such profundity, it is a nice thing to say. Bon-Bon, as far
as I can learn, did not think the subject adapted to minute investigation – nor do I. Yet in the indulgence of a propensity so truly
classical, it is not to be supposed that the *restaurateur* would lose sight
of that intuitive discrimination which was wont to characterise, at one

and the same time, his *essais* and his *omelettes*. In his seclusions the Vin de Bourgogne had its allotted hour, and there were appropriate moments for the Côtes du Rhone. With him Sauterne was to Medoc what Catullus was to Homer. He would sport with a syllogism in sipping St. Peray, but unravel an argument over Clos Vougeot, and upset a theory in a torrent of Chambertin. Well had it been if the same quick sense of propriety had attended him in the peddling propensity to which I have formerly alluded – but this was by no means the case. Indeed, to say the truth, *that* trait of mind in the philosophic Bon-Bon *did* begin at length to assume a character of strange intensity and mysticism, and appeared deeply tinctured with the *diablerie* of his favourite German studies.

To enter the little *Café* in the *Cul-de-Sac* Le Febvre was, at the period of our tale, to enter the *sanctum* of a man of genius. Bon-Bon was a man of genius. There was not a *sous-cuisinier* in Rouen who could not have told you that Bon-Bon was a man of genius. His very cat knew it, and forbore to whisk her tail in the presence of the man of genius. His large water-dog was acquainted with the fact, and upon the approach of his master betrayed his sense of inferiority by a sanctity of deportment, a debasement of the ears, and a dropping of the lower jaw not altogether unworthy of a dog. It is, however, true that much of this habitual respect might have been attributed to the personal appearance of the metaphysician. A distinguished exterior will, I am constrained to say, have its weight even with a beast; and I am willing to allow much in the outward man of the *restaurateur* calculated to impress the imagination of the quadruped. There is a peculiar majesty about the atmosphere of the little great – if I may be permitted so equivocal an expression – which mere physical bulk alone will be found at all times inefficient in creating. If, however, Bon-Bon was barely three feet in height, and if his head was diminutively small, still it was impossible to behold the rotundity of his stomach without a sense of magnificence nearly bordering upon the sublime. In its size both dogs and men must have seen a type of his acquirements – in its immensity a fitting habitation for his immortal soul.

I might here, if it so pleased me, dilate upon the matter of

habiliment, and other mere circumstances of the external metaphysician. I might hint that the hair of our hero was worn short, combed
smoothly over his forehead, and surmounted by a conical-shaped
white flannel cap and tassels – that his pea-green jerkin was not after
the fashion of those worn by the common class of *restaurateurs* at that
day – that the sleeves were something fuller than the reigning costume
permitted – that the cuffs were turned up, not, as usual in that
barbarous period, with cloth of the same quality and colour as the
garment, but faced in a more fanciful manner with the particoloured
velvet of Genoa – that his slippers were of a bright purple, curiously
filigreed, and might have been manufactured in Japan but for the
exquisite pointing of the toes and the brilliant tints of the binding and
embroidery – that his breeches were of the yellow satin-like material
called *amiable* – that his sky-blue cloak, resembling in form a dressing-
wrapper, and richly bestudded all over with crimson devices, floated
cavalierly upon his shoulders like a mist of the morning – and that his
tout ensemble gave rise to the remarkable words of Benevenuta, the
Improvisatrice of Florence, 'that it was difficult to say whether Pierre
Bon-Bon was indeed a bird of Paradise, or the rather a very Paradise of
perfection.' I might, I say, expatiate upon all these points if I pleased;
but I forbear: merely personal details may be left to historical
novelists; they are beneath the moral dignity of matter-of-fact.

I have said that 'to enter the *Café* in the *Cul-de-Sac* Le Febvre was
to enter the *sanctum* of a man of genius' – but then it was only the man
of genius who could duly estimate the merits of the *sanctum*. A sign,
consisting of a vast folio, swung before the entrance. On one side of the
volume was painted a bottle; on the reverse a *pâté*. On the back were
visible in large letters *Œuvres de Bon-Bon*. Thus was delicately
shadowed forth the twofold occupation of the proprietor.

Upon stepping over the threshold, the whole interior of the
building presented itself to view. A long, low-pitched room, of antique
construction, was indeed all the accommodation afforded by the *Café*.
In a corner of the apartment stood the bed of the metaphysician. An
array of curtains, together with a canopy *à la Greque*, gave it an air at
once classic and comfortable. In the corner diagonally opposite

appeared, in direct family communion, the properties of the kitchen and the *bibliothèque*. A dish of polemics stood peacefully upon the dresser. Here lay an oven-full of the latest ethics, there a kettle of duodecimo *mélanges*. Volumes of German morality were hand-and-glove with the gridiron – a toasting-fork might be discovered by the side of Eusebius – Plato reclined at his ease in the frying-pan – and contemporary manuscripts were filed away upon the spit.

In other respects the *Café de Bon-Bon* might be said to differ little from the usual *restaurants* of the period. A large fireplace yawned opposite the door. On the right of the fireplace an open cupboard displayed a formidable array of labelled bottles.

It was here, about twelve o'clock one night during the severe winter of ——, that Pierre Bon-Bon, after having listened some time to the comments of his neighbours upon his singular propensity – that Pierre Bon-Bon, I say, having turned them all out of his house, locked the door upon them with an oath, and betook himself in no very pacific mood to the comforts of a leather-bottomed arm-chair and a fire of blazing faggots.

It was one of those terrific nights which are only met with once or twice during a century. It snowed fiercely, and the house tottered to its centre with the floods of wind that, rushing through the crannies of the wall, and pouring impetuously down the chimney, shook awfully the curtains of the philosopher's bed, and disorganised the economy of his *pâté* pans and papers. The huge folio sign that swung without, exposed to the fury of the tempest, creaked ominously, and gave out a moaning sound from its stanchions of solid oak.

It was in no placid temper, I say, that the metaphysician drew up his chair to its customary station by the hearth. Many circumstances of a perplexing nature had occurred during the day to disturb the serenity of his meditations. In attempting *des œufs à la Princesse* he had unfortunately perpetrated an *omelette à la Reine*; the discovery of a principle in ethics had been frustrated by the overturning of a stew; and last, not least, he had been thwarted in one of those admirable bargains which he at all times took such especial delight in bringing to a successful termination. But in the chafing of his mind at these unaccountable vicissitudes there did not fail to be mingled some degree of that nervous anxiety which the fury of a boisterous night is so well calculated to produce. Whistling to his more immediate vicinity the large black water-dog we have spoken of before, and settling himself uneasily in his chair, he could not help casting a wary and unquiet eye towards those distant recesses of the apartment whose inexorable shadows not even the red firelight itself could more than partially succeed in overcoming. Having completed a scrutiny whose exact purpose was perhaps unintelligible to himself, he drew close to his seat a small table covered with books and papers, and soon became absorbed in the task of re-touching a voluminous manuscript intended for publication on the morrow.

He had been thus occupied for some minutes, when 'I am in no hurry, Monsieur Bon-Bon,' suddenly whispered a whining voice in the apartment.

'The devil!' ejaculated our hero, starting to his feet, overturning the table at his side, and staring around him in astonishment.

'Very true,' calmly replied the voice.

'Very true! – what is very true? – how came you here?' vociferated the metaphysician, as his eye fell upon something which lay stretched at full length upon the bed.

'I was saying,' said the intruder, without attending to the interrogatories, 'I was saying that I am not at all pushed for time – that the business upon which I took the liberty of calling is of no pressing importance – in short, that I can very well wait until you have finished your Exposition.'

'My Exposition! – there now! – how do *you* know? – how came *you* to understand that I was writing an Exposition – good God!'

'Hush!' replied the figure, in a shrill undertone; and, arising quickly from the bed, he made a single step towards our hero, while an iron lamp that depended overhead swung convulsively back from his approach.

The philosopher's amazement did not prevent a narrow scrutiny of the stranger's dress and appearance. The outline of his figure, exceedingly lean, but much above the common height, were rendered minutely distinct by means of a faded suit of black cloth which fitted tight to the skin, but was otherwise cut very much in the style of a century ago. These garments had evidently been intended for a much shorter person than their present owner. His ankles and wrists were left naked for several inches. In his shoes, however, a pair of very brilliant buckles gave the lie to the extreme poverty implied by the other portions of his dress. His head was bare, and entirely bald, with the exception of the hinder-part, from which depended a *queue* of considerable length. A pair of green spectacles, with side glasses, protected his eyes from the influence of the light, and at the same time prevented our hero from ascertaining either their colour or their conformation. About the entire person there was no evidence of a shirt; but a white cravat, of filthy appearance, was tied with extreme precision around the throat, and the ends, hanging down formally side by side, gave (although I dare say unintentionally) the idea of an ecclesiastic. Indeed many other points both in his appearance and demeanour might have very well sustained a conception of that nature. Over his left ear he carried, after the fashion of a modern clerk, an instrument resembling the *stylus* of the ancients. In a breastpocket of his coat appeared conspicuously a small black volume fastened with clasps of steel. This book, whether accidentally or not, was so turned outwardly from the person as to discover the words '*Rituel Catholique*' in white letters upon the back. His entire physiognomy was interestingly saturnine – even cadaverously pale. The forehead was lofty, and deeply furrowed with the ridges of contemplation. The corners of the mouth were drawn down into an expression of the most submissive humility. There was also a clasping of the hands, as he stepped towards our hero – a deep sigh – and altogether a look of such utter sanctity as could not have failed to be unequivocally prepossessing. Every shadow of anger faded from the countenance of the metaphysician, as, having completed a satisfactory survey of his visitor's person, he shook him cordially by the hand, and conducted him to a seat.

There would, however, be a radical error in attributing this instantaneous transition of feeling in the philosopher, to any one of those causes which might naturally be supposed to have had an influence. Indeed, Pierre Bon-Bon, from what I have been able to understand of his disposition, was of all men the least likely to be imposed upon by any speciousness of exterior deportment. It was impossible that so accurate an observer of men and things should have failed to discover, upon the moment, the real character of the personage who had thus intruded upon his hospitality. To say no more, the conformation of his visitor's feet was sufficiently remarkable – he maintained lightly upon his head an inordinately tall hat – there was a tremulous swelling about the hinder part of his breeches – and the vibration of his coat-tail was a palpable fact. Judge, then, with what feelings of satisfaction our hero found himself thrown thus at once into the society of a person for whom he had at all times entertained the most unqualified respect. He was, however, too much of the diplomatist to let escape him any intimation of his suspicions in regard to the true state of affairs. It was not his cue to appear at all conscious of the high honour he thus unexpectedly enjoyed; but, by leading his guest into conversation, to elicit some important ethical ideas, which might, in obtaining a place in his contemplated publication, enlighten the human race, and at the same time immortalise himself – ideas which, I should have added, his visitor's great age, and well-known proficiency in the science of morals, might very well have enabled him to afford.

Actuated by these enlightened views, our hero bade the gentleman sit down, while he himself took occasion to throw some faggots upon the fire, and place upon the now re-established table some bottles of *Mousseux*. Having quickly completed these operations, he drew his chair *vis-à-vis* to his companion's, and waited until the latter should open the conversation. But plans, even the most skilfully matured, are often thwarted in the outset of their application – and the *restaurateur* found himself *nonplussed* by the very first words of his visitor's speech.

'I see you know me, Bon-Bon,' said he: 'ha! ha! ha! – he! he! he! – hi! hi! hi! – ho! ho! ho! – hu! hu! hu!' – and the devil, dropping at once the sanctity of his demeanour, opened to its fullest extent a mouth from ear to ear, so as to display a set of jagged and fang-like teeth; and throwing back his head, laughed long, loudly, wickedly, and uproariously, while the black dog, crouching down upon his haunches, joined lustily in the chorus, and the tabby cat, flying off at a tangent, stood up on end, and shrieked in the fartherest corner of the apartment.

Not so the philosopher: he was too much a man of the world either to laugh like the dog, or by shrieks to betray the indecorous trepidation of the cat. It must be confessed he felt a little astonishment to see the white letters which formed the worlds '*Rituel Catholique*' on the book in his guest's pocket, momently changing both their colour and their import, and in a few seconds, in place of the original title, the words, '*Registre des Condamnés*' blaze forth in characters of red. This startling circumstance, when Bon-Bon replied to his visitor's remark, imparted to his manner an air of embarrassment which probably might not otherwise have been observed.

'Why, sir,' said the philosopher, 'why sir, to speak sincerely – I believe you are – upon my word – the d—dest – that is to say, I think – I imagine – I *have* some faint – some *very* faint idea – of the remarkable honour'——

'Oh! – ah! – yes! – very well!' interrupted his Majesty; 'say no more – I see how it is.' And hereupon, taking off his green spectacles, he wiped the glasses carefully with the sleeve of his coat, and deposited them in his pocket.

If Bon-Bon had been astonished at the incident of the book, his amazement was now much increased by the spectacle which here presented itself to view. In raising his eyes, with a strong feeling of curiosity, to ascertain the colour of his guest's, he found them by no means black, as he had anticipated – nor grey, as might have been imagined – nor yet hazel nor blue – nor indeed yellow nor red – nor purple – nor white – nor green – nor any other colour in the heavens above, or in the earth beneath, or in the waters under the earth. In short, Pierre Bon-Bon not only saw plainly that his Majesty had no eyes whatsoever, but could discover no indications of their having existed at any previous period – for the space where eyes should naturally have been, was, I am constrained to say, simply a dead level of flesh.

It was not in the nature of the metaphysician to forbear making some inquiry into the sources of so strange a phenomenon; and the reply of his Majesty was at once prompt, dignified and satisfactory.

'Eyes! my dear Bon-Bon – eyes! did you say? – oh! – ah! – I perceive! The ridiculous prints, eh, which are in circulation, have given you a false idea of my personal appearance? Eyes! – true. Eyes, Pierre Bon-Bon, are very well in their proper place – *that*, you would say, is the head? – right – the head of a worm. To *you* likewise these optics are indispensable – yet I will convince you that my vision is more penetrating than your own. There is a cat I see in the corner – a pretty cat – look at her – observe her well. Now, Bon-Bon, do you behold the thoughts – the thoughts, I say – the ideas – the reflections – which are being engendered in her pericranium? There it is, now – you do not! She is thinking we admire the length of her tail and the profundity of her mind. She has just concluded that I am the most distinguished of ecclesiastics, and that you are the most superficial of metaphysicians. Thus you see I am not altogether blind; but to one of my profession, the eyes you speak of would be merely an incumbrance, liable at any time to be put out by a toasting-iron or a pitchfork. To you, I allow, these optical affairs are indispensable. Endeavour, Bon-Bon, to use them well; – *my* vision is the soul.'

Hereupon the guest helped himself to the wine upon the table, and pouring out a bumper for Bon-Bon, requested him to drink it without scruple, and make himself perfectly at home.

'A clever book that of yours, Pierre,' resumed his Majesty, tapping our friend knowingly upon the shoulder, as the latter put down his glass after a thorough compliance with his visitor's injunction. 'A clever book that of yours, upon my honour. It's a work after my own heart. Your arrangement of the matter, I think, however, might be improved, and many of your notions remind me of Aristotle. That philosopher was one of my most intimate acquaintances. I liked him as much for his terrible ill-temper, as for his happy knack at making a blunder. There is only one solid truth in all that he has written, and for that I gave him the hint out of pure compassion for his absurdity. I suppose, Pierre Bon-Bon, you very well know to what divine moral truth I am alluding?'

'Cannot say that I'——

'Indeed! – why, it was I who told Aristotle that, by sneezing, men expelled superfluous ideas through the proboscis.'

'Which is – hiccup! – undoubtedly the case,' said the metaphysician, while he poured out for himself another bumper of Mousseux, and offered his snuff-box to the fingers of his visitor.

'There was Plato,' continued his Majesty, modestly declining the snuff-box and the compliment it implied – 'there was Plato, too, for whom I at one time felt all the affection of a friend. You knew Plato, Bon-Bon? – ah, no, I beg a thousand pardons. He met me at Athens one day in the Parthenon, and told me he was distressed for an idea. I bade him write down that o $\nu o \upsilon \varsigma$ $\epsilon \sigma \tau \iota \nu$ $a \upsilon \lambda o \varsigma$. He said that he would do so, and went home, while I stepped over to the pyramids. But my conscience smote me for having uttered a truth, even to aid a friend, and hastening back to Athens, I **arrived** behind the philosopher's chair as he was inditing the "$a \upsilon \lambda o \varsigma$." Giving the lamma a fillip with my finger, I turned it upside down. So the sentence now reads "o $\nu o \upsilon \varsigma$ $\epsilon o \tau \iota \nu$ $a \upsilon \gamma o \varsigma$," and is, you perceive, the fundamental doctrine in his metaphysics.'

'Were you ever at Rome!' asked the *restaurateur*, as he finished his second bottle of Mousseux, and drew from the closet a larger supply of Chambertin.

'But once, Monsieur Bon-Bon, but once. There was a time,' said the devil, as if reciting some passage from a book – 'There was a time when occurred an anarchy of five years, during which the republic, bereft of all its officers, had no magistracy besides the tribunes of the people, and these were not legally vested with any degree of executive power – at that time, Monsieur Bon-Bon – at that time *only* I was in Rome, and I have no earthly acquaintance, consequently, with any of its philosophy.*

'What do you think of – what do you think of – hiccup! – Epicurus?'

* Ils ecrivaient sur la Philosophie (*Cicero, Lucretius, Seneca*), mais c'était la Philosophie Grecque. – *Condorcet.*

'What do I think of *whom?*' said the devil, in astonishment, 'you cannot surely mean to find any fault with Epicurus! What do I think of Epicurus! Do you mean me, sir? – *I* am Epicurus! I am the same philosopher who wrote each of the three hundred treatises commemorated by Diogenes Laertes.'

'That's a lie!' said the metaphysician, for the wine had gotten a little into his head.

'Very well! – very well, sir! – very well, indeed, sir!' said his Majesty, apparently much flattered.

'That's a lie!' repeated the *restaurateur*, dogmatically, 'that's a – hiccup! – a lie!'

'Well, well, have it your own way!' said the devil pacifically; and Bon-Bon, having beaten his Majesty at an argument, thought it his duty to conclude a second bottle of Chambertin.

'As I was saying,' resumed the visitor, 'as I was observing a little while ago, there are some very *outré* notions in that book of yours, Monsieur Bon-Bon. What, for instance, do you mean by all that humbug about the soul? Pray, sir, what *is* the soul?'

'The – hiccup! – soul,' replied the metaphysician, referring to his MS., 'is undoubtedly'——

'No, sir.'

'Indubitably'——

'No, sir!'

'Indisputably'——

'No, sir!'

'Evidently'——

'No, sir!'

'Incontrovertibly'——

'No, sir!'

'Hiccup!'

'No, sir!'

'And beyond all question, a'——

'No, sir, the soul is no such thing!' Here the philosopher, looking daggers, took occasion to make an end upon the spot of his third bottle of Chambertin.

'Then – hiccup! – pray, sir – what – what is it?'

'That is neither here nor there, Monsieur Bon-Bon,' replied his Majesty, musingly. 'I have tasted – that is to say, I have known some very bad souls, and some, too – pretty good ones.' Here he smacked his lips, and, having unconsciously let fall his hand upon the volume in his pocket, was seized with a violent fit of sneezing.

He continued:–

'There was the soul of Cratinus – passable: Aristophanes – racy: Plato – exquisite – not *your* Plato, but Plato the comic poet: your Plato would have turned the stomach of Cerberus – faugh! Then let me see! there were Nævius, and Andronicus, and Plautus, and Terentius. Then there were Lucilius, and Catullus, and Naso, and Quintus Flaccus, – dear Quinty! as I called him when he sang a *seculare* for my amusement, while I toasted him, in pure good-humour, on a fork. But they want *flavour* these Romans. One fat Greek is worth a dozen of them, and besides, will *keep*, which cannot be said of a Quirite. – Let us taste your Sauterne.'

Bon-Bon had by this time made up his mind to the *nil admirari*, and endeavoured to hand down the bottles in question. He was, however, conscious of a strange sound in the room like the wagging of a tail. Of this, although extremely indecent in his Majesty, the philosopher took no notice; – simply kicking the dog, and requesting him to be quiet. The visitor continued:

'I found that Horace tasted very much like Aristotle; – You know I am fond of variety. Terentius I could not have told from Menander. Naso, to my astonishment, was Nicander in disguise. Virgilius had a strong twang of Theocritus. Martial put me much in mind of Archilochus and Titus Livius was positively Polybius, and none other.'

'Hiccup!' here replied Bon-Bon, and his Majesty proceeded:

'But if I *have* a *penchant*, Monsieur Bon-Bon – if I *have* a *penchant*, it is for a philosopher. Yet, let me tell you, it is not every dev – I mean it is not every gentleman, who knows how to *choose* a philosopher. Long ones are *not* good; and the best, if not carefully shelled, are apt to be a little rancid on account of the gall.'

'Shelled!'

'I mean, taken out of the carcase.'

'What do you think of a – hiccup! – physician?'

'*Don't* mention them! – ugh! – ugh!' (Here his Majesty retched violently.) 'I never tasted but one – that rascal Hippocrates! – smelt of asafœtida – ugh! ugh! ugh! – caught a wretched cold washing him in the Styx – and after all he gave me the cholera morbus.'

'The – hiccup! – wretch!' ejaculated Bon-Bon, 'the – hiccup! – abortion of a pill-box!' – and the philosopher dropped a tear.

'After all,' continued the visitor, 'after all, if a dev – if a gentleman wishes to *live*, he must have more talents than one or two; and with us a fat face is an evidence of diplomacy.'

'How so?'

'Why, we are sometimes exceedingly pushed for provisions. You must know that, in a climate so sultry as mine, it is frequently impossible to keep a spirit alive for more than two or three hours; and after death, unless pickled immediately (and a pickled spirit is *not* good), they will – smell – you understand, eh? Putrefaction is always to be apprehended when the souls are consigned to us in the usual way.'

'Hiccup – hiccup! – good God! how *do* you manage?'

Here the iron lamp commenced swinging with redoubled violence, and the devil half started from his seat; – however, with a slight sigh, he recovered his composure, merely saying to our hero in a low tone, 'I tell you what, Pierre Bon-Bon, we *must* have no more swearing.'

The host swallowed another bumper, by way of denoting thorough comprehension and acquiescence, and the visitor continued:

'Why, there are *several* ways of managing. The most of us starve: some put up with the pickle; for my part I purchase my spirits *vivente corpore*, in which case I find they keep very well.'

'But the body! – hiccup! – the body!!!'

'The body, the body – well, what of the body? – oh! ah! I perceive. Why, sir, the body is not *at all* affected by the transaction. I have made innumerable purchases of the kind in my day, and the parties never experienced any inconvenience. There were Cain and Nimrod, and Nero, and Caligula, and Dionysius, and Pisistratus, and – and a thousand others, who never knew what it was to have a soul during the latter part of their lives; yet, sir, these men adorned society. Why, isn't there A—— now, whom you know as well as I! Is *he* not in possession of all his faculties, mental and corporeal? Who writes a keener epigram? Who reasons more wittily? Who—— but stay! I have his agreement in my pocket-book.'

Thus saying, he produced a red leather wallet, and took from it a number of papers. Upon some of these Bon-Bon caught a glimpse of the letters *Machi – Maza – Robesp* – with the words *Caligula, George, Elizabeth*. His Majesty selected a narrow slip of parchment, and from it read aloud the following words:–

'In consideration of certain mental endowments which it is unnecessary to specify, and in further consideration of one thousand louis d'or, I, being aged one year and one month, do hereby make over to the bearer of this agreement all my right, title, and appurtenance in the shadow called my soul.' (Signed) A——* (Here his Majesty repeated a name which I do not feel myself justified in indicating more unequivocally.)

'A clever fellow that,' resumed he; 'but like you, Monsieur Bon-Bon, he was mistaken about the soul. The soul a shadow, truly! The soul a shadow! Ha! ha! ha! – he! he! he! – hu! hu! hu! Only think of a fricasséed shadow!'

'*Only* think – hiccup! – of a fricasséed shadow!' exclaimed our hero, whose faculties were becoming much illuminated by the profundity of his Majesty's discourse.

'*Only* think of a – hiccup! – fricasséed shadow!! Now, damme! – hiccup! – hump! If *I* would have been such a – hiccup! – nincompoop. *My* soul, – Mr. – humph!'

'*Your* soul, Monsieur Bon-Bon!'

'Yes, sir – hiccup! – *my* soul is!'——

'*No* shadow, damme!'

'What sir?'

'Did you mean to say'——

'Yes, sir, *my* soul is – hiccup! – hump! – yes, sir.'

* *Quere* – Arouet?

'Did you intend to assert'——

'*My* soul is – hiccup! – peculiarly qualified for – hiccup! – a'——

'What, sir?'

'Stew.'

'Ha!'

'Soufflée.'

'Eh?'

'Fricassée.'

'Indeed!'

'Ragout and fricandeau – and see here, my good fellow! I'll let you have it – hiccup! – a bargain.' Here the philosopher slapped his Majesty upon the back.

'Couldn't think of such a thing,' said the latter calmly, at the same time rising from his seat. The metaphysician stared.

'Am supplied at present,' said his Majesty.

'Hic-cup! – e-h?' said the philosopher.

'Have no funds on hand.'

'What?'

'Besides, very unhandsome in me'——

'Sir!'

'To take advantage of'——

'Hic-cup!'

'Your present disgusting and ungentlemanly situation.'

Here the visitor bowed and withdrew – in what manner could not precisely be ascertained – but in a well-concerted effort to discharge a bottle at 'the villain,' the slender chain was severed that depended from the ceiling, and the metaphysician prostrated by the downfall of the lamp.

The Tell-Tale Heart

True! nervous, very, very dreadfully nervous I had been and am; but why *will* you say that I am mad? The disease had sharpened my senses, not destroyed, not dulled them. Above all was the sense of hearing acute. I heard all things in the heaven and in the earth. I heard many things in hell. How then am I mad? Hearken! and observe how healthily, how calmly, I can tell you the whole story.

It is impossible to say how first the idea entered my brain, but, once conceived, it haunted me day and night. Object there was none. Passion there was none. I loved the old man. He had never wronged me. He had never given me insult. For his gold I had no desire. I think it was his eye! Yes, it was this! One of his eyes resembled that of a vulture – a pale blue eye with a film over it. Whenever it fell upon me my blood ran cold, and so by degrees, very gradually, I made up my mind to take the life of the old man, and thus rid myself of the eye for ever.

Now this is the point. You fancy me mad. Madmen know nothing. But you should have seen *me*. You should have seen how wisely I proceeded – with what caution – with what foresight, with what dissimulation, I went to work! I was never kinder to the old man than during the whole week before I killed him. And every night about midnight I turned the latch of his door and opened it – oh, so gently! And then, when I had made an opening sufficient for my head, I put in a dark lantern all closed, closed so that no light shone out, and then I thrust in my head. Oh, you would have laughed to see how cunningly I thrust it in! I moved it slowly, very, very slowly, so that I might not disturb the old man's sleep. It took me an hour to place my whole head within the opening so far that I could see him as he lay upon his bed. Ha! would a madman have been so wise as this? And then when my head was well in the room I undid the lantern cautiously – oh, so cautiously – cautiously (for the hinges creaked), I undid it just so much that a single thin ray fell upon the vulture eye. And this I did for seven long nights, every night just at midnight, but I found the eye always closed, and so it was impossible to do the work, for it was not the old man who vexed me but his Evil Eye. And every morning, when the day broke, I went boldly into the chamber and spoke courageously to him, calling him by name in a hearty tone, and inquiring how he had passed the night. So you see he would have been a very profound old man, indeed, to suspect that every night, just at twelve, I looked in upon him while he slept.

Upon the eighth night I was more than usually cautious in opening the door. A watch's minute hand moves more quickly than did mine. Never before that night had I *felt* the extent of my own powers, of my sagacity. I could scarcely contain my feelings of triumph. To think that there I was opening the door little by little, and he not even to dream of my secret deeds or thoughts. I fairly chuckled at the idea, and perhaps he heard me, for he moved on the bed suddenly as if startled. Now you may think that I drew back – but no. His room was as black as pitch with the thick darkness (for the shutters were close fastened through fear of robbers), and so I knew that he could not see the opening of the door, and I kept pushing it on steadily, steadily.

I had my head in, and was about to open the lantern, when my thumb slipped upon the tin fastening, and the old man sprang up in the bed, crying out, 'Who's there?'

I kept quite still and said nothing. For a whole hour I did not move a muscle, and in the meantime I did not hear him lie down. He was still sitting up in the bed, listening; just as I have done night after night hearkening to the death watches in the wall.

Presently, I heard a slight groan, and I knew it was the groan of mortal terror. It was not a groan of pain or of grief – oh, no! it was the low stifled sound that arises from the bottom of the soul when overcharged with awe. I knew the sound well. Many a night, just at midnight, when all the world slept, it has welled up from my own bosom, deepening, with its dreadful echo, the terrors that distracted me. I say I knew it well. I knew what the old man felt, and pitied him although I chuckled at heart. I knew that he had been lying awake ever since the first slight noise when he had turned in the bed. His fears had been ever since growing upon him. He had been trying to fancy them causeless, but could not. He had been saying to himself, 'It is nothing but the wind in the chimney, it is only a mouse crossing the floor,' or, 'It is merely a cricket which had made a single chirp.' Yes, he had been trying to comfort himself with these suppositions; but he had found all in vain. *All in vain*, because Death in approaching him had stalked with his black shadow before him and enveloped the victim. And it was the mournful influence of the unperceived shadow that caused him to feel, although he neither saw nor heard, to *feel* the presence of my head within the room.

When I had waited a long time very patiently without hearing him lie down, I resolved to open a little – a very, very little crevice in the lantern. So I opened it – you cannot imagine how stealthily, stealthily – until at length a single dim ray like the thread of the spider shot out from the crevice and fell upon the vulture eye.

It was open, wide, wide open, and I grew furious as I gazed upon it. I saw it with perfect distinctness – all a dull blue with a hideous veil over it that chilled the very marrow in my bones, but I could see nothing else of the old man's face or person, for I had directed the ray as if by instinct precisely upon the damned spot.

And now have I not told you that what you mistake for madness is but over-acuteness of the senses? now, I say, there came to my ears a low, dull, quick sound, such as a watch makes when enveloped in cotton. I knew *that* sound well, too. It was the beating of the old man's heart. It increased my fury as the beating of a drum stimulates the soldier into courage.

But even yet I refrained and kept still. I scarcely breathed. I held the lantern motionless. I tried how steadily I could maintain the ray upon the eye. Meantime the hellish tattoo of the heart increased. It grew quicker and quicker, and louder and louder, every instant. The old man's terror *must* have been extreme! It grew louder, I say, louder every moment! – do you mark me well? I have told you that I am nervous: so I am. And now at the dead hour of the night, amid the dreadful silence of that old house, so strange a noise as this excited me to uncontrollable terror. Yet, for some minutes longer I refrained and stood still. But the beating grew louder, louder! I thought the heart must burst. And now a new anxiety seized me – the sound would be heard by a neighbour! The old man's hour had come! With a loud yell, I threw open the lantern and leaped into the room. He shrieked once – once only. In an instant I dragged him to the floor, and pulled the heavy bed over him. I then smiled gaily, to find the deed so far done. But for many minutes the heart beat on with a muffled sound. This, however, did not vex me; it would not be heard through the wall. At length it ceased. The old man was dead. I removed the bed and examined the corpse. Yes, he was stone, stone dead. I placed my hand upon the heart and held it there many minutes. There was no pulsation. He was stone dead. His eye would trouble me no more.

If still you think me mad, you will think so no longer when I describe the wise precautions I took for the concealment of the body. The night waned, and I worked hastily, but in silence.

I took up three planks from the flooring of the chamber, and deposited all between the scantlings. I then replaced the boards so cleverly, so cunningly, that no human eye – not even *his* – could have detected anything wrong. There was nothing to wash out – no stain of any kind – no blood-spot whatever. I had been too wary for that.

When I had made an end of these labours, it was four o'clock – still dark as midnight. As the bell sounded the hour, there came a knocking at the street door. I went down to open it with a light heart, – for what had I *now* to fear? There entered three men, who introduced

But, for many minutes, the heart beat on with a muffled sound

themselves, with perfect suavity, as officers of the police. A shriek had been heard by a neighbour during the night; suspicion of foul play had been aroused; information had been lodged at the police office, and they (the officers) had been deputed to search the premises.

I smiled, – for *what* had I to fear? I bade the gentlemen welcome. The shriek, I said, was my own in a dream. The old man, I mentioned, was absent in the country. I took my visitors all over the house. I bade them search – search *well*. I led them, at length, to *his* chamber. I showed them his treasures, secure, undisturbed. In the enthusiasm of my confidence, I brought chairs into the room, and desired them *here* to rest from their fatigues, while I myself, in the wild audacity of my perfect triumph, placed my own seat upon the very spot beneath which reposed the corpse of the victim.

The officers were satisfied. My *manner* had convinced them. I was singularly at ease. They sat, and while I answered cheerily, they chatted of familiar things. But, ere long, I felt myself getting pale and wished them gone. My head ached, and I fancied a ringing in my ears; but still they sat, and still chatted. The ringing became more distinct: I talked more freely to get rid of the feeling: but it continued and gained definitiveness – until, at length, I found that the noise was *not* within my ears.

No doubt I now grew *very* pale; but I talked more fluently, and with a heightened voice. Yet the sound increased – and what could I do? It was *a low, dull, quick sound – much such a sound as a watch makes when enveloped in cotton*. I gasped for breath, and yet the officers heard it not. I talked more quickly, more vehemently; but the noise steadily increased. I arose and argued about trifles, in a high key and with violent gesticulations; but the noise steadily increased. Why *would* they not be gone? I paced the floor to and fro with heavy strides, as if excited to fury by the observations of the men, but the noise steadily increased. O God! what *could* I do? I foamed – I raved – I swore! I swung the chair upon which I had been sitting, and grated it upon the boards, but the noise arose over all and continually increased. It grew louder – louder – *louder*! And still the men chatted pleasantly, and smiled. Was it possible they heard not? Almighty God! – no, no? They heard! – they suspected! – they *knew*! – they were making a mockery of my horror! – this I thought, and this I think. But anything was better than this agony! Anything was more tolerable than this derision! I could bear those hypocritical smiles no longer! I felt that I must scream or die! – and now – again! hark! louder! louder! louder! *louder*! –

'Villains!' I shrieked, 'dissemble no more! I admit the deed! – tear up the planks! – here, here! – it is the beating of his hideous heart!'

The Oblong Box

Some years ago I engaged a passage from Charleston, S.C., to the city of New York, in the fine packet-ship *Independence*, Captain Hardy. We were to sail on the fifteenth of the month (June), weather permitting; and on the fourteenth I went on board to arrange some matters in my state-room.

I found that we were to have a great many passengers, including a more than usual number of ladies. On the list were several of my acquaintances; and among other names, I was rejoiced to see that of Mr. Cornelius Wyatt, a young artist, for whom I entertained feelings of warm friendship. He had been with me a fellow-student at C—— University, where we were very much together. He had the ordinary temperament of genius, and was a compound of misanthropy, sensibility, and enthusiasm. To these qualities he united the warmest and truest heart which ever beat in a human bosom.

I observed that his name was carded upon *three* state-rooms; and upon again referring to the list of passengers, I found that he had engaged passage for himself, wife, and two sisters – his own. The state-rooms were sufficiently roomy, and each had two berths, one above the other. These berths, to be sure, were so exceedingly narrow as to be insufficient for more than one person; still I could not comprehend why there were *three* state-rooms for these four persons. I was just at that epoch, in one of those moody frames of mind which make a man abnormally inquisitive about trifles, and I confess with shame that I busied myself in a variety of ill-bred and preposterous conjectures about this matter of the supernumerary state-room. It was no business of mine, to be sure; but with none the less pertinacity did I occupy my self in attempts to resolve the enigma. At last I reached a conclusion which wrought in me great wonder why I had not arrived at it before. 'It is a servant, of course,' I said, 'what a fool I am not sooner to have thought of so obvious a solution!' And then I again repaired to the list – but here I saw distinctly that *no* servant was to come with the party; although, in fact, it had been the original design to bring one – for the words 'and servant,' had been first written and then overscored. 'Oh, extra baggage to be sure,' I now said to myself – 'something he wishes not to be put in the hold – something to be kept under his own eye – ah, I have it – a painting or so – and this is what he has been bargaining about with Nicolino, the Italian Jew.' This idea satisfied me, and I dismissed my curiosity for the nonce.

Wyatt's two sisters I knew very well, and most amiable and clever girls they were. His wife he had newly married, and I had never yet seen her. He had often talked about her in my presence, however, and in his usual style of enthusiasm. He described her as of surpassing beauty, wit, and accomplishment. I was therefore quite anxious to make her acquaintance.

On the day in which I visited the ship (the fourteenth) Wyatt and party were also to visit it – so the captain informed me – and I waited on board an hour longer than I had designed, in hope of being presented to the bride; but then an apology came. 'Mrs. W. was a little indisposed, and would decline coming on board until to-morrow, at the hour of sailing.'

The morrow having arrived, I was going from my hotel to the wharf, when Captain Hardy met me and said that, 'owing to circumstances' (a stupid but convenient phrase) 'he rather thought the *Independence* would not sail for a day or two, and that when all was ready he would send up and let me know.' This I thought strange, for there was a stiff southerly breeze: but as 'the circumstances' were not forthcoming, although I pumped for them with much perseverance, I had nothing to do but to return home and digest my impatience at leisure.

I did not receive the expected message from the captain for nearly a week. It came at length, however, and I immediately went on board; the ship was crowded with passengers, and everything was in the bustle attendant upon making sail. Wyatt's party arrived about ten minutes after myself. There were the two sisters, the bride, and the artist – the latter in one of his customary fits of moody misanthropy. I was too well used to these, however, to pay them any special attention. He did not even introduce me to his wife – this courtesy devolving, per force, upon his sister Marian – a very sweet and intelligent girl, who, in a few hurried words, made us acquainted.

Mrs. Wyatt had been closely veiled; and when she raised her veil, in acknowledging my bow, I confess that I was very profoundly astonished. I should have been much more so, however, had not long experience advised me not to trust, with too implicit a reliance, the enthusiastic descriptions of my friend the artist when indulging in comments upon the loveliness of woman. When beauty was the theme, I well knew with what facility he soared into the regions of the purely ideal.

The truth is, I could not help regarding Mrs. Wyatt as a decidedly plain-looking woman. If not positively ugly, she was not, I think, very far from it. She was dressed, however, in exquisite taste – and then I had no doubt that she had captivated my friend's heart by the more enduring graces of the intellect and soul. She said very few words, and passed at once into her state-room with Mr. W.

My old inquisitiveness now returned. There was *no* servant – *that* was a settled point. I looked, therefore, for the extra baggage. After some delay, a cart arrived at the wharf, with an oblong pine box, which was everything that seemed to be expected. Immediately upon its arrival we made sail, and in a short time were safely over the bar and standing out to sea.

The box in question was, as I say, oblong. It was about six feet in length by two and a half in breadth; I observed it attentively, and like to be precise. Now this shape was *peculiar*; and no sooner had I seen it than I took credit to myself for the accuracy of my guessing. I had reached the conclusion, it will be remembered, that the extra baggage of my friend the artist would prove to be pictures, or at least a picture; for I knew he had been for several weeks in conference with Nicolino; and now here was a box which, from its shape, *could* possibly contain nothing in the world but a copy of Leonardo's 'Last Supper;' and a copy of this very 'Last Supper,' done by Rubini the younger at Florence, I had known for some time to be in the possession of Nicolino. This point therefore I considered as sufficiently settled. I chuckled excessively when I thought of my acumen. It was the first time I had ever known Wyatt to keep from me any of his artistical secrets, but here he evidently intended to steal a march upon me, and smuggle a fine picture to New York under my very nose, expecting me to know nothing of the matter. I resolved to quiz him *well*, now and hereafter.

One thing, however, annoyed me not a little. The box did *not* go into the extra state-room. It was deposited in Wyatt's own; and there, too, it remained, occupying very nearly the whole of the floor – no doubt to the exceeding discomfort of the artist and his wife; this the more especially as the tar or paint with which it was lettered in sprawling capitals emitted a strong, disagreeable, and, to *my* fancy, a peculiarly disgusting odour. On the lid were painted the words – '*Mrs. Adelaide Curtis, Albany, New York. Charge of Cornelius Wyatt, Esq. This side up. To be handled with care.*'

Now, I was aware that Mrs. Adelaide Curtis, of Albany, was the artist's wife's mother; but then I looked upon the whole address as a mystification, intended especially for myself. I made up my mind of course that the box and contents would never get farther north than the studio of my misanthropic friend in Chambers Street, New York.

For the first three or four days we had fine weather, although the wind was dead ahead; having chopped round to the northward immediately upon our losing sight of the coast. The passengers were consequently in high spirits, and disposed to be social. I *must* except,

314 The Oblong Box

however, Wyatt and his sisters, who behaved stiffly, and I could not help thinking uncourteously to the rest of the party. *Wyatt's* conduct I did not so much regard. He was gloomy, even beyond his usual habit – in fact he was *morose* – but in him I was prepared for eccentricity. For the sisters, however, I could make no excuse. They secluded themselves in their state-rooms during the greater part of the passage, and absolutely refused, although I repeatedly urged them, to hold communication with any person on board.

Mrs. Wyatt herself was far more agreeable. That is to say, she was *chatty*; and to be chatty is no slight recommendation at sea. She became *excessively* intimate with most of the ladies; and, to my profound astonishment, evinced no equivocal disposition to coquet with the men. She amused us all very much. I say 'amused' – and scarcely know how to explain myself. The truth is, I soon found that Mrs. W. was far oftener laughed *at* than *with*. The gentlemen said little about her; but the ladies, in a little while pronounced her 'a good-hearted thing, rather indifferent-looking, totally uneducated, and decidedly vulgar.' The great wonder was how Wyatt had been entrapped into such a match. Wealth was the general solution – but this I knew to be no solution at all; for Wyatt had told me that she neither brought him a dollar, nor had any expectations from any source whatever. 'He had married,' he said, 'for love, and for love only; and, his bride was far more than worthy of his love.' When I thought of these expressions on the part of my friend, I confess that I felt indescribably puzzled. Could it be possible that he was taking leave of his senses? What else could I think? *He*, so refined, so intellectual, so fastidious, with so exquisite a perception of the faulty, and so keen an appreciation of the beautiful! To be sure, the lady seemed especially fond of *him* – particularly so in his absence – when she made herself ridiculous by frequent quotations of what had been said by her 'beloved husband, Mr. Wyatt.' The word 'husband' seemed for ever – to use one of her own delicate expressions – for ever 'on the tip of her tongue.' In the meantime, it was observed by all on board, that he avoided *her* in the most pointed manner, and for the most part shut himself up alone in his state-room, where, in fact, he might have been said to live altogether, leaving his wife at full liberty to amuse herself as she thought best in the public society of the main cabin.

My conclusion, from what I saw and heard, was that the artist, by some unaccountable freak of fate, or perhaps in some fit of enthusiastic and fanciful passion, had been induced to unite himself with a person altogether beneath him, and that the natural result, entire and speedy disgust, had ensued. I pitied him from the bottom of my heart – but could not, for that reason, quite forgive his incommunicativeness in the matter of the 'Last Supper.' For this I resolved to have my revenge.

One day he came upon deck, and taking his arm as had been my wont, I sauntered with him backwards and forwards. His gloom, however (which I considered quite natural under the circumstances), seemed entirely unabated. He said little, and that moodily, and with evident effort. I ventured a jest or two, and he made a sickening attempt at a smile. Poor fellow! – as I thought of *his wife*, I wondered that he could have heart to put on even the semblance of mirth. At last I ventured a home thrust. I determined to commence a series of covert insinuations or innuendoes about the oblong box – just to let him perceive gradually that I was *not* altogether the butt or victim of his little bit of pleasant mystification. My first observation was by way of opening a masked battery. I said something about the 'peculiar shape of *that* box;' and, as I spoke the words, I smiled knowingly, winked, and touched him gently with my fore-finger in the ribs.

The manner in which Wyatt received this harmless pleasantry convinced me at once that he was mad. At first he stared at me as if he found it impossible to comprehend the witticism of my remark; but as its point seemed slowly to make its way into his brain, his eyes in the same proportion seemed protruding from their sockets. Then he grew very red, then hideously pale, then, as if highly amused with what I had insinuated, he began a loud and boisterous laugh, which to my astonishment, he kept up with gradually increasing vigour for ten minutes or more. In conclusion he fell flat and heavily upon the deck. When I ran to uplift him to all appearance he was *dead*.

I called assistance, and with much difficulty we brought him to himself. Upon reviving he spoke incoherently for some time. At length we bled him and put him to bed. The next morning he was quite recovered, so far as regarded his mere bodily health. Of his mind I say nothing, of course. I avoided him during the rest of the passage by advice of the captain, who seemed to coincide with me altogether in my views of his insanity, but cautioned me to say nothing on this head to any person on board.

Several circumstances occurred immediately after this fit of Wyatt's which contributed to heighten the curiosity with which I was already possessed. Among other things, this: I had been nervous – drank too much strong green tea, and slept ill at night – in fact, for two nights I could not be properly said to sleep at all. Now, my state-room opened into the main cabin, or dining-room, as did those of all the single men on board. Wyatt's three rooms were in the after-cabin, which was separated from the main one by a slight sliding-door, never locked even at night. As we were almost constantly on a wind, and the breeze was not a little stiff, the ship heeled to leeward very considerably; and whenever her starboard was to leeward, the sliding-door between the cabins slid open, and so remained, no-body taking the trouble to get up and shut it. But my berth was in such a position that when my own state-room door was open, as well as the sliding-door in question (and my own door was *always* open on account of the heat) I could see into the after-cabin quite distinctly, and just at that portion of it, too, where were situated the state-rooms of Mr. Wyatt. Well, during two nights (*not* consecutive) while I lay awake, I clearly saw Mrs. W., about eleven o'clock upon each night, steal cautiously from the state-room of Mr. W., and enter the extra room, where she remained until daybreak, when she was called by her husband and went back. That they were virtually separated was clear. They had separate apartments – no doubt in contemplation of a more permanent divorce; and here, after all, I thought, was the mystery of the extra state-room.

There was another circumstance, too, which interested me much. During the two wakeful nights in question, and immediately after the

disappearance of Mrs. Wyatt into the extra state-room, I was attracted
by certain singular, cautious, subdued noises in that of her husband.
After listening to them for some time with thoughtful attention, I at
length succeeded perfectly in translating their import. They were
sounds occasioned by the artist in prying open the oblong box by
means of a chisel and mallet, the latter being apparently muffled or
deadened by some soft woollen or cotton substance in which its head
was enveloped.

In this manner I fancied I could distinguish the precise moment
when he fairly disengaged the lid – also, that I could determine when
he removed it altogether, and when he deposited it upon the lower
berth in his room; this latter point I knew, for example, by certain
slight taps which the lid made in striking against the wooden edges of
the berth as he endeavoured to lay it down *very* gently, there being no
room for it on the floor. After this there was a dead stillness, and I
heard nothing more upon either occasion until nearly daybreak; unless
perhaps, I may mention a low sobbing or murmuring sound, so very
much suppressed as to be nearly inaudible, if indeed the whole of this
latter noise were not rather produced by my own imagination. I say it
seemed to *resemble* sobbing or sighing, but of course it could not have
been either. I rather think it was a ringing in my own ears. Mr. Wyatt,
no doubt, according to custom, was merely giving the rein to one of his
hobbies, indulging in one of his fits of artistic enthusiasm. He had
opened his oblong box in order to feast his eyes on the pictorial
treasure within. There was nothing in this, however, to make him *sob*.
I repeat therefore that it must have been simply a freak of my own
fancy, distempered by good Captain Hardy's green tea. Just before
dawn, on each of the two nights of which I speak, I distinctly heard
Mr. Wyatt replace the lid upon the oblong box and force the nails into
their old places by means of the muffled mallet. Having done this, he
issued from his state-room, fully dressed, and proceeded to call Mrs.
W. from hers.

We had been at sea seven days, and were now off Cape Hatteras,
when there came a tremendously heavy blow from the south-west. We
were in a measure prepared for it, however, as the weather had been

holding out threats for some time. Everything was made snug, alow and aloft; and as the wind steadily freshened we lay-to, at length, under spanker and foretopsail, both double-reefed.

In this trim we rode safely enough for forty-eight hours – the ship proving herself an excellent sea-boat in many respects, and shipping no water of any consequence. At the end of this period, however, the gale freshened into a hurricane, and our after-sail split into ribbons, bringing us so much in the trough of the water that we shipped several prodigious seas, one immediately after the other. By this accident we lost three men overboard, with the caboose and nearly the whole of the larboard bulwarks. Scarcely had we recovered our senses before the foretopsail went into shreds, when we got up a storm stay-sail, and with this did pretty well for some time, the ship heading the sea much more steadily than before.

The gale still held on, however, and we saw no signs of its abating. The rigging was found to be ill-fitted, and greatly strained; and on the third day of the blow, about five in the afternoon, our mizzenmast, in a heavy lurch to windward, went by the board. For an hour or more we tried in vain to get rid of it, on account of the prodigious rolling of the ship, and before we had succeeded, the carpenter came aft and announced four feet water in the hold. To add to our dilemma, we found the pumps choked and nearly useless.

All was now confusion and despair – but an effort was made to lighten the ship by throwing overboard as much of her cargo as could be reached, and by cutting away the two masts that remained. This we at last accomplished – but we were still unable to do anything at the pumps; and in the meantime the leak gained on us very fast.

At sundown the gale had sensibly diminished in violence, and as the sea went down with it, we still entertained faint hopes of saving ourselves in the boats. At eight P.M. the clouds broke away to windward, and we had the advantage of a full moon – a piece of good fortune which served wonderfully to cheer our drooping spirits.

After incredible labour we succeeded at length in getting the long-boat over the side without material accident, and into this we crowded the whole of the crew and most of the passengers. This party made off immediately, and after undergoing much suffering finally arrived in safety at Ocracoke Inlet on the third day after the wreck.

Fourteen passengers, with the captain, remained on board, resolving to trust their fortunes to the jolly-boat at the stern. We lowered it without difficulty, although it was only by a miracle that we prevented it from swamping as it touched the water. It contained when afloat, the captain and his wife, Mr. Wyatt and party, a Mexican officer, wife, four children, and myself, with a negro valet.

We had no room, of course, for anything except a few positively necessary instruments, some provisions, and the clothes upon our backs. No one had thought of even attempting to save anything more. What must have been the astonishment of all then, when, having proceeded a few fathoms from the ship, Mr. Wyatt stood up in the stern-sheets, and coolly demanded of Captain Hardy that the boat should be put back for the purpose of taking in his oblong box!

'Sit down, Mr. Wyatt,' replied the Captain, somewhat sternly; 'you will capsize us if you do not sit quite still. Our gunwale is almost in the water now.'

'The box!' vociferated Mr. Wyatt, still standing – 'the box, I say! Captain Hardy, you cannot, you *will* not refuse me. Its weight will be but a trifle – it is nothing – mere nothing. By the mother who bore you – for the love of Heaven – by your hope of salvation, I *implore* you to put back for the box!'

The captain, for a moment, seemed touched by the earnest appeal of the artist, but he regained his stern composure, and merely said –

'Mr. Wyatt, you are *mad*. I cannot listen to you. Sit down, I say, or you will swamp the boat. Stay – hold him – seize him! – he is about to spring overboard! There – I knew it – he is over!'

As the captain said this, Mr. Wyatt, in fact, sprang from the boat, and as we were yet in the lee of the wreck, succeeded by almost superhuman exertion in getting hold of a rope which hung from the fore-chains. In another moment he was on board, and rushing frantically down into the cabin.

In the meantime, we had been swept astern of the ship, and being quite out of her lee, were at the mercy of the tremendous sea which was still running. We made a determined effort to put back, but out little boat was like a feather in the breath of the tempest. We saw at a glance that the doom of the unfortunate artist was sealed.

As our distance from the wreck rapidly increased, the madman (for as such only could we regard him) was seen to emerge from the companion-way, up which, by dint of a strength that appeared gigantic, he dragged bodily the oblong box. While we gazed in the extremity of astonishment, he passed rapidly several turns of a three-inch rope, first around the box and then around his body. In another instant both body and box were in the sea – disappearing suddenly, at once and for ever.

We lingered a while sadly upon our oars, with our eyes riveted upon the spot. At length we pulled away. The silence remained unbroken for an hour. Finally, I hazarded a remark.

'Did you observe, Captain, how suddenly they sank? Was not that an exceedingly singular thing? I confess that I entertained some feeble hope of his final deliverance, when I saw him lash himself to the box, and commit himself to the sea.'

'They sank as a matter of course,' replied the captain, 'and that like a shot. They will soon rise again, however, *but not till the salt melts.*'

'The salt!' I ejaculated.

'Hush!' said the captain, pointing to the wife and sisters of the deceased. 'We must talk of these things at some more appropriate time.'

We suffered much, and made a narrow escape; but fortune befriended *us*, as well as our mates in the long-boat. We landed, in fine, more dead than alive, after four days of intense distress, upon the beach opposite Roanoke Island. We remained here a week, were not ill-treated by the wreckers, and at length obtained a passage to New York.

About a month after the loss of the *Independence*, I happened to meet Captain Hardy in Broadway. Our conversation turned, naturally, upon the disaster, and especially upon the sad fate of poor Wyatt. I thus learned the following particulars.

The artist had engaged passage for himself, wife, two sisters, and a servant. His wife was, indeed, as she had been represented, a most lovely and most accomplished woman. On the morning of the fourteenth of June (the day in which I first visited the ship), the lady suddenly sickened and died. The young husband was frantic with grief, but circumstances imperatively forbade the deferring his voyage to New York. It was necessary to take to her mother the corpse of his adored wife, and on the other hand, the universal prejudice which would prevent his doing so openly was well known. Nine-tenths of the passengers would have abandoned the ship rather than take passage with a dead body.

In this dilemma, Captain Hardy arranged that the corpse, being first partially embalmed, and packed with a large quantity of salt, in a box of suitable dimensions, should be conveyed on board as merchandise. Nothing was to be said of the lady's decease; and as it was well understood that Mr. Wyatt had engaged passage for his wife, it became necessary that some person should personate her during the voyage. This the deceased's lady's maid was easily prevailed on to do. The extra state-room, originally engaged for this girl during her mistress's life, was now merely retained. In this state-room the pseudo wife slept every night. In the day-time she performed, to the best of her ability, the part of her mistress – whose person, it had been carefully ascertained, was not known to any of the passengers on board. My own mistakes arose, naturally enough, through too careless, too inquisitive, and too impulsive a temperament. But of late, it is a rare thing that I sleep soundly at night. There is a countenance which haunts me, turn as I will. There is an hysterical laugh which will for ever ring within my ears.

The Thousand-and-Second Tale of Scheherazade

Truth is stranger than fiction. – Old Saying.

Having had occasion lately, in the course of some Oriental investigations, to consult the *Tellmenow Isitsoörnot*, a work which (like the Zohar of Simeon Jochaides) is scarcely known at all, even in Europe, and which has never been quoted to my knowledge by any American – if we except, perhaps, the author of the 'Curiosities of American Literature' – having had occasion, I say, to turn over some pages of the first-mentioned very remarkable work, I was not a little astonished to discover that the literary world has hitherto been strangely in error respecting the fate of the vizier's daughter, Scheherazade, as that fate is depicted in the 'Arabian Nights;' and that the *dénouement* there given, if not altogether inaccurate as far as it goes, is at least to blame in not having gone very much farther.

For full information on this interesting topic I must refer the inquisitive reader to the 'Isitsoörnot' itself; but in the meantime I shall be pardoned for giving a summary of what I there discovered.

It will be remembered that in the usual version of the tales, a certain monarch having good cause to be jealous of his queen, not only puts her to death, but makes a vow by his beard and the prophet to espouse each night the most beautiful maiden in his dominions, and the next morning to deliver her up to the executioner.

Having fulfilled this vow for many years to the letter, and with a religious punctuality and method that conferred great credit upon him as a man of devout feelings and excellent sense, he was interrupted one afternoon (no doubt at his prayers) by a visit from his grand vizier, to whose daughter it appears there had occurred an idea.

Her name was Scheherazade, and her idea was that she would either redeem the land from the depopulating tax upon its beauty, or perish, after the approved fashion of all heroines, in the attempt.

Accordingly, and although we do not find it to be leap-year (which makes the sacrifice more meritorious), she deputes her father, the grand vizier, to make an offer to the king of her hand. This hand the king eagerly accepts – (he had intended to take it at all events, and had put off the matter from day to day only through fear of the vizier) – but in accepting it now he gives all parties very distinctly to understand that, grand vizier or no grand vizier, he has not the slightest design of giving up one iota of his vow or of his privileges. When, therefore, the fair Scheherazade insisted upon marrying the king, and did actually marry him despite her father's excellent advice not to do anything of the kind – when she would and did marry him, I say, will I nill I, it was with her beautiful black eyes as thoroughly open as the nature of the case would allow.

It seems, however, that this politic damsel (who had been reading Machiavelli beyond doubt) had a very ingenious little plot in her mind. On the night of the wedding she contrived, upon I forget what specious pretence, to have her sister occupy a couch sufficiently near that of the royal pair to admit of easy conversation from bed to bed; and a little before cock-crowing she took care to awaken the good monarch, her husband (who bore her none the worse will because he intended to wring her neck on the morrow) – she managed to awaken him, I say (although, on account of a capital conscience and an easy digestion, he slept well), by the profound interest of a story (about a rat and a black cat, I think), which she was narrating (all in an under tone, of course) to her sister. When the day broke, it so happened that this history was not altogether finished, and that Scheherazade, in the nature of things, could not finish it just then, since it was high time for her to get up and be bow-strung – a thing very little more pleasant than hanging, only a trifle more genteel!

The king's curiosity however, prevailing, I am sorry to say, even over his sound religious principles, induced him for this once to postpone the fulfilment of his vow until next morning, for the purpose and with the hope of hearing that night how it fared in the end with the black cat (a black cat, I think it was) and the rat.

The night having arrived, however, the lady Scheherazade not only put the finishing stroke to the black cat and the rat (the rat was blue), but before she well knew what she was about, found herself deep in the intricacies of a narration, having reference (if I am not altogether mistaken) to a pink horse (with green wings) that went in a violent manner by clockwork, and was wound up with an indigo key. With this history the king was even more profoundly interested than with the other; and as the day broke before its conclusion (notwithstanding all the queen's endeavours to get through with it in time for the bowstring), there was again no recourse but to postpone that ceremony as before for twenty-four hours. The next night there happened a similar accident with a similar result; and then the next – and then again the next; so that, in the end, the good monarch having been unavoidably deprived of all opportunity to keep his vow during a period of no less than one thousand and one nights, either forgets it altogether by the expiration of this time, or gets himself absolved of it in the regular way, or (what is more probable) breaks it outright, as well as the head of his father confessor. At all events Scheherazade, who, being lineally descended from Eve, fell heir perhaps to the whole seven baskets of talk, which the latter lady, we all know, picked up from under the trees in the garden of Eden; Scheherazade, I say, finally triumphed, and the tariff upon beauty was repealed.

Now this conclusion (which is that of the story as we have it upon record) is, no doubt, excessively proper and pleasant – but, alas! like a great many pleasant things, is more pleasant than true; and I am indebted altogether to the 'Isitsoörnot' for the means of correcting the error. 'Le mieux,' says a French proverb, 'est l'ennemi du bien,' and in mentioning that Scheherazade had inherited the seven baskets of talk, I should have added that she put them out at compound interest until they amounted to seventy-seven.

'My dear sister,' said she, on the thousand-and-second night (I quote the language of the 'Isitsoörnot' at this point *verbatim*), 'my dear sister,' said she, 'now that all this little difficulty about the bowstring has blown over, and that this odious tax is so happily repealed, I feel that I have been guilty of great indiscretion in withholding from you and the king (who, I am sorry to say, snores – a thing no gentleman would do), the full conclusion of the history of Sinbad the sailor. This person went through numerous other and more interesting adventures than those which I related; but the truth is I felt sleepy on the particular night of their narration, and so was seduced into cutting them short – a grievous piece of misconduct for which I only trust that Allah will forgive me. But even yet it is not too late to remedy my great neglect, and as soon as I have given the king a pinch or two in order to wake him up so far that he may stop making that horrible noise, I will forthwith entertain you (and him if he pleases) with the sequel of this very remarkable story.

Hereupon the sister of Scheherazade, as I have it from the 'Isitsoörnot,' expressed no very particular intensity of gratification; but the king having been sufficiently pinched, at length ceased snoring, and finally said 'Hum!' and then 'Hoo!' when the queen understanding these words (which are no doubt Arabic) to signify that he was all attention, and would do his best not to snore any more – the queen, I say, having arranged these matters to her satisfaction, re-entered thus, at once into the history of Sinbad the sailor:

' "At length, in my old age" (these are the words of Sinbad himself, as retailed by Scheherazade) – "at length, in my old age, and after enjoying many years of tranquillity at home, I became once more possessed with a desire of visiting foreign countries; and one day, without acquainting any of my family with my design, I packed up some bundles of such merchandise as was most precious and least bulky, and engaging a porter to carry them, went with him down to the sea-shore, to await the arrival of any chance vessel that might convey me out of the kingdom into some region which I had not as yet explored.

'"Having deposited the packages upon the sands, we sat down beneath some trees, and looked out into the ocean in the hope of perceiving a ship, but during several hours we saw none whatever. At length I fancied that I could hear a singular buzzing or humming sound, and the porter, after listening awhile, declared that he also could distinguish it. Presently it grew louder, and then still louder, so that we could have no doubt that the object which caused it was approaching us. At length, on the edge of the horizon we discovered a black speck, which rapidly increased in size until we made it out to be a vast monster, swimming with a great part of its body above the surface of the sea. It came towards us with inconceivable swiftness, throwing up huge waves of foam around its breast, and illuminating all that part of the sea through which it passed with a long line of fire that extended far off into the distance.

'"As the thing drew near we saw it very distinctly. Its length was equal to that of three of the loftiest trees that grow, and it was as wide as the great hall of audience in your palace, O most sublime and munificent of the caliphs! Its body, which was unlike that of ordinary fishes, was as solid as a rock, and of a jetty blackness throughout all that portion of it which floated above the water, with the exception of a narrow blood-red streak that completely begirdled it. The belly, which floated beneath the surface, and of which we could get only a glimpse now and then as the monster rose and fell with the billows, was entirely covered with metallic scales of a colour like that of the moon in misty weather. The back was flat and nearly white, and from it there extended upwards six spines, about half the length of the whole body.

'"This horrible creature had no mouth that we could perceive; but, as if to make up for this deficiency, it was provided with at least fourscore of eyes, that protruded from their sockets like those of the green dragon-fly, and were arranged all around the body in two rows, one above the other, and parallel to the blood-red streak, which seemed to answer the purpose of an eyebrow. Two or three of these dreadful eyes were much larger than the others, and had the appearance of solid gold.

"'Although this beast approached us, as I have before said, with the greatest rapidity, it must have been moved altogether by necromancy – for it had neither fins like a fish, nor web-feet like a duck, nor wings like the sea-shell, which is blown along in the manner of a vessel; nor yet did it writhe itself forward as do the eels. Its head and its tail were shaped precisely alike, only, not far from the latter were two small holes that served for nostrils, and through which the monster puffed out its thick breath with prodigious violence, and with a shrieking disagreeable noise.

"'Our terror at beholding this hideous thing was very great, but it was even surpassed by our astonishment, when, upon getting a nearer look, we perceived upon the creature's back a vast number of animals about the size and shape of men, and altogether much resembling them, except that they wore no garments (as men do), being supplied (by nature no doubt), with an ugly uncomfortable covering a good deal like cloth, but fitting so tight to the skin as to render the poor wretches laughably awkward, and put them apparently to severe pain. On the very tips of their heads were certain square-looking boxes, which, at first sight, I thought might have been intended to answer as turbans, but I soon discovered that they were excessively heavy and solid, and I therefore concluded they were contrivances designed, by their great weight, to keep the heads of the animals steady and safe upon their shoulders. Around the necks of the creatures were fastened black collars (badges of servitude no doubt), such as we keep on our dogs, only much wider and infinitely stiffer – so that it was quite impossible for these poor victims to move their heads in any direction without moving the body at the same time; and thus they were doomed to perpetual contemplation of their noses – a view puggish and snubby in a wonderful if not positively in an awful degree.

"'When the monster had nearly reached the shore where we stood, it suddenly pushed out one of its eyes to a great extent, and emitted from it a terrible flash of fire, accompanied by a dense cloud of smoke, and a noise that I can compare to nothing but thunder. As the smoke cleared away, we saw one of the odd man-animals standing near the head of the large beast with a trumpet in his hand, through which (putting it to his mouth) he presently addressed us in loud, harsh, and disagreeable accents, that perhaps we should have mistaken for language had they not come altogether through the nose.

' "Being thus evidently spoken to, I was at a loss how to reply, as I could in no manner understand what was said; and in this difficulty I turned to the porter, who was near swooning through affright, and demanded of him his opinion as to what species of monster it was, what it wanted, and what kind of creatures those were that so swarmed upon his back. To this the porter replied, as well as he could for trepidation, that he had once before heard of this sea-beast; that it was a cruel demon, with bowels of sulphur and blood of fire, created by evil genii as the means of inflicting misery upon mankind; that the things upon its back were vermin, such as sometimes invest cats and dogs, only a little larger and more savage; and that these vermin had their uses, however evil – for, through the torture they caused the beast by their nibblings and stingings, it was goaded into that degree of wrath which was requisite to make it roar and commit ill, and so fulfil the vengeful and malicious designs of the wicked genii.

' "This account determined me to take to my heels, and without once even looking behind me I ran at full speed up into the hills, while the porter ran equally fast, although nearly in an opposite direction, so that by these means he finally made his escape with my bundles, of which, I have no doubt, he took excellent care, although this is a point I cannot determine, as I do not remember that I ever beheld him again.

' "For myself, I was so hotly pursued by a swarm of the men-vermin (who had come to the shore in boats) that I was very soon overtaken, bound hand and foot, and conveyed to the beast, which immediately swam out again into the middle of the sea.

' "I now bitterly repented my folly in quitting a comfortable home to imperil my life in such adventures as these; but regret being useless, I made the best of my condition, and exerted myself to secure the goodwill of the man-animal that owned the trumpet, and who appeared to exercise authority over its fellows. I succeeded so well in this endeavour that in a few days the creature bestowed upon me various tokens of its favour, and in the end even went to the trouble of teaching me the rudiments of what it was vain enough to denominate its language; so that at length I was enabled to converse with it readily, and came to make it comprehend the ardent desire I had of seeing the world.

'"*Washish squashish squeak, Sinbad, hey-diddle diddle grunt unt grumble, hiss, fiss, whiss,*" said he to me one day after dinner – but I beg a thousand pardons, I had forgotten that your majesty is not conversant with the dialect of the Cock-neighs (so the man-animals were called; I presume because their language formed the connecting link between that of the horse and that of the rooster). With your permission I will translate. "*Washish squashish,*" and so forth:– that is to say, "I am happy to find, my dear Sinbad, that you are really a very excellent fellow; we are now about doing a thing which is called circumnavigating the globe; and since you are so desirous of seeing the world, I will strain a point and give you a free passage upon the back of the beast."'

When the Lady Scheherazade had proceeded thus far, relates the 'Isitsoörnt,' the king turned over from his left side to his right, and said –

'It is in fact *very* surprising, my dear queen, that you omitted hitherto these latter adventures of Sinbad. Do you know, I think them exceedingly entertaining and strange?'

The king having thus expressed himself, we are told, the fair Scheherazade resumed her history in the following words:–

'Sinbad went on in this manner with his narrative – "I thanked the man-animal for its kindness, and soon found myself very much at home on the beast which swam at a prodigious rate through the ocean, although the surface of the latter is, in that part of the world, by no means flat, but round like a pomegranate, so that we went, so to say, either up hill or down hill all the time."'

'That, I think, was very singular,' interrupted the king.

'Nevertheless, it is quite true,' replied Scheherazade.

'I have my doubts,' rejoined the king; 'but, pray, be so good as go on with the story.'

'I will,' said the queen. '"The beast," continued Sinbad, "swam, as I have related, up hill and down hill, until at length we arrived at an island many hundreds of miles in circumference, but which, nevertheless, had been built in the middle of the sea by a colony of little things like caterpillars."'*

'Hum!' said the king.

'"Leaving this island," said Sinbad – (for Scheherazade, it must be understood took no notice of her husband's ill-mannered ejaculation) – "leaving this island, we came to another where the forests were of solid stone, and so hard that they shivered to pieces the finest-tempered axes with which we endeavoured to cut them down."'†

* The coralites.

† 'One of the most remarkable natural curiosities in Texas is a petrified forest, near the head of Pasigno river. It consists of several hundred trees, in an erect position, all turned to stone. Some trees, now growing, are partly petrified. This is a startling fact for natural philosophers, and must cause them to modify the existing theory of petrifaction.' – *Kennedy*.

This account, at first discredited, has since been corroborated by the discovery of a completely petrified forest near the head waters of the Chayenne, or Chienne river, which has its source in the Black Hills of the Rocky chain.

There is scarcely, perhaps, a spectacle on the surface of the globe more remarkable, either in a geological or picturesque point of view, than that presented by the petrified forest near Cairo. The traveller, having passed the tombs of the caliphs, just beyond the gates of the city, proceeds to the southward, nearly at right angles to the road across the desert to Suez, and, after having travelled some ten miles up a low barren valley, covered with sand, gravel, and sea-shells, fresh as if the tide had retired but yesterday, crosses a low range of sandhills, which has for some distance run parallel to his path. The scene now presented to him is beyond conception singular and desolate. A mass of fragments of trees, all converted into stone, and when struck by his horse's hoof ringing like cast-iron, is seen to extend itself for miles and miles around him in the form of a decayed and prostrate forest. The wood is of a dark brown hue, but retains its form in perfection, the pieces being from one to fifteen feet in length, and from half-a-foot to three feet in thickness, strewed so closely together, as far as the eye can reach, that an Egyptian donkey can scarcely thread its way through amongst them, and so natural that, were it in Scotland or Ireland, it might pass without remark for some enormous drained bog on which the exhumed trees lay rotting in the

'Hum!' said the king again; but Scheherazade, paying him no attention, continued in the language, of Sinbad.

'"Passing beyond this last island, we reached a country where there was a cave that ran to the distance of thirty or forty miles within the bowels of the earth, and that contained a greater number of far more spacious and more magnificent palaces than are to be found in all Damascus and Bagdad. From the roofs of these palaces there hung myriads of gems, like diamonds, but larger than men; and in among the streets of towers and pyramids and temples, there flowed immense rivers as black as ebony, and swarming with fish that had no eyes."'*

'Hum!' said the king.

' "We then swam into a region of the sea where we found a lofty mountain, down whose sides there streamed torrents of melted metal, some of which were twelve miles wide and sixty miles long;† while from an abyss on the summit issued so vast a quantity of ashes that the sun was entirely blotted out from the heavens, and it became darker than the darkest midnight, so that when we were even at the distance of a hundred and fifty miles from the mountain, it was impossible to see the whitest object, however close we held it to our eyes."'‡

---

sun. The roots and rudiments of the branches are in many cases nearly perfect, and in some the worm holes eaten under the bark are readily recognisable. The most delicate of the sap vessels, and all the finer portions of the centre of the wood, are perfectly entire, and bear to be examined with the strongest magnifiers. The whole are so thoroughly silicified as to scratch glass and be capable of receiving the highest polish. – *Asiatic Magazine.*

* The Mammoth Cave of Kentucky.

† In Iceland, 1783.

‡ 'During the eruption of Hecla in 1766 clouds of this kind produced such a degree of darkness that at Glaumba, which is more than fifty leagues from the mountain, people could only find their way by groping. During the eruption of Vesuvius in 1794 at Caserta, four leagues distant, people could only walk by the light of torches. On the first of May 1812 a cloud of volcanic ashes and sand, coming from a volcano in the island of St. Vincent, covered the whole of Barbadoes, spreading over it so intense a darkness that at mid-day, in the open air, one could not perceive the trees or other objects near him, or even a white handkerchief placed at the distance of six inches from the eye.' – *Murray*, p. 215, *Phil. edit.*

'Hum!' said the king.

' "After quitting this coast, the beast continued his voyage until we met with a land in which the nature of things seemed reversed – for we here saw a great lake, at the bottom of which, more than a hundred feet beneath the surface of the water, there flourished in full leaf a forest of tall and luxuriant trees." '*

'Hoo!' said the king.

' "Some hundred miles farther on brought us to a climate where the atmosphere was so dense as to sustain iron or steel, just as our own does feathers." '†

'Fiddle de dee,' said the king.

' "Proceeding still in the same direction, we presently arrived at the most magnificent region in the whole world. Through it there meandered a glorious river for several thousands of miles. This river was of unspeakable depth, and of a transparency richer than that of amber. It was from three to six miles in width, and its banks, which arose on either side to twelve hundred feet in perpendicular height, were crowned with ever-blossoming trees and perpetual sweet-scented flowers that made the whole territory one gorgeous garden, but the name of this luxuriant land was the kingdom of Horror, and to enter it was inevitable death." '‡

'Humph!' said the king.

' "We left this kingdom in great haste, and after some days came to another, where we were astonished to perceive myriads of monstrous animals, with horns resembling scythes upon their heads. These

---

* 'In the year 1790, in the Caraccas, during an earthquake, a portion of the granite soil sank and left a lake eight hundred yards in diameter and from eighty to a hundred feet deep. It was a part of the forest of Aripao which sank, and the trees remained green for several months under the water.' – *Murray*, p. 221.

† The hardest steel ever manufactured may, under the action of a blow-pipe, be reduced to an impalpable powder, which will float readily in the atmospheric air.

‡ The region of the Niger. See *Simmonds' 'Colonial Magazine.'*

hideous beasts dig for themselves vast caverns in the soil, of a funnel shape, and line the sides of them with rocks, so disposed one upon the other that they fall instantly when trodden upon by other animals, thus precipitating them into the monsters dens, where their blood is immediately sucked, and their carcases afterwards hurled contemptuously out to an immense distance from 'the caverns of death.'"*

'Pooh!' said the king.

'"Continuing our progress, we perceived a district abounding with vegetables that grew not upon any soil, but in the air.† There were others that sprang from the substance of other vegetables,‡ others that derived their sustenance from the bodies of living animals;§ and then, again, there were others that glowed all over with intense fire;|| others that moved from place to place at pleasure;¶ and what is

---

* The *Myrmeleon* – lion-ant. The term 'monster' is equally applicable to small abnormal things and to great, while such epithets as 'vast' are merely comparative. The cavern of the myrmeleon is *vast* in comparison with the hole of the common red ant. A grain of silex is also a 'rock.'

† The *Epidendron*, *Flos Aeris*, of the family of the *Orchideæ*, grows with merely the surface of its roots attached to a tree or other object, from which it derives no nutriment – subsisting altogether upon air.

‡ The *Parasites*, such as the wonderful *Rafflesia Arnaldii*.

§ *Schouw* advocates a class of plants that grow upon living animals – the plant *Plantæ Epizoæ*. Of this class are some *Fuci* and *Algæ*.

Mr. *J. B. Williams, of Salem., Mass.*, presented the 'National Institute' with an insect from New Zealand, with the following description: '"*The Hotte*, a decided caterpillar or worm, is found growing at the root of the *Rata* tree, with a plant growing out of its head. This most peculiar and most extraordinary insect travels up both the *Rata* and *Perriri* trees, and, entering into the top, eats its way, perforating the trunk of the tree until it reaches the root, it then comes out of the root and dies, or remains dormant, and the plant propagates out of its head; the body remains perfect and entire, of a harder substance than when alive. From this insect the natives make a colouring for tattooing."'

|| In mines and natural caves we find a species of cryptogamous *fungus* emits an intense phosphorescence.

¶ The orchis, scabious, and vallisneria.

still more wonderful, we discovered flowers that lived and breathed and moved their limbs at will, and had, moreover, the detestable passion of mankind for enslaving other creatures, and confining them in horrid and solitary prisons until the fulfilment of appointed tasks."'*

'Pshaw!' said the king.

'"Quitting this land, we soon arrived at another in which the bees and the birds are mathematicians of such genius and erudition, that they give daily instructions in the science of geometry to the wise men of the empire. The king of the place having offered a reward for the solution of two very difficult problems, they were solved upon the spot – the one by the bees and the other by the birds; but the king keeping their solutions a secret, it was only after the most profound researches and labour, and a writing of an infinity of big books during a long series of years, that the men-mathematicians at length arrived at the identical

---

* 'The corolla of this flower (*Aristolochia Clematitis*), which is tubular, but terminating upwards in a ligulate limb, is inflated into a globular figure at the base. The tubular part is internally beset with stiff hairs, pointing downwards. The globular part contains the pistil, which consists merely of a germen and stigma, together with the surrounding stamens. But the stamens being shorter than even the germen, cannot discharge the pollen so as to throw it upon the stigma, as the flower stands always upright till after impregnation. And hence, without some additional and peculiar aid, the pollen must necessarily fall down to the bottom of the flower. Now, the aid that nature has furnished in this case is that of the *Tiputa Pennicornis*, a small insect, which, entering the tube of the corolla in quest of honey, descends to the bottom, and rummages about till it becomes quite covered with pollen; but not being able to force its way out again, owing to the downward position of the hairs, which converge to a point like the wires of a mouse-trap, and being somewhat impatient of its confinement, it brushes backwards and forwards, trying every corner, till after repeatedly traversing the stigma, it covers it with pollen sufficient for its impregnation, in consequence of which the flower soon begins to droop, and the hairs to shrink to the side of the tube, effecting an easy passage for the escape of the insect.' – *Rev. P. Keith – System of Physiological Botany.*

solutions which had been given upon the spot by the bees and by the birds."'*

'O my!' said the king.

'"We had scarcely lost sight of this empire, when we found ourselves close upon another, from whose shores there flew over our heads a flock of fowls a mile in breadth, and two hundred and forty miles in length; so that although they flew a mile during every minute, it required no less than four hours for the whole flock to pass over us in which there were several millions of millions of fowls."'†

'O fy!' said the king.

'"No sooner had we got rid of these birds, which occasioned us great annoyance, than we were terrified by the appearance of a fowl of another kind, and infinitely larger than even the rocs which I met in my former voyages; for it was bigger than the biggest of the domes upon your seraglio, O most munificent of caliphs. This terrible fowl had no head that we could perceive, but was fashioned entirely of belly,

---

* The bees – ever since bees were – have been constructing their cells with just such sides, in just such number, and at just such inclinations, as it has been demonstrated (in a problem involving the profoundest mathematical principles) are the very sides, in the very number, and at the very angles, which will afford the creatures the most room that is compatible with the greatest stability of structure.

During the latter part of the last century, the question arose among mathematicians – 'to determine the best form that can be given to the sails of a windmill, according to their varying distances from the revolving vanes, and likewise from the centres of the revolution.' This is an excessively complex problem; for it is, in other words, to find the best possible position at an infinity of varied distances, and at an infinity of points on the arm. There were a thousand futile attempts to answer the query on the part of the most illustrious mathematicians; and when, at length, an undeniable solution was discovered, men found that the wings of a bird had given it with absolute precision ever since the first bird had traversed the air.

† 'He observed a flock of pigeons passing betwixt Frankfort and the Indiana territory one mile at least in breadth; it took up four hours in passing, which, at the rate of one mile per minute, gives a length of 240 miles; and, supposing three pigeons to each square yard, gives 2,230,272,000 pigeons.' – *Travels in Canada and the United States,* by *Lieut F. Hall.*

which was of a prodigious fatness and roundness, of a soft-looking substance, smooth, shining, and striped with various colours. In its talons the monster was bearing away to its eyrie in the heavens a house from which it had knocked off the roof, and in the interior of which we distinctly saw human beings, who, beyond doubt, were in a state of frightful despair at the horrible fate which awaited them. We shouted with all our might in the hope of frightening the bird into letting go of its prey, but it merely gave a snort or puff as if of rage, and then let fall upon our heads a heavy sack which proved to be filled with sand."'

'Stuff!' said the king.

'"It was just after this adventure that we encountered a continent of immense extent and of prodigious solidity, but which, nevertheless, was supported entirely upon the back of a sky-blue cow that had no fewer than four hundred horns."'*

'*That*, now, I believe,' said the king, 'because I have read something of the kind before in a book.'

'"We passed immediately beneath this continent, (swimming in between the legs of the cow), and after some hours found ourselves in a wonderful country indeed, which, I was informed by the man-animal, was his own native land, inhabited by things of his own species. This elevated the man-animal very much in my esteem, and in fact I now began to feel ashamed of the contemptuous familiarity with which I had treated him; for I found that the man-animals in general were a nation of the most powerful magicians who lived with worms in their brains,† which no doubt served to stimulate them by their painful writhings and wrigglings to the most miraculous efforts of imagination."'

'Nonsense!' said the king.

'"Among the magicians were domesticated several animals of very singular kinds; for example, there was a huge horse whose bones were

---

* 'The earth is upheld by a cow of a blue colour, having horns four hundred in number.' – *Sale's Koran*.

† 'The *Entozoa* or intestinal worms have repeatedly been observed in the muscles and in the cerebral substances of men.' – *See Wyatt's Physiology*, p. 143.

iron and whose blood was boiling water. In place of corn, he had black stones for his usual food; and yet, in spite of so hard a diet, he was so strong and swift that he would drag a load more weighty than the grandest temple in this city, at a rate surpassing that of the flight of most birds.'"*

'Twaddle!' said the king.

'"I saw also among these people a hen without feathers, but bigger than a camel; instead of flesh and bone she had iron and brick; her blood, like that of the horse (to whom in fact she was nearly related), was boiling water, and like him she ate nothing but wood or black stones. This hen brought forth very frequently a hundred chickens in the day, and after birth they took up their residence for several weeks within the stomach of their mother.'"†

'Fal lal!' said the king.

'"One of this nation of mighty conjurors created a man out of brass and wood and leather, and endowed him with such ingenuity that he would have beaten at chess all the race of mankind with the exception of the great Caliph Haroun Alraschid.‡ Another of these magi constructed (of like material) a creature that put to shame even the genius of him who made it; for so great were its reasoning powers that in a second it performed calculations of so vast an extent that they would have required the united labour of fifty thousand fleshly men for a year.§ But a still more wonderful conjuror fashioned for himself a mighty thing that was neither man nor beast, but which had brains of lead intermixed with a black matter like pitch, and fingers that it employed with such incredible speed and dexterity that it would have had no trouble in writing out twenty thousand copies of the Koran in an hour; and this with so exquisite a precision, that in all the copies there should not be found one to vary from another by the breadth of the finest hair. This thing was of prodigious strength, so that it erected

* On the Great Western Railway, between London and Exeter, a speed of 71 miles per hour has been attained. A train weighing 90 tons was whirled from Paddington to Didcot (53 miles) in 51 minutes.

† The *Eccolabeion*.   ‡ Maelzel's Automaton Chess-player.

§ Babbage's Calculating Machine.

or overthrew the mightiest empires at a breath; but its powers were exercised equally for evil and for good."'

'Ridiculous!' said the king.

'"Among this nation of necromancers there was also one who had in his veins the blood of the salamanders; for he made no scruple of sitting down to smoke his chibouc in a red-hot oven until his dinner was thoroughly roasted upon its floor.* Another had the faculty of converting the common metals into gold without even looking at them during the process.† Another had such a delicacy of touch that he made a wire so fine as to be invisible.‡ Another had such quickness of perception that he counted all the separate motions of an elastic body while it was springing backwards and forwards at the rate of nine hundred millions of times in a second."'§

'Absurd!' said the king.

'"Another of these magicians, by means of a fluid that nobody ever yet saw, could make the corpses of his friends brandish their arms, kick out their legs, fight, or even get up and dance at his will.|| Another had cultivated his voice to so great an extent that he could have made himself heard from one end of the earth to the other. ¶ Another had so long an arm that he could sit down in Damascus and indite a letter at Bagdad, or indeed at any distance whatsoever.** Another commanded the lightning to come down to him out of the heavens, and it came at his call, and served him for a plaything when it came. Another took two loud sounds and out of them made a silence. Another constructed a

* *Chabert*, and since him a hundred others.
† The Electrotype.
‡ *Wollaston* made of platinum for the field of view in a telescope, a wire one eighteen-thousandth part of an inch in thickness. It could be seen only by means of the microscope.
§ Newton demonstrated that the retina, beneath the influence of the violet ray of the spectrum, vibrated 900,000,000 of times in a second.
|| The Voltaic pile.
¶ The Electric Telegraph transmits intelligence instantaneously – at least so far as regards any distance upon the earth.
** The Electric Telegraph Printing Apparatus.

deep darkness out of two brilliant lights.* Another made ice in a red-hot furnace.† Another directed the sun to paint his portrait, and the sun did.‡ Another took this luminary with the moon and the planets, and having first weighed them with a scrupulous accuracy, probed into their depths and found out the solidity of the substance of which they are made. But the whole nation is indeed of so surprising a necromantic ability that not even their infants nor their commonest cats and dogs have any difficulty in seeing objects that do not exist at all, or that for twenty millions of years before the birth of the nation itself had been blotted out from the face of creation.'''§

* Common experiments in Natural Philosophy. If two red rays from two luminous points be admitted into a dark chamber so as to fall on a white surface, and differ in their length by .00000258 of an inch, their intensity is doubled. So, also, if the difference in length be any whole-number multiple of that fraction. A multiple by $2\frac{1}{4}$, $3\frac{1}{4}$, etc., gives an intensity equal to one ray only; but a multiple by $2\frac{1}{2}$, $3\frac{1}{2}$, etc., gives the result of total darkness. In violet rays similar effects arise when the difference in length is .00000167 of an inch; and with all other rays the results are the same – the difference varying with a uniform increase from the violet to the red.

Analogous experiments in respect to sound produce analogous results.

† Place a platina crucible over a spirit-lamp and keep it a red heat; pour in some sulphuric acid, which, though the most volatile of bodies at a common temperature, will be found to become completely fixed in a hot crucible, and not a drop evaporates   being surrounded by an atmosphere of its own, it does not, in fact, touch the sides. A few drops of water are now introduced, when the acid immediately coming in contact with the heated sides of the crucible, flies off in sulphurous acid vapour, and so rapid is its progress that the caloric of the water passes off with it, which falls a lump of ice to the bottom; by taking advantage of the moment before it is allowed to re-melt it may be turned out a lump of ice from a red-hot vessel.

‡ The Daguerreotype.

§ Although light travels 167,000 miles in a second, the distance of 61 Cygni (the only star whose distance is ascertained) is so inconceivably great that its rays would require more than ten years to reach the earth. For stars beyond this, 20 – or even 1,000 years – would be a moderate estimate. Thus, if they had been annihilated 20 or 1,000 years ago we might still see them to-day by the light which *started* from their surfaces 20 or 1,000 years in the past time. That many which we see daily are really extinct is not impossible, not even improbable.

'Preposterous!' said the king.

'"The wives and daughters of these incomparably great and wise magi," continued Scheherazade, without being in any manner disturbed by these frequent and most ungentlemanly interruptions on the part of her husband – ' "the wives and daughters of these eminent conjurors are everything that is accomplished and refined, and would be everything that is interesting and beautiful but for an unhappy fatality that besets them, and from which not even the miraculous powers of their husbands and fathers has hitherto been adequate to save them. Some fatalities come in certain shapes and some in others, but this of which I speak has come in the shape of a crotchet."'

'A what?' said the king.

'"A crotchet,"' said Scheherazade. '"One of the evil genii who are perpetually upon the watch to inflict ill, has put it into the heads of these accomplished ladies that the thing which we describe as personal beauty consists altogether in the protuberance of the region which lies not very far below the small of the back. Perfection of loveliness they say is in the direct ratio of the extent of this hump. Having been long possessed of this idea, and bolsters being cheap in that country, the days have long gone by since it was possible to distinguish a woman from a dromedary——"'

'Stop!' said the king – 'I can't stand that, and I won't. You have already given me a dreadful headache with your lies. The day, too, I perceive, is beginning to break. How long have we been married? – my conscience is getting to be troublesome again. And then that dromedary touch – do you take me for a fool? Upon the whole you might as well get up and be throttled.'

These words, as I learn from the Isitsoörnot, both grieved and astonished Scheherazade; but as she knew the king to be a man of scrupulous integrity, and quite unlikely to forfeit his word, she

---

The elder Herschel maintains that the light of the faintest nebulæ seen through his great telescope must have taken 3,000,000 years in reaching the earth. Some, made visible by Lord Rosse's instrument must then have required at least 20,000,000.

submitted to her fate with a good grace. She derived, however, great consolation (during the tightening of the bowstring) from the reflection that much of the history remained still untold, and that the petulance of her brute of a husband had reaped for him a most righteous reward in depriving him of many inconceivable adventures.

The Masque of the Red Death

The 'Red Death' had long devastated the country. No pestilence had ever been so fatal or so hideous. Blood was its Avatar and its seal – the redness and the horror of blood. There were sharp pains, and sudden dizziness, and then profuse bleeding at the pores, with dissolution. The scarlet stains upon the body, and especially upon the face of the victim, were the pest ban which shut him out from the aid and from the sympathy of his fellow-men; and the whole seizure, progress, and termination of the disease, were the incidents of half-an-hour.

But the Prince Prospero was happy and dauntless and sagacious. When his dominions were half-depopulated, he summoned to his presence a thousand hale and light-hearted friends from among the knights and dames of his court, and with these retired to the deep seclusion of one of his castellated abbeys. This was an extensive and magnificent structure, the creation of the prince's own eccentric yet august taste. A strong and lofty wall girdled it in. This wall had gates of iron. The courtiers, having entered, brought furnaces and massy hammers and welded the bolts. They resolved to leave means neither of ingress or egress to the sudden impulses of despair from without or of frenzy from within. The abbey was amply provisioned. With such precautions the courtiers might bid defiance to contagion. The external world could take care of itself. In the meantime it was folly to grieve or to think. The prince had provided all the appliances of pleasure. There were buffoons, there were improvisatori, there were ballet-dancers, there were musicians, there was beauty, there was wine. All these and security were within. Without was the 'Red Death.'

It was towards the close of the fifth or sixth month of his seclusion, and while the pestilence raged most furiously abroad, that the Prince Prospero entertained his thousand friends at a masked ball of the most unusual magnificence.

It was a voluptuous scene that masquerade. But first let me tell of the rooms in which it was held. There were seven – an imperial suite, In many palaces, however, such suites form a long and straight vista, while the folding doors slide back nearly to the walls on either hand, so that the view of the whole extent is scarcely impeded. Here the case was very different, as might have been expected from the duke's love of the *bizarre*. The apartments were so irregularly disposed that the vision embraced but little more than one at a time. There was a sharp turn at every twenty or thirty yards, and at each turn a novel effect. To the right and left, in the middle of each wall, a tall and narrow Gothic window looked out upon a closed corridor which pursued the windings of the suite. These windows were of stained glass whose colour varied in accordance with the prevailing hue of the decorations of the chamber into which it opened. That at the eastern extremity was hung, for example, in blue, and vividly blue were its windows. The second chamber was purple in its ornaments and tapestries, and here the panes were purple. The third was green throughout, and so were the casements. The fourth was furnished and lighted with orange, the fifth with white, the sixth with violet. The seventh apartment was closely shrouded in black velvet tapestries that hung all over the ceiling and down the walls, falling in heavy folds upon a carpet of the same material and hue. But in this chamber only the colour of the windows failed to correspond with the decorations. The panes here were scarlet – a deep blood-colour. Now in no one of the seven apartments was there any lamp or candelabrum amid the profusion of golden ornaments that lay scattered to and fro or depended from the roof. There was no light of any kind emanating from lamp or candle within the suite of chambers; but in the corridors that followed the suite there stood opposite to each window a heavy tripod bearing a brazier of fire that projected its rays through the tinted glass and so glaringly illumined the room. And thus were produced a multitude of gaudy and fantastic appearances. But in the western or black chamber the effect of the fire-light that streamed upon the dark hangings, through the blood-tinted panes, was ghastly in the extreme, and produced so wild a look upon the countenances of those who entered that there were few of the company bold enough to set foot within its precincts at all.

It was in this apartment also that there stood against the western wall a gigantic clock of ebony. Its pendulum swung to and fro with a dull, heavy, monotonous clang; and when the minute hand made the circuit of the face, and the hour was to be stricken, there came from the brazen lungs of the clock a sound which was clear and loud, and deep, and exceedingly musical, but of so peculiar a note and emphasis that, at each lapse of an hour, the musicians of the orchestra were constrained to pause momentarily in their performance to hearken to the sound; and thus the waltzers perforce ceased their evolutions, and there was a brief disconcert of the whole gay company, and while the chimes of the clock yet rang it was observed that the giddiest grew pale, and the more aged and sedate passed their hands over their brows as if in confused reverie or meditation; but when the echoes had fully ceased a light laughter at once pervaded the assembly; the musicians looked at each other and smiled as if at their own nervousness and folly, and made whispering vows each to the other that the next chiming of the clock should produce in them no similar emotion, and then, after the lapse of sixty minutes (which embrace three thousand and six hundred seconds of the time that flies), there came yet another chiming of the clock, and then were the same disconcert and tremulousness and meditation as before.

But in spite of these things it was a gay and magnificent revel. The tastes of the duke were peculiar. He had a fine eye for colours and effects. He disregarded the *decora* of mere fashion. His plans were bold and fiery, and his conceptions glowed with barbaric lustre. There are some who would have thought him mad. His followers felt that he was not. It was necessary to hear, and see, and touch him to be *sure* that he was not.

He had directed, in great part, the moveable embellishments of the seven chambers, upon occasion of this great *fête*; and it was his own guiding taste which had given character to the masqueraders. Be sure they were grotesque. There was much glare and glitter and piquancy and phantasm – much of what has been since seen in 'Hernani.' There were arabesque figures with unsuited limbs and appointments. There were delirious fancies such as the madman fashions. There was much of the beautiful, much of the wanton, much of the *bizarre*, something of the terrible, and not a little of that which might have excited disgust. To and fro in the seven chambers there stalked, in fact, a multitude of dreams. And these – the dreams – writhed in and about, taking hue from the rooms, and causing the wild music of the orchestra to seem as the echo of their steps. And anon, there strikes the ebony clock which stands in the hall of the velvet; and then, for a moment, all is still, and all is silent save the voice of the clock. The dreams are stiff-frozen as they stand. But the echoes of the chime die away – they have endured but an instant – and a light, half-subdued laughter floats after them as they depart. And now again the music swells, and the dreams live, and writhe to and fro more merrily than ever, taking hue from the many tinted windows through which stream the rays from the tripods. But to the chamber which lies most westwardly of the seven, there are now none of the maskers who venture; for the night is waning away; and there flows a ruddier light through the blood-coloured panes; and the blackness of the sable drapery appals; and to him whose foot falls upon the sable carpet, there comes from the near clock of ebony a muffled peal more solemnly emphatic than any which reaches *their* ears who indulge in the more remote gaieties of the other apartments.

But these other apartments were densely crowded, and in them beat feverishly the heart of life. And the revel went whirlingly on, until at length there commenced the sounding of midnight upon the clock.

And then the music ceased, as I have told; and the evolutions of the waltzers were quieted; and there was an uneasy cessation of all things as before. But now there were twelve strokes to be sounded by the bell of the clock; and thus it happened, perhaps that more of thought crept, with more of time, into the meditations of the thoughtful among those who revelled. And thus, too, it happened, perhaps, that before the last echoes of the last chime had utterly sunk into silence, there were many individuals in the crowd who had found leisure to become aware of the presence of a masked figure which had arrested the attention of no single individual before. And the rumour of this new presence having spread itself whisperingly around, there arose at length from the whole company a buzz, or murmur, expressive of disapprobation and surprise – then, finally, of terror, of horror, and of disgust.

In an assembly of phantasms such as I have painted, it may well be supposed that no ordinary appearance could have excited such sensation. In truth the masquerade license of the night was nearly unlimited; but the figure in question had out-Heroded Herod, and gone beyond the bounds of even the prince's indefinite decorum. There are chords in the hearts of the most reckless which cannot be touched without emotion. Even with the utterly lost, to whom life and death are equally jests, there are matters of which no jest can be made. The whole company indeed seemed now deeply to feel that in the costume and bearing of the stranger neither wit nor propriety existed. The figure was tall and gaunt, and shrouded from head to foot in the habiliments of the grave. The mask which concealed the visage was made so nearly to resemble the countenance of a stiffened corpse that the closest scrutiny must have had difficulty in detecting the cheat. And yet all this might have been endured, if not approved, by the mad revellers around. But the mummer had gone so far as to assume the type of the Red Death. His vesture was dabbled in *blood* – and his broad brow with all the features of the face, was besprinkled with the scarlet horror.

When the eyes of Prince Prospero fell upon this spectral image (which with a slow and solemn movement, as if more fully to sustain its *rôle*, stalked to and fro among the waltzers) he was seen to be convulsed in the first moment with a strong shudder either of terror or distaste; but in the next his brow reddened with rage.

'Who dares?' he demanded hoarsely of the courtiers who stood near him – 'who dares insult us with this blasphemous mockery? Seize him and unmask him, that we may know whom we have to hang at sunrise from the battlements!'

It was in the eastern or blue chamber in which stood the Prince Prospero as he uttered these words. They rang throughout the seven rooms loudly and clearly – for the prince was a bold and robust man, and the music had become hushed at the waving of his hand.

It was in the blue room where stood the prince, with a group of pale courtiers by his side. At first, as he spoke, there was a slight rushing movement of this group in the direction of the intruder, who, at the moment was also near at hand, and now, with deliberate and stately step, made closer approach to the speaker. But, from a certain nameless awe with which the mad assumptions of the mummer had inspired the whole party, there were found none who put forth hand to seize him; so that unimpeded he passed within a yard of the prince's person; and while the vast assembly, as if with one impulse, shrank from the centres of the rooms to the walls, he made his way uninterruptedly, but with the same solemn and measured step which had distinguished him from the first, through the blue chamber to the purple – through the purple to the green – through the green to the orange – through this again to the white – and even thence to the violet, ere a decided movement had been made to arrest him. It was then, however, that the Prince Prospero, maddening with rage and the shame of his own momentary cowardice, rushed hurriedly through the six chambers while none followed him on account of a deadly terror that had seized upon all. He bore aloft a drawn dagger, and had approached in rapid impetuosity, to within three or four feet of the retreating figure, when the latter, having attained the extremity of the velvet apartment, turned suddenly and confronted his pursuer. There was a sharp cry – and the dagger dropped gleaming upon the sable carpet upon which, instantly afterwards, fell prostrate in death the Prince Prospero. Then, summoning the wild courage of despair, a

The dagger dropped gleaming upon the sable carpet

throng of the revellers at once threw themselves into the black apartment, and, seizing the mummer, whose tall figure stood erect and motionless within the shadow of the ebony clock, gasped in unutterable horror at finding the grave cerements and corpse-like mask which they handled with so violent a rudeness, untenanted by any tangible form.

And now was acknowledged the presence of the Red Death. He had come like a thief in the night; and one by one dropped the revellers in the blood-bedewed halls of their revel, and died each in the despairing posture of his fall; and the life of the ebony clock went out with that of the last of the gay; and the flames of the tripods expired; and darkness and decay, and the Red Death held illimitable dominion over all.

The Imp of the Perverse

In the consideration of the faculties and impulses – of the *prima mobilia* of the human soul, the phrenologists have failed to make room for a propensity which, although obviously existing as a radical, primitive, irreducible sentiment, has been equally overlooked by all the moralists who have preceded them. In the pure arrogance of the reason, we have all overlooked it. We have suffered its existence to escape our senses solely through want of belief – of faith; whether it be faith in revelation, or faith in the Kabbala. The idea of it has never occurred to us, simply because of its supererogation. We saw no *need* of the impulse – for the propensity. We could not perceive its necessity. We could not understand, that is to say, we could not have understood had the notion of this *primum mobile* ever obtruded itself; we could not have understood in what manner it might be made to further the objects of humanity, either temporal or eternal. It cannot be denied that phrenology, and in a great measure, all metaphysician-ism, have been concocted *à priori*. The intellectual or logical man, rather than the understanding or observant man, sets himself to imagine designs – to dictate purposes to God. Having thus fathomed to his satisfaction the intentions of Jehovah, out of these intentions he built his innumerable systems of mind. In the matter of phrenology, for example, we first determined, naturally enough, that it was the design of the Deity that man should eat. We then assigned to man an organ of alimentiveness, and this organ is the scourge with which the Deity compels man, will I nill I, into eating. Secondly, having settled it to be God's will that man should continue his species, we discovered an organ of amativeness, forthwith; and so with combativeness, with ideality, with causality, with constructiveness, – so, in short, with every organ, whether representing a propensity, a moral sentiment, or a faculty of the pure intellect. And in these arrangements of the *principia* of human action, the Spurzheimites, whether right or wrong, in part or upon the whole, have but followed in principle the footsteps of their predecessors, deducing and establishing everything from the preconceived destiny of man, and upon the ground of the objects of his Creator.

It would have been wiser, it would have been safer to classify (if classify we must), upon the basis of what man usually or occasionally did, and was always occasionally doing, rather than upon the basis of what we took it for granted the Deity intended him to to do. If we cannot comprehend God in his visible works, how then in his inconceivable thoughts that call the works into being? If we cannot understand him in his objective creatures, how then in his substantive moods and phases of creation?

Induction, *a posteriori*, would have brought phrenology to admit, as an innate and primitive principle of human action, a paradoxical something, which we may call *perverseness*, for want of a more characteristic term. In the sense I intend, it is, in fact, a *mobile* without motive, a motive not *motivirt*. Through its promptings we act without comprehensible object; or, if this shall be understood as a contradiction in terms, we may so far modify the proposition as to say that through its promptings we act, for the reason that we should *not*. In theory, no reason can be more unreasonable; but, in fact, there is none more strong. With certain minds, under certain conditions, it becomes absolutely irresistible. I am not more certain that I breathe than that the assurance of the wrong or error of any action is often the one unconquerable *force* which impels us, and alone impels us to its prosecution. Nor will this overwhelming tendency to do wrong for the wrong's sake admit of analysis or resolution into ulterior elements. It is a radical, a primitive impulse – elementary. It will be said, I am aware, that when we persist in acts because we feel we should *not* persist in them, our conduct is but a modification of that which ordinarily springs from the *combativeness* of phrenology. But a glance will show the fallacy of this idea. The phrenological combativeness has for its essence the necessity of self-defence. It is our safeguard against injury. Its principle regards our well-being; and thus the desire to be well is excited simultaneously with its development. It follows that the desire to be well must be excited simultaneously with any principle which shall be merely a modification of combativeness, but in the case of that something which I term *perverseness*, the desire to be well is not only not aroused, but a strongly antagonistical sentiment exists.

An appeal to one's own heart is after all the best reply to the sophistry just noticed. No one who trustingly consults and thoroughly questions his own soul, will be disposed to deny the entire radicalness of the propensity in question. It is not more incomprehensible than distinctive. There lives no man who at some period has not been tormented, for example, by an earnest desire to tantalise a listener by circumlocution. The speaker is aware that he displeases; he has every intention to please; he is usually curt, precise, and clear; the most laconic and luminous language is struggling for utterance upon his tongue; it is only with difficulty that he restrains himself from giving it flow; he dreads and deprecates the anger of him whom he addresses; yet the thought strikes him that, by certain involutions and paren-thesis, this anger may be engendered. That single thought is enough. The impulse increases to a wish, the wish to a desire, the desire to an uncontrollable longing, and the longing (to the deep regret and mortification of the speaker, and in defiance of all consequences) is indulged.

We have a task before us which must be speedily performed. We know that it will be ruinous to make delay. The most important crisis of our life calls, trumpet-tongued, for immediate energy and action.

We glow, we are consumed with eagerness to commence the work, with the anticipation of whose glorious result our whole souls are on fire. It must, it shall be undertaken to-day, and yet we put it off until to-morrow; and why? There is no answer except that we feel *perverse*, using the word with no comprehension of the principle. To-morrow arrives, and with it a more impatient anxiety to do our duty, but with this very increase of anxiety arrives, also, a nameless, a positively fearful, because unfathomable craving for delay. This craving gathers strength as the moments fly. The last hour for action is at hand. We tremble with the violence of the conflict within us – of the definite with the indefinite – of the substance with the shadow. But, if the contest have proceeded thus far, it is the shadow which prevails – we struggle in vain. The clock strikes, and is the knell of our welfare. At the same time, it is the chanticleer-note to the ghost that has so long overawed us. It flies – it disappears – we are free. The old energy returns. We will labour *now*. Alas, it is *too late!*

We stand upon the brink of a precipice. We peer into the abyss – we grow sick and dizzy. Our first impulse is to shrink from the danger. Unaccountably we remain. By slow degrees our sickness, and dizziness, and horror, become merged in a cloud of unnameable feeling. By gradations, still more imperceptible, this cloud assumes shape, as did the vapour from the bottle out of which arose the genius in the Arabian Nights. But out of this *our* cloud upon the precipice's edge there grows into palpability a shape, far more terrible than any genius, or any demon of a tale, and yet it is but a thought, although a fearful one, and one which chills the very marrow of our bones with the fierceness of the delight of its horror. It is merely the idea of what would be our sensations during the sweeping precipitancy of a fall from such a height; and this fall – this rushing annihilation – for the very reason that it involves that one most ghastly and loathsome of all the most ghastly and loathsome images of death and suffering which have ever presented themselves to our imagination – for this very cause do we now the most vividly desire it; and because our reason violently deters us from the brink, *therefore* do we the more impetuously approach it. There is no passion in nature so demoniacally impatient as that of him who, shuddering upon the edge of a precipice, thus meditates a plunge. To indulge for a moment in any attempt at *thought* is to be inevitably lost; for reflection but urges us to forbear, and *therefore* it is I say that we *cannot*. If there be no friendly arm to check us, or if we fail in a sudden effort to prostrate ourselves backward from the abyss, we plunge and are destroyed.

Examine these and similar actions as we will, we shall find them resulting solely from the spirit of the *perverse*. We perpetrate them merely because we feel that we should *not*. Beyond or behind this there is no intelligible principle; and we might indeed deem this perverseness a direct instigation of the arch-fiend, were it not occasionally known to operate in furtherance of good.

I have said thus much, that in some measure I may answer your question – that I may explain to you why I am here – that I may assign to you something that shall have at least the faint aspect of a cause for my wearing these fetters, and for my tenanting this cell of the condemned. Had I not been thus prolix, you might either have misunderstood me altogether, or with the rabble have fancied me mad. As it is, you will easily perceive that I am one of the many uncounted victims of the Imp of the Perverse.

It is impossible that any deed could have been wrought with a more thorough deliberation. For weeks, for months, I pondered upon the means of the murder. I rejected a thousand schemes because their accomplishment involved a *chance* of detection. At length, in reading some French memoirs, I found an account of a nearly fatal illness that occurred to Madame Pilau, through the agency of a candle accidentally poisoned. The idea struck my fancy at once. I knew my victim's habit of reading in bed. I knew, too, that his apartment was narrow and ill-ventilated. But I need not vex you with inpertinent details. I need not describe the easy artifices by which I substituted in his bedroom candlestand, a wax light of my own making for the one which I there found. The next morning he was discovered dead in his bed and the coroner's verdict was – 'Death by the visitation of God.'

Having inherited his estate all went well with me for years. The idea of detection never once entered my brain. Of the remains of the fatal taper, I had myself carefully disposed. I had left no shadow of a clue by which it would be possible to convict, or even to suspect me of the crime. It is inconceivable how rich a sentiment of satisfaction arose in my bosom as I reflected upon my absolute security. For a very long period of time I was accustomed to revel in this sentiment. It afforded me more real delight than all the mere worldly advantages accruing from my sin. But there arrived at length an epoch from which the pleasurable feeling grew, by scarcely perceptible gradations, into a haunting and harassing thought. It harassed because it haunted. I could scarcely get rid of it for an instant. It is quite a common thing to be thus annoyed with the ringing in our ears, or rather in our memories, of the burthen of some ordinary song or some unimpressive snatches from an opera. Nor will we be the less tomented if the song in itself be good, or the opera air meritorious. In this manner, at last, I would perpetually catch myself pondering upon my security, and repeating in a low undertone the phrase, 'I am safe.'

One day whilst sauntering along the streets, I arrested myself in the act of murmuring half-aloud these customary syllables. In a fit of petulance I re-modelled them thus:– 'I am safe – I am safe – yes, if I be not fool enough to make open confession!'

No sooner had I spoken these words than I felt an icy chill creep to my heart. I had had some experience in these fits of perversity (whose nature I have been at some trouble to explain), and I remembered well that in no instance had I successfully resisted their attacks; and now my own casual self-suggestion that I might possibly be fool enough to confess the murder of which I had been guilty confronted me, as if with the very ghost of him whom I had murdered – and beckoned me on to death.

At first I made an effort to shake off this nightmare of the soul. I walked vigorously, faster, still faster, at length I ran. I felt a maddening desire to shriek aloud. Every succeeding wave of thought over-whelmed me with new terror, for, alas! I well, too well, understood that to *think* in my situation was to be lost. I still quickened my pace. I bounded like a madman through the crowded thoroughfares. At length the populace took the alarm and pursued me. I felt *then* the consummation of my fate. Could I have torn out my tongue I would have done it – but a rough voice resounded in my ears – a rougher grasp seized me by the shoulder. I turned – I gasped for breath. For a moment I experienced all the pangs of suffocation; I became blind, and deaf, and giddy; and then some invisible fiend, I thought, struck me with his broad palm upon the back. The long-imprisoned secret burst forth from my soul.

They say that I spoke with a distinct enunciation, but with marked emphasis and passionate hurry, as if in dread of interruption before concluding the brief but pregnant sentences that consigned me to the hangman and to hell.

Having related all that was necessary for the fullest judicial conviction, I fell prostrate in a swoon.

But why shall I say more? To-day I wear these chains and am *here*! To-morrow I shall be fetterless! – *but where?*

The Mystery of Marie Rogêt*

A Sequel to 'The Murders in the Rue Morgue'

Es giebt eine Reihe idealischer Begebenheiten, die der Wirklichkeit
parallel lauft. Selten fallen sie zusammen. Menschen und Zufälle modificiren
gewöhnlich die idealische Begebenheit, so dass sie unvollkommen erscheint,
und ihre Folgen gleichfalls unvollkommen sind. So bei der Reformation; statt
des Protestantismus kam das Lutherthum hervor.

There are ideal series of events which run parallel with the real ones.
They rarely coincide. Men and circumstances generally modify the ideal train
of events, so that it seems imperfect, and its consequences are equally
imperfect. Thus with the Reformation; instead of Protestantism came
Lutheranism. NOVALIS – *Moral Ansichten.*

There are few persons, even among the calmest thinkers, who have not
occasionally been startled into a vague yet thrilling half-credence in
the supernatural, by *coincidences* of so seemingly marvellous a
character that, as *mere* coincidences, the intellect has been unable to
receive them. Such sentiments – for the half-credences of which I
speak have never the full force of *thought* – such sentiments are seldom

*Upon the original publication of 'Marie Rogêt,' the footnotes now
appended were considered unnecessary; but the lapse of several years since
the tragedy upon which the tale is based, renders it expedient to give them,
and also to say a few words in explanation of the general design. A young girl
Mary Cecilia Rogers, was murdered in the vicinity of New York; and although

thoroughly stifled unless by reference to the doctrine of chance, or as it is technically termed, the Calculus of Probabilities. Now this Calculus is in its essence purely mathematical; and thus we have the anomaly of the most rigidly exact in science applied to the shadow and spirituality of the most intangible in speculation.

The extraordinary details which I am now called upon to make public will be found to form, as regards sequence of time, the primary branch of a series of scarcely intelligible *coincidences*, whose secondary or concluding branch will be recognised by all readers in the late murder of MARY CECILIA ROGERS, at New York.

When, in an article entitled 'The Murders in the Rue Morgue,' I endeavoured, about a year ago, to depict some very remarkable features in the mental character of my friend, the Chevalier C. Auguste Dupin, it did not occur to me that I should ever resume the subject. This depicting of character constituted my design; and this design was thoroughly fulfilled in the wild train of circumstances brought to instance Dupin's idiosyncrasy. I might have adduced other examples, but I should have proved no more. Late events, however, in their surprising development, have startled me into some further details, which will carry with them the air of extorted confession.

---

her death occasioned an intense and long-enduring excitement, the mystery attending it had remained unsolved at the period when the present paper was written and published (November 1842). Herein, under pretence of relating the fate of a Parisian *grisette*, the author has followed in minute detail, the essential, while merely paralleling the inessential facts of the real murder of Mary Rogers. Thus all argument founded upon the fiction is applicable to the truth; and the investigation of the truth was the object.

The 'Mystery of Marie Rogêt' was composed at a distance from the scene of the atrocity, and with no other means of investigation than the newspapers afforded. Thus, much escaped the writer of which he could have availed himself had he been upon the spot, and visited the localities. It may not be improper to record, nevertheless, that the confessions of *two* persons (one of them the Madame Deluc of the narrative), made at different periods, long subsequent to the publication, confirmed in full, not only the general conclusion, but absolutely *all* the chief hypothetical details by which that conclusion was attained.

Hearing what I have lately heard, it would be indeed strange should I remain silent in regard to what I both heard and saw so long ago.

Upon the winding up of the tragedy involved in the deaths of Madame L'Espanaye and her daughter, the Chevalier dismissed the affair at once from his attention, and relapsed into his old habits of moody reverie. Prone, at all times, to abstraction, I readily fell in with his humour; and continuing to occupy our chambers in the Faubourg Saint Germain, we gave the Future to the winds, and slumbered tranquilly in the Present, weaving the dull world around us into dreams.

But these dreams were not altogether uninterrupted. It may readily be supposed that the part played by my friend in the drama at the Rue Morgue, had not failed of its impression upon the fancies of the Parisian police. With its emissaries, the name of Dupin had grown into a household word. The simple character of those inductions by which he had disentangled the mystery never having been explained even to the Prefect, or to any other individual than myself, of course it is not surprising that the affair was regarded as little less than miraculous, or that the Chevalier's analytical abilities acquired for him the credit of intuition. His frankness would have led him to disabuse every inquirer of such prejudice; but his indolent humour forbade all further agitation of a topic whose interest to himself had long ceased. It thus happened that he found himself the cynosure of the policial eyes; and the cases were not few in which attempt was made to engage his services at the Prefecture. One of the most remarkable instances was that of the murder of a young girl named Marie Rogêt.

This event occurred about two years after the atrocity in the Rue Morgue. Marie, whose Christian and family name will at once arrest attention from their resemblance to those of the unfortunate 'cigar-girl,' was the only daughter of the widow Estelle Rogêt. The father had died during the child's infancy, and from the period of his death, until within eighteen months before the assassination which forms the subject of our narrative, the mother and daughter had dwelt together in the Rue Pavée Saint Andrée;* Madame there keeping a

* Nassau Street

pension, assisted by Marie. Affairs went on thus until the latter had attained her twenty-second year, when her great beauty attracted the notice of a perfumer, who occupied one of the shops in the basement of the Palais Royal, and whose custom lay chiefly among the desperate adventurers infesting that neighbourhood. Monsieur Le Blanc* was not unaware of the advantages to be derived from the attendance of the fair Marie in his perfumery; and his liberal proposals were accepted eagerly by the girl, although with somewhat more of hesitation by Madame.

The anticipations of the shopkeeper were realised, and his rooms soon became notorious through the charms of the sprightly *grisette*. She had been in his employ about a year, when her admirers were thrown into confusion by her sudden disappearance from the shop. Monsieur Le Blanc was unable to account for her absence, and Madame Rogêt was distracted with anxiety and terror. The public papers immediately took up the theme, and the police were upon the point of making serious investigations, when, one fine morning, after the lapse of a week, Marie, in good health, but with a somewhat saddened air, made her reappearance at her usual counter in the perfumery. All inquiry, except that of a private character, was of course immediately hushed. Monsieur Le Blanc professed total ignorance, as before. Marie, with Madame, replied to all questions, that the last week had been spent at the house of a relation in the country. Thus the affair died away and was generally forgotten, for the girl, ostensibly to relieve herself from the impertinence of curiosity, soon bade a final adieu to the perfumer, and sought the shelter of her mother's residence in the Rue Pavée St. Andrée.

It was about five months after this return home, that her friends were alarmed by her sudden disappearance for the second time. Three days elapsed, and nothing was heard of her. On the fourth her corpse was found floating in the Seine,† near the shore which is opposite the Quartier of the Rue Saint Andrée, and at a point not very far distant from the secluded neighbourhood of the Barrière du Roule.‡

The atrocity of this murder (for it was at once evident that

* Anderson.   † The Hudson.   ‡ Weehawken.

murder had been committed), the youth and beauty of the victim, and, above all, her previous notoriety, conspired to produce intense excitement in the minds of the sensitive Parisians. I can call to mind no similar occurrence producing so general and so intense an effect. For several weeks, in the discussion of this one absorbing theme even the momentous political topics of the day were forgotten. The Prefect made unusual exertions; and the powers of the whole Parisian police were of course tasked to the utmost extent.

Upon the first discovery of the corpse it was not supposed that the murderer would be able to elude, for more than a very brief period, the inquisition which was immediately set on foot. It was not until the expiration of a week that it was deemed necessary to offer a reward; and even then this reward was limited to a thousand francs. In the meantime the investigation proceeded with vigour, if not always with judgment, and numerous individuals were examined to no purpose; while, owing to the continued absence of all clue to the mystery, the popular excitement greatly increased. At the end of the tenth day it was thought advisable to double the sum originally proposed; and, at length, the second week having elapsed without leading to any discoveries, and the prejudice which always exists in Paris against the Police having given vent to itself in several serious *émeutes*, the Prefect took it upon himself to offer the sum of twenty thousand francs 'for the conviction of the assassin', or, if more than one should prove to have been implicated, 'for the conviction of any one of the assassins.' In the proclamation setting forth this reward, a full pardon was promised to any accomplice who should come forward in evidence against his fellow; and to the whole was appended, wherever it appeared, the private placard of a committee of citizens, offering ten thousand francs in addition to the amount proposed by the Prefecture. The entire reward thus stood at no less than thirty thousand francs, which will be regarded as an extraordinary sum when we consider the humble condition of the girl, and the great frequency in large cities of such atrocities as the one described.

No one doubted now that the mystery of this murder would be immediately brought to light. But although, in one or two instances, arrests were made which promised elucidation, yet nothing was elicited which could implicate the parties suspected, and they were discharged forthwith. Strange as it may appear, the third week from the discovery of the body had passed, and passed without any light being thrown upon the subject, before even a rumour of the events which had so agitated the public mind reached the ears of Dupin and myself. Engaged in researches which had absorbed our whole attention, it had been nearly a month since either of us had gone abroad, or received a visitor, or more than glanced at the leading political articles in one of the daily papers. The first intelligence of the murder was brought us by G——, in person. He called upon us early in the afternoon of the thirteenth of July 18 –, and remained with us until late in the night. He had been piqued by the failure of all his endeavours to ferret out the assassins. His reputation – so he said with a peculiarly Parisian air – was at stake. Even his honour was concerned. The eyes of the public were upon him; and there was really no sacrifice which he would not be willing to make for the development of the mystery. He concluded a somewhat droll speech with a compliment upon what he was pleased to term the *tact* of Dupin, and made him a direct and certainly a liberal proposition, the precise nature of which I do not feel myself at liberty to disclose, but which has no bearing upon the proper subject of my narrative.

The compliment my friend rebutted as best he could, but the proposition he accepted at once, although its advantages were altogether provisional. This point being settled, the Prefect broke forth at once into explanations of his own views, interspersing them with long comments upon the evidence; of which latter we were not yet in possession. He discoursed much, and, beyond doubt, learnedly; while I hazarded an occasional suggestion as the night wore drowsily away. Dupin, sitting steadily in his accustomed arm-chair, was the embodiment of respectful attention. He wore spectacles during the whole interview, and an occasional glance beneath their green glasses sufficed to convince me that he slept not the less soundly, because silently, throughout the seven or eight leaden-footed hours which immediately preceded the departure of the Prefect.

In the morning I procured at the Prefecture a full report of all the evidence elicited, and, at the various newspaper offices, a copy of every paper in which, from first to last, had been published any decisive information in regard to this sad affair. Freed from all that was positively disproved, this mass of information stood thus:–

Marie Rogêt left the residence of her mother, in the Rue Pavée St. Andrée, about nine o'clock in the morning of Sunday, June the twenty-second, 18—. In going out, she gave notice to a Monsieur Jacques St. Eustache,* and to him only, of her intention to spend the day with an aunt who resided in the Rue des Drômes. The Rue des Drômes is a short and narrow but populous thoroughfare, not far from the banks of the river, and at a distance of some two miles, in the most direct course possible, from the *pension* of Madame Rogêt. St. Eustache was the accepted suitor of Marie, and lodged, as well as took his meals, at the *pension*. He was to have gone for his betrothed at dusk, and to have escorted her home. In the afternoon, however, it came on to rain heavily; and, supposing that she would remain all night at her aunt's (as she had done under similar circumstances before), he did not think it necessary to keep his promise. As night drew on, Madame Rogêt (who was an infirm old lady, seventy years of age) was heard to express a fear 'that she should never see Marie again;' but this observation attracted little attention at the time.

On Monday, it was ascertained that the girl had not been to the Rue des Drômes; and when the day elapsed without tidings of her, a tardy search was instituted at several points in the city and its environs. It was not, however, until the fourth day from the period of her disappearance that anything satisfactory was ascertained respecting her. On this day (Wednesday, the twenty-fifth of June), a Monsieur Beauvais,† who, with a friend, had been making inquiries for Marie near the Barrière du Roule, on the shore of the Seine which is opposite the Rue Pavée St. Andrée, was informed that a corpse had just been towed ashore by some fishermen, who had found it floating in the river. Upon seeing the body, Beauvais, after some hesitation,

* Payne.
† Crommelin.

identified it as that of the perfumery-girl. His friend recognised it more promptly.

The face was suffused with dark blood, some of which issued from the mouth. No foam was seen, as in the case of the merely drowned. There was no discoloration in the cellular tissue. About the throat were bruises and impressions of fingers. The arms were bent over on the chest and were rigid. The right hand was clenched; the left partially open. On the left wrist were two circular excoriations, apparently the effect of ropes, or of a rope in more than one volution. A part of the right wrist, also, was much chafed, as well as the back throughout its extent, but more especially at the shoulderblades. In bringing the body to the shore the fishermen had attached to it a rope, but none of the excoriations had been effected by this. The flesh of the neck was much swollen. There were no cuts apparent, or bruises which appeared the effect of blows. A piece of lace was found tied so tightly around the neck as to be hidden from sight; it was completely buried in the flesh, and was fastened by a knot which lay just under the left ear. This alone would have sufficed to produce death. The medical testimony spoke confidently of the virtuous character of the deceased. She had been subjected, it said, to brutal violence. The corpse was in such condition when found that there could have been no difficulty in its recognition by friends.

The dress was much torn and otherwise disordered. In the outer garment a slip, about a foot wide, had been torn upward from the bottom hem to the waist, but not torn off. It was wound three times around the waist, and secured by a sort of hitch in the back. The dress immediately beneath the frock was of fine muslin; and from this a slip eighteen inches wide had been torn entirely out – torn very evenly and with great care. It was found around her neck, fitting loosely, and secured with a hard knot. Over this muslin slip and the slip of lace, the strings of a bonnet were attached; the bonnet being appended. The knot by which the strings of the bonnet were fastened was not a lady's, but a slip or sailor's knot.

After the recognition of the corpse, it was not, as usual, taken to the Morgue (this formality being superfluous), but hastily interred not far from the spot at which it was brought ashore. Through the exertions of Beauvais, the matter was industriously hushed up, as far as possible; and several days had elapsed before any public emotion resulted. A weekly paper,* however, at length, took up the theme; the corpse was disinterred, and a re-examination instituted, but nothing was elicited beyond what has been already noted. The clothes, however, were now submitted to the mother and friends of the deceased, and fully identified as those worn by the girl upon leaving home.

Meantime, the excitement increased hourly. Several individuals were arrested and discharged. St. Eustache fell especially under suspicion, and he failed at first to give an intelligible account of his whereabouts during the Sunday on which Marie left home. Subsequently, however, he submitted to Monsieur G—— affidavits, accounting satisfactorily for every hour of the day in question. As time passed and no discovery ensued, a thousand contradictory rumours were circulated, and journalists busied themselves in *suggestions*. Among these, the one which attracted the most notice was the idea that Marie Rogêt still lived – that the corpse found in the Seine was that of some other unfortunate. It will be proper that I submit to the reader some passages which embody the suggestion alluded to. These passages are *literal* translations from 'L'Etoile,'† a paper conducted, in general, with much ability.

'Mademoiselle Rogêt left her mother's house on Sunday morning, June the twenty-second, 18——, with the ostensible purpose of going to see her aunt, or some other connection, in the Rue des Drômes. From that hour nobody is proved to have seen her. There is no trace or tidings of her at all. . . . There has no person whatever come forward so far, who saw her at all on that day after she left her mother's door. . . . Now, though we have no evidence that Marie Rogêt was in the land of the living after nine o'clock on Sunday, June the twenty-second, we have proof that up to that hour she was alive. On Wednesday at noon, a female body was discovered afloat on the shore of the Barrière du

* 'The New York Mercury.'
† 'The New York Brother Jonathan.'

Roule. This was, even if we presume that Marie Rogêt was thrown into the river within three hours after she left her mother's house, only three days from the time she left her home – three days to an hour. But it is folly to suppose that the murder, if murder was committed on her body, could have been consummated soon enough to have enabled her murderers to throw the body into the river before midnight. Those who are guilty of such horrid crimes choose darkness rather than light. . . . Thus we see that if the body found in the river *was* that of Marie Rogêt, it could only have been in the water two and a half days, or three at the outside. All experience has shown that drowned bodies, or bodies thrown into the water immediately after death by violence, require from six to ten days for sufficient decomposition to take place to bring them to the top of the water. Even where a cannon is fired over a corpse, and it rises before at least five or six days' immersion, it sinks again if let alone. Now, we ask, what was there in this case to cause a departure from the ordinary course of nature? . . . If the body had been kept in its mangled state on shore until Tuesday night, some trace would be found on shore of the murderers. It is a doubtful point, also, whether the body would be so soon afloat, even were it thrown in after having been dead two days. And, furthermore, it is exceedingly improbable that any villains who had committed such a murder as is here supposed, would have thrown the body in without weight to sink it, when such a precaution could have so easily been taken.'

The editor here proceeds to argue that the body must have been in the water 'not three days merely, but at least five times three days,' because it was so far decomposed that Beauvais had great difficulty in recognising it. This latter point, however, was fully disproved. I continue the translation:

'What then are the facts on which M. Beauvais says that he has no doubt the body was that of Marie Rogêt? He ripped up the gown sleeve, and says he found marks which satisfied him of the identity. The public generally supposed those marks to have consisted of some description of scars. He rubbed the arm and found *hair* upon it –

something as indefinite, we think, as can readily be imagined – as little conclusive as finding an arm in the sleeve. M. Beauvais did not return that night, but sent word to Madame Rogêt at seven o'clock on Wednesday evening that an investigation was still in progress respecting her daughter. If we allow that Madame Rogêt, from her age and grief, could not go over (which is allowing a great deal), there certainly must have been some one who would have thought it worth while to go over and attend the investigation, if they thought the body was that of Marie. Nobody went over. There was nothing said or heard about the matter in the Rue Pavée St. Andrée that reached even the occupants of the same building. M. St. Eustache, the lover and intended husband of Marie, who boarded in her mother's house, deposes that he did not hear of the discovery of the body of his intended until the next morning, when M. Beauvais came into his chamber and told him of it. For an item of news like this, it strikes us it was very coolly received.'

In this way the journal endeavoured to create the impression of an apathy on the part of the relatives of Marie, inconsistent with the supposition that these relatives believed the corpse to be hers. Its insinuations amount to this: that Marie with the connivance of her friends, had absented herself from the city for reasons involving a charge against her chastity, and that these friends, upon the discovery of a corpse in the Seine, somewhat resembling that of the girl, had availed themselves of the opportunity to impress the public with the belief of her death. But 'L'Etoile' was again over-hasty. It was distinctly proved that no apathy, such as was imagined, existed: that the old lady was exceedingly feeble, and so agitated as to be unable to attend to any duty: that St. Eustache, so far from receiving the news coolly, was distracted with grief, and bore himself so frantically that M. Beauvais prevailed upon a friend and relative to take charge of him, and prevent his attending the examination at the disinterment. Moreover, although it was stated by 'L'Etoile' that the corpse was reinterred at the public expense, that an advantageous offer of private sepulture was absolutely declined by the family, and that no member of the family attended the ceremonial: although, I say, all this was asserted by 'L'Etoile' in furtherance of the impression it designed to convey – yet *all* this was satisfactorily disproved. In a subsequent number of the paper, an attempt was made to throw suspicion upon Beauvais himself. The editor says:

'Now, then, a change comes over the matter. We are told that on one occasion, while a Madame B—— was at Madame Rogêt's house, M. Beauvais, who was going out, told her that a *gendarme* was expected there, and that she, Madame B——, must not say anything to the *gendarme* until he returned, but let the matter be for him. . . . In the present posture of affairs M. Beauvais appears to have the whole matter locked up in his head. A single step cannot be taken without M. Beauvais, for go which way you will you run against him. . . . For some reason he determined that nobody shall have anything to do with the proceedings but himself, and he has elbowed the male relatives out of the way, according to their representations, in a very singular manner. He seems to have been very much averse to permitting the relatives to see the body.'

By the following fact some colour was given to the suspicion thus thrown upon Beauvais. A visitor at his office a few days prior to the girl's disappearance, and during the absence of its occupant, had observed *a rose* in the keyhole of the door, and the name '*Marie*' inscribed upon a slate which hung near at hand.

The general impression, so far as we were enabled to glean it from the newspapers, seemed to be that Marie had been the victim of *a gang* of desperadoes, that by these she had been borne across the river, maltreated, and murdered. 'Le Commerciel,'* however, a print of extensive influence, was earnest in combating this popular idea. I quote a passage or two from its columns:

'We are persuaded that pursuit has hitherto been on a false scent, so far as it has been directed to the Barrière du Roule. It is impossible

* New York 'Journal of Commerce.'

that a person so well known to thousands as this young woman was, should have passed three blocks without some one having seen her; and any one who saw her would have remembered it, for she interested all who knew her. It was when the streets were full of people that she went out.... It is impossible that she could have gone to the Barrière du Roule or to the Rue des Drômes without being recognised by a dozen persons, yet no one has come forward who saw her outside of her mother's door, and there is no evidence, except the testimony concerning her *expressed intentions*, that she did go out at all. Her gown was torn and bound round her, and tied, and by that the body was carried as a bundle. If the murder had been committed at the Barrière du Roule there would have been no necessity for any such arrangement. The fact that the body was found floating near the Barrière is no proof as to where it was thrown into the water.... A piece of one of the unfortunate girl's petticoats, two feet long and one foot wide, was torn out and tied under her chin around the back of her head, probably to prevent screams. This was done by fellows who had no pocket handkerchiefs.'

A day or two before the Prefect called upon us, however, some important information reached the police, which seemed to overthrow, at least, the chief portion of 'Le Commerciel's' argument.

Two small boys, sons of a Madame Deluc, while roaming among the woods near the Barrière du Roule, chanced to penetrate a close thicket, within which were three or four large stones, forming a kind of seat, with a back and footstool. On the upper stone lay a white petticoat, on the second a silk scarf. A parasol, gloves, and a pocket handkerchief were also here found. The handkerchief bore the name 'Marie Rogêt.' Fragments of dress were discovered on the brambles around. The earth was trampled, the bushes were broken, and there was every evidence of a struggle. Between the thicket and the river the fences were found taken down, and the ground bore evidence of some heavy burden having been dragged along it.

A weekly paper, 'Le Soleil,'* had the following comments upon

* Philadelphia 'Saturday Evening Post.'

this discovery – comments which merely echoed the sentiment of the whole Parisian press:

'The things had all evidently been there at least three or four weeks; they were all mildewed down hard with the action of the rain, and stuck together from mildew. The grass had grown around and over some of them. The silk on the parasol was strong, but the threads of it were run together within. The upper part, where it had been doubled and folded, was all mildewed and rotten, and tore on its being opened...... The pieces of her frock torn out by the bushes were about three inches wide and six inches long. One part was the hem of the frock, and it had been mended; the other piece was part of the skirt, not the hem. They looked like strips torn off, and were on the thorn bush, about a foot from the ground...... There can be no doubt, therefore, that the spot of this appalling outrage has been discovered.

Consequent upon this discovery, new evidence appeared. Madame Deluc testified that she keeps a roadside inn not far from the bank of the river, opposite the Barrière du Roule. The neighbourhood is secluded – particularly so. It is the usual Sunday resort of blackguards from the city, who cross the river in boats. About three o'clock in the afternoon of the Sunday in question a young girl arrived at the inn accompanied by a young man of dark complexion. The two remained here for some time. On their departure, they took the road to some thick woods in the vicinity. Madame Deluc's attention was called to the dress worn by the girl on account of its resemblance to one worn by a deceased relative. A scarf was particularly noticed. Soon after the departure of the couple a gang of miscreants made their appearance, behaved boisterously, ate and drank without making payment, followed in the route of the young man and the girl, returned to the inn about dusk, and re-crossed the river as if in great haste.

It was soon after dark, upon this same evening, that Madame Deluc, as well as her eldest son, heard the screams of a female in the vicinity of the inn. The screams were violent but brief. Madame D. recognised not only the scarf which was found in the thicket, but the dress which was discovered upon the corpse. An omnibus-driver, Valence,* now also testified that he saw Marie Rogêt cross a ferry on the Seine, on the Sunday in question, in company with a young man of dark complexion. He, Valence, knew Marie, and could not be mistaken in her identity. The articles found in the thicket were fully identified by the relatives of Marie.

The items of evidence and information thus collected by myself from the newspapers, at the suggestion of Dupin, embraced only one more point – but this was a point of seemingly vast consequence. It appears that, immediately after the discovery of the clothes as above described, the lifeless, or nearly lifeless body of St. Eustache, Marie's betrothed, was found in the vicinity of what all now supposed the scene of the outrage. A phial labelled 'laudanum,' and emptied, was found near him. His breath gave evidence of the poison. He died without speaking. Upon his person was found a letter, briefly stating his love for Marie, with his design of self-destruction.

'I need scarcely tell you,' said Dupin, as he finished the perusal of my notes, 'that this is a far more intricate case than that of the Rue Morgue, from which it differs in one important respect. This is an *ordinary*, although an atrocious instance of crime. There is nothing peculiarly *outré* about it. You will observe that, for this reason, the mystery has been considered easy, when, for this reason, it should have been considered difficult of solution. Thus, at first, it was thought unnecessary to offer a reward. The myrmidons of G—— were able at once to comprehend how and why such an atrocity *might have been* committed. They could picture to their imaginations a mode – many modes – and a motive – many motives; and because it was not impossible that either of these numerous modes and motives *could* have been the actual one, they have taken it for granted that one of them *must*. But the ease with which these variable fancies were entertained, and the very plausibility which each assumed, should have been understood as indicative rather of the difficulties than of the facilities which must attend elucidation. I have before observed that it is by prominences above the plane of the ordinary, that reason feels her

* Adam.

way, if at all, in her search for the true, and that the proper question in cases such as this, is not so much "what has occurred?" as "what has occurred that has never occurred before?" In the investigations at the house of Madame L'Espanaye,* the agents of G—— were discouraged and confounded by that very *unusualness* which, to a properly regulated intellect, would have afforded the surest omen of success; while this same intellect might have been plunged in despair at the ordinary character of all that met the eye in the case of the perfumery-girl, and yet told of nothing but easy triumph to the functionaries of the Prefecture.

'In the case of Madame L'Espanaye and her daughter, there was, even at the beginning of our investigation, no doubt that murder had been committed. The idea of suicide was excluded at once. Here, too, we are freed at the commencement from all supposition of self-murder. The body found at the Barrière du Roule was found under such circumstances as to leave us no room for embarrassment upon this important point. But it has been suggested that the corpse discovered is not that of the Marie Rogêt, for the conviction of whose assassin, or assassins, the reward is offered, and respecting whom, solely, our agreement has been arranged with the Prefect. We both know this gentleman well. It will not do to trust him too far. If, dating our inquiries from the body found, and then tracing a murderer, we yet discover this body to be that of some other individual than Marie; or, if starting from the living Marie, we find her, yet find her unassassinated – in either case we lose our labour, since it is Monsieur —— with whom we have to deal. For our own purpose, therefore, if not for the purpose of justice, it is indispensable that our first step should be the determination of the identity of the corpse with the Marie Rogêt who is missing.

'With the public, the arguments of "L'Etoile" have had weight; and that the journal itself is convinced of their importance would appear from the manner in which it commences one of its essays upon the subject – "Several of the morning papers of the day," it says, "speak of the *conclusive* article in Monday's 'Etoile.'" To me, this

* See 'Murders in the Rue Morgue.'

article appears conclusive of little beyond the zeal of its inditer. We should bear in mind, that in general it is the object of our newspapers rather to create a sensation – to make a point – than to further the cause of truth. The latter end is only pursued when it seems coincident with the former. The print which merely falls in with ordinary opinion (however well founded this opinion may be) earns for itself no credit with the mob. The mass of the people regard as profound only him who suggests *pungent contradictions* of the general idea. In ratiocination, not less than in literature, it is the *epigram* which is the most immediately and the most universally appreciated. In both, it is of the lowest order of merit.

'What I mean to say is, that it is the mingled epigram and melodrama of the idea, that Marie Rogêt still lives, rather than any true plausibility in this idea, which have suggested it to "L'Etoile," and secured it a favourable reception with the public. Let us examine the heads of this journal's argument; endeavouring to avoid the incoherence with which it is originally set forth.

'The first aim of the writer is to show, from the brevity of the interval between Marie's disappearance and the finding of the floating corpse, that this corpse cannot be that of Marie. The reduction of this interval to its smallest possible dimension, becomes thus, at once, an object with the reasoner. In the rash pursuit of this object he rushes into mere assumption at the outset. "It is folly to suppose," he says, "that the murder, if murder was committed on her body, could have been consummated soon enough to have enabled her murderers to throw the body into the river before midnight? We demand at once, and very naturally *why?* Why is it folly to suppose that the murder was committed *within five minutes* after the girl's quitting her mother's house?" Why is it folly to suppose that the murder was committed at any given period of the day? There have been assassinations at all hours. But, had the murder taken place at any moment between nine o'clock in the morning of Sunday, and a quarter before midnight, there would still have been time enough "to throw the body into the river before midnight." This assumption then, amounts precisely to this – that the murder was not committed on Sunday at all; and, if we allow "L'Etoile" to assume this, we may permit it any liberties whatever. The paragraph beginning, "It is folly to suppose that the murder, etc.," however it appears as printed in "L'Etoile," may be imagined to have existed actually *thus* in the brain of its inditer – "It is folly to suppose that the murder, if murder was committed on the body, could have been committed soon enough to have enabled her murderers to throw the body into the river before midnight. It is folly, we say, to suppose all this, and, to suppose at the same time (as we are resolved to suppose), that the body was *not* thrown in until *after* midnight" – a sentence sufficiently inconsequential in itself, but not so utterly preposterous as the one printed.

'Were it my purpose,' continued Dupin, 'merely to *make out a case* against this passage of "L'Etoile's" argument, I might safely leave it where it is. It is not, however, with "L'Etoile" that we have to do, but with the truth. The sentence in question has but one meaning as it stands, and this meaning I have fairly stated; but it is material that we go behind the mere words for an idea which these words have obviously intended – and failed – to convey. It was the design of the journalist to say that, at whatever period of the day or night of Sunday this murder was committed, it was improbable that the assassins would have ventured to bear the corpse to the river before midnight. And herein lies, really, the assumption of which I complain. It is assumed that the murder was committed at such a position, and under such circumstances, that *the bearing it* to the river became necessary. Now, the assassination might have taken place upon the river's brink or on the river itself; and, thus, the throwing the corpse in the water might have been resorted to at any period of the day or night as the most obvious and most immediate mode of disposal. You will understand that I suggest nothing here as probable, or as coincident with my own opinion. My design, so far, has no reference to the *facts* of the case. I wish merely to caution you against the whole tone of "L'Etoile's" *suggestion*, by calling your attention to its *ex parte* character at the outset.

'Having prescribed thus a limit to suit its own preconceived notions; having assumed that, if this were the body of Marie, it could have been in the water but a very brief time; the journal goes on to say:–

"All experience has shown that drowned bodies, or bodies thrown into the water immediately after death by violence, require from six to ten days for sufficient decomposition to take place to bring them to the top of the water. Even when a cannon is fired over a corpse, and it rises before at least five or six days' immersion, it sinks again if let alone."

'These assertions have been tacitly received by every paper in Paris with the exception of "Le Moniteur."* This latter print endeavours to combat that portion of the paragraph which has reference to "drowned bodies" only, by citing some five or six instances in which the bodies of individuals known to be drowned were found floating after the lapse of less time than is insisted upon by "L'Etoile." But there is something excessively unphilosophical in the attempt on the part of "Le Moniteur" to rebut the general assertion of "L'Etoile," by a citation of particular instances militating against that assertion. Had it been possible to adduce fifty instead of five examples of bodies found floating at the end of two or three days, these fifty examples could still have been properly regarded only as exceptions to "L'Etoile's" rule until such time as the rule itself should be confuted. Admitting the rule (and this "Le Moniteur" does not deny, insisting merely upon its exceptions), the argument of "L'Etoile" is suffered to remain in full force; for this argument does not pretend to involve more than a question of the *probability* of the body having risen to the surface in less than three days; and this probability will be in favour of "L'Etoile's" position until the instances so childishly adduced shall be sufficient in number to establish an antagonistical rule.

'You will see at once that all argument upon this head should be urged, if at all, against the rule itself; and for this end we must examine the *rationale* of the rule. Now the human body, in general, is neither much lighter nor much heavier than the water of the Seine; that is to say, the specific gravity of the human body, in its natural condition, is about equal to the bulk of fresh water which it displaces. The bodies of

* The New York 'Commercial Advertiser.'

fat and fleshy persons, with small bones, and of women generally, are lighter than those of the lean and large-boned, and of men; and the specific gravity of the water of a river is somewhat influenced by the presence of the tide from sea. But, leaving this tide out of question, it may be said that *very* few human bodies will sink at all, even in fresh water, *of their own accord*. Almost any one, falling into a river, will be enabled to float, if he suffer the specific gravity of the water fairly to be adduced in comparison with his own – that is to say, if he suffer his whole person to be immersed, with as little exception as possible. The proper position for one who cannot swim, is the upright position of the walker on land, with the head thrown fully back, and immersed; the mouth and nostrils alone remaining above the surface. Thus circumstanced, we shall find that we float without difficulty and without exertion. It is evident, however, that the gravities of the body, and of the bulk of water displaced, are very nicely balanced, and that a trifle will cause either to preponderate. An arm, for instance, uplifted from the water, and thus deprived of its support, is an additional weight sufficient to immerse the whole head, while the accidental aid of the smallest piece of timber will enable us to elevate the head so as to look about. Now, in the struggles of one unused to swimming, the arms are invariably thrown upwards, while an attempt is made to keep the head in its usual perpendicular position. The result is the immersion of the mouth and nostrils, and the reception, during efforts to breathe while beneath the surface, of water into the lungs. Much is also received into the stomach, and the whole body becomes heavier by the difference between the weight of the air originally distending these cavities, and that of the fluid which now fills them. This difference is sufficient to cause the body to sink, as a general rule; but is insufficient in the cases of individuals with small bones and an abnormal quantity of flaccid or fatty matter. Such individuals float even after drowning.

'The corpse, being supposed at the bottom of the river, will there remain until, by some means, its specific gravity again becomes less than that of the bulk of water which it displaces. This effect is brought about by decomposition, or otherwise. The result of decomposition is the generation of gas, distending the cellular tissues and all the cavities, and giving the *puffed* appearance which is so horrible. When this distension has so far progressed that the bulk of the corpse is materially increased without a corresponding increase of *mass* or weight, its specific gravity becomes less than that of the water displaced, and it forthwith makes its appearance at the surface. But decomposition is modified by innumerable circumstances – is hastened or retarded by innumerable agencies; for example, by the heat or cold of the season, by the mineral impregnation or purity of the water, by its depth or shallowness, by its currency or stagnation, by the temperament of the body, by its infection or freedom from disease before death. Thus it is evident that we can assign no period, with anything like accuracy, at which the corpse shall rise through decomposition. Under certain conditions this result would be brought about within an hour; under others, it might not take place at all. There are chemical infusions by which the animal frame can be preserved *for ever* from corruption; the bi-chloride of mercury is one. But, apart from decomposition, there may be, and very usually is, a generation of gas within the stomach from the acetous fermentation of vegetable matter (or within other cavities from other causes) sufficient to induce a distension which will bring the body to the surface. The effect produced by the firing of a cannon is that of simple vibration. This may either loosen the corpse from the soft mud or ooze in which it is imbedded, thus permitting it to rise when other agencies have already prepared it for so doing; or it may overcome the tenacity of some putrescent portions of the cellular tissue; allowing the cavities to distend under the influence of the gas.

'Having thus before us the whole philosophy of this subject, we can easily test by it the assertions of "L'Etoile." "All experience shows," says this paper, "that drowned bodies, or bodies thrown into the water immediately after death by violence, require from six to ten days for sufficient decomposition to take place to bring them to the top of the water. Even when a cannon is fired over a corpse, and it rises before at least five or six days' immersion, it sinks again if let alone."

'The whole of this paragraph must now appear a tissue of inconsequence and incoherence. All experience does *not* show that "drowned bodies" *require* from six to ten days for sufficient decomposition to take place to bring them to the surface. Both science and experience show that the period of their rising is, and necessarily must be indeterminate. If, moreover, a body has risen to the surface through firing of cannon, it will *not* "sink again if let alone," until decomposition has so far progressed as to permit the escape of the generated gas. But I wish to call your attention to the distinction which is made between "drowned bodies," and "bodies thrown into the water immediately after death by violence." Although the writer admits the distinction, he yet includes them all in the same category. I have shown how it is that the body of a drowning man becomes specifically heavier than its bulk of water, and that he would not sink at all, except for the struggles by which he elevates his arms above the surface, and his gasps for breath while beneath the surface – gasps which supply by water the place of the original air in the lungs. But these struggles and these gasps would not occur in the body "thrown into the water immediately after death by violence." Thus, in the latter instance, *the body, as a general rule, would not sink at all* – a fact of which "L'Etoile" is evidently ignorant. When decomposition had proceeded to a very great extent – when the flesh had in a great measure left the bones – then, indeed, but not *till* then, should we lose sight of the corpse.

'And now what are we to make of the argument that the body found could not be that of Marie Rogêt because, three days only having elapsed, this body was found floating? If drowned, being a woman, she might never have sunk; or, having sunk, might have reappeared in twenty-four hours, or less. But no one supposes her to have been drowned; and, dying before being thrown into the river, she might have been found floating at any period afterwards whatever.

' "But," says "L'Etoile," "if the body had been kept in its mangled state on shore until Tuesday night, some trace would be found on shore of the murderers." Here it is at first difficult to perceive the intention of the reasoner. He means to anticipate what he imagines would be an objection to his theory – viz., that the body was kept on shore two days, suffering rapid decomposition – *more* rapid than if immersed in water. He supposes that, had this been the case, it *might* have appeared at the surface on the Wednesday, and thinks that *only* under such circumstances it could so have appeared. He is accordingly in haste to show that it *was not* kept on shore; for, if so, "some trace would be found on shore of the murderers." I presume you smile at the *sequitur.* You cannot be made to see how the mere *duration* of the corpse on the shore could operate to *multiply traces* of the assassins. Nor can I.

' "And, furthermore, it is exceedingly improbable," continues our journal, "that any villains who had committed such a murder as is here supposed, would have thrown the body in without weight to sink it, when such a precaution could have so easily been taken." Observe, here, the laughable confusion of thought. No one – not even "L'Etoile" – disputes the murder committed *on the body found.* The marks of violence are too obvious. It is our reasoner's object merely to show that this body is not Marie's. He wishes to prove that *Marie* is not assassinated – not that the corpse was not. Yet his observation proves only the latter point. Here is a corpse without weight attached. Murderers, casting it in, would not have failed to attach a weight. Therefore it was not thrown in by murderers. This is all which is proved, if anything is. The question of identity is not even approached, and "L'Etoile" has been at great pains merely to gainsay now what it has admitted only a moment before. "We are perfectly convinced," it says, "that the body was that of a murdered female."

'Nor is this the sole instance, even in this division of his subject, where our reasoner unwittingly reasons against himself. His evident object, I have already said, is to reduce, as much as possible, the interval between Marie's disappearance and the finding of the corpse. Yet we find him *urging* the point that no person saw the girl from the moment of her leaving her mother's house. "We have no evidence," he says, "that Marie Rogêt was in the land of the living after nine o'clock on Sunday June the twenty-second." As his argument is obviously an *ex parte* one, he should, at least, have left this matter out of sight; for had any one been known to see Marie, say on Monday, or on Tuesday, the interval in question would have been much reduced, and by his own ratiocination, the probability much diminished of the corpse being that of the *grisette*. It is, nevertheless, amusing to observe that "L'Etoile" insists upon its point in the full belief of its furthering its general argument.

'Reperuse now that portion of this argument which has reference to the identification of the corpse by Beauvais. In regard to the *hair* upon the arm, "L'Etoile" has been obviously disingenuous. M. Beauvais, not being an idiot, could never have urged, in identification of the corpse, simply *hair upon its arm*. No arm is *without* hair. The *generality* of the expression of "L'Etoile" is a mere perversion of the witness's phraseology. He must have spoken of some *peculiarity* in this hair. It must have been a peculiarity of colour, of quantity, of length, or of situation.

' "Her foot," says the journal, "was small, – so are thousands of feet. Her garter is no proof whatever, nor is her shoe, for shoes and garters are sold in packages. The same may be said of the flowers in her hat. One thing upon which M. Beauvais strongly insists is that the clasp on the garter found had been set back to take it in. This amounts to nothing; for most women find it proper to take a pair of garters home and fit them to the size of the limbs they are to encircle, rather than to try them in the store where they purchase." Here it is difficult to suppose the reasoner in earnest. Had M. Beauvais, in his search for the body of Marie, discovered a corpse corresponding in general size and appearance to the missing girl, he would have been warranted (without reference to the question of habiliment at all) in forming an opinion that his search had been successful. If, in addition to the point of general size and contour, he had found upon the arm a peculiar hairy appearance which he had observed upon the living Marie, his opinion might have been justly strengthened, and the increase of positiveness might well have been in the ratio of the peculiarity or unusualness of the hairy mark. If the feet of Marie being small, those of the corpse were also small, the increase of probability that the body was that of Marie would not be an increase in a ratio merely arithmetical, but in one highly geometrical, or accumulative. Add to all this shoes such as she had been known to wear upon the day of her disappearance, and although these shoes may be "sold in packages," you so far augment the probability as to verge upon the certain. What of itself would be no evidence of identity, becomes, through its corroborative position, proof most sure. Give us, then, flowers in the hat corresponding to those worn by the missing girl, and we seek for nothing further. If only *one* flower, we seek for nothing further – what then if two or three, or more? Each successive one is multiple evidence – proof not *added* to proof, but *multiplied* by hundreds or thousands. Let us now discover upon the deceased garters such as the living used, and it is almost folly to proceed. But these garters are found to be tightened by the setting back of a clasp, in just such a manner as her own had been tightened by Marie, shortly previous to her leaving home. It is now madness or hypocrisy to doubt. What "l'Etoile" says in respect to this abbreviation of the garters being a usual occurrence, shows nothing beyond its own pertinacity in error. The elastic nature of the clasp-garter is self-demonstration of the *unusualness* of the abbreviation. What is made to adjust itself must of necessity require foreign adjustment but rarely. It must have been by an accident, in its strictest sense, that these garters of Marie needed the tightening described. They alone would have amply established her identity. But it is not that the corpse was found to have the garters of the missing girl, or found to have her shoes, or her bonnet, or the flowers of her bonnet, or her feet, or a peculiar mark upon the arm, or her general size and appearance – it is that the corpse had each, and *all collectively*. Could it be proved that the editor of "L'Etoile" *really* entertained a doubt, under the circumstances, there would be no need, in his case, of a commission *de lunatico inquirendo*. He has thought it sagacious to echo the small talk of the lawyers, who, for the most part, content themselves with echoing the rectangular precepts of the courts. I would here observe that very much of what is rejected as evidence by a court is the best of evidence to the intellect. For the court, guiding itself by the general principles of evidence – the recognised and *booked* principles – is averse from swerving at particular instances. And this steadfast adherence to principle, with rigorous disregard of the conflicting exception, is a sure mode of attaining the *maximum* of attainable truth in any long sequence of time. The practice, *in mass*, is therefore philosophical; but it is not the less certain that it engenders vast individual error.*

'In respect to the insinuations levelled at Beauvais, you will be willing to dismiss them in a breath. You have already fathomed the true character of this good gentleman. He is a *busybody*, with much of romance and little of wit. Any one so constituted will readily so conduct himself, upon occasion of *real* excitement as to render himself liable to suspicion on the part of the over-acute or the ill-disposed. M. Beauvais (as it appears from your notes) had some personal interviews with the editor of "L'Etoile," and offended him by venturing an opinion that the corpse, notwithstanding the theory of the editor, was in sober fact, that of Marie. "He persists," says the paper, "in asserting the corpse to be that of Marie, but cannot give a circumstance, in addition to those which we have commented upon, to make others believe." Now, without readverting to the fact that stronger evidence "to make others believe" could *never* have been adduced, it may be remarked that a man may very well be understood to believe, in a case of this kind, without the ability to advance a single reason for the belief of a second party. Nothing is more vague than impressions of individual identity. Each man recognises his neighbour, yet there are few instances in which any one is prepared to *give a reason* for his recognition. The editor of "L'Etoile" had no right to be offended at M. Beauvais' unreasoning belief.

'The suspicious circumstances which invest him, will be found to tally much better with my hypothesis of *romantic busybodyism*, than with the reasoner's suggestion of guilt. Once adopting the more

---

* 'A theory based on the qualities of an object will prevent its being unfolded according to its objects; and he who arranges topics in reference to their causes will cease to value them according to their results. Thus the jurisprudence of every nation will show that, when law becomes a science and a system, it ceases to be justice. The errors into which a blind devotion to *principles* of classification has led the common law will be seen by observing how often the legislature has been obliged to come forward to restore the equity its scheme had lost.' – *Landor*.

charitable interpretation we shall find no difficulty in comprehending the rose in the keyhole; the "Marie" upon the slate; the "elbowing the male relatives out of the way;" the "aversion to permitting them to see the body;" the caution given to Madame B——, that she must hold no conversation with the *gendarme* until his return (Beauvais'); and, lastly his apparent determination "that nobody should have anything to do with the proceedings except himself." It seems to me unquestionable that Beauvais was a suitor of Marie's; that she coquetted with him; and that he was ambitious of being thought to enjoy her fullest intimacy and confidence. I shall say nothing more upon this point; and, as the evidence fully rebuts the assertion of "L'Etoile," touching the matter of *apathy* on the part of the mother and other relatives – an apathy inconsistent with the supposition of their believing the corpse to be that of the perfumery-girl – we shall now proceed as if the question of *identity* were settled to our perfect satisfaction.'

'And what,' I here demanded, 'do you think of the opinions of "Le Commerciel"?'

'That, in spirit, they are far more worthy of attention than any which have been promulgated upon the subject. The deductions from the premises are philosophical and acute; but the premises, in two instances at least, are founded in imperfect observation. "Le Commerciel" wishes to intimate that Marie was seized by some gang of low ruffians not far from her mother's door. "It is impossible," it urges, "that a person so well known to thousands as this young woman was, should have passed three blocks without some one having seen her." This is the idea of a man long resident in Paris – a public man – and one whose walks to and fro in the city have been mostly limited to the vicinity of the public offices. He is aware that *he* seldom passes so far as a dozen blocks from his own *bureau*, without being recognised and accosted. And, knowing the extent of his personal acquaintance with others, and of others with him, he compares his notoriety with that of the perfumery-girl, finds no great difference between them, and reaches at once the conclusion that she in her walks, would be equally liable to recognition with himself in his. This could only be the case were her walks of the same unvarying, methodical character and within the same *species* of limited region as are his own. He passes to and fro at regular intervals, within a confined periphery, abounding in individuals who are led to observation of his person through interest in the kindred nature of his occupation with their own. But the walks of Marie may, in general, be supposed discursive. In this particular instance it will be understood as most probable, that she proceeded upon a route of more than average diversity from her accustomed ones. The parallel which we imagine to have existed in the mind of "Le Commerciel" would only be sustained in the event of the two individuals traversing the whole city. In this case, granting the personal acquaintances to be equal, the chances would be also equal that an equal number of personal encounters would be made. For my own part, I should hold it not only as possible, but as very far more than probable, that Marie might have proceeded, at any given period, by any one of the many routes between her own residence and that of her aunt, without meeting a single individual whom she knew, or by whom she was known. In viewing this question in its full and proper light, we must hold steadily in mind the great disproportion between the personal acquaintances of even the most noted individual in Paris and the entire population of Paris itself.

'But whatever force there may still appear to be in the suggestion of "Le Commerciel" will be much diminished when we take into consideration *the hour* at which the girl went abroad. "It was when the streets were full of people," says "Le Commerciel," "that she went out." But not so. It was at nine o'clock in the morning. Now at nine o'clock of every morning in the week, *with the exception of Sunday*, the streets of the city are, it is true, thronged with people. At nine on Sunday the populace are chiefly within doors, *preparing for church*. No observing person can have failed to notice the peculiarly deserted air of the town from about eight until ten on the morning of every Sabbath. Between ten and eleven the streets are thronged, but not at so early a period as that designated.

'There is another point at which there seems a deficiency of *observation* on the part of "Le Commerciel." "A piece," it says, "of one of the unfortunate girl's petticoats, two feet long, and one foot wide, was torn out and tied under her chin, and around the back of her head, probably to prevent screams. This was done by fellows who had no pocket-handkerchiefs." Whether this idea is or is not well founded we will endeavour to see hereafter; but "by fellows who have no pocket-handkerchiefs," the editor intends the lowest class of ruffians. These, however, are the very description of people who will always be found to have handkerchiefs even when destitute of shirts. You must have had occasion to observe how absolutely indispensable, of late years, to the thorough blackguard, has become the pocket-handkerchief.'

'And what are we to think,' I asked, 'of the article in "Le Soleil"?'

'That it is a vast pity its inditer was not born a parrot – in which case he would have been the most illustrious parrot of his race. He has merely repeated the individual items of the already published opinion; collecting them, with a laudable industry, from this paper and from that. "The things had all *evidently* been there," he says, "at least three or four weeks, and there can be *no doubt* that the spot of this appalling outrage has been discovered." The facts here re-stated by "Le Soleil" are very far indeed from removing my own doubts upon this subject, and we will examine them more particularly hereafter in connection with another division of the theme.

'At present we must occupy ourselves with other investigations. You cannot fail to have remarked the extreme laxity of the examination of the corpse. To be sure, the question of identity was readily determined, or should have been, but there were other points to be ascertained. Had the body been in any respect *despoiled*? Had the deceased any articles of jewellery about her person upon leaving home? If so, had she any when found? These are important questions utterly untouched by the evidence; and there are others of equal moment which have met with no attention. We must endeavour to satisfy ourselves by personal inquiry. The case of St. Eustache must be re-examined. I have no suspicion of this person, but let us proceed methodically. We will ascertain beyond a doubt the validity of the *affidavits* in regard to his whereabouts on the Sunday. Affidavits of this character are readily made matter of mystification. Should there be nothing wrong here, however, we will dismiss St. Eustache from our investigations. His suicide, however corroborative of suspicion, were there found to be deceit in the affidavits, is, without such deceit, in no respect an unaccountable circumstance, or one which need cause us to deflect from the line of ordinary analysis.

'In that which I now propose, we will discard the interior points of this tragedy, and concentrate our attention upon its outskirts. Not the least usual error, in investigations such as this, is the limiting of inquiry to the immediate, with total disregard of the collateral or circumstantial events. It is the mal-practice of the courts to confine evidence and discussion to the bounds of apparent relevancy. Yet experience has shown, and a true philosophy will always show, that a vast, perhaps the larger portion of truth, arises from the seemingly irrelevant. It is through the spirit of this principle, if not precisely through its letter, that modern science has resolved to *calculate upon the unforeseen*. But perhaps you do not comprehend me. The history of human knowledge has so uninterruptedly shown that to collateral, or incidental, or accidental events, we are indebted for the most numerous and most valuable discoveries, that it has at length become necessary, in any prospective view of improvement, to make not only large, but the largest allowances for inventions that shall arise by chance, and quite out of the range of ordinary expectation. It is no longer philosophical to base upon what has been a vision of what is to be. *Accident* is admitted as a portion of the substructure. We make chance a matter of absolute calculation. We subject the unlooked for and unimagined to the mathematical *formulæ* of the schools.

'I repeat that it is no more than fact that the *larger* portion of all truth has sprung from the collateral; and it is but in accordance with the spirit of the principle involved in this fact that I would divert inquiry in the present case, from the trodden and hitherto unfruitful ground of the event itself, to the contemporary circumstances which surround it. While you ascertain the validity of the affidavits, I will examine the newspapers more generally than you have as yet done. So far, we have only reconnoitred the field of investigation; but it will be strange indeed if a comprehensive survey, such as I propose, of the public prints will not afford us some minute points which shall establish a *direction* for inquiry.'

In pursuance of Dupin's suggestion, I made a scrupulous examination of the affair of the affidavits. The result was a firm conviction of their validity, and of the consequent innocence of St. Eustache. In the meantime my friend occupied himself with what seemed to me a minuteness altogether objectless in a scrutiny of the various newspaper files. At the end of a week he placed before me the following extracts:–

'About three years and a half ago a disturbance very similar to the present was caused by the disappearance of this same Marie Rogêt from the *parfumerie* of Monsieur Le Blanc in the Palais Royal. At the end of a week, however, she re-appeared at her customary *comptoir* as well as ever, with the exception of a slight paleness not altogether usual. It was given out by Monsieur Le Blanc and her mother that she had merely been on a visit to some friend in the country, and the affair was speedily hushed up. We presume that the present absence is a freak of the same nature, and that, at the expiration of a week, or perhaps a month, we shall have her among us again.' – *Evening Paper – Monday, June 23.**

'An evening journal of yesterday refers to a former mysterious disappearance of Mademoiselle Rogêt. It is well known that during the week of her absence from Le Blanc's *parfumerie* she was in the company of a young naval officer much noted for his debaucheries. A quarrel, it is supposed, providentially led to her return home. We have the name of the Lothario in question, who is at present stationed in Paris, but, for obvious reasons, forbear to make it public.' – *Le Mercurie – Tuesday Morning, June 24.*†

'An outrage of the most atrocious character was perpetrated near this city the day before yesterday. A gentleman, with his wife and daughter, engaged about dusk the services of six young men, who were idly rowing a boat to and fro near the banks of the Seine, to convey him

* New York 'Express.'
† New York 'Herald.'

across the river. Upon reaching the opposite shore, the three passengers stepped out, and had proceeded so far as to be beyond the view of the boat, when the daughter discovered that she had left in it her parasol. She returned for it, was seized by the gang, carried out into the stream, gagged, brutally treated, and finally taken to the shore at a point not far from that at which she had originally entered the boat with her parents. The villains have escaped for the time, but the police are upon their trail, and some of them will soon be taken.' – *Morning Paper* – *June 25.**

'We have received one or two communications, the object of which is to fasten the crime of the late atrocity upon Mennais;† but as this gentleman has been fully exonerated by a legal inquiry, and as the arguments of our several correspondents appear to be more zealous than profound, we do not think it advisable to make them public.' – *Morning Paper* – *June 28.*‡

'We have received several forcibly written communications, apparently from various sources, and which go far to render it a matter of certainty that the unfortunate Marie Rogêt has become a victim of one of the numerous bands of blackguards which infest the vicinity of the city upon Sunday. Our own opinion is decidedly in favour of this supposition. We shall endeavour to make room for some of these arguments hereafter.' – *Evening Paper* – *Tuesday, June 31.*§

'On Monday, one of the bargemen connected with the revenue service saw an empty boat floating down the Seine. Sails were lying in the bottom of the boat. The bargemen towed it under the barge office. The next morning it was taken from thence without the knowledge of any of the officers. The rudder is now at the barge office.' – *Le Diligence* – *Thursday, June 26.*||

*New York 'Courier and Inquirer.'
† Mennais was one of the parties originally suspected and arrested, but discharged through total lack of evidence.
‡ New York 'Courier and Inquirer.'
§ New York 'Evening Post.'
|| New York 'Standard.'

Upon reading these various extracts, they not only seemed to me irrelevant, but I could perceive no mode in which any one of them could be brought to bear upon the matter in hand. I waited for some explanation from Dupin.

'It is not my present design,' he said, 'to *dwell* upon the first and second of these extracts. I have copied them chiefly to show you the extreme remissness of the police, who, as far as I can understand from the Prefect, have not troubled themselves in any respect with an examination of the naval officer alluded to. Yet it is mere folly to say that between the first and second disappearance of Marie, there is no *supposable* connection. Let us admit the first elopement to have resulted in a quarrel between the lovers, and the return home of the betrayed. We are now prepared to view a second *elopement* (if we *know* that an elopement has again taken place) as indicating a renewal of the betrayer's advances, rather than as the result of new proposals by a second individual – we are prepared to regard it as a "making up" of the old *amour* rather than as the commencement of a new one. The chances are ten to one that he who had once eloped with Marie would again propose an elopement rather than that she to whom proposals of elopement had been made by one individual should have them made to her by another. And here let me call your attention to the fact that the time elapsing between the first ascertained, and the second supposed elopement, is a few months more than the general period of the cruises of our men-of-war. Had the lover been interrupted in his first villainy by the necessity of departure to sea, and had he seized the first moment of his return to renew the base designs not yet altogether accomplished, or not yet altogether accomplished *by him?* Of all these things we know nothing.

'You will say, however, that, in the second instance, there was *no* elopement as imagined. Certainly not – but are we prepared to say that there was not the frustrated design? Beyond St. Eustache, and perhaps Beauvais, we find no recognised, no open, no honourable suitors of Marie. Of none other is there anything said. Who, then, is the secret lover of whom the relatives (*at least most of them*) know nothing, but whom Marie meets upon the morning of Sunday, and who is so deeply in her confidence that she hesitates not to remain with him until the shades of the evening descend amid the solitary groves of the Barrière du Roule? Who is that secret lover, I ask, of whom, at least, *most* of the relatives know nothing? And what means the singular prophecy of Madame Rogêt on the morning of Marie's departure? – "I fear that I shall never see Marie again."

'But if we cannot imagine Madame Rogêt privy to the design of elopement, may we not at least suppose this design entertained by the girl? Upon quitting home, she gave it to be understood that she was about to visit her aunt in the Rue des Drômes, and St. Eustache was requested to call for her at dark. Now, at first glance, this fact strongly militates against my suggestion, but let us reflect. That she *did* meet some companion, and proceed with him across the river, reaching the Barrière du Roule at so late an hour as three o'clock in the afternoon, is known. But in consenting so to accompany this individual (*for whatever purpose – to her mother known or unknown*), she must have thought of her expressed intention when leaving home, and of the surprise and suspicion aroused in the bosom of her affianced suitor, St. Eustache, when, calling for her at the hour appointed in the Rue des Drômes, he should find that she had not been there, and when, moreover, upon returning to the *pension* with this alarming intelligence, he should become aware of her continued absence from home. She must have thought of these things, I say. She must have foreseen the chagrin of St. Eustache, the suspicion of all. She could not have thought of returning to brave this suspicion; but the suspicion becomes a point of trivial importance to her if we suppose her *not* intending to return.

'We may imagine her thinking thus – "I am to meet a certain person for the purpose of elopement, or for certain other purposes known only to myself. It is necessary that there be no chance of interruption – there must be sufficient time given us to elude pursuit – I will give it to be understood that I shall visit and spend the day with my aunt at the Rue des Drômes – I will tell St. Eustache not to call for me until dark – in this way, my absence from home for the longest possible period, without causing suspicion or anxiety, will be accounted for, and I shall gain more time than in any other manner. If I bid St. Eustache call for me at dark, he will be sure not to call before; but, if I wholly neglect to bid him call, my time for escape will be diminished, since it will be expected that I return the earlier, and my absence will the sooner excite anxiety. Now, if it were my design to return *at all* – if I had in contemplation merely a stroll with the individual in question – it would not be my policy to bid St. Eustache call; for, calling, he will be *sure* to ascertain that I have played him false – a fact of which I might keep him for ever in ignorance, by leaving home without notifying him of my intention, by returning before dark, and by then stating that I had been to visit my aunt in the Rue des Drômes. But, as it is my design *never* to return – or not for some weeks – or not until certain concealments are effected – the gaining of time is the only point about which I need give myself any concern."

'You have observed in your notes, that the most general opinion in relation to this sad affair is, and was from the first, that the girl had been the victim of *a gang* of blackguards. Now, the popular opinion, under certain conditions, is not to be disregarded. When arising of itself – when manifesting itself in a strictly spontaneous manner – we should look upon it as analogous with that *intuition* which is the idiosyncrasy of the individual man of genius. In ninety-nine cases from the hundred I would abide by its decision. But it is important that we find no palpable traces of *suggestion*. The opinion must be rigorously *the public's own*; and the distinction is often exceedingly difficult to perceive and to maintain. In the present instance, it appears to me that this "public opinion," in respect to *a gang*, has been superinduced by the collateral event which is detailed in the third of my extracts. All Paris is excited by the discovered corpse of Marie, a girl young, beautiful, and notorious. This corpse is found, bearing marks of violence, and floating in the river. But it is now made known that, at the very period, or about the very period in which it is supposed that the girl was assassinated, an outrage similar in nature to that endured by the deceased, although less in extent, was perpetrated, by a gang of young ruffians, upon the person of a second young female. Is it wonderful that the one known atrocity should influence the popular judgment in regard to the other unknown? This judgment awaited direction, and the known outrage seemed so opportunely to afford it! Marie, too, was found in the river; and upon this very river was this known outrage committed. The connection of the two events had about it so much of the palpable, that the true wonder would have been a *failure* of the populace to appreciate and to seize it. But, in fact, the one atrocity, known to be so committed, is, if anything, evidence that the other, committed at a time nearly coincident, was *not* so committed. It would have been a miracle indeed, if, while a gang of ruffians were perpetrating, at a given locality, a most unheard-of wrong, there should have been another similar gang, in a similar locality, in the same city, under the same circumstances, with the same means and appliances, engaged in a wrong of precisely the same aspect, at precisely the same period of time! Yet in what, if not in this marvellous train of coincidence, does the accidentally *suggested* opinion of the populace call upon us to believe?

'Before proceeding further, let us consider the supposed scene of the assassination in the thicket at the Barrière du Roule. This thicket, although dense, was in the close vicinity of a public road. Within were three or four large stones, forming a kind of seat with a back and footstool. On the upper stone was discovered a white petticoat; on the second, a silk scarf. A parasol, gloves, and a pocket-handkerchief, were also here found. The handkerchief bore the name "Marie Rogêt." Fragments of dress were seen on the branches around. The earth was trampled, the bushes were broken, and there was every evidence of a violent struggle.

'Notwithstanding the acclamation with which the discovery of this thicket was received by the press, and the unanimity with which it was supposed to indicate the precise scene of the outrage, it must be admitted that there was some very good reason for doubt. That it *was* the scene, I may or I may not believe – but there was excellent reason for doubt. Had the *true* scene been, as "Le Commerciel" suggested, in the neighbourhood of the Rue Pavée St. Andrée, the perpetrators of the crime, supposing them still resident in Paris, would naturally have been stricken with terror at the public attention thus acutely directed into the proper channel; and in certain classes of minds there would have arisen at once a sense of the necessity of some exertion to re-divert this attention. And thus the thicket of the Barrière du Roule having been already suspected, the idea of placing the articles where they were found might have been naturally entertained. There is no real evidence, although "Le Soleil" so supposes, that the articles discovered had been more than a very few days in the thicket; while there is much circumstantial proof that they could not have remained there, without attracting attention, during the twenty days elapsing between the fatal Sunday and the afternoon upon which they were found by the boys. "They were all *mildewed* down hard," says "Le Soleil," adopting the opinions of its predecessors, "with the action of the rain, and stuck together from *mildew*. The grass had grown around and over some of them. The silk of the parasol was strong, but the threads of it were run together within. The upper part, where it had been doubled and folded, was all *mildewed* and rotten, and tore on being opened." In respect to the grass having "grown around and over some of them," it is obvious that the fact could only have been ascertained from the words, and thus from the recollections, of two small boys; for these boys removed the articles and took them home before they had been seen by a third party. But grass will grow, especially in warm and damp weather (such as was that of the period of the murder), as much as two or three inches in a single day. A parasol lying upon a newly-turfed ground might in a single week be entirely concealed from sight by the upspringing grass. And touching that *mildew*, upon which the editor of "Le Soleil" so pertinaciously insists, that he employs the word no less than three times in the brief paragraph just quoted, is he really unaware of the nature of this *mildew*? Is he to be told that it is one of the many classes of *fungus*, of which the most ordinary feature is its upspringing and decadence within twenty-four hours?

'Thus we see at a glance that what has been most triumphantly adduced in support of the idea that the articles had been "for at least three or four weeks" in the thicket is most absurdly null as regards any evidence of that fact. On the other hand, it is exceedingly difficult to believe that these articles could have remained in the thicket specified for a longer period than a single week – for a longer period than from one Sunday to the next. Those who know anything of the vicinity of Paris know the extreme difficulty of finding *seclusion*, unless at a great distance from its suburbs. Such a thing as an unexplored, or even an unfrequently visited recess, amid its woods or groves, is not for a moment to be imagined. Let any one, who, being at heart a lover of nature, is yet chained by duty to the dust and heat of this great metropolis – let any such one attempt, even during the week-days, to slake his thirst for solitude amid the scenes of natural loveliness which immediately surround us – at every second step he will find the growing charm dispelled by the voice and personal intrusion of some ruffian or party of carousing blackguards. He will seek privacy amid the densest foliage all in vain. Here are the very nooks where the unwashed most abound – here are the temples most desecrate. With sickness of the heart the wanderer will flee back to the polluted Paris as to a less odious, because less incongruous, sink of pollution. But if the vicinity of the city is so beset during the working days of the week, how much more so on the Sabbath! It is now especially that, released from the claims of labour, or deprived of the customary opportunities of crime, the town blackguard seeks the precincts of the town, not through love of the rural, which in his heart he despises, but by way of escape from the restraints and conventionalities of society. He desires less the fresh air and the green trees than the utter *license* of the country. Here, at the roadside inn or beneath the foliage of the woods, he indulges, unchecked by an eye except those of his boon companions, in all the mad excess of a counterfeit hilarity – the joint offspring of liberty and of rum. I say nothing more than what must be obvious to every dispassionate observer, when I repeat that the circumstance of the articles in question having remained undiscovered for a longer period than from one Sunday to another, in *any* thicket in the immediate neighbourhood of Paris, is to be looked upon as little less than miraculous.

'But there are not wanting other grounds for the suspicion that the articles were placed in the thicket with the view of diverting attention from the real scene of the outrage. And, first, let me direct your notice to the *date* of the discovery of the articles. Collate this with the date of the fifth extract made by myself from the newspapers. You will find that the discovery followed, almost immediately, the urgent communications sent to the evening newspaper. These communications, although various, and apparently from various sources, tended all to the same point – viz., the directing of attention to *a gang* as the perpetrators of the outrage, and to the neighbourhood of the Barrière du Roule as its scene. Now here, of course, the suspicion is not that, in consequence of these communications, or of the public attention by them directed, the articles were found by the boys; but the suspicion might and may well have been, that the articles were not *before* found by the boys for the reason that the articles had not before been in the thicket; having been deposited there only at so late a period as at the date or shortly prior to the date of the communications, by the guilty authors of these communications themselves.

'This thicket was a singular – an exceedingly singular one. It was unusually dense. Within its naturally walled enclosure were three extraordinary stones, *forming a seat with a back and footstool*. And this thicket, so full of a natural art, was in the immediate vicinity, *within a few rods*, of the dwelling of Madame Deluc, whose boys were in the habit of closely examining the shrubberies about them in search of the bark of the sassafras. Would it be a rash wager, a wager of one thousand to one, that *a day* never passed over the heads of these boys without finding at least one of them ensconced in the umbrageous hall, and enthroned upon its natural throne? Those who would hesitate at such a wager have either never been boys themselves or have forgotten the boyish nature. I repeat, it is exceedingly hard to comprehend how the articles could have remained in this thicket undiscovered for a longer period than one or two days; and that thus there is good ground for suspicion, in spite of the dogmatic ignorance of "Le Soleil," that they were, at a comparatively late date, deposited where found.

'But there are still other and stronger reasons for believing them so deposited, than any which I have as yet urged. And, now, let me beg your notice to the highly artificial arrangement of the articles. On the *upper* stone lay a white petticoat; on the *second* a silk scarf; scattered around, were a parasol, gloves, and a pocket-handkerchief bearing the name of "Marie Rogêt." Here is just such an arrangement as would *naturally* be made by a not-over-acute person wishing to dispose the articles *naturally*. But it is by no means a *really* natural arrangement. I should rather have looked to see the things *all* lying on the ground and trampled under foot. In the narrow limits of that bower, it would have been scarcely possible that the petticoat and scarf should have retained a position upon the stones, when subjected to the brushing to and fro of many struggling persons. "There was evidence," it is said, "of a struggle; and the earth was trampled, the bushes were broken," but the petticoat and scarf are found deposited as if upon shelves. "The pieces of the frock torn out by the bushes were about three inches wide and six inches long. One part was the hem of the frock, and it had been mended. They *looked* like strips torn off." Here inadvertently "Le Soleil" has employed an exceedingly suspicious phrase. The pieces, as described, do indeed "look like strips torn off," but purposely and by hand. It is one of the rarest of accidents that a piece is "torn off" from any garment such as is now in question, by the agency *of a thorn*. From the very nature of such fabrics, a thorn or nail becoming entangled in them tears them rectangularly, divides them into two longitudinal rents, at right angles with each other, and meeting at an apex where the thorn enters, but it is scarcely possible to conceive the piece "torn off." I never so knew it, nor did you. To tear a piece *off* from such fabric, two distinct forces, in different directions, will be in almost every case required. If there be two edges to the fabric – if, for example, it be a pocket-handkerchief and it is desired to tear from it a slip, then, and then only will the one force serve the purpose. But in the present case, the question is of a dress presenting but one edge. To tear a piece from the interior, where no edge is presented, could only be effected by a miracle through the agency of thorns, and no *one* thorn could accomplish it. But, even where an edge is presented, two thorns will be necessary, operating, the one in two distinct directions, and the other in one. And this in the supposition that the edge is unhemmed. If hemmed, the matter is nearly out of the question. We thus see the numerous and great obstacles in the way of pieces being "torn off" through the simple agency of "thorns;" yet we are required to believe not only that one piece but that many have been so torn. "And one part," too, *was the hem of the frock!*" Another piece was "*part of the skirt not the hem,*" – that is to say, was torn completely out, through the agency of thorns, from the unedged interior of the dress! These, I say, are things which one may well be pardoned for disbelieving; yet, taken collectedly, they form, perhaps, less of reasonable ground for suspicion than the one startling circumstance of the articles having been left in this thicket at all by any *murderers* who had enough precaution to think of removing the corpse. You will not have apprehended me rightly, however, if you suppose it my design to *deny* this thicket as the scene of the outrage. There might have been a wrong *here*, or, more possibly, an accident at Madame Deluc's. But, in fact, this is a point of minor importance. We are not engaged in an attempt to discover the scene, but to produce the perpetrators of the murder. What I have adduced, notwithstanding the minuteness with which I have adduced it, has been with the view, first, to show the folly of the positive and headlong assertions of "Le Soleil," but secondly and chiefly, to bring you by the most natural route to a further contemplation of the doubt whether this assassination has, or has not been, the work of a *gang*.

'We will resume this question by mere allusion to the revolting details of the surgeon examined at the inquest. It is only necessary to say that his published *inferences*, in regard to the number of the ruffians, have been properly ridiculed as unjust and totally baseless by all the reputable anatomists of Paris. Not that the matter *might not* have been as inferred, but that there was no ground for the inference:– was there not much for another?

'Let us reflect now upon "the traces of a struggle;" and let me ask what these traces have been supposed to demonstrate. A gang. But do they not rather demonstrate the absence of a gang? What *struggle* could have taken place – what struggle so violent and so enduring as to have left its "traces" in all directions – between a weak and defenceless girl and the *gang* of ruffians imagined? The silent grasp of a few rough arms and all would have been over. The victim must have been absolutely passive at their will. You will here bear in mind that the arguments urged against the thicket as the scene, are applicable, in chief part, only against it as the scene of an outrage committed by *more than a single individual*. If we imagine but *one* violator, we can conceive, and thus only conceive, the struggle of so violent and so obstinate a nature as to have left the "traces" apparent.

'And again. I have already mentioned the suspicion to be excited by the fact that the articles in question were suffered to remain at all in the thicket where discovered. It seems almost impossible that these evidences of guilt should have been accidentally left where found. There was sufficient presence of mind (it is supposed) to remove the corpse; and yet a more positive evidence than the corpse itself (whose features might have been quickly obliterated by decay) is allowed to lie conspicuously in the scene of the outrage – I allude to the handkerchief with the name of the deceased. If this was accident, it was not the accident of a gang. We can imagine it only the accident of an individual. Let us see. An individual has committed the murder. He is alone with the ghost of the departed. He is appalled by what lies motionless before him. The fury of his passion is over, and there is abundant room in his heart for the natural awe of the deed. His is none of that confidence which the presence of numbers inevitably inspires. He is *alone* with the dead. He trembles and is bewildered. Yet there is a necessity for disposing of the corpse. He bears it to the river, but leaves behind him the other evidences of guilt; for it is difficult, if not impossible, to carry all the burden at once, and it will be easy to return for what is left. But in his toilsome journey to the water his fears redouble within him. The sounds of life encompass his path. A dozen times he hears or fancies the step of an observer. Even the very lights from the city bewilder him. Yet, in time, and by long and frequent pauses of deep agony, he reaches the river's brink, and disposes of his ghastly charge – perhaps through the medium of a boat. But *now* what treasure does the world hold – what threat of vengeance could it hold out – which would have power to urge the return of that lonely murderer over that toilsome and perilous path to the thicket and its blood-chilling recollections? He returns *not*, let the consequences be

In his toilsome journey to the water his fears redouble within him

what they may. He *could* not return if he would. His sole thought is immediate escape. He turns his back *for ever* upon those dreadful shrubberies, and flees as from the wrath to come.

'But how with a gang? Their number would have inspired them with confidence; if, indeed, confidence is ever wanting in the breast of the arrant blackguard; and of arrant blackguards alone are the supposed *gangs* ever constituted. Their number, I say, would have prevented the bewildering and unreasoning terror which I have imagined to paralyse the single man. Could we suppose an oversight in one, or two, or three, this oversight would have been remedied by a fourth. They would have left nothing behind them; for their number would have enabled them to carry *all* at once. There would have been no need of *return*.

'Consider now the circumstance that, in the outer garment of the corpse when found, "a slip, about a foot wide, had been torn upward from the bottom hem to the waist, wound three times round the waist, and secured by a sort of hitch in the back." This was done with the obvious design of affording *a handle* by which to carry the body. But would any *number* of men have dreamed of resorting to such an expedient? To three or four, the limbs of the corpse would have afforded not only a sufficient, but the best possible hold. The device is that of a single individual; and this brings us to the fact that "between the thicket and the river, the rails of the fences were found taken down, and the ground bore evident traces of some heavy burden having been dragged along it!" But would a *number* of men have put themselves to the superfluous trouble of taking down a fence for the purpose of dragging through it a corpse which they might have *lifted over* any fence in an instant? Would a *number* of men have so *dragged* a corpse at all as to have left evident *traces* of the dragging?

'And here we must refer to an observation of "Le Commerciel," an observation upon which I have already, in some measure, commented. "A piece," says this journal, "of one of the unfortunate girl's petticoats was torn out and tied under her chin, and around the back of her head, probably to prevent screams. This was done by fellows who had no pocket-handkerchiefs."

'I have before suggested that a genuine blackguard is never *without* a pocket-handkerchief. But it is not to this fact that I now especially advert. That it was not through want of a handkerchief for the purpose imagined by "Le Commerciel" that this bandage was employed, is rendered apparent by the handkerchief left in the thicket; and that the object was not "to prevent screams" appears, also, from the bandage having been employed in preference to what would so much better have answered the purpose. But the language of the evidence speaks of the strip in question as "found around the neck, fitting loosely, and secured with a hard knot." These words are sufficiently vague, but differ materially from those of "Le Commerciel." The slip was eighteen inches wide, and therefore, although of muslin, would form a strong band when folded or rumpled longitudinally. And thus rumpled it was discovered. My inference is this. The solitary murderer, having borne the corpse for some distance (whether from the thicket or elsewhere by means of the bandage hitched around its middle), found the weight in this mode of procedure too much for his strength. He resolved to drag the burden – the evidence goes to show that it *was* dragged. With this object in view, it became necessary to attach something like a rope to one of the extremities. It could be best attached about the neck, where the head would prevent its slipping off. And now the murderer bethought him, unquestionably, of the bandage about the loins. He would have used this, but for its volution about the corpse, the hitch which embarrassed it, and the reflection that it had not been "torn off" from the garment. It was easier to tear a new slip from the petticoat. He tore it, made it fast about the neck, and so *dragged* his victim to the brink of the river. That this "bandage," only attainable with trouble and delay, and but imperfectly answering its purpose – that this bandage was employed *at all*, demonstrates that the necessity for its employment sprang from circumstances arising at a period when the handkerchief was no longer attainable, that is to say, arising, as we have imagined, after quitting the thicket (if the thicket it was), and on the road between the thicket and the river.

'But the evidence, you will say, of Madame Deluc (!) points especially to the presence of *a gang*, in the vicinity of the thicket, at or about the epoch of the murder. This I grant. I doubt if there were not a *dozen* gangs, such as described by Madame Deluc, in and about the vicinity of the Barrière du Roule at *or about* the period of this tragedy. But the gang which has drawn upon itself the pointed animadversion, although the somewhat tardy and very suspicious evidence of Madame Deluc, is the *only* gang which is represented by that honest and scrupulous old lady as having eaten her cakes and swallowed her brandy without putting themselves to the trouble of making her payment. *Et hinc illæ iræ?*

'But what *is* the precise evidence of Madame Deluc? A gang of miscreants made their appearance, behaved boisterously, ate and drank without making payment, followed in the route of the young man and girl, returned to the inn *about dusk*, and recrossed the river as if in great haste.

'Now this "great haste" very possibly seemed *greater* haste in the eyes of Madame Deluc since she dwelt lingeringly and lamentingly upon her violated cakes and ale – cakes and ale for which she might still have entertained a faint hope of compensation. Why, otherwise, since it was *about dusk*, should she make a point of the haste? It is no cause for wonder, surely, that even a gang of blackguards should make *haste* to get home, when a wide river is to be crossed in small boats, when storm impends, and when night *approaches*.

'I say *approaches*; for the night had *not yet arrived*. It was only *about dusk* that the indecent haste of these "miscreants" offended the sober eyes of Madame Deluc. But we are told it was upon this very evening that Madame Deluc, as well as her eldest son "heard the screams of a female in the vicinity of the inn." And in what words does Madame Deluc designate the period of the evening at which these screams were heard? "It was *soon after dark*," she says. But "soon *after dark*" is, at least, *dark*; and, "*about dusk*" is as certainly daylight. Thus, it is abundantly clear that the gang quitted the Barrière du Roule *prior* to the screams overheard (?) by Madame Deluc. And although, in all the many reports of the evidence, the relative expressions in question are distinctly and invariably employed just as I have employed them in this conversation with yourself, no notice whatever of the gross discrepancy has as yet been taken by any of the public journals, or by any of the myrmidons of police.

'I shall add but one to the arguments against *a gang*; but this *one* has, to my own understanding at least, a weight altogether irresistible. Under the circumstances of large reward offered, and full pardon to any King's evidence, it is not to be imagined for a moment, that some member of *a gang* of low ruffians, or of any body of men, would not long ago have betrayed his accomplices. Each one of a gang so placed is not so much greedy of reward, or anxious for escape, as *fearful of betrayal*. He betrays eagerly and early that *he may not himself be betrayed*. That the secret has not been divulged is the very best of proof that it is in fact a secret. The horrors of this dark deed are known only to *one* or two living human beings and to God.

'Let us sum up now the meagre, yet certain fruits of our long analysis. We have attained the idea either of a fatal accident under the roof of Madame Deluc, or of a murder perpetrated in the thicket at the Barrière du Roule, by a lover, or at least by an intimate and secret associate of the deceased. This associate is of swarthy complexion. This complexion, the "hitch" in the bandage, and the sailor's "knot" with which the bonnet-ribbon is tied, point to a seaman. His companionship with the deceased, a gay, but not an abject young girl, designates him as above the grade of the common sailor. Here the well-written and urgent communications to the journals are much in the way of corroboration. The circumstance of the first elopement, as mentioned by "Le Mercurie," tends to blend the idea of this seaman with that of the "naval officer" who is first known to have led the unfortunate into crime.

'And here most fitly comes the consideration of the continued absence of him of the dark complexion. Let me pause to observe that the complexion of this man is dark and swarthy; it was no common swarthiness which constituted the *sole* point of remembrance, both as regards Valence and Madame Deluc. But why is this man absent? Was he murdered by the gang? If so, why are there only *traces* of the assassinated *girl*? The scene of the two outrages will naturally be supposed identical. And where is his corpse? The assassins would most probably have disposed of both in the same way. But it may be said that this man lives, and is deterred from making himself known through dread of being charged with the murder. This consideration might be supposed to operate upon him now – at this late period – since it has been given in evidence that he was seen with Marie – but it would have had no force at the period of the deed. The first impulse of an innocent man would have been to announce the outrage, and to aid in identifying the ruffians. This *policy* would have suggested. He had been seen with the girl. He had crossed the river with her in an open ferry-boat. The denouncing of the assassins would have appeared, even to an idiot, the surest and sole means of relieving himself from suspicion. We cannot suppose him on the night of the fatal Sunday both innocent himself and incognisant of an outrage committed. Yet only under such circumstances is it possible to imagine that he would have failed, if alive, in the denouncement of the assassins.

'And what means are ours of attaining the truth? We shall find these means multiplying and gathering distinctness as we proceed. Let us sift to the bottom this affair of the first elopement. Let us know the full history of "the officer," with his present circumstances, and his whereabouts at the precise period of the murder. Let us carefully compare with each other the various communications sent to the evening paper, in which the object was to inculpate a *gang*. This done, let us compare these communications, both as regards style and MS., with those sent to the morning paper, at a previous period, and insisting so vehemently upon the guilt of Mennais. And all this done, let us again compare these various communications with the known MSS. of the officer. Let us endeavour to ascertain by repeated questionings of Madame Deluc and her boys, as well as of the omnibus-driver, Valence, something more of the personal appearance and bearing of the "man of dark complexion." Queries, skilfully directed will not fail to elicit from some of these parties information on this particular point (or upon others) – information which the parties themselves may not even be aware of possessing. And let us now trace *the boat* picked up by the bargeman on the morning of Monday the twenty-third of June, and which was removed from the barge-office without the cognisance of the officer in attendance, and *without the rudder*, at some period prior to the discovery of the corpse. With a proper caution and perseverance we shall infallibly trace this boat; for not only can the bargeman who picked it up identify it, but the *rudder is at hand*. The rudder *of a sail-boat* would not have been abandoned, without inquiry, by one altogether at ease in heart. And here let me pause to insinuate a question. There was no *advertisement* of the picking up of this boat. It was silently taken to the barge office, and as silently removed. But its owner or employer – how *happened* he, at so early a period as Tuesday morning, to be informed without the agency of advertisement, of the locality of the boat taken up on Monday, unless we imagine some connection with the *navy* – some personal permanent connection leading to cognisance of its minute interests – its petty local news?

'In speaking of the lonely assassin dragging his burden to the shore, I have already suggested the probability of his availing himself *of a boat*. Now we are to understand that Marie Rogêt *was* precipitated from a boat. This would naturally have been the case. The corpse could not have been trusted to the shallow waters of the shore. The peculiar marks on the back and shoulders of the victim tell of the bottom ribs of a boat. That the body was found without weight is also corroborative of the idea. If thrown from the shore a weight would have been attached. We can only account for its absence by supposing the murderer to have neglected the precaution of supplying himself with it before pushing off. In the act of consigning the corpse to the water, he would unquestionably have noticed his oversight; but then no remedy would have been at hand. Any risk would have been preferred to a return to that accursed shore. Having rid himself of his ghastly charge, the murderer would have hastened to the city. There, at some obscure wharf he would have leaped on land. But the boat – would he have secured it? He would have been in too great haste for such things as securing a boat. Moreover, in fastening it to the wharf he would have felt as if securing evidence against himself. His natural thought would have been to cast from him as far as possible, all that had held connection with his crime. He would not only have fled from the wharf, but he would not have permitted *the boat* to remain. Assuredly he would have cast it adrift. Let us pursue our fancies. – In the morning the wretch is stricken with unutterable horror at finding that the boat has been picked up and detained at a locality which he is in the daily habit of frequenting – at a locality, perhaps, which his duty compels him to frequent. The next night *without daring to ask for the rudder* he removes it. Now *where* is that rudderless boat? Let it be one of our first purposes to discover. With the first glimpse we obtain of it, the dawn of our success shall begin. This boat shall guide us with a rapidity which will surprise even ourselves, to him who employed it in the midnight of the fatal Sabbath. Corroboration will rise upon corroboration, and the murderer will be traced.'

[For reasons which we shall not specify, but which to many readers will appear obvious, we have taken the liberty of here omitting, from the MSS. placed in our hands, such portion as details the *following up* of the apparently slight clue obtained by Dupin. We feel it advisable only to state, in brief, that the result desired was brought to pass; and that the Prefect fulfilled punctually, although with reluctance, the terms of his compact with the Chevalier. Mr Poe's article concludes with the following words. – *Eds.**]

It will be understood that I speak of coincidences *and no more*. What I have said above upon this topic must suffice. In my own heart there dwells no faith in preter-nature. That nature and its God are two, no man who thinks will deny. That the latter, creating the former, can, at will, control or modify it, is also unquestionable. I say 'at will'; for the question is of will, and not, as the insanity of logic has assumed, of power. It is not that the Deity *cannot* modify his laws, but that we insult Him in imagining a possible necessity for modification. In their origin these laws were fashioned to embrace *all* contingencies which *could* lie in the Future. With God all is *Now*.

I repeat, then, that I speak of these things only as of coincidences. And further: in what I relate it will be seen that between the fate of the unhappy Mary Cecilia Rogers, so far as that fate is known, and the fate of one Marie Rogêt up to a certain epoch in her history, there has

* Of the Magazine in which the article was originally published.

existed a parallel in the contemplation of whose wonderful exactitude the reason becomes embarrassed. I say all this will be seen. But let it not for a moment be supposed that, in proceeding with the sad narrative of Marie from the epoch just mentioned, and in tracing to its *dénouement* the mystery which enshrouded her, it is my covert design to hint at an extension of the parallel, or even to suggest that the measures adopted in Paris for the discovery of the assassin of a *grisette*, or measures founded in any similar ratiocination, would produce any similar result.

For, in respect to the latter branch of the supposition, it should be considered that the most trifling variation in the facts of the two cases might give rise to the most important miscalculations, by diverting thoroughly the two courses of events; very much as, in arithmetic, an error which, in its own individuality, may be inappreciable, produces, at length, by dint of multiplication at all points of the process, a result enormously at variance with truth. And, in regard to the former branch, we must not fail to hold in view that the very Calculus of Probabilities to which I have referred, forbids all idea of the extension of the parallel:– forbids it with a positiveness strong and decided just in proportion as this parallel has already been long-drawn and exact. This is one of those anomalous propositions which, seemingly appealing to thought altogether apart from the mathematical, is yet one which only the mathematician can fully entertain. Nothing, for example, is more difficult than to convince the merely general reader that the fact of sixes having been thrown twice in succession by a player at dice, is sufficient cause for betting the largest odds that sixes will not be thrown in the third attempt. A suggestion to this effect is usually rejected by the intellect at once. It does not appear that the two throws which have been completed, and which lie now absolutely in the Past, can have influence upon the throw which exists only in the Future. The chance for throwing sixes seems to be precisely as it was at any ordinary time – that is to say, subject only to the influence of the various other throws which may be made by dice. And this is a reflection which appears so exceedingly obvious that attempts to controvert it are received more frequently with a derisive smile than with anything like respectful attention. The error here involved – a gross error redolent of mischief – I cannot pretend to expose within the limits assigned me at present; and with the philosophical it needs no exposure. It may be sufficient here to say that it forms one of an infinite series of mistakes which arise in the path of Reason through her propensity for seeking truth *in detail*.

The Balloon-Hoax

[Astounding News by Express, *via* Norfolk! – The Atlantic crossed in Three Days! Signal Triumph of Mr. Monck Mason's Flying Machine! – Arrival at Sullivan's Island, near Charleston, S.C., of Mr. Mason, Mr. Robert Holland, Mr. Henson, Mr. Harrison Ainsworth, and four others, in the Steering Balloon, 'Victoria,' after a passage of Seventy-five Hours from Land to Land! Full Particulars of the Voyage!

The subjoined *jeu d'esprit*, with the preceding heading in magnificent capitals, well interspersed with notes of admiration, was originally published, as matter of fact, in the 'New York Sun,' a daily newspaper, and therein fully subserved the purpose of creating indigestible aliment for the *quidnuncs* during the few hours intervening between a couple of the Charleston mails. The rush for the 'sole paper which had the news' was something beyond even the prodigious: and, in fact, if (as some assert) the 'Victoria' *did* not absolutely accomplish the voyage recorded, it will be difficult to assign a reason why she *should* not have accomplished it.]

The great problem is at length solved! The air, as well as the earth and the ocean, has been subdued by science, and will become a common and convenient highway for mankind. *The Atlantic has been actually crossed in a balloon!* and this too without difficulty – without any great apparent danger – with thorough control of the machine – and in the inconceivably brief period of seventy-five hours from shore to shore!

By the energy of an agent at Charleston, S.C., we are enabled to be the first to furnish the public with a detailed account of this most extraordinary voyage, which was performed between Saturday, the 6th instant, at 11 A.M., and 2 P.M., on Tuesday, the 9th instant, by Sir Everard Bringhurst; Mr. Osborne, a nephew of Lord Bentinck's; Mr. Monck Mason and Mr. Robert Holland, the well-known æronauts; Mr. Harrison Ainsworth, author of 'Jack Sheppard,' etc.; and Mr. Henson, the projector of the late unsuccessful flying-machine, with two seamen from Woolwich; in all, eight persons. The particulars furnished below may be relied on as authentic and accurate in every respect, as, with a slight exception, they are copied *verbatim* from the joint diaries of Mr. Monck Mason and Mr. Harrison Ainsworth, to whose politeness our agent is also indebted for much verbal information respecting the balloon itself, its construction, and other matters of interest. The only alteration in the MS. received, has been made for the purpose of throwing the hurried account of our agent, Mr. Forsyth, into a connected and intelligible form.

THE BALLOON

Two very decided failures of late – those of Mr. Henson and Sir George Cayley – had much weakened the public interest in the subject of aerial navigation. Mr. Henson's scheme (which at first was considered very feasible even by men of science) was founded upon the principle of an inclined plane, started from an eminence by an extrinsic force, applied and continued by the revolution of impinging vanes, in form and number resembling the vanes of a windmill. But, in all the experiments made with models at the Adelaide Gallery, it was found that the operation of these fans not only did not propel the machine, but actually impeded its flight. The only propelling force it ever exhibited was the mere *impetus* acquired from the descent of the inclined plane; and this *impetus* carried the machine farther when the vanes were at rest than when they were in motion, a fact which sufficiently demonstrates their inutility; and in the absence of the propelling, which was also the *sustaining* power, the whole fabric would necessarily descend. This consideration led Sir George Cayley to think only of adapting a propeller to some machine having of itself an independent power of support – in a word, to a balloon; the idea, however, being novel, or original, with Sir George, only so far as regards the mode of its application to practice. He exhibited a model of his invention at the Polytechnic Institution. The propelling principle or power was here also applied to interrupted surfaces or vanes put in revolution. These vanes were four in number, but were found entirely ineffectual in moving the balloon, or in aiding its ascending power. The whole project was thus a complete failure.

It was at this juncture that Mr. Monck Mason (whose voyage from Dover to Weilburg in the balloon, 'Nassau,' occasioned so much excitement in 1837) conceived the idea of employing the principle of the Archimedean screw for the purpose of propulsion through the air – rightly attributing the failure of Mr. Henson's scheme, and of Sir George Cayley's, to the interruption of surface in the independent vanes. He made the first public experiment at Willis's Rooms, but afterwards removed his model to the Adelaide Gallery.

Like Sir George Cayley's balloon, his own was an ellipsoid. Its length was thirteen feet six inches – height, six feet eight inches. It contained about three hundred and twenty cubic feet of gas, which, if pure hydrogen, would support twenty-one pounds upon its first inflation, before the gas has time to deteriorate or escape. The weight of the whole machine and apparatus was seventeen pounds – leaving about four pounds to spare. Beneath the centre of the balloon, was a frame of light wood about nine feet long, and rigged on to the balloon itself with a network in the customary manner. From this framework was suspended a wicker basket or car.

The screw consists of an axis of hollow brass tube, eighteen inches in length, through which, upon a semi-spiral inclined at fifteen degrees, pass a series of a steel wire radii, two feet long, and thus projecting a foot on either side. These radii are connected at the outer extremities by two bands of flattened wire – the whole in this manner forming the framework of the screw, which is completed by a covering of oiled silk cut into gores, and tightened so as to present a tolerably uniform surface. At each end of its axis this screw is supported by pillars of hollow brass tube descending from the hoop. In the lower ends of these tubes are holes in which the pivots of the axis revolve. From the end of the axis which is next the car, proceeds a shaft of steel, connecting the screw with the pinion of a piece of spring machinery fixed in the car. By the operation of this spring, the screw is made to revolve with great rapidity, communicating a progressive motion to the whole. By means of the rudder, the machine was readily turned in any direction. The spring was of great power compared with its dimensions, being capable of raising forty-five pounds upon a barrel of four inches diameter after the first turn, and gradually increasing as it was wound up. It weighed altogether eight pounds six ounces. The rudder was a light frame of cane covered with silk, shaped somewhat like a battledore, and was about three feet long, and at the widest one foot. Its weight was about two ounces. It could be turned *flat*, and directed upwards or downwards, as well as to the right or left; and thus enabled the æronaut to transfer the resistance of the air, which in an inclined position it must generate in its passage, to any side upon which he might desire to act, thus determining the balloon in the opposite direction.

This model (which, through want of time, we have necessarily described in an imperfect manner) was put in action at the Adelaide Gallery, where it accomplished a velocity of five miles per hour; although, strange to say, it excited very little interest in comparison with the previous complex machine of Mr. Henson – so resolute is the world to despise anything which carries with it an air of simplicity. To accomplish the great desideratum of aerial navigation, it was very generally supposed that some exceedingly complicated application must be made of some unusually profound principle in dynamics.

So well satisfied, however, was Mr. Mason of the ultimate success of his invention, that he determined to construct immediately, if possible, a balloon of sufficient capacity to test the question by a voyage of some extent – the original design being to cross the British Channel as before in the Nassau balloon. To carry out his views, he solicited and obtained the patronage of Sir Everard Bringhurst and Mr. Osborne, two gentlemen well known for scientific acquirement, and especially for the interest they have exhibited in the progress of ærostation. The project, at the desire of Mr. Osborne, was kept a profound secret from the public – the only persons entrusted with the design being those actually engaged in the construction of the machine, which was built (under the superintendence of Mr. Mason, Mr. Holland, Sir Everard Bringhurst, and Mr. Osborne) at the seat of the latter gentleman near Penstruthal, in Wales. Mr. Henson, accompanied by his friend Mr. Ainsworth, was admitted to a private view of the balloon on Saturday last – when the two gentlemen made final arrangements to be included in the adventure. We are not informed for what reason the two seamen were also included in the party – but, in the course of a day or two, we shall put our readers in possession of the minutest particulars respecting this extraordinary voyage.

The balloon is composed of silk, varnished with the liquid gum caoutchouc. It is of vast dimensions, containing more than 40,000 cubic feet of gas; but as coal-gas was employed in place of the more expensive and inconvenient hydrogen, the supporting power of the machine when fully inflated, and immediately after inflation, is not more than about 2500 pounds. The coal-gas is not only much less costly, but is easily procured and managed.

For its introduction into common use for purposes of aerostation we are indebted to Mr. Charles Green. Up to his discovery, the process of inflation was not only exceedingly expensive, but uncertain. Two, and even three days, have frequently been wasted in futile attempts to procure a sufficiency of hydrogen to fill a balloon, from which it had great tendency to escape, owing to its extreme subtlety, and its affinity for the surrounding atmosphere. In a balloon sufficiently perfect to retain its contents of coal-gas unaltered in quality or amount for six months, an equal quantity of hydrogen could not be maintained in equal purity for six weeks.

The supporting power being estimated at 2500 pounds, and the united weights of the party amounting only to about 1200, there was left a surplus of 1300, of which again 1200 was exhausted by ballast, arranged in bags of different sizes, with their respective weights marked upon them; by cordage, barometers, telescopes, barrels containing provision for a fortnight, water-casks, cloaks, carpet-bags, and various other indispensable matters, including a coffee-warmer, contrived for warming coffee by means of slacklime, so as to dispense altogether with fire, if it should be judged prudent to do so. All these articles, with the exception of the ballast and a few trifles, were suspended from the hoop overhead. The car is much smaller and lighter in proportion than the one appended to the model. It is formed of a light wicker, and is wonderfully strong for so frail-looking a machine. Its rim is about four feet deep. The rudder is also very much larger in proportion than that of the model; and the screw is considerably smaller. The balloon is furnished besides with a grapnel and a guide-rope; which latter is of the most indispensable importance. A few words in explanation will here be necessary for such of our readers as are not conversant with the details of aerostation.

As soon as the balloon quits the earth it is subjected to the influence of many circumstances tending to create a difference in its weight, augmenting or diminishing its ascending power. For example, there may be a deposition of dew upon the silk to the extent even of several hundred pounds; ballast has then to be thrown out, or the machine may descend. This ballast being discarded, and a clear sunshine evaporating the dew, and at the same time expanding the gas in the silk, the whole will again rapidly ascend. To check this ascent, the only resource is (or rather *was*, until Mr. Green's invention of the guide-rope) the permission of the escape of gas from the valve; but, in the loss of gas, is a proportionate general loss of ascending power; so that in a comparatively brief period the best constructed balloon must necessarily exhaust all its resources and come to the earth. This was the great obstacle to voyages of length.

The guide-rope remedies the difficulty in the simplest manner conceivable. It is merely a very long rope which is suffered to trail from the car, and the effect of which is to prevent the balloon from changing its level in any material degree. If, for example, there should be a deposition of moisture upon the silk, and the machine begins to descend in consequence, there will be no necessity for discharging ballast to remedy the increase of weight, for it is remedied or counteracted in an exactly just proportion by the deposit on the ground of just so much of the end of the rope as is necessary. If, on the other hand, any circumstances should cause undue levity, and consequent ascent, this levity is immediately counteracted by the additional weight of rope upraised from the earth. Thus, the balloon can neither ascend nor descend, except within very narrow limits, and its resources, either in gas or ballast, remain comparatively unimpaired. When passing over an expanse of water it becomes necessary to employ small kegs of copper or wood filled with liquid ballast of a lighter nature than water. These float, and serve all the purposes of a mere rope on land. Another most important office of the guide-rope is to point out the *direction* of the balloon. The rope *drags*, either on land or sea, while the balloon is free; the latter, consequently, is always in advance when any progress whatever is made; a comparison, therefore, by means of the compass of the relative positions of the two objects will always indicate the *course*. In the same way, the angle formed by the rope with the vertical axis of the machine indicates the *velocity*. When there is *no* angle – in other words, when the rope hangs perpendicularly, the whole apparatus is stationary; but the larger the angle, that is to say, the farther the balloon precedes the end of the rope, the greater the velocity; and the converse.

As the original design was to cross the British Channel, and alight as near Paris as possible, the voyagers had taken the precaution to prepare themselves with passports directed to all parts of the Continent, specifying the nature of the expedition, as in the case of the Nassau voyage, and entitling the adventurers to exemption from the usual formalities of office. Unexpected events, however, rendered these passports superfluous.

The inflation was commenced very quietly at daybreak, on Saturday morning, the 6th instant in the courtyard of Weal-Vor House, Mr. Osborne's seat, about a mile from Penstruthal, in North Wales; and at 7 minutes past 11, everything being ready for departure, the balloon was set free, rising gently but steadily in a direction nearly south, no use being made for the first half-hour of either the screw or the rudder. We proceed now with the journal as transcribed by Mr. Forsyth from the joint MSS. of Mr. Monck Mason and Mr. Ainsworth. The body of the journal, as given, is in the hand-writing of Mr. Mason, and a P.S. is appended each day by Mr. Ainsworth, who has in preparation, and will shortly give the public, a more minute and, no doubt, a thrillingly interesting account of the voyage.

THE JOURNAL

Saturday, April the 6th. – Every preparation likely to embarrass us having been made over night, we commenced the inflation this morning at daybreak; but owing to a thick fog, which encumbered the folds of the silk and rendered it unmanageable, we did not get through before nearly 11 o'clock. Cut loose then, in high spirits, and rose gently but steadily, with a light breeze at north, which bore us in the direction of the British Channel. Found the ascending force greater than we had expected; and as we arose higher and so got clear of the cliffs, and more in the sun's rays, our ascent became very rapid. I did not wish, however, to lose gas at so early a period of the adventure, and so concluded to ascend for the present. We soon ran out our guide-rope; but even when we had raised it clear of the earth, we still went up very rapidly. The balloon was unusually steady, and looked beautifully. In about ten minutes after starting the barometer indicated an altitude of 15,000 feet. The weather was remarkably fine, and the view of the subjacent country – a most romantic one when seen from any point – was now especially sublime. The numerous deep gorges presented the appearance of lakes, on account of the dense vapours with which they were filled, and the pinnacles and crags to the south-east, piled in inextricable confusion, resembled nothing so much as the giant cities of eastern fable. We were rapidly approaching the mountains in the south, but our elevation was more than sufficient to enable us to pass them in safety. In a few minutes we soared over them in fine style; and

Mr. Ainsworth, with the seamen, were surprised at their apparent want of altitude when viewed from the car, the tendency of great elevation in a balloon being to reduce inequalities of the surface below to nearly a dead level. At half-past eleven, still proceeding nearly south, we obtained our first view of the Bristol Channel; and, in fifteen minutes afterwards, the line of breakers on the coast appeared immediately beneath us, and we were fairly out at sea. We now resolved to let off enough gas to bring our guide-rope, with the buoys affixed, into the water. This was immediately done, and we commenced a gradual descent. In about twenty minutes our first buoy dipped, and at the touch of the second soon afterwards we remained stationary as to elevation. We were all now anxious to test the efficiency of the rudder and screw, and we put them both into requisition forthwith, for the purpose of altering our direction more to the eastward, and in a line for Paris. By means of the rudder we instantly effected the necessary change of direction, and our course was brought nearly at right angles to that of the wind, when we set in motion the spring of the screw, and were rejoiced to find it propel us readily as desired. Upon this we gave nine hearty cheers, and dropped in the sea a bottle, enclosing a slip of parchment with a brief account of the principle of the invention. Hardly, however, had we done with our rejoicings, when an unforeseen accident occurred which discouraged us in no little degree. The steel rod connecting the spring with the propeller was suddenly jerked out of place at the car end (by a swaying of the car through some movement of one of the two seamen we had taken up), and in an instant hung dangling out of reach from the pivot of the axis of the screw. While we were endeavouring to regain it, our attention being completely absorbed, we became involved in a strong current of wind from the east, which bore us with rapidly increasing force towards the Atlantic. We soon found ourselves driving out to sea at the rate of not less, certainly, than fifty or sixty miles an hour, so that we came up with Cape Clear, at some forty miles to our north, before we had secured the rod and had time to think what we were about. It was now that Mr. Ainsworth made an extraordinary, but, to my fancy, a by no means unreasonable or chimerical proposition, in which he was instantly seconded by Mr. Holland – viz., that we should take advantage of the strong gale which bore us on, and in place of beating back to Paris, make an attempt to reach the coast of North America. After slight reflection I gave a willing ascent to this bold proposition, which (strange to say) met with objection from the two seamen only. As the stronger party, however, we overruled their fears, and kept resolutely upon our course. We steered due west; but as the trailing of the buoys materially impeded our progress, and we had the balloon abundantly at command, either for ascent or descent, we first threw out fifty pounds of ballast, and then wound up (by means of a windlass), so much of a rope as brought it quite clear of the sea. We perceived the effect of this manœuvre immediately in a vastly increased rate of progress; and, as the gale freshened, we flew with a velocity nearly inconceivable – the guide-rope flying out behind the car like a streamer from a vessel. It is needless to say that a very short time sufficed us to lose sight of the coast. We passed over innumerable vessels of all kinds, a few of which were endeavouring to beat up, but the most of them lying to. We occasioned the greatest excitement on board all – an excitement greatly relished by ourselves, and especially by our two men, who, now under the influence of a dram of Geneva, seemed resolved to give all scruple or fear to the wind. Many of the vessels fired signal guns; and in all we were saluted with loud cheers (which we heard with surprising distinctness) and the waving of caps and handkerchiefs. We kept on in this manner throughout the day with no material incident, and as the shades of night closed around us we made a rough estimate of the distance traversed. It could not have been less than five hundred miles, and was probably much more. The propeller was kept in constant operation, and no doubt aided our progress materially. As the sun went down, the gale freshened into an absolute hurricane, and the ocean beneath was clearly visible on account of its phosphorescence. The wind was from the east all night, and gave us the brightest omen of success. We suffered no little from cold, and the dampness of the atmosphere was most unpleasant; but the ample space in the car enabled us to lie down, and by means of cloaks and a few blankets, we did sufficiently well.

P.S. [By Mr. Ainsworth.] The last nine hours have been unquestionably the most exciting of my life. I can conceive nothing more
sublimating than the strange peril and novelty of an adventure such as
this. May God grant that we succeed! I ask not success for mere safety
to my insignificant person, but for the sake of human knowledge, and
for the vastness of the triumph. And yet the feat is only so evidently
feasible that the sole wonder is why men have scrupled to attempt it
before. One single gale such as now befriends us – let such a tempest
whirl forward a balloon for four or five days (these gales often last
longer), and the voyager will be easily borne in that period from coast
to coast. In view of such a gale the broad Atlantic becomes a mere lake.
I am more struck just now with the supreme silence which reigns in the
sea beneath us, notwithstanding its agitation, than with any other
phenomenon presenting itself. The waters give up no voice to the
heavens. The immense flaming ocean writhes and is tortured uncom-
plainingly. The mountainous surges suggest the idea of innumerable
dumb gigantic fiends struggling in impotent agony. In a night such as
is this to me, a man *lives* – lives a whole century of ordinary life – nor
would I forego this rapturous delight for that of a whole century of
ordinary existence.

Sunday, the 7th. [Mr. Mason's MS.] This morning the gale, by 10,
had subsided to an eight or nine knot breeze (for a vessel at sea), and
bears us, perhaps, thirty miles per hour or more. It has veered,
however, very considerably to the north; and now, at sundown, we are
holding our course due west, principally by the screw and rudder,
which answer their purposes to admiration. I regard the project as
thoroughly successful, and the easy navigation of the air in any
direction (not exactly in the teeth of a gale) as no longer problematical.
We could not have made head against the strong wind of yesterday;
but, by ascending, we might have got out of its influence if requisite.
Against a pretty stiff breeze, I feel convinced we can make our way
with the propeller. At noon to-day, ascended to an elevation of nearly
25,000 feet by discharging ballast. Did this to search for a more direct
current, but found none so favourable as the one we are now in. We
have an abundance of gas to take us across this small pond even should

the voyage last three weeks. I have not the slightest fear for the result. The difficulty has been strangely exaggerated and misapprehended. I can choose my current, and should I find *all* currents against me, I can make very tolerable headway with the propeller. We have had no incidents worth recording. The night promises fair.

P.S. [By Mr. Ainsworth.] I have little to record, except the fact (to me quite a surprising one) that, at an elevation equal to that of Cotopaxi, I experienced neither very intense cold, nor headache, nor difficulty of breathing; neither, I find, did Mr. Mason, nor Mr. Holland, nor Sir Everard. Mr. Osborne complained of constriction of the chest – but this soon wore off. We have flown at a great rate during the day, and we must be more than half way across the Atlantic. We have passed over some twenty or thirty vessels of various kinds, and all seem to be delightfully astonished. Crossing the ocean in a balloon is not so difficult a feat after all. *Omne ignotum pro magnifico. Mem.* – At 25,000 feet elevation the sky appears nearly black, and the stars are distinctly visible; while the sea does not seem convex (as one might suppose), but absolutely and most unequivocally *concave.**

Monday, the 8th. [Mr. Mason's MS.] This morning we had again some little trouble with the rod of the propeller, which must be entirely remodelled for fear of serious accident – I mean the steel rod,

---

* Mr. Ainsworth has not attempted to account for this phenomena, which, however, is quite susceptible of explanation. A line dropped from an elevation of 25,000 feet perpendicularly to the surface of the earth (or sea) would form the perpendicular of a right-angled triangle, of which the base would extend from the right angle to the horizon, and the hypothenuse from the horizon to the balloon. But the 25,000 feet of altitude is little or nothing in comparison with the extent of the prospect. In other words, the base and hypothenuse of the supposed triangle would be so long when compared with the perpendicular, that the two former may be regarded as nearly parallel. In this manner the horizon of the aeronaut would appear to be *on a level* with the car. But as the point immediately beneath seems, and is, at a great distance below him, it seems, of course, also at a great distance below the horizon. Hence the impression of *concavity*; and this impression must remain until the elevation shall bear so great a proportion to the extent of prospect, that the apparent parallelism of the base and hypothenuse disappears – when the earth's real convexity must become apparent.

not the vanes. The latter could not be improved. The wind has been blowing steadily and strongly from the north-east all day; and so far fortune seems bent upon favouring us. Just before day we were all somewhat alarmed at some odd noises and concussions in the balloon, accompanied with the apparent rapid subsidence of the whole machine. These phenomena were occasioned by the expansion of the gas, through increase of heat in the atmosphere, and the consequent disruption of the minute particles of ice with which the network had become encrusted during the night. Threw down several bottles to the vessels below. Saw one of them picked up by a large ship – seemingly one of the New York line packets. Endeavoured to make out her name, but could not be sure of it. Mr. Osborne's telescope made it out something like 'Atalanta.' It is now twelve at night, and we are still going nearly west at a rapid pace. The sea is peculiarly phosphorescent.

P.S. [By Mr. Ainsworth.] It is now 2 A.M., and nearly calm, as well as I can judge – but it is very difficult to determine this point, since we move *with* the air so completely. I have not slept since quitting Wheal-Vor, but can stand it no longer, and must take a nap. We cannot be far from the American coast.

Tuesday, the 9th. [Mr. Ainsworth's MS.] 1 P.M. *We are in full view of the low coast of South Carolina.* The great problem is accomplished. We have crossed the Atlantic – fairly and *easily* crossed it in a balloon! God be praised! Who shall say that anything is impossible hereafter?

The Journal here ceases. Some particulars of the descent were communicated, however, by Mr. Ainsworth to Mr. Forsyth. It was nearly dead calm when the voyagers first came in view of the coast, which was immediately recognised by both the seamen, and by Mr. Osborne. The latter gentleman having acquaintances at Fort Moultrie, it was immediately resolved to descend in its vicinity. The balloon was brought over the beach (the tide being out and the sand hard, smooth, and admirably adapted for a descent), and the grapnel let go, which took firm hold at once. The inhabitants of the island and of the fort thronged out of course to see the balloon; but it was with the greatest difficulty that any one could be made to credit the actual voyage – *the crossing of the Atlantic*. The grapnel caught at 2 P.M. precisely; and thus the whole voyage was completed in seventy-five hours, or rather less, counting from shore to shore. No serious accident occurred. No real danger was at any time apprehended. The balloon was exhausted and secured without trouble; and when the MS. from which this narrative is compiled was despatched from Charleston the party was still at Fort Moultrie. Their further intentions were not ascertained but we can safely promise our readers some additional information either on Monday or in the course of the next day at furthest.

This is unquestionably the most stupendous, the most interesting, and the most important undertaking ever accomplished or even attempted by man. What magnificent events may ensue it would be useless now to think of determining.

Some Words with a Mummy

The *symposium* of the preceding evening had been a little too much for my nerves. I had a wretched headache, and was desperately drowsy. Instead of going out therefore to spend the evening as I had proposed, it occurred to me that I could not do a wiser thing than just eat a mouthful of supper and go immediately to bed.

A *light* supper of course. I am exceedingly fond of Welsh rabbit. More than a pound at once, however, may not at all times be advisable. Still, there can be no material objection to two. And really between two and three, there is merely a single unit of difference. I ventured, perhaps, upon four. My wife will have it five; – but, clearly, she has confounded two very distinct affairs. The abstract number, five, I am willing to admit; but, concretely, it has reference to bottles of brown stout, without which, in the way of condiment, Welsh rabbit is to be eschewed.

Having thus concluded a frugal meal, and donned my night-cap, with the serene hope of enjoying it till noon the next day, I placed my head upon the pillow, and, through the aid of a capital conscience, fell into a profound slumber forthwith.

But when were the hopes of humanity fulfilled? I could not have completed my third snore when there came a furious ringing at the street-door bell, and then an impatient thumping at the knocker, which awakened me at once. In a minute afterwards, and while I was still rubbing my eyes, my wife thrust in my face a note from an old friend, Doctor Ponnonner. It ran thus:

'Come to me, by all means, my dear good friend, as soon as you receive this. Come and help us to rejoice. At last, by long persevering diplomacy, I have gained the assent of the Directors of the City Museum, to my examination of the mummy – you know the one I mean. I have permission to unswathe it and open it if desirable. A few friends only will be present – you of course. The mummy is now at my house, and we shall begin to unroll it at eleven to-night. – Yours, ever,
'PONNONNER.'

By the time I had reached the 'Ponnonner' it struck me that I was as wide awake as a man need be. I leaped out of bed in an ecstasy, overthrowing all in my way, dressed myself with a rapidity truly marvellous, and set off at the top of my speed for the doctor's.

There I found a very eager company assembled. They had been awaiting me with much impatience; the mummy was extended upon the dining-table, and the moment I entered its examination was commenced.

It was one of a pair brought, several years previously, by Captain Arthur Sabretash, a cousin of Ponnonner's, from a tomb near Eleithias, in the Lybian Mountains, a considerable distance above Thebes on the Nile. The grottoes at this point, although less magnificent than the Theban sepulchres, are of higher interest, on account of affording more numerous illustrations of the private life of the Egyptians. The chamber from which our specimen was taken was said to be very rich in such illustrations, the walls being completely covered with fresco paintings and bas-reliefs, while statues, vases, and mosaic work of rich patterns, indicated the vast wealth of the deceased.

The treasure had been deposited in the museum precisely in the same condition in which Captain Sabretash had found it; – that is to say, the coffin had not been disturbed. For eight years it had thus stood, subject only externally to public inspection. We had now, therefore, the complete mummy at our disposal, and to those who are aware how very rarely the unransacked antique reaches our shores, it will be evident at once that we had great reason to congratulate ourselves upon our good fortune.

Approaching the table I saw on it a large box or case nearly seven feet long, and perhaps three feet wide, by two feet and a half deep. It was oblong, not coffin-shaped. The material was at first supposed to be the wood of the sycamore (*platanus*), but upon cutting into it we found it to be pasteboard or, more properly, *papier maché*, composed of papyrus. It was thickly ornamented with paintings representing funeral scenes and other mournful subjects, interspersed among which, in every variety of position, were certain series of hieroglyphical characters, intended no doubt for the name of the departed. By good luck, Mr. Gliddon formed one of our party, and he had no difficulty in translating the letters, which were simply phonetic, and represented the word *Allamistakeo*.

We had some difficulty in getting this case open without injury, but having at length accomplished the task we came to a second, coffin-shaped, and very considerably less in size than the exterior one, but resembling it precisely in every other respect. The interval between the two was filled with resin, which had in some degree defaced the colours of the interior box.

Upon opening this latter (which we did quite easily) we arrived at a third case, also coffin-shaped and varying from the second one in no particular except in that of its material, which was cedar, and still emitted the peculiar and highly aromatic odour of that wood. Between the second and the third case there was no interval, the one fitting accurately within the other.

Removing the third case, we discovered and took out the body itself. We had expected to find it, as usual, enveloped in frequent rolls or bandages of linen, but in place of these we found a sort of sheath made of papyrus and coated with a layer of plaster thickly gilt and painted. The paintings represented subjects connected with the various supposed duties of the soul, and its presentation to different divinities, with numerous identical human figures, intended very probably as portraits of the person embalmed. Extending from head to foot was a columnar or perpendicular inscription, in phonetic hieroglyphics, giving again his name and titles, and the names and titles of his relations.

Around the neck thus unsheathed was a collar of cylindrical glass beads, diverse in colour, and so arranged as to form images of deities, of the scarabæus, etc., with the winged globe. Around the small of the waist was a similar collar or belt.

Stripping off the papyrus we found the flesh in excellent preservation, with no perceptible odour. The colour was reddish. The skin was hard, smooth, and glossy. The teeth and hair were in good condition. The eyes (it seemed) had been removed, and glass ones substituted, which were very beautiful and wonderfully life-like, with the exception of somewhat too determined a stare. The fingers and the nails were brilliantly gilded.

Mr. Gliddon was of opinion, from the redness of the epidermis, that the embalment had been effected altogether by asphaltum; but, on scraping the surface with a steel instrument, and throwing into the fire some of the powder thus obtained, the flavour of camphor and other sweet-scented gums became apparent.

We searched the corpse very carefully for usual openings through which the entrails are extracted, but to our surprise we could discover none. No member of the party was at that period aware that entire or unopened mummies are not unfrequently met. The brain it was customary to withdraw through the nose; the intestines through an incision in the side; the body was then shaved, washed and salted; then laid aside for several weeks, when the operation of embalming, properly so called, began.

As no trace of an opening could be found, Dr. Ponnonner was preparing his instruments for dissection, when I observed that it was then past two o'clock. Hereupon it was agreed to postpone the internal examination until the next evening; and we were about to separate for the present, when some one suggested an experiment or two with the Voltaic pile. The application of electricity to a mummy three or four thousand years old at the least was an idea, if not very sage, still sufficiently original, and we all caught it at once. About one-tenth in earnest and nine-tenths in jest, we arranged a battery in the doctor's study, and conveyed thither the Egyptian.

It was only after much trouble that we succeeded in laying bare some portions of the temporal muscle, which appeared of less stony rigidity than other parts of the frame, but which, as we had anticipated, of course, gave no indication of galvanic susceptibility when brought in contact with the wire. This, the first trial, indeed, seemed decisive, and, with a hearty laugh at our own absurdity, we were bidding each other good-night, when my eyes happening to fall upon those of the mummy, were there immediately rivetted in amazement. My brief glance, in fact, had sufficed to assure me that the orbs which we had all supposed to be glass, and which were originally noticeable for a certain wild stare, were now so far covered by the lids that only a small portion of the *tunica albuginea* remained visible.

With a shout I called attention to the fact, and it became immediately obvious to all.

I cannot say that I was *alarmed* at the phenomenon, because 'alarmed' is, in my case, not exactly the word. It is possible, however, that, but for the brown stout, I might have been a little nervous. As for the rest of the company, they really made no attempt at concealing the downright fright which possessed them. Doctor Ponnonner was a man to be pitied. Mr. Gliddon by some peculiar process, rendered himself invisible. Mr. Silk Buckingham, I fancy, will scarcely be so bold as to deny that he made his way, upon all fours, under the table.

After the first shock of astonishment, however, we resolved, as a matter of course, upon further experiment forthwith. Our operations were now directed against the great toe of the right foot. We made an incision over the outside of the exterior *os sesamoideum pollicis pedis*, and thus got at the root of the *abductor* muscle. Re-adjusting the battery we now applied the fluid to the bisected nerves – when, with a movement of exceeding life-likeness, the mummy first drew up its right knee so as to bring it nearly in contact with the abdomen, and then, straightening the limb with inconceivable force, bestowed a kick upon Doctor Ponnonner, which had the effect of discharging that gentleman, like an arrow from a catapult, through a window into the street below.

We rushed out *en masse* to bring in the mangled remains of the victim, but had the happiness to meet him upon the staircase, coming up in an unaccountable hurry, brimful of the most ardent philosophy, and more than ever impressed with the necessity of prosecuting our experiments with rigour and with zeal.

It was by his advice, accordingly, that we made upon the spot a profound incision into the tip of the subject's nose, while the Doctor himself laying violent hands upon it pulled it into vehement contact with the wire.

Morally and physically – figuratively and literally – was the effect electric. In the first place, the corpse opened its eyes and winked very rapidly for several minutes, as does Mr. Barnes in the pantomime; in the second place, it sneezed: in the third, it sat upon end; in the fourth, it shook its fist in Doctor Ponnonner's face; in the fifth, turning to Messieurs Gliddon and Buckingham, it addressed them, in very capital Egyptian, thus:–

'I must say, gentlemen, that I am as much surprised as I am mortified at your behaviour. Of Doctor Ponnonner nothing better was to be expected. He is a poor little fat fool who *knows* no better. I pity and forgive him. But you, Mr. Gliddon – and you, Silk – who have travelled and resided in Egypt until one might imagine you to the manner born – you, I say, who have been so much among us that you speak Egyptian fully as well, I think, as you write your mother tongue – you, whom I have always been led to regard as the firm friend of the mummies – I really did anticipate more gentlemanly conduct from *you*. What am I to think of your standing quietly by and seeing me thus unhandsomely used? What am I to suppose by your permitting Tom, Dick, and Harry to strip me of my coffins, and my clothes, in this wretchedly cold climate? In what light (to come to the point) am I to regard your aiding and abetting that miserable little villain, Doctor Ponnonner, in pulling me by the nose?'

It will be taken for granted, no doubt, that upon hearing this speech under the circumstances, we all either made for the door, or fell into violent hysterics, or went off in a general swoon. One of these three things was, I say, to be expected. Indeed each and all of these lines of conduct might have been very plausibly pursued. And upon my word, I am at a loss to know how or why it was that we pursued neither the one nor the other. But perhaps, the true reason is to be sought in the spirit of the age, which proceeds by the rule of contraries altogether, and is now usually admitted as the solution of everything in the way of paradox and impossibility. Or perhaps, after all, it was only the mummy's exceedingly natural and matter-of-course air that divested his words of the terrible. However this may be, the facts are clear, and no member of our party betrayed any very particular trepidation, or seemed to consider that anything had gone very especially wrong.

For my part I was convinced it was all right, and merely stepped aside, out of the range of the Egyptian's fist. Doctor Ponnonner thrust his hands into his breeches' pockets, looked hard at the mummy, and grew excessively red in the face. Mr. Gliddon stroked his whiskers and drew up the collar of his shirt. Mr. Buckingham hung down his head, and put his right thumb into the left corner of his mouth.

The Egyptian regarded him with a severe countenance for some minutes, and at length, with a sneer, said:

'Why don't you speak, Mr. Buckingham? Did you hear what I asked you, or not? *Do* take your thumb out of your mouth!'

Mr. Buckingham, hereupon, gave a slight start, took his right thumb out of the left corner of his mouth, and, by way of indemnification, inserted his left thumb in the right corner of the aperture above-mentioned.

Not being able to get an answer from Mr. B., the figure turned peevishly to Mr. Gliddon, and, in a peremptory tone, demanded in general terms what we all meant.

Mr. Gliddon replied at great length, in phonetics; and but for the deficiency of American printing-offices in hieroglyphical type, it would afford me much pleasure to record here, in the original, the whole of his very excellent speech.

I may as well take this occasion to remark that all the subsequent conversation in which the mummy took a part was carried on in primitive Egyptian, through the medium (so far as concerned myself and other untravelled members of the company) – through the medium, I say, of Messieurs Gliddon and Buckingham, as interpreters. These gentlemen spoke the mother-tongue of the mummy with inimitable fluency and grace; but I could not help observing that (owing, no doubt, to the introduction of images entirely modern, and of course entirely novel to the stranger), the two travellers were reduced occasionally to the employment of sensible forms for the purpose of conveying a particular meaning. Mr. Gliddon, at one period, for example, could not make the Egyptian comprehend the term 'politics' until he sketched upon the wall, with a bit of charcoal, a little carbuncle-nosed gentleman, out at elbows, standing upon a stump, with his left leg drawn back, his right arm thrown forward, with fist shut, the eyes rolled up towards heaven, and the mouth open at an angle of ninety degrees. Just in the same way Mr. Buckingham failed to convey the absolutely modern idea, 'whig,' until (at Doctor Ponnonner's suggestion), he grew very pale in the face, and consented to take off his own.

It will be readily understood that Mr Gliddon's discourse turned chiefly upon the vast benefits accruing to science from the unrolling and disembowelling of mummies; apologising, upon this score, for any disturbance that might have been occasioned *him*, in particular, the individual mummy called Allamistakeo; and concluding with a mere hint (for it could scarcely be considered more), that, as these little matters were now explained, it might be as well to proceed with the investigation intended. Here Doctor Ponnonner made ready his instruments.

In regard to the latter suggestions of the orator, it appears that Allamistakeo had certain scruples of conscience, the nature of which I did not distinctly learn; but he expressed himself satisfied with the apologies tendered, and getting down from the table, shook hands with the company all round.

When this ceremony was at an end, we immediately busied

ourselves in repairing the damages which our subject had sustained
from the scalpel. We sewed up the wound in his temple, bandaged his
foot, and applied a square inch of black plaster to the tip of his nose.

It was now observed that the Count (this was the title, it seems, of
Allamistakeo), had a slight fit of shivering – no doubt from the cold.
The Doctor immediately repaired to his wardrobe, and soon returned
with a black dress coat, made in Jennings' best manner, a pair of sky-
blue plaid pantaloons with straps, a pink gingham *chemise*, a flapped
vest of brocade, a white sac overcoat, a walking cane with a hook, a hat
with no brim, patent-leather boots, straw-coloured kid gloves, an eye-
glass, a pair of whiskers, and a waterfall cravat. Owing to the disparity
of size between the Count and the Doctor (the proportion being as two
to one), there was some little difficulty in adjusting these habiliments
upon the person of the Egyptian; but when all was arranged, he might
have been said to be dressed. Mr. Gliddon therefore gave him his arm,
and led him to a comfortable chair by the fire, while the Doctor rang
the bell upon the spot and ordered a supply of cigars and wine.

The conversation soon grew animated. Much curiosity was of
course expressed in regard to the somewhat remarkable fact of
Allamistakeo's still remaining alive.

'I should have thought,' observed Mr. Buckingham, 'that it is high
time you were dead.'

'Why,' replied the Count, very much astonished, 'I am little more
than seven hundred years old! My father lived a thousand, and was by
no means in his dotage when he died.'

Here ensued a brisk series of questions and computations, by
means of which it became evident that the antiquity of the mummy
had been grossly misjudged. It had been five thousand and fifty years,
and some months, since he had been consigned to the catacombs at
Eleithias.

'But my remark,' resumed Mr. Buckingham, 'had no reference to
your age at the period of interment (I am willing to grant, in fact, that
you are still a young man), and my allusion was to the immensity of
time during which, by your own showing, you must have been done up
in asphaltum.'

'In what?' said the Count.

'In asphaltum,' persisted Mr. B.

'Ah, yes; I have some faint notion of what you mean; it might be made to answer, no doubt, but in my time we employed scarcely anything else than the bichloride of mercury.'

'But what we are especially at a loss to understand,' said Doctor Ponnonner, 'is how it happens that, having been dead and buried in Egypt five thousand years ago, you are here to-day all alive, and looking so delightfully well.'

'Had I been as you say, *dead*,' replied the Count, 'it is more than probable that dead I should still be; for I perceive you are yet in the infancy of galvanism, and cannot accomplish with it what was a common thing among us in the old days. But the fact is, I fell into catilepsy, and it was considered by my best friends that I was either dead or should be; they accordingly embalmed me at once – I presume you are aware of the chief principle of the embalming process?'

'Why, not altogether.'

'Ah, I perceive; – a deplorable condition of ignorance! Well, I cannot enter into details just now; but it is necessary to explain that to embalm (properly speaking) in Egypt, was to arrest indefinitely *all* the animal functions subjected to the process. I use the word "animal" in its widest sense, as including the physical not more than the moral and *vital* being. I repeat that the leading principle of embalment consisted with us in the immediately arresting, and holding in perpetual *abeyance*, *all* the animal functions subjected to the process. To be brief, in whatever condition the individual was at the period of embalment in that condition he remained. Now, as it is my good fortune to be of the blood of the Scarabæus, I was embalmed *alive* as you see me at present.'

'The blood of the Scarabæus!' exclaimed Doctor Ponnonner.

'Yes. The Scarabæus was the *insignium*, or the "arms," of a very distinguished and very rare patrician family. To be "of the blood of the Scarabæus," is merely to be one of that family of which the Scarabæus is the *insignium*. I speak figuratively.'

'But what has this to do with your being alive?'

'Why, it is the general custom in Egypt to deprive a corpse before embalment of its bowels and brains; the race of Scarabæi alone did not coincide with the custom. Had I not been a Scarabæus, therefore, I should have been without bowels and brains; and without either it is inconvenient to live.'

'I perceive that,' said Mr. Buckingham, 'and I presume that all the *entire* mummies that come to hand are of the race of the Scarabæi.'

'Beyond doubt.'

'I thought,' said Mr. Gliddon, very meekly, 'that the Scarabæus was one of the Egyptian gods.'

'One of the Egyptian *what?*' exclaimed the Mummy, starting to its feet.

'Gods!' repeated the traveller.

'Mr. Gliddon, I really am astonished to hear you talk in this style,' said the Count, resuming his chair. 'No nation upon the face of the earth has ever acknowledged more than *one god*. The Scarabæus, the Ibis, etc., were with us (as similar creatures have been with others) the symbols or *media* through which we offered worship to the Creator too august to be more directly approached.'

There was here a pause. At length the colloquy was renewed by Doctor Ponnonner.

'It is not improbable, then, from what you have explained,' said he, 'that among the catacombs near the Nile, there may exist other mummies of the Scarabæus tribe in a condition of vitality.'

'There can be no question of it,' replied the Count; 'all the Scarabæi embalmed accidentally while alive are alive. Even some of those *purposely* so embalmed may have been overlooked by their executors, and still remain in the tombs.'

'Will you be kind enough to explain,' I said, 'what you mean by "purposely so embalmed?"'

'With great pleasure,' answered the Mummy, after surveying me leisurely through his eye-glass – for it was the first time I had ventured to address him a direct question.

'With great pleasure,' he said. 'The usual duration of man's life in my time was about eight hundred years. Few men died, unless by most extraordinary accident before the age of six hundred; few lived longer than a decade of centuries; but eight were considered the natural term. After the discovery of the embalming principle, as I have already described it to you, it occurred to our philosophers that a laudable curiosity might be gratified, and at the same time the interests of science much advanced by living this natural term in instalments. In the case of history, indeed, experience demonstrated that something of this kind was indispensable. An historian, for example, having attained the age of five hundred, would write a book with great labour and then get himself carefully embalmed, leaving instructions to his executors *pro tem.*, that they should cause him to be revivified after the lapse of a certain period – say five or six hundred years. Resuming existence at the expiration of this time, he would invariably find his great work converted into a species of hap-hazard notebook – that is to say, into a kind of literary arena for the conflicting guesses, riddles, and personal squabbles of whole herds of exasperated commentators. These guesses, etc., which passed under the name of annotations, or emendations, were found so completely to have enveloped, distorted, and overwhelmed the text, that the author had to go about with a lantern to discover his own book. When discovered, it was never worth the trouble of the search. After rewriting it throughout, it was regarded as the bounden duty of the historian to set himself to work immediately in correcting from his own private knowledge and experience the traditions of the day concerning the epoch at which he had originally lived. Now this process of re-scription and personal rectification, pursued by various individual sages from time to time had the effect of preventing our history from degenerating into absolute fable.'

'I beg your pardon,' said Doctor Ponnonner at this point, laying his hand gently upon the arm of the Egyptian – 'I beg your pardon, sir, but may I presume to interrupt you for one moment?'

'By all means, *sir*,' replied the Count, drawing up.

'I merely wished to ask you a question,' said the Doctor. 'You mentioned the historian's personal correction of *traditions* respecting his own epoch. Pray, sir, upon an average, what proportion of these

Kabbala were usually found to be right?'

'The Kabbala as you properly term them, sir, were generally discovered to be precisely on a par with the facts recorded in the unrewritten histories themselves; – that is to say, not one individual iota of either was ever known under any circumstances, to be not totally and radically wrong.'

'But since it is quite clear,' resumed the Doctor, 'that at least five thousand years have elapsed since your entombment, I take it for granted that your histories at that period, if not your traditions, were sufficiently explicit on that one topic of universal interest, the creation, which took place, as I presume you aware, only about ten centuries before.'

'Sir!' said the Count Allamistakeo.

The Doctor repeated his remarks, but it was only after much additional explanation that the foreigner could be made to comprehend them. The latter at length said, hesitatingly:

'The ideas you have suggested are to me, I confess, utterly novel. During my time I never knew any one to entertain so singular a fancy as that the universe (or this world if you will have it so), ever had a beginning at all. I remember once, and once only, hearing something remotely hinted by a man of many speculations concerning the origin *of the human race*; and by this individual, the very word *Adam* (or Red Earth), which you make use of, was employed. He employed it, however, in a generical sense, with reference to the spontaneous germination from rank soil (just as a thousand of the lower *genera* of creatures are germinated) – the spontaneous germination, I say, of five vast hordes of men, simultaneously upspringing in five distinct and nearly equal divisions of the globe.'

Here, in general, the company shrugged their shoulders, and one or two of us touched our foreheads with a very significant air. Mr. Silk Buckingham, first glancing slightly at the occiput and then at the sinciput of Allamistakeo, spoke as follows:–

'The long duration of human life in your time, together with the occasional practice of passing it, as you have explained, in instalments, must have had indeed a strong tendency to the general development and conglomeration of knowledge. I presume, therefore, that we are to attribute the marked inferiority of the old Egyptians in all particulars of science, when compared with the moderns, and more especially with the Yankees, altogether to the superior solidity of the Egyptian skull.'

'I confess again,' replied the Count, with much suavity, 'that I am somewhat at a loss to comprehend you: pray, to what particulars of science do you allude?'

Here our whole party, joining voices, detailed at great length the assumptions of phrenology and the marvels of animal magnetism.

Having heard us to an end, the Count proceeded to relate a few anecdotes, which rendered it evident that prototypes of Gall and Spurzheim had flourished and faded in Egypt so long ago as to have been nearly forgotten, and that the manœuvres of Mesmer were really very contemptible tricks when put in collation with the positive miracles of the Theban *savans*, who created lice and a great many other similar things.

I here asked the Count if his people were able to calculate eclipses. He smiled rather contemptuously, and said they were.

This put me a little out, but I began to make other inquiries in regard to his astronomical knowledge, when a member of the company, who had never as yet opened his mouth, whispered in my ear that for information on this head, I had better consult Ptolemy (whoever Ptolemy is), as well as one Plutarch *de facie lunœ*.

I then questioned the Mummy about burning-glasses and lenses, and, in general, about the manufacture of glass; but I had not made an end of my queries before the silent member again touched me quietly on the elbow, and begged me for God's sake to take a peep at Diodorus Siculus. As for the Count, he merely asked me, in the way of reply, if we moderns possessed any such microscopes as would enable us to cut cameos in the style of the Egyptians. While I was thinking how I should answer this question, little Doctor Ponnonner committed himself in a very extraordinary way.

'Look at our architecture!' he exclaimed, greatly to the indignation of both the travellers, who pinched him black and blue to no purpose.

'Look,' he cried with enthusiasm, 'at the Bowling-Green Fountain in New York! or if this be too vast a contemplation, regard for a moment the Capitol at Washington, D.C.!' – and the good little medical man went on to detail, very minutely, the proportion of the fabric to which he referred. He explained that the portico alone was adorned with no less than four and twenty columns, five feet in diameter, and ten feet apart.

The Count said that he regretted not being able to remember, just at that moment, the precise dimensions of any one of the principal buildings of the city of Aznac, whose foundations were laid in the night of Time, but the ruins of which were still standing, at the epoch of his entombment, in a vast plain of sand to the westward of Thebes. He recollected, however (talking of porticoes), that one affixed to an inferior palace in a kind of suburb called Carnac, consisted of one hundred and forty-four columns, thirty-seven feet each in circumference and twenty-five feet apart. The approach of this portico from the Nile was through an avenue two miles long, composed of sphynxes, statues, and obelisks, twenty, sixty, and a hundred feet in height. The palace itself (as well as he could remember) was, in one direction, two miles long, and might have been altogether about seven in circuit. Its walls were richly painted all over, within and without, with hieroglyphics. He would not pretend to *assert* that even fifty or sixty of the Doctor's Capitols might have been built within these walls, but he was by no means sure that two or three hundred of them might not have been squeezed in with some trouble. That palace at Carnac was an insignificant little building after all. He (the Count) however, could not conscientiously refuse to admit the ingenuity, magnificence, and superiority of the Fountain at the Bowling-Green, as described by the Doctor. Nothing like it, he was forced to allow, had ever been seen in Egypt or elsewhere.

I here asked the Count what he had to say to our railroads.

'Nothing,' he replied, 'in particular.' They were rather slight, rather ill-conceived, and clumsily put together. They could not be compared, of course, with the vast, level, direct, iron-grooved causeways upon which the Egyptians conveyed entire temples and solid obelisks of a hundred and fifty feet in altitude.

I spoke of our gigantic mechanical forces.

He agreed that we knew something in that way, but inquired how I should have gone to work in getting up the imposts on the lintels of even the little palace at Carnac.

This question I concluded not to hear, and demanded if he had any idea of Artesian wells; but he simply raised his eye-brows; while Mr. Gliddon winked at me very hard, and said in a low tone, that one had been recently discovered by the engineers employed to bore for water in the Great Oasis.

I then mentioned our steel; but the foreigner elevated his nose, and asked me if our steel could have executed the sharp carved works seen on the obelisks, and which was wrought altogether by edge-tools of copper.

This disconcerted us so greatly that we thought it advisable to vary the attack to metaphysics. We sent for a copy of a book called the 'Dial,' and read out of it a chapter or two about something which is not very clear, but which the Bostonians call the great movement or progress.

The Count merely said that great movements were awfully common things in his day, and as for progress, it was at one time quite a nuisance, but it never progressed.

We then spoke of the great beauty and importance of democracy, and were at much trouble in impressing the Count with a due sense of the advantages we enjoyed in living where there was suffrage *ad libitum*, and no king.

He listened with marked interest, and in fact seemed not a little amused. When we had done, he said that, a great while ago, there had occurred something of a very similar sort. Thirteen Egyptian provinces determined all at once to be free, and so set a magnificent example to the rest of mankind. They assembled their wise men, and concocted the most ingenious constitution it is possible to conceive. For a while they managed remarkably well, only their habit of bragging was prodigious. The thing ended, however, in the con- solidation of the thirteen states, with some fifteen or twenty others, in the most odious and insupportable despotism that ever was heard of upon the face of the earth.

I asked what was the name of the usurping tyrant.

As well as the Count could recollect it was *Mob*.

Not knowing what to say to this, I raised my voice, and deplored the Egyptian ignorance of steam.

The Count looked at me with much astonishment, but made no answer. The silent gentleman, however, gave me a violent nudge in the ribs with his elbows – told me I had sufficiently exposed myself for once – and demanded if I was really such a fool as not to know that the modern steam-engine is derived from the invention of Hero, through Solomon de Caus.

We were now in imminent danger of being discomfited; but, as good luck would have it, Doctor Ponnonner, having rallied, returned to our rescue, and inquired if the people of Egypt would seriously pretend to rival the moderns in the all-important particular of dress.

The Count, at this, glanced downwards to the straps of his pantaloons, and then taking hold of the end of one of his coat-tails, held it up close to his eyes for some minutes. Letting it fall at last, his mouth extended itself very gradually from ear to ear; but I do not remember that he said anything in the way of reply.

Hereupon we recovered our spirits, and the Doctor, approaching the mummy with great dignity, desired it to say candidly, upon its honour as a gentleman, if the Egyptians had comprehended, at *any* period, the manufacture of either Ponnonner's lozenges or Brandreth's pills.

We looked with profound anxiety for an answer, but in vain. It was not forthcoming. The Egyptian blushed and hung down his head. Never was triumph more consummate; never was defeat borne with so ill a grace. Indeed, I could not endure the spectacle of the poor mummy's mortification. I reached my hat, bowed to him stiffly, and took leave.

Upon getting home I found it past four o'clock, and went immediately to bed. It is now ten A.M. I have been up since seven, penning these memoranda for the benefit of my family and of mankind. The former I shall behold no more. My wife is a shrew. The truth is, I am heartily sick of this life and of the nineteenth century in general. I am convinced that everything is going wrong. Besides, I am anxious to know who will be President in 2045. As soon, therefore, as I have shaved and swallowed a cup of coffee, I shall just step over to Ponnonner's and get embalmed for a couple of hundred years.

The Premature Burial

There are certain themes of which the interest is all-absorbing, but which are too entirely horrible for the purposes of legitimate fiction. These the mere romanticist must eschew, if he do not wish to offend or to disgust. They are with propriety handled only when the severity and majesty of truth sanctify and sustain them. We thrill, for example, with the most intense of 'pleasurable pain' over the accounts of the Passage of the Beresina, of the Earthquake at Lisbon, of the Plague at London, of the Massacre of St. Bartholomew, or of the stifling of the hundred and twenty-three prisoners in the Black Hole at Calcutta. But in these accounts it is the fact – it is the reality – it is the history which excites. As inventions, we should regard them with simple abhorrence.

I have mentioned some few of the more prominent and august calamities on record; but in these it is the extent, not less than the character of the calamity, which so vividly impresses the fancy. I need not remind the reader that, from the long and weird catalogue of human miseries, I might have selected many individual instances more replete with essential suffering than any of these vast generalities of disaster. The true wretchedness, indeed – the ultimate woe – is particular, not diffuse. That the ghastly extremes of agony are endured by man the unit, and never by man the mass – for this let us thank a merciful God!

To be buried while alive is beyond question the most terrific of these extremes which has ever fallen to the lot of mere mortality. That it has frequently, very frequently, so fallen, will scarcely be denied by those who think. The boundaries which divide life from death are at best shadowy and vague. Who shall say where the one ends and where the other begins? We know that there are diseases in which occur total cessations of all the apparent functions of vitality, and yet in which these cessations are merely suspensions, properly so called. They are only temporary pauses in the incomprehensible mechanism. A certain period elapses, and some unseen mysterious principle again sets in motion the magic pinions and the wizard wheels. The silver cord was not for ever loosed, nor the golden bowl irreparably broken. But where meantime was the soul?

Apart, however, from the inevitable conclusion, *a priori*, that such causes must produce such effects – that the well-known occurrence of such cases of suspended animation must naturally give rise now and then to premature interments – apart from this consideration, we have the direct testimony of medical and ordinary experience to prove that a vast number of such interments have actually taken place. I might refer at once, if necessary, to a hundred well authenticated instances. One of very remarkable character, and of which the circumstances may be fresh in the memory of some of my readers, occurred not very long ago in the neighbouring city of Baltimore, where it occasioned a painful, intense, and widely extended excitement. The wife of one of the most respectable citizens – a lawyer of eminence and a member of Congress – was seized with a sudden and unaccountable illness, which completely baffled the skill of her physicians. After much suffering she died, or was supposed to die. No one suspected, indeed, or had reason to suspect, that she was not actually dead. She presented all the ordinary appearances of death. The face assumed the usual pinched and sunken outline. The lips were of the usual marble pallor. The eyes were lustreless. There was no warmth. Pulsation had ceased. For three days the body was preserved unburied, during which it had acquired a stony rigidity. The funeral, in short, was hastened, on account of the rapid advance of what was supposed to be decomposition.

The lady was deposited in her family vault, which for three subsequent years was undisturbed. At the expiration of this term it was opened for the reception of a sarcophagus; – but alas! how fearful a shock awaited the husband, who personally threw open the door. As its portals swung outwardly back, some white-apparelled object fell rattling within his arms. It was the skeleton of his wife in her yet unmouldered shroud.

A careful investigation rendered it evident that she had revived within two days after her entombment – that her struggles within the coffin had caused it to fall from a ledge or shelf to the floor, where it was so broken as to permit her escape. A lamp which had been accidentally left full of oil within the tomb was found empty; it might have been exhausted, however, by evaporation. On the uppermost of the steps which led down into the dread chamber was a large fragment of the coffin, with which it seemed that she had endeavoured to arrest attention by striking the iron door. While thus occupied she probably swooned, or possibly died, through sheer terror; and in falling, her shroud became entangled in some iron-work which projected interiorly. Thus she remained, and thus she rotted, erect.

In the year 1810, a case of living inhumation happened in France, attended with circumstances which go far to warrant the assertion that truth is indeed stranger than fiction. The heroine of the story was a Mademoiselle Victorine Lafourcade, a young girl of illustrious family, of wealth, and of great personal beauty. Among her numerous suitors was Julien Bossuet, a poor *litterateur*, or journalist, of Paris. His talents and general amiability had recommended him to the notice of the heiress, by whom he seems to have been truly beloved; but her pride of birth decided her finally to reject him, and to wed a Monsieur Renelle, a banker, and a diplomatist of some eminence. After marriage, however, this gentleman neglected, and perhaps even more positively ill-treated her. Having passed with him some wretched years, she died – at least her condition so closely resembled death as to deceive every one who saw her. She was buried – not in a vault – but in an ordinary grave in the village of her nativity. Filled with despair, and still inflamed by the memory of a profound attachment, the lover journeys from the capital to the remote province in which the village lies, with the romantic purpose of disinterring the corpse and possessing himself of its luxuriant tresses. He reaches the grave. At midnight he unearths the coffin, opens it, and is in the act of detaching the hair, when he is arrested by the unclosing of the beloved eyes. In fact the lady had been buried alive. Vitality had not altogether departed; and she was aroused by the caresses of her lover from the lethargy which had been mistaken for death. He bore her frantically to his lodgings in the village. He employed certain powerful restoratives suggested by no little medical learning. In fine, she revived. She recognised her preserver. She remained with him until by slow degrees she fully recovered her original health. Her woman's heart was not adamant, and this last lesson of love sufficed to soften it. She bestowed it upon Bossuet. She returned no more to her husband, but concealing from him her resurrection, fled with her lover to America. Twenty years afterwards the two returned to France, in the persuasion that time had so greatly altered the lady's appearance that her friends would be unable to recognise her. They were mistaken, however; for at the first meeting Monsieur Renelle did actually recognise and make claim to his wife. This claim she resisted; and a judicial tribunal sustained her in her resistance, deciding that the peculiar circumstances, with the long lapse of years, had extinguished, not only equitably but legally, the authority of the husband.

'The "Chirurgical Journal" of Leipsic – a periodical of high authority and merit, which some American bookseller would do well to translate and republish – records in a late number a very distressing event of the character in question.

An officer of artillery, a man of gigantic stature and of robust health, being thrown from an unmanageable horse, received a very severe contusion upon the head, which rendered him insensible at once; the skull was slightly fractured, but no immediate danger was apprehended. Trepanning was accomplished successfully. He was bled, and many other of the ordinary means of relief were adopted. Gradually, however, he fell into a more and more hopeless state of stupor, and, finally, it was thought that he died.

The weather was warm, and he was buried with indecent haste in one of the public cemeteries. His funeral took place on Thursday. On the Sunday following the grounds of the cemetery were as usual much thronged with visitors; and about noon an intense excitement was created by the declaration of a peasant that, while sitting upon the grave of the officer he had distinctly felt a commotion of the earth, as if occasioned by some one struggling beneath. At first little attention was paid to the man's asseveration; but his evident terror, and the dogged obstinacy with which he persisted in his story, had at length their natural effect upon the crowd. Spades were hurriedly procured, and the grave, which was shamefully shallow, was in a few minutes so far thrown open that the head of its occupant appeared. He was then seemingly dead, but he sat nearly erect within his coffin, the lid of which, in his furious struggles, he had partially uplifted.

He was forthwith conveyed to the nearest hospital, and there pronounced to be still living, although in an asphyctic condition. After some hours he revived, recognised individuals of his acquaintance, and in broken sentences spoke of his agonies in the grave.

From what he related it was clear that he must have been conscious of life for more than an hour, while inhumed, before lapsing into insensibility. The grave was carelessly and loosely filled with an exceedingly porous soil, and thus some air was necessarily admitted. He heard the footsteps of the crowd overhead, and endeavoured to make himself heard in turn. It was the tumult within the grounds of the cemetery, he said, which appeared to awaken him from a deep sleep, but no sooner was he awake than he became fully aware of the awful horrors of his position.

This patient it is recorded was doing well, and seemed to be in a fair way of ultimate recovery, but fell a victim to the quackeries of medical experiment. The galvanic battery was applied, and he suddenly expired in one of those ecstatic paroxysms which occasionally it superinduces.

The mention of the galvanic battery, nevertheless, recalls to my memory a well-known and very extraordinary case in point, where its action proved the means of restoring to animation a young attorney of

London, who had been interred for two days. This occurred in 1831, and created at the time a very profound sensation wherever it was made the subject of converse.

The patient, Mr. Edward Stapleton, had died apparently of typhus fever, accompanied with some anomalous symptoms which had excited the curiosity of his medical attendants. Upon his seeming decease his friends were requested to sanction a *post mortem* examination, but declined to permit it. As often happens when such refusals are made, the practitioners resolved to disinter the body and dissect it at leisure in private. Arrangements were easily effected with some of the numerous corps of body snatchers with which London abounds; and upon the third night after the funeral, the supposed corpse was unearthed from a grave eight feet deep, and deposited in the operating chamber of one of the private hospitals.

An incision of some extent had been actually made in the abdomen, when the fresh and undecayed appearance of the subject suggested an application of the battery. One experiment succeeded another, and the customary effects supervened, with nothing to characterise them in any respect except upon one or two occasions a more than ordinary degree of life-likeness in the convulsive action.

It grew late. The day was about to dawn, and it was thought expedient at length to proceed at once to the dissection. A student, however, was especially desirous of testing a theory of his own, and insisted upon applying the battery to one of the pectoral muscles. A rough gash was made, and a wire hastily brought in contact, when the patient with a hurried but quite unconvulsive movement, arose from the table, stepped into the middle of the floor, gazed about him uneasily for a few seconds, and then spoke. What he said was unintelligible; but the words were uttered; the syllabification was distinct. Having spoken, he fell heavily to the floor.

For some moments all were paralysed with awe – but the urgency of the case soon restored them to their presence of mind. It was seen that Mr. Stapleton was alive, although in a swoon. Upon exhibition of ether he revived and was rapidly restored to health, and to the society of his friends – from whom, however, all knowledge of his resuscitation was withheld, until a relapse was no longer to be apprehended. Their wonder – their rapturous astonishment – may be conceived.

The most thrilling peculiarity of this incident, nevertheless, is involved in what Mr. S. himself asserts. He declares that at no period was he altogether insensible – that, dully and confusedly he was aware of everything which happened to him, from the moment in which he was pronounced *dead* by his physicians, to that in which he fell swooning to the floor of the hospital. 'I am alive,' were the uncomprehended words which, upon recognising the locality of the dissecting-room, he had endeavoured in his extremity to utter.

It were an easy matter to multiply such histories as these, but I forbear, for, indeed, we have no need of such to establish the fact that premature interments occur. When we reflect how very rarely, from the nature of the case, we have it in our power to detect them, we must admit that they may *frequently* occur without our cognisance. Scarcely, in truth, is a graveyard encroached upon for any purpose, to any great extent, that skeletons are not found in postures which suggest the most fearful of suspicions.

Fearful indeed the suspicion, but more fearful the doom! It may be asserted, without hesitation, that *no* event is so terribly well adapted to inspire the supremeness of bodily and of mental distress as is burial before death. The unendurable oppression of the lungs – the stifling fumes of the damp earth – the clinging to the death garments – the rigid embrace of the narrow house – the blackness of the absolute night – the silence like a sea that overwhelms – the unseen but palpable presence of the conqueror worm – these things, with thoughts of the air and grass above, with memory of dear friends who would fly to save us if but informed of our fate, and with consciousness that of this fate they can *never* be informed – that our hopeless portion is that of the really dead – these considerations, I say, carry into the heart which still palpitates a degree of appalling and intolerable horror: from which the most daring imagination must recoil. We know of nothing so agonising upon earth – we can dream of nothing half so hideous in the realms of the nethermost hell; and thus all narratives upon this topic have an interest so profound; an interest, nevertheless, which, through the sacred awe of the topic itself, very properly and very peculiarly depends upon our conviction of the *truth* of the matter narrated. What I have now to tell is of my own actual knowledge – of my own positive and personal experience.

For several years I have been subject to attacks of the singular disorder which physicians have agreed to term catalepsy in default of a more definitive title. Although both the immediate and the predisposing causes, and even the actual diagnosis of this disease, are still mysterious, its obvious and apparent character is sufficiently well understood. Its variations seem to be chiefly of degree. Sometimes the patient lies for a day only, or even for a shorter period, in a species of exaggerated lethargy. He is senseless and externally motionless, but the pulsation of the heart is still faintly perceptible; some traces of warmth remain; a slight colour lingers within the centre of the cheek; and upon application of a mirror to the lips we can detect a torpid, unequal, and vacillating action of the lungs. Then again the duration of the trance is for weeks – even for months; while the closest scrutiny, and the most rigorous medical tests, fail to establish any material distinction between the state of the sufferer and what we conceive of absolute death. Very usually he is saved from premature interment solely by the knowledge of his friends that he has been previously subject to catalepsy, by the consequent suspicion excited, and, above all, by the non-appearance of decay. The advances of the malady are, luckily, gradual. The first manifestations, although marked, are unequivocal. The fits grow successively more and more distinctive, and endure each for a longer term than the preceding. In this lies the principal security from inhumation. The unfortunate whose *first* attack should be of the extreme character which is occasionally seen would almost inevitably be consigned alive to the tomb.

My own case differed in no important particular from those mentioned in medical books. Sometimes, without any apparent cause, I sank, little by little, into a condition of semi-syncope or half-swoon; and in this condition, without pain, without ability to stir, or, strictly speaking, to think, but with a dull lethargic consciousness of life and of the presence of those who surrounded my bed, I remained, until the crisis of the disease restored me, suddenly, to perfect sensation. At other times I was quickly and impetuously smitten. I grew sick, and numb, and chilly, and dizzy, and so fell prostrate at once. Then for weeks all was void, and black, and silent, and Nothing became the universe. Total annihilation could be no more. From these latter attacks I awoke, however, with a gradation slow in proportion to the suddenness of the seizure. Just as the day dawns to the friendless and houseless beggar who roams the street throughout the long desolate winter night – just so tardily – just so wearily – just so cheerily came back the light of the soul to me.

Apart from the tendency to trance, however, my general health appeared to be good; nor could I perceive that it was at all affected by the one prevalent malady – unless, indeed, an idiosyncrasy in my ordinary *sleep* may be looked upon as superinduced. Upon awaking from slumber, I could never gain at once thorough possession of my senses, and always remained for many minutes in much bewilderment and perplexity; the mental faculties in general, but the memory in especial, being in a condition of absolute abeyance.

In all that I endured there was no physical suffering, but of moral distress an infinitude. My fancy grew charnel. I talked 'of worms, of tombs, and epitaphs.' I was lost in reveries of death, and the idea of premature burial held continual possession of my brain. The ghastly danger to which I was subjected haunted me day and night. In the former, the torture of meditation was excessive – in the latter, supreme. When the grim darkness overspread the earth, then, with very horror of thought, I shook – shook as the quivering plumes upon the hearse. When nature could endure wakefulness no longer, it was with a struggle that I consented to sleep – for I shuddered to reflect that upon awaking I might find myself the tenant of a grave. And when, finally, I sank into slumber, it was only to rush at once into a world of phantasms, above which, with vast, sable, overshadowing wings, hovered predominant the one sepulchral idea.

From the innumerable images of gloom which thus oppressed me in dreams, I select for record but a solitary vision. Methought I was immersed in a cataleptic trance of more than usual duration and profundity. Suddenly there came an icy hand upon my forehead, and an impatient gibbering voice whispered the word 'arise!' within my ear.

I sat erect. The darkness was total. I could not see the figure of him who had aroused me. I could call to mind neither the period at which I had fallen into the trance, nor the locality in which I then lay. While I remained motionless, and busied in endeavours to collect my thoughts, the cold hand grasped me fiercely by the wrist, shaking it petulantly, while the gibbering voice said again:

'Arise! did I not bid thee arise?'

'And who,' I demanded, 'art thou?'

'I have no name in the regions which I inhabit,' replied the voice, mournfully; 'I was mortal, but am fiend. I was merciless, but am pitiful. Thou dost feel that I shudder. My teeth chatter as I speak, yet it is not with the chilliness of the night – of the night without end. But this hideousness is insufferable. How canst *thou* tranquilly sleep? I cannot rest for the cry of these great agonies. These sights are more than I can bear. Get thee up! Come with me into the outer night, and let me unfold to thee the graves. Is not this a spectacle of woe? – Behold!'

I looked; and the unseen figure, which still grasped me by the wrist, had caused to be thrown open the graves of all mankind, and from each issued the faint phosphoric radiance of decay, so that I could see into the innermost recesses, and there view the shrouded bodies in their sad and solemn slumbers with the worm. But, alas! the real sleepers were fewer by many millions than those who slumbered not at all; and there was a feeble struggling; and there was a general sad unrest; and from out the depths of the countless pits there came a melancholy rustling from the garments of the buried; and of those who seemed tranquilly to repose I saw that a vast number had changed, in a greater or less degree, the rigid and uneasy position in which they had originally been entombed. And the voice again said to me as I gazed:

'Is it not – O, is it *not* a pitiful sight?' But before I could find word to reply the figure had ceased to grasp my wrist, the phosphoric lights expired, and the graves were closed with a sudden violence, while from out them arose a tumult of despairing cries, saying again, 'Is it not – O, God! is it *not* a very pitiful sight?'

Phantasies such as these presenting themselves at night extended their terrific influence far into my waking hours. My nerves became thoroughly unstrung, and I fell a prey to perpetual horror. I hesitated to ride, or to walk, or to indulge in any exercise that would carry me from home. In fact, I no longer dared trust myself out of the immediate presence of those who were aware of my proneness to catalepsy, lest, falling into one of my usual fits, I should be buried before my real condition could be ascertained. I doubted the care, the fidelity of my dearest friends. I dreaded that, in some trance of more than customary duration, they might be prevailed upon to regard me as irrecoverable. I even went so far as to fear that, as I occasioned much trouble, they might be glad to consider any very protracted attack as sufficient excuse for getting rid of me altogether. It was vain they endeavoured to reassure me by the most solemn promises. I exacted the most sacred oaths that under no circumstances they would bury me until decomposition had so materially advanced as to render further preservation impossible; and even then my mortal terrors would listen to no reason, would accept no consolation. I entered into a series of elaborate precautions. Among other things, I had the family vault so remodelled as to admit of being readily opened from within. The slightest pressure upon a long lever that extended far into the tomb would cause the iron portals to fly back. There were arrangements also for the free admission of air and light, and convenient receptacles for food and water, within immediate reach of the coffin intended for my reception. This coffin was warmly and softly padded, and was provided with a lid, fashioned upon the principle of the vault-door, with the addition of springs so contrived that the feeblest movement of the body would be sufficient to set it at liberty. Besides all this, there was suspended from the roof of the tomb a large bell, the rope of which, it was designed, should extend through a hole in the coffin, and so be fastened to one of the hands of the corpse. But, alas! what avails the vigilance against the destiny of man? Not even these well contrived securities sufficed to save from the uttermost agonies of living inhumation a wretch to these agonies foredoomed!

There arrived an epoch – as often before there had arrived – in which I found myself emerging from total unconsciousness into the first feeble and indefinite sense of existence. Slowly – with a tortoise gradation – approached the faint grey dawn of the psychal day. A torpid uneasiness. An apathetic endurance of dull pain. No care – no hope – no effort. Then, after long interval, a ringing in the ears; then, after a lapse still longer, a pricking or tingling sensation in the extremities; then a seemingly eternal period of pleasurable quiescence, during which the awakening feelings are struggling into thought; then a brief re-sinking into nonentity; then a sudden recovery. At length the slight quivering of an eyelid, and immediately thereupon an electric shock of a terror, deadly and indefinite, which sends the blood in torrents from the temples to the heart. And now the first positive effort to think. And now the first endeavour to remember. And now a partial and evanescent success. And now the memory has so far regained its dominion that, in some measure, I am cognisant of my state. I feel that I am not awaking from ordinary sleep. I recollect that I have been subject to catalepsy. And now, at last, as if by the rush of an ocean, my shuddering spirit is overwhelmed by the one grim danger – by the one spectral and ever-prevalent idea.

For some minutes after this fancy possessed me, I remained without motion. And why? I could not summon courage to move. I dared not make the effort which was to satisfy me of my fate; and yet there was something at my heart which whispered me it *was sure*. Despair – such as no other species of wretchedness ever calls into being – despair alone urged me after long irresolution to uplift the heavy lids of my eyes. I uplifted them. It was dark – all dark. I knew that the fit was over. I knew that the crisis of my disorder had long passed. I knew that I had now fully recovered the use of my visual faculties – and yet it was dark – all dark – the intense and utter raylessness of the night that endureth for evermore.

I endeavoured to shriek, and my lips and my parched tongue moved convulsively together in the attempt – but no voice issued from the cavernous lungs, which, oppressed as if by the weight of some incumbent mountain, gasped and palpitated with the heart, at every elaborate and struggling inspiration.

The movement of the jaws in this effort to cry aloud showed me that they were bound up, as usual with the dead. I felt too that I lay upon some hard substance; and by something similar my sides were also closely compressed. So far I had not ventured to stir any of my limbs – but now I violently threw up my arms, which had been lying at length with the wrists crossed. They struck a solid wooden substance which extended above my person at an elevation of not more than six inches from my face. I could no longer doubt that I reposed within a coffin at last.

And now amid all my infinite miseries came sweetly the cherub hope – for I thought of my precautions. I writhed and made spasmodic exertions to force open the lid; it would not move. I felt my wrists for the bell-rope; it was not to be found. And now the comforter fled for ever, and a still sterner despair reigned triumphant; for I could not help perceiving the absence of the paddings which I had so carefully prepared; and then too there came suddenly to my nostrils the strong peculiar odour of moist earth. The conclusion was irresistible. I was *not* within the vault. I had fallen into a trance while absent from home – while among strangers – when or how I could not remember; and it was they who had buried me as a dog – nailed up in some common coffin – and thrust deep, deep and for ever, into some ordinary and nameless *grave*.

As this awful conviction forced itself thus into the innermost chambers of my soul, I once again struggled to cry aloud; and in this second endeavour I succeeded. A long, wild, and continuous shriek, or yell of agony resounded through the realms of the subterrene night.

'Hillo! hillo, there!' said a gruff voice, in reply.

'What the devil's the matter now?' said a second.

'Get out o' that!' said a third.

'What do you mean by yowling in that ere kind of style like a cattymount?' said a fourth; and hereupon I was seized and shaken without ceremony for several minutes by a junto of very rough-looking

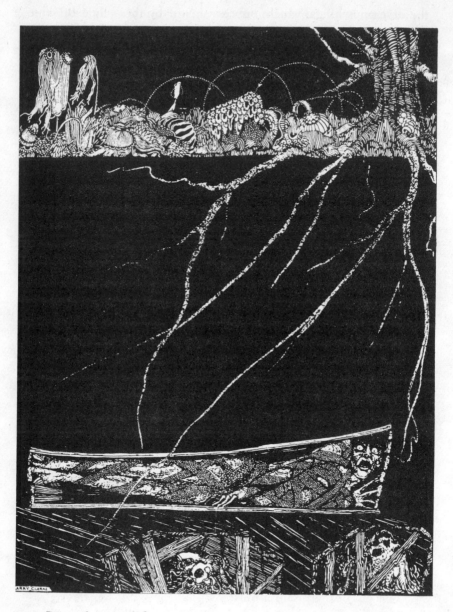

Deep, deep, and for ever, into some ordinary and nameless grave individuals. They did not arouse me from my slumber – for I was wide awake when I screamed – but they restored me to the full possession of my memory.

This adventure occurred near Richmond, in Virginia. Accompanied by a friend I had proceeded upon a gunning expedition some miles down the banks of James River. Night approached, and we were overtaken by a storm. The cabin of a small sloop lying at anchor in the stream, and laden with garden mould, afforded us the only available shelter. We made the best of it, and passed the night on board. I slept in one of the only two berths in the vessel – and the berths of a sloop of sixty or seventy tons need scarcely be described. That which I occupied had no bedding of any kind. Its extreme width was eighteen inches. The distance of its bottom from the deck overhead was precisely the same. I found it a matter of exceeding difficulty to squeeze myself in. Nevertheless, I slept soundly; and the whole of my vision – for it was no dream, and no nightmare – arose naturally from the circumstances of my position – from my ordinary bias of thought, and from the difficulty, to which I have alluded, of collecting my senses, and especially of regaining my memory for a long time after awaking from slumber. The men who shook me were the crew of the sloop and some labourers engaged to unload it. From the load itself came the earthy smell. The bandage about the jaws was a silk handkerchief in which I had bound up my head in default of my customary nightcap.

The tortures endured, however, were indubitably quite equal for the time to those of actual sepulture. They were fearfully – they were inconceivably hideous; but out of evil proceeded good, for their very excess wrought in my spirit an inevitable revulsion. My soul acquired tone – acquired temper. I went abroad. I took vigorous exercise. I breathed the free air of heaven. I thought upon other subjects than death. I discarded my medical books. 'Buchan' I burned. I read no 'Night Thoughts' – no fustian about churchyards – no bugaboo tales – *such as this*. In short I became a new man and lived a man's life.

From that memorable night I dismissed for ever my charnel apprehensions, and with them vanished the cataleptic disorder of which perhaps they had been less the consequence than the cause.

There are moments when, even to the sober eye of reason, the world of our sad humanity may assume the semblance of a hell; but the imagination of man is no Carathis to explore with impunity its every cavern. Alas! the grim legion of sepulchral terrors cannot be regarded as altogether fanciful, but, like the demons in whose company Afrasiab made his voyage down the Oxus, they must sleep or they will devour us – they must be suffered to slumber or we perish.

The Literary Life of Thingum Bob, Esq.

Late Editor of the 'Goosetherumfoodle.'

BY HIMSELF.

I am now growing in years, and – since I understand that Shakespeare and Mr. Emmons are deceased – it is not impossible that I may even die. It has occurred to me, therefore, that I may as well retire from the field of Letters and repose upon my laurels. But I am ambitious of signalising my abdication of the literary sceptre by some important bequest to posterity; and perhaps I cannot do a better thing than just pen for it an account of my earlier career. My name, indeed, has been so long and so constantly before the public eye, that I am not only willing to admit the naturalness of the interest which it has everywhere excited, but ready to satisfy the extreme curiosity which it has inspired. In fact, it is no more than the duty of him who achieves greatness, to leave behind him, in his ascent, such landmarks as may guide others to be great. I propose, therefore, in the present paper (which I had some idea of calling 'Memoranda to serve for the Literary History of America'), to give a detail of those important, yet feeble and tottering first steps, by which, at length, I attained the high road to the pinnacle of human renown.

Of one's *very* remote ancestors it is superfluous to say much. My father, Thomas Bob, Esq., stood for many years at the summit of his profession, which was that of a merchant-barber in the city of Smug. His warehouse was the resort of all the principal people of the place, and especially of the editorial corps – a body which inspires all about it with profound veneration and awe. For my own part, I regarded them as gods, and drank in with avidity the rich wit and wisdom which continuously flowed from their august mouths during the process of what is styled 'lather.' My first moment of positive inspiration must be dated from that ever-memorable epoch, when the brilliant conductor of the 'Gad-Fly,' in the intervals of the important process just mentioned, recited aloud, before a conclave of our apprentices, an inimitable poem in honour of the 'Only Genuine Oil-of-Bob' (so called from its talented inventor, my father), and for which effusion the editor of the 'Fly' was remunerated, with a regal liberality, by the firm of Thomas Bob and Company, merchant-barbers.

The genius of the stanzas to the 'Oil-of-Bob' first breathed into me, I say, the divine *afflatus*. I resolved at once to become a great man, and to commence by becoming a great poet. That very evening I fell upon my knees at the feet of my father.

'Father,' I said, 'pardon me! – but I have a soul above lather. It is my firm intention to cut the shop. I would be an editor – I would be a poet – I would pen stanzas to the "Oil-of-Bob." Pardon me and aid me to be great!'

'My dear Thingum,' replied my father (I had been christened Thingum after a wealthy relative so surnamed), 'My dear Thingum,' he said, raising me from my knees by the ears – 'Thingum, my boy, you're a trump, and take after your father in having a soul. You have an immense head, too, and it must hold a great many brains. This I have long seen, and therefore had thoughts of making you a lawyer. The business, however, has grown ungenteel, and that of a politician don't pay. Upon the whole you judge wisely – the trade of editor is best; and if you can be a poet at the same time, as most of the editors are, by-the-by – why, you will kill two birds with one stone. To encourage you in the beginning of things, I will allow you a garret, pen, ink, and paper, a rhyming dictionary, and a copy of the "Gad-Fly." I suppose you would scarcely demand any more.'

'I would be an ungrateful villain if I did,' I replied with enthusiasm. 'Your generosity is boundless. I will repay it by making you the father of a genius.'

Thus ended my conference with the best of men, and immediately upon its termination I betook myself with zeal to my poetical labours, as upon these, chiefly, I founded my hopes of ultimate elevation to the editorial chair.

In my first attempts at composition I found the stanzas to the 'Oil-of-Bob' rather a drawback than otherwise. Their splendour dazzled more than they enlightened me. The contemplation of their excellence tended naturally to discourage me, by comparison with my own abortions, so that for a long time I laboured in vain. At length there came into my head one of those exquisitely original ideas which now and then *will* permeate the brain of a man of genius. It was this, – or rather, thus was it carried into execution. From the rubbish of an old book-stall, in a very remote corner of the town I got together several antique and altogether unknown or forgotten volumes. The bookseller sold them to me for a song. From one of these, which purported to be a translation of one Dante's 'Inferno,' I copied with remarkable neatness a long passage about a man named Ugolino, who had a parcel of brats. From another, which contained a good many old plays by some person whose name I forget, I extracted in the same manner, and with the same care, a great number of lines about 'angels' and 'ministers saying grace,' and 'goblins damned,' and more besides of that sort. From a third, which was the composition of some blind man or other, either a Greek or a Choctaw – I cannot be at the pains of remembering every trifle exactly – I took about fifty verses beginning with 'Achilles' wrath,' and 'grease,' and something else. From a fourth, which I recollect was also the work of a blind man, I selected a page or two all about 'hail' and 'holy light;' and although a blind man has no business to write about light, still the verses were sufficiently good in their way.

Having made fair copies of these poems, I signed every one of them

'Oppodeldoc' (a fine sonorous name), and doing each up nicely in a separate envelope, I despatched one to each of the four principal Magazines, with a request for speedy insertion and prompt pay. The result of this well-conceived plan, however (the success of which would have saved me much trouble in after life), served to convince me that some editors are not to be bamboozled, and gave the *coup-de-grâce* (as they say in France) to my nascent hopes (as they say in the city of the transcendentals).

The fact is, that each and every one of the Magazines in question gave Mr. 'Oppodeldoc' a complete using-up, in the 'Monthly Notices to Correspondents.' The 'Hum-Drum' gave him a dressing after this fashion:

'Oppodeldoc' (whoever he is) has sent us a long *tirade* concerning a Bedlamate whom he styles 'Ugolino,' who had a great many children that should have been all whipped and sent to bed without their suppers. The whole affair is exceedingly tame – not to say *flat*. "Oppodeldoc" (whoever he is) is entirely devoid of imagination – and imagination, in our humble opinion, is not only the soul of Poesy, but also its very heart. "Oppodeldoc" (whoever he is) has the audacity to demand of us, for his twaddle, a "speedy insertion and prompt pay." We neither insert nor purchase any stuff of the sort. There can be no doubt, however, that he would meet with a ready sale for all the balderdash he can scribble at the office of either the "Rowdy-Dow," the "Lollipop," or the "Goosetherumfoodle."'

All this, it must be acknowledged, was very severe upon 'Oppodeldoc' – but the unkindest cut was putting the word Poesy in small caps. In those five pre-eminent letters what a world of bitterness is there not involved!

But 'Oppodeldoc' was punished with equal severity in the 'Rowdy-Dow,' which spoke thus:

'We have received a most singular and insolent communication from a person (whoever he is) signing himself "Oppoldedoc" – thus desecrating the greatness of the illustrious Roman Emperor so named. Accompanying the letter of "Oppodeldoc" (whoever he is) we find sundry lines of most disgusting and unmeaning rant about "angels and ministers of grace" – rant such as no madman short of a Nat Lee, or an "Oppodeldoc," could possibly perpetrate. And for this trash of trash, we are modestly requested to "pay promptly." No, sir – no! We pay for nothing of *that* sort. Apply to the "Hum Drum," the "Lollipop," or the "Goosetherumfoodle.' These *periodicals* will undoubtedly accept any literary offal you may send them – and as undoubtedly *promise* to pay for it.'

This was bitter indeed upon poor 'Oppodeldoc;' but, in this instance, the weight of the satire falls upon the 'Hum-Drum,' the 'Lollipop,' and the 'Goosetherumfoodle,' who are pungently styled 'periodicals' – in italics, too – a thing that must have cut them to the heart.

Scarcely less savage was the 'Lollipop,' which thus discoursed:

'Some *individual*, who rejoices in the appellation "Oppodeldoc" (to what low uses are the names of the illustrious dead too often applied), has enclosed us some fifty or sixty *verses* commencing after this fashion:

> "Achilles' wrath, to Greece the direful spring
>   Of woes unnumbered," etc. etc. etc. etc.

'"Oppodeldoc" (whoever he is) is respectfully informed that there is not a printer's devil in our office who is not in the daily habit of composing better *lines*. Those of "Oppodeldoc" will not *scan*. "Oppodeldoc" should learn to *count*. But why he should have received the idea that *we* (of all others, *we!*) would disgrace our pages with his ineffable nonsense is utterly beyond comprehension. Why, the absurd twaddle is scarcely good enough for the "Hum-Drum," the "Rowdy-Dow," the "Goosetherumfoodle" – things that are in the practice of publishing "Mother Goose's Melodies" as original lyrics. And

"Oppodeldoc" (whoever he is) has even the assurance to demand *pay* for this drivel. Does "Oppodeldoc" (whoever he is) know – is he aware that we could not be paid to insert it?'

As I perused this I felt myself growing gradually smaller and smaller, and when I came to the point at which the editor sneered at the poem as 'verses,' there was little more than an ounce of me left. As for 'Oppodeldoc,' I began to experience compassion for the poor fellow. But the 'Goosetherumfoodle' showed, if possible, less mercy than the 'Lollipop.' It was the 'Goosetherumfoodle' that said:

'A wretched poetaster, who signs himself "Oppodeldoc," is silly enough to fancy that *we* will print and *pay for* a medley of incoherent and ungrammatical bombast which he has transmitted to us, and which commences with the following most *intelligible* line:

"Hail, Holy Light! Offspring of Heaven, first born."

'We say, "most *intelligible*." "Oppodeldoc" (whoever he is) will be kind enough to tell us, perhaps, how *"hail"* can be *"holy light."* We always regarded it as *frozen rain*. Will he inform us also, how frozen rain can be at one and the same time both "holy light" (whatever that is) and an "offspring"? – which latter term (if we understand anything about English) is only employed with propriety in reference to small babies of about six weeks old. But it is preposterous to descant upon such absurdity – although "Oppodeldoc" (whoever he is) has the unparalleled effrontery to suppose that we will not only "insert" his ignorant ravings, but (absolutely) *pay for them!*'

'Now this is fine – it is rich! – and we have half a mind to punish this young scribbler for his egotism by really publishing his effusion *verbatim et literatim*, as he has written it. We could inflict no punishment so severe, and we *would* inflict it, but for the boredom which we should cause our readers in so doing.

'Let "Oppodeldoc" (whoever he is) send any future *composition* of like character to the "Hum-Drum," the "Lollipop," or the "Rowdy-

Dow." *They* will "insert" it. *They* "insert" every month just such stuff. Send it to them. WE are not to be insulted with impunity.'

This made an end of me; and as for the 'Hum-Drum,' the 'Rowdy-Dow,' and the 'Lollipop,' I never could comprehend how they survived it. The putting *them* in the smallest possible *minion* (that was the rub – thereby insinuating their lowness – their baseness), while WE stood looking down upon them in gigantic capitals! oh it was *too* bitter! – it was wormwood – it was gall. Had I been either of these periodicals I would have spared no pains to have the 'Goose-therumfoodle' prosecuted. It might have been done under the Act for the 'Prevention of Cruelty to Animals.' As for 'Oppodeldoc' (whoever he was), I had by this time lost all patience with the fellow, and sympathised with him no longer. He was a fool beyond doubt (whoever he was), and got not a kick more than he deserved.

The result of my experiment with the old books convinced me, in the first place, that 'honesty is the best policy,' and in the second, that if I could not write better than Mr. Dante and the two blind men, and the rest of the old set, it would at least be a difficult matter to write worse. I took heart, therefore, and determined to prosecute the 'entirely original' (as they say on the covers of the magazines) at whatever cost of study and pains. I again placed before my eyes, as a model, the billiant stanzas on 'The Oil-of-Bob' by the editor of the 'Gad-Fly,' and resolved to construct an Ode on the same sublime theme, in rivalry of what had already been done.

With my first verse I had no material difficulty. It ran thus:–

> '*To pen an Ode upon the "Oil-of-Bod."*'

Having carefully looked out, however, all the legitimate rhymes to 'Bob,' I found it impossible to proceed. In this dilemma I had recourse to paternal aid; and after some hours of mature thought, my father and myself thus constructed the poem:–

> '*To pen an Ode upon the "Oil-of-Bob"*
> *Is all sorts of a job.*
>
> (Signed) SNOB.'

To be sure this composition was of no very great length – but I 'have yet to learn,' as they say in the 'Edinburgh Review,' that the mere extent of a literary work has anything to do with its merit. As for the Quarterly cant about 'sustained effort,' it is impossible to see the sense of it. Upon the whole, therefore, I was satisfied with the success of my maiden attempt, and now the only question regarded the disposal I should make of it. My father suggested that I should send it to the 'Gad-Fly' – but there were two reasons which operated to prevent me from so doing. I dreaded the jealousy of the editor – and I had ascertained that he did not pay for original contributions. I therefore, after due deliberation, consigned the article to the more dignified pages of the 'Lollipop,' and awaited the event in anxiety, but with resignation.

In the very next published number I had the proud satisfaction of seeing my poem printed at length as the leading article, with the following significant words, prefixed in italics and between brackets:–

[*We call the attention of our readers to the subjoined admirable stanzas on 'The Oil-of-Bob.' We need say nothing of their sublimity or of their pathos:– it is impossible to peruse them without tears. Those who have been nauseated with a sad dose on the same august topic from the goose-quill of the editor of the 'Gad-Fly,' will do well to compare the two compositions.*

P.S. – We are consumed with anxiety to probe the mystery which envelops the pseudonym 'Snob.' May we hope for a personal interview?]

All this was scarcely more than justice, but it was, I confess, rather more than I had expected – I acknowledged this, be it observed, to the everlasting disgrace of my country and of mankind. I lost no time, however, in calling upon the editor of the 'Lollipop,' and had the good fortune to find this gentleman at home. He saluted me with an air of profound respect, slightly blended with a fatherly and patronising admiration, wrought in him no doubt by my appearance of extreme youth and inexperience. Begging me to be seated, he entered at once upon the subject of my poem:– but modesty will ever forbid me to repeat the thousand compliments which he lavished upon me. The eulogies of Mr. Crab (such was the editor's name) were, however, by no means fulsomely indiscriminate. He analysed my composition with much freedom and great ability – not hesitating to point out a few trivial defects – a circumstance which elevated him highly in my esteem. The 'Gad-Fly' was, of course, brought upon the *tapis*, and I hope never to be subjected to a criticism so searching, or to rebukes so withering, as were bestowed by Mr. Crab upon that unhappy effusion. I had been accustomed to regard the editor of the 'Gad-Fly' as something superhuman; but Mr. Crab soon disabused me of that idea. He set the literary as well as the personal character of the Fly (so Mr. C. satirically designated the rival editor) in its true light. He, the Fly, was very little better than he should be. He had written infamous things. He was a penny-a-liner, and a buffoon. He was a villain. He had composed a tragedy which set the whole country in a guffaw, and a farce which deluged the universe in tears. Besides all this, he had the impudence to pen what he meant for a lampoon upon himself (Mr. Crab), and the temerity to style him 'an ass.' Should I at any time wish to express my opinion of Mr. Fly, the pages of the 'Lollipop,' Mr. Crab assured me, were at my unlimited disposal. In the meantime, as it was very certain that I would be attacked in the Fly for my attempt at composing a rival poem on the 'Oil-of-Bob,' he (Mr. Crab) would take it upon himself to attend, pointedly, to my private and personal interests. If I were not made a man of at once, it should not be the fault of himself (Mr. Crab).

Mr. Crab having now paused in his discourse (the latter portion of which I found it impossible to comprehend), I ventured to suggest something about the remuneration which I had been taught to expect for my poem, by an announcement on the cover of the 'Lollipop,' declaring that it (the 'Lollipop') 'insisted upon being permitted to pay exorbitant prices for all accepted contributions, frequently expending more money for a single brief poem than the whole annual cost of the "Hum-Drum," the "Rowdy-Dow," and the "Goosetherumfoodle" combined.'

As I mentioned the word 'remuneration' Mr. Crab first opened his eyes, and then his mouth, to quite a remarkable extent; causing his personal appearance to resemble that of a highly-agitated elderly duck in the act of quacking – and in this condition he remained (ever and anon pressing his hands tightly to his forehead, as if in a state of desperate bewilderment), until I had nearly made an end of what I had to say.

Upon my conclusion, he sank back into his seat, as if much overcome, letting his arms fall lifelessly by his side, but keeping his mouth still rigorously open, after the fashion of the duck. While I remained in speechless astonishment at behaviour so alarming, he suddenly leaped to his feet and made a rush at the bell-rope; but just as he reached this, he appeared to have altered his intention, whatever it was, for he dived under the table and immediately re-appeared with a cudgel. This he was in the act of uplifting (for what purpose I am at a loss to imagine), when, all at once, there came a benign smile over his features, and he sank placidly back in his chair.

'Mr. Bob,' he said (for I had sent up my card before ascending myself), 'Mr. Bob, you are a young man, I presume – *very?*'

I assented; adding that I had not yet concluded my third lustrum.

'Ah!' he replied, 'very good! I see how it is – say no more! Touching this matter of compensation, what you observe is very just: in fact it is excessively so. But ah – ah – the *first* contribution – the *first*, I say – it is never the Magazine custom to pay for – you comprehend, eh? The truth is, we are usually the *recipients* in such case.' [Mr. Crab smiled blandly as he emphasised the word 'recipients.'] 'For the most part we are *paid* for the insertion of a maiden attempt – especially in verse. In the second place, Mr. Bob, the Magazine rule is never to disburse what we term in France the *argent comptant*. I have no doubt you understand. In a quarter or two after the publication of the article – or in a year or two – we make no objection to giving our note at nine months – provided always that we can so arrange our affairs as to be quite certain of a "burst-up" in six. I really *do* hope, Mr. Bob, that you will look upon this explanation as satisfactory.' Here Mr. Crab concluded, and the tears stood in his eyes.

Grieved to the soul at having been, however innocently, the cause of pain to so eminent and so sensitive a man, I hastened to apologise, and to reassure him, by expressing my perfect coincidence with his views, as well as my entire appreciation of the delicacy of his position. Having done all this in a neat speech, I took leave.

One fine morning, very shortly afterwards, 'I awoke and found myself famous.' The extent of my renown will be best estimated by reference to the editorial opinions of the day. These opinions, it will be seen, were embodied in critical notices of the number of the 'Lollipop' containing my poem, and are perfectly satisfactory, conclusive, and clear, with the exception, perhaps, of the hieroglyphical marks, '*Sept. 15–1 t.*' appended to each of the critiques.

The 'Owl,' a journal of profound sagacity, and well known for the deliberate gravity of its literary decisions – the 'Owl,' I say, spoke as follows:–

'"THE LOLLIPOP!" The October number of this delicious magazine surpasses its predecessors, and sets competition at defiance. In the beauty of its typography and paper – in the number and excellence of its steel plates – as well as in the literary merit of its contributions – the "Lollipop" compares with its slow-paced rivals as Hyperion with a Satyr. The "Hum-Drum," the "Rowdy-Dow," and the "Goosetherumfoodle," excel, it is true, in braggadocio, but in all other points give us the "Lollipop!" How this celebrated journal can sustain its evidently tremendous expenses is more than we can understand. To be sure it has a circulation of 100,000, and its subscription-list has increased one-fourth during the last month; but, on the other hand, the sums it disburses constantly for contributions are inconceivable. It is reported that Mr. Slyass received no less than thirty-seven and a half cents for his inimitable paper on "Pigs." With Mr. CRAB as editor, and with such names upon the list of contributors as SNOB and Slyass, there can be no such word as "fail" for the "Lollipop." Go and subscribe. – *Sept.* 15–1 *t.*'

I must say that I was gratified with this high-toned notice from a paper so respectable as the 'Owl.' The placing my name – that is to say, my *nom de guerre* – in priority of station to that of the great Slyass, was a compliment as happy as I felt it to be deserved.

My attention was next arrested by these paragraphs in the 'Toad' – a print highly distinguished for its uprightness and independence – for its entire freedom from sycophancy and subservience to the givers of dinners:–

'The "Lollipop" for October is out in advance of all its contemporaries, and infinitely surpasses them of course in the splendour of its embellishments, as well as in the richness of its literary contents. The "Hum-Drum," the "Rowdy-Dow," and the "Goose-therumfoodle" excel, we admit, in braggadocio, but in all other points give us the "Lollipop." How this celebrated magazine can sustain its evidently tremendous expenses is more than we can understand. To be sure it has a circulation of 200,000, and its subscription-list has increased one-third during the last fortnight, but, on the other hand, the sums it disburses monthly for contributions are fearfully great. We learn that Mr. Mumblethumb received no less than fifty cents for his late "Monody in a Mud-Puddle."

'Among the original contributors to the present numbers we notice (besides the eminent editor, Mr. CRAB) such men as SNOB, Slyass, and Mumblethumb. Apart from the editorial matter, the most valuable paper, nevertheless, is, we think, a poetical gem by "Snob, on the Oil-of-Bob" – but our readers must not suppose from the title of this incomparable *bijou*, that it bears any similitude to some balderdash on the same subject by a certain contemptible individual whose name is unmentionable to ears polite. The *present* poem "On the Oil-of-Bob," has excited universal anxiety and curiosity in respect to the owner of the evident pseudonym, "Snob" – a curiosity which, happily, we have it in our power to satisfy. "Snob" is the *nom-de-plume* of Mr. Thingum Bob, of this city – a relative of the great Mr. Thingum (after whom he is named), and otherwise connected with the most illustrious families of the State. His father, Thomas Bob, Esq., is an opulent merchant in Smug. *Sept.* 15–1 *t.*'

This generous approbation touched me to the heart – the more especially as it emanated from a source so avowedly – so proverbially pure as the 'Toad.' The word 'balderdash,' as applied to the 'Oil-of-Bob' of the Fly, I considered singularly pungent and appropriate. The words 'gem' and '*bijou*,' however, used in reference to my composition, struck me as being in some degree feeble. They seemed to me to be deficient in force. They were not sufficiently *prononcés* (as we have it in France).

I had hardly finished reading the 'Toad,' when a friend placed in my hands a copy of the 'Mole,' a daily, enjoying high reputation for the keenness of its perception about matters in general, and for the open, honest, above-ground style of its editorials. The 'Mole' spoke of the 'Lollipop' as follows:–

'We have just received the "Lollipop" for October, and *must* say that never before have we perused any single number of any periodical which afforded us a felicity so supreme. We speak advisedly. The "Hum-Drum," the "Rowdy-Dow," and the "Goosetherumfoodle," must look well to their laurels. These prints, no doubt, surpass everything in loudness of pretension, but, in all other points, give us the "Lollipop!" How this celebrated Magazine can sustain its evidently tremendous expenses, is more than we can comprehend. To be sure it has a circulation of 300,000; and its subscription list has increased one-half within the last week, but then the sum it disburses monthly for contributions is astoundingly enormous. We have it upon good authority that Mr. Fatquack received no less than sixty-two cents and a half for his late Domestic Nouvelette, the "Dish-Clout."

'The contributors to the number before us are Mr. CRAB (the eminent editor), SNOB, Mumblethumb, Fatquack, and others; but, after the inimitable compositions of the editor himself, we prefer a diamond-like effusion from the pen of a rising poet who writes over the signature "Snob" a *nom-de-guerre* which we predict will one day extinguish the radiance of "BOZ." "SNOB," we learn, is a THINGUM BOB, Esq., sole heir of a wealthy merchant of this city, Thomas Bob, Esq., and a near relative of the distinguished Mr. Thingum. The title of Mr. B.'s admirable poem is the "Oil-of-Bob" – a somewhat unfortunate name by-the-by, as some contemptible vagabond connected with the penny press has already disgusted the town with a great deal of drivel upon the same topic. There will be no danger, however, of confounding the compositions. *Sept.* 15–1 *t.*'

The generous approbation of so clear-sighted a journal as the 'Mole' penetrated my soul with delight. The only objection which occurred to me was, that the terms 'contemptible vagabond' might have been better written '*odius and* contemptible, *wretch, villain,* and vagabond.' This would have sounded more gracefully, I think. 'Diamond-like,' also, was scarcely, it will be admitted, of sufficient intensity to express what the 'Mole' evidently *thought* of the brilliancy of the 'Oil-of-Bob.'

On the same afternoon in which I saw these notices in the 'Owl,' the 'Toad,' and the 'Mole,' I happened to meet with a copy of the 'Daddy-Long-Legs,' a periodical proverbial for the extreme extent of its understanding. And it was the 'Daddy-Long-Legs' which spoke thus:–

'The "Lollipop"!! This gorgeous magazine is already before the public for October. The question of pre-eminence is for ever put to rest, and hereafter it will be excessively preposterous in the "Hum-Drum," the "Rowdy-Dow," or the "Goosetherumfoodle," to make any farther spasmodic attempts at competition. These journals may excel the "Lollipop!" in outcry, but in all other points give us the "Lollipop!" How this celebrated magazine can sustain its evidently tremendous expenses is past comprehension. To be sure it has a circulation of precisely half-a-million, and its subscription-list has increased seventy-five per cent. within the last couple of days; but then the sums it disburses monthly for contributions are scarcely credible; we are cognisant of the fact, that Mademoiselle Cribalittle received no less than eighty-seven cents and a half for her late valuable Revolutionary Tale, entitled "The York-Town Katy-Did, and the Bunker-Hill Katy-Didn't."

'The most able papers in the present number are of course those furnished by the editor (the eminent Mr. CRAB), but there are numerous magnificent contributions from such names as SNOB, Mademoiselle Cribalittle, Slyass, Mrs. Fibalittle, Mumblethumb, Mrs. Squibalittle, and last, though not least, Fatquack. The world may well be challenged to produce so rich a galaxy of genius.

'The poem over the signature "SNOB" is, we find, attracting universal commendation, and we are constrained to say, deserves, if possible, even more applause than it has received. The "Oil-of-Bob" is the title of this masterpeice of eloquence and art. One or two of our readers *may* have a *very* faint, although sufficiently disgusting, recollection of a poem (?) similarly entitled, the perpetration of a miserable penny-a-liner, mendicant, and cut-throat, connected in the capacity of scullion, we believe, with one of the indecent prints about the purlieus of the city; we beg them, for God's sake, not to confound the compositions. The author of *the* "Oil-of-Bob" is, we hear, THINGUM BOB, Esq., a gentleman of high genius, and a scholar. "Snob" is merely a *nom-de-guerre. Sept.* 15–1 *t.*'

I could scarcely restrain my indignation while I perused the concluding portions of this diatribe. It was clear to me that the yea-nay manner – not to say the gentleness – the positive forbearance with which the 'Daddy-Long-Legs' spoke of that pig, the editor of the 'Gad-Fly' – it was evident to me, I say, that this gentleness of speech could proceed from nothing else than a partiality for the Fly – whom it was clearly the intention of the 'Daddy-Long-Legs' to elevate into reputation at my expense. Any one, indeed, might perceive, with half an eye, that, had the real design of the 'Daddy' been what it wished to appear, it (the 'Daddy') might have expressed itself in terms more direct, more pungent, and altogether more to the purpose. The words 'penny-a-liner,' 'mendicant,' 'scullion,' and 'cut-throat,' were epithets so intentionally inexpressive and equivocal, as to be worse than nothing when applied to the author of the very worst stanzas ever penned by one of the human race. We all know what is meant by 'damning with faint praise,' and, on the other hand, who could fail seeing through the covert purpose of the 'Daddy' – that of glorifying with feeble abuse?

What the 'Daddy' chose to say of the Fly, however, was no business of mine. What it said of myself *was*. After the noble manner in which the 'Owl,' the 'Toad,' the 'Mole,' had expressed themselves in respect to my ability, it was rather too much to be coolly spoken of by a thing like the 'Daddy-Long-Legs,' as merely 'a gentleman of high genius and a scholar.' Gentleman indeed! I made up my mind at once, either to get a written apology from the 'Daddy-Long-Legs,' or to call it out.

Full of this purpose, I looked about me to find a friend whom I could entrust with a message to his Daddyship, and as the editor of the 'Lollipop' had given me marked tokens of regard, I at length concluded to seek assistance upon the present occasion. I have never yet been able to account, in a manner satisfactory to my own understanding, for the *very* peculiar countenance and demeanour with which Mr. Crab listened to me, as I unfolded to him my design. He again went through the scene of the bell-rope and cudgel, and did not omit the duck. At one period I thought he really intended to quack. His fit, nevertheless, finally subsided as before, and he began to act and speak in a rational way. He declined bearing the cartel, however, and, in fact, dissuaded me from sending it at all; but was candid enough to admit that the 'Daddy-Long-Legs' had been disgracefully in the wrong – more especially in what related to the epithets 'gentleman and scholar.'

Towards the end of this interview with Mr. Crab, who really appeared to take a paternal interest in my welfare, he suggested to me that I might turn an honest penny, and at the same time advance my reputation, by occasionally playing Thomas Hawk for the 'Lollipop.'

I begged Mr. Crab to inform me who was Mr. Thomas Hawk, and how it was expected that I should play him.

Here Mr. Crab again 'made great eyes' (as we say in Germany), but at length, recovering himself from a profound attack of astonishment, he assured me that he employed the words 'Thomas Hawk' to avoid the colloquialism Tommy, which was low – but that the true idea was Tommy Hawk or tomahawk – and that by 'playing tomahawk' he referred to scalping, brow-beating, and otherwise using-up the herd of poor-devil authors.

I assured my patron that, if this was all, I was perfectly resigned to the task of playing Thomas Hawk. Hereupon Mr. Crab desired me to use-up the editor of the 'Gad-Fly' forthwith, in the fiercest style within the scope of my ability, and as a specimen of my power. This I did upon the spot, in a review of the original 'Oil-of-Bob,' occupying thirty-six pages of the 'Lollipop.' I found playing Thomas Hawk, indeed, a far less onerous occupation than poetising; for I went upon *system* altogether, and thus it was easy to do the thing thoroughly and well. My practice was this. I bought auction copies (cheap) of 'Lord Brougham's Speeches,' 'Cobbett's Complete Works,' the 'New Slang-Syllabus,' the 'Whole Art of Snubbing,' 'Prentice's Billingsgate' (folio edition), and 'Lewis G. Clarke on Tongue.' These works I cut up thoroughly with a curry-comb, and then, throwing the shreds into a sieve, shifted out carefully all that might be thought decent (a mere trifle); reserving the hard phrases, which I threw into a large tin pepper-castor with longitudinal holes, so that an entire sentence could get through without material injury. The mixture was then ready for use. When called upon to play Thomas Hawk, I anointed a sheet of foolscap with the white of a gander's egg; then shredding the thing to be reviewed as I had previously shredded the books – only with more care, so as to get every word separate – I threw the latter shreds in with the former, screwed on the lid of the castor, gave it a shake, and so dusted out the mixture upon the egged foolscap; where it stuck. The effect was beautiful to behold. It was captivating. Indeed, the reviews I brought to pass by this simple expedient have never been approached, and were the wonder of the world. At first, through bashfulness – the result of inexperience – I was a little put out by a certain inconsistency – a certain air of the *bizarre* (as we say in France) worn by the composition as a whole. All the phrases did not *fit* (as we say in the Anglo-Saxon). Many were quite awry. Some, even, were upside-down; and there were none of them which were not in some measure injured in regard to effect, by this latter species of accident when it occurred; – with the exception of Mr. Lewis Clarke's paragraphs, which were so vigorous, and altogether stout, that they seemed not particularly disconcerted by any extreme of position, but looked equally happy and satisfactory whether on their heads or on their heels.

What became of the editor of the 'Gad-Fly,' after the publication of my criticism on his 'Oil-of-Bob,' it is somewhat difficult to determine. The most reasonable conclusion is that he wept himself to death. At all events he disappeared instantaneously from the face of the earth, and no man has seen even the ghost of him since.

This matter having been properly accomplished, and the Furies appeased, I grew at once into high favour with Mr. Crab. He took me into his confidence, gave me a permanent situation as Thomas Hawk of the 'Lollipop,' and, as for the present he could afford me no salary, allowed me to profit, at discretion, by his advice.

'My dear Thingum,' said he to me one day after dinner, 'I respect your abilities and love you as a son. You shall be my heir. When I die I will bequeath you the "Lollipop." In the meantime I will make a man of you – I *will* – provided always that you follow my counsel. The first thing to do is to get rid of the old bore.'

'Boar?' said I inquiringly – 'pig, eh? – *oper* (as we say in Latin) – who? – where?'

'Your father,' said he.

'Precisely,' I replied, – 'pig.'

'You have your fortune to make, Thingum,' resumed Mr. Crab, 'and that governor of yours is a millstone about your neck. We must cut him at once' [Here I took out my knife.] 'We must cut him,' continued Mr. Crab, 'decidedly and for ever. He won't do – he *won't*. Upon second thoughts, you had better kick him, or cane him, or something of that kind.'

'What do you say,' I suggested modestly, 'to my kicking him the first instance, caning him afterwards, and winding up by tweaking his nose?'

Mr. Crab looked at me musingly for some moments, and then answered:

'I think, Mr. Bob, that what you propose would answer sufficiently well – indeed remarkably well – that is to say, as far as it went – but barbers are exceedingly hard to cut, and I think, upon the whole, that, having performed upon Thomas Bob the operations you suggest, it would be advisable to blacken, with your fists, both his eyes, very carefully and thoroughly, to prevent his ever seeing you again in fashionable promenades. After doing this, I really do not perceive that you can do any more. However – it might be just as well to roll him once or twice in the gutter, and then put him in charge of the police. Any time the next morning you can call at the watch-house and swear an assault.'

I was much affected by the kindness of feeling towards me personally which was evinced in this excellent advice of Mr. Crab, and I did not fail to profit by it forthwith. The result was that I got rid of the old bore, and began to feel a little independent and gentleman-like. The want of money, however, was for a few weeks a source of some discomfort; but at length, by carefully putting to use my two eyes, and observing how matters went just in front of my nose, I perceived how the thing was to be brought about. I say 'thing' – be it observed – for they tell me the Latin for it is *rem*. By the way, talking of Latin, can any one tell me the meaning of *quocunque* – or what is the meaning of *modo*.

My plan was exceedingly simple. I bought, for a song, a sixteenth of the 'Snapping-Turtle' – that was all. The thing was *done*, and I put money in my purse. There were some trivial arrangements afterwards, to be sure; but these formed no portion of the plan. They were a consequence – a result. For example, I bought pen, ink, and paper, and put them into furious activity. Having thus completed a magazine article, I gave it, for appellation, 'FOL-LOL, *by the author of* 'THE OIL-OF-BOB,'' and enveloped it to the 'Goosetherumfoodle.' That journal, however, having pronounced it 'twaddle' in the 'Monthly Notices to Correspondents,' I re-headed the paper '"Hey-Diddle-Diddle," by THINGUM BOB, Esq., Author of the Ode on "The Oil-of-Bob," *and* Editor of the "Snapping-Turtle."' With this amendment, I re-enclosed it to the 'Goosetherumfoodle,' and, while I awaited a reply, published daily, in the 'Turtle,' six columns of what may be termed philosophical and analytical investigation of the literary merits of the

'Goosetherumfoodle,' as well as of the personal character of the editor of the 'Goosetherumfoodle.' At the end of a week the 'Goosetherumfoodle' discovered that it had, by some odd mistake, 'confounded a stupid article headed "Hey-Diddle-Diddle," and composed by some unknown ignoramus, with a gem of splendid lustre similarly entitled, the work of Thingum Bob, Esq., the celebrated author of "Oil-of-Bob." ' The 'Goosetherumfoodle' deeply 'regretted this very natural accident,' and promised, moreover, an insertion of the *genuine* 'Hey-Diddle-Diddle' in the very next number of the magazine.

The fact is I *thought* – I *really* thought – I thought at the time – I thought *then* – and have no reason for thinking otherwise *now* – that the 'Goosetherumfoodle' *did* make a mistake. With the best intentions in the world, I never knew anything that made as many singular mistakes as the 'Goosetherumfoodle.' From that day I took a liking to the 'Goosetherumfoodle,' and the result was I soon saw into the very depths of its literary merits, and did not fail to expatiate upon them in the 'Turtle' whenever a fitting opportunity occurred. And it is to be regarded as a very peculiar coincidence – as one of those positively *remarkable* coincidences which set a man to serious thinking – that just such a total revolution of opinion – just such entire *bouleversement* (as we say in French), – just such thorough *topsiturviness* (if I may be permitted to employ a rather forcible term of Choctaws), as happened, *pro* and *con*, between myself on the one part, and the 'Goose-therumfoodle' on the other, did actually again happen, in a brief period afterwards, and with precisely similar circumstances, in the case of myself and the 'Rowdy-Dow,' and in the case of myself and the 'Hum-Drum.'

Thus it was that, by a master-stroke of genius, I at length consummated my triumphs by 'putting money in my purse,' and thus may be said really and fairly to have commenced that brilliant and eventful career which rendered me illustrious, and which now enables me to say, with Chateaubriand, 'I have made history' '*J'ai fait l' histoire.*'

I have indeed 'made history.' From the bright epoch which I now record, my actions – my works – are the property of mankind. They are familiar to the world. It is, then, needless for me to detail how, soaring rapidly, I fell heir to the 'Lollipop' – how I merged this journal in the 'Hum-Drum' – how again I made purchase of the 'Rowdy-Dow,' thus combining the three periodicals – how, lastly, I effected a bargain for the sole remaining rival, and united all the literature of the country in one magnificent magazine, known everywhere as the

'Rowdy-Dow, Lollipop, Hum-Drum,
and
GOOSETHERUMFOODLE.'

Yes; I have made history. My fame is universal. It extends to the uttermost ends of the earth. You cannot take up a common newspaper in which you shall not see some allusion to the immortal THINGUM BOB. It is Mr. Thingum Bob said so, and Mr. Thingum Bob wrote this, and Mr. Thingum Bob did that. But I am meek and expire with an humble heart. After all, what is it? – this indescribable something which men will persist in terming 'genius?' I agree with Buffon – with Hogarth – it is but *diligence* after all.

'Look at *me*! how I laboured – how I toiled – how I wrote! Ye gods, did I *not* write? I knew not the word 'ease.' By day I adhered to my desk, and at night, a pale student, I consumed the midnight oil. You should have seen me – you *should*. I leaned to the right. I leaned to the left. I sat forward. I sat backward. I sat upon end. I sat *tête baissée* (as they have it in the Kickapoo), bowing my head close to the alabaster page. And, through all, I – *wrote*. Through joy and through sorrow, I – *wrote*. Through hunger and through thirst, I – *wrote*. Through good report and ill report, I – *wrote*. Through sunshine and through moonshine, I – *wrote*. *What* I wrote it is unnecessary to say. The *style!* – that was the thing. I caught it from Fatquack – whizz! – fizz! – and I am giving you a specimen of it now.

The Fall of the House of Usher

Son cœur est un luth suspendu;
Sitôt qu'on le touche il résonne.

DE BÉRANGER.

During the whole of a dull, dark, and soundless day in the autumn of
the year, when the clouds hung oppressively low in the heavens, I had
been passing alone, on horseback, through a singularly dreary tract of
country, and at length found myself, as the shades of evening drew on,
within view of the melancholy House of Usher. I know not how it was
– but, with the first glimpse of the building, a sense of insufferable
gloom pervaded my spirit. I say insufferable; for the feeling was
unrelieved by any of that half-pleasurable, because poetic, sentiment,
with which the mind usually receives even the sternest natural images
of the desolate or terrible. I looked upon the scene before me – upon
the mere house, and the simple landscape features of the domain –
upon the bleak walls – upon the vacant eye-like windows – upon a few
rank sedges – and upon a few white trunks of decayed trees – with an
utter depression of soul, which I can compare to no earthly sensation
more properly than to the after-dream of the reveller upon opium – the
bitter lapse into every-day life – the hideous dropping of the veil. There
was an iciness, a sinking, a sickening of the heart – an unredeemed

dreariness of thought, which no goading of the imagination could torture into aught of the sublime. What was it – I paused to think – what was it that so unnerved me in the contemplation of the House of Usher? It was a mystery all insoluble; nor could I grapple with the shadowy fancies that crowded upon me as I pondered. I was forced to fall back upon the unsatisfactory conclusion, that while, beyond doubt, there *are* combinations of very simple natural objects which have the power of thus affecting us, still the analysis of this power lies among considerations beyond our depth. It was possible, I reflected, that a mere different arrangement of the particulars of the scene, of the details of the picture, would be sufficient to modify, or perhaps to annihilate its capacity for sorrowful impression; and, acting upon this idea, I reined my horse to the precipitous brink of a black and lurid tarn that lay in unruffled lustre by the dwelling, and gazed down – but with a shudder more thrilling than before – upon the remodelled and inverted images of the grey sedge, and the ghastly tree-stems, and the vacant and eye-like windows.

Nevertheless, in this mansion of gloom I now proposed to myself a sojourn of some weeks. Its proprietor, Roderick Usher, had been one of my boon companions in boyhood; but many years had elapsed since our last meeting. A letter, however, had lately reached me in a distant part of the country – a letter from him – which, in its wildly importunate nature, had admitted of no other than a personal reply. The MS. gave evidence of nervous agitation. The writer spoke of acute bodily illness – of a mental disorder which oppressed him – and of an earnest desire to see me, as his best, and indeed his only personal friend, with a view of attempting, by the cheerfulness of my society, some alleviation of his malady. It was the manner in which all this, and much more, was said – it was the apparent *heart* that went with his request – which allowed me no room for hesitation, and I accordingly obeyed forthwith what I still considered a very singular summons.

Although, as boys, we had been even intimate associates, yet I really knew little of my friend. His reserve had been always excessive and habitual. I was aware, however, that his very ancient family had been noted, time out of mind, for a peculiar sensibility of temperament, displaying itself through long ages in many works of exalted art, and manifested of late in repeated deeds of munificent yet unobtrusive charity, as well as in a passionate devotion to the intricacies, perhaps even more than to the orthodox and easily-recognisable beauties of musical science. I had learned, too, the very remarkable fact that the stem of the Usher race, all time-honoured as it was, had put forth at no period any enduring branch; in other words, that the entire family lay in the direct line of descent, and had always, with very trifling and very temporary variation, so lain. It was this deficiency, I considered, while running over in thought the perfect keeping of the character of the premises with the accredited character of the people, and while speculating upon the possible influence which the one, in the long lapse of centuries, might have exercised upon the other – it was this deficiency perhaps of collateral issue, and the consequent undeviating transmission from sire to son of the patrimony with the name, which had at length so identified the two as to merge the original title of the estate in the quaint and equivocal appellation of the 'House of Usher' – an appellation which seemed to include, in the minds of the peasantry who used it, both the family and the family mansion.

I have said that the sole effect of my somewhat childish experiment – that of looking down within the tarn – had been to deepen the first singular impression. There can be no doubt that the consciousness of the rapid increase of my superstition – for why should I not so term it? – served mainly to accelerate the increase itself. Such, I have long known, is the paradoxical law of all sentiments having terror as a basis; and it might have been for this reason only that, when I again uplifted my eyes to the house itself from its image in the pool, there grew in my mind a strange fancy – a fancy so ridiculous indeed that I but mention it to show the vivid force of the sensations which oppressed me. I had so worked upon my imagination as really to believe that about the whole mansion and domain there hung an atmosphere peculiar to themselves and their immediate vicinity – an atmosphere which had no affinity with the air of heaven, but which had reeked up from the decayed trees, and the grey wall, and the silent tarn – a pestilent and mystic vapour, dull, sluggish, faintly discernible, and leaden-hued.

Shaking off from my spirit what *must* have been a dream, I scanned more narrowly the real aspect of the building. Its principal feature seemed to be that of an excessive antiquity. The discoloration of ages had been great. Minute fungi overspread the whole exterior, hanging in a fine tangled webwork from the eaves. Yet all this was apart from any extraordinary dilapidation. No portion of the masonry had fallen, and there appeared to be a wild inconsistency between its still perfect adaptation of parts and the crumbling condition of the individual stones. In this there was much that reminded me of the spacious totality of old woodwork which has rotted for long years in some neglected vault with no disturbance from the breath of the external air. Beyond this indication of extensive decay, however, the fabric gave little token of instability. Perhaps the eye of a scrutinising observer might have discovered a barely perceptible fissure, which, extending from the roof of the building in front, made its way down the wall in a zigzag direction, until it became lost in the sullen waters of the tarn.

Noticing these things, I rode over a short causeway to the house. A servant in waiting took my horse, and I entered the Gothic archway of the hall. A valet, of stealthy step, thence conducted me in silence through many dark and intricate passages in my progress to the *studio* of his master. Much that I encountered on the way contributed, I know not how, to heighten the vague sentiments of which I have already spoken. While the objects around me – while the carvings of the ceilings, the sombre tapestries of the walls, the ebony blackness of the floors, and the phantasmagoric armorial trophies which rattled as I strode, were but matters to which, or to such as which, I had been accustomed from my infancy – while I hesitated not to acknowledge how familiar was all this – I still wondered to find how unfamiliar were the fancies which ordinary images were stirring up. On one of the staircases I met the physician of the family. His countenance, I thought, wore a mingled expression of low cunning and perplexity. He accosted me with trepidation and passed on. The valet now threw open a door and ushered me into the presence of his master.

The room in which I found myself was very large and lofty. The windows were long, narrow, and pointed, and at so vast a distance from the black oaken floor as to be altogether inaccessible from within. Feeble gleams of encrimsoned light made their way through the trellissed panes, and served to render sufficiently distinct the more prominent objects around; the eye, however, struggled in vain to reach the remoter angles of the chamber, or the recesses of the vaulted and fretted ceiling. Dark draperies hung upon the walls. The general furniture was profuse, comfortless, antique, and tattered. Many books and musical instruments lay scattered about, but failed to give any vitality to the scene. I felt that I breathed an atmosphere of sorrow. An air of stern, deep, and irredeemable gloom hung over and pervaded all.

Upon my entrance, Usher arose from a sofa on which he had been lying at full length, and greeted me with a vivacious warmth which had much in it, I at first thought, of an overdone cordiality – of the constrained effort of the *ennuyé* man of the world. A glance, however, at his countenance convinced me of his perfect sincerity. We sat down; and for some moments, while he spoke not, I gazed upon him with a feeling half of pity, half of awe. Surely man had never before so terribly altered, in so brief a period, as had Roderick Usher! It was with difficulty that I could bring myself to admit the identity of the wan being before me with the companion of my early boyhood. Yet the character of his face had been at all times remarkable. A cadaverousness of complexion; an eye large, liquid, and luminous beyond comparison; lips somewhat thin and very pallid, but of a surpassingly beautiful curve; a nose of a delicate Hebrew model, but with a breadth of nostril unusual in similar formations; a finely moulded chin, speaking, in its want of prominence, of a want of moral energy; hair of a more than web-like softness and tenuity; these features, with an inordinate expansion above the regions of the temple, made up altogether a countenance not easily to be fogotten. And now in the mere exaggeration of the prevailing character of these features, and of the expression they were wont to convey, lay so much of change that I doubted to whom I spoke. The now ghastly pallor of the skin, and the now miraculous lustre of the eye, above all things startled and even awed me. The silken hair, too, had been suffered to grow all unheeded, and as, in its wild gossamer texture, it floated rather than fell about the face, I could not, even with effort, connect its Arabesque expression with any idea of simple humanity.

In the manner of my friend I was at once struck with an incoherence – an inconsistency; and I soon found this to arise from a series of feeble and futile struggles to overcome an habitual trepidancy – an excessive nervous agitation. For something of this nature I had indeed been prepared, no less by his letter than by reminiscences of certain boyish traits, and by conclusions deduced from his peculiar physical conformation and temperament. His action was alternately vivacious and sullen. His voice varied rapidly from a tremulous indecision (when the animal spirits seemed utterly in abeyance) to that species of energetic concision – that abrupt, weighty, unhurried, and hollow-sounding enunciation – that leaden, self-balanced and perfectly modulated guttural utterance which may be observed in the lost drunkard, or the irreclaimable eater of opium, during the periods of his most intense excitement.

It was thus that he spoke of the object of my visit, of his earnest desire to see me, and of the solace he expected me to afford him. He entered at some length into what he conceived to be the nature of his malady. It was, he said, a constitutional and a family evil, and one for which he despaired to find a remedy – a mere nervous affection, he immediately added, which would undoubtedly soon pass off. It displayed itself in a host of unnatural sensations. Some of these as he detailed them, interested and bewildered me; although perhaps the terms and the general manner of the narration had their weight. He suffered much from a morbid acuteness of the senses; the most insipid food was alone endurable; he could wear only garments of certain texture; the odours of all flowers were oppressive; his eyes were tortured by even a faint light; and there were but peculiar sounds, and these from stringed instruments, which did not inspire him with horror.

To an anomalous species of terror I found him a bounden slave. 'I shall perish,' said he, 'I *must* perish in this deplorable folly. Thus, thus, and not otherwise, shall I be lost. I dread the events of the future, not in themselves, but in their results. I shudder at the thought of any, even the most trivial incident, which may operate upon this intolerable agitation of soul. I have indeed no abhorrence of danger, except in its absolute effect – in terror. In this unnerved – in this pitiable condition – I feel that the period will sooner or later arrive when I must abandon life and reason together in some struggle with the grim phantasm, FEAR.'

I learned, moreover, at intervals, and through broken and equivocal hints, another singular feature of his mental condition. He was enchained by certain superstitious impressions in regard to the dwelling which he tenanted, and whence, for many years, he had never ventured forth – in regard to an influence whose supposititious force was conveyed in terms too shadowy here to be re-stated – an influence which some peculiarities in the mere form and substance of his family mansion, had, by dint of long sufferance, he said, obtained over his spirit – an effect which the *physique* of the grey walls and turrets, and of the dim tarn into which they all looked down, had at length brought about upon the *morale* of his existence.

He admitted, however, although with hesitation, that much of the peculiar gloom which thus afflicted him could be traced to a more natural and far more palpable origin – to the severe and long continued illness – indeed to the evidently approaching dissolution – of a tenderly beloved sister – his sole companion for long years – his last and only relative on earth. 'Her decease,' he said, with a bitterness which I can never forget, 'would leave him (him the hopeless and the frail) the last of the ancient race of the Ushers.' While he spoke, the lady Madeline (for so was she called) passed slowly through a remote part of the apartment, and, without having noticed my presence, disappeared. I regarded her with an utter astonishment not unmingled with dread – and yet I found it impossible to account for such feelings. A sensation of stupor oppressed me as my eyes followed her retreating steps. When a door at length closed upon her, my glance sought instinctively and eagerly the countenance of the brother – but he had buried his face in his hands, and I could only perceive that a far more than ordinary wanness had overspread the emaciated fingers through which trickled many passionate tears.

The disease of the lady Madeline had long baffled the skill of her physicians. A settled apathy, a gradual wasting away of the person, and frequent although transient affections of a partially cataleptical character, were the unusual diagnosis. Hitherto she had steadily borne up against the pressure of her malady, and had not betaken herself finally to bed; but, on the closing in of the evening of my arrival at the house, she succumbed (as her brother told me at night with inexpressible agitation) to the prostrating power of the destroyer; and I learned that the glimpse I had obtained of her person would thus probably be the last I should obtain – that the lady, at least while living, would be seen by me no more.

For several days ensuing her name was unmentioned by either Usher or myself; and during this period I was busied in earnest endeavours to alleviate the melancholy of my friend. We painted and read together, or I listened, as if in a dream, to the wild improvisations of his speaking guitar. And thus, as a closer and still closer intimacy admitted me more unreservedly into the recesses of his spirit, the more bitterly did I perceive the futility of all attempts at cheering a mind from which darkness, as if an inherent positive quality, poured forth upon all objects of the moral and physical universe in one unceasing radiation of gloom.

I shall ever bear about me a memory of the many solemn hours I thus spent alone with the master of the House of Usher. Yet I should fail in any attempt to convey an idea of the exact character of the studies, or of the occupations in which he involved me or led me the way. An excited and highly distempered ideality threw a sulphureous lustre over all. His long improvised dirges will ring forever in my ears. Among other things, I hold painfully in mind a certain singular perversion and amplification of the wild air of the last waltz of Von Weber. From the paintings over which his elaborate fancy brooded, and which grew, touch by touch, into vaguenesses at which I shuddered the more thrillingly, because I shuddered knowing not why – from these paintings (vivid as their images now are before me) I would in vain endeavour to educe more than a small portion which should lie within the compass of merely written words. By the utter simplicity, by the nakedness of his designs, he arrested and overawed attention. If ever mortal painted an idea that mortal was Roderick Usher. For me at least – in the circumstances then surrounding me – there arose out of the pure abstractions which the hypochondriac contrived to throw upon his canvas an intensity of intolerable awe, no shadow of which felt I ever yet in the contemplation of the certainly glowing yet too concrete reveries of Fuseli.

One of the phantasmagoric conceptions of my friend, partaking not so rigidly of the spirit of abstraction, may be shadowed forth, although feebly, in words. A small picture presented the interior of an immensely long and rectangular vault or tunnel, with low walls, smooth, white, and without interruption or device. Certain accessory points of the design served well to convey the idea that this excavation lay at an exceeding depth below the surface of the earth. No outlet was observed in any portion of its vast extent, and no torch, or other artificial source of light was discernible, yet a flood of intense rays rolled throughout, and bathed the whole in a ghastly and inappropriate splendour.

I have just spoken of that morbid condition of the auditory nerve which rendered all music intolerable to the sufferer, with the exception of certain effects of stringed instruments. It was perhaps the narrow limits to which he thus confined himself upon the guitar which gave birth, in great measure, to the fantastic character of his performances. But the fervid *facility* of his *impromptus* could not be so accounted for. They must have been and were, in the notes, as well as in the words of his wild fantasias (for he not unfrequently accompanied himself with rhymed-verbal improvisations), the result of that intense mental collectedness and concentration to which I have previously alluded as observable only in particular moments of the highest artifical excitement. The words of one of these rhapsodies I have easily remembered. I was perhaps the more forcibly impressed with it as he gave it, because, in the under or mystic current of its meaning, I fancied that I perceived, and for the first time, a full consciousness on the part of Usher, of the tottering of his lofty reason upon her throne. The verses, which were entitled 'The Haunted Palace,' ran very nearly, if not accurately, thus:

In the greenest of our valleys,
    By good angels tenanted,
Once a fair and stately palace –
    Radiant palace – reared its head.
In the monarch Thought's dominion –
    It stood there!
Never seraph spread a pinion
    Over fabric half so fair.

Banners yellow, glorious, golden,
    On its roof did float and flow;
(This – all this – was in the olden
    Time long ago)
And every gentle air that dallied,
    In that sweet day,
Along the ramparts plumed and pallid,
    A winged odour went away.

Wanderers in that happy valley
    Through two luminous windows saw
Spirits moving musically
    To a lute's well-tunéd law,
Round about a throne, where sitting
    (Porphyrogene!)
In state his glory well befitting,
    The ruler of the realm was seen.

And all with pearl and ruby glowing
    Was the fair palace door,
Through which came flowing, flowing, flowing,
    And sparkling evermore,
A troop of Echoes whose sweet duty
    Was but to sing,
In voices of surpassing beauty,
    The wit and wisdom of their king.

But evil things, in robes of sorrow,
　　Assailed the monarch's high estate;
(Ah, let us mourn, for never morrow
　　Shall dawn upon him, desolate!)
And, round about his home, the glory
　　That blushed and bloomed
Is but a dim-remembered story
　　Of the old time entombed.

And travellers now within that valley,
　　Through the red-litten windows, see
Vast forms that move fantastically
　　To a discordant melody;
While, like a rapid ghastly river,
　　Through the pale door,
A hideous throng rush out for ever,
　　And laugh – but smile no more.

I well remember that suggestions arising from this ballad led us into a train of thought wherein there became manifest an opinion of Usher's, which I mention not so much on account of its novelty (for other men* have thought thus), as on account of the pertinacity with which he maintained it. This opinion, in its general form, was that of the sentience of all vegetable things. But, in his disordered fancy, the idea had assumed a more daring character, and trespassed, under certain conditions, upon the kingdom of inorganisation. I lack words to express the full extent, or the earnest *abandon* of his persuasion. The belief, however, was connected (as I have previously hinted) with the grey stones of the home of his forefathers. The conditions of the sentience had been here, he imagined, fulfilled in the method of collocation of these stones – in the order of their arrangement, as well as in that of the many *fungi* which overspread them, and of the decayed trees which stood around – above all, in the long undisturbed endurance of this arrangement, and in its reduplication in the still

* Watson, Dr. Percival, Spallanzani, and especially the Bishop of Llandaff. – See 'Chemical Essays,' vol. v.

waters of the tarn. Its evidence — the evidence of the sentience, was to be seen, he said (and I here started as he spoke), in the gradual yet certain condensation of an atmosphere of their own about the waters and the walls. The result was discoverable, he added, in that silent yet importunate and terrible influence which for centuries had moulded the destinies of his family, and which made *him* what I now saw him — what he was. Such opinions need no comment, and I will make none.

Our books — the books which for years had formed no small portion of the mental existence of the invalid — were, as might be supposed, in strict keeping with this character of phantasm. We pored together over such works as the Ververt et Chartreuse of Gresset; the Belphegor of Machiavelli; the Heaven and Hell of Swedenborg; the Subterranean Voyage of Nicholas Klimm by Holberg; the Chiromancy of Robert Flud, of Jean D'Indaginé, and of De la Chambre; the Journey into the Blue Distance of Tieck; and the City of the Sun of Campanella. One favourite volume was a small octavo edition of the *Directorium Inquisitorium*, by the Dominican Eymeric de Gironne; and there were passages in Pomponius Mela, about the old African Satyrs and Œgipans, over which Usher would sit dreaming for hours. His chief delight, however, was found in the perusal of an exceedingly rare and curious book in quarto Gothic — the manual of a forgotten church the *Vigiliae Mortuorum secundum Chorum Ecclesiae Maguntinae.*

I could not help thinking of the wild ritual of this work, and of its probable influence upon the hypochondriac, when, one evening, having informed me abruptly that the lady Madeline was no more, he stated his intention of preserving her corpse for a fortnight (previously to its final interment), in one of the numerous vaults within the main walls of the building. The worldly reason, however, assigned for this singular proceeding was one which I did not feel at liberty to dispute. The brother had been led to his resolution (so he told me) by consideration of the unusual character of the malady of the deceased, of certain obtrusive and eager inquiries on the part of her medical men, and of the remote and exposed situation of the burial-ground of the family. I will not deny that when I called to mind the sinister countenance of the person whom I met upon the staircase on the day of my arrival at the house, I had no desire to oppose what I regarded as at best but a harmless and by no means an unnatural precaution.

At the request of Usher, I personally aided him in the arrangements for the temporary entombment. The body having been encoffined, we two alone bore it to its rest. The vault in which we placed it (and which had been so long unopened that our torches, half smothered in its oppressive atmosphere, gave us little opportunity for investigation) was small, damp, and entirely without means of admission for light, lying at great depth immediately beneath that portion of the building in which was my own sleeping apartment. It had been used apparently in remote feudal times for the worst purposes of a donjon-keep, and in later days as a place of deposit for powder or some other highly combustible substance, as a portion of its floor, and the whole interior of a long archway through which we reached it, were carefully sheathed with copper. The door, of massive iron, had been also similarly protected. Its immense weight caused an unusually sharp grating sound as it moved upon its hinges.

Having deposited our mournful burden upon tressels within this region of horror, we partially turned aside the yet unscrewed lid of the coffin and looked upon the face of the tenant. A striking similitude between the brother and sister now first arrested my attention, and Usher, divining perhaps my thoughts, murmured out some few words from which I learned that the deceased and himself had been twins, and that sympathies of a scarcely intelligible nature had always existed between them. Our glances, however, rested not long upon the dead for we could not regard her unawed. The disease which had thus entombed the lady in the maturity of youth had left, as usual in all maladies of a strictly cataleptical character, the mockery of a faint blush upon the bosom and the face, and that suspiciously lingering smile upon the lip which is so terrible in death. We replaced and screwed down the lid, and having secured the door of iron, made our way with toil into the scarcely less gloomy apartments of the upper portion of the house.

And now, some days of bitter grief having elapsed, an observable change came over the features of the mental disorder of my friend. His ordinary manner had vanished. His ordinary occupations were neglected or forgotten. He roamed from chamber to chamber with hurried, unequal, and objectless step. The pallor of his countenance had assumed if possible a more ghastly hue – but the luminousness of his eye had utterly gone out. The once occasional huskiness of his tone was heard no more, and a tremulous quaver, as if of extreme terror, habitually characterised his utterance. There were times indeed when I thought his unceasingly agitated mind was labouring with some oppressive secret, to divulge which he struggled for the necessary courage. At times again I was obliged to resolve all into the mere inexplicable vagaries of madness, for I beheld him gazing upon vacancy for long hours in an attitude of the profoundest attention, as if listening to some imaginary sound. It was no wonder that his condition terrified – that it infected me. I felt creeping upon me, by slow yet certain degrees, the wild influences of his own fantastic yet impressive superstitions.

It was especially upon retiring to bed late in the night of the seventh or eighth day after the placing of the lady Madeline within the donjon that I experienced the full power of such feelings. Sleep came not near my couch – while the hours waxed and waned away. I struggled to reason off the nervousness which had dominion over me. I endeavoured to believe that much if not all of what I felt was due to the bewildering influence of the gloomy furniture of the room – of the dark and tattered draperies which, tortured into motion by the breath of a rising tempest, swayed fitfully to and fro upon the walls, and rustled uneasily about the decorations of the bed. But my efforts were fruitless. An irrepressible tremor gradually pervaded my frame, and at length there sat upon my very heart an incubus of utterly causeless alarm. Shaking this off with a gasp and a struggle I uplifted myself upon the pillows, and peering earnestly within the intense darkness of the chamber, hearkened – I know not why, except that an instinctive spirit prompted me – to certain low and indefinite sounds which came, through the pauses of the storm, at long intervals I knew not whence.

Overpowered by an intense sentiment of horror, unaccountable yet unendurable, I threw on my clothes with haste (for I felt that I should sleep no more during the night), and endeavoured to arouse myself from the pitiable condition into which I had fallen, by pacing rapidly to and fro through the apartment.

I had taken but few turns in this manner, when a light step on an adjoining staircase arrested my attention. I presently recognised it as that of Usher. In an instant afterward he rapped with a gentle touch at my door, and entered, bearing a lamp. His countenance was as usual cadaverously wan – but, moreover, there was a species of mad hilarity in his eyes – an evidently restrained *hysteria* in his whole demeanour. His air appalled me – but anything was preferable to the solitude which I had so long endured, and I even welcomed his presence as a relief.

'And you have not seen it?' he said abruptly, after having stared about him for some moments in silence – 'you have not then seen it? – but, stay! you shall.' Thus speaking, and having carefully shaded his lamp, he hurried to one of the casements, and threw it freely open to the storm.

The impetuous fury of the entering gust nearly lifted us from our feet. It was indeed a tempestuous yet sternly beautiful night, and one wildly singular in its terror and its beauty. A whirlwind had apparently collected its force in our vicinity, for there were frequent and violent alterations in the direction of the wind, and the exceeding density of the clouds (which hung so low as to press upon the turrets of the house) did not prevent our perceiving the life-like velocity with which they flew careering from all points against each other without passing away into the distance.

I say that even their exceeding density did not prevent our perceiving this – yet we had no glimpse of the moon or stars – nor was there any flashing forth of the lightning. But the under surfaces of the huge masses of agitated vapour, as well as all terrestrial objects immediately around us, were glowing in the unnatural light of a faintly luminous and distinctly visible gaseous exhalation which hung about and enshrouded the mansion.

'You must not – you shall not behold this!' said I, shudderingly, to Usher, as I led him with a gentle violence from the window to a seat. 'These appearances which bewilder you are merely electrical pheno-mena not uncommon, or it may be that they have their ghastly origin in the rank miasma of the tarn. Let us close this casement; the air is chilling and dangerous to your frame. Here is one of your favourite romances. I will read, and you shall listen; and so we will pass away this terrible night together.'

The antique volume which I had taken up was the 'Mad Trist' of Sir Launcelot Canning, but I had called it a favourite of Usher's, more in sad jest than in earnest; for, in truth, there is little in its uncouth and unimaginative prolixity which could have had interest for the lofty and spiritual ideality of my friend. It was, however, the only book immediately at hand, and I indulged a vague hope that the excitement which now agitated the hypochondriac might find relief (for the history of mental disorder is full of similar anomalies) even in the extremeness of the folly which I should read. Could I have judged, indeed, by the wild overstrained air of vivacity with which he hearkened, or apparently hearkened, to the words of the tale, I might well have congratulated myself upon the success of my design.

I had arrived at that well-known portion of the story where Ethelred, the hero of the Trist, having sought in vain for peaceable admission into the dwelling of the hermit, proceeds to make good an entrance by force. Here, it will be remembered, the words of the narrative run thus:

'And Ethelred, who was by nature of a doughty heart, and who was now mighty withal, on account of the powerfulness of the wine which he had drunken, waited no longer to hold parley with the hermit, who in sooth was of an obstinate and maliceful turn, but feeling the rain upon his shoulders, and fearing the rising of the tempest, uplifted his mace outright, and with blows made quickly room in the plankings of the door for his gauntleted hand; and now pulling therewith sturdily, he so cracked and ripped, and tore all asunder, that the noise of the dry and hollow-sounding wood alarummed and reverberated throughout the forest.'

At the termination of this sentence I started, and for a moment paused, for it appeared to me (although I at once concluded that my excited fancy had deceived me) that from some very remote portion of the mansion there came indistinctly to my ears what might have been, in its exact similarity of character, the echo (but a stifled and dull one certainly) of the very cracking and ripping sound which Sir Launcelot had so particularly described. It was beyond doubt the coincidence alone which had arrested my attention; for amid the rattling of the sashes of the casements, and the ordinary commingled noises of the still increasing storm, the sound in itself had nothing surely which should have interested or disturbed me. I continued the story:

'But the good champion Ethelred, now entering within the door, was soon enraged and amazed to perceive no signal of the maliceful hermit; but in the stead thereof, a dragon of a scaly and prodigious demeanour, and of a fiery tongue, which sate in guard before a palace of gold, with a floor of silver; and upon the wall there hung a shield of shining brass with this legend enwritten –

'Who entereth herein, a conqueror hath bin;
Who slayeth the dragon, the shield he shall win.

And Ethelred uplifted his mace, and struck upon the head of the dragon, which fell before him, and gave up his pesty breath, with a shriek so horrid and harsh, and withal so piercing, that Ethelred had fain to close his ears with his hands against the dreadful noise of it, the like whereof was never before heard.'

Here again I paused abruptly, and now with a feeling of wild amazement – for there could be no doubt whatever that in this instance I did actually hear (although from what direction it proceeded I found it impossible to say) a low and apparently distant, but harsh, protracted, and most unusual screaming or grating sound – the exact counterpart of what my fancy had already conjured up for the dragon's unnatural shriek as described by the romancer.

Oppressed, as I certainly was upon the occurrence of this second and most extraordinary coincidence, by a thousand conflicting sensations, in which wonder and extreme terror were predominate, I still retained sufficient presence of mind to avoid exciting by any observation the sensitive nervousness of my companion. I was by no means certain that he had noticed the sounds in question, although, assuredly, a strange alteration had during the last few minutes taken place in his demeanour. From a position fronting my own, he had gradually brought round his chair, so as to sit with his face to the door of the chamber; and thus I could but partially perceive his features, although I saw that his lips trembled as if he were murmuring inaudibly. His head had dropped upon his breast, yet I knew that he was not asleep, from the wide and rigid opening of the eye, as I caught a glance of it in profile. The motion of his body too, was at variance with this idea, – for he rocked from side to side with a gentle yet constant and uniform sway. Having rapidly taken notice of all this I resumed the narrative of Sir Launcelot which thus proceeded:

'And now, the champion having escaped from the terrible fury of the dragon, bethinking himself of the brazen shield, and of the breaking up of the enchantment which was upon it, removed the carcase from out of the way before him, and approached valorously over the silver pavement of the castle to where the shield was upon the wall; which in sooth tarried not for his full coming, but fell down at his feet upon the silver floor with a mighty great and terrible ringing sound.'

No sooner had these syllables passed my lips, than – as if a shield of brass had indeed at the moment fallen heavily upon a floor of silver – I became aware of a distinct, hollow, metallic, and clangorous, yet apparently muffled, reverberation. Completely unnerved, I leaped to my feet, but the measured rocking movement of Usher was undisturbed. I rushed to the chair in which he sat. His eyes were bent fixedly before him, and throughout his whole countenance there reigned a stony rigidity. But, as I placed my hand upon his shoulder, there came a strong shudder over his whole person; a sickly smile quivered about his lips, and I saw that he spoke in a low, hurried, and gibbering murmur, as if unconscious of my presence. Bending closely over him, I at length drank in the hideous import of his words.

'Not hear it? – yes, I hear it, and *have* heard it. Long – long – long – many minutes, many hours, many days, have I heard it – yet I dared not – oh, pity me, miserable wretch that I am! – I dared not – I *dared* not speak! *We have put her living in the tomb!* Said I not that my senses were acute? I *now* tell you that I heard her first feeble movements in the hollow coffin. I heard them – many, many days ago – yet I dared not – *I dared not speak!* And now – to-night – Ethelred – ha! ha! – the breaking of the hermit's door, and the death-cry of the dragon, and the clangour of the shield! – say, rather, the rending of her coffin, and the grating of the iron hinges of her prison, and her struggles within the coppered archway of the vault. O whither shall I fly? Will she not be here anon? Is she not hurrying to upbraid me for my haste? Have I not heard her footstep on the stair? Do I not distinguish that heavy and horrible beating of her heart? Madman!' Here he sprang furiously to his feet, and shrieked out his syllables, as if in the effort he were giving up his soul – '*Madman! I tell you that she now stands without the door!*'

As if in the superhuman energy of his utterance there had been found the potency of a spell – the huge antique panels to which the speaker pointed, threw slowly back, upon the instant, their ponderous and ebony jaws. It was the work of the rushing gust – but then without those doors there *did* stand the lofty and enshrouded figure of the lady Madeline of Usher. There was blood upon her white robes, and the evidence of some bitter struggle upon every portion of her emaciated frame. For a moment she remained trembling and reeling to and fro upon the threshold – then, with a low moaning cry, fell heavily inward upon the person of her brother, and in her violent and now final death-agonies, bore him to the floor a corpse, and a victim to the terrors he had anticipated.

From that chamber and from that mansion I fled aghast. The storm was still abroad in all its wrath as I found myself crossing the old causeway. Suddenly there shot along the path a wild light, and I turned to see whence a gleam so unusual could have issued, for the vast house and its shadows were alone behind me. The radiance was that of the full, setting, and blood-red moon, which now shone vividly through that once barely-discernible fissure, of which I have before

*But then without those doors there DID stand the lofty and enshrouded
figure of the Lady Madeline of Usher*

spoken as extending from the roof of the building in a zigzag direction to the base. While I gazed, this fissure rapidly widened; there came a fierce breath of the whirlwind; the entire orb of the satellite burst at once upon my sight; my brain reeled as I saw the mighty walls rushing asunder; there was a long tumultuous shouting sound like the voice of a thousand waters, and the deep and dark tarn at my feet closed sullenly and silently over the fragments of the '*House of Usher.*'

The Man that was Used Up

A Tale of the late Bugaboo and Kickapoo Campaign

Pleurez, pleurez, mes yeux, et fondez vous en eau!
La moitié de ma vie a mis l'autre au tombeau.
                                                CORNEILLE.

I cannot just now remember when or where I first made the
acquaintance of that truly fine-looking fellow, Brevet Brigadier-
General John A. B. C. Smith. Some one *did* introduce me to the
gentleman, I am sure – at some public meeting, I know very well –
held about something of great importance, no doubt – at some place or
other, I feel convinced, – whose name I have unaccountably forgotten.
The truth is – that the introduction was attended, upon my part, with a
degree of anxious embarrassment which operated to prevent any
definite impressions of either time or place. I am constitutionally
nervous – this, with me, is a family failing, and I can't help it. In
especial, the slightest appearance of mystery – or any point I cannot
exactly comprehend – puts me at once into a pitiable state of agitation.
There was something, as it were, remarkable – yes, *remarkable,*

although this is but a feeble term to express my full meaning – about the entire individuality of the personage in question. He was, perhaps, six feet in height, and of a presence singularly commanding. There was an *air distingué* pervading the whole man, which spoke of high breeding, and hinted at high birth. Upon this topic – the topic of Smith's personal appearance – I have a kind of melancholy satisfaction in being minute. His head of hair would have done honour to a Brutus; nothing could be more richly flowing, or possess a brighter gloss. It was of a jetty black; which was also the colour, or more properly the no colour, of his unimaginable whiskers. You perceive I cannot speak of these latter without enthusiasm; it is not too much to say that they were the handsomest pair of whiskers under the sun. At all events, they encircled, and at times partially overshadowed, a mouth utterly unequalled. Here were the most entirely even, and the most brilliantly white of all conceivable teeth. From between them, upon every proper occasion, issued a voice of surpassing cleanness, melody, and strength. In the matter of eyes, also, my acquaintance was pre-eminently endowed. Either one of such a pair was worth a couple of the ordinary ocular organs. They were of deep hazel, exceedingly large and lustrous; and there was perceptible about them, ever and anon, just that amount of interesting obliquity which gives pregnancy to expression.

The bust of the General was unquestionably the finest bust I ever saw. For your life you could not have found a fault with its wonderful proportion. This rare peculiarity set off to great advantage a pair of shoulders which would have called up a blush of conscious inferiority in to the countenance of the marble Apollo. I have a passion for fine shoulders, and may say that I never beheld them in perfection before. The arms altogether were admirably modelled. Nor were the lower limbs less superb. These were, indeed, the *ne plus ultra* of good legs. Every connoisseur in such matters admitted the legs to be good. There was neither too much flesh, nor too little, neither rudeness nor fragility. I could not imagine a more graceful curve than that of the *os femoris*, and there was just that due gentle prominence in the rear of the *fibula* which goes to the conformation of a properly-proportioned calf.

I wish to God my young and talented friend Chiponchipino, the sculptor, had but seen the legs of Brevet Brigadier-General John A. B. C. Smith.

But although men so absolutely fine-looking are neither as plenty as raisins or blackberries, still I could not bring myself to believe that *the remarkable* something to which I alluded just now, – that the odd air of *je ne sais quoi* which hung about my new acquaintance, – lay altogether, or indeed at all, in the supreme excellence of his bodily endowments. Perhaps it might be traced to the *manner*; yet here again I could not pretend to be positive. There *was* a primness, not to say stiffness, in his carriage – a degree of measured, and, if I may so express it, of rectangular precision, attending his every movement, which, observed in a more diminutive figure, would have had the least little savour in the world of affectation, pomposity, or constraint, but which, noticed in a gentleman of his undoubted dimensions, was readily placed to the account of reserve, *hauteur* – of a commendable sense, in short, of what is due to the dignity of colossal proportion.

The kind friend who presented me to General Smith whispered in my ear some few words of comment upon the man. 'He was a *remarkable* man – a *very* remarkable man – indeed one of the *most* remarkable men of the age. He was an especial favourite, too, with the ladies, chiefly on account of his high reputation for courage.

'In *that* point he is unrivalled, indeed he is a perfect desperado, a downright fire-eater, and no mistake,' said my friend, here dropping his voice excessively low, and thrilling me with the mystery of his tone.

'A downright fire-eater, and *no* mistake. Showed *that*, I should say, to some purpose in the late tremendous swamp-fight away down South with the Bugaboo and Kickapoo Indians.' (Here my friend opened his eyes to some extent.) 'Bless my soul! – blood and thunder, and all that! – *prodigies* of valour! – heard of him of course? – you know he's the man'——

'Man alive, how *do* you do? why how *are* ye? *very* glad to see ye indeed!' here interrupted the General himself, seizing my companion by the hand as he drew near, and bowing stiffly but profoundly as I was presented. I then thought (and I think so still) that I never heard a clearer nor a stronger voice, nor beheld a finer set of teeth, but I *must* say that I was sorry for the interruption just at that moment as, owing to the whispers and insinuations aforesaid, my interest had been greatly excited in the hero of the Bugaboo and Kickapoo campaign.

However, the delightfully luminous conversation of Brevet Brigadier-General John A. B. C. Smith soon completely dissipated this chagrin. My friend leaving us immediately, we had quite a long *tête-à-tête*, and I was not only pleased but *really* instructed. I never heard a more fluent talker, or a man of greater general information. With becoming modesty he forbore, nevertheless, to touch upon the theme I had just then most at heart – I mean the mysterious circumstances attending the Bugaboo war, and on my own part, what I conceive to be a proper sense of delicacy forbade me to broach the subject, although, in truth, I was exceedingly tempted to do so. I perceived, too, that the gallant soldier preferred topics of philosophical interest, and that he delighted especially in commenting upon the rapid march of mechanical invention. Indeed, lead him where I would, this was a point to which he invariably came back.

'There is nothing at all like it,' he would say; 'we are a wonderful people, and live in a wonderful age. Parachutes and rail-roads, man-traps and spring-guns! Our steamboats are upon every sea, and the Nassau balloon packet is about to run regular trips (fare either way only twenty pounds sterling) between London and Timbuctoo. And who shall calculate the immense influence upon social life, upon arts, upon commerce, upon literature, which will be the immediate result of the great principles of electro-magnetics! Nor is this all, let me assure you! There is really no end to the march of invention. The most wonderful, the most ingenious, and let me add, Mr. – Mr. – Thompson, I believe is your name – let me add, I say, the most *useful*, the most truly *useful* mechanical contrivances, are daily springing up like mushrooms, if I may so express myself, or more figuratively, like – ah – grasshoppers – like grasshoppers, Mr. Thompson – about us and ah – ah – ha around us!'

Thompson, to be sure, is not my name; but it is needless to say that I left General Smith with a heightened interest in the man, with an exalted opinion of his conversational powers, and a deep sense of the valuable privileges we enjoy in living in this age of mechanical invention. My curiosity, however, had not been altogether satisfied, and I resolved to prosecute immediate inquiry among my acquaintances, touching the Brevet Brigadier-General himself, and particularly respecting the tremendous events *quorum pars magna fuit*, during the Bugaboo and Kickapoo campaign.

The first opportunity which, presented itself, and which (*horresco referens*) I did not in the least scruple to seize, occurred at the church of the Reverend Doctor Drummummupp, where I found myself established one Sunday just at sermon-time, not only in the pew, but by the side of that worthy and communicative little friend of mine, Miss Tabitha T. Thus seated, I congratulated myself, and with much reason, upon the very flattering state of affairs. If any person knew anything about Brevet Brigadier-General John A. B. C. Smith, that person it was clear to me, was Miss Tabitha T. We telegraphed a few signals, and then commenced, *sotto voce*, a brisk *tête-à-tête*.

'Smith!' said she, in reply to my very earnest inquiry; 'Smith! – why, not General John A. B. C.? Bless me, I thought you *knew* all about *him*! This is a wonderfully inventive age! Horrid affair that! – a bloody set of wretches, those Kickapoos! – fought like a hero – prodigies of valour – immortal renown. Smith! Brevet Brigadier-General John A. B. C.! – why, you know he's the man'——

'Man,' here broke in Doctor Drummummupp, at the top of his voice, and with a thump that came near knocking the pulpit about our ears; 'man that is born of a woman hath but a short time to live; he cometh up and is cut down like a flower!' I started to the extremity of the pew, and perceived by the animated looks of the divine, that the wrath which had nearly proved fatal to the pulpit had been excited by the whispers of the lady and myself. There was no help for it; so I submitted with a good grace, and listened in all the martyrdom of dignified silence to the balance of that very capital discourse.

Next evening found me a somewhat late visitor at the Rantipole Theatre, where I felt sure of satisfying my curiosity at once, by merely stepping into the box of those exquisite specimens of affability and omniscience, the Misses Arabella and Miranda Cognoscenti. That fine tragedian, Climax, was doing Iago to a very crowded house, and I experienced some little difficulty in making my wishes understood; especially as our box was next the slips, and completely overlooked the stage.

'Smith!' said Miss Arabella, as she at length comprehended the purport of my query; 'Smith? – why, not General John A. B. C.?'

'Smith?' inquired Miranda, musingly. 'God bless me, did you ever behold a finer figure?'

'Never, madam, but *do* tell me'——

'Or such inimitable grace?'

'Never, upon my word! – but pray inform me'——

'Or so just an appreciation of stage effect?'

'Madam!'

'Or a more delicate sense of the true beauties of Shakespeare! Be so good as to look at that leg!'

'The devil!' and I turned again to her sister.

'Smith?' said she, 'why, not General John A. B. C.? Horrid affair that, wasn't it? – great wretches, those Bugaboos – savage and so on, but we live in a wonderfully inventive age! – Smith! – O yes! great man! – perfect desperado – immortal renown – prodigies of valour! *Never heard!*' (This was given in a scream.) 'Bless my soul! – why he's the man'——

'——Man-dragora
Nor all the drowsy syrups of the world
Shall ever medicine thee to that sweet sleep
Which thou owd'st yesterday!'

here roared out Climax just in my ear, and shaking his fist in my face all the time, in a way that I *couldn't* stand, and I *wouldn't*. I left the Misses Cognoscenti immediately, went behind the scenes forthwith, and gave the beggarly scoundrel such a thrashing as I trust he will remember to the day of his death.

At the *soirée* of the lovely widow Mrs. Kathleen O'Trump, I was confident that I should meet with no similar disappointment. Accordingly, I was no sooner seated at the card-table, with my pretty hostess for a *vis-à-vis*, than I propounded those questions the solution of which had become a matter so essential to my peace.

'Smith?' said my partner, 'why, not General John A. B. C.? Horrid affair that, wasn't it? – diamonds, did you say? – terrible wretches those Kickapoos! – we are playing *whist*, if you please, Mr. Tattle – however, this is the age of invention, most certainly *the age*, one may say – *the* age *par excellence* – speak French! – oh, quite a hero – perfect desperado! *no hearts*, Mr. Tattle? – I don't believe it! – immortal renown and all that – prodigies of valour! – *Never heard!!* – why, bless me, he's the man'——

'Mann –? *Captain* Mann?' here screamed some little feminine interloper from the farthest corner of the room. 'Are you talking about Captain Mann and the duel? – oh, I *must* hear – do tell – go on Mrs. O'Trump! – do now go on!' And go on Mrs. O'Trump did – all about a certain Captain Mann, who was either shot or hung, or should have been both shot and hung. Yes! Mrs. O'Trump, she went on, and I – I went off. There was no chance of hearing anything farther that evening in regard to Brevet Brigadier-General John A. B. C. Smith.

Still I consoled myself with the reflection that the tide of ill luck would not run against me for ever, and so determined to make a bold push for information at the rout of that bewitching little angel, the graceful Mrs. Pirouette.

'Smith?' said Mrs. P., as we twirled about together in a *pas de zéphyr*, 'Smith? – why not General John A. B. C.? Dreadful business that of the Bugaboos, wasn't it? – terrible creatures those Indians! *do* turn out your toes! I really am ashamed of you – man of great courage, poor fellow! – but this is a wonderful age of invention – O dear me, I'm out of breath – quite a desperado – prodigies of valour – *never heard!* – I can't believe it – I shall have to sit down and enlighten you – Smith! why he's the man'——

'Man-*Fred*, I tell you!' here bawled out Miss Bas-Bleu, as I led Mrs. Pirouette to a seat. 'Did ever anybody hear the like? It's Man-*Fred* I say, and not at all by any means Man-*Friday*.' Here Miss Bas-

Bleu beckoned to me in a very peremptory manner; and I was obliged, will I nill I, to leave Mrs. P., for the purpose of deciding a dispute touching the title of a certain poetical drama of Lord Byron's. Although I pronounced, with great promptness, that the true title was Man-*Friday*, and not by any means Man-*Fred*, yet when I returned to seek Mrs. Pirouette she was not to be discovered, and I made my retreat from the house in a very bitter spirit of animosity against the whole race of the Bas-Bleus.

Matters had now assumed a really serious aspect, and I resolved to call at once upon my particular friend Mr. Theodore Sinivate; for I knew that here at least I should get something like definite information.

'Smith?' said he, in his well-known peculiar way of drawling out his syllables; 'Smith! – why, not General John A. B. C.? Savage affair that with the Kickapo-o-o-os, wasn't it? Say, don't you think so? – perfect despera-a-ado – great pity, 'pon my honour! – wonderfully inventive age! – pro-o-odigies of valour! By-the-by, did you ever hear about Captain Ma-a-a-an?'

'Captain Mann be d—d!' said I, 'please to go on with your story.'

'Hem! oh well! – quite *la même cho-o-ose*, as we say in France. Smith, eh? Brigadier-General John A – B – C.? I say?' – (here Mr. S. thought proper to put his finger to the side of his nose) 'I say, you don't mean to insinuate now, really and truly, and conscientiously, that you don't know all about that affair of Smith's, as well as I do, eh? Smith? John A – B – C.? Why, bless me, he's the ma-a-an'——

'*Mr.* Sinivate,' said I, imploringly, '*is* he the man in the mask?'

'No-o-o!' said he, looking wise, 'nor the man in the mo-o-on.' This reply I considered a pointed and positive insult, and so left the house at once in high dudgeon, with a firm resolve to call my friend Mr. Sinivate to a speedy account for his ungentlemanly conduct and ill-breeding.

In the meantime, however, I had no notion of being thwarted touching the information I desired. There was one resource left me yet. I would go to the fountain-head. I would call forthwith upon the General himself, and demand, in explicit terms, a solution of this abominable piece of mystery. Here, at least, there should be no chance for equivocation. I would be plain, positive, peremptory – as short as pie-crust – as concise as Tacitus or Montesquieu.

It was early when I called, and the General was dressing; but I pleaded urgent business, and was shown at once into his bed-room by an old negro valet, who remained in attendance during my visit. As I entered the chamber, I looked about of course for the occupant, but did not immediately perceive him. There was a large and exceedingly odd-looking bundle of something which lay close by my feet on the floor, and as I was not in the best humour in the world, I gave it a kick out of the way.

'Hem! ahem! rather civil that, I should say!' said the bundle, in one of the smallest, and altogether the funniest little voices, between a squeak and a whistle, that I ever heard in all the days of my existence.

'Ahem! rather civil that, I should observe.'

I fairly shouted with terror, and made off at a tangent, into the farthest extremity of the room.

'God bless me! my dear fellow,' here again whistled the bundle, 'what – what – what – why, what *is* the matter? I really believe you don't know me at all.'

What *could* I say to all this – what *could* I? I staggered into an arm-chair, and with staring eyes and open mouth, awaited the solution of the wonder.

'Strange you shouldn't know me though, isn't it?' presently re-squeaked the nondescript, which I now perceived was performing upon the floor some inexplicable evolution, very analogous to the drawing on of a stocking. There was only a single leg, however, apparent.

'Strange, you shouldn't know me though, isn't it? Pompey, bring me that leg!' Here Pompey handed the bundle a very capital cork leg, already dressed, which it screwed on in a trice; and then it stood up before my eyes.

'And a bloody action it *was*,' continued the thing, as if in a soliloquy; but then one mustn't fight with the Bugaboos and Kickapoos, and think of coming off with a mere scratch. Pompey, I'll thank you now for that arm. Thomas' (turning to me) 'is decidedly the best hand at a cork leg; but if you should ever want an arm, my dear fellow, you must really let me recommend you to Bishop.' Here Pompey screwed on an arm.

'We had rather hot work of it, that you may say. Now you dog, slip on my shoulders and bosom! Pettitt makes the best shoulders, but for a bosom you will have to go to Ducrow.'

'Bosom!' said I.

'Pompey, will you *never* be ready with that wig? Scalping is a rough process after all; but then you can procure such a capital scratch at De L'Orme's.'

'Scratch!'

'Now you nigger, my teeth! For a *good* set of these you had better go to Parmly's at once; high prices but excellent work. I swallowed some very capital articles, though, when the big Bugaboo rammed me down with the butt end of his rifle.'

'Butt end! ram down!! my eye!!'

'O yes, by-the-by, my eye – her Pompey, you scamp, screw it in! Those Kickapoos are not so very slow at a gouge, but he's a belied man that Dr. Williams after all; you can't imagine how well I see with the eyes of his make.'

I now began very clearly to perceive that the object before me was nothing more nor less than my new acquaintance, Brevet Brigadier-General John A. B. C. Smith. The manipulations of Pompey had made, I must confess, a very striking difference in the appearance of the personal man. The voice, however, still puzzled me no little; but even this apparent mystery was speedily cleared up.

'Pompey, you black rascal,' squeaked the General, 'I really do believe you would let me go out without my palate.'

Hereupon the negro, grumbling out an apology went up to his master, opened his mouth with the knowing air of a horse-jockey, and adjusted therein a somewhat singular-looking machine, in a very dexterous manner, that I could not altogether comprehend. The alteration, however, in the entire expression of the General's counten-ance was instantaneous and surprising. When he again spoke, his voice had resumed all that rich melody and strength which I had noticed upon our original introduction.

'D—n the vagabonds!' said he, in so clear a tone that I positively started at the change, 'D—n the vagabonds! they not only knocked in the roof of my mouth, but took the trouble to cut off at least seven-eighths of my tongue. There isn't Bonfanti's equal, however, in America, for really good articles of this description. I can recommend you to him with confidence' (here the General bowed), 'and assure you that I have the greatest pleasure in so doing.'

I acknowledged his kindness in my best manner, and took leave of him at once, with a perfect understanding of the true state of affairs – with a full comprehension of the mystery which had troubled me so long. It was evident. It was a clear case. Brevet Brigadier-General John A. B. C. Smith was the man – was *the man that was used up*.

Loss of Breath

A Tale neither in nor out of 'Blackwood'

O breathe not, etc. – *Moore's Melodies.*

The most notorious ill-fortune must in the end yield to the untiring courage of philosophy – as the most stubborn city to the ceaseless vigilance of an enemy. Shalmanezer, as we have it in the holy writings, lay three years before Samaria; yet it fell. Sardanapalus – see Diodorus – maintained himself seven in Nineveh; but to no purpose. Troy expired at the close of the second lustrum; and Azoth, as Aristæus declares upon his honour as a gentleman, opened at last her gates to Psammetichus, after having barred them for the fifth part of a century. . . .

'Thou wretch! – thou vixen! – thou shrew!' said I to my wife on the morning after our wedding, 'thou witch! – thou hag! – thou whipper-snapper! – thou sink of iniquity! – thou fiery-faced quintessence of all that is abominable! – thou – thou' – here standing upon tiptoe, seizing her by the throat, and placing my mouth close to her ear, I was preparing to launch forth a new and more decided epithet of opprobrium, which should not fail, if ejaculated, to convince her of her insignificance, when to my extreme horror and astonishment I discovered that *I had lost my breath.*

The phrases 'I am out of breath,' 'I have lost my breath,' etc., are often enough repeated in common conversation; but it had never occurred to me that the terrible accident of which I speak could *bona fide* and actually happen! Imagine – that is if you have a fanciful turn – imagine, I say, my wonder – my consternation – my despair!

There is a good genius, however, which has never entirely deserted me. In my most ungovernable moods I still retain a sense of propriety, *et le chemin de passions me conduit* – as Lord Edouard in the 'Julie' says it did him – *à la philosophie veritable.*

Although I could not at first precisely ascertain to what degree the occurrence had affected me, I determined at all events to conceal the matter from my wife until further experience should discover to me the extent of this my unheard of calamity. Altering my countenance, therefore, in a moment, from its bepuffed and distorted appearance to an expression of arch and coquettish benignity, I gave my lady a pat on the one cheek, and a kiss on the other, and without saying one syllable (Furies! I could not), left her astonished at my drollery, as I pirouetted out of the room, in a *Pas de Zéphyr.*

Behold me then safely ensconced in my private *boudoir*, a fearful instance of the ill consequences attending upon irascibility – alive, with the qualifications of the dead – dead, with the propensities of the living – an anomaly on the face of the earth – being very calm, yet breathless.

Yes! breathless. I am serious in asserting that my breath was entirely gone. I could not have stirred with it a feather if my life had been at issue, or sullied even the delicacy of a mirror. Hard fate! yet there was some alleviation to the first overwhelming paroxysm of my sorrow. I found, upon trial, that the powers of utterance which, upon my inability to proceed in the conversation with my wife, I then concluded to be totally destroyed, were in fact only partially impeded, and I discovered that had I at that interesting crisis, dropped my voice to a singularly deep guttural, I might still have continued to her the communication of my sentiments; this pitch of voice (the guttural) depending. I find, not upon the current of the breath, but upon a certain spasmodic action of the muscles of the throat.

Throwing myself upon a chair, I remained for some time absorbed in meditation. My reflections, to be sure, were of no consolatory kind. A thousand vague and lachrymatory fancies took possession of my soul – and even the idea of suicide flitted across my brain; but it is a trait in the perversity of human nature to reject the obvious and the ready for the far-distant and equivocal. Thus I shuddered at self-murder as the most decided of atrocities, while the tabby cat purred strenuously upon the rug, and the very water-dog wheezed assiduously under the table; each taking to itself much merit for the strength of its lungs, and all obviously done in derision of my own pulmonary incapacity.

Oppressed with a tumult of vague hopes and fears, I at length heard the footsteps of my wife descending the staircase. Being now assured of her absence, I returned with a palpitating heart to the scene of my disaster.

Carefully locking the door on the inside, I commenced a vigorous search. It was possible, I thought that, concealed in some obscure corner, or lurking in some closet or drawer, might be found the lost object of my inquiry. It might have a vapoury – it might even have a tangible form. Most philosophers, upon many points of philosophy, are still very unphilosophical. William Godwin, however, says in his 'Mandeville,' that 'invisible things are the only realities,' and this, all will allow, is a case in point. I would have the judicious reader pause before accusing such asseverations of an undue quantum of absurdity. Anaxagoras, it will be remembered, maintained that snow is black, and this I have since found to be the case.

Long and earnestly did I continue the investigation: but the contemptible reward of my industry and perseverance proved to be only a set of false teeth, two pairs of hips, an eye, and a bundle of *billet-doux* from Mr. Windenough to my wife. I might as well here observe that this confirmation of my lady's partiality for Mr. W. occasioned me little uneasiness. That Mrs. Lackobreath should admire anything so dissimilar to myself was a natural and necessary evil. I am, it is well known, of a robust and corpulent appearance, and at the same time somewhat diminutive in stature. What wonder then that the lath-like tenuity of my acquaintance, and his altitude, which has grown into a proverb, should have met with all due estimation in the eyes of Mrs. Lackobreath. But to return.

My exertions, as I have before said, proved fruitless. Closet after closet – drawer after drawer – corner after corner – were scrutinised to no purpose. At one time, however, I thought myself sure of my prize, having, in rummaging a dressing-case, accidentally demolished a bottle of Grandjean's Oil of Archangels – which, as an agreeable perfume, I here take the liberty of recommending.

With a heavy heart I returned to my *boudoir* – there to ponder upon some method of eluding my wife's penetration, until I could make arrangements prior to my leaving the country, for to this I had already made up my mind. In a foreign climate, being unknown, I might, with some probability of success, endeavour to conceal my unhappy calamity – a calamity calculated, even more than beggary, to estrange the affections of the multitude, and to draw down upon the wretch the well-merited indignation of the virtuous and the happy. I was not long in hesitation. Being naturally quick, I committed to memory the entire tragedy of 'Metamora.' I had the good fortune to recollect that in the accentuation of this drama, or at least of such portion of it as is allotted to the hero, the tones of voice in which I found myself deficient were altogether unnecessary, and that the deep guttural was expected to reign monotonously throughout.

I practised for some time by the borders of a well-frequented marsh; – herein, however, having no reference to a similar proceeding of Demosthenes, but from a design peculiarly and conscientiously my own. Thus armed at all points, I determined to make my wife believe that I was suddenly smitten with a passion for the stage. In this I succeeded to a miracle; and to every question or suggestion found myself at liberty to reply in my most frog-like and sepulchral tones with some passage from the tragedy – any portion of which, as I soon took great pleasure in observing, would apply equally well to any particular subject. It is not to be supposed, however, that in the delivery of such passages I was found at all deficient in the looking asquint – the showing my teeth – the working my knees – the shuffling my feet – or in any of those unmentionable graces which are now justly considered the characteristics of a popular performer. To be sure they spoke of confining me in a strait-jacket – but, Good God! they never suspected me of having lost my breath.

Having at length put my affairs in order, I took my seat very early one morning in the mail stage for ———, giving it to be understood among my acquaintances that business of the last importance required my immediate personal attendance in that city.

The coach was crammed to repletion; but in the uncertain twilight the features of my companions could not be distinguished. Without making any effectual resistance, I suffered myself to be placed between two gentlemen of colossal dimensions; while a third, of a size larger, requesting pardon for the liberty he was about to take, threw himself upon my body at full length, and falling asleep in an instant, drowned all my guttural ejaculations for relief, in a snore which would have put to blush the roarings of the bull of Phalaris. Happily the state of my respiratory faculties rendered suffocation an accident entirely out of the question.

As however, the day broke more distinctly in our approach to the outskirts of the city, my tormentor, arising and adjusting his shirt-collar, thanked me in a very friendly manner for my civility. Seeing that I remained motionless (all my limbs were dislocated and my head twisted on one side,) his apprehensions began to be excited; and arousing the rest of the passengers, he communicated in a very decided manner, his opinion that a dead man had been palmed upon them during the night for a living and responsible fellow-traveller; here giving me a thump on the right eye, by way of demonstrating the truth of his suggestion.

Hereupon all, one after another (there were nine in company), believed it their duty to pull me by the ear. A young practising physician, too, having applied a pocket-mirror to my mouth, and found me without breath, the assertion of my persecutor was pronounced a true bill; and the whole party expressed a determination to endure tamely no such impositions for the future, and to proceed no farther with any such carcases for the present.

I was here, accordingly, thrown out at the sign of the 'Crow' (by which tavern the coach happened to be passing) without meeting with any farther accident than the breaking of both my arms under the left hind wheel of the vehicle. I must besides do the driver the justice to state that he did not forget to throw after me the largest of my trunks, which unfortunately falling on my head, fractured my skull in a manner at once interesting and extraordinary.

The landlord of the 'Crow,' who is a hospitable man, finding that my trunk contained sufficient to indemnify him for any little trouble he might take in my behalf, sent forthwith for a surgeon of his acquaintance, and delivered me to his care with a bill and receipt for ten dollars.

The purchaser took me to his apartments and commenced operations immediately. Having cut off my ears, however, he discovered signs of animation. He now rang the bell, and sent for a neighbouring apothecary with whom to consult in the emergency. In case of his suspicions with regard to my existence proving ultimately correct, he, in the meantime, made an incision in my stomach, and removed several of my viscera for private dissection.

The apothecary had an idea that I was actually dead. This idea I endeavoured to confute, kicking and plunging with all my might, and making the most furious contortions – for the operations of the surgeon had, in a measure, restored me to the possession of my faculties. All, however, was attributed to the effects of a new galvanic battery, wherewith the apothecary, who is really a man of information, performed several curious experiments, in which, from my personal share in their fulfilment, I could not help feeling deeply interested. It was a source of mortification to me, nevertheless, that although I made several attempts at conversation, my powers of speech were so entirely in abeyance that I could not even open my mouth; much less than make reply to some ingenious but fanciful theories of which under other circumstances my minute acquaintance with the Hippocratian pathology would have afforded me a ready confutation.

Not being able to arrive at a conclusion, the practitioners remanded me for farther examination. I was taken up into a garret; and the surgeon's lady having accommodated me with drawers and stockings, the surgeon himself fastened my hands, and tied up my jaws with a pocket-handkerchief – then bolted the door on the outside as he hurried to his dinner, leaving me alone to silence and to meditation.

I now discovered to my extreme delight that I could have spoken had not my mouth been tied up by the pocket-handkerchief. Consoling myself with this reflection, I was mentally repeating some passages of the 'Omnipresence of the Deity,' as is my custom before resigning myself to sleep, when two cats, of a greedy and vituperative turn entering at a hole in the wall, leaped up with a flourish *à la Catalani*, and alighting opposite one another on my visage, betook themselves of indecorous contention for the paltry consideration of my nose.

But, as the loss of his ears proved the means of elevating to the throne of Cyrus, the Magian or Mige-Gush of Persia, and as the cutting off his nose gave Zopyrus possession of Babylon, so the loss of a few ounces of my countenance proved the salvation of my body. Aroused by the pain, and burning with indignation, I burst, at a single effort, the fastenings and the bandage. Stalking across the room I cast a glance of contempt at the belligerents, and throwing open the sash to their extreme horror and disappointment, precipitated myself very dexterously from the window.

The mail-robber W——, to whom I bore a singular resemblance, was at this moment passing from the city jail to the scaffold erected for his execution in the suburbs. His extreme infirmity and long continued ill health had obtained him the privilege of remaining unmanacled; and habited in his gallows costume – one very similar to my own – he lay at full length in the bottom of the hangman's cart (which happened to be under the windows of the surgeon at the moment of my precipitation) without any other guard than the driver who was asleep, and two recruits of the sixth infantry who were drunk.

As ill-luck would have it, I alit upon my feet within the vehicle. W——, who was an acute fellow, perceived his opportunity. Leaping up immediately, he bolted out behind, and turning down an alley, was out of sight in the twinkling of an eye. The recruits, aroused by the bustle could not exactly comprehend the merits of the transaction. Seeing, however, a man, the precise counterpart of the felon, standing upright in the cart before their eyes, they were of opinion that the rascal (meaning W——) was after making his escape (so they expressed themselves), and, having communicated this opinion to one another, they took each a dram, and then knocked me down with the butt-ends of their muskets.

It was not long ere we arrived at the place of destination. Of course nothing could be said in my defence. Hanging was my inevitable fate. I resigned myself thereto with a feeling half stupid, half acrimonious. Being little of a cynic, I had all the sentiments of a dog. The hangman, however, adjusted the noose about my neck. The drop fell.

I forbear to depict my sensations upon the gallows; although here undoubtedly, I could speak to the point, and it is a topic upon which nothing has been well said. In fact, to write upon such a theme it is necessary to have been hanged. Every author should confine himself to matters of experience. Thus Mark Antony composed a treatise upon getting drunk.

I may just mention, however, that die I did not. My body *was*, but I had no breath *to be* suspended; and but for the knot under my left ear (which had the feel of a military stock) I dare say that I should have experienced very little inconvenience. As for the jerk given to my neck upon the falling of the drop, it merely proved a corrective to the twist afforded me by the fat gentleman in the coach.

For good reasons, however, I did my best to give the crowd the worth of their trouble. My convulsions were said to be extraordinary. My spasms it would have been difficult to beat. The populace *encored*. Several gentlemen swooned; and a multitude of ladies were carried home in hysterics. Pinxit availed himself of the opportunity to retouch, from a sketch taken upon the spot, his admirable painting of the 'Marsyas flayed alive.'

When I had afforded sufficient amusement, it was thought proper to remove my body from the gallows; – this the more especially as the real culprit had in the meantime been retaken and recognised; a fact which I was so unlucky as not to know.

Much sympathy was of course exercised in my behalf, and as no one made claim to my corpse, it was ordered that I should be interred in a public vault.

Here after due interval I was deposited. The sexton departed, and I was left alone. A line of Marston's 'Malcontent' –

'Death's a good fellow and keeps open house' –

struck me at that moment as a palpable lie.

I knocked off, however, the lid of my coffin, and stepped out. The place was dreadfully dreary and damp, and I became troubled with *ennui*. By way of amusement, I felt my way among the numerous coffins ranged in order around. I lifted them down one by one, and breaking open their lids, busied myself in speculations about the mortality within.

'This,' I soliloquised, tumbling over a carcase, puffy, bloated and rotund – 'this has been, no doubt, in every sense of the word, an unhappy – an unfortunate man. It has been his terrible lot not to walk but to waddle – to pass through life not like a human being, but like an elephant – not like a man but like a rhinoceros.

'His attempts at getting on have been mere abortions, and his circumgyratory proceedings a palpable failure. Taking a step forward, it has been his misfortune to take two towards the right, and three towards the left. His studies have been confined to the poetry of Crabbe. He can have had no idea of the wonder of a *pirouette*. To him a *pas de papillon* has been an abstract conception. He has never ascended the summit of a hill. He has never viewed from any steeple the glories of a metropolis. Heat has been his mortal enemy. In the dog-days his days have been the days of a dog. Therein, he has dreamed of flames and suffocation – of mountains upon mountains – of Pelion upon Ossa. He was short of breath – to say all in a word, he was short of breath. He thought it extravagant to play upon wind instruments. He was the inventor of self-moving fans, wind-sails, and ventilators. He patronised Du Pont the bellows-maker, and died miserably in attempting to smoke a cigar. His was a case in which I feel a deep interest – a lot in which I sincerely sympathise. But here,' – said I – 'here' – and I dragged spitefully from its receptacle a gaunt tall, and peculiar-looking form, whose remarkable appearance struck me with a sense of unwelcome familiarity – 'here is a wretch entitled to no earthly commiseration.' Thus saying in order to obtain a more distinct view of my subject, I applied my thumb and forefinger to its nose, and causing it to assume a sitting position upon the ground, held it thus, at the length of my arm, while I continued my soliloquy.

– 'Entitled,' I repeated, 'to no earthly commiseration. Who indeed would think of compassionating a shadow? Besides, has he not had his full share of the blessings of mortality? He was the originator of tall monuments – shot towers – lightning rods – Lombardy-poplars. His treatise upon "Shades and Shadows" has immortalised him. He edited with distinguished ability the last edition of "South on the Bones." He went early to college and studied pneumatics. He then came home, talked eternally, and played upon the French horn. He patronised the bagpipes. Captain Barclay, who walked against Time, would not walk against *him*. Windham and Allbreath were his favourite writers – his favourite artist, Phiz. He died gloriously while inhaling gas – *levique flatu corrupitur*, like the *fama pudicitiæ* in Hieronymus.* He was indubitably a' –

'How *can* you? – how – *can* – you?' – interrupted the object of my animadversions, gasping for breath, and tearing off, with a desperate exertion, the bandage around its jaws – 'how *can* you, Mr. Lackobreath, be so infernally cruel as to pinch me in that manner by the nose? Did you not see how they had fastened up my mouth – and you *must* know – if you know anything – how vast a superfluity of breath I have to dispose of! If you do *not* know, however, sit down and you shall see. – In my situation it is really a great relief to be able to open one's mouth – to be able to expatiate – to be able to communicate

---

* *Tenera res in feminis fama pudicitiæ, et quasi flos pulcherrimus cito ad levem marcessit auram, levique flatu corrupitur, maxime etc.* – Hieronymus ad Salvinam.

with a person like yourself, who do not think yourself called upon at every period to interrupt the thread of a gentleman's discourse. — Interruptions are annoying and should undoubtedly be abolished — don't you think so? — no reply. I beg you, — one person is enough to be speaking at a time. — I shall be done by-and-by, and then you may begin. — How the devil, sir, did you get into this place? — not a word I beseech you — been here sometime myself — terrible accident! — heard of it I suppose — awful calamity! — walking under your windows — some short while ago — about the time you were stage struck — horrible occurrence! — heard of "catching one's breath," eh? — hold your tongue, I tell you! I caught somebody else's! — had always too much of my own — met Blab at the corner of the street — wouldn't give me a chance for a word — couldn't get in a syllable edgeways — attacked, consequently, with epilepsis — Blab made his escape — damn all fools! — they took me up for dead, and put me in this place — pretty doings all of them! — heard all you said about me — every word a lie — horrible! — wonderful! — outrageous! — hideous! — incomprehensible! — et cetera — et cetera — et cetera — et cetera——'

It is impossible to conceive my astonishment at so unexpected a discourse; or the joy with which I became gradually convinced that the breath so fortunately caught by the gentleman (whom I soon recognised as my neighbour Windenough) was, in fact, the identical expiration mislaid by myself in the conversation with my wife. Time, place, and circumstance rendered it a matter beyond question. I did not, however, immediately release my hold upon Mr. W.'s proboscis — not at least during the long period in which the inventor of Lombardy-poplars continued to favour me with his explanations.

In this respect I was actuated by that habitual prudence which has ever been my predominating trait. I reflected that many difficulties might still lie in the path of preservation which only extreme exertion on my part would be able to surmount. Many persons, I considered, are prone to estimate commodities in their possession — however valueless to the then proprietor — however troublesome, or distressing — in direct ratio with the advantages to be derived by others from their attainment, or by themselves from their abandonment.

Might not this be the case with Mr. Windenough? In displaying anxiety for the breath of which he was at present so willing to get rid, might I not lay myself open to the exactions of his avarice? There are scoundrels in this world, I remembered with a sigh, who will not scruple to take unfair opportunities with even a next door neighbour, and (this remark is from Epictetus) it is precisely at that time when men are most anxious to throw off the burden of their own calamities that they feel the least desirous of relieving them in others.

Upon considerations similar to these, and still retaining my grasp upon the nose of Mr. W., I accordingly thought proper to model my reply.

'Monster!' I began in a tone of the deepest indignation, 'monster; and double-winded idiot! – dost *thou*, whom for thine iniquities it has pleased heaven to accurse with a two-fold respiration – dost *thou*, I say, presume to address me in the familiar language of an old acquaintance? – "I lie," forsooth! – and "hold my tongue," to be sure! – pretty conversation indeed to a gentleman with a single breath! – all this too, when I have it in my power to relieve the calamity under which thou dost so justly suffer, to curtail the superfluities of thine unhappy respiration.'

Like Brutus, I paused for a reply, with which, like a tornado, Mr. Windenough immediately overwhelmed me. Protestation followed upon protestation, and apology upon apology. There were no terms with which he was unwilling to comply, and there were none of which I failed to take the fullest advantage.

Preliminaries being at length arranged, my acquaintance delivered me the respiration; for which (having carefully examined it) I gave him afterwards a receipt. I am aware that by many I shall be held to blame for speaking, in a manner so cursory, of a transaction so impalpable. It will be thought that I should have entered more minutely into the details of an occurrence by which – and this is very true – much new light might be thrown upon a highly interesting branch of physical philosophy.

To all this I am sorry that I cannot reply. A hint is the only answer which I am permitted to make. There were *circumstances* – but I think it much safer upon consideration to say as little as possible about an affair *so delicate*? I repeat, and at the time involving the interests of a third party whose sulphurous resentment I have not the least desire at this moment of incurring.

We were not long after this necessary arrangement in effecting an escape from the dungeons of the sepulchre. The united strength of our resuscitated voices was soon sufficiently apparent. Scissors, the Whig Editor, republished a treatise upon 'the nature and origin of sub-terranean noises.' A reply – rejoinder – confutation – and justification – followed in the columns of a Democratic Gazette. It was not until the opening of the vault to decide the controversy that the appearance of Mr. Windenough and myself proved both parties to have been decidedly in the wrong.

I cannot conclude these details of some very singular passages in a life at all times sufficiently eventful, without again recalling to the attention of the reader the merits of that indiscriminate philosophy which is a sure and ready shield against those shafts of calamity which can neither be seen, felt, nor fully understood. It was in the spirit of this wisdom that, among the Ancient Hebrews, it was believed the gates of Heaven would be inevitably opened to that sinner, or saint, who with good lungs and implicit confidence should vociferate the word '*Amen!*' It was in the spirit of this wisdom that, when a great plague raged at Athens, and every means had been in vain attempted for its removal, Epimenides, as Laertius relates in his second book of that philosopher, advised the erection of a shrine and temple 'to the proper God.'

LYTTLETON BARRY.

A Descent into the Maelström

The ways of God in Nature, as in Providence, are not as *our* ways; nor are the models that we frame any way commensurate to the vastness, profundity, and unsearchableness of His works, *which have a depth in them greater than the well of Democritus.*

Joseph Glanville.

We had now reached the summit of the loftiest crag. For some minutes the old man seemed too much exhausted to speak. 'Not long ago,' said he at length, 'and I could have guided you on this route as well as the youngest of my sons; but, about three years past, there happened to me an event such as never happened before to mortal man – or at least such as no man ever survived to tell of – and the six hours of deadly terror which I then endured have broken me up body and soul. You suppose me a *very* old man – but I am not. It took less than a single day to change these hairs from a jetty black to white, to weaken my limbs, and to unstring my nerves, so that I tremble at the least exertion, and am frightened at a shadow. Do you know I can scarcely look over this little cliff without getting giddy?'

The 'little cliff,' upon whose edge he had so carelessly thrown himself down to rest that the weightier portion of his body hung over it, while he was only kept from falling by the tenure of his elbow on its extreme and slippery edge – this 'little cliff' arose, a sheer unobstructed precipice of black shining rock, some fifteen or sixteen hundred feet from the world of crags beneath us. Nothing would have tempted me to within half-a-dozen yards of its brink. In truth, so deeply was I excited by the perilous position of my companion, that I fell at full length upon the ground, clung to the shrubs around me, and dared not even glance upward at the sky – while I strugged in vain to divest myself of the idea that the very foundations of the mountain were in danger from the fury of the winds. It was long before I could reason myself into sufficient courage to sit up and look out into the distance.

'You must get over these fancies,' said the guide, 'for I have brought you here that you might have the best possible view of the scene of that event I mentioned – and to tell you the whole story with the spot just under your eye.

'We are now,' he continued in that particularising manner which distinguished him – 'we are now close upon the Norwegian coast – in the sixty-eighth degree of latitude – in the great province of Nordland – and in the dreary district of Lofoden. The mountain upon whose top we sit is Helseggen, the Cloudy. Now raise yourself up a little higher – hold on to the grass if you feel giddy – so – and look out, beyond the belt of vapour beneath us, into the sea.'

I looked dizzily, and beheld a wide expanse of ocean, whose waters wore so inky a hue as to bring at once to my mind the Nubian geographer's account of the *Mare Tenebrarum*. A panorama more deplorably desolate no human imagination can conceive. To the right and left, as far as the eye could reach, there lay outstretched, like ramparts of the world, lines of horridly black and beetling cliff, whose character of gloom was but the more forcibly illustrated by the surf which reared high up against its white and ghastly crest, howling and shrieking for ever. Just opposite the promontory upon whose apex we were placed, and at a distance of some five or six miles out at sea, there was visible a small, bleak-looking island; or, more properly, its position was discernible through the wilderness of surge in which it was enveloped. About two miles nearer the land arose another of smaller size, hideously craggy and barren, and encompassed at various intervals by a cluster of dark rocks.

The appearance of the ocean, in the space between the more distant island and the shore, had something very unusual about it. Although at the time so strong a gale was blowing landward that a brig in the remote offing lay to under a double-reefed try-sail, and constantly plunged her whole hull out of sight, still there was here nothing like a regular swell, but only a short, quick, angry cross dashing of water in every direction – as well in the teeth of the wind as otherwise. Of foam there was little except in the immediate vicinity of the rocks.

'The island in the distance,' resumed the old man, 'is called by the Norwegians Vurrgh. The one midway is Moskoe. That a mile to the northward is Ambaaren. Yonder are Islesen, Hotholm, Keildhelm, Suarven, and Buckholm. Farther off – between Moskoe and Vurrgh – are Otterholm, Flimen, Sandflesen, and Stockholm. These are the true names of the places – but why it has been thought necessary to name them at all, is more than either you or I can understand. Do you hear anything? Do you see any change in the water?'

We had now been about ten minutes upon the top of Helseggen, to which we had ascended from the interior of Lofoden, so that we had caught no glimpse of the sea until it had burst upon us from the summit. As the old man spoke, I became aware of a loud and gradually increasing sound, like the moaning of a vast herd of buffaloes upon an American prairie; and at the same moment I perceived that what seamen term the *chopping* character of the ocean beneath us, was rapidly changing into a current which set to the eastward. Even while I gazed this current acquired a monstrous velocity. Each moment added to its speed – to its headlong impetuosity. In five minutes the whole sea as far as Vurrgh was lashed into ungovernable fury: but it was between Moskoe and the coast that the main uproar held its sway. Here the vast bed of the waters, seamed and scarred into a thousand conflicting channels, burst suddenly into frenzied convulsion – heaving, boiling, hissing, – gyrating in gigantic and innumerable vortices, and all whirling and plunging on to the eastward with a rapidity which water never elsewhere assumes except in precipitous descents.

In a few minutes more, there came over the scene another radical alteration. The general surface grew somewhat more smooth, and the whirlpools one by one disappeared, while prodigious streaks of foam became apparent where none had been seen before. These streaks, at length, spreading out to a great distance, and entering into combination, took unto themselves the gyratory motion of the subsided vortices, and seemed to form the germ of another more vast. Suddenly – very suddenly – this assumed a distinct and definite existence in a circle of more than a mile in diameter. The edge of the whirl was represented by a broad belt of gleaming spray; but no particle of this slipped into the mouth of the terrific funnel, whose interior, as far as the eye could fathom it, was a smooth, shining, and jet-black wall of water, inclined to the horizon at an angle of some forty-five degrees, speeding dizzily round and round with a swaying and sweltering motion, and sending forth to the winds an appalling voice, half-shriek, half-roar, such as not even the mighty cataract of Niagara ever lifts up in its agony to Heaven.

The mountain trembled to its very base, and the rock rocked. I threw myself upon my face, and clung to the scant herbage in an excess of nervous agitation.

'This,' said I at length, to the old man – 'this *can* be nothing else than the great whirlpool of the Maelström.'

'So it is sometimes termed,' said he. 'We Norwegians call it the Moskoe-ström, from the island of Moskoe in the midway.'

The ordinary accounts of this vortex had by no means prepared me for what I saw. That of Jonas Ramus, which is perhaps the most circumstantial of any, cannot impart the faintest conception either of the magnificence, or of the horror of the scene – or of the wild bewildering sense of *the novel* which confounds the beholder. I am not sure from what point of view the writer in question surveyed it, nor at what time; but it could neither have been from the summit of Helseggen, nor during a storm. There are some passages of his description, nevertheless, which may be quoted for their details, although their effect is exceedingly feeble in conveying an impression of the spectacle.

'Between Lofoden and Moskoe,' he says, 'the depth of the water is between thirty-five and forty fathoms; but on the other side, towards Ver (Vurrgh) this depth decreases so as not to afford a convenient passage for a vessel, without the risk of splitting on the rocks, which happens even in the calmest weather. When it is in flood, the stream runs up the country between Lofoden and Moskoe with a boisterous rapidity, but the roar of its impetuous ebb to the sea is scarce equalled by the loudest and most dreadful cataracts – the noise being heard several leagues off, and the vortices or pits are of such an extent and depth, that if a ship comes within its attraction it is inevitably absorbed and carried down to the bottom and there beaten to pieces against the rocks, and when the water relaxes the fragments thereof are thrown up again. But these intervals of tranquillity are only at the turn of the ebb and flood, and in calm weather, and last but a quarter of an hour, its violence gradually returning. When the stream is most boisterous, and its fury heightened by a storm, it is dangerous to come within a Norway mile of it. Boats, yachts, and ships have been carried away by not guarding against it before they were within in its reach. It likewise happens frequently that whales come too near the stream, and are overpowered by its violence, and then it is impossible to describe their howlings and bellowings in their fruitless struggles to disengage themselves. A bear once, attempting to swim from Lofoden to Moskoe, was caught by the stream and borne down, while he roared terribly, so as to be heard on shore. Large stocks of firs and pine trees, after being absorbed by the current, rise again broken and torn to such a degree as if bristles grew upon them. This plainly shows the bottom to consist of craggy rocks, among which they are whirled to and fro. This stream is regulated by the flux and reflux of the sea – it being constantly high and low water every six hours. In the year 1645, early in the morning of Sexagesima Sunday, it raged with such noise and impetuosity that the very stones of the houses on the coast fell to the ground.'

In regard to the depth of the water, I could not see how this could have been ascertained at all in the immediate vicinity of the vortex. The 'forty fathoms' must have reference only to portions of the channel close upon the shore either of Moskoe or Lofoden. The depth in the centre of the Moskoe-ström must be immeasurably greater; and no better proof of this fact is necessary than can be obtained from even the sidelong glance into the abyss of the whirl which may be had from the highest crag of Helseggen. Looking down from this pinnacle upon the howling Phlegethon below, I could not help smiling at the simplicity with which the honest Jonas Ramus records, as a matter difficult of belief, the anecdotes of the whales and the bears; for it appeared to me, in fact, a self-evident thing that the largest ship of the line in existence coming within the influence of that deadly attraction could resist it as little as a feather the hurricane, and must disappear bodily and at once.

The attempts to account for the phenomenon – some of which I remember seemed to me sufficiently plausible in persual, now wore a very different and unsatisfactory aspect. The idea generally received is that this, as well as three smaller vortices among the Ferroe Islands, 'have no other cause than the collision of waves rising and falling at flux and reflux against a ridge of rocks and shelves, which confines the water so that it precipitates itself like a cataract; and thus the higher the flood rises the deeper must the fall be, and the natural result of all is as a whirlpool or vortex, the prodigious suction of which is sufficiently known by lesser experiments.' These are the words of the Encyclopædia Britannica. – Kircher and others imagine that in the centre of the channel of the Maelström is an abyss penetrating the globe, and issuing in some very remote part – the Gulf of Bothnia being somewhat decidedly named in one instance. This opinion, idle in itself, was the one to which, as I gazed, my imagination most readily assented; and, mentioning it to the guide, I was rather surprised to hear him say that, although it was the view almost universally entertained of the subject by the Norwegians, it nevertheless was not his own. As to the former notion he confessed his inability to comprehend it; and here I agreed with him – for, however conclusive on paper, it becomes altogether unintelligible, and even absurd, amid the thunder of the abyss.

'You have had a good look at the whirl now,' said the old man, 'and if you will creep round this crag so as to get in its lee, and deaden the roar of the water, I will tell you a story that will convince you I ought to know something of the Moskoe-ström.'

I placed myself as desired, and he proceeded.

'Myself and my two brothers once owned a schooner-rigged smack of about seventy tons burden, with which we were in the habit of fishing among the islands, beyond Moskoe, nearly to Vurrgh. In all violent eddies at sea there is good fishing at proper opportunities if one has only the courage to attempt it, but among the whole of the Lofoden coastmen, we three were the only ones who made a regular business of going out to the islands, as I tell you. The usual grounds are a great way lower down to the southward. There fish can be got at all hours, without much risk, and therefore these places are preferred. The choice spots over here among the rocks, however, not only yield the finest variety, but in far greater abundance, so that we often got in a single day what the more timid of the craft could not scrape together in a week. In fact, we made it a matter of desperate speculation – the risk of life standing instead of labour, and courage answering for capital.

'We kept the smack in a cove about five miles higher up the coast than this; and it was our practice, in fine weather, to take advantage of the fifteen minutes' slack to push across the main channel of the Moskoe-ström, far above the pool, and then drop down upon anchorage somewhere near Otterholm, or Sandflesen, where the eddies are not so violent as elsewhere. Here we used to remain until nearly time for slack-water again when we weighed and made for home. We never set out upon this expedition without a steady side wind for going and coming – one that we felt sure would not fail us before our return – and we seldom made a miscalculation upon this point. Twice during six years we were forced to stay all night at anchor on account of a dead calm, which is a rare thing indeed just about here; and once we had to remain on the grounds nearly a week, starving to death, owing to a gale which blew up shortly after our arrival, and made the channel too boisterous to be thought of. Upon this occasion we should have been driven out to sea in spite of everything (for the whirlpools threw us round and round so violently that at length we fouled our anchor and dragged it) if it had not been that we drifted into one of the innumerable cross currents – here to-day and gone to-morrow – which drove us under the lee of Flimen, where, by good luck, we brought up.

'I could not tell you the twentieth part of the difficulties we encountered "on the grounds" – it is a bad spot to be in, even in good weather – but we made shift always to run the gauntlet of the Moskoe-ström itself without accident; although at times my heart has been in my mouth when we happened to be a minute or so behind or before the slack. The wind sometimes was not as strong as we thought it at starting, and then we made rather less way than we could wish, while the current rendered the smack unmanageable. My eldest brother had a son eighteen years old, and I had two stout boys of my own. These would have been of great assistance at such times in using the sweeps, as well as afterward in fishing, but somehow, although we ran the risk ourselves, we had not the heart to let the young ones get into the danger – for, after all is said and done, it *was* a horrible danger, and that is the truth.

'It is now within a few days of three years since what I am going to tell you occurred. It was on the tenth day of July 18—, a day which the people of this part of the world will never forget – for it was one in which blew the most terrible hurricane that ever came out of the heavens; and yet all the morning, and indeed until late in the afternoon, there was a gentle and steady breeze from the south-west, while the sun shone brightly, so that the oldest seaman among us could not have foreseen what was to follow.

'The three of us – my two brothers and myself – had crossed over to the islands about 2 o'clock P.M., and had soon nearly loaded the smack with fine fish, which, we all remarked, were more plentiful that day than we had ever known them. It was just seven *by my watch* when we weighed and started for home, so as to make the worst of the Ström at slack water, which we knew would be at eight.

'We set out with a fresh wind on our starboard quarter, and for some time spanked along at a great rate, never dreaming of danger, for indeed we saw not the slightest reason to apprehend it. All at once we were taken aback by a breeze from over Helseggen. This was most unusual – something that had never happened to us before – and I began to feel a little uneasy without exactly knowing why. We put the boat on the wind, but could make no headway at all for the eddies, and I was just upon the point of proposing to return to the anchorage, when, looking astern, we saw the whole horizon covered with a singular copper-coloured cloud that rose with the most amazing velocity.

'In the meantime the breeze that had headed us off fell away, and we were dead becalmed, drifting about in every direction. This state of things however, did not last long enough to give us time to think about it. In less than a minute the storm was upon us – in less than two the sky was entirely overcast – and what with this and the driving spray it became suddenly so dark that we could not see each other in the smack.

'Such a hurricane as then blew it is folly to attempt describing. The oldest seaman in Norway never experienced anything like it. We had let our sails go by the run before it cleverly took us; but, at the first puff, both our masts went by the board as if they had been sawed off – the mainmast taking with it my youngest brother, who had lashed himself to it for safety.

'Our boat was the lightest feather of a thing that ever sat upon water. It had a complete flush deck, with only a small hatch near the bow, and this hatch it had always been our custom to batten down when about to cross the Ström by way of precaution against the chopping seas. But for this circumstance we should have foundered at once – for we lay entirely buried for some moments. How my elder brother escaped destruction I cannot say, for I never had an opportunity of ascertaining. For my part, as soon as I had let the foresail run, I threw myself flat on deck, with my feet against the narrow gunwale of the bow, and with my hands grasping a ring-bolt near the foot of the fore-mast. It was mere instinct that prompted me to do this – which was undoubtedly the very best thing I could have done – for I was too much flurried to think.

'For some moments we were completely deluged, as I say, and all this time I held my breath, and clung to the bolt. When I could stand it no longer I raised myself upon my knees, still keeping hold with my hands, and thus got my head clear. Presently our little boat gave herself a shake, just as a dog does in coming out of the water, and thus rid herself in some measure of the seas. I was now trying to get the better of the stupor that had come over me, and to collect my senses so as to see what was to be done, when I felt somebody grasp my arm. It was my elder brother, and my heart leaped for joy, for I had made sure that he was overboard – but the next moment all this joy was turned into horror – for he put his mouth close to my ear, and screamed out the word *"Moskoe-ström!"*

'No one ever will know what my feelings were at that moment. I shook from head to foot, as if I had had the most violent fit of the ague. I knew what he meant by that one word well enough – I knew what he wished to make me understand. With the wind that now drove us on, we were bound for the whirl of the Ström, and nothing could save us!

'You perceive that in crossing the Ström *channel*, we always went a long way up above the whirl, even in the calmest weather, and then had to wait and watch carefully for the slack – but now we were driving right upon the pool itself, and in such a hurricane as this! "To be sure," I thought, "we shall get there just about the slack – there is some little hope in that" – but in the next moment I cursed myself for being so great a fool as to dream of hope at all. I knew very well that we were doomed had we been ten times a ninety-gun ship.

'By this time the first fury of the tempest had spent itself, or perhaps we did not feel it so much as we scudded before it, but at all events the seas, which at first had been kept down by the wind and lay flat and frothing now got up into absolute mountains. A singular change, too, had come over the heavens. Around in every direction it was still as black as pitch, but nearly overhead there burst out, all at once, a circular rift of clear sky – as clear as I ever saw, and of a deep bright blue – and through it there blazed forth the full moon with a lustre that I never before knew her to wear. She lit up everything about us with the greatest distinctness – but, O God, what a scene it was to light up!

'I now made one or two attempts to speak to my brother – but, in some manner which I could not understand, the din had so increased that I could not make him hear a single word, although I screamed at the top of my voice in his ear. Presently he shook his head, looking as pale as death, and held up one of his fingers, as if to say *"listen!"*

'At first I could not make out what he meant, but soon a hideous thought flashed upon me. I dragged my watch from its fob. It was not going. I glanced at its face by the moonlight, and then burst into tears as I flung it far away into the ocean. *It had run down at seven o'clock! We were behind the time of the slack, and the whirl of the Ström was in full fury!*

'When a boat is well built, properly trimmed, and not deep laden, the waves in a strong gale, when she is going large, seem always to slip from beneath her – which appears very strange to a landsman – and this is what is called *riding*, in sea-phrase. Well, so far we had ridden the swells very cleverly, but presently a gigantic sea happened to take us right under the counter, and bore us with it as it rose – up – up – as if into the sky. I would not have believed that any wave could rise so high. And then down we came with a sweep, a slide, and a plunge, that made me feel sick and dizzy, as if I was falling from some lofty mountain-top in a dream. But while we were up I had thrown a quick glance around – and that one glance was all sufficient. I saw our exact position in an instant. The Moskoe-ström whirlpool was about a quarter of a mile dead ahead, but no more like the everyday Moskoe-ström than the whirl as you now see it is like a mill-race. If I had not known where we were, and what we had to expect, I should not have recognised the place at all. As it was, I involuntarily closed my eyes in horror. The lids clenched themselves together as if in a spasm.

'It could not have been more than two minutes afterwards until we suddenly felt the waves subside, and were enveloped in foam. The boat made a sharp half turn to larboard, and then shot off in its new direction like a thunderbolt. At the same moment the roaring noise of the water was completely drowned in a kind of shrill shriek – such a sound as you might imagine given out by the wastepipes of many thousand steam-vessels letting off their steam all together. We were now in the belt of surf that always surrounds the whirl; and I thought of course that another moment would plunge us into the abyss – down which we could only see indistinctly on account of the amazing velocity with which we were borne along. The boat did not seem to sink into the water at all, but to skim like an air-bubble upon the surface of the surge. Her starboard side was next the whirl, and on the larboard arose the world of ocean we had left. It stood like a huge writhing wall between us and the horizon.

'It may appear strange, but now, when we were in the very jaws of the gulf, I felt more composed than when we were only approaching it. Having made up my mind to hope no more, I got rid of a great deal of that terror which unmanned me at first. I suppose it was despair that strung my nerves.

'It may look like boasting – but what I tell you is truth – I began to reflect how magnificent a thing it was to die in such a manner, and how foolish it was in me to think of so paltry a consideration as my own individual life in view of so wonderful a manifestation of God's power. I do believe that I blushed with shame when this idea crossed my mind. After a little while I became possessed with the keenest curiosity about the whirl itself. I positively felt a *wish* to explore its depths, even at the sacrifice I was going to make; and my principal grief was that I should never be able to tell my old companions on shore about the mysteries I should see. These no doubt were singular fancies to occupy a man's mind in such extremity, and I have often thought since that the revolution of the boat around the pool might have rendered me a little light-headed.

'There was another circumstance which tended to restore my self-possession, and this was the cessation of the wind, which could not reach us in our present situation – for, as you saw yourself, the belt of surf is considerably lower than the general bed of the ocean, and this latter now towered above us, a high, black, mountainous ridge. If you have never been at sea in a heavy gale you can form no idea of the confusion of mind occasioned by the wind and spray together. They blind, deafen, and strangle you, and take away all power of action or reflection. But we were now, in a great measure, rid of these annoyances – just as death-condemned felons in prison are allowed petty indulgences, forbidden them while their doom is yet uncertain.

'How often we made the circuit of the belt it is impossible to say. We careered round and round for perhaps an hour, flying rather than floating, getting gradually more and more into the middle of the surge, and then nearer and nearer to its horrible inner edge. All this time I had never let go of the ring-bolt. My brother was at the stern, holding on to a small empty water-cask which had been securely lashed under the coop of the counter, and was the only thing on deck that had not been swept overboard when the gale first took us. As we approached the brink of the pit he let go his hold upon this, and made for the ring, from which, in the agony of his terror, he endeavoured to force my hands, as it was not large enough to afford us both a secure grasp. I never felt deeper grief than when I saw him attempt this act – although I knew he was a madman when he did it – a raving maniac through sheer fright. I did not care, however, to contest the point with him. I knew it could make no difference whether either of us held on at all, so I let him have the bolt, and went astern to the cask. This there was no great difficulty in doing, for the smack flew round steadily enough, and upon an even keel, only swaying to and fro with the immense sweeps and swelters of the whirl. Scarcely had I secured myself in my new position when we gave a wild lurch to starboard, and rushed headlong into the abyss. I muttered a hurried prayer to God, and thought all was over.

'As I felt the sickening sweep of the descent I had instinctively tightened my hold upon the barrel, and closed my eyes. For some seconds I dared not open them, while I expected instant destruction, and wondered that I was not already in my death-struggles with the water. But moment after moment elapsed. I still lived. The sense of falling had ceased; and the motion of the vessel seemed much as it had been before while in the belt of foam, with the exception that she now lay more along. I took courage, and looked once again upon the scene.

'Never shall I forget the sensations of awe, horror, and admiration with which I gazed about me. The boat appeared to be hanging, as if by magic, midway down, upon the interior surface of a funnel vast in circumference, prodigious in depth, and whose perfectly smooth sides might have been mistaken for ebony but for the bewildering rapidity with which they spun around, and for the gleaming and ghastly radiance they shot forth, as the rays of the full moon, from that circular rift amid the clouds which I have already described, streamed in a flood of golden glory along the black walls, and far away down into the inmost recesses of the abyss.

'At first I was too much confused to observe anything accurately. The general burst of terrific grandeur was all that I beheld. When I recovered myself a little, however, my gaze fell instinctively downward. In this direction I was able to obtain an unobstructed view from the manner in which the smack hung on the inclined surface of the pool. She was quite upon an even keel – that is to say, her deck lay in a plane parallel with that of the water – but this latter sloped at an angle of more than forty-five degrees, so that we seemed to be lying upon our beam-ends. I could not help observing, nevertheless, that I had scarcely more difficulty in maintaining my hold and footing in this situation than if we had been upon a dead level, and this, I suppose, was owing to the speed at which we revolved.

'The rays of the moon seemed to search the very bottom of the profound gulf; but still I could make out nothing distinctly, on account of a thick mist in which everything there was enveloped, and over which there hung a magnificent rainbow, like that narrow and tottering bridge which Mussulmen say is the only pathway between Time and Eternity. This mist or spray was no doubt occasioned by the clashing of the great walls of the funnel as they all met together at the bottom, but the yell that went up to the Heavens from out of that mist I dare not attempt to describe.

'Our first slide into the abyss itself, from the belt of foam above, had carried us a great distance down the slope, but our farther descent was by no means proportionate. Round and round we swept – not with any uniform movement – but in dizzying swings and jerks, that sent us sometimes only a few hundred yards – sometimes nearly the complete

The boat appeared to be hanging, as if by magic, ... upon the interior surface of a funnel

circuit of the whirl. Our progress downward at each revolution was slow but very perceptible.

'Looking about me upon the wide waste of liquid ebony on which we were thus borne, I perceived that our boat was not the only object in the embrace of the whirl. Both above and below us were visible fragments of vessels, large masses of building timber and trunks of trees, with many smaller articles, such as pieces of house furniture, broken boxes, barrels, and staves. I have already described the unnatural curiosity which had taken the place of my original terrors. It appeared to grow upon me as I drew nearer and nearer to my dreadful doom. I now began to watch, with a strange interest, the numerous things that floated in our company. I *must* have been delirious, for I even sought *amusement* in speculating upon the relative velocities of their several descents towards the foam below. 'This fir-tree,' I found myself at one time saying, 'will certainly be the next thing that takes the awful plunge and disappears,' – and then I was disappointed to find that the wreck of a Dutch merchant ship overtook it and went down before. At length, after making several guesses of this nature, and being deceived in all, this fact – the fact of my invariable mis-calculation – set me upon a train of reflection that made my limbs again tremble, and my heart beat heavily once more.

'It was not a new terror that thus affected me, but the dawn of a more exciting *hope*. This hope arose partly from memory and partly from present observation. I called to mind the great variety of buoyant matter that strewed the coast of Lofoden, having been absorbed and then thrown forth by the Moskoe-ström. By far the greater number of the articles were shattered in the most extraordinary way – so chafed and roughened as to have the appearance of being stuck full of splinters – but then I distinctly recollected that there were *some* of them which were not disfigured at all. Now I could not account for this difference except by supposing that the roughened fragments were the only ones which had been *completely absorbed* – that the others had entered the whirl at so late a period of the tide, or, for some reason, had descended so slowly after entering, that they did not reach the bottom before the turn of the flood came, or of the ebb, as the case might be. I conceived it possible, in either instance, that they might thus be whirled up again to the level of the ocean, without undergoing the fate of those which had been drawn in more early, or absorbed more rapidly. I made also three important observations. The first was that, as a general rule, the larger the bodies were the more rapid their descent; the second, that, between two masses of equal extent, the one spherical and the other *of any other shape*, the superiority in speed of descent was with the sphere; the third, that, between two masses of equal size, the one cylindrical and the other of any other shape, the cylinder was absorbed the more slowly. Since my escape I have had several conversations on this subject with an old schoolmaster of the district, and it was from him that I learned the use of the words "cylinder" and "sphere." He explained to me – although I have forgotten the explanation – how what I observed was in fact the natural consequence of the forms of the floating fragments, and showed me how it happened that a cylinder swimming in a vortex offered more resistance to its suction, and was drawn in with greater difficulty than an equally bulky body of any form whatever.*

'There was one startling circumstance which went a great way in enforcing these observations and rendering me anxious to turn them to account, and this was that at every revolution we passed something like a barrel, or else the yard or the mast of a vessel, while many of these things which had been on our level when I first opened my eyes upon the wonders of the whirlpool were now high up above us, and seemed to have moved but little from their original station.

'I no longer hesitated what to do. I resolved to lash myself securely to the water-cask upon which I now held, to cut it loose from the counter, and to throw myself with it into the water. I attracted my brother's attention by signs, pointed to the floating barrels that came near us, and did everything in my power to make him understand what I was about to do. I thought at length that he comprehended my design, but, whether this was the case or not, he shook his head despairingly, and refused to move from his station by the ring-bolt. It was impossible to reach him, the emergency admitted of no delay, and so, with a bitter

* See Archimedes *'De Incidentibus in Fluido.'* – lib. 2.

struggle, I resigned him to his fate, fastened myself to the cask by means of the lashings which secured it to the counter, and precipitated myself with it into the sea without another moment's hesitation.

'The result was precisely what I had hoped it might be. As it is myself who now tell you this tale – as you see that I *did* escape – and as you are already in possession of the mode in which this escape was effected, and must therefore anticipate all that I have further to say, I will bring my story quickly to conclusion. It might have been an hour or thereabout after my quitting the smack, when, having descended to a vast distance beneath me; it made three or four wild gyrations in rapid succession and, bearing my loved brother with it, plunged headlong at once and for ever into the chaos of foam below. The barrel to which I was attached sunk very little farther than half the distance between the bottom of the gulf and the spot at which I leaped overboard, before a great change took place in the character of the whirlpool. The slope of the sides of the vast funnel became momently less and less steep. The gyrations of the whirl grew gradually less and less violent. By degrees the froth and the rainbow disappeared, and the bottom of the gulf seemed slowly to uprise. The sky was clear, the winds had gone down, and the full moon was setting radiantly in the west, when I found myself on the surface of the ocean, in full view of the shores of Lofoden, and above the spot where the pool of the Moskoe-ström *had been*. It was the hour of the slack – but the sea still heaved in mountainous waves from the effects of the hurricane. I was borne violently into the channel of the Ström, and in a few minutes was hurried down the coast into the "grounds" of the fishermen. A boat picked me up, exhausted from fatigue and (now that the danger was removed) speechless from the memory of its horror. Those who drew me on board were my old mates and daily companions, but they knew me no more than they would have known a traveller from the spirit-land. My hair which had been raven black the day before, was as white as you see it now. They say, too, that the whole expression of my countenance had changed. I told them my story – they did not believe it. I now tell it to *you*, and I can scarcely expect you to put more faith in it than did the merry fishermen of Lofoden.'

'Thou art the Man'

I will now play the Œdipus to the Rattleborough enigma. I will expound to you – as I alone can – the secret of the enginery that effected the Rattleborough miracle – the one, the true, the admitted, the undisputed, the indisputable miracle, which put a definite end to infidelity among the Rattleburghers, and converted to the orthodoxy of the grandames all the carnal-minded who had ventured to be sceptical before.

This event – which I should be sorry to discuss in a tone of unsuitable levity – occurred in the summer of 18—. Mr. Barnabas Shuttleworthy – one of the wealthiest and most respectable citizens of the borough – had been missing for several days under circumstances which gave rise to suspicion of foul play. Mr. Shuttleworthy had set out from Rattleborough very early one Saturday morning on horseback, with the avowed intention of proceeding to the city of ——, about fifteen miles distant, and of returning the night of the same day. Two hours after his departure, however, his horse returned without him, and without the saddle-bags which had been strapped on his back at starting. The animal was wounded, too, and covered with mud. These circumstances naturally gave rise to much alarm among the friends of the missing man; and when it was found on Sunday morning that he had not yet made his appearance, the whole borough arose *en masse* to go and look for his body.

The foremost and most energetic in instituting this search was the bosom friend of Mr. Shuttleworthy – a Mr. Charles Goodfellow, or, as he was universally called, 'Charley Goodfellow,' or 'Old Charley Goodfellow.' Now, whether it is a marvellous coincidence, or whether it is that the name itself has an imperceptible effect upon the character, I have never yet been able to ascertain; but the fact is unquestionable, that there never yet was any person named Charles who was not an open, manly, honest, good-natured, and frank-hearted fellow, with a rich, clear voice, that did you good to hear it, and an eye that looked you always straight in the face, as much as to say, 'I have a clear conscience myself; am afraid of no man, and am altogether above doing a mean action.' And thus all the hearty, careless, 'walking gentlemen' of the stage are very certain to be called Charles.

Now, 'Old Charley Goodfellow,' although he had been in Rattleborough not longer than six months or thereabouts, and although nobody knew anything about him before he came to settle in the neighbourhood, had experienced no difficulty in the world in making the acquaintance of all the respectable people in the borough. Not a man of them but would have taken his bare word for a thousand at any moment; and as for the women there is no saying what they would not have done to oblige him. And all this came of his having been christened Charles, and of his possessing, in consequence, that ingenuous face which is proverbially the very 'best letter of recommendation.'

I have already said that Mr. Shuttleworthy was one of the most respectable, and, undoubtedly, he was the most wealthy man in Rattleborough, while 'Old Charley Goodfellow' was upon as intimate terms with him as if he had been his own brother. The two old gentlemen were next-door neighbours, and although Mr. Shuttleworthy seldom if ever visited 'Old Charley,' and never was known to take a meal in his house, still this did not prevent the two friends from being exceedingly intimate, as I have just observed; for 'Old Charley' never let a day pass without stepping in three or four times to see how his neighbour came on, and very often he would stay to breakfast or tea, and almost always to dinner; and then the amount of wine that was made away with by the two cronies at a sitting it would really be a difficult thing to ascertain. Old Charley's favourite beverage was *Château Margaux*, and it appeared to do Mr. Shuttleworthy's heart good to see the old fellow swallow it as he did, quart after quart; so that one day when the wine was *in* and the wit, as a natural consequence, somewhat *out*, he said to his crony, as he slapped him upon the back, 'I tell you what it is, Old Charley, you are, by all odds, the heartiest old fellow I ever came across in all my born days; and since you love to guzzle the wine at that fashion I'll be darned if I don't have to make thee a present of a big box of the Château Margaux. Od rot me' (Mr. Shuttleworthy had a sad habit of swearing, although he seldom went beyond 'Od rot me,' or 'By gosh,' or 'By the jolly golly'), 'Od rot me,' says he, 'if I don't send an order to town this very afternoon for a double box of the best that can be got, and I'll make ye a present of it, I will! – ye needn't say a word now – I *will*, I tell ye, and there's an end of it; so look out for it – it will come to hand some of these fine days, precisely when ye are looking for it the least!' I mention this little bit of liberality on the part of Mr. Shuttleworthy just by way of showing you how *very* intimate an understanding existed between the two friends.

Well, on the Sunday morning in question, when it came to be fairly understood that Mr. Shuttleworthy had met with foul play, I never saw any one so profoundly affected as 'Old Charley Goodfellow.' When he first heard that the horse had come home without his master, and without his master's saddle-bags, and all bloody from a pistol-shot that had gone through and through the poor animal's chest without quite killing him – when he heard all this he turned as pale as if the missing man had been his own dear brother or father, and shivered and shook all over as if he had had a fit of the ague.

At first he was too much overpowered with grief to be able to do anything at all, or to decide upon any plan of action; so that for a long time he endeavoured to dissuade Mr. Shuttleworthy's other friends from making a stir about the matter, thinking it best to wait awhile – say for a week or two, or a month or two – to see if something wouldn't turn up, or if Mr. Shuttleworthy wouldn't come in the natural way and explain his reasons for sending his horse on before. I daresay you have often observed this disposition to temporise, or to procrastinate, in people who are labouring under any very poignant sorrow. Their powers of mind seem to be rendered torpid, so that they have a horror of anything like action, and like nothing in the world so well as to lie quietly in bed and 'nurse their grief,' as the old ladies express it – that is to say, ruminate over their trouble.

The people of Rattleborough had, indeed, so high an opinion of the wisdom and discretion of 'Old Charley,' that the greater part of them felt disposed to agree with him, and not make a stir in the business 'until something should turn up,' as the honest old gentleman worded it; and I believe that, after all, this would have been the general determination, but for the very suspicious interference of Mr. Shuttleworthy's nephew, a young man of very dissipated habits, and otherwise of rather bad character. This nephew, whose name was Pennifeather, would listen to nothing like reason in the matter of 'lying quiet,' but insisted upon making immediate search for the 'corpse of the murdered man.' This was the expression he employed; and Mr. Goodfellow acutely remarked at the time that it was 'a *singular* expression, to say no more.' This remark of 'Old Charley's,' too, had great effect upon the crowd; and one of the party was heard to ask very impressively, 'how it happened that young Mr. Pennifeather was so intimately cognisant of all the circumstances connected with his wealthy uncle's disappearance as to feel authorised to assert, distinctly and unequivocally, that his uncle *was* "a murdered man."' Hereupon some little squibbing and bickering occurred among various members of the crowd, and especially between 'Old Charley' and Mr. Pennifeather – although this latter occurrence was indeed by no means a novelty, for little good will had subsisted between the parties for the last three or four months, and matters had even gone so far that Mr. Pennifeather had actually knocked down his uncle's friend for some alleged access of liberty that the latter had taken in the uncle's house, of which the nephew was an inmate. Upon this occasion, 'Old Charley' is said to have behaved with exemplary moderation and Christian charity. He arose from the blow, adjusted his clothes, and made no attempt at retaliation at all – merely muttering a few words about 'taking summary vengeance at the first convenient opportunity' – a natural and very justifiable ebullition of anger, which meant nothing, however, and beyond doubt was no sooner given vent to than forgotten.

However these matters may be (which have no reference to the point now at issue), it is quite certain that the people of Rattleborough, principally through the persuasion of Mr. Pennifeather, came at length to the determination of dispersing over the adjacent country in search of the missing Mr. Shuttleworthy. I say they came to this determination in the first instance. After it had been fully resolved that a search should be made, it was considered almost a matter of course that the seekers should disperse – that is to say, distribute themselves in parties – for the more thorough examination of the region round about. I forget, however, by what ingenious train of reasoning it was that 'Old Charley' finally convinced the assembly that this was the most injudicious plan that could be pursued. Convince them, however, he did – all except Mr. Pennifeather – and in the end it was arranged that a search should be instituted, carefully and very thoroughly, by the burghers *en masse*, 'Old Charley' himself leading the way.

As for the matter of that, there could have been no better pioneer than 'Old Charley,' whom everybody knew to have the eye of a lynx; but although he led them into all manner of out-of-the-way holes and corners, by routes that nobody had ever suspected of existing in the neighbourhood, and although the search was incessantly kept up day and night for nearly a week, still no trace of Mr. Shuttleworthy could be discovered. When I say no trace, however, I must not be understood to speak literally, for trace to some extent there certainly was. The poor gentleman had been tracked by his horse's shoes (which were peculiar) to a spot about three miles to the east of the borough, on the main road leading to the city. Here the track made off into a bye-path through a piece of woodland, the path coming out again into the main road, and cutting off about half-a-mile of the regular distance.

Following the shoe-marks down this lane, the party came at length to a pool of stagnant water, half hidden by the brambles to the right of the lane, and opposite this pool all vestige of the track was lost sight of. It appeared, however, that a struggle of some nature had here taken place; and it seemed as if some large and heavy body, much larger and heavier than a man, had been drawn from the bye-path to the pool. This latter was carefully dragged twice, but nothing was found; and the party were upon the point of going away in despair of coming to any result, when Providence suggested to Mr. Goodfellow the expediency of draining the water off altogether. This project was received with cheers and many high compliments to 'Old Charley' upon his sagacity and consideration. As many of the burghers had brought spades with them, supposing that they might possibly be called upon to disinter a corpse, the drain was easily and speedily effected; and no sooner was the bottom visible than right in the middle of the mud that remained was discovered a black silk velvet waistcoat, which nearly every one present immediately recognised as the property of Mr. Pennifeather. This waistcoat was much torn and stained with blood, and there were several persons among the party who had a distinct remembrance of its having been worn by its owner on the very morning of Mr. Shuttleworthy's departure for the city; while there were others, again, ready to testify upon oath, if required, that Mr. P. did *not* wear the garment in question at any period during the *remainder* of that memorable day; nor could any one be found to say that he had seen it upon Mr. P.'s person at any period at all subsequent to Mr. Shuttleworthy's disappearance.

Matters now wore a very serious aspect for Mr. Pennifeather, and it was observed, as an indubitable confirmation of the suspicions which were excited against him, that he grew exceedingly pale, and when asked what he had to say for himself was utterly incapable of saying a word. Hereupon, the few friends his riotous mode of living had left him deserted him at once to a man, and were even more clamorous than his ancient and avowed enemies for his instantaneous arrest. But on the other hand, the magnanimity of Mr. Goodfellow shone forth with only the more brilliant lustre through contrast. He made a warm and intensely eloquent defence of Mr. Pennifeather, in which he alluded more than once to his own sincere forgiveness of that wild young gentleman – 'the heir of the worthy Mr. Goodfellow,' for the insult which he (the young gentleman) had, no doubt in the heat of passion, thought proper to put upon him (Mr. Goodfellow). He forgave him for it, he said, from the very bottom of his heart; and for himself (Mr. Goodfellow), so far from pushing the suspicious circumstances to extremity, which, he was sorry to say, really *had* arisen against Mr. Pennifeather, he (Mr. Goodfellow) would make every exertion in his power, would employ all the little eloquence in his possession to – to – to – soften down, as much as he could conscientiously do so, the worst features of this really exceedingly perplexing piece of business.

Mr. Goodfellow went on for some half-hour longer in this strain, very much to the credit both of his head and of his heart; but your warm-hearted people are seldom apposite in their observations – they run into all sorts of blunders, *contre-temps* and *mal âpropos-isms*, in the hot-headedness of their zeal to serve a friend – thus, often with the kindest intentions in the world, doing infinitely more to prejudice his cause than to advance it.

So in the present instance, it turned out with all the eloquence of 'Old Charley'; for, although he laboured earnestly in behalf of the suspected, yet it so happened, somehow or other, that every syllable he uttered of which the direct but unwitting tendency was not to exalt the speaker in the good opinion of his audience, had the effect of deepening the suspicion already attached to the individual whose cause he pled, and of arousing against him the fury of the mob.

One of the most unaccountable errors committed by the orator was his allusion to the suspected as 'the heir of the worthy old gentleman Mr. Shuttleworthy.' The people had really never thought of this before. They had only remembered certain threats of disinheritance uttered a year or two previously by the uncle (who had no living relative except the nephew); and they had, therefore, always looked upon this disinheritance as a matter that was settled – so single-minded a race of beings were the Rattleburghers; but the remark of

'Old Charley' brought them at once to a consideration of this point, and thus gave them to see the possibility of the threats having been nothing *more* than threats. And straightway hereupon arose the natural question of *Cui bono?* a question that tended even more than the waistcoat to fasten the terrible crime upon the young man. And here, lest I be misunderstood, permit me to digress for one moment merely to observe that the exceedingly brief and simple Latin phrase which I have employed, is invariably mistranslated and misconceived. '*Cui bono*,' in all the crack novels and elsewhere, – in those of Mrs. Gore, for example, the author of 'Cecil,' a lady who quotes all tongues from the Chaldæan to Chickasaw, and is helped to her learning, 'as needed,' upon a systematic plan by Mr. Beckford – in *all* the crack novels, I say, from those of Bulwer and Dickens to those of Turnapenny and Ainsworth, the two little Latin words *cui bono* are rendered 'to what purpose,' or (as if *quo bono*) 'to what good.' Their true meaning, nevertheless, is 'for whose advantage.' *Cui*, to whom; *bono*, is it for a benefit. It is a purely legal phrase, and applicable precisely in cases such as we have now under consideration, where the probability of the doer of a deed hinges upon the probability of the benefit accruing to this individual or to that from the deed's accomplishment. Now in the present instance, the question *cui bono* very pointedly implicated Mr. Pennifeather. His uncle had threatened him, after making a will in his favour, with disinheritance. But the threat had not been actually kept; the original will, it appeared, had not been altered. *Had* it been altered, the only supposable motive for murder on the part of the suspected would have been the ordinary one of revenge, and even this would have been counteracted by the hope of reinstation into the good graces of the uncle. But the will being unaltered, while the threat to alter remained suspended over the nephew's head, there appears at once the very strongest possible inducement for the atrocity: and so concluded, very sagaciously, the worthy citizens of the borough of Rattle.

Mr. Pennifeather was accordingly arrested upon the spot, and the crowd, after some further search, proceeded homewards, having him in custody. On the route, however, another circumstance occurred tending to confirm the suspicion entertained. Mr. Goodfellow, whose zeal led him to be always a little in advance of the party, was seen suddenly to run forward a few paces, stoop, and then apparently to pick up some small object from the grass. Having quickly examined it, he was observed, too, to make a sort of half attempt at concealing it in his coat pocket; but this action was noticed, as I say, and consequently prevented, when the object picked up was found to be a Spanish knife which a dozen persons at once recognised as belonging to Mr. Pennifeather. Moreover, his initials were engraved upon the handle. The blade of this knife was open and bloody.

No doubt now remained of the guilt of the nephew, and immediately upon reaching Rattleborough he was taken before a magistrate for examination.

Here matters again took a most unfavourable turn. The prisoner being questioned as to his whereabouts on the morning of Mr. Shuttleworthy's disappearance, had absolutely the audacity to acknowledge that on that very morning he had been out with his rifle deer-stalking in the immediate neighbourhood of the pool where the blood-stained waistcoat had been discovered through the sagacity of Mr. Goodfellow.

This latter now came forward, and with tears in his eyes, asked permission to be examined. He said that a stern sense of the duty he owed his Maker, not less than his fellow-men, would permit him no longer to remain silent. Hitherto, the sincerest affection for the young man (notwithstanding the latter's ill-treatment of himself, Mr. Goodfellow), had induced him to make every hypothesis which imagination could suggest, by way of endeavouring to account for what appeared suspicious in the circumstances that told so seriously against Mr. Pennifeather; but these circumstances were now altogether *too* convincing – *too* damning; he would hesitate no longer – he would tell all he knew, although his heart (Mr. Goodfellow's) should absolutely burst asunder in the effort. He then went on to state that on the afternoon of the day previous to Mr. Shuttleworthy's departure for the city, that worthy old gentleman had mentioned to his nephew in *his* hearing (Mr. Goodfellow's) that his object in going to town on the morrow was to make a deposit of an unusually large sum of money in the 'Farmers and Mechanics' Bank,' and that then and there the said Mr. Shuttleworthy had distinctly avowed to the said nephew his irrevocable determination of rescinding the will originally made, and of cutting him off with a shilling. He (the witness) now solemnly called upon the accused to state whether what he (the witness) had just stated was or was not the truth in every substantial particular. Much to the astonishment of every one present, Mr. Pennifeather frankly admitted that *it was.*

The magistrate now considered it his duty to send a couple of constables to search the chamber of the accused in the house of his uncle. From this search they almost immediately returned with the well-known steel-bound, russet leather pocket-book which the old gentleman had been in the habit of carrying for years. Its valuable contents, however, had been abstracted, and the magistrate in vain endeavoured to extort from the prisoner the use which had been made of them, or the place of their concealment. Indeed he obstinately denied all knowledge of the matter. The constables also discovered between the bed and sacking of the unhappy man a shirt and neck-handkerchief, both marked with the initials of his name, and both hideously besmeared with the blood of the victim.

At this juncture, it was announced that the horse of the murdered man had just expired in the stable, from the effects of the wound he had received; and it was proposed by Mr. Goodfellow that a *post mortem* examination of the beast should be immediately made, with the view, if possible, of discovering the ball. This was accordingly done; and, as if to demonstrate beyond a question the guilt of the accused, Mr. Goodfellow, after considerable searching in the cavity of the chest, was enabled to detect and to pull forth a bullet of very extraordinary size, which, upon trial, was found to be exactly adapted to the bore of Mr. Pennifeather's rifle, while it was far too large for that of any other person in the borough or its vicinity. To render the matter even surer yet, however, this bullet was discovered to have a flaw or seam at right angles to the usual suture; and upon examination, this seam corresponded precisely with an accidental ridge or elevation in a pair of moulds acknowledged by the accused himself to be his own property. Upon the finding of this bullet, the examining magistrate refused to listen to any further testimony, and immediately committed the prisoner for trial, declining resolutely to take any bail in the case, although against this severity Mr. Goodfellow very warmly remonstrated, and offered to become surety in whatever amount might be required. This generosity on the part of 'Old Charley' was only in accordance with the whole tenor of his amiable and chivalrous conduct during the entire period of his sojourn in the borough of Rattle. In the present instance, the worthy man was so entirely carried away by the excessive warmth of his sympathy that he seemed to have quite forgotten, when he offered to go bail for his young friend, that he himself (Mr. Goodfellow) did not possess a single dollar's worth of property upon the face of the earth.

The result of the committal may be readily foreseen. Mr. Pennifeather, amid the loud execrations of all Rattleborough, was brought to trial at the next criminal sessions, when the chain of circumstantial evidence (strengthened as it was by some additional damning facts, which Mr. Goodfellow's sensitive conscientiousness forbade him to withhold from the court), was considered so unbroken and so thoroughly conclusive that the jury, without leaving their seats, returned an immediate verdict of *'Guilty of murder in the first degree.'* Soon afterwards the unhappy wretch received sentence of death, and was remanded to the county jail to await the inexorable vengeance of the law.

In the meantime, the noble behaviour of 'Old Charley Goodfellow' had doubly endeared him to the honest citizens of the borough. He became ten times a greater favourite than ever; and, as a natural result of the hospitality with which he was treated, he relaxed, as it were, perforce, the extremely parsimonious habits which his poverty had hitherto impelled him to observe, and very frequently had little *réunions* at his own house, when wit and jollity reigned supreme, dampened a little *of course*, by the occasional remembrance of the untoward and melancholy fate which impended over the nephew of the late lamented bosom friend of the generous host.

One fine day this magnanimous old gentleman was agreeably surprised at the receipt of the following letter:

Charles Goodfellow, Esquire—

DEAR SIR—In Conformity with an order transmitted to our firm about two months since, by our esteemed correspondent Mr. Barnabas Shuttleworthy, we have the honour of forwarding this morning, to your address, a double box of Château-Margaux, of the antelope brand, violet seal. Box numbered and marked as per margin.

We remain, Sir,

Your most ob'nt. ser'ts.,

HOGGS, FROGS, BOGS & CO.

City of——, June, 21, 18—

P.S.—The box will reach you, by waggon, on the day after your receipt of this letter. Our respects to Mr. Shuttleworthy.

H., F., B. & Co.

Charles Goodfellow, Esq., Rattleborough.
From H, F, B. & Co.
Chât. Mar. A. – No. 1. – 6 doz. bottles (½ Gross.)

The fact is, that Mr. Goodfellow had, since the death of Mr. Shuttleworthy, given over all expectation of ever receiving the promised Château-Margaux, and he therefore looked upon it *now* as a sort of especial dispensation of Providence in his behalf. He was highly delighted of course, and in the exuberance of his joy invited a large party of friends to a *petit souper* on the morrow, for the purpose of broaching the good old Mr. Shuttleworthy's present. Not that he *said* anything about 'the good old Mr. Shuttleworthy' when he issued the invitations. The fact is, he thought much and concluded to say nothing at all. He did *not* mention to anyone – if I remember aright – that he had received a *present* of Château-Margaux. He merely asked his friends to come and help him drink some of a remarkably fine quality and rich flavour that he had ordered up from the city a couple of months ago, and of which he would be in the receipt upon the morrow. I have often puzzled myself to imagine *why* it was that 'Old Charley' came to the conclusion to say nothing about having received the wine from his old friend, but I could never precisely understand his reason for the silence, although he had *some* excellent and very magnanimous reason, no doubt.

The morrow at length arrived, and with it a very large and highly respectable company at Mr. Goodfellow's house. Indeed, half the borough was there – I myself among the number – but much to the vexation of the host, the Château-Margaux did not arrive until a late hour, and when the sumptuous supper supplied by 'Old Charley' had been done very ample justice by the guests. It came at length, however – a monstrously big box of it there was, too – and as the whole party were in excessively good humour, it was decided, *nem. con.*, that it should be lifted upon the table and its contents disembowelled forthwith.

No sooner said than done. I lent a helping hand, and in a trice we had the box upon the table, in the midst of all the bottles and glasses, not a few of which were demolished in the scuffle. 'Old Charley,' who was pretty much intoxicated, and excessively red in the face, now took a seat, with an air of mock dignity, at the head of the board, and thumped furiously upon it with a decanter, calling upon the company to keep order 'during the ceremony of disinterring the treasure.'

After some vociferation, quiet was at length fully restored, and, as very often happens in similar cases, a profound and remarkable silence ensued. Being then requested to force open the lid, I complied, of course, 'with an infinite deal of pleasure.' I inserted a chisel, and giving it a few slight taps with a hammer, the top of the box flew suddenly and violently off, and, at the same instant, there sprang up into a sitting position, directly facing the host, the bruised, bloody, and nearly putrid corpse of the murdered Mr. Shuttleworthy himself. It gazed for a few moments fixedly and sorrowfully, with its decaying and lack-lustre eyes, full into the countenance of Mr. Goodfellow, uttered slowly but clearly and impressively the words 'Thou art the man!' and then, falling over the side of the chest as if thoroughly satisfied, stretched out its limbs quiveringly upon the table.

The scene that ensued is altogether beyond description. The rush for the doors and windows was terrific, and many of the most robust men in the room fainted outright through sheer horror. But after the first wild shrieking burst of affright all eyes were directed to Mr. Goodfellow. If I live a thousand years I can never forget the more than mortal agony which was depicted in that ghastly face of his, so lately rubicund with triumph and wine. For several minutes he sat rigidly as a statue of marble, his eyes seeming in the intense vacancy of their gaze to be turned inwards and absorbed in the contemplation of his own miserable, murderous soul. At length their expression appeared to flash suddenly out into the external world, when with a quick leap he sprang from his chair, and falling heavily with his head and shoulders upon the table, and in contact with the corpse, poured out rapidly and vehemently a detailed confession of the hideous crime for which Mr. Pennifeather was then imprisoned and doomed to die.

What he recounted was in substance this:– He followed his victim to the vicinity of the pool; there shot his horse with a pistol; despatched the rider with its butt end; possessed himself of the pocket-book: and, supposing the horse dead, dragged it with great labour to the brambles by the pond. Upon his own beast he slung the corpse of Mr. Shuttleworthy, and thus bore it to a secure place of concealment a long distance off through the woods.

The waistcoat, the knife, the pocket-book and bullet, had been placed by himself where found, with the view of avenging himself upon Mr. Pennifeather. He had also contrived the discovery of the stained handkerchief and shirt.

Towards the end of the blood-chilling recital, the words of the guilty wretch faltered and grew hollow. When the record was finally exhausted, he arose, staggered backwards from the table, and fell – *dead*.

The means by which this happily-timed confession was extorted, although efficient, were simple indeed. Mr. Goodfellow's excess of frankness had disgusted me, and excited my suspicions from the first. I was present when Mr. Pennifeather had struck him, and the fiendish expression which then arose upon his countenance, although momentary, assured me that his threat of vengeance would, if possible, be rigidly fulfilled. I was thus prepared to view the *manœuvring* of 'Old Charley' in a very different light from that in which it was regarded by the good citizens of Rattleborough. I saw at once that all the criminating discoveries arose, either directly or indirectly, from himself. But the fact which clearly opened my eyes to the true state of the case was the affair of the bullet *found* by Mr. G. in the carcase of the horse. *I* had not forgotten, although the Rattleburghers *had*, that there was a hole where the ball had entered the horse, and another where it *went out*. If it were found in the animal then, after having made its exit, I saw clearly that it must have been deposited by the person who found it. The bloody shirt and handkerchief confirmed the idea suggested by the bullet; for the blood upon examination proved to be capital claret, and no more. When I came to think of these things, and also of the late increase of liberality and expenditure on the part of Mr. Goodfellow, I entertained a suspicion which was none the less strong because I kept it altogether to myself.

In the meantime I instituted a rigorous private search for the corpse of Mr. Shuttleworthy, and, for good reasons searched in quarters as divergent as possible from those to which Mr. Goodfellow conducted his party. The result was that after some days, I came across an old dry well, the mouth of which was nearly hidden by brambles; and here, at the bottom, I discovered what I sought.

Now, it so happened that I had overheard the colloquy between the two cronies, when Mr. Goodfellow had contrived to cajole his host into the promise of a box of Château-Margaux. Upon this hint I acted. I procured a stiff piece of whalebone, thrust it down the throat of the corpse, and deposited the latter in an old wine box — taking care so to double the body up as to double the whalebone with it. In this manner I had to press forcibly upon the lid to keep it down while I secured it with nails; and I anticipated, of course, that as soon as these latter were removed, the top would fly *off* and the body *up*.

Having thus arranged the box, I marked, numbered, and addressed it as already told; and then writing a letter in the name of the wine merchants with whom Mr. Shuttleworthy dealt, I gave instructions to my servant to wheel the box to Mr. Goodfellow's door, in a barrow, at a given signal from myself. For the words which I intended the corpse to speak, I confidently depended upon my ventriloquial abilities; for their effect I counted upon the conscience of the murderous wretch.

I believe there is nothing more to be explained. Mr. Pennifeather was released upon the spot, inherited the fortune of his uncle, profited by the lessons of experience, turned over a new leaf, and led happily ever afterwards a new life.

The Devil In The Belfry

What o'clock is it? – *Old Saying.*

Everybody knows, in a general way, that the finest place in the world is – or, alas, *was* – the Dutch borough of Vondervotteimittiss. Yet as it lies some distance from any of the main roads, being in a somewhat out-of-the-way situation, there are perhaps very few of my readers who have ever paid it a visit. For the benefit of those who have *not*, therefore, it will be only proper that I should enter into some account of it. And this is indeed the more necessary, as with the hope of enlisting public sympathy in behalf of the inhabitants, I design here to give a history of the calamitous events which have so lately occurred within its limits. No one who knows me will doubt that the duty thus self-imposed will be executed to the best of my ability, with all that rigid impartiality, all that cautious examination into facts, and diligent collation of authorities, which should ever distinguish him who aspires to the title of historian.

By the united aid of medals, manuscripts, and inscriptions, I am enabled to say, positively, that the borough of Vondervotteimittiss has existed, from its origin, in precisely the same condition which it at present preserves. Of the date of this origin, however, I grieve that I can only speak with that species of indefinite definiteness which mathematicians are at times forced to put up with in certain algebraic formulæ. The date, I may thus say, in regard to the remoteness of its antiquity, cannot be less than any assignable quantity whatsoever.

Touching the derivation of the name Vondervotteimittiss, I confess myself with sorrow equally at fault. Among a multitude of opinions upon this delicate point – some acute, some learned, some sufficiently the reverse – I am able to select nothing which ought to be considered satisfactory. Perhaps the idea of Grogswigg – nearly coincident with that of Kroutaplenttey – is to be cautiously pre-ferred:– It runs:– '*Vondervotteimittiss* – *Vonder, lege Donder* – *Votteimittiss, quasi und Bleitziz* – *Bleitziz, obsol: pro Blitzen.*' This derivation, to say the truth, is still countenanced by some traces of the electric fluid evident on the summit of the steeple of the House of the Town-Council. I do not choose however, to commit myself on a theme of such importance, and must refer the reader desirous of information to the '*Oratiunculæ de Rebus Præteritis,*' of Dundergutz. See also Blunderbuzzard '*De Derivationibus,*' pp. 27 to 5010, Folio, Gothic edit., Red and Black character, Catchword and no Cypher; – wherein consult also marginal notes in the autograph of Stuffundpuff, with the Sub-Commentaries of Gruntundguzzel.

Notwithstanding the obscurity which thus envelops the date of the foundation of Vondervotteimittiss, and the derivation of its name, there can be no doubt, as I said before, that it has always existed as we find it at this epoch. The oldest man in the borough can remember not the slightest difference in the appearance of any portion of it; and indeed the very suggestion of such a possibility is considered an insult. The site of the village is in a perfectly circular valley, about a quarter of a mile in circumference, and entirely surrounded by gentle hills, over whose summit the people have never yet ventured to pass. For this they assign the very good reason that they do not believe there is anything at all on the other side.

Round the skirts of the valley (which is quite level, and paved throughout with flat tiles), extends a continuous row of sixty little houses. These, having their backs on the hills, must look of course to the centre of the plain, which is just sixty yards from the front door of each dwelling. Every house has a small garden before it, with a circular path, a sun-dial, and twenty-four cabbages. The buildings themselves are so precisely alike that one can in no manner be distinguished from the other. Owing to the vast antiquity, the style of architecture is somewhat odd, but it is not for that reason the less strikingly picturesque. They are fashioned of hard burned little bricks, red, with black ends, so that the walls look like a chess-board upon a great scale. The gables are turned to the front, and there are cornices as big as all the rest of the house over the eaves and over the main doors. The windows are narrow and deep, with very tiny panes and a great deal of sash. On the roof is a vast quantity of tiles with long curly ears. The wood-work throughout is of a dark hue, and there is much carving about it, with but a trifling variety of pattern; for time out of mind, the carvers of Vondervotteimittiss have never been able to carve more than two objects – a time-piece and a cabbage. But these they do exceedingly well, and intersperse them, with singular ingenuity, wherever they find room for the chisel.

The dwellings are as much alike inside as out, and the furniture is all upon one plan. The floors are of square tiles, the chairs and tables of black-looking wood, with thin crooked legs and puppy feet. The mantelpieces are wide and high, and have not only time-pieces and cabbages sculptured over the front, but a real time-piece, which makes a prodigious ticking, on the top in the middle, with a flower-pot containing a cabbage standing on each extremity by way of outrider. Between each cabbage and the time-piece, again, is a little China man having a large stomach with a great round hole in it, through which is seen the dial-plate of a watch.

The fireplaces are large and deep, with fierce crooked-looking fire-dogs. There is constantly a rousing fire, and a huge pot over it, full of sauerkraut and pork, to which the good woman of the house is always busy in attending. She is a little fat old lady, with blue eyes and a red face, and wears a huge cap like a sugar-loaf, ornamented with purple and yellow ribbons. Her dress is of orange-coloured linsey-woolsey, made very full behind and very short in the waist, and indeed very short in other respects, not reaching below the middle of her leg. This is somewhat thick, and so are her ankles, but she has a fine pair of green stockings to cover them. He shoes – of pink leather – are fastened each with a bunch of yellow ribbons puckered up in the shape of a cabbage. In her left hand she has a little heavy Dutch watch; in her right she wields a ladle for the sauerkraut and pork. By her side there stands a fat tabby cat, with a gilt toy repeater tied to its tail, which 'the boys' have fastened there by way of a quiz.

The boys themselves are, all three of them, in the garden attending the pig. They are each two feet in height. They have three-cornered cocked hats, purple waistcoats reaching down to their thighs, buckskin kneebreeches, red woollen stockings, heavy shoes with big silver buckles, and long surtout coats with large buttons of mother-of-pearl. Each, too, has a pipe in his mouth, and a little dumpy watch in his right hand. He takes a puff and a look, and then a look and a puff. The pig – which is corpulent and lazy – is occupied now in picking up the stray leaves that fall from the cabbages, and now in giving a kick behind at the gilt repeater, which the urchins have also tied to *his* tail in order to make him look as handsome as the cat.

Right at the front door, in a high-backed leather-bottomed arm chair, with crooked legs and puppy feet like the tables, is seated the old man of the house himself. He is an exceedingly puffy little old gentleman, with big circular eyes and a huge double chin. His dress resembles that of the boys, and I need say nothing farther about it. All the difference is, that his pipe is somewhat bigger than theirs, and he can make a greater smoke. Like them, he has a watch, but he carries his watch in his pocket. To say the truth, he has something of more importance than a watch to attend to, and what that is I shall presently explain. He sits with his right leg upon his left knee, wears a grave countenance, and always keeps one of his eyes at least resolutely bent upon a certain remarkable object in the centre of the plain.

This object is situated in the steeple of the House of the Town-Council. The Town-Council are all very little, round, oily, intelligent men, with big saucer eyes and fat double chins, and have their coats much longer and their shoe-buckles much bigger than the ordinary inhabitants of Vondervotteimittiss. Since my sojourn in the borough, they have had several special meetings, and have adopted these three important resolutions:—

'That it is wrong to alter the good old course of things:'
'That there is nothing tolerable out of Vondervotteimittiss:' and –
'That we will stick by our clocks and our cabbages.'

Above the session room of the Council is the steeple, and in the steeple is the belfry, where exists, and has existed time out of mind, the pride and wonder of the village – the great clock of the borough of Vondervotteimittiss. And this is the object to which the eyes of the old gentlemen are turned who sit in the leather-bottomed arm-chairs.

The great clock has seven faces – one in each of the seven sides of the steeple – so that it can be readily seen from all quarters. Its faces are large and white, and its hands heavy and black. There is a belfry-man whose sole duty is to attend to it; but this duty is the most perfect of sinecures – for the clock of Vondervotteimittiss was never yet known to have anything the matter with it. Until lately, the bare supposition of such a thing was considered heretical. From the remotest period of antiquity to which the archives have reference, the hours have been regularly struck by the big bell. And, indeed, the case was just the same with all the other clocks and watches in the borough. Never was such a place for keeping the true time. When the large clapper thought proper to say 'Twelve o'clock!' all its obedient followers opened their throats simultaneously and responded like a very echo. In short, the good burghers were fond of their sauerkraut, but then they were proud of their clocks.

All people who hold sinecure offices are held in more or less respect, and as the belfry-man of Vondervotteimittiss has the most perfect of sinecures, he is the most perfectly respected of any man in the world. He is the chief dignitary of the borough, and the very pigs look up to him with a sentiment of reverence. His coat-tail is *very* far longer – his pipe, his shoe-buckles, his eyes, and his stomach, *very* far bigger – than those of any other old gentleman in the village; and as to his chin, it is not only double, but triple.

I have thus painted the happy estate of Vondervotteimittiss: alas, that so fair a picture should ever experience a reverse!

There has been long a saying among the wisest inhabitants, that 'no good can come from over the hills,' and it really seemed that the words had in them something of the spirit of prophecy. It wanted five minutes of noon, on the day before yesterday, when there appeared a very odd-looking object on the summit of the ridge to the eastward. Such an occurrence of course attracted universal attention, and every little old gentleman who sat in a leather-bottomed arm-chair turned one of his eyes with a stare of dismay upon the phenomenon, still keeping the other upon the clock in the steeple.

By the time that it wanted only three minutes to noon the droll object in question was perceived to be a very diminutive foreign-looking young man. He descended the hills at a great rate, so that everybody had soon a good look at him. He was really the most finnicky little personage that had ever been seen in Vonder-votteimittiss. His countenance was of a dark snuff-colour, and he had a long hooked nose, pea eyes, a wide mouth, and an excellent set of teeth, which latter he seemed anxious of displaying, as he was grinning from ear to ear. What with mustachios and whiskers, there was none of the rest of his face to be seen. His head was uncovered, and his hair neatly done up in *papillotes*. His dress was a tight-fitting swallow-tailed black coat (from one of whose pockets dangled a vast length of white handkerchief), black kerseymere knee-breeches, black stockings, and stumpy-looking pumps, with huge bunches of black satin ribbon for bows. Under one arm he carried a huge *chapeau-de-bras*, and under the other a fiddle nearly fives times as big as himself. In his left hand was a gold snuff-box, from which, as he capered down the hill, cutting all manner of fantastical steps, he took snuff incessantly with an air of the greatest possible self-satisfaction. God bless me! – here was a sight for the honest burghers of Vondervotteimittiss.

To speak plainly, the fellow had, in spite of his grinning, an audacious and sinister kind of face; and as he curvetted right into the village, the odd stumpy appearance of his pumps excited no little suspicion; and many a burgher who beheld him that day would have given a trifle for a peep beneath the white cambric handkerchief which hung so obtrusively from the pocket of his swallow-tailed coat. But what mainly occasioned a righteous indignation was that the scoundrelly popinjay, while he cut a fandango here and a whirligig there, did not seem to have the remotest idea in the world of such a thing as *keeping time* in his steps.

The good people of the borough had scarcely a chance, however, to get their eyes thoroughly open, when, just as it wanted half-a-minute of noon, the rascal bounced, as I say, right into the midst of them; gave a *chassez* here, and a *balancez* there; and then, after a *pirouette* and a *pas-de-zephyr*, pigeon-winged himself right up into the belfry of the House of the Town-Council, where the wonder-stricken belfry-man sat smoking in a state of dignity and dismay. But the little chap seized him at once by the nose; gave it a swing and a pull; clapped the big *chapeau-de-bras* upon his head; knocked it down over his eyes and mouth; and then, lifting up the big fiddle, beat him with it so long and so soundly that, what with the belfry-man being so fat and the fiddle being to hollow, you would have sworn that there was a regiment of double bass drummers all beating the devil's tattoo up in the belfry of the steeple of Vondervotteimittiss.

There is no knowing to what desperate act of vengeance this unprincipled attack might have aroused the inhabitants but for the important fact that it now wanted only half-a-second of noon. The bell was about to strike, and it was a matter of absolute and pre-eminent necessity that everybody should look well at his watch. It was evident, however, that just at this moment the fellow in the steeple was doing something that he had no business to do with the clock. But as it now began to strike nobody had any time to attend to his manœuvres, for they had all to count the strokes of the bell as it sounded.

'One!' said the clock.

'Von!' echoed every little old gentleman in every leather-bottomed arm-chair in Vondervotteimittiss. 'Von!' said his watch also; 'von!' said the watch on his vrow, and 'von!' said the watches of the boys, and the little gilt repeaters on the tails of the cat and pig.

'Two!' continued the big bell; and

'Doo!' repeated all the repeaters.

'Three! Four! Five ! Six! Seven! Eight! Nine! Ten!' said the bell.

'Dree! Vour! Fibe! Sax! Seben! Aight! Noin! Den!' answered the others.

'Eleven!' said the big one.

'Eleben!' assented the little fellows.

'Twelve!' said the bell.

'Dvelf!' they replied, perfectly satisfied, and dropping their voices.

'Und dvelf it iss!' said all the little old gentlemen, putting up their watches. But the big bell had not done with them yet.

'*Thirteen!*' said he.

'Der Teufel!' gasped the little old gentlemen, turning pale, dropping their pipes, and putting down all their right legs from over their left knees.

'Der Teufel!' groaned they, 'Dirteen! Dirteen!! – Mein Gott, it is Dirteen o'clock!!'

Why attempt to describe the terrible scene which ensued? All Vondervotteimittiss flew at once into a lamentable state of uproar.

'Vot is cum'd to mein pelly?' roared all the boys. – 'I've been ongry for dis hour!'

'Vot is cum'd to mein kraut?' screamed all the vrows. 'It has been done to rags for dis hour!'

'Vot is cum'd to mein pipe?' swore all the little old gentlemen. 'Donder and Blitzen! it has been smoked out for dis hour!' – and they filled them up again in a great rage, and, sinking back in their arm-chairs, puffed away so fast and so fiercely that the whole valley was immediately filled with impenetrable smoke.

Meantime the cabbages all turned very red in the face, and it seemed as if Old Nick himself had taken possession of everything in the shape of a timepiece. The clocks carved upon the furniture took to dancing as if bewitched, while those upon the mantelpieces could scarcely contain themselves for fury, and kept such a continual striking of thirteen, and such a frisking and wriggling of their pendulums as was really horrible to see. But, worse than all, neither the cats nor the pigs could put up any longer with the behaviour of the little repeaters tied to their tails, and resented it by scampering all over the place, scratching and poking, and squeaking and screetching, and caterwauling and squalling, and flying into the faces, and running under the petticoats of the people, and creating altogether the most abominable din and confusion which it is possible for a reasonable person to conceive. And to make matters still more distressing, the rascally little scrapegrace in the steeple was evidently exerting himself to the utmost. Every now and then one might catch a glimpse of the scoundrel through the smoke. There he sat in the belfry upon the belfry-man, who was lying flat upon his back. In his teeth the villain held the bell-rope, which he kept jerking about with his head, raising such a clatter that my ears ring again even to think of it. On his lap lay the big fiddle at which he was scraping out of all time and tune with both hands, making a great show, the nincompoop! of playing 'Judy O'Flannagan and Paddy O'Rafferty.'

Affairs being thus miserably situated I left the place in disgust, and now appeal for aid to all lovers of correct time and fine kraut. Let us proceed in a body to the borough, and restore the ancient order of things in Vondervotteimittiss by ejecting that little fellow from the steeple.

The Murders in the Rue Morgue

What song the Sirens sang, or what name Achilles assumed when
 he hid himself among women, although puzzling questions are not
 beyond *all* conjecture. – *Sir Thomas Browne.*

The mental features discoursed of as the analytical are, in themselves,
but little susceptible of analysis. We appreciate them only in their
effects. We know of them, among other things, that they are always to
their possessor, when inordinately possessed a source of the liveliest
enjoyment. As the strong man exults in his physical ability, delighting
in such exercises as call his muscles into action, so glories the analyst in
that moral activity which *disentangles*. He derives pleasure from even
the most trivial occupations bringing his talent into play. He is fond of
enigmas, of conundrums, of hieroglyphics; exhibiting in his solutions
of each a degree of *acumen* which appears to the ordinary apprehension
preternatural. His results, brought about by the very soul and
essence of method, have, in truth, the whole air of intuition.

 The faculty of re-solution is possibly much invigorated by
mathematical study, and especially by the highest branch of it which,
unjustly, and merely on account of its retrograde operations, has been
called, as if *par excellence*, analysis. Yet to calculate is not in itself to

analyse. A chess-player, for example, does the one without effort at the other. It follows that the game of chess, in its effects upon mental character, is greatly misunderstood. I am not now writing a treatise, but simply prefacing a somewhat peculiar narrative by observations very much at random; I will therefore take occasion to assert that the higher powers of the reflective intellect are more decidedly and more usefully tasked by the unostentatious game of draughts than by all the elaborate frivolity of chess. In this latter, where the pieces have different and *bizarre* motions, with various and variable values, what is only complex is mistaken (a not unusual error) for what is profound. The *attention* is here called powerfully into play. If it flag for an instant, an oversight is committed, resulting in injury or defeat. The possible moves being not only manifold but involute, the chances of such oversights are multiplied; and in nine cases out of ten it is the more concentrative rather than the more acute player who conquers. In draughts, on the contrary, where the moves are *unique* and have but little variation, the probabilities of inadvertence are diminished, and the mere attention being left comparatively unemployed, what advantages are obtained by either party are obtained by superior *acumen*. To be less abstract – let us suppose a game of draughts where the pieces are reduced to four kings, and where, of course, no oversight is to be expected. It is obvious that here the victory can be decided (the players being at all equal) only by some *recherché* movement, the result of some strong exertion of the intellect. Deprived of ordinary resources, the analyst throws himself into the spirit of his opponent, identifies himself therewith, and not unfrequently sees thus, at a glance, the sole methods (sometimes indeed absurdly simple ones) by which he may seduce into error or hurry into miscalculation.

Whist has long been noted for its influence upon what is termed the calculating power; and men of the highest order of intellect have been known to take an apparently unaccountable delight in it, while eschewing chess as frivolous. Beyond doubt there is nothing of a similar nature, so greatly tasking the faculty of analysis. The best chess-player in Christendom *may* be little more than the best player of chess; but proficiency in whist implies capacity for success in all those more important undertakings where mind struggles with mind. When I say proficiency, I mean that perfection in the game which includes a comprehension of *all* the sources whence legitimate advantage may be derived. These are not only manifold but multiform, and lie frequently among recesses of thought, altogether inaccessible to the ordinary understanding. To observe attentively is to remember distinctly; and, so far, the concentrative chess-player will do very well at whist; while the rules of Hoyle (themselves based upon the mere mechanism of the game) are sufficiently and generally comprehensible. Thus to have a retentive memory, and to proceed by 'the book,' are points commonly regarded as the sum total of good playing. But it is in matters beyond the limits of mere rule that the skill of the analyst is evinced. He makes in silence, a host of observations and inferences. So, perhaps, do his companions; and the difference in the extent of the information obtained lies not so much in the validity of the inference as in the quality of the observation. The necessary knowledge is that of *what* to observe. Our player confines himself not at all; nor, because the game is the object, does he reject deductions from things external to the game. He examines the countenance of his partner, comparing it carefully with that of each of his opponents. He considers the mode of assorting the cards in each hand; often counting trump by trump, and honour by honour, through the glances bestowed by their holders upon each. He notes every variation of face as the play progresses, gathering a fund of thought from the differences in the expression of certainty, of surprise, of triumph, or of chagrin. From the manner of gathering up a trick he judges whether the person taking it can make another in the suit. He recognises what is played through feint, by the air with which it is thrown upon the table. A casual or inadvertent word; the accidental dropping or turning of a card, with the accompanying anxiety or carelessness in regard to its concealment; the counting of the tricks, with the order of their arrangement; embarrassment, hesitation, eagerness or trepidation – all afford, to his apparently intuitive perception, indications of the true state of affairs. The first two or three rounds having been played, he is in full possession of the contents of each hand, and thenceforward puts down his cards with as absolute a precision of purpose as if the rest of the party had turned outward the faces of their own.

The analytical power should not be confounded with simple ingenuity; for while the analyist is necessarily ingenious, the ingenious man is often remarkably incapable of analysis. The constructive or combining power, by which ingenuity is usually manifested, and to which the phrenologists (I believe erroneously) have assigned a separate organ, supposing it a primitive faculty, has been so frequently seen in those whose intellect bordered otherwise upon idiocy, as to have attracted general observation among writers on morals. Between ingenuity and the analytic ability there exists a difference far greater indeed, than that between the fancy and the imagination, but of a character very strictly analogous. It will be found, in fact, that the ingenious are always fanciful, and the *truly* imaginative never otherwise than analytic.

The narrative which follows will appear to the reader somewhat in the light of a commentary upon the propositions just advanced.

Residing in Paris during the spring and part of the summer of 18—, I there became acquainted with a Monsieur C. Auguste Dupin. This young gentleman was of an excellent – indeed of an illustrious family, but, by a variety of untoward events, had been reduced to such poverty that the energy of his character succumbed beneath it, and he ceased to bestir himself in the world, or to care for the retrieval of his fortunes. By courtesy of his creditors, there still remained in his possession a small remnant of his patrimony; and upon the income arising from this, he managed by means of a rigorous economy to procure the necessaries of life, without troubling himself about its superfluities. Books, indeed, were his sole luxuries, and in Paris these are easily obtained.

Our first meeting was at an obscure library in the Rue Montmartre, where the accident of our both being in search of the same very rare and very remarkable volume brought us into closer communion. We saw each other again and again. I was deeply interested in the little family history which he detailed to me with all that candour which a Frenchman indulges whenever mere self is his theme. I was astonished, too, at the vast extent of his reading; and, above all, I felt my soul enkindled within me by the wild fervour, and the vivid freshness of his imagination. Seeking in Paris the objects I then sought, I felt that the society of such a man would be to me a treasure beyond price; and this feeling I frankly confided to him. It was at length arranged that we should live together during my stay in the city; and as my worldly circumstances were somewhat less embarrassed than his own, I was permitted to be at the expense of renting and furnishing, in a style which suited the rather fantastic gloom of our common temper, a time-eaten and grotesque mansion, long deserted through superstitions into which we did not inquire, and tottering to its fall in a retired and desolate portion of the Faubourg St. Germain.

Had the routine of our life at this place been known to the world, we should have been regarded as madmen – although, perhaps, as madmen of a harmless nature. Our seclusion was perfect. We admitted no visitors. Indeed the locality of our retirement had been carefully kept a secret from my own former associates; and it had been many years since Dupin had ceased to know or be known in Paris. We existed within ourselves alone.

It was a freak of fancy in my friend (for what else shall I call it?) to be enamoured of the Night for her own sake; and into this *bizarrerie*, as into all his others, I quietly fell; giving myself up to his wild whims with a perfect *abandon*. The sable divinity would not herself dwell with us always; but we could counterfeit her presence. At the first dawn of the morning we closed all the massive shutters of our old building; lighting a couple of tapers which, strongly perfumed, threw out only the ghastliest and feeblest of rays. By the aid of these we then busied our souls in dreams – reading, writing, or conversing, until warned by the clock of the advent of the true Darkness. Then we sailed forth into the streets, arm in arm, continuing the topics of the day, or roaming far and wide until a late hour, seeking amid the wild lights and shadows of the populous city, that infinity of mental excitement which quiet observation can afford.

At such times I could not help remarking and admiring (although from his rich ideality I had been prepared to expect it) a peculiar analytic ability in Dupin. He seemed, too, to take an eager delight in its exercise – if not exactly in its display – and did not hesitate to confess the pleasure thus derived. He boasted to me, with a low chuckling laugh, that most men, in respect to himself, wore windows in their bosoms, and was wont to follow up such assertions by direct and very startling proofs of his intimate knowledge of my own. His manner at these moments was frigid and abstract; his eyes were vacant in expression; while his voice, usually a rich tenor, rose into a treble which would have sounded petulantly but for the deliberateness and entire distinctness of the enunciation. Observing him in these moods, I often dwelt meditatively upon the old philosophy of the Bi-Part Soul, and amused myself with the fancy of a double Dupin – the creative and the resolvent.

Let it not be supposed from what I have just said that I am detailing any mystery, or penning any romance. What I have described in the Frenchman was merely the result of an excited or perhaps of a diseased intelligence. But of the character of his remarks at the periods in question an example will best convey the idea.

We were strolling one night down a long dirty street, in the vicinity of the Palais Royal. Being both apparently occupied with thought, neither of us had spoken a syllable for fifteen minutes at least. All at once Dupin broke forth with these words:

'He is a very little fellow, that's true, and would do better for the *Théâtre des Variétés*.'

'There can be no doubt of that,' I replied unwittingly, and not at first observing (so much had I been absorbed in reflection) the extraordinary manner in which the speaker had chimed in with my meditations. In an instant afterwards I recollected myself, and my astonishment was profound.

'Dupin,' said I gravely, 'this is beyond my comprehension. I do not hesitate to say that I am amazed, and can scarcely credit my senses. How was it possible you should know I was thinking of – ?' Here I paused, to ascertain beyond a doubt whether he really knew of whom I thought.

'Of Chantilly,' said he, 'why do you pause! You were remarking to yourself that his dimunitive figure unfitted him for tragedy.'

This was precisely what had formed the subject of my reflections. Chantilly was a *quondam* cobbler of the Rue St. Denis, who, becoming stage mad, had attempted the *rôle* of Xerxes, in Crébillon's tragedy so-called, and been notoriously pasquinaded for his pains.

'Tell me, for Heaven's sake,' I exclaimed, 'the method – if method there is – by which you have been enabled to fathom my soul in this matter.' In fact I was even more startled than I would have been willing to express.

'It was the fruiterer,' replied my friend, 'who brought you to the conclusion that the mender of soles was not of sufficient height for Xerxes *et id genus omne.*'

'The fruiterer! – you astonish me – I know no fruiterer whomsoever.'

'The man who ran up against you as we entered the street – it may have been fifteen minutes ago.'

I now remembered that, in fact, a fruiterer, carrying upon his head a large basket of apples, had nearly thrown me down by accident as we passed from the Rue C—— into the thoroughfare where we stood; but what this had to do with Chantilly I could not possibly understand.

There was not a particle of *charlatanerie* about Dupin. 'I will explain,' he said, 'and that you may comprehend all clearly, we will first retrace the course of your meditations from the moment in which I spoke to you until that of the *rencontre* with the fruiterer in question. The larger links of the chain run thus – Chantilly, Orion, Doctor Nichols, Epicurus, Stereotomy, the street stones, the fruiterer.'

There are few persons who have not at some period of their lives amused themselves in retracing the steps by which particular conclusions of their own minds have been attained. The occupation is often full of interest; and he who attempts it for the first time is astonished by the apparently illimitable distance and incoherence between the starting-point and the goal. What then must have been my amazement when I heard the Frenchman speak what he had just spoken, and when I could not help acknowledging that he had spoken the truth. He continued:

'We had been talking of horses, if I remember aright, just before leaving the Rue C——. This was the last subject we discussed. As we crossed into this street, a fruiterer, with a large basket upon his head, brushing quickly past us, thrust you upon a pile of paving-stones collected at a spot where the causeway is undergoing repair. You stepped upon one of the loose fragments, slipped, slightly sprained your ankle, appeared vexed or sulky, muttered a few words, turned to look at the pile, and then proceeded in silence. I was not particularly attentive to what you did; but observation has become with me, of late, a species of necessity.

'You kept your eyes upon the ground – glancing, with a petulant expression, at the holes and ruts in the pavement (so that I saw you were still thinking of the stones), until we reached the little alley called Lamartine, which has been paved, by way of experiment, with the overlapping and riveted blocks. Here your countenance brightened up, and, perceiving your lips move, I could not doubt that you murmured the word "stereotomy," a term very affectedly applied to this species of pavement. I knew that you could not say to yourself "stereotomy" without being brought to think of atomies, and thus of the theories of Epicurus; and since, when we discussed this subject not very long ago, I mentioned to you how singularly, yet with how little notice, the vague guesses of that noble Greek had met with confirmation in the late nebular cosmogony, I felt that you could not avoid casting your eyes upward to the great *nebula* in Orion, and I certainly expected that you would do so. You did look up; and I was now assured that I had correctly followed your steps. But in that bitter *tirade* upon Chantilly, which appeared in yesterday's *Musée*, the satirist, making some disgraceful allusions to the cobbler's change of name upon assuming the buskin, quoted a Latin line about which we have often conversed. I mean the line –

Perdidit antiquum litera prima sonum.

I had told you that this was in reference to Orion, formerly written

Urion, and from certain pungencies connected with this explanation I was aware that you could not have forgotten it. It was clear, therefore, that you would not fail to combine the two ideas of Orion and Chantilly. That you did combine them I saw by the character of the smile which passed over your lips. You thought of the poor cobbler's immolation. So far you had been stooping in your gait, but now I saw you draw yourself up to your full height. I was then sure that you reflected upon the diminutive figure of Chantilly. At this point I interrupted your meditations to remark that as, in fact, he *was* a very little fellow – that Chantilly – he would do better at the *Théâtre des Variétés*.'

Not long after this we were looking over an evening edition of the 'Gazette des Tribunaux,' when the following paragraphs arrested our attention.

'EXTRAORDINARY MURDERS. – This morning about three o'clock the inhabitants of the Quartier St. Roch were aroused from sleep by a succession of terrific shrieks, issuing, apparently from the fourth storey of a house in the Rue Morgue, known to be in the sole occupancy of one Madame L'Espanaye, and her daughter, Mademoiselle Camille L'Espanaye. After some delay, occasioned by a fruitless attempt to procure admission in the usual manner, the gateway was broken in with a crowbar, and eight or ten of the neighbours entered, accompanied by two *gendarmes*. By this time the cries had ceased, but as the party rushed up the first flight of stairs, two or more rough voices in angry contention were distinguished, and seemed to proceed from the upper part of the house. As the second landing was reached these sounds also had ceased, and everything remained perfectly quiet. The party spread themselves and hurried from room to room. Upon arriving at a large back chamber in the fourth storey (the door of which, being found locked with the key inside, was forced open) a spectacle presented itself which struck every one present not less with horror than with astonishment.

'The apartment was in the wildest disorder, the furniture broken and thrown about in all directions. There was only one bedstead, and from this the bed had been removed and thrown into the middle of the floor. On a chair lay a razor besmeared with blood. On the hearth were two or three long and thick tresses of grey human hair, also dabbled in blood, and seeming to have been pulled out by the roots. Upon the floor were found four Napoleons, an earring of topaz, three large silver spoons, three smaller of *métal d'Alger*, and two bags containing nearly four thousand francs in gold. The drawers of a *bureau* which stood in one corner were open, and had been apparently rifled, although many articles still remained in them. A small iron safe was discovered under the *bed* (not under the bedstead). It was open, with the key still in the door. It had no contents beyond a few old letters and other papers of little consequence.

'Of Madame L'Espanaye no traces were here seen, but an unusual quantity of soot being observed in the fireplace, a search was made in the chimney and (horrible to relate!) the corpse of the daughter, head downward, was dragged therefrom, it having been thus forced up the narrow aperture for a considerable distance. The body was quite warm. Upon examining it many excoriations were perceived, no doubt occasioned by the violence with which it had been thrust up and disengaged. Upon the face were many severe scratches, and upon the throat, dark bruises and deep indentations of finger nails, as if the deceased had been throttled to death.

'After a thorough investigation of every portion of the house without further discovery, the party made its way into a small paved yard in the rear of the building, where lay the corpse of the old lady, with her throat so entirely cut that, upon an attempt to raise her, the head fell off. The body as well as the head was fearfully mutilated, the former so much so as scarcely to retain any semblance of humanity.

'To this horrible mystery there is not as yet, we believe, the slightest clue.'

The next day's paper had these additional particulars.

'*The Tragedy in the Rue Morgue.* – Many individuals have been examined in relation to this most extraordinary and frightful affair' [the word "*affaire*" has not yet in France that levity of import which it conveys with us], 'but nothing whatever has transpired to throw light upon it. We give below all the material testimony elicited.

'*Pauline Dubourg*, laundress, deposes that she has known both the deceased for three years, having washed for them during that period. The old lady and her daughter seemed on good terms – very affectionate towards each other. They were excellent pay. Could not speak in regard to their mode or means of living. Believed that Madame L. told fortunes for a living. Was reputed to have money put by. Never met any persons in the house when she called for the clothes or took them home. Was sure that they had no servant in employ. There appeared to be no furniture in any part of the building except in the fourth storey.

'*Pierre Moreau*, tobacconist, deposes that he has been in the habit of selling small quantities of tobacco and snuff to Madame L'Espanaye for nearly four years. Was born in the neighbourhood, and has always resided there. The deceased and her daughter had occupied the house in which the corpses were found for more than six years. It was formerly occupied by a jeweller, who underlet the upper rooms to various persons. The house was the property of Madame L. She became dissatisfied with the abuse of the premises by her tenant, and moved into them herself, refusing to let any portion. The old lady was childish. Witness had seen the daughter some five or six times during the six years. The two lived an exceedingly retired life – were reputed to have money. Had heard it said among the neighbours that Madame L. told fortunes – did not believe it. Had never seen any person enter the door except the old lady and her daughter, a porter once or twice, and a physician some eight or ten times.

'Many other persons, neighbours, gave evidence to the same effect. No one was spoken of as frequenting the house. It was not known whether there were any living connections of Madame L. and her daughter. The shutters of the front windows were seldom opened. Those in the rear were always closed with the exception of the large back room, fourth storey. The house was a good house, not very old.

'*Isidore Musèt, gendarme*, deposes that he was called to the house about three o'clock in the morning, and found some twenty or thirty persons at the gateway endeavouring to gain admittance. Forced it open at length with a bayonet – not with a crowbar. Had but little difficulty in getting it open on account of its being a double or folding gate, and bolted neither at bottom nor top. The shrieks were continued until the gate was forced, and then suddenly ceased. They seemed to be screams of some person (or persons) in great agony, were loud and drawn out, not sharp and quick. Witness led the way up stairs. Upon reaching the first landing, heard two voices in loud and angry contention – the one a gruff voice, the other much shriller – a very strange voice. Could distinguish some words of the former, which was that of a Frenchman. Was positive it was not a woman's voice. Could distinguish the words "*sacré*" and "*diable*." The shrill voice was that of a foreigner. Could not be sure whether it was the voice of a man or of a woman. Could not make out what was said, but believed the language to be Spanish. The state of the room and of the bodies was described by this witness as we described them yesterday.

'*Henri Duval*, a neighbour, and by trade a silversmith, deposes that he was one of the party who first entered the house. Corroborates the testimony of Musèt in general. As soon as they forced an entrance they reclosed the door to keep out the crowd, which collected very fast, notwithstanding the lateness of the hour. The shrill voice, this witness thinks, was that of an Italian. Was certain it was not French. Could not be sure that it was a man's voice. It might have been a woman's. Was not acquainted with the Italian language. Could not distinguish the words, but was convinced by the intonation that the speaker was an Italian. Knew Madame L. and her daughter. Had conversed with both frequently. Was sure that the shrill voice was not that of either of the deceased.

'—— *Odenheimer, restaurateur*. – This witness volunteered his testimony. Not speaking French, was examined through an interpreter. Is a native of Amsterdam. Was passing the house at the time of the shrieks. They lasted for several minutes – probably ten. They were long and loud – very awful and distressing. Was one of those who entered the building. Corroborated the previous evidence in every respect but one. Was sure that the shrill voice was that of a man – of a Frenchman. Could not distinguish the words uttered. They were loud and quick – unequal – spoken apparently in fear as well as in anger.

The voice was harsh – not so much shrill as harsh. Could not call it a shrill voice. The gruff voice said repeatedly, "*sacré*," "*diable*," and once "*mon Dieu.*"

'*Jules Mignaud*, banker, of the firm of Mignaud et Fils, Rue Deloraine. – Is the elder Mignaud. Madame L'Espanaye had some property. Had opened an account with his banking house in the spring of the year —— (eight years previously). Made frequent deposits in small sums. Had checked for nothing until the third day before her death, when she took out in person the sum of 4000 francs. This sum was paid in gold, and a clerk sent home with the money.

'*Adolphe Le Bon*, clerk to Mignaud et Fils, deposes that on the day in question, about noon, he accompanied Madame L'Espanaye to her residence with the 4000 francs, put up on two bags. Upon the door being opened, Mademoiselle L. appeared and took from his hands one of the bags, while the old lady relieved him of the other. He then bowed and departed. Did not see any person in the street at the time. It is a by-street – very lonely.

'*William Bird*, tailor, deposes that he was one of the party who entered the house. Is an Englishman. Has lived in Paris two years. Was one of the first to ascend the stairs. Heard the voices in contention. The gruff voice was that of a Frenchman. Could make out several words, but cannot now remember all. Heard distinctly "*sacré*" and "*mon Dieu.*" There was a sound at the moment as if of several persons struggling – a scraping and scuffling sound. The shrill voice was very loud – louder than the gruff one. Is sure that it was not the voice of an Englishman. Appeared to be that of a German. Might have been a woman's voice. Does not understand German.

'Four of the above named witnesses, being recalled, deposed that the door of the chamber in which was found the body of Mademoiselle L. was locked on the inside when the party reached it. Everything was perfectly silent – no groans or noises of any kind. Upon forcing the door no person was seen. The windows, both of the back and front room, were down and firmly fastened from within. A door between the two rooms was closed, but not locked. The door leading from the front room into the passage was locked, with the key on the inside. A small room in the front of the house, on the fourth storey, at the head of the passage, was open, the door being ajar. This room was crowded with old beds, boxes, and so forth. These were carefully removed and searched. There was not an inch of any portion of the house which was not carefully searched. Sweeps were sent up and down the chimneys. The house was a four storey one, with garrets (*mansardes*). A trap-door on the roof was nailed down very securely – did not appear to have been opened for years. The time elapsing between the hearing of the voices in contention and the breaking open of the room door was variously stated by the witnesses. Some made it as short as three minutes – some as long as five. The door was opened with difficulty.

'*Alfonzo Garcio*, undertaker, deposes that he resides in the Rue Morgue. Is a native of Spain. Was one of the party who entered the house. Did not proceed up stairs. Is nervous, and was apprehensive of the consequences of agitation. Heard the voices in contention. The gruff voice was that of a Frenchman. Could not distinguish what was said. The shrill voice was that of an Englishman – is sure of this. Does not understand the English language, but judges by the intonation.

'*Alberto Montani*, confectioner, deposes that he was among the first to ascend the stairs. Heard the voices in question. The gruff voice was that of a Frenchman. Distinguished several words. The speaker appeared to be expostulating. Could not make out the words of the shrill voice. Spoke quick and unevenly. Thinks it the voice of a Russian. Corroborates the general testimony. Is an Italian. Never conversed with a native of Russia.

'Several witnesses, recalled, here testified that the chimneys of all the rooms on the fourth storey were too narrow to admit the passage of a human being. By "sweeps" were meant cylindrical sweeping-brushes, such as are employed by those who clean chimneys. These brushes were passed up and down every flue in the house. There is no back passage by which any one could have descended while the party proceeded upstairs. The body of Mademoiselle L'Espanaye was so firmly wedged in the chimney that it could not be got down until four or five of the party united their strength.

'*Paul Dumas*, physician, deposes that he was called to view the bodies about daybreak. They were both then lying on the sacking of the bedstead in the chamber where Mademoiselle L. was found. The corpse of the young lady was much bruised and excoriated. The fact that it had been thrust up the chimney would sufficiently account for these appearances. The throat was greatly chafed. There were several deep scratches just below the chin, together with a series of livid spots which were evidently the impression of fingers. The face was fearfully discoloured, and the eye-balls protruded. The tongue had been partially bitten through. A large bruise was discovered upon the pit of the stomach, produced apparently by the pressure of a knee. In the opinion of M. Dumas, Mademoiselle L'Espanaye had been throttled to death by some person or persons unknown. The corpse of the mother was horribly mutilated. All the bones of the right leg and arm were more or less shattered. The left *tibia* much splintered, as well as all the ribs of the left side. Whole body dreadfully bruised and discoloured. It was not possible to say how the injuries had been inflicted. A heavy club of wood, or a broad bar of iron – a chair – any large, heavy, and obtuse weapon would have produced such results if wielded by the hands of a very powerful man. No woman could have inflicted the blows with any weapon. The head of the deceased, when seen by witnesses, was entirely separated from the body, and was also greatly shattered. The throat had evidently been cut with some very sharp instrument – probably with a razor.

'*Alexandre Etienne*, surgeon, was called with M. Dumas to view the bodies. Corroborated the testimony and the opinions of M. Dumas.

'Nothing further of importance was elicited, although several other persons were examined. A murder so mysterious, and so perplexing in all its particulars, was never before committed in Paris – if indeed a murder has been committed at all. The police are entirely at fault – an unusual occurrence in affairs of this nature. There is not, however, the shadow of a clue apparent.'

The evening edition of the paper stated that the greatest excitement still continued in the Quartier St. Roch – that the premises in question had been carefully re-searched, and fresh examinations of witnesses instituted, but all to no purpose. A postscript, however, mentioned that Adolphe Le Bon had been arrested and imprisoned – although nothing appeared to criminate him beyond the facts already detailed.

Dupin seemed singularly interested in the progress of this affair – at least so I judged from his manner, for he made no comments. It was only after the announcement that Le Bon had been imprisoned that he asked me my opinion respecting the murders.

I could merely agree with all Paris in considering them an insoluble mystery. I saw no means by which it would be possible to trace the murderer.

'We must not judge of the means,' said Dupin, 'by this shell of an examination. The Parisian police, so much extolled for *acumen*, are cunning, but no more. There is no method in their proceedings, beyond the method of the moment. They make a vast parade of measures; but, not unfrequently, these are so ill-adapted to the objects proposed as to put us in mind of Monsieur Jordain's calling for his *robé-de-chambre – pour mieux entendre la musique*. The results attained by them are not unfrequently surprising, but for the most part are brought about by simple diligence and activity. When these qualities are unavailing, their schemes fail. Vidocq, for example, was a good guesser, and a persevering man. But, without educated thought, he erred continually by the very intensity of his investigations. He impaired his vision by holding the object too close. He might see, perhaps, one or two points with unusual clearness, but in so doing, he necessarily lost sight of the matter as a whole. Thus there is such a thing as being too profound. Truth is not always in a well. In fact as regards the more important knowledge, I do believe that she is invariably superficial. The truth lies not in the valleys where we seek her, but upon the mountain-tops where she is found. The modes and sources of this kind of error are well typified in the contemplation of the heavenly bodies. To look at a star by glances – to view it in a side-long way, by turning towards it the exterior portions of the *retina* (more susceptible of feeble impressions of light than the interior), is to behold the star distinctly – is to have the best appreciation of its lustre

– a lustre which grows dim just in proportion as we turn our vision *fully* upon it. A greater number of rays actually fall upon the eye in the latter case, but in the former there is the more refined capacity for comprehension. By undue profundity we perplex and enfeeble thought; and it is possible to make even Venus herself vanish from the firmament by a scrutiny too sustained, too concentrated, or too direct.

'As for these murders, let us enter into some examinations for ourselves before we make up an opinion respecting them. An inquiry will afford us amusement' (I thought this an odd term so applied, but said nothing), 'and besides, Le Bon once rendered me a service for which I am not ungrateful. We will go and see the premises with our own eyes. I know G——, the Prefect of Police, and shall have no difficulty, in obtaining the necessary permission.'

The permission was obtained, and we proceeded at once to the Rue Morgue. This is one of those miserable thoroughfares which intervene between the Rue Richelieu and the Rue St. Roch. It was late in the afternoon when we reached it, as this quarter is at a great distance from that in which we resided. The house was readily found; for there were still many persons gazing up at the closed shutters, with an objectless curiosity, from the opposite side of the way. It was an ordinary Parisian house, with a gateway, on one side of which was a glazed watch-box, with a sliding panel in the window, indicating a *loge de concierge*. Before going in we walked up the street, turned down an alley, and then, again turning, passed in the rear of the building – Dupin, meanwhile, examining the whole neighbourhood, as well as the house, with a minuteness of attention for which I could see no possible object.

Retracing our steps, we came again to the front of the dwelling, rang, and, having shown our credentials, were admitted by the agents in charge. We went upstairs – into the chamber where the body of Mademoiselle L'Espanaye had been found, and where both the deceased still lay. The disorders of the room had, as usual, been suffered to exist. I saw nothing beyond what had been stated in the 'Gazette des Tribunaux.' Dupin scrutinised everything – not excepting the bodies of the victims. We then went into the other rooms, and into the yard; a *gendarme* accompanying us throughout. The examination occupied us until dark, when we took our departure. On our way home my companion stepped in for a moment at the office of one of the daily papers.

I have said that the whims of my friend were manifold, and that *Je les ménageais* – for this phrase there is no English equivalent. It was his humour now to decline all conversation on the subject of the murder, until about noon the next day. He then asked me suddenly, if I had observed anything *peculiar* at the scene of the atrocity.

There was something in his manner of emphasising the word 'peculiar,' which caused me to shudder, without knowing why.

'No, nothing *peculiar*,' I said; 'nothing more, at least, than we both saw stated in the paper.'

'The "Gazette,"' he replied, 'has not entered, I fear, into the unusual horror of the thing. But dismiss the idle opinions of this print. It appears to me that this mystery is considered insoluble for the very reason which should cause it to be regarded as easy of solution – I mean for the *outré* character of its features. The police are confounded by the seeming absence of motive – not for the murder itself, but for the atrocity of the murder. They are puzzled, too, by the seeming impossibility of reconciling the voices heard in contention, with the facts that no one was discovered upstairs but the assassinated Mademoiselle L'Espanaye, and that there were no means of egress without the notice of the party ascending. The wild disorder of the room; the corpse thrust, with the head downward, up the chimney; the frightful mutilation of the body of the old lady; these considerations, with those just mentioned, and others which I need not mention, have sufficed to paralyse the powers, by putting completely at fault the boasted *acumen* of the government agents. They have fallen into the gross but common error of confronting the unusual with the abstruse. But it is by these deviations from the plane of the ordinary that reason feels its way, if at all, in its search for the true. In investigations such as we are now pursuing it should not be so much asked "what has occurred," as "what has occurred that has never occurred before." In fact, the facility with which I shall arrive, or have arrived at the solution of this mystery, is in the direct ratio of its apparent insolubility in the eyes of the police.'

I stared at the speaker in mute astonishment.

'I am now awaiting,' continued he, looking towards the door of our apartment – 'I am now awaiting a person, who, although perhaps not the perpetrator of these butcheries, must have been in some measure implicated in their perpetration. Of the worst portion of the crimes committed, it is probable that he is innocent. I hope that I am right in this supposition; for upon it I build my expectation of reading the entire riddle. I look for the man here – in this room – every moment. It is true that he may not arrive; but the probability is that he will. Should he come, it will be necessary to detain him. Here are pistols; and we both know how to use them when occasion demands their use.'

I took the pistols, scarcely knowing what I did, or believing what I heard, while Dupin went on, very much as if in a soliloquy. I have already spoken of his abstract manner at such times. His discourse was addressed to myself; but his voice, although by no means loud, had that intonation which is commonly employed in speaking to some one at a great distance. His eyes, vacant in expression, regarded only the wall.

'That the voices heard in contention,' he said, 'by the party upon the stairs, were not the voices of the women themselves, was fully proved by the evidence. This relieves us of all doubt upon the question whether the old lady could have first destroyed the daughter, and afterwards have committed suicide. I speak of this point chiefly for the sake of method; for the strength of Madame L'Espanaye would have been utterly unequal to the task of thrusting her daughter's corpse up the chimney as it was found; and the nature of the wounds upon her own person entirely preclude the idea of self-destruction. Murder, then, has been committed by some third party; and the voices of this third party were those heard in contention. Let me now advert – not to the whole testimony respecting these voices – but to what was *peculiar* in that testimony. Did you observe anything peculiar about it?'

I remarked that, while all the witnesses agreed in supposing the gruff voice to be that of a Frenchman, there was much disagreement in regard to the shrill, or, as one individual termed it, the harsh voice.

'That was the evidence itself,' said Dupin, 'but it was not the peculiarity of the evidence. You have observed nothing distinctive. Yet there *was* something to be observed. The witnesses, as you remark, agreed about the gruff voice; they were here unanimous. But in regard to the shrill voice, the peculiarity is – not that they disagreed – but that, while an Italian, an Englishman, a Spaniard, a Hollander, and a Frenchman attempted to describe it, each one spoke of it as that *of a foreigner*. Each is sure that it was not the voice of one of his own countrymen. Each likens it – not to the voice of an individual of any nation with whose language he is conversant – but the converse. The Frenchman supposes it the voice of a Spaniard, and "might have distinguished some words *had he been acquainted with the Spanish*." The Dutchman maintains it to have been that of a Frenchman; but we find it stated that "*not understanding French this witness was examined through an interpreter*." The Englishman thinks it the voice of a German, and "*does not understand German*." The Spaniard "is sure" that it was that of an Englishman, but "judges by the intonation" altogether, "*as he has no knowledge of the English*." The Italian believes it the voice of a Russian, but "*has never conversed with a native of Russia*." A second Frenchman differs, moreover, with the first, and is positive that the voice was that of an Italian; but, *not being cognisant of that tongue*, is, like the Spaniard, "convinced by the intonation." Now, how strangely unusual must that voice have really been, about which such testimony as this *could* have been elicited! – in whose *tones*, even, denizens of the five great divisions of Europe could recognise nothing familiar! You will say that it might have been the voice of an Asiatic – of an African. Neither Asiatics nor Africans abound in Paris; but, without denying the inference, I will now merely call your attention to three points. The voice is termed by one witness "harsh rather than shrill." It is represented by two others to have been "quick and *unequal*." No words – no sounds resembling words – were by any witness mentioned as distinguishable.

'I know not,' continued Dupin, 'what impression I may have

made, so far, upon your own understanding, but I do not hesitate to say that legitimate deductions even from this portion of the testimony – the portion respecting the gruff and shrill voices – are in themselves sufficient to engender a suspicion which should give direction to all further progress in the investigation of the mystery. I said "legitimate deductions," but my meaning is not thus fully expressed. I designed to imply that the deductions are the *sole* proper ones, and that the suspicion arises *inevitably* from them as the single result. What the suspicion is, however, I will not say just yet. I merely wish you to bear in mind that, with myself, it was sufficiently forcible to give a definite form – a certain tendency – to my inquiries in the chamber.

'Let us now transport ourselves, in fancy, to this chamber. What shall we first seek here? The means of egress employed by the murderers. It is not too much to say that neither of us believe in preternatural events. Madame and Mademoiselle L'Espanaye were not destroyed by spirits. The doers of the deed were material, and escaped materially. Then how? Fortunately there is but one mode of reasoning upon the point, and that mode *must* lead us to a definite decision. Let us examine, each by each, the possible means of egress. It is clear that the assassins were in the room where Mademoiselle L'Espanaye was found, or at least in the room adjoining, when the party ascended the stairs. It is then only from these two apartments that we have to seek issues. The police have laid bare the floors, the ceilings, and the masonry of the walls in every direction. No *secret* issues could have escaped their vigilance. But, not trusting to *their* eyes, I examined with my own. There were, then, *no* secret issues. Both doors leading from the rooms into the passage were securely locked, with the keys inside. Let us turn to the chimneys. These, although of ordinary width for some eight or ten feet above the hearths, will not admit, throughout their extent, the body of a large cat. The impossibility of egress, by means already stated, being thus absolute, we are reduced to the windows. Through those of the front room no one could have escaped without notice from the crowd in the street. The murderers *must* have passed, then, through those of the back room. Now, brought to this conclusion in so unequivocal a manner as we are, it is not our part, as reasoners, to reject it on account of apparent impossibilities. It is only left for us to prove that these apparent "impossibilities" are, in reality, not such.

'There are two windows in the chamber. One of them is unobstructed by furniture, and is wholly visible. The lower portion of the other is hidden from view by the head of the unwieldy bedstead which is thrust close up against it. The former was found securely fastened from within. It resisted the utmost force of those who endeavoured to raise it. A large gimlet-hole had been pierced in its frame to the left, and a very stout nail was found fitted therein, nearly to the head. Upon examining the other window a similar nail was seen similarly fitted in it; and a vigorous attempt to raise this sash failed also. The police were now entirely satisfied that egress had not been in these directions. And, *therefore*, it was thought a matter of super-erogation to withdraw the nails and open the windows.

'My own examination was somewhat more particular, and was so for the reason I have just given – because here it was, I knew, that all apparent impossibilites *must* be proved to be not such in reality.

'I proceeded to think thus – *a posteriori*. The murderers *did* escape from one of these windows. This being so, they could not have re-fastened the sashes from the inside, as they were found fastened – the consideration which puts a stop, through its obviousness, to the scrutiny of the police in this quarter. Yet the sashes *were* fastened. They *must*, then, have the power of fastening themselves. There was no escape from this conclusion. I stepped to the unobstructed casement, withdrew the nail with some difficulty, and attempted to raise the sash. It resisted all my efforts, as I had anticipated. A concealed spring must, I now knew, exist; and this corroboration of my idea convinced me that my premises, at least, were correct, however mysterious still appeared the circumstances attending the nails. A careful search soon brought to light the hidden spring. I pressed it, and, satisfied with the discovery, forbore to upraise the sash.

'I now replaced the nail and regarded it attentively. A person passing out through this window might have reclosed it, and the spring would have caught; but the nail could not have been replaced. The conclusion was plain, and again narrowed in the field of my investigations. The assassins *must* have escaped through the other window. Supposing, then, the springs upon each sash to be the same, as was probable, there *must* be found a difference between the nails, or at least between the modes of their fixture. Getting upon the sacking of the bedstead, I looked over the head-board minutely at the second casement. Passing my hand down behind the board, I readily discovered and pressed the spring, which was, as I had supposed, identical in character with its neighbour. I now looked at the nail. It was as stout as the other, and apparently fitted in the same manner, driven in nearly up to the head.

'You will say that I was puzzled; but if you think so you must have misunderstood the nature of the inductions. To use a sporting phrase, I had not been once "at fault." The scent had never for an instant been lost. There was no flaw in any link of the chain. I had traced the secret to its ultimate result; and that result was *the nail*. It had, I say, in every respect the appearance of its fellow in the other window; but this fact was an absolute nullity (conclusive as it might seem to be) when compared with the consideration that here at this point terminated the clue. "There *must* be something wrong," I said, "about the nail." I touched it, and the head, with about a quarter of an inch of the shank, came off in my fingers. The rest of the shank was in the gimlet-hole, where it had been broken off. The fracture was an old one (for its edges were incrusted with rust), and had apparently been accomplished by the blow of a hammer, which had partially imbedded in the top of the bottom sash the head portion of the nail. I now carefully replaced this head portion in the indentation whence I had taken it, and the resemblance to a perfect nail was complete – the fissure was invisible. Pressing the spring, I gently raised the sash for a few inches; the head went up with it, remaining firm in its bed. I closed the window, and the semblance of the whole nail was again perfect.

'The riddle, so far, was now unriddled. The assassin had escaped through the window which looked upon the bed. Dropping of its own accord upon his exit (or perhaps purposely closed), it had become fastened by the spring; and it was the retention of this spring which had been mistaken by the police for that of the nail, further inquiry being thus considered unnecessary.

'The next question is that of the mode of descent. Upon this point I had been satisfied in my walk with you around the building. About five feet and a-half from the casement in question there runs a lightning-rod. From this rod it would have been impossible for any one to reach the window itself, to say nothing of entering it. I observed, however, that the shutters of the fourth storey were of the peculiar kind called by Parisian carpenters, *ferrades*, a kind rarely employed at the present day, but frequently seen upon very old mansions at Lyons and Bordeaux. They are in the form of an ordinary door (a single, not a folding door), except that the lower half is latticed or worked in open trellis, thus affording an excellent hold for the hands. In the present instance these shutters are fully three feet and-a-half broad. When we saw them from the rear of the house they were both about half-open, that is to say, they stood off at right angles from the wall. It is probable that the police, as well as myself, examined the back of the tenement; but if so, in looking at these *ferrades* in the line of their breadth (as they must have done), they did not perceive this great breadth itself, or, at all events, failed to take it into due consideration. In fact, having once satisfied themselves that no egress could have been made in this quarter, they would naturally bestow here a very cursory examination. It was clear to me, however, that the shutter belonging to the window at the head of the bed would, if swung fully back to the wall, reach to within two feet of the lightning-rod. It was also evident that by exertion of a very unusual degree of activity and courage an entrance into the window from the rod might have been thus effected. By reaching to the distance of two feet and-a-half (we now suppose the shutter open to its whole extent) a robber might have taken a firm grasp upon the trellis-work. Letting go, then, his hold upon the rod, placing his feet securely against the wall, and springing boldly from it, he might have swung the shutter so as to close it, and, if we imagine the window open at the time, might even have swung himself into the room.

'I wish you to bear especially in mind that I have spoken of a *very* unusual degree of activity as requisite to success in so hazardous and so difficult a feat. It is my design to show you, first, that the thing might possibly have been accomplished; but, secondly and *chiefly*, I wish to impress upon your understanding the *very extraordinary*, the almost preternatural, character of that agility which could have accomplished it.

'You will say, no doubt, using the language of the law, that "to make out my case" I should rather undervalue than insist upon a full estimation of the activity required in this matter. This may be the practice in law, but it is not the usage of reason. My ultimate object is only the truth. My immediate purpose is to lead you to place in juxtaposition that *very unusual* activity of which I have just spoken with that *very peculiar* shrill (or harsh) and *unequal* voice, about whose nationality no two persons could be found to agree, and in whose utterance no syllabification could be detected.'

At these words a vague and half-formed conception of the meaning of Dupin flitted over my mind. I seemed to be upon the verge of comprehension, without power to comprehend, as men at times find themselves upon the brink of remembrance, without being able in the end to remember. My friend went on with his discourse.

'You will see,' he said, 'that I have shifted the question from the mode of egress to that of ingress. It was my design to convey the idea that both were effected in the same manner at the same point. Let us now revert to the interior of the room. Let us survey the appearances here. The drawers of the bureau, it is said, had been rifled, although many articles of apparel still remained within them. The conclusion here is absurd. It is a mere guess – a very silly one – and no more. How are we to know that the articles found in the drawers were not all these drawers had originally contained? Madame L'Espanaye and her daughter lived an exceedingly retired life – saw no company, seldom went out – had little use for numerous changes of habiliment. Those found were at least of as good quality as any likely to be possessed by these ladies. If a thief had taken any, why did he not take the best – why did he not take all? In a word, why did he abandon four thousand francs in gold to encumber himself with a bundle of linen? The gold *was* abandoned. Nearly the whole sum mentioned by Monsieur Mignaud, the banker, was discovered in bags upon the floor. I wish you, therefore, to discard from your thoughts the blundering idea of *motive*, engendered in the brains of the police by that portion of the evidence which speaks of money delivered at the door of the house. Coincidences ten times as remarkable as this (the delivery of the money, and murder committed within three days upon the party receiving it), happen to all of us every hour of our lives, without attracting even momentary notice. Coincidences, in general, are great stumbling-blocks in the way of that class of thinkers who have been educated to know nothing of the theory of probabilities – that theory to which the most glorious objects of human research are indebted for the most glorious of illustration. In the present instance, had the gold been gone, the fact of its delivery three days before would have formed something more than a coincidence. It would have been corroborative of this idea of motive. But, under the real circumstances of the case, if we are to suppose gold the motive of this outrage, we must also imagine the perpetrator so vacillating an idiot as to have abandoned his gold and his motive together.

'Keeping now steadily in mind the points to which I have drawn your attention – that peculiar voice, that unusual agility, and that startling absence of motive in a murder so singularly atrocious as this – let us glance at the butchery itself. Here is a woman strangled to death by manual strength, and thrust up a chimney, head downward. Ordinary assassins employ no such modes of murder as this. Least of all do they dispose of the murdered. In the manner of thrusting the corpse up the chimney, you will admit that there was something *excessively outré* – something altogether irreconcilable with our common notions of human action, even when we suppose the actors the most depraved of men. Think, too, how great must have been that strength which could have thrust the body *up* such an aperture so forcibly that the united vigour of several persons was found barely sufficient to drag it *down!*

'Turn, now, to other indications of the employment of a vigour most marvellous. On the hearth were thick tresses – very thick tresses – of grey human hair. These had been torn out by the roots. You are aware of the great force necessary in tearing thus from the head even twenty or thirty hairs together. You saw the locks in question as well as myself. Their roots (a hideous sight) were clotted with fragments of the flesh of the scalp – sure token of the prodigious power which had been exerted in uprooting perhaps half-a-million of hairs at a time. The throat of the old lady was not merely cut, but the head absolutely severed from the body – the instrument was a mere razor. I wish you also to look at the *brutal* ferocity of these deeds. Of the bruises upon the body of Madame L'Espanaye I do not speak. Monsieur Dumas, and his worthy coadjutor, Monsieur Etienne, have pronounced that they were inflicted by some obtuse instrument; and so far these gentlemen are very correct. The obtuse instrument was clearly the stone pavement in the yard upon which the victim had fallen from the window which looked in upon the bed. This idea, however simple it may now seem, escaped the police for the same reason that the breadth of the shutters escaped them – because, by the affair of the nails, their perceptions had been hermetically sealed against the possibility of the windows having ever been opened at all.

'If, now, in addition to all these things, you have properly reflected upon the odd disorder of the chamber, we have gone so far as to combine the ideas of an agility astounding, a strength super-human, a ferocity brutal, a butchery without motive, a *grotesquerie* in horror absolutely alien from humanity, and a voice foreign in tone to the ears of men of many nations, and devoid of all distinct or intelligible syllabification. What result, then, has ensued? What impression have I made upon your fancy?'

I felt a creeping of the flesh as Dupin asked me the question. 'A madman,' I said, 'has done this deed – some raving maniac escaped from a neighbouring *maison de santé*.'

'In some respects,' he replied, 'your idea is not irrelevant; but the voices of madmen, even in their wildest paroxysms, are never found to tally with that peculiar voice heard upon the stairs. Madmen are of some nation, and their language, however incoherent in its words, has always the coherence of syllabification. Besides, the hair of a madman is not such as I now hold in my hand. I disentangled this little tuft from the rigidly clutched fingers of Madame L'Espanaye. Tell me what you can make of it?'

'Dupin!' I said, completely unnerved, 'this hair is most unusual – this is no *human* hair.'

'I have not asserted that it is,' said he; 'but, before we decide this point, I wish you to glance at the little sketch I have here traced upon this paper. It is a *facsimile* drawing of what has been described in one portion of the testimony as "dark bruises, and deep indentations of finger nails," upon the throat of Mademoiselle L'Espanaye, and in another (by Messrs. Dumas and Etienne), as a "series of livid spots evidently the impression of fingers."

'You will perceive,' continued my friend, spreading out the paper upon the table before us, 'that this drawing gives the idea of a firm and fixed hold. There is no *slipping* apparent. Each finger has retained – possibly until the death of the victim – the fearful grasp by which it originally enbedded itself. Attempt, now, to place all your fingers at the same time, in the respective impressions as you see them.'

I made the attempt in vain.

'We are possibly not giving this matter a fair trial,' he said. 'The paper is spread out upon a plane surface; but the human throat is cylindrical. Here is a billet of wood, the circumference of which is about that of the throat. Wrap the drawing around it, and try the experiment again.'

I did so; but the difficulty was even more obvious than before. 'This,' I said, 'is the mark of no human hand.'

'Read now,' replied Dupin, 'this passage from Cuvier.'

It was a minute anatomical and generally descriptive account of the large fulvous Ourang-outang of the East Indian Islands. The gigantic stature, the prodigious strength and activity, the wild ferocity, and the imitative propensities of these mammalia are sufficiently well known to all. I understood the full horrors of the murder at once.

'The description of the digits,' said I, as I made an end of reading, 'is in exact accordance with this drawing. I see that no animal but an Ourang-outang, of the species here mentioned, could have impressed the indentations as you have traced them. This tuft of tawny hair, too, is identical in character with that of the beast of Cuvier. But I cannot possibly comprehend the particulars of this frightful mystery. Besides, there were *two* voices heard in contention, and one of them was unquestionably the voice of a Frenchman.'

'True; and you will remember an expression attributed almost unanimously, by the evidence, to this voice, – the expression "*Mon Dieu!*" This, under the circumstances, has been justly characterised by one of the witnesses (Montani, the confectioner) as an expression of remonstrance or expostulation. Upon these two words, therefore, I have mainly built my hopes of a full solution of the riddle. A Frenchman was cognisant of the murder. It is possible – indeed it is far more than probable – that he was innocent of all participation in the bloody transactions which took place. The Ourang-outang may have escaped from him. He may have traced it to the chamber; but, under the agitating circumstances which ensued, he could never have recaptured it. It is still at large. I will not pursue these guesses – for I have no right to call them more – since the shades of reflection upon which they are based are scarcely of sufficient depth to be appreciable by my own intellect and since I could not pretend to make them intelligible to the understanding of another. We will call them guesses, then, and speak of them as such. If the Frenchman in question is indeed, as I suppose, innocent of this atrocity, this advertisement, which I left last night, upon our return home, at the office of "Le Monde" (a paper devoted to the shipping interests, and much sought by sailors) will bring him to our residence.'

He handed me a paper, and I read thus:

'CAUGHT. – *In the Bois de Boulogne, early in the morning of the ——— inst. (the morning of the murder), a very large, tawny Ourang-outang of the Bornese species. The owner (who is ascertained to be a sailor, belonging to a Maltese vessel) may have the animal again, upon identifying it satisfactorily, and paying a few charges arising from its capture and keeping. Call at No. —, Rue ——, Faubourg St. Germain – au troisième.'*

'How was it possible,' I asked, 'that you should know the man to be a sailor, and belonging to a Maltese vessel?'

'I do *not* know it,' said Dupin. 'I am not *sure* of it. Here, however, is a small piece of ribbon, which from its form, and from its greasy appearance, has evidently been used in tying the hair in one of those long *queues* of which sailors are so fond. Moreover, this knot is one which few besides sailors can tie, and is peculiar to the Maltese. I picked the ribbon up at the foot of the lightning-rod. It could not have belonged to either of the deceased. Now if, after all, I am wrong in my induction from this ribbon, that the Frenchman was a sailor belonging to a Maltese vessel, still I can have done no harm in saying what I did in the advertisement. If I am in error, he will merely suppose that I have been misled by some circumstance into which he will not take the trouble to inquire. But if I am right, a great point is gained. Cognisant, altogether innocent, of the murder, the Frenchman will naturally hesitate about replying to the advertisement – about demanding the Ourang-outang. He will reason thus: "I am innocent; I am poor; my Ourang-outang is of great value – to one in my circumstances a fortune of itself – why should I lose it through idle apprehensions of danger? Here it is, within my grasp. It was found in the Bois de Boulogne, at a vast distance from the scene of that butchery. How can it ever be suspected that a brute beast should have done the deed? The police are at fault, they have failed to procure the slightest clue. Should they even trace the animal, it would be impossible to prove me cognisant of the murder, or to implicate me in guilt on account of that cognisance. Above all, *I am known*. The advertiser designates me as the possessor of the beast. I am not sure to what limit his knowledge may extend. Should I avoid claiming a property of so great value, which it is known that I possess, I will render the animal at least, liable to suspicion. It is not my policy to attract attention either to myself or to the beast. I will answer the advertisement, get the Ourang-outang and keep it close until this matter has blown over."'

At this moment we heard a step upon the stairs.

'Be ready,' said Dupin, 'with your pistols, but neither use them nor show them until at a signal from myself.'

The front door of the house had been left open, and the visitor had entered without ringing, and advanced several steps upon the staircase. Now, however, he seemed to hesitate. Presently we heard him descending. Dupin was moving quickly to the door, when we again heard him coming up. He did not turn back a second time, but stepped up with decision, and rapped at the door of our chamber.

'Come in,' said Dupin, in a cheerful and hearty tone.

A man entered. He was a sailor, evidently, – a tall, stout, and muscular-looking person, with a certain dare-devil expression of countenance, not altogether unprepossessing. His face, greatly sunburnt, was more than half hidden by whisker and *mustachio*. He had with him a huge oaken cudgel, but appeared to be otherwise unarmed. He bowed awkwardly, and bade us 'Good evening' in French accents, which, although somewhat Neufchatelish, were still sufficiently indicative of a Parisian origin.

'Sit down, my friend,' said Dupin. 'I suppose you have called about the Ourang-outang. Upon my word I almost envy you the possession of him; a remarkably fine, and no doubt a very valuable animal. How old do you suppose him to be?'

The sailor drew a long breath, with the air of a man relieved of some intolerable burden, and then replied in an assured tone.

'I have no way of telling, but he can't be more than four or five years old. Have you got him here?'

'Oh no; we had no conveniences for keeping him here. He is at a livery stable in the Rue Dubourg, just by. You can get him in the morning. Of course you are prepared to identify the property?'

'To be sure I am, sir.'

'I shall be sorry to part with him,' said Dupin.

'I don't mean that you should be at all this trouble for nothing, sir,' said the man. 'Couldn't expect it. Am very willing to pay a reward for the finding of the animal, that is to say, anything in reason.'

'Well,' replied my friend, 'that is all very fair, to be sure. Let me think! what should I have? Oh! I will tell you. My reward shall be this. You shall give me all the information in your power about these murders in the Rue Morgue.'

Dupin said the last words in a very low tone, and very quietly. Just as quietly, too, he walked towards the door, locked it, and put the key in his pocket. He then drew a pistol from his bosom and placed it, without the least flurry, upon the table.

The sailor's face flushed up as if he were struggling with suffocation. He started to his feet and grasped his cudgel; but the next moment he fell back into his seat, trembling violently, and with the countenance of death itself. He spoke not a word. I pitied him from the bottom of my heart.

'My friend,' said Dupin in a kind tone, 'you are alarming yourself unnecessarily – you are indeed. We mean you no harm whatever. I pledge you the honour of a gentleman, and of a Frenchman, that we intend you no injury. I perfectly well know that you are innocent of the atrocities in the Rue Morgue. It will not do, however, to deny that you are in some measure implicated in them. From what I have already said, you must know that I have had means of information about this matter – means of which you could never have dreamed. Now the thing stands thus. You have done nothing which you could have avoided – nothing, certainly, which renders you culpable. You were not even guilty of robbery, when you might have robbed with impunity. You have nothing to conceal. You have no reason for concealment. On the other hand, you are bound by every principle of honour to confess all you know. An innocent man is now imprisoned, charged with that crime of which you can point out the perpetrator.'

The sailor had recovered his presence of mind, in a great measure, while Dupin uttered these words; but his original boldness of bearing was all gone.

'So help me God,' said he, after a brief pause, 'I *will* tell you all I know about this affair; – but I do not expect you to believe one-half I say – I would be a fool indeed if I did. Still I *am* innocent, and I will make a clean breast if I die for it.'

What he stated was in substance this. He had lately made a voyage to the Indian Archipelago. A party, of which he formed one, landed at Borneo and passed into the interior on an excursion of pleasure. Himself and a companion had captured the Ourang-outang. This companion dying, the animal fell into his own exclusive possession.

After great trouble, occasioned by the intractable ferocity of his captive during the home voyage, he at length succeeded in lodging it safely at his own residence in Paris, where, not to attract towards himself the unpleasant curiosity of his neighbours, he kept it carefully secluded until such time as it should recover from a wound in the foot received from a splinter on board ship. His ultimate design was to sell it.

Returning home from some sailors' frolic on the night, or rather in the morning of the murder, he found the beast occupying his own bed-room, into which it had broken from a closet adjoining, where it had been, as was thought, securely confined. Razor in hand, and fully lathered, it was sitting before a looking-glass attempting the operation of shaving, in which it had no doubt previously watched its master through the key-hole of the closet. Terrified at the sight of so dangerous a weapon in the possession of an animal so ferocious and so well able to use it, the man, for some moments, was at a loss what to do. He had been accustomed, however, to quiet the creature, even in its fiercest moods, by the use of a whip, and to this he now resorted. Upon sight of it, the Ourang-outang sprang at once through the door of the chamber, down the stairs, and thence through a window, unfortunately open, into the street.

The Frenchman followed in despair; the ape, razor still in hand, occasionally stopping to look back and gesticulate at its pursuer, until the latter had nearly come up with it. It then again made off. In this manner the chase continued for a long time. The streets were profoundly quiet, as it was nearly three o'clock in the morning. In passing down an alley in the rear of the Rue Morgue, the fugitive's attention was arrested by a light gleaming from the open window of Madame L'Espanaye's chamber, in the fourth storey of her house. Rushing to the building, it perceived the lightning-rod, clambered up with inconceivable agility, grasped the shutter, which was thrown fully back against the wall, and, by its means, swung itself directly upon the headboard of the bed. The whole feat did not occupy a minute. The shutter was kicked open again by the Ourang-outang as it entered the room.

The sailor, in the meantime, was both rejoiced and perplexed. He had strong hopes of now recapturing the brute, as it could scarcely escape from the trap into which it had ventured except by the rod, where it might be intercepted as it came down. On the other hand, there was much cause for anxiety as to what it might do in the house. This latter reflection urged the man still to follow the fugitive. A lightning-rod is ascended without difficulty, especially by a sailor; but when he had arrived as high as the window, which lay far to his left, his career was stopped; the most that he could accomplish was to reach over so as to obtain a glimpse of the interior of the room. At this glimpse he nearly fell from his hold through excess of horror. Now it was that those hideous shrieks arose upon the night which had startled from slumber the inmates of the Rue Morgue. Madame L'Espanaye and her daughter, habited in their night-clothes, had apparently been occupied in arranging some papers in the iron chest already mentioned, which had been wheeled into the middle of the room. It was open, and its contents lay beside it on the floor. The victims must have been sitting with their backs towards the window; and, from the time elapsing between the ingress of the beast and the screams, it seems probable that it was not immediately perceived. The flapping to of the shutter would naturally have been attributed to the wind.

As the sailor looked in, the gigantic animal had seized Madame L'Espanaye by the hair (which was loose as she had been combing it), and was flourishing the razor about her face in imitation of the motions of a barber. The daughter lay prostrate and motionless; she had swooned. The screams and struggles of the old lady (during which the hair was torn from her head) had the effect of changing the probably pacific purposes of the Ourang-outang into those of wrath. With one determined sweep of its muscular arm it nearly severed her head from her body. The sight of blood inflamed its anger into frenzy. Gnashing

Gnashing its teeth, and flashing fire from its eyes,
it flew upon the body of the girl

its teeth and flashing fire from its eyes, it flew upon the body of the girl, and imbedded its fearful talons in her throat, retaining its grasp until she expired. Its wandering and wild glances fell at this moment upon the head of the bed, over which the face of its master, rigid with horror, was just discernible. The fury of the beast, which no doubt bore still in mind the dreaded whip, was instantly converted into fear. Conscious of having deserved punishment, it seemed desirous of concealing its bloody deeds, and skipped about the chamber in an agony of nervous agitation, throwing down and breaking the furniture as it moved, and dragging the bed from the bedstead. In conclusion, it seized first the corpse of the daughter and thrust it up the chimney, as it was found; then that of the old lady, which it immediately hurled through the window headlong.

As the ape approached the casement with its mutilated burden, the sailor shrank aghast to the rod, and, rather gliding than clambering down it, hurried at once home – dreading the consequences of the butchery, and gladly abandoning, in his terror, all solicitude about the fate of the Ourang-outang. The words heard by the party upon the staircase were the Frenchman's exclamations of horror and affright, commingled with the fiendish jabberings of the brute.

I have scarcely anything to add. The Ourang-outang must have escaped from the chamber by the rod, just before the breaking of the door. I must have closed the window as it passed through it. It was subsequently caught by the owner himself, who obtained for it a very large sum at the *Jardin des Plantes*. Le Bon was instantly released, upon our narration of the circumstances (with some comments from Dupin) at the *bureau* of the Prefect of Police. This functionary, however well disposed to my friend, could not altogether conceal his chagrin at the turn which affairs had taken, and was fain to indulge in a sarcasm or two about the propriety of every person minding his own business.

'Let him talk,' said Dupin, who had not thought it necessary to reply. 'Let him discourse; it will ease his conscience. I am satisfied with having defeated him in his own castle. Nevertheless, that he failed in the solution of this mystery is by no means that matter for wonder which he supposes it; for, in truth, our friend the Prefect is somewhat too cunning to be profound. In his wisdom is no *stamen*. It is all head and no body, like the pictures of the Goddess Laverna, – or, at best, all head and shoulders, like a codfish. But he is a good creature after all. I like him especially for one master stroke of cant, by which he has attained his reputation for ingenuity. I mean the way he has "*de nier ce qui est, et d'expliquer ce qui n'est pas.*"*

* ROUSSEAU – *Nouvelle Heloise*.

The System of Doctor Tarr and Professor Fether

During the autumn of 18—, while on a tour through the extreme southern provinces of France, my route led me within a few miles of a certain *Maison de Santé* or private Madhouse, about which I had heard much in Paris from my medical friends. As I had never visited a place of the kind, I thought the opportunity too good to be lost; and so proposed to my travelling companion (a gentleman with whom I had made casual acquaintance a few days before) that we should turn aside for an hour or so and look through the establishment. To this he objected – pleading haste in the first place, and in the second, a very usual horror at the sight of a lunatic. He begged me, however, not to let any mere courtesy towards himself interfere with the gratification of my curiosity, and said that he would ride on leisurely, so that I might overtake him during the day, or at all events, during the next. As he bade me good-bye, I bethought me that there might be some difficulty in obtaining access to the premises, and mentioned my fears on this point. He replied that, in fact, unless I had personal knowledge of the superintendent, Monsieur Maillard, or some credential in the way of a letter, a difficulty might be found to exist, as the regulations of these private mad-houses were more rigid than the public hospital laws. For himself, he added, he had some years since made the acquaintance of

Maillard, and would so far assist me as to ride up to the door and introduce me, although his feelings on the subject of lunacy would not permit his entering the house.

I thanked him, and turning from the main-road we entered a grass-grown by-path, which, in half-an-hour, nearly lost itself in a dense forest closing the base of a mountain. Through this dank and gloomy wood we rode some two miles, when the *Maison de Santé* came in view. It was a fantastic *château*, much delapidated, and indeed scarcely tenantable through age and neglect. Its aspect inspired me with absolute dread, and checking my horse, I half resolved to turn back. I soon, however, grew ashamed of my weakness and proceeded.

As we rode up to the gateway, I perceived it slightly open, and the visage of a man peering through. In an instant afterward, this man came forth, accosted my companion by name, shook him cordially by the hand and begged him to alight. It was Monsieur Maillard himself. He was a portly fine-looking gentleman of the old school, with a polished manner, and a certain air of gravity, dignity, and authority, which was very impressive.

My friend having presented me, mentioned my desire to inspect the establishment, and received Monsieur Maillard's assurance that he would show me all attention, now took leave, and I saw him no more.

When he had gone, the superintendent ushered me into a small and exceedingly neat parlour, containing, among other indications of refined taste, many books, drawings, pots of flowers, and musical instruments. A cheerful fire blazed upon the hearth. At a piano, singing an aria from Bellini sat a young and very beautiful woman, who, at my entrance, paused in her song, and received me with graceful courtesy. Her voice was low, and her whole manner subdued. I thought, too, that I perceived the traces of sorrow in her countenance, which was excessively, although to my taste not unpleasingly pale. She was attired in deep mourning, and excited in my bosom a feeling of mingled respect, interest, and admiration.

I had heard at Paris that the institution of Monsieur Maillard was managed upon what is vulgarly termed the 'system of soothing' – that all punishments were avoided – that even confinement was seldom resorted to – that the patients, while secretly watched, were left much apparent liberty, and that most of them were permitted to roam about the house and grounds in the ordinary apparel of persons in right mind.

Keeping these impressions in view, I was cautious in what I said before the young lady, for I could not be sure that she was sane; and in fact there was a certain restless brilliancy about her eyes which half led me to imagine she was not. I confined my remarks, therefore, to general topics, and to such as I thought would not be displeasing or exciting even to a lunatic. She replied in a perfectly rational manner to all that I said, and even her original observations were marked with the soundest good sense; but a long acquaintance with the metaphysics of *mania* had taught me to put no faith in such evidence of sanity, and I continued to practise, throughout the interview, the caution with which I commenced it.

Presently a smart footman in livery brought in a tray with fruit, wine, and other refreshments, of which I partook, the lady soon afterwards leaving the room. As she departed I turned my eyes in an inquiring manner towards my host.

'No,' he said, 'oh, no – a member of my family – my niece, and a most accomplished woman.'

'I beg a thousand pardons for the suspicion,' I replied, 'but of course you will know how to excuse me. The excellent administration of your affairs here is well understood in Paris, and I thought it just possible, you know——'

'Yes, yes – say no more – or rather it is myself who should thank you for the commendable prudence you have displayed. We seldom find so much of forethought in young men, and, more than once, some unhappy *contre-temps* has occurred in consequence of thoughtlessness on the part of our visitors. While my former system was in operation and my patients were permitted the privilege of roaming to and fro at will, they were often aroused to a dangerous frenzy by injudicious persons who called to inspect the house. Hence I was obliged to enforce a rigid system of exclusion; and none obtained access to the premises upon whose discretion I could not rely.'

'While your *former* system was in operation!' I said, repeating his words – 'do I understand you, then, to say that the "soothing system" of which I have heard so much, is no longer in force?'

'It is now,' he replied, 'several weeks since we have concluded to renounce it for ever.'

'Indeed! you astonish me!'

'We found it, sir,' he said with a sigh, 'absolutely necessary to return to the old usages. The *danger* of the soothing system was at all times appalling, and its advantages have been much overrated. I believe, sir, that in this house it has been given a fair trial, if ever in any. We did everything that rational humanity could suggest. I am sorry that you could not have paid us a visit at an earlier period, that you might have judged for yourself. But I presume you are conversant with the soothing practice – with its details.'

'Not altogether. What I have heard has been at third or fourth hand.'

'I may state the system then, in general terms, as one in which the patients were *ménagés*, humoured. We contradicted *no* fancies which entered the brains of the mad. On the contrary, we not only indulged but encouraged them; and many of our most permanent cures have been thus effected. There is no argument which so touches the feeble reason of the madman as the *reductio ad absurdum*. We have had men, for example, who fancied themselves chickens. The cure was, to insist upon the thing as a fact – to accuse the patient of stupidity in not sufficiently perceiving it to be a fact – and thus to refuse him any other diet for a week than that which properly appertains to a chicken. In this manner a little corn and gravel were made to perform wonders.'

'But was this species of acquiesence all?'

'By no means. We put much faith in amusements of a simple kind, such as music, dancing, gymnastic exercises generally, cards, certain classes of books, and so forth. We affected to treat each individual as if for some ordinary physical disorder, and the word "lunacy" was never employed. A great point was to set each lunatic to guard the actions of all the others. To repose confidence in the understanding or discretion of a madman is to gain him body and soul. In this way we were enabled to dispense with an expensive body of keepers.'

'And you had no punishments of any kind?'

'None.'

'And you never confined your patients?'

'Very rarely. Now and then, the malady of some individual growing to a crisis, or taking a sudden turn of fury, we conveyed him to a secret cell, lest his disorder should infect the rest, and there kept him until we could dismiss him to his friends; for with the raging maniac we have nothing to do. He is usually removed to the public hospitals.'

'And you have now changed all this – and you think for the better?'

'Decidedly. The system had its disadvantages, and even its dangers. It is now, happily, exploded throughout all the *Maisons de Santé* of France.'

'I am very much surprised,' I said, 'at what you tell me; for I made sure that, at this moment, no other method of treatment for mania existed in any portion of the country.'

'You are young yet, my friend,' replied my host, 'but the time will arrive when you will learn to judge for yourself of what is going on in the world without trusting to the gossip of others:– Believe nothing you hear, and only one half that you see. Now, about our *Maisons de Santé*, it is clear that some ignoramus has misled you. After dinner, however, when you have sufficiently recovered from the fatigue of your ride, I will be happy to take you over the house, and introduce to you a system which, in my opinion, and in that of every one who has witnessed its operation, is incomparably the most effectual as yet devised.'

'Your own,' I inquired – 'one of your own invention?'

'I am proud,' he replied, 'to acknowledge that it is – at least in some measure.'

In this manner I conversed with Monsieur Maillard for an hour or two, during which he showed me the gardens and conservatories of the place.

'I cannot let you see my patients,' he said, 'just at present. To a sensitive mind there is always more or less of the shocking in such exhibitions; and I do not wish to spoil your appetite for dinner. We will dine. I can give you some veal *à la Sainte Ménehould*, with cauliflowers in *velouté* sauce – after that a glass of *Clos Vougeot* – then your nerves will be sufficiently steadied.'

At six dinner was announced; and my host conducted me into a large *salle à manger*, where a very numerous company were assembled – twenty-five or thirty in all. They were, apparently, people of rank – certainly of high breeding – although their habiliments, I thought, were extravagantly rich, partaking somewhat too much of the ostentatious finery of the *vieille cour*. I noticed that at least two-thirds of these guests were ladies; and some of the latter were by no means accoutred in what a Parisian would consider good taste at the present day. Many females, for example, whose age could not have been less than seventy, were bedecked with a profusion of jewellery, such as rings, bracelets, and ear-rings, and wore their bosoms and arms shamefully bare. I observed, too, that very few of the dresses were well made – or, at least, that very few of them fitted the wearers. In looking about I discovered the interesting girl to whom Monsieur Maillard had presented me in the little parlour; but my surprise was great to see her wearing a hoop and farthingale, with high-heeled shoes, and a dirty cap of Brussels lace, so much too large for her that it gave her face a ridiculously diminutive expression. When I had first seen her she was attired, most becomingly, in deep mourning. There was an air of oddity, in short, about the dress of the whole party, which, at first, caused me to recur to my original idea of the 'soothing system,' and to fancy that Monsieur Maillard had been willing to deceive me until after dinner, that I might experience no uncomfortable feelings during the repast at finding myself dining with lunatics; but I remembered having been informed in Paris that the southern provincialists were a peculiarly eccentric people, with a vast number of antiquated notions; and then, too, upon conversing with several members of the company, my apprehensions were immediately and fully dispelled.

The dining-room itself, although perhaps sufficiently comfortable and of good dimensions, had nothing too much of elegance about it. For example, the floor was uncarpeted; in France, however, a carpet is frequently dispensed with. The windows, too, were without curtains;

the shutters, being shut, were securely fastened with iron bars, applied diagonally, after the fashion of our ordinary shop-shutters. The apartment, I observed, formed in itself a wing of the *château*, and thus the windows were on three sides of the parallelogram – the door being at the other. There were no less than ten windows in all.

The table was superbly set out. It was loaded with plate, and more than loaded with delicacies. The profusion was absolutely barbaric. There were meats enough to have feasted the Anakim. Never in all my life had I witnessed so lavish, so wasteful an expenditure of the good things of life. There seemed very little taste, however, in the arrangements; and my eyes, accustomed to quiet lights, were sadly offended by the prodigious glare of a multitude of wax candles which, in silver *candelabra*, were deposited upon the table and all about the room, wherever it was possible to find a place. There were several active servants in attendance; and upon a large table at the farther end of the apartment were seated seven or eight people with fiddles, fifes, trombones, and a drum. These fellows annoyed me very much at intervals during the repast, by an infinite variety of noises, which were intended for music, and which appeared to afford much entertainment to all present with the exception of myself.

Upon the whole, I could not help thinking that there was much of the *bizarre* about everything I saw – but then the world is made up of all kinds of persons, with all modes of thought, and all sorts of conventional customs. I had travelled, too, so much as to be quite an adept in the *nil admirari*, so I took my seat very coolly at the right hand of my host, and having an excellent appetite, did justice to the good cheer set before me.

The conversation in the meantime was spirited and general. The ladies, as usual, talked a great deal. I soon found that nearly all the company were well educated; and my host was a world of good-humoured anecdote in himself. He seemed quite willing to speak of his position as superintendent of a *Maison de Santé*, and, indeed, the topic of lunacy was, much to my surprise, a favourite one with all present. A great many amusing stories were told having reference to the *whims* of the patients.

'We had a fellow here once,' said a fat little gentleman, who sat at my right – 'a fellow that fancied himself a tea-pot; and, by the way, is it not especially singular how often this particular crotchet has entered the brain of the lunatic? There is scarcely an insane asylum in France which cannot supply a human tea-pot. *Our* gentleman was a Britannia-ware tea-pot, and was careful to polish himself every morning with buckskin and whiting.'

'And then,' said a tall man, just opposite, 'we had here, not long ago, a person who had taken it into his head that he was a donkey – which, allegorically speaking, you will say, was quite true. He was a troublesome patient, and we had much ado to keep him within bounds. For a long time he would eat nothing but thistles; but of this idea we soon cured him by insisting upon his eating nothing else. Then he was perpetually kicking out his heels——so——so'——

'Mr. de Kock! I will thank you to behave yourself!' here interrupted an old lady, who sat next to the speaker. 'Please keep your feet to yourself! You have spoiled my brocade! Is it necessary, pray, to illustrate a remark in so practical a style? Our friend, here, can surely comprehend you without all this. Upon my word you are nearly as great a donkey as the poor unfortunate imagined himself. Your acting is very natural, as I live.'

'*Mille pardons! Ma'mselle!*' replied Monsieur de Kock, thus addressed – 'a thousand pardons! I had no intention of offending. Ma'mselle Laplace – Monsieur de Kock will do himself the honour of taking wine with you.'

Here Monsieur de Kock bowed low, kissed his hand with much ceremony, and took wine with Ma'mselle Laplace.

'Allow me, *mon ami*,' now said Monsieur Maillard, addressing myself, 'allow me to send you a morsel of this veal *á la Ste. Ménéhould* – you will find it particularly fine.'

At this instant three sturdy waiters had just succeeded in depositing safely upon the table an enormous dish or trencher, containing what I supposed to be the '*monstrum horrendum, informe, ingens, cui lumen, ademptum.*' A closer scrutiny assured me, however, that it was only a small calf roasted whole, and set upon its knees, with an apple in its mouth, as is the English fashion of dressing a hare.

'Thank you, no,' I replied; 'to say the truth, I am not particularly partial to veal *à la Ste.* – what is it? – for I do not find that it altogether agrees with me. I will change my plate, however, and try some of the rabbit.'

There were several side-dishes on the table containing what appeared to be the ordinary French rabbit – a very delicious *morceau*, which I can recommend.

'Pierre,' cried the host, 'change this gentleman's plate, and give him a side-piece of this rabbit *au-chat*.'

'This what?'

'This rabbit *au-chat*.'

'Why, thank you – upon second thoughts, no. I will just help myself to some of the ham.'

There is no knowing what one eats, thought I to myself, at the tables of these people of the province. I will have none of their rabbit *au-chat* – and, for the matter of that, none of their *cat-au-rabbit* either.

'And then,' said a cadaverous-looking personage, near the foot of the table, taking up the thread of the conversation where it had been broken off – 'and then, among other oddities, we had a patient once upon a time who very pertinaciously maintained himself to be a Cordova cheese, and went about with a knife in his hand soliciting his friends to try a small slice from the middle of his leg.'

'He was a great fool, beyond doubt,' interposed some one, 'but not to be compared with a certain individual whom we all know, with the exception of this strange gentleman. I mean the man who took himself for a bottle of champagne, and always went off with a pop and a fizz, in this fashion.'

Here the speaker, very rudely, as I thought, put his right thumb in his left cheek, withdrew it with a sound resembling the popping of a cork, and then, by a dexterous movement of the tongue upon the teeth, created a sharp hissing and fizzing which lasted for several minutes, in imitation of the frothing of champagne. This behaviour, I saw plainly, was not very pleasing to Monsieur Maillard; but that gentleman said nothing, and the conversation was resumed by a very lean little man in a big wig.

'And then there was an ignoramus,' said he, 'who mistook himself for a frog; which, by the way, he resembled in no little degree. I wish you could have seen him, sir' – here the speaker addressed myself – 'it would have done your heart good to see the natural airs that he put on. Sir, if that man was *not* a frog, I can only observe that it is a pity he was not. His croak thus – o-o-o-o-gh – o-o-o-o-gh! was the finest note in the world – B flat; and when he put his elbows upon the table thus – after taking a glass or two of wine – and distended his mouth thus, and rolled up his eyes thus, and winked them with excessive rapidity thus, why then, sir, I take it upon myself to say positively, that you would have been lost in admiration of the genius of the man.'

'I have no doubt of it,' I said.

'And then,' said somebody else, 'then there was Petit Gaillard, who thought himself a pinch of snuff, and was truly distressed because he could not take himself between his own finger and thumb.'

'And then there was Jules Desoulières, who was a very singular genius indeed, and went mad with the idea that he was a pumpkin. He persecuted the cook to make him up into pies – a thing which the cook indignantly refused to do. For my part, I am by no means sure that a pumpkin pie *à la Desoulières* would not have been very capital eating indeed!'

'You astonish me!' said I; and I looked inquisitively at Monsieur Maillard.

'Ha! ha! ha!' said that gentleman – 'he! he! he! – hi! hi! hi! – ho! ho! ho! – hu! hu! hu! – very good indeed! You must not be astonished *mon ami*, our friend here is a wit – a *drôle* – you must not understand him to the letter.'

'And then,' said some other one of the party, 'then there was Bouffon le Grand – another extraordinary personage in his way. He grew deranged through love, and fancied himself possessed of two heads. One of these he maintained to be the head of Cicero; the other he imagined a composite one, being Demosthenes from the top of the forehead to the mouth, and Lord Brougham from the mouth to the chin. It is not impossible that he was wrong; but he would have convinced you of his being in the right; for he was a man of great eloquence. He had an absolute passion for oratory, and could not refrain from display. For example, he used to leap upon the dinner-table thus, and – and'——

Here a friend, at the side of the speaker, put a hand upon his shoulder, and whispered a few words in his ear; upon which he ceased talking with great suddenness, and sank back within his chair.

'And then,' said the friend who had whispered, 'there was Boullard, the tee-totum. I call him the tee-totum, because, in fact, he was seized with the droll, but not altogether irrational crotchet that he had been converted into a tee-totum. You would have roared with laughter to see him spin. He would turn round upon one heel by the hour, in this manner – so'——

Here the friend whom he had just interrupted by a whisper, performed an exactly similar office for himself.

'But then,' cried an old lady, at the top of her voice, 'your Monsieur Boullard was a madman, and a very silly madman at best; for who, allow me to ask you, ever heard of a human tee-totum? The thing is absurd. Madame Joyeuse was a more sensible person, as you know. She had a crotchet, but it was instinct with common sense, and gave pleasure to all who had the honour of her acquaintance She found, upon mature deliberation, that by some accident she had been turned into a chicken-cock; but, as such, she behaved with propriety. She flapped her wings with prodigious effect – so – so – so – and as for her crow, it was delicious! Cock-a-doodle-doo! – cock-a-doodle-doo cock-a-doodle-de-doo-doo-dooo-do-o-o-o-o-o-o!'

'Madame Joyeuse, I will thank you to behave yourself!' here interrupted our host, very angrily. 'You can either conduct yourself as a lady should do, or you can quit the table forthwith – take your choice.'

The lady (whom I was much astonished to hear addressed as Madame Joyeuse, after the description of Madame Joyeuse she had just given) blushed up to the eyebrows, and seemed exceedingly abashed at the reproof. She hung down her head, and said not a syllable in reply. But another and younger lady resumed the theme. It was my beautiful girl of the little parlour!

'Oh, Madame Joyeuse *was* a fool!' she exclaimed, 'but there was really much sound sense, after all, in the opinion of Eugénie Salsafette. She was a very beautiful and painfully modest young lady, who thought the ordinary mode of habilment indecent, and wished to dress herself, always, by getting outside, instead of inside of her clothes. It is a thing very easily done, after all. You have only to do so – and then so – so – so – and then so – so – so – and then'——

'Mon Dieu! Ma'mselle Salsafette!' here cried a dozen voices at once. 'What *are* you about? – forbear? – that is sufficient! – we see, very plainly, how it is done! – hold! hold!' and several persons were already leaping from their seats to withhold Ma'mselle Salsafette from putting herself upon a par with the Medicean Venus, when the point was very effectually and suddenly accomplished by a series of loud screams, or yells from some portion of the main body of the château.

My nerves were very much affected indeed by these yells; but the rest of the company I really pitied. I never saw any set of reasonable people so thoroughly frightened in my life. They all grew as pale as so many corpses, and, shrinking within their seats, sat quivering and gibbering with terror, and listening for a repetition of the sound. It came again – louder and seemingly nearer – and then a third time *very* loud, and then a fourth time with a vigour evidently diminished. At this apparent dying away of the noise, the spirits of the company were immediately regained, and all was life and anecdote as before. I now ventured to inquire the cause of the disturbance.

'A mere *bagatelle*,' said Monsieur Maillard. 'We are used to these things, and care really very little about them. The lunatics, every now and then, get up a howl in concert; one starting another, as is sometimes the case with a bevy of dogs at night. It occasionally happens, however, that the *concerto* yells are succeeded by a simultaneous effort at breaking loose; when, of course, some little danger is to be apprehended.'

'And how many have you in charge?'

'At present we have not more than ten altogether.'

'Principally females, I presume?'

'Oh, no – every one of them men, and stout fellows, too, I can tell you.'

'Indeed! I have always understood that the majority of lunatics were of the gentler sex.'

'It is generally so, but not always. Some time ago there were about twenty-seven patients here, of that number no less than eighteen were women; but, lately, matters have changed very much, as you see.'

'Yes – have changed very much, as you see,' here interrupted the gentleman who had broken the shins of Ma'mselle Laplace.

'Yes – have changed very much, as you see,' chimed in the whole company at once.

'Hold your tongues, every one of you!' said my host, in a great rage. Whereupon the whole company maintained a dead silence for nearly a minute. As for one lady she obeyed Monsieur Maillard to the letter, and thrusting out her tongue, which was an excessively long one, held it very resignedly, with both hands, until the end of the entertainment.

'And this gentlewoman,' said I to Monsieur Maillard, bending over and addressing him in a whisper – 'this good lady who has just spoken, and who gives us the cock-a-doodle-de-doo – she, I presume, is harmless – quite harmless, eh?'

'Harmless!' ejaculated he, in unfeigned surprise, 'why – why, what *can* you mean?'

'Only slightly touched?' said I, touching my head. 'I take it for granted that she is not particularly – not dangerously affected, eh?'

'*Mon Dieu!* what *is* it you imagine? This lady, my particular old friend, Madame Joyeuse, is as absolutely sane as myself. She has her little eccentricities, to be sure – but then, you know, all old women – all *very* old women are more or less eccentric!'

'To be sure,' said I – 'to be sure – and then the rest of these ladies and gentlemen——'

'Are my friends and keepers,' interrupted Monsieur Maillard, drawing himself up with *hauteur* – 'my very good friends and assistants.'

'What! all of them?' I asked – 'the women and all?'

'Assuredly,' he said – 'we could not do at all without the women; they are the best lunatic nurses in the world; they have a way of their own, you know; their bright eyes have a marvellous effect; – something like the fascination of the snake, you know.'

'To be sure,' said I – 'to be sure! They behave a little odd, eh? – they are a little *queer*, eh? – don't you think so?'

'Odd! – queer! – why, do you *really* think so? We are not very prudish, to be sure, here in the South – do pretty much as we please – enjoy life, and all that sort of thing, you know'——

'To be sure,' said I; 'to be sure.'

'And then, perhaps, this *Clos de Vougeot* is a little heady, you know, – a little *strong* – you understand, eh?'

'To be sure,' said I; 'to be sure. By-the-by, monsieur, did I understand you to say that the system you have adopted, in place of the celebrated soothing system, was one of very rigorous severity?'

'By no means. Our confinement is necessarily close; but the treatment – the medical treatment, I mean – is rather agreeable to the patients than otherwise.'

'And the new system is one of your own invention?'

'Not altogether. Some portions of it are referable to Doctor Tarr, of whom you have necessarily heard; and, again, there are modifications in my plan which I am happy to acknowledge as belonging of right to the celebrated Fether, with whom, if I mistake not, you have the honour of an intimate acquaintance.'

'I am quite ashamed to confess,' I replied, 'that I have never even heard the name of either gentleman before.'

'Good Heavens!' ejaculated my host, drawing back his chair abruptly, and uplifting his hands. 'I surely do not hear you aright! You did not intend to say, eh? that you had never *heard* either of the learned Doctor Tarr, or of the celebrated Professor Fether?'

'I am forced to acknowledge my ignorance,' I replied; 'but the truth should be held inviolate above all things. Nevertheless, I feel humbled to the dust, not to be acquainted with the works of these, no doubt, extraordinary men. I will seek out their writings forthwith, and peruse them with deliberate care. Monsieur Maillard, you have really

– I must confess it – you have *really* – made me ashamed of myself!'

And this was the fact.

'Say no more, my good young friend,' he said kindly, pressing my hand – 'join me now in a glass of Sauterne.'

We drank. The company followed our example, without stint. They chatted – they jested – they laughed – they perpetuated a thousand absurdities – the fiddles shrieked – the drum row-de-dowed – the trombones bellowed like so many brazen bulls of Phalaris – and the whole scene, growing gradually worse and worse as the wines gained the ascendancy, became at length a sort of Pandemonium *in petto*. In the meantime, Monsieur Maillard and myself, with some bottles of Sauterne and Clos Vougeot between us, continued our conversation at the top of the voice. A word spoken in an ordinary key stood no more chance of being heard than the voice of a fish from the bottom of Niagara Falls.

'And, sir,' said I, screaming in his ear, 'you mentioned something before dinner about the danger incurred in the old system of soothing. How is that?'

'Yes,' he replied, 'there was occasionally very great danger indeed. There is no accounting for the caprices of madmen; and, in my opinion, as well as in that of Doctor Tarr and Professor Fether, it is *never* safe to permit them to run at large unattended. A lunatic may be "soothed," as it is called, for a time, but in the end he is very apt to become obstreperous. His cunning, too, is proverbial and great. If he has a project in view, he conceals his design with a marvellous wisdom; and the dexterity with which he counterfeits sanity, presents to the metaphysician one of the most singular problems in the study of mind. When a madman appears *thoroughly* sane, indeed, it is high time to put him in a strait jacket.'

'But the *danger*, my dear sir, of which you were speaking – in your own experience – during your control of this house – have you had practical reason to think liberty hazardous in the case of a lunatic?'

'Here? – in my own experience? – why, I may say yes. For example:– no *very* long while ago, a singular circumstance occurred in this very house. The "soothing system," you know, was then in operation, and the patients were at large. They behaved remarkably well – especially so – any one of sense might have known that some devilish scheme was brewing from that particular fact, that the fellows behaved so *remarkably* well. And, sure enough, one fine morning the keepers found themselves pinioned hand and foot, and thrown into the cells, where they were attended, as if *they* were the lunatics themselves, who had usurped the offices of the keepers.'

'You don't tell me so! I never heard of anything so absurd in my life!'

'Fact – it all came to pass by means of a stupid fellow – a lunatic – who, by some means had taken it into his head that he had invented a better system of government than any ever heard of before – of lunatic government, I mean. He wished to give his invention a trial, I suppose, and so he persuaded the rest of the patients to join him in a conspiracy for the overthrow of the reigning powers.'

'And he really succeeded?'

'No doubt of it. The keepers and kept were soon made to exchange places. Not that exactly either, for the madmen had been free, but the keepers were shut up in cells forthwith, and treated, I am sorry to say, in a very cavalier manner.'

'But I presume a counter-revolution was soon effected. This condition of things could not have long existed. The country people in the neighbourhood – visitors coming to see the establishment – would have given the alarm.'

'There you are out. The head rebel was too cunning for that. He admitted no visitors at all – with the exception, one day, of a very stupid-looking young gentleman of whom he had no reason to be afraid. He let him in to see the place – just by way of variety – to have a little fun with him. As soon as he had gammoned him sufficiently, he let him out, and set him about his business.'

'And *how* long, then, did the madmen reign?'

'Oh, a very long time indeed – a month, certainly – how much longer I can't precisely say. In the meantime the lunatics had a jolly season of it – that you may swear. They doffed their own shabby clothes, and made free with the family wardrobe and jewels. The cellars of the *château* were well stocked with wine; and these madmen are just the devils that know how to drink it. They lived well, I can tell you.'

'And the treatment – what was the particular species of treatment which the leader of the rebels put into operation?'

'Why, as for that, a madman is not necessarily a fool, as I have already observed; and it is my honest opinion that his treatment was a much better treatment than that which it superseded. It was a very capital system indeed – simple – neat – no trouble at all, in fact it was delicious – it was'——

Here my host's observations were cut short by another series of yells, of the same character as those which had previously disconcerted us. This time, however, they seemed to proceed from persons rapidly approaching.

'Gracious heavens!' I ejaculated – 'the lunatics have undoubtedly broken loose.'

'I very much fear it is so,' replied Monsieur Maillard, now becoming excessively pale. He had scarcely finished the sentence before loud shouts and imprecations were heard beneath the windows; and immediately afterwards it became evident that some persons outside were endeavouring to gain entrance into the room. The door was beaten with what appeared to be a sledge-hammer, and the shutters were wrenched and shaken with prodigious violence.

A scene of the most terrible confusion ensued. Monsieur Maillard, to my excessive astonishment, threw himself under the sideboard. I had expected more resolution at his hands. The members of the orchestra, who for the last fifteen minutes had been seemingly too much intoxicated to do duty, now sprang all at once to their feet and to their instruments, and, scrambling upon their table, broke out with one accord into 'Yankee Doodle,' which they performed, if not exactly in tune, at least with an energy superhuman, during the whole of the uproar.

Meantime, upon the main dining-table, among the bottles and glasses, leaped the gentleman who with such difficulty had been restrained from leaping there before. As soon as he fairly settled himself he commenced an oration, which no doubt was a very capital one if it could only have been heard. At the same moment, the man with the tee-totum predilections set himself to spinning around the apartment with immense energy, and with arms outstretched at right angles with his body, so that he had all the air of a tee-totum in fact, and knocked everybody down that happened to get in his way. And now, too, hearing an incredible popping and fizzing of champagne, I discovered at length that it proceeded from the person who performed the bottle of that delicate drink during dinner. And then again, the frog-man croaked away as if the salvation of his soul depended upon every note that he uttered. And in the midst of all this, the continuous braying of a donkey arose over all. As for my old friend Madame Joyeuse, I really could have wept for the poor lady, she appeared so terribly perplexed. All she did, however, was to stand up in a corner by the fireplace, and sing out incessantly, at the top of her voice, 'Cock-a-doodle-de-dooooooh!'

And now came the climax – the catastrophe of the drama. As no resistance beyond whooping and yelling and cock-a-doodling was offered to the encroachments of the party without, the ten windows were very speedily and almost simultaneously broken in. But I shall never forget the emotions of wonder and horror with which I gazed, when, leaping through these windows and down among us *pêle-mêle*, fighting, stamping, scratching and howling, there rushed a perfect army of what I took to be Chimpanzees, Ourang-Outangs, or big black baboons of the Cape of Good Hope.

I received a terrible beating, after which I rolled under a sofa and lay still. After lying there some fifteen minutes, however, during which time I listened with all my ears to what was going on in the room, I came to some satisfactory *dénouement* of this tragedy. Monsieur Maillard, it appeared, in giving me the account of the lunatic who had excited his fellows to rebellion, had been merely relating his own exploits. This gentleman had, indeed, some two or three years before been the superintendent of the establishment, but grew crazy himself, and so became a patient. This fact was unknown to the travelling companion who introduced me. The keepers, ten in number, having been suddenly overpowered, were first well tarred, then carefully feathered, and then shut up in underground cells. They had been so imprisoned for more than a month, during which period Monsieur Maillard had generously allowed them not only the tar and feather (which constituted his system), but some bread and abundance of water. The latter was pumped on them daily. At length, one escaping through a sewer, gave freedom to all the rest.

The 'soothing system,' with important modifications, has been resumed at the *château*; yet I cannot help agreeing with Monsieur Maillard that his own 'treatment' was a very capital one of its kind. As he justly observed, it was 'simple, neat, and gave no trouble at all – not the least.'

I have only to add that, although I have searched every library in Europe for the works of Doctor *Tarr* and Professor *Fether*, I have, up to the present day, utterly failed in my endeavours at procuring an edition.

The Pit and the Pendulum

Impia tortorum longas hic turba furores
Sanguinis innocui, non satiata, aluit.
Sospite nunc patria, fracto nunc funeris antro,
Mors ubi dira fuit vita salusque patent.

*[Quatrain composed for the gates of a market to be erected upon the site of the
Jacobin Club House at Paris.]*

I was sick, sick unto death, with that long agony, and when they at
length unbound me, and I was permitted to sit, I felt that my senses
were leaving me. The sentence, the dread sentence of death, was the
last of distinct accentuation which reached my ears. After that, the
sound of the inquisitorial voices seemed merged in one dreamy
indeterminate hum. It conveyed to my soul the idea of *revolution*,
perhaps from its association in fancy with the burr of a mill-wheel.
This only for a brief period, for presently I heard no more. Yet, for a
while, I saw, but with how terrible an exaggeration! I saw the lips of
the black-robed judges. They appeared to me white – whiter than the
sheet upon which I trace these words – and thin even to grotesqueness;
thin with the intensity of their expression of firmness, of immovable
resolution, of stern contempt of human torture. I saw that the decrees

of what to me was fate were still issuing from those lips. I saw them writhe with a deadly locution. I saw them fashion the syllables of my name, and I shuddered, because no sound succeeded. I saw, too, for a few moments of delirious horror, the soft and nearly imperceptible waving of the sable draperies which enwrapped the walls of the apartment; and then my vision fell upon the seven tall candles upon the table. At first they wore the aspect of charity, and seemed white slender angels who would save me: but then all at once there came a most deadly nausea over my spirit, and I felt every fibre in my frame thrill, as if I had touched the wire of a galvanic battery, while the angel forms became meaningless spectres, with heads of flame, and I saw that from them there would be no help. And then there stole into my fancy, like a rich musical note, the thought of what sweet rest there must be in the grave. The thought came gently and stealthily, and it seemed long before it attained full appreciation; but just as my spirit came at length properly to feel and entertain it, the figures of the judges vanished, as if magically, from before me; the tall candles sank into nothingness; their flames went out utterly; the blackness of darkness supervened; all sensations appeared swallowed up in a mad rushing descent as of the soul into Hades. Then silence, and stillness, and night were the universe.

I had swooned; but still will not say that all of consciousness was lost. What of it there remained I will not attempt to define, or even to describe; yet all was not lost. In the deepest slumber – no! In delirium – no! In a swoon – no! In death – no! Even in the grave all *is not* lost. Else there is no immortality for man. Arousing from the most profound of slumbers, we break the gossamer web of *some* dream. Yet in a second afterwards (so frail may that web have been) we remember not that we have dreamed. In the return to life from the swoon there are two stages; first, that of the sense of mental or spiritual; secondly, that of the sense of physical existence. It seems probable that if, upon reaching the second stage, we could recall the impressions of the first, we should find these impressions eloquent in memories of the gulf beyond. And that gulf is, what? How at least shall we distinguish its shadows from those of the tomb? But if the impressions of what I have termed the first stage are not at will recalled, yet, after long interval, do they not come unbidden, while we marvel whence they come? He who has never swooned is not he who finds strange palaces and wildly familiar faces in coals that glow; is not he who beholds floating in mid-air the sad visions that the many may not view; is not he who ponders over the perfume of some novel flower; is not he whose brain grows bewildered with the meaning of some musical cadence which has never before arrested his attention.

Amid frequent and thoughtful endeavours to remember, amid earnest struggles to regather some token of the state of seeming nothingness into which my soul had lapsed, there have been moments when I have dreamed of success; there have been brief, very brief periods when I have conjured up remembrances which the lucid reason of a later epoch assures me could have had reference only to that condition of seeming unconsciousness. These shadows of memory tell indistinctly of tall figures that lifted and bore me in silence down – down – still – down – till a hideous dizziness oppressed me at the mere idea of the interminableness of the descent. They tell also of a vague horror at my heart on account of that heart's unnatural stillness. Then comes a sense of sudden motionlessness throughout all things; as if those who bore me (a ghastly train!) had outrun, in their descent, the limits of the limitless, and paused from the wearisomeness of their toil. After this I call to mind flatness and dampness; and then all is *madness* – the madness of a memory which busies itself among forbidden things.

Very suddenly there came back to my soul motion and sound – the tumultuous motion of the heart, and in my ears the sound of its beating. Then a pause in which all is blank. Then again sound, and motion, and touch, a tingling sensation pervading my frame. Then the mere consciousness of existence, without thought, a condition which lasted long. Then, very suddenly, *thought*, and shuddering terror, and earnest endeavour to comprehend my true state. Then a strong desire to lapse into insensibility. Then a rushing revival of soul and a successful effort to move. And now a full memory of the trial, of the judges, of the sable draperies, of the sentence, of the sickness, of the swoon. Then entire forgetfulness of all that followed; of all that a later day and much earnestness of endeavour have enabled me vaguely to recall.

So far I had not opened my eyes. I felt that I lay upon my back unbound. I reached out my hand, and it fell heavily upon something damp and hard. There I suffered it to remain for may minutes, while I strove to imagine where and *what* I could be. I longed, yet dared not, to employ my vision. I dreaded the first glance at objects around me. It was not that I feared to look upon things horrible, but that I grew aghast lest there should be *nothing* to see. At length, with a wild desperation at heart, I quickly inclosed my eyes. My worst thoughts, then, were confirmed. The blackness of eternal night encompassed me. I struggled for breath. The intensity of the darkness seemed to oppress and stifle me. The atmosphere was intolerably close. I still lay quietly, and made effort to exercise my reason. I brought to mind the inquisitorial proceedings, and attempted from that point to deduce my real condition. The sentence had passed, and it appeared to me that a very long interval of time had since elapsed. Yet not for a moment did I suppose myself actually dead. Such a supposition, notwithstanding what we read in fiction, is altogether inconsistent with real existence; – but where and in what state was I? The condemned to death, I knew, perished usually at the *auto-da-fes*, and one of these had been held on the very night of the day of my trial. Had I been remanded to my dungeon, to await the next sacrifice, which would not take place for many months? This I at once saw could not be. Victims had been in immediate demand. Moreover my dungeon, as well as all the condemned cells at Toledo, had stone floors, and light was not altogether excluded.

A fearful idea now suddenly drove the blood in torrents upon my heart, and for a brief period I once more relapsed into insensibility. Upon recovering, I at once started to my feet, trembling convulsively in every fibre. I thrust my arms wildly above and around me in all directions. I felt nothing; yet dreaded to move a step, lest I should be impeded by the walls of a *tomb*. Perspiration burst from every pore, and stood in cold big beads upon my forehead. The agony of suspense grew at length intolerable, and I cautiously moved forward, with my arms extended, and my eyes straining from their sockets, in the hope of catching some faint ray of light. I proceeded for many paces, but still all was blackness and vacancy. I breathed more freely. It seemed evident that mine was not, at least, the most hideous of fates.

And now, as I still continued to step cautiously onward, there came thronging upon my recollection a thousand vague rumours of the horrors of Toledo. Of the dungeons there had been strange things narrated – fables I had always deemed them – but yet strange, and too ghastly to repeat, save in a whisper. Was I left to perish of starvation in this subterranean world of darkness; or what fate perhaps even more fearful awaited me? That the result would be death, and a death of more than customary bitterness, I knew too well the character of my judges to doubt. The mode and the hour were all that occupied or distracted me.

My outstretched hands at length encountered some solid obstruction. It was a wall, seemingly of stone masonry – very smooth, slimy, and cold. I followed it up; stepping with all the careful distrust with which certain antique narratives had inspired me. This process, however, afforded me no means of ascertaining the dimensions of my dungeon; as I might make its circuit, and return to the point whence I set out, without being aware of the fact, so perfectly uniform seemed the wall. I therefore sought the knife which had been in my pocket when led into the inquisitorial chamber, but it was gone; my clothes had been exchanged for a wrapper of coarse serge. I had thought of forcing the blade in some minute crevice of the masonry, so as to identify my point of departure. The difficulty, nevertheless, was but trivial, although, in the disorder of my fancy, it seemed at first insuperable. I tore a part of the hem from the robe, and placed the fragment at full length, and at right angles to the wall. In groping my way around the prison, I could not fail to encounter this rag upon completing the circuit. So, at least, I thought, but I had not counted upon the extent of the dungeon, or upon my own weakness. The ground was moist and slippery. I staggered onward for some time, when I stumbled and fell. My excessive fatigue induced me to remain prostrate, and sleep soon overtook me as I lay.

Upon awaking, and stretching forth an arm, I found beside me a loaf and a pitcher with water. I was too much exhausted to reflect upon this circumstance, but ate and drank with avidity. Shortly afterwards I resumed my tour around the prison, and with much toil came at last upon the fragment of the serge. Up to the period when I fell I had counted fifty-two paces, and upon resuming my walk I had counted forty-eight more, when I arrived at the rag. There were in all, then, a hundred paces; and, admitting two paces to the yard, I presumed the dungeon to be fifty yards in circuit. I had met, however, with many angles in the wall, and thus I could form no guess at the shape of the vault, for vault I could not help supposing it to be.

I had little object – certainly no hope – in these researches, but a vague curiosity prompted me to continue them. Quitting the wall, I resolved to cross the area of the enclosure. At first I proceeded with extreme caution, for the floor although seemingly of solid material was treacherous with slime. At length, however, I took courage and did not hesitate to step firmly – endeavouring to cross in as direct a line as possible. I had advanced some ten or twelve paces in this manner, when the remnant of the torn hem of my robe became entangled between my legs. I stepped on it, and fell violently on my face.

In the confusion attending my fall, I did not immediately apprehend a somewhat startling circumstance, which yet, in a few seconds afterward, and while I still lay prostrate, arrested my attention. It was this: my chin rested upon the floor of the prison, but my lips, and the upper portion of my head, although seemingly at a less elevation than the chin, touched nothing. At the same time, my forehead seemed bathed in a clammy vapour, and the peculiar smell of decayed fungus arose to my nostrils. I put forward my arm, and shuddered to find that I had fallen at the very brink of a circular pit, whose extent of course I had no means of ascertaining at the moment. Groping about the masonry just below the margin, I succeeded in dislodging a small fragment, and let it fall into the abyss. For many seconds I hearkened to its reverberations as it dashed against the sides of the chasm in its descent; at length there was a sullen plunge into water, succeeded by loud echoes. At the same moment there came a sound resembling the quick opening, and as rapid closing of a door overhead, while a faint gleam of light flashed suddenly through the gloom, and as suddenly faded away.

I saw clearly the doom which had been prepared for me, and congratulated myself upon the timely accident by which I had escaped. Another step before my fall, and the world had seen me no more; and the death just avoided was of that very character which I had regarded as fabulous and frivolous in the tales respecting the Inquisition. To the victims of its tyranny, there was the choice of death with its direst physical agonies, or death with its most hideous moral horrors. I had been reserved for the latter. By long suffering my nerves had been unstrung, until I trembled at the sound of my own voice, and had become in every respect a fitting subject for the species of torture which awaited me.

Shaking in every limb, I groped my way back to the wall – resolving there to perish rather than risk the terrors of the wells, of which my imagination now pictured many in various positions about the dungeon. In other conditions of mind I might have had courage to end my misery at once by a plunge into one of these abysses; but now I was the veriest of cowards. Neither could I forget what I had read of these pits – that the *sudden* extinction of life formed no part of their most horrible plan.

Agitation of spirit kept me awake for many long hours; but at length I again slumbered. Upon arousing, I found by my side, as before, a loaf and a pitcher of water. A burning thirst consumed me, and I emptied the vessel at a draught. It must have been drugged, for scarcely had I drunk before I became irresistibly drowsy. A deep sleep fell upon me – a sleep like that of death. How long it lasted of course I know not; but when once again I unclosed my eyes the objects around me were visible. By a wild sulphurous lustre, the origin of which I could not at first determine, I was enabled to see the extent and aspect of the prison.

In its size I had been greatly mistaken. The whole circuit of its walls did not exceed twenty-five yards. For some minutes this fact occasioned me a world of vain trouble; vain indeed – for what could be of less importance, under the terrible circumstances which environed me, than the mere dimensions of my dungeon? But my soul took a wild interest in trifles, and I busied myself in endeavours to account for the error I had committed in my measurement. The truth at length flashed upon me. In my first attempt at exploration I had counted fifty-two paces up to the period when I fell; I must then have been within a pace or two of the fragment of serge; in fact I had nearly performed the circuit of the vault. I then slept, and upon awaking, I must have returned upon my steps, thus supposing the circuit nearly double what it actually was. My confusion of mind prevented me from observing that I began my tour with the wall to the left, and ended it with the wall to the right.

I had been deceived too in respect to the shape of the enclosure. In feeling my way I had found many angles, and thus deduced an idea of great irregularity, so potent is the effect of total darkness upon one arousing from lethargy or sleep! The angles were simply those of a few slight depressions or niches at odd intervals. The general shape of the prison was square. What I had taken for masonry seemed now to be iron, or some other metal in huge plates, whose sutures or joints occasioned the depression. The entire surface of this metallic enclosure was rudely daubed in all the hideous and repulsive devices to which the charnel superstition of the monks has given rise. The figures of fiends in aspects of menace, with skeleton forms and other more really fearful images, overspread and disfigured the walls. I observed that the outlines of these monstrosities were sufficiently distinct, but that the colours seemed faded and blurred, as if from the effects of a damp atmosphere. I now noticed the floor, too, which was of stone. In the centre yawned the circular pit from whose jaws I had escaped; but it was the only one in the dungeon.

All this I saw indistinctly and by much effort, for my personal condition had been greatly changed during slumber. I now lay upon my back, and at full length, on a species of low framework of wood. To this I was securely bound by a long strap resembling a surcingle. It passed in many convolutions about my limbs and body, leaving at liberty only my head, and my left arm to such extent that I could by dint of much exertion supply myself with food from an earthen dish which lay by my side on the floor. I saw to my horror that the pitcher had been removed. I say to my horror, for I was consumed with intolerable thirst. This thirst it appeared to be the design of my persecutors to stimulate, for the food in the dish was meat pungently seasoned.

Looking upward, I surveyed the ceiling of my prison. It was some thirty or forty feet overhead, and constructed much as the side walls. In one of its panels a very singular figure riveted my whole attention. It was the painted figure of Time as he is commonly represented, save that in lieu of a scythe he held what at a casual glance I supposed to be the pictured image of a huge pendulum, such as we see on antique clocks. There was something, however, in the appearance of this machine which caused me to regard it more attentively. While I gazed directly upward at it (for its position was immediately over my own), I fancied that I saw it in motion. In an instant afterward the fancy was confirmed. Its sweep was brief, and of course slow. I watched it for some minutes, somewhat in fear but more in wonder. Wearied at length with observing its dull movement, I turned my eyes upon the other objects in the cell.

A slight noise attracted my notice, and looking to the floor, I saw several enormous rats traversing it. They had issued from the well which lay just within view to my right. Even then while I gazed, they came up in troops hurriedly, with ravenous eyes, allured by the scent of the meat. From this it required much effort and attention to scare them away.

It might have been half-an-hour, perhaps even an hour (for I could take but imperfect note of time) before I again cast my eyes upward. What I then saw confounded and amazed me. The sweep of the pendulum had increased in extent by nearly a yard. As a natural consequence, its velocity was also much greater. But what mainly disturbed me was the idea that it had perceptibly *descended*. I now observed, with that horror it is needless to say, that its nether extremity was formed of a crescent of glittering steel, about a foot in length from horn to horn; the horns upward, and the under edge evidently as keen as that of a razor. Like a razor also it seemed massy and heavy, tapering from the edge into a solid and broad structure above. It was appended to a weighty rod of brass, and the whole *hissed* as it swung through the air.

I could no longer doubt the doom prepared for me by monkish ingenuity in torture. My cognisance of the pit had become known to the inquisitorial agents – *the pit*, whose horrors had been destined for so bold a recusant as myself, *the pit*, typical of hell, and regarded by rumour as the Ultima Thule of all their punishments. The plunge into this pit I had avoided by the merest of accidents, and I knew that surprise or entrapment into torment formed an important portion of all the grotesquerie of these dungeon deaths. Having failed to fall, it was no part of the demon plan to hurl me into the abyss, and thus (there being no alternative) a different and a milder destruction awaited me. Milder! I half smiled in my agony as I thought of such application of such a term.

What boots it to tell of the long, long hours of horror more than mortal, during which I counted the rushing oscillations of the steel! Inch by inch – line by line – with a descent only appreciable at intervals that seemed ages – down and still down it came! Days passed – it might have been that many days passed – ere it swept so closely over me as to fan me with its acrid breath. The odour of the sharp steel forced itself into my nostrils. I prayed – I wearied heaven with my prayer for its more speedy descent. I grew frantically mad, and struggled to force myself upward against the sweep of the fearful scimitar. And then I fell suddenly calm and lay smiling at the glittering death as a child at some rare bauble.

There was another interval of utter insensibility; it was brief, for upon again lapsing into life there had been no perceptible descent in the pendulum. But it might have been long – for I knew there were demons who took note of my swoon, and who could have arrested the vibration at pleasure. Upon my recovery, too, I felt very – oh! inexpressibly – sick and weak, as if through long inanition. Even amid the agonies of that period the human nature craved food. With painful effort I outstretched my left arm as far as my bonds permitted, and took possession of the small remnant which had been spared me by the rats. As I put a portion of it within my lips there rushed to my mind a half-formed thought of joy – of hope. Yet what business had *I* with hope? It was, as I say, a half-formed thought – man has many such, which are never completed. I felt that it was of joy – of hope; but I felt also that it had perished in its formation. In vain I struggled to perfect – to regain it. Long suffering had nearly annihilated all my ordinary powers of mind. I was an imbecile – an idiot.

The vibration of the pendulum was at right angles to my length. I saw that the crescent was designed to cross the region of the heart. It would fray the serge of my robe; it would return and repeat its operations – again – and again. Notwithstanding its terrifically wide sweep (some thirty feet or more) and the hissing vigour of its descent, sufficient to sunder these very walls of iron, still the fraying of my robe would be all that, for several minutes, it would accomplish; and at this thought I paused. I dared not go farther than this reflection. I dwelt upon it with a pertinacity of attention – as if, in so dwelling, I could arrest *here* the descent of the steel. I forced myself to ponder upon the sound of the crescent as it should pass across the garment – upon the peculiar thrilling sensation which the friction of cloth produces on the nerves. I pondered upon all this frivolity until my teeth were on edge.

Down – steadily down it crept. I took a frenzied pleasure in contrasting its downward with its lateral velocity. To the right – to the left – far and wide – with the shriek of a damned spirit! to my heart with the stealthy pace of the tiger! I alternately laughed and howled, as the one or the other idea grew predominant.

Down – certainly, relentlessly down! It vibrated within three inches of my bosom! I struggled violently – furiously – to free my left arm. This was free only from the elbow to the hand. I could reach the latter, from the platter beside me to my mouth with great effort, but no farther. Could I have broken the fastenings above the elbow, I would have seized and attempted to arrest the pendulum. I might as well have attempted to arrest an avalanche!

Down – still unceasingly – still inevitably down! I gasped and struggled at each vibration. I shrunk convulsively at its every sweep. My eyes followed its outward or upward whirls with the eagerness of the most unmeaning despair; they closed themselves spasmodically at the descent, although death would have been a relief. O, how unspeakable! Still I quivered in every nerve to think how slight a sinking of the machinery would precipitate that keen glistening axe upon my bosom. It was *hope* that prompted the nerve to quiver – the frame to shrink. It was *hope* – the hope that triumphs on the rack – that whispers to the death-condemned even in the dungeons of the Inquisition.

I saw that some ten or twelve vibrations would bring the steel in actual contact with my robe, and with this observation there suddenly came over my spirit all the keen, collected calmness of despair. For the first time during many hours, or perhaps days, I *thought*. It now occurred to me that the bandage or surcingle which enveloped me was *unique*. I was tied by no separate cord. The first stroke of the razor-like crescent athwart any portion of the band would so detach it that it might be unwound from my person by means of my left hand. But how fearful, in that case, the proximity of the steel! The result of the slightest struggle, how deadly! Was it likely, moreover, that the minions of the torturer had not foreseen and provided for this possibility! Was it probable that the bandage crossed my bosom in the track of the pendulum? Dreading to find my faint, and, as it seemed, my last hope frustrated, I so far elevated my head as to obtain a distinct view of my breast. The surcingle enveloped my limbs and body close in all directions *save in the path of the destroying crescent*.

Scarcely had I dropped my head back into its original position when there flashed upon my mind what I cannot better describe then as the unformed half of that idea of deliverance to which I have previously alluded, and of which a moiety only floated indeterminately through my brain when I raised food to my burning lips. The whole thought was now present – feeble, scarcely sane, scarcely definite, but still entire. I proceeded at once, with the nervous energy of despair, to attempt its execution.

For many hours the immediate vicinity of the low framework upon which I lay had been literally swarming with rats. They were wild, bold, ravenous, their red eyes glaring upon me as if they waited but for motionlessness on my part to make me their prey. 'To what food,' I thought, 'have they been accustomed in the well?'

They had devoured, in spite of all my efforts to prevent them, all but a small remnant of the contents of the dish. I had fallen into an habitual see-saw or wave of the hand about the platter; and at length the unconscious uniformity of the movement deprived it of effect. In their voracity the vermin frequently fastened their sharp fangs in my fingers. With the particles of the oily and spicy viand which now remained, I thoroughly rubbed the bandage wherever I could reach it; then, raising my hand from the floor, I lay breathlessly still.

At first the ravenous animals were startled and terrified at the change – at the cessation of movement. They shrank alarmedly back; many sought the well. But this was only for a moment. I had not counted in vain upon their voracity. Observing that I remained without motion, one or two of the boldest leaped upon the framework and smelt at the surcingle. This seemed the signal for a general rush. Forth from the well they hurried in fresh troops. They clung to the wood, they overran it, and leaped in hundreds upon my person. The measured movement of the pendulum disturbed them not at all. Avoiding its strokes, they busied themselves with the annointed bandage. They pressed, they swarmed upon me in ever accumulating heaps. They writhed upon my throat; their cold lips sought my own; I was half stifled by their thronging pressure; disgust, for which the world has no name, swelled my bosom, and chilled with heavy clamminess my heart. Yet one minute and I felt that the struggle would be over. Plainly I perceived the loosening of the bandage. I knew that in more than one place it must be already severed. With a more than human resolution I lay *still*.

Nor had I erred in my calculations, nor had I endured in vain. I at length felt that I was *free*. The surcingle hung in ribands from my body. But the stroke of the pendulum already pressed upon my bosom. It had divided the serge of the robe. It had cut through the linen

'*They swarmed upon me in ever-accumulating heaps*'

beneath. Twice again it swung, and a sharp sense of pain shot through every nerve. But the moment of escape had arrived. At a wave of my hand my deliverers hurried tumultuously away. With a steady movement, cautious, sidelong, shrinking, and slow, I slid from the embrace of the bandage and beyond the reach of the scimitar. For the moment, at least *I was free*.

Free! and in the grasp of the Inquisition! I had scarcely stepped from my wooden bed of horror upon the stone floor of the prison, when the motion of the hellish machine ceased and I beheld it drawn up by some invisible force through the ceiling. This was a lesson which I took desperately to heart. My every motion was undoubtedly watched. Free! I had but escaped death in one form of agony to be delivered unto worse than death in some other. With that thought I rolled my eyes nervously around on the barriers of iron that hemmed me in. Something unusual – some change which at first I could not appreciate distinctly – it was obvious had taken place in the apartment. For many minutes of a dreamy and trembling abstraction I busied myself in vain, unconnected conjecture. During this period I became aware, for the first time, of the origin of the sulphurous light which illumined the cell. It proceeded from a fissure about half-an-inch in width extending entirely around the prison at the base of the walls which thus appeared, and were completely separated from the floor. I endeavoured, but of course in vain, to look through the aperture.

As I arose from the attempt, the mystery of the alteration in the chamber broke at once upon my understanding. I have observed that although the outlines of the figures upon the walls were sufficiently distinct, yet the colours seemed blurred and indefinite. These colours had now assumed, and were momentarily assuming, a startling and most intense brilliancy, that give to the spectral and fiendish portraitures an aspect that might have thrilled even firmer nerves than my own. Demon eyes, of a wild and ghastly vivacity, glared upon me in a thousand directions where none had been visible before, and gleamed with the lurid lustre of a fire that I could not force my imagination to regard as unreal.

Unreal! – Even while I breathed there came to my nostrils the breath of the vapour of heated iron! A suffocating odour pervaded the prison! A deeper glow settled each moment in the eyes that glared at my agonies! A richer tint of crimson diffused itself over the pictured horrors of blood. I panted! I gasped for breath! There could be no doubt of the design of my tormentors – oh, most unrelenting! oh, most demoniac of men! I shrank from the glowing metal to the centre of the cell. Amid the thought of the fiery destruction that impended, the idea of the coolness of the well came over my soul like balm. I rushed to its deadly brink. I threw my straining vision below. The glare from the enkindled roof illumined its inmost recesses. Yet, for a wild moment, did my spirit refuse to comprehend the meaning of what I saw. At length it forced – it wrestled its way into my soul – it burned itself in upon my shuddering reason. O for a voice to speak! – oh, horror! – oh, any horror but this! With a shriek I rushed from the margin and buried my face in my hands – weeping bitterly.

The heat rapidly increased, and once again I looked up, shuddering as if with a fit of the ague. There had been a second change in the cell – and now the change was obviously in the *form*. As before, it was in vain that I at first endeavoured to appreciate or understand what was taking place. But not long was I left in doubt. The inquisitorial vengeance had been hurried by my two-fold escape, and there was to be no more dallying with the King of Terrors. The room had been square. I saw that two of its iron angles were now acute – two, consequently, obtuse. The fearful difference quickly increased with a low rumbling or moaning sound. In an instant the apartment had shifted its form into that of a lozenge. But the alteration stopped not here – I neither hoped nor desired it to stop. I could have clasped the red walls to my bosom as a garment of eternal peace. 'Death,' I said 'any death but that of the pit!' Fool! might I not have known that *into the pit* it was the object of the burning iron to urge me? Could I resist its glow? or if even that, could I withstand its pressure? And now, flatter and flatter grew the lozenge, with a rapidity that left me no time for contemplation. Its centre, and of course, its greatest width, came just over the yawning gulf. I shrank back – but the closing walls pressed me resistlessly onward. At length for my seared and writhing body there was no longer an inch of foothold on the firm floor of the prison. I struggled no more, but the agony of my soul found vent in one loud, long, and final scream of despair. I felt that I tottered upon the brink – I averted my eyes——

There was a discordant hum of human voices! There was a loud blast as of many trumpets! There was a harsh grating as of a thousand thunders! The fiery walls rushed back! An outstretched arm caught my own as I fell fainting into the abyss. It was that of General Lasalle. The French army had entered Toledo. The Inquisition was in the hands of its enemies.